The sweet far thing

Author: Bray, Libba
Reading Level: 4.8 UG
Point Value: 30.0
ACCELERATED READER QUIZ 119499

At Spence Academy, 16-year old Gemma Doyle continues preparing for her London debut while struggling to determine how best to use magic to resolve a power struggle in the enchanted world of the realms, and to protect her own world and loved ones.

THE SWEET FAR THING

THE
SWEET
FAR
THING

Libba Bray

DELACORTE PRESS

Published by Delacorte Press
an imprint of Random House Children's Books
a division of Random House, Inc.
New York

Visit us on the Web! www.randomhouse.com/teens

Educators and librarians, for a variety of teaching tools, visit us at
www.randomhouse.com/teachers

Library of Congress Cataloging-in-Publication Data

Bray, Libba.
    The sweet far thing / Libba Bray. — 1st ed.
        p. cm.
    Summary: At Spence Academy, sixteen-year-old Gemma Doyle continues preparing for her London debut while struggling to determine how best to use magic to resolve a power struggle in the enchanted world of the realms, and to protect her own world and loved ones.
    ISBN 978-0-385-73030-3 (hardcover)—ISBN 978-0-385-90295-3 (Gibraltar lib. bdg.)—ISBN 978-0-440-23777-8 (trade pbk.) [1. Magic—Fiction. 2. Supernatural—Fiction. 3. Boarding schools—Fiction. 4. Schools—Fiction. 5. England—Social life and customs—19th century—Fiction. I. Title.
    PZ7.B7386Swe 2007
    [Fic]—dc22
                                2007031302

The text of this book is set in 13-point Adobe Jensen.

Book design by Trish Parcell Watts

Printed in the United States of America

10 9 8 7 6

First Edition

For Barry and Josh, with love

And for all who believe that peace
is not an ideal or a pipe dream but a necessity

The essence of nonviolence is love.
Out of love and the willingness to act selflessly,
strategies, tactics, and techniques
for a nonviolent struggle arise naturally.
Nonviolence is not a dogma; it is a process.
—THICH NHAT HANH

Peace is not only better than war,
but infinitely more arduous.
—GEORGE BERNARD SHAW

ACKNOWLEDGMENTS

They say it takes a village to raise a child. I've discovered that that's largely true. (Well, that and a truckload of M&M's.) But to write the last book in a trilogy, it takes more than a village. At last count, it takes a great coffee shop; lots of caffeine and chocolate; Guitar Hero (curse you, "Bark at the Moon" on medium!); a drool cup; Kleenex; and many, many understanding friends, family members, editors, publishers, and other writers to nod and pass you the Ben & Jerry's and occasionally pull on the bungee cord of your self-esteem to snap you back from the Perpetual Night of the I Suck Abyss. (Perpetual Night of the I Suck Abyss—new band name. I call dibs.)

I went through so many revisions on this book that I was reminded of the movie *Airplane!*: "Look—I can make a hat or a brooch or a pterodactyl. . . ." Also, I think I lost a lot of what was left of my brain cells, and since I'm afraid of forgetting someone here, let me just issue a blanket "You rock—here's a big old fruit basket" to everyone I might have shared oxygen with in the past eighteen months. I am sure you helped me enormously. Seriously. So extra high fives to the following:

My editor, St. Wendy of Loggia, who deserves to have her face on a prayer card, for calling me with a calm, cool "Let me just show you how the dates back out" rather than screaming into the phone, "If you miss another deadline, I will put your head on a pike outside my office as a warning to other authors!" You da best, babe.

Pam Bobowicz, aka the Lifeline, for letting me stroll into her office sporting an eye twitch and say, "Hey, got a minute?" only to release her from my grip two hours later, having told her every single possible plot thread until I'm convinced she kept a bottle of Scotch hidden behind her computer monitor. Love you, Pam.

My long-suffering agent/husband, Barry Goldblatt (that sounds so *Chinatown*, doesn't it? "My agent [*slap!*], my husband [*slap!*]"), who tolerated unbelievable amounts of whining and handled that plus the child care with aplomb.

Beverly Horowitz—sometimes it takes a village; sometimes it takes the best Jewish mother in publishing. Big kiss.

Chip Gibson, for prying my fingers off the keys and forcing me to come eat cake and laugh at people doing Jell-O shots.

The cool folks at Random House, who let me crash there for three months and who would sometimes drop by with chocolate like the Keebler Elves of Publishing.

Holly Black, Cassandra Clare, and Emily Lauer, the Holy Trinity of Awesome, Badass, Magic Systems R Us Writers-in-Arms, for *everything*. Lunch on me, ladies. And Holly, I will seriously birth your child for you, that's how much I love you. (I've done natural childbirth, and let me tell you—piece of cake compared to the third book in a trilogy.)

Rachel Cohn, for the espresso balls (still vibrating), the CDs, the writing dates, and the company.

Maureen Johnson, Justine Larbalestier, Dani Bennett, and Jaida Jones, for doing the world's fastest read on the last draft and offering invaluable insights.

My peeps, Cecil Castellucci, Margaret Crocker, and Diana Peterfreund, for being there with grace, style, and snark.

Über-librarians Jen Hubert and Phil Swann, for the research help, and for continuing to take my increasingly desperate calls.

Delia Sherman, Ellen Kushner, Jo Knowles, Tracie Vaughn Zimmer, Cynthia and Greg Letitch-Smith, Nancy Werlin, YA Writers, Tony Tallent, and Chaundra Wall, for the support and inspiration.

Cheryl Levine, Susanna Schrobsdorff, Pam Carden, and Lori Lebovitch, for talking me off the ledge and just generally being lovely.

My pals at Kensington Publishing, for letting me take the time off I needed.

The fabulous baristas of Tea Lounge in Brooklyn—Aimee, Alma, Amanda, Asia, Beth, Brigid, Geri, Kevin, Rachel—for keeping the caffeine and the hilarity coming.

Ben Jones and Christine Kenneally, for being so incredibly funny and supportive, and the Gang on the Couch—Jeff Strickland, Nicola Behrman, Matt Schwartz, Kyle Smith, and Jonathan Hafner-Layton (or is it Layton-Hafner?), for making sure to tell me a joke when I started to look like Jack Nicholson in *The Shining*.

My mother, Nancy Bray, for the poetry help. Thanks, Mom.

My readers, who kept me going.

David Levithan, for the boffo title suggestion. Unfortunately, marketing felt that *Lick My Sweat* was perhaps not quite what we were looking for.

And last, but definitely not least, my wonderful son, Joshua, for being so patient about "the book" (insert eye-rolling here) when the least I could have done was write something about ninja bunnies or dragons. Next time, sweetie. Next time.

Rose of all Roses, Rose of all the World!
You, too, have come where the dim tides are hurled
Upon the wharves of sorrow, and heard ring
The bell that calls us on; the sweet far thing.
Beauty grown sad with its eternity
Made you of us, and of the dim grey sea.
Our long ships loose thought-woven sails and wait,
For God has bid them share an equal fate;
And when at last, defeated in His wars,
They have gone down under the same white stars,
We shall no longer hear the little cry
Of our sad hearts, that may not live nor die.

—from THE ROSE OF BATTLE, W. B. Yeats

ACT I

Before Dawn

Nothing is easier than self-deceit.
For what each man wishes,
that he also believes to be true.

—DEMOSTHENES

PROLOGUE

1893
LONDON

THE NIGHT WAS COLD AND DISMAL, AND OUT ON THE
Thames, the rivermen cursed their luck. Skulking through the
shadows of London's great river for profit wasn't a cheery occu-
pation, but it paid for a meal here and there, and the damp that
stiffened your bones, put the ache in your back, was a part of it,
like it or not.

"See anyfin', Archie?"

"Nuffin'," Archie called to his friend, Rupert. "'S as foul a
night as I've seen."

They'd been at it for an hour now, with nothing to show for
it but a bit of clothing taken from the body of a sailor. That,
they could sell to the rag-and-bone men come morning. But a
pocketful of coins would put food and ale in their bellies tonight, and for rivermen like Archie and Rupert, the here and

now was what counted; hoping to see beyond tomorrow was a cockeyed optimism best left to people who didn't spend their lives scouring the Thames for the dead.

The boat's single lantern wasn't much use against the infernal fog. The gloom haunted the banks. Across the river, the unlit houses were skulls of dark. The rivermen navigated the shallows of the Thames, poking their long hooks into the filthy water, looking for the bodies of anyone who'd met with misfortune on this night—sailors or dockworkers too drunk to save themselves from drowning; the sorry victims of knife fights, or of cutpurses and murderers; the mud larks carried away by a sudden strong tide, their aprons heavy with prized coal, that same coal that pulled them under to their deaths.

Archie's hook hit something solid. "Oi, slow there, Rupert. I got sumfin'."

Rupert grabbed the lantern from its perch and shone it over the water where a body bobbed. They fished the corpse out, dropping it onto the deck and rolling it over onto its back.

"Blimey," Rupert said. "It's a lady."

"Was," Archie said. "Check 'er pockets."

The rivermen set about their grisly task. The lady was well heeled, in a fine lavender silk dress that could not have been cheap. She wasn't what they were used to finding in these waters.

Archie smiled. "Oh, 'ello!" He drew four coins from the lady's coat pocket and bit each.

"Wot you got, then, Archie? 'Nuff to buy us a pint?"

Archie looked closely at the coins. Not pounds. Shillings. "Aye, and not much more from the looks o' it," he grumbled. "Take the necklace."

"Righ'." Rupert removed it from the woman's neck. It was an

odd thing—metal fashioned into the shape of an eye with a crescent moon dangling below it. There were no jewels to speak of; he couldn't imagine anyone wanting it.

"Wot's this, then?" Archie called. He peeled back the woman's stiff fingers. She tightly clutched a scrap of sodden paper.

Rupert nudged his partner. "Whassit say?"

Archie shoved it at him. "Dunno. Can't read, now, can I?"

"I 'ad schoolin' till I was eight," Rupert said, taking it. "'The Tree of All Souls lives.'"

Archie nudged Rupert. "Wot's that supposed to mean?"

Rupert shook his head. "Dunno. What should we do wif it?"

"Leave it. There's no profit in words, Rupert, m'boy. Take the clothes and toss 'er over."

Rupert shrugged and did as he was told. Archie was right that there was no money to be gotten from an old letter. Still, it was sad when the deceased's last words were lost with her, but, he reasoned, if this lady had anyone to care about her at all, she wouldn't be floating facedown in the Thames on a rough night. With a sharp shove, the riverman dropped the dead woman overboard. She made only the slightest splash.

Her body slid slowly under, the bloated white hands remaining on the surface for a few seconds more as if they were reaching for something. The rivermen pressed their hooks against the muddy bottom and cast off with the current, looking for treasure that might make a night in the cold worth the ache.

Archie gave the woman's head a last prod with his hook, a violent benediction, and she slipped below the filth and muck of the mighty Thames. The river swallowed her up, accepting her flesh, taking her final warning down with her to a murky grave.

CHAPTER ONE

March 1896
SPENCE ACADEMY FOR YOUNG LADIES

THERE IS A PARTICULAR CIRCLE OF HELL NOT MENTIONED in Dante's famous book. It is called comportment, and it exists in schools for young ladies across the empire. I do not know how it feels to be thrown into a lake of fire. I am sure it isn't pleasant. But I can say with all certainty that walking the length of a ballroom with a book upon one's head and a backboard strapped to one's back while imprisoned in a tight corset, layers of petticoats, and shoes that pinch is a form of torture even Mr. Alighieri would find too hideous to document in his *Inferno*.

"Let us keep our eyes trained toward heaven, girls," our head-mistress, Mrs. Nightwing, pleads as we attempt our slow march across the floor, heads held high, arms out like ballerinas.

The loops of the backboard chafe the sides of my arms. The

block of wood is unyielding, and I am forced to stand as stiff as the guards at Buckingham Palace. My neck aches with the effort. Come May, I shall make my debut a full year early, for it has been decided by all parties involved that at nearly seventeen I am ready and that it would do me good to have my season now. I shall wear beautiful gowns, attend lavish parties, and dance with handsome gentlemen—if I survive my training. At present, that outcome is very much in doubt.

Mrs. Nightwing paces the length of the ballroom. Her stiff skirts *whisk-whisk* across the floor as if to rebuke it for lying there. All the while she barks orders like Admiral Nelson himself. "Heads held high! Do not smile, Miss Hawthorne! Serene, somber expressions! Empty your minds!"

I strain to keep my face a blank canvas. My spine aches. My left arm, held out to the side for what seems hours, trembles with the effort.

"And curtsy . . ."

Like falling soufflés, we drop low, trying desperately not to lose our balance. Mrs. Nightwing does not give the order to rise. My legs shake with exhaustion. I cannot manage it. I stumble forward. The book tumbles from my head and lands on the floor with a resounding thud. We have done this four times, and four times I have failed in some fashion. Mrs. Nightwing's boots stop inches from my disgraced form.

"Miss Doyle, may I remind you that this is the court, and you are curtsying to your sovereign, not performing in the Folies Bergère?"

"Yes, Mrs. Nightwing," I say sheepishly.

It is hopeless. I shall never curtsy without falling. I shall lie sprawled upon the gleaming floors of Buckingham Palace like a disgraceful stain of a girl, my nose resting upon the boot of the Queen. I shall be the talk of the season, whispered about behind open fans. No doubt every man will avoid me like typhus.

"Miss Temple, perhaps you will demonstrate the proper curtsy for us?"

Without ado, Cecily Temple, She Who Can Do No Wrong, settles to the floor in a long, slow, graceful arc that seems to defy gravity. It is a thing of beauty. I am hideously jealous.

"Thank you, Miss Temple."

Yes, thank you, you little demon beast. May you marry a man who eats garlic with every meal.

"Now, let us—" Mrs. Nightwing is interrupted by loud banging. She closes her eyes tightly against the noise.

"Mrs. Nightwing," Elizabeth whines. "How can we possibly concentrate on our form with such a terrible racket coming from the East Wing?"

Mrs. Nightwing is in no humor for our complaining. She takes a deep breath and clasps her hands at her waist, her head held high.

"We shall carry on, like England herself. If she could withstand Cromwell, the Wars of the Roses, and the French, surely you may overlook a bit of hammering. Think how lovely the East Wing shall be when it is completed. We shall try again— steady! All eyes are upon you! It won't do to scurry to Her Majesty like a timid church mouse."

I often imagine what sort of position Nightwing might seek out were she not currently torturing us as headmistress of Spence Academy for Young Ladies. *Dear Sirs,* her letter might begin. *I am writing to inquire about your advert for the position of*

Balloon Popper. I have a hatpin that will do the trick neatly and bring about the wails of small children everywhere. My former charges will attest to the fact that I rarely smile, never laugh, and can steal the joy from any room simply by entering and bestowing upon it my unique sense of utter gloom and despair. My references in this matter are impeccable. If you have not fallen into a state of deep melancholia simply by reading my letter, please respond to Mrs. Nightwing (I have a Christian name but no one ever has leave to use it) in care of Spence Academy for Young Ladies. If you cannot be troubled to find the address on your own, you are not trying your very best. Sincerely, Mrs. Nightwing.

"Miss Doyle! What is that insipid smile you're wearing? Have I said something that amuses you?" Mrs. Nightwing's admonishment brings a flush to my cheeks. The other girls giggle.

We glide across the floor, trying our best to ignore the hammering and the shouts. The noise isn't what distracts us. It is the knowledge that there are men here, one floor above us, that keeps us jittery and light.

"Perhaps we could see the progress they've made, Mrs. Nightwing? How extraordinary it must be," Felicity Worthington suggests with a sweetness bordering on pure syrup. Only Felicity would be so bold as to suggest this. She is too daring by half. She is also one of my only allies here at Spence.

"The workmen do not need girls underfoot, as they are already behind schedule," Mrs. Nightwing says. "Heads up, if you please! And—"

A loud bang sounds from above. The sudden noise makes us jump. Even Mrs. Nightwing lets out a "Merciful heavens!"

Elizabeth, who is nothing more than a nervous condition disguised as a debutante, yelps and grabs hold of Cecily.

"Oh, Mrs. Nightwing!" Elizabeth cries.

We look to our headmistress hopefully.

Mrs. Nightwing exhales through disapproving lips. "Very well. We shall adjourn for the present. Let us take the air to restore the roses to our cheeks."

"Might we bring our paper and sketch the progress on the East Wing?" I suggest. "It would make a fine record."

Mrs. Nightwing favors me with a rare smile. "A most excellent suggestion, Miss Doyle. Very well, then. Gather your paper and pencils. I shall send Brigid with you. Don your coats. And walk, if you please."

We abandon our backboards along with our decorum, racing for the stairs and the promise of freedom, however temporary it may be.

"Walk!" Mrs. Nightwing shouts. When we cannot seem to heed her advice, she bellows after us that we are savages not fit for marriage. She adds that we shall be the shame of the school and something else besides, but we are down the first flight of stairs, and her words cannot touch us.

CHAPTER TWO

THE LONG EXPANSE OF THE EAST WING STRETCHES OUT like the skeleton of a great wooden bird. The framing is in place, but the men spend most of their effort on restoring the dilapidated turret that joins the East Wing to the rest of the school. Since the fire that ravaged it twenty-five years ago, it has been nothing more than a beautiful ruin. But it shall be resurrected with stone and brick and mortar, and it promises to be a magnificent tower—tall and wide and imposing—once it is complete.

Since January, swarms of men have come from the neighboring villages to work in the cold and damp, every day but Sunday, to make our school whole again. We girls are not allowed near the East Wing during its reconstruction. The official reason given for this is that it is far too dangerous: we might be hit by an errant beam or impaled by a rusty nail. The various ways in which we could meet a terrible end have been detailed so thoroughly by Mrs. Nightwing that every hammer stroke makes the nervous among us as jumpy as a bagful of cats.

But the truth is that she doesn't want us near the men. Her orders have been clear on this point: We are not to speak to the workers at all, and they are not to speak to us. A careful distance is maintained. The workers have pitched their tents a half mile from the school. They are under the watchful eye of Mr. Miller, their foreman, while we are never without a chaperone. Every care has been taken to keep us apart.

This is precisely what compels us to seek them out.

Our coats buttoned up against the still-formidable March chill, we walk quickly through the woods behind Spence with our housekeeper, Brigid, huffing and puffing to keep pace. It is not kind of us to walk faster than necessary, but it is the only way to have a few moments of privacy. When we race up the hill and secure a spot with a commanding view of the construction, Brigid lags far behind, affording us precious time.

Felicity thrusts out a hand. "The opera glasses, if you please, Martha."

Martha pulls the binoculars from her coat pocket, and they are passed from girl to girl, to Felicity's waiting hands. She puts them to her eyes.

"Very impressive, indeed," Felicity purrs. Somehow, I do not think she means the East Wing. From where we sit, I can see six handsomely formed men in shirtsleeves hoisting a giant beam into place. I'm sure that had I the opera glasses, I could see the outline of their every muscle.

"Oh, do let me see, Fee," Cecily moans. She reaches for the glasses, but Felicity pulls away.

"Wait your turn!"

Cecily pouts. "Brigid will be here any moment. I shan't *have* a turn!"

Felicity drops the glasses quickly and reaches for her sketch pad. "Don't look now, but I believe we've caught the eye of one of the men."

Elizabeth jumps up, craning her neck this way and that. "Which one? Which one?" Felicity steps on Elizabeth's foot, and she falls back.

"Ow! What did you do that for?"

"I said, don't look now," Felicity hisses through clenched teeth. "The key is to make it seem as if you do not notice their attention."

"Ohhh," Elizabeth says in understanding.

"That one on the end, in the shirt with the unfortunate red patching," Felicity says, feigning interest in her sketch. Her coolness is a talent I wish I could manage. Instead, every day, I search the horizon for some sign of another young man, one I've not heard a word from since I left him in London three months ago.

Elizabeth steals a peek through the opera glasses. "Oh, my!" she says, dropping them. "He winked at me! The cheek of him! I should report him to Mrs. Nightwing at once," she protests, but the breathless excitement in her voice betrays her.

"By all the saints." Brigid has finally reached us. Hurriedly, Felicity hands the opera glasses to Martha, who squeaks and drops them in the grass before shoving them into the pocket of her cape.

Brigid takes a seat on a rock to catch her breath. "You're too quick for your old Brigid. Have you no shame, leaving me so?"

Felicity smiles sweetly. "Oh, we are sorry, Brigid. We didn't know you'd fallen so behind." Under her breath she adds, "You old battle-ax."

Brigid narrows her eyes at our tittering. "Here now, wot are you on about? Making sport of your Brigid, are you?"

"Not at all."

"Oh, this is no good." Cecily sighs. "How can we possibly draw the East Wing from so far a distance?" She looks hopefully at Brigid.

"You'll sketch it from here and not an inch closer, miss. You've 'eard wot Missus Nightwing 'as to say on the matter." Brigid stares at the timber spine, the masons cutting stone. She shakes her head. "It ain't right putting that cursed place back together. They should leave well enough alone."

"Oh, but it's thrilling!" Elizabeth argues.

"And think how lovely Spence will look once the East Wing has been restored!" Martha echoes. "How could you say it's not right, Brigid?"

"Because I remember," Brigid says, tapping the side of her head. "There was something not right about that place, the turret in particular. Somethin' you could feel. I could tell you stories . . ."

"Yes, I'm sure you could, Brigid, and fine stories they'd be," Felicity says, as sweetly as a mother placating her irritable child. "But I do worry that the chill will put the ache in your back."

"Well," Brigid says, rubbing her sides. " 'Tis a bother. And m'knees ain't gettin' no younger."

We nod in concerned agreement.

"We'll only step a fraction closer," Felicity coos. "Just enough for a proper sketch."

We do our best to look as innocent as a choir of angels.

Brigid gives us a quick nod. "Off you go, then. Don't go gettin' too close! And don't think I won't be watching!"

"Thank you, Brigid!" we shout gleefully. We move quickly down the hill before she can change her mind.

"And be quick about it! Looks like rain!"

A sudden gust of brisk late-March wind blows across the brittle lawn. It rattles the weary tree limbs like bone necklaces and whips our skirts up till we have to push them down. The girls squeal in surprise—and delight—for it has brought us the attention of every man's eyes for one unguarded, forbidden moment. The gust is the last charge of winter's army. Already the leaves are shaking off sleep and arming themselves. Soon they will mount their attack of green, forcing winter's retreat. I pull my shawl about my neck. Spring is coming, but I cannot yet shake the cold.

"Are they looking?" Elizabeth asks excitedly, stealing glances at the men.

"Steady," Felicity says under her breath.

Martha's curls hang limply at her neck. She gives them a hopeful push, but they will not spring back into shape. "Tell me truthfully, has the damp made a ruin of my hair?"

"No," Elizabeth lies at the precise moment I say, "Yes, it has."

Martha purses her lips. "I might have known you'd be unkind, Gemma Doyle."

The other girls give me frosty stares. It would appear that "Tell me truthfully" is a carefully coded message which means "Lie at all costs." I shall make a note of it. It often seems that there is a primer on all things Polite and Ladylike and that I have not had the good guidance of its pages. Perhaps this is why Cecily, Martha, and Elizabeth loathe me so and only tolerate my presence when Felicity is around. For my part, I find their minds to be as corseted as their waists, with conversations limited to parties, dresses, and the misfortunes or shortcomings of others. I should rather take my chances with the lions of Rome's ancient Colosseum than endure another tea chat with the likes of them. At least the lions are honest about their desire to eat you and make no effort to hide it.

Felicity glances at the men. "Here we go."

We edge closer to the work site.

The workers have caught the fever of us now. They stop what they are doing and quickly doff their caps. The gesture is all politeness, but their smiles hint at less mannerly thoughts. I find I am blushing.

"Oi, gents. Keep to the work if you want to keep working," the foreman warns. Mr. Miller is a burly man with arms the size of small hams. To us, he is courteous. "Good day, ladies."

"Good day," we murmur.

"There's trinkets for the taking, if you'd like a souvenir of the old girl." He nods toward a rubbish pile where discarded lumber lies along with the broken, soot-smudged glass of decades-old lamps. It is the very sort of thing Mrs. Nightwing would place on her To Be Avoided for Fear of Injury, Death, or Disgrace list. "Take any souvenirs you like."

"Thank you," Cecily mumbles, backing away. Elizabeth continues to blush and smile and glance shyly at the man with the red-patched shirt, who appraises her longingly.

"Yes, thank you," Felicity says, taking control of the situation as she always does. "We shall do that."

We set about scavenging through the remains of the old East Wing. The great school's past is told here in splintered, charred wood and remnants of paper. To some, it is the story of a tragic fire that took the lives of two girls. But I know better. The true story of this place is one of magic and mystery, of devotion and betrayal, of wickedness and unspeakable sacrifice. Most of all, it is the story of two girls—best friends turned bitter enemies—both of them thought dead in the fire twenty-five years ago. The truth was so much worse.

One of the girls, Sarah Rees-Toome, chose a path of darkness under the name Circe. Years later, she hunted down the other girl, her former friend, Mary Dowd, who had become someone new, Virginia Doyle—my mother. With an evil spirit at her disposal, Circe murdered my mother and set my life on a different course. The story whispered in these walls is my story as well.

All around me, the girls jump about in merry treasure hunting. But I can't feel happy here. This is a place of ghosts, and I don't believe that new beams and a warm fire in a marble hearth will change that. I want no souvenirs of the past.

A fresh round of hammering sets a family of birds squawking toward the safety of the sky. I stare at the pile of discarded remnants and think of my mother. Did she touch that pillar there? Does her scent still linger in a fragment of glass or a splinter of wood? A terrible emptiness settles into my chest. No matter how much I go about living, there are always small reminders that make the loss fresh again.

"Oi, there's a beauty." It's the man with the red patch on his shirt. He points to a jagged wooden pillar eaten through at one end with rot. But much of it has managed to survive the wrath of the fire and the years of neglect. Carved into it is an assortment of girls' names. I run my fingers over the grooves and the fanciful scrapings. So many names. Alice. Louise. Theodora. Isabel. Mina. My fingers move across the bumpy wood, feeling it like a blind person's. I know that her name must be here, and I am not disappointed. Mary. I flatten my palm against the years-worn carving, hoping to feel my mother's presence beneath my skin. But it is only dead wood. I blink against the tears that sting my eyes.

"Miss?" The man is looking at me curiously.

Quickly, I wipe my cheeks. "It's the wind. It's blown cinders into my eyes."

"Aye, wind's strong. More rain comin'. Maybe a storm."

"Oh, here comes Mrs. Nightwing!" Cecily hisses. "Please, let's go! I don't want to get in trouble."

Quickly, we gather our sketches and sit a safe distance away on a stone bench by the still-hibernating rose garden, our heads bent in desperate concentration. But Mrs. Nightwing takes no note. She appraises the progress on the building. The wind carries her voice to us.

"I had hoped to be farther along by now, Mr. Miller."

"We're putting in a ten-hour day, missus. And then there's the rain. Can't blame a man for nature." Mr. Miller makes the grave error of smiling at Mrs. Nightwing in a charming way. She does not succumb to charm. But it is too late for me to warn him. Mrs. Nightwing's withering glare sends the men's heads down over their lumber. The sound of hammers and saws hard at work is deafening. Mr. Miller's smile vanishes.

"If you cannot finish the job in a timely manner, Mr. Miller, I shall be forced to seek other workers."

"There's building all over London, mum. You won't find the likes of us growing on trees."

By my count, there are at least twenty men working day in and day out, and still Mrs. Nightwing isn't satisfied. She clucks and fusses and badgers Mr. Miller daily. It is very queer. For if the old building has lain hollowed out for this long, what do a few months more matter?

I try to capture the likeness of the new turret on my paper. When completed, it will be the tallest part of Spence, perhaps five stories high. It is wide as well. A man stands near the top, pressed against the gathering rain clouds like a weather vane.

"Do you not find it odd that Nightwing's in such haste to complete the East Wing?" I ask Felicity.

Cecily overhears and is compelled to give her opinion. "It's not a moment too soon, if you ask me. It's a disgrace they've let it go so long."

"I hear it's only now they've secured the funds," Elizabeth reports.

"No, no, no!" Mrs. Nightwing strides toward the masons with purpose, as if they were her charges. "I've told you—these stones must be placed in order, here and here."

She points to an outline made in chalk.

"Begging your pardon, missus, but what does it matter? She's goin' up sturdy and strong."

"It is a restoration," she sniffs as if speaking to a simpleton. "The plans are to be followed exactly, without deviation."

A worker calls down from atop the turret's third floor. "'Ere comes the rain, sir!"

A splat hits my cheek in warning. A rhythm of drops follows. They splatter across my page, turning my sketch of the East Wing into rivulets of charcoal. The men look to the sky with upturned palms as if asking it for mercy, and the sky answers: *No quarter.*

Quickly, the men scamper down the turret's side and race to cover their tools and save them from rust. With sketch pads held over our heads, we girls dash through the trees like frightened geese, squawking and squealing at the indignity of such a soaking. Brigid waves us in, her arms a promise of safety and a warm fire. Felicity pulls me behind a tree.

"Fee! The rain!" I protest.

"Ann returns this evening. We could try to enter the realms."

"And what if I can't make the door appear?"

"You only need to put your mind to it," she insists.

"Do you think I didn't put my mind to it last week or last month or the time before that?" The rain is coming down harder now. "Perhaps I am to be punished. For what I did to Nell and Miss Moore."

"Miss Moore!" Felicity spits. "Circe—that's her name. She was a murderer. Gemma, she killed your mother and countless other girls to get to you and your power, and she would surely have destroyed you had you not dispatched her first."

I want to believe that this is true, that I did right to imprison Miss Moore in the realms forever. I want to believe that binding the magic to myself was the only way to save it. I want to believe that Kartik is alive and well and making his way to me here at Spence, that in these woods at any moment I shall see him wearing a smile meant only for me. But these days, I'm not certain of anything.

"I don't know that she's dead," I mumble.

"She's dead and good riddance to her." Life is ever so much simpler in Fee's world. And for once, I wish I could crawl into the solid lines of it and live without question. "I have to know what happened to Pippa. Tonight we'll try again. Look at me."

She turns my face to hers so that I cannot avoid her eyes. "Promise."

"I promise," I say, and I hope she cannot see my doubt turning to fear.

CHAPTER THREE

THE RAIN HAS LOOSED ITS WRATH IN FULL. IT SOAKS THE sleeping rose garden and the lawn, the yellow green of the leaves struggling to be born. It has also found my friend Ann Bradshaw. She stands in the foyer in a plain brown wool coat and a drab hat dotted with droplets. Her small suitcase rests at her feet. She has spent the week with her cousins in Kent. Come May, when Felicity and I make our debuts, Ann will go to work for them as governess to their two children. Our only hope for changing her prospects was to enter the realms and attempt to bind the magic to all of us. But no matter how hard I try, I cannot enter the realms. And without the realms, I cannot make the magic flare to life. Not since Christmas have I seen that enchanted world, though in these past few months I have tried dozens of times to get back. There have been moments when I've felt a spark, but it is short-lived, no more consequential than a single drop of rain in a drought. Day by day, our hopes dim, and our futures seem as fixed as the stars.

"Welcome home," I say, helping Ann out of her wet coat.

"Thank you." Her nose runs, and her hair, the color of a field mouse's fur, slips loose of its moorings. Long, thin strands of it hang over her blue eyes and plaster themselves to her full cheeks.

"How was your stay with your cousins?"

Ann does not smile at all. "Tolerable."

"And the children? Are you fond of them?" I ask, hopefully.

"Lottie locked me in a cupboard for an hour. Little Carrie kicked my leg and called me a pudding." She wipes her nose. "That was the first day."

"Oh." We stand uncertainly under the glare of Spence's infamous brass snake chandelier.

Ann lowers her voice to a whisper. "Have you managed to return to the realms?"

I shake my head, and Ann looks as if she might cry. "But we'll try again tonight," I say quickly.

A glimmer of a smile lights Ann's face for a moment. "There's hope yet," I add.

Without a word, Ann follows me to the great hall, past the roaring fires and the ornately carved columns, the girls playing whist. Brigid thrills a small circle of younger girls with tales of fairies and pixies she swears live in the woods behind Spence.

"They don't!" one girl protests, but in her eyes I see she wants to be proven wrong.

"Aye, they do, miss. And more creatures besides. You'd best not go out past dark. That's their time. Stay safe in your beds and you'll not wake to find you've been carried away in the company of the Others," Brigid warns.

The girls rush to the windows to peer into the vast expanse

of night, hoping for a glimpse of fairy queens and sprites. I could tell them they won't see them there. They'd have to travel with us through the door of light to the world beyond this one to keep company with such fantastical creatures. And they might not like all that they see.

"Our Ann has returned," I announce, parting the curtains to Felicity's private tent. Ever the dramatic one, Felicity has cordoned off one corner of the enormous room with silk curtains. It is like a pasha's home, and she lords over it as if it were an empire of her own.

Felicity takes in the sight of Ann's damp, mud-caked skirt hem. "Mind the carpets."

Ann wipes her soiled skirts, dropping crumbs of dried mud onto the floor, and Felicity sighs in irritation. "Oh, Ann, really."

"Sorry," Ann mumbles. She pulls her skirts close to her body and takes a seat on the floor, trying not to dirty it further. Without asking, she reaches into the open chocolate box and takes three, much to Felicity's annoyance.

"You needn't take them all," Fee grumbles.

Ann puts two back. They are imprinted with her hand. Felicity sighs. "You've touched them now; you might as well eat them."

Guiltily, Ann shoves all three into her mouth at once. She cannot possibly be enjoying their taste. "What do you have there?"

"This?" Felicity holds out a white card with beautiful black lettering. "I've received an invitation to Lady Tatterhall's tea for a Miss Hurley. It shall have an Egyptian theme."

"Oh," Ann says dully. Her hand lingers over the chocolate box. "I suppose you've gotten one, too, Gemma."

"Yes," I say guiltily. I hate that Ann's not included—it is beastly unfair—but I can't help wishing she didn't make me feel quite so horrid about it.

"And of course there is the ball at Yardsley Hall," Felicity continues. "That promises to be quite grand. Did you hear about young Miss Eaton?"

I shake my head.

"She wore diamonds before evening!" Felicity nearly squeals with delight. "It was the talk of London. She'll never make that mistake again. Oh, you should see the gloves Mother sent round for the Collinsworth ball. They're exquisite!"

Ann pulls a thread on the hem of her dress. She won't attend the Collinsworth ball or any other unless it is as chaperone to Lottie or Carrie someday. She will not have a season or dance with handsome suitors. She will not wear ostrich feathers in her hair and bow to Her Majesty. She is here at Spence as a scholarship student, sponsored by her wealthy cousins so that she might make an appropriate governess to their children.

I clear my throat. Felicity catches my eye.

"Ann," she says, far too cheerfully. "How was your time in Kent? Is it as lovely in the spring as they say?"

"Little Carrie called me a pudding."

Felicity tries not to laugh. "Ahem. Well, she's only a child. You'll have her in hand soon enough."

"There's a small room for me at the top of the stairs. It looks out on the stables."

"A window. Yes, well, quite nice to have a view," Felicity says, missing the point entirely. "Oh, what do you have there?"

Ann shows us a program for a production of *Macbeth* at the Drury Lane Theatre, starring the great American actress Lily

Trimble. Ann gazes longingly at the dramatic drawing of Miss Trimble as Lady Macbeth.

"Did you attend?" I ask.

Ann shakes her head. "My cousins went."

Without her. Everyone who knows Ann at all knows how much she adores plays.

"But they let you keep the program," Felicity says. "That's quite nice."

Yes, just as a cat that lets a mouse keep its tail is nice. Felicity can be so beastly at times.

"Did you have a fine birthday?" Ann says.

"Yes, ever so enjoyable," Felicity purrs. "Eighteen. What a glorious age. Now I shall come into my inheritance. Well, not straightaway, mind. My grandmother did insist I make my debut as a condition of her will. The moment I curtsy before the Queen and back away again, I shall be a rich woman, and I may do as I please."

"Once you make your debut," Ann repeats, swallowing the last of her chocolate.

Felicity takes a chocolate for herself. "Lady Markham has already announced her intention to sponsor me. So it's as good as done. Felicity Worthington, heiress." Fee's good spirits vanish. "I only wish Pippa were here to share it."

Ann and I exchange glances at the mention of Pip. Once, she was one of us. Now she is somewhere in the realms, most likely lost to the Winterlands. Who knows what she has become? But Fee still clings to the hope that she might be found, might yet be saved.

The tent opens. Cecily, Elizabeth, and Martha crowd inside. It is far too close with all of us here. Elizabeth falls into Felicity while Martha and Cecily take a seat next to me. Ann is pushed to the very back of the tent.

"I've just had an invitation to a ball hosted by the Duchess of Crewesbury," Cecily says. She settles herself on the floor like a spoiled Persian cat.

"And I as well," Elizabeth adds.

Felicity does her best to look bored. "My mother received ours ages ago."

I haven't received such an invitation, and I hope no one will ask me if I have.

Martha fans herself, grimacing. "Oh, dear. It is rather close in here, isn't it? I'm afraid we cannot all fit." She glances at Ann. Cecily and her lot have never treated Ann as more than a servant, but since our unfortunate attempt to pass her off in society as a duke's daughter of Russian blood last Christmas, Ann has become a complete pariah. The gossip has spread in letters and whispers and now there isn't a girl at Spence who doesn't know the story.

"We shall miss you dearly, Cecily," I say, smiling brightly. I should like to kick her squarely in the teeth.

Cecily makes it quite clear she won't be the one to leave. She spreads out her skirts, taking up even more space. Martha whispers in Elizabeth's ear and they break into tittering. I could ask what they are laughing about, but they won't tell me, so there's no point.

"What is that smell?" Martha asks, making a face.

Cecily sniffs dramatically. "Caviar, perhaps? All the way from Russia! Why, it must be from the czar himself!"

The venal little trolls. Ann's cheeks blaze and her lips quiver. She stands so quickly she nearly topples over as she rushes for the tent's flaps. "If you'll excuse me, I've needlework to finish."

"Please do give my best to your uncle, the duke," Cecily calls after her, and the others snicker.

"Why must you taunt her so?" I ask.

"She doesn't deserve to be here," Cecily says with easy certainty.

"That isn't true," I say.

"Isn't it? Some people simply don't belong." Cecily fixes me with a haughty stare. "I've recently heard your father is unwell and resting at Oldham. How worried you must be. Pray, what is his affliction?"

All Cecily lacks is a forked tongue, for she is certainly a snake beneath that beautiful dress.

"Influenza," I say, the lie tasting sharp in my mouth.

"Influenza," she repeats, glancing slyly at the others.

"But he is much improved, and I shall pay him a visit tomorrow."

Cecily doesn't yield just yet. "I am glad to know it, for one hears such unsavory stories at times—gentlemen being found in opium dens and forced into sanitariums for it. Scandalous."

"Cecily Temple, I shall not hear slander this evening," Felicity warns.

"It is influenza," I repeat, but my voice has lost its steadiness.

Cecily's smile is triumphant. "Yes, of course it is."

I hurry after Ann, calling her name, but she doesn't stop. Instead, she quickens her pace till she's nearly running, desperate to be away from us and our talk of parties and teas. All that glittering promise close enough to touch but not to have.

"Ann, please," I say, stopping at the bottom of the stairs. She's halfway up. "Ann, you mustn't pay them any mind. They're not true girls. They are hideous fiends—troglodytes in ringlets!"

If I'd hoped to make Ann laugh, I'd missed my mark. "But

they are the ones who rule," she says without looking up. "They always have and they always shall."

"But, Ann, they've not seen the things you have in the realms. They don't know what you've done. You turned rocks to butterflies and sailed through a curtain of gold. You saved us from the water nymphs with your song."

"Once," she says flatly. "What does any of it matter? It won't change my fate, will it? Come May, you and Felicity will have your season. I shall go to work for my cousins. It will end, and we'll never see each other again."

For a moment, she looks into my eyes, obviously hoping to find comfort there. *Tell me I am wrong; tell me you've got another trick up your sleeve, Gemma,* her eyes plead. But she isn't wrong, and I'm not quick or glib enough to lie. Not tonight.

"Don't let them win, Ann. Come back to the tent."

She doesn't look at me, but I can feel her disgust. "You don't understand, do you? They've already won." And with that, she retreats into the shadows.

I could return to Fee and the others, but I'm in no humor for it. A melancholy has settled over my heart and will not yield, and I want solitude. I find a proper reading chair in the great hall far away from the chatter of girls. I've read no more than a few pages when I notice that I am only an arm's length away from the infamous column. It is one of the many odd touches at Spence. There is the chandelier of carved snakes in the foyer. The leering gargoyles upon the roof. The ridiculous ostrich-feather paper on the walls. The portrait of Spence's founder, Eugenia Spence, looming at the top of the stairs, her piercing blue eyes seeing all. I would count among these oddities the giant hearths that seem less like mantels and more like the open maws of terrible beasts. And then there is this column in the center of the great room. It boasts carvings of fairies, satyrs, sprites, nymphs, and imps of all sorts.

It is also alive.

Or it was once. Those "carvings" are realms creatures stuck here for eternity. Once, we foolishly brought them to life with the magic, and we were nearly destroyed by it. Some of the mischievous creatures tried to escape; others attempted to compromise our virtue. In the end, we forced them back to their prison.

I peer closely at those tiny bodies frozen in stone. The creatures' mouths are open in a scream of anger. Their eyes stare through me. If they got loose, I shouldn't want to be here. Though it frightens me, I'm compelled to touch the column. My fingers come to rest on a fairy's rigid wings, stopped in midflight. A shudder passes through me, and I lay my palm elsewhere. It lands on a satyr's snarling lips, and my heartbeat quickens, for I feel a curious mixture of fascination and repulsion. I close my eyes and allow my fingers to explore the rough grooves and rises of its threatening mouth, the tongue, the lips, the teeth.

My fingers slip on the stone; a harsh edge cuts my skin. I gasp at the pain. Blood beads in the slim crevice. I've no handkerchief, so I plunge my finger into my mouth, tasting the bitter tang of it. The column is silent, but I can feel its menace in the throb of my injury. I move my chair closer to Brigid's comforting patter, her motherly maxims, and far away from the column's dangerous beauty.

At ten o'clock, our eyes heavy and our bodies longing for the warmth of blankets and the forgetting of sleep, we girls climb the stairs to our rooms for the night.

Felicity squeezes past me. "Half past twelve. The usual spot," she whispers. She does not wait for my nod. She has given the order and that is all.

The lamps still burn softly in my room. Ann is asleep, but she has left the sewing scissors where I can see them. The blades are closed, but I know they have done their work marking the insides of her arms. I know she is covered in fresh welts that will soon blend into the tapestry of old scars woven into her flesh. If I had a way into the realms again, a way to the magic, I might be able to help her. But for now, I cannot change her fate. I can only wonder if she will.

CHAPTER FOUR

When I first arrived at the Spence Academy for Young Ladies, I knew nothing of its past and its relation to my life. I had come in mourning weeds, my mother having died only months before. Cholera was the official explanation for her death. But I knew better. In a vision I had seen her die, hunted by a hideous wraith from another world, a tracker, that meant to take her soul had she not taken her own life in self-defense.

It was the first of my visions but not the last. I came to have many of them. I had inherited a power; a lineage passed from my mother to me, a gift in some ways, a curse in others. It was here at Spence that I learned of my bond to a world beyond this one, a world of extraordinary power called the realms.

For centuries, the realms were ruled by a powerful tribe of priestesses called the Order. Together, they used the realms magic to help the dead complete their souls' tasks when needed and cross the river. Over time, their power grew. They could cast grand illusions, influence people and events in the mortal world. But their greatest duty was to keep the balance between good and evil within the realms. For there are many tribes there, and some of them—the malevolent creatures of the Winterlands—would do anything to seize control of the magic, that they might rule the realms and perhaps our world as well. To keep the magic safe, the Order sealed it in a circle of runes. Only they could draw upon its power then. The other tribes of the realms grew disenchanted and resentful. They wanted to have equal say.

Even the Order's allies became untrustworthy over time. The Order was once united in protecting the realms with the Rakshana. These men kept law there and watched over the priestesses. They were also their lovers. But they, too, grew resentful of the Order's control over the realms and its great magic.

And so it had been for ages: every side grappling to hold the magic—until the fire twenty-five years ago. On that night, my mother and her best friend offered a sacrifice—a young Gypsy girl—to the Winterlands creatures in exchange for power. But something went wrong. The child was accidentally killed, and thus her soul could not be taken. Enraged, the creatures demanded the girls themselves, for they had foolishly entered into the bargain, and now it would be honored, one way or another. To save the lives of my mother and Sarah, Eugenia Spence, the Order's great teacher and the founder of Spence Academy, gave herself to the Winterlands creatures in payment for the girls' terrible deed. Her last act was to throw her amulet to my mother. Eugenia closed the realms, sealed them so that no one and nothing could go in or come out until a powerful priestess was born, one who could open the realms again and chart a new course for the magical world.

I am that girl. And no one seems at all happy about it. The Order thinks me headstrong and foolish. The Rakshana find me dangerous. They sent one of their own, a young man named Kartik, to watch me, to warn me not to enter the realms, and when that did not work, they told him to kill me. Instead, he betrayed his brotherhood and saved my life, putting a price on his own head.

They may not like it, but the facts are these: I was the one who was able to open the realms again, and so far, no one may enter without my help. I was the one who broke the seal on the magic by shattering the runes. And I was the one to find the source of the magic, in a protected place called the Temple. It was at the Temple that I fought Circe, my mother's foe and an enemy of the Order, to keep the magic safe. In so doing, I killed her and bound the magic to myself for safekeeping. I promised to join hands with my friends, with Kartik, and with the tribes of the realms to make an alliance, with a share of magic for all.

But since that time, I've had no visions and no way to enter the realms. I haven't a clue why this has happened. I know only that each time I have tried to make the door of light that leads into the other world, it has not come. Instead, I am tormented by a momentary glimpse of Circe, as I left her, trapped beneath the surface of the well of eternity inside the Temple. Lost forever in that magical well turned watery grave.

I am the one who must decide the future of the realms and their power, and I haven't the slightest idea how to get back.

Right.

But tonight will be a different story. We'll find our way in. I shall find my courage. I shall feel the magic spark in my veins again. My friends and I will step into the fragrant gardens of the realms, and a new chapter will begin.

For if not, I fear that the realms are lost to us for good.

When the school is dark and silent, and the day's merry schoolgirl chatter is no more than an echo's echo in Spence's halls, Ann and I tiptoe to meet Felicity near the stairs. The East Wing sleeps tonight—no hammers to disturb us. Yet it has a power all its own.

Be silent, East Wing. I shall not listen to your whispers this evening.

Felicity has something cupped in her hand.

"What do you have there?" I ask.

She opens her hand to show us a dainty lace handkerchief. "It's for Pippa, if we see her."

"It's very nice. She'll adore it," I say, because I shan't be the one to take Felicity's hope away.

We follow her down the long staircase. Our shadows stretch taller as we descend, as if they would reach for the safety of our beds. We slip into the great hall, to Felicity's tent, and sit on the floor, legs crossed, as we have so many times before.

Ann chews her bottom lip and watches me.

"Ready?" Felicity asks.

I take a shaky breath and let it out. "Yes. Let's begin."

We clasp hands, and I do my best to clear my mind, to think of nothing but the realms. I see the green of the garden, the Caves of Sighs rising high over the singing river. That enchanted world begins to take shape behind my eyes.

"Do you see it yet?" Ann interrupts.

The view of the garden fades like a wisp of smoke. "Ann!"

"Sorry," she mumbles.

"You mustn't unsettle her nerves!" Felicity scolds. She squeezes my hands. "Just remember, Gemma, the whole of our futures rests with you."

Yes, thank you. I'm ever so calmed by that. "I shall need absolute quiet, if you please."

Dutifully, they bow their heads and shut their mouths, and, already, it is like a stroke of magic.

Come now, Gemma. You mustn't think you can't. Imagine the door. It will come. Make it come. Will it to be.

The door doesn't appear. I see nothing, feel nothing. Panic takes hold, whispering now-familiar questions through my soul: What if the gift was only borrowed? What if I've lost it forever? What if it's all been a mistake and I'm only ordinary after all?

I open my eyes, try to steady my breathing. "I need a moment."

"We shouldn't have waited so long to try," Felicity grouses. "We should have gone in straightaway, in January. Why did we wait?"

"I wasn't ready to return then," I say.

"You were waiting for him to come back," Felicity says. "Well, he's not coming."

"I wasn't waiting for Kartik," I snap, stung through and through. She's partly right, of course. But only partly. An image of Miss Moore drifts into my head. I see her determined jaw, the pocket watch in her hand, the way she looked when she was our beloved teacher, before we knew her to be Circe. Before I killed her. "I . . . I wasn't ready yet. That's all."

Felicity fixes me with a cool stare. "You did nothing to be sorry for. She deserved to die."

"Let's try again," Ann says. She offers her hands, and I see the bumpy welts of this evening's little cuts.

"Right. Third time's the charm," I joke, though I'm anything but lighthearted.

I close my eyes and slow my breathing, trying again to clear my mind of everything but the realms and a way in. Heat pools in my stomach, teasing. It is like repeatedly striking a dull match that will not burn. *Come on, come on.* For a moment, it flares to life, the familiar fire catching on the tinder of my desires. I see the softly swaying olive trees in the garden. The sweet river. And I see the door of light. Ha! Oh, yes! I have missed this! Now I need only to make it stay. . . .

The image fades, and in its place, I see Circe's ghostly face beneath the cold water of the well. Her eyes snap open. "Gemma . . ."

With a gasp, I break off, and the power is gone. I can feel the realms receding like a tide I'm helpless to pull to the shore. No matter how much I try to get it back, I can't.

Ann lets go first. She's accustomed to disappointment and quicker to recognize defeat. "I'm going to bed."

"I'm sorry," I whisper. The weight of their unhappiness makes it hard to breathe. "I don't know what has happened."

Felicity shakes her head. "I don't understand how this could be. You bound the magic to yourself. We should be able to get it without any trouble at all."

We should, but we can't. I can't. And with each failed attempt, my confidence wanes. What if I should never get back?

Long after my friends have gone to sleep, I sit in my bed, hugging my knees to my chest with my eyes closed tight. I beg the door of light to appear with a single repeated word. *Please, please, please* . . . I beg until my voice is raspy with tears and desperation, till the early dawn casts its unforgiving light on me, till I am left with only what I cannot bring myself to say—that I have lost my magic, and that I am nothing without it.

CHAPTER FIVE

THE OLDHAM SANITARIUM, AN HOUR'S TRAIN RIDE FROM London, is a large white estate surrounded by a vast, pleasing lawn. Several chairs have been set out so that the residents may take some sun as often as they like.

As promised, Tom and I have come to visit Father. I've not wanted to see him in this place. I prefer to think of him always in his study by a robust fire, his pipe in one hand, a twinkle in his eye and a fantastic tale at the ready to entertain all. But I suppose even the Oldham Sanitarium is a far better memory than the one I have of my father in an East London opium den, so lost on the drug that he'd bartered even his wedding ring for more.

No, I shan't think about that. Not today.

"Remember, Gemma, you're to be cheerful and light," Tom—my older, yet sadly not wiser, brother—advises as we stroll down the great expanse of lawn past neatly trimmed hedges with nary a stray branch or errant weed to disturb their careful symmetry. I smile brightly at a passing nurse. "I think I shall remember how to behave without your good counsel, Thomas," I say through clenched teeth.

"I do wonder."

Honestly, what use are brothers except to torment and irritate at equal turns?

"Really, Thomas, you should take more care at breakfast. You've an egg stain big as life on your shirt."

Tom paws at himself, panicked. "I don't see it!"

"Right"—I tap the side of his head—"here."

"What?"

"April Fools'."

His mouth twists into a smirk. "But it's not yet April."

"Yes," I say, marching ahead at a good clip. "And yet you are still a fool."

A nurse in a starched white pinafore points us toward a small sitting area near a gazebo. A man sits stretched out on a reclining caned-back chair, a plaid blanket across his legs. I don't recognize Father at first. He is so very thin.

Tom clears his throat. "Hello, Father. You're looking well."

"Yes, better each day. Gemma, pet, you've grown more beautiful, I think."

He only glances at me as he says this. We don't look at each other anymore. Not really. Not since I pulled him from that opium den. Now when I look at him, I see the addict. And when he looks at me, he sees what he would rather not remember. I wish I could be his adored little girl again, sitting at his side.

"You're too kind, Father." *Light and cheerful, Gemma.* I give a pained smile. He is so thin.

"Fine day, is it not?" Father says.

"Indeed. A very fine day."

"The gardens here are quite lovely," I say.

"Yes. Quite," Tom seconds.

Father nods absently. "Ah."

I perch on the edge of my seat, ready to go at a moment's notice. I offer him a box wrapped in elaborate gold foil and garnished with a big red bow. "I've brought you those peppermints you're so fond of."

"Ah," he says, taking them without enthusiasm. "Thank you, pet. Thomas, have you given any thought to the Hippocrates Society?"

Tom scowls.

"What is the Hippocrates Society?" I ask.

"A fine gentlemen's club of scientists and physicians, great thinkers all. They've expressed an interest in our Thomas."

This seems a fine match for Tom, as he's a clinical assistant at Bethlem Royal Hospital—Bedlam—and, despite his many faults, a gifted healer. Medicine and science are his twin passions, so I cannot understand his sneer at the Hippocrates Society.

"I have no interest in them," Tom says firmly.

"Why not?"

"Most of their members are between the ages of forty and death," Tom sniffs.

"There is great wisdom in those halls, Thomas. You'd be wise to honor that."

Tom takes one of the peppermints. "It is not the Athenaeum Club."

"Setting your sights a bit high, aren't you, old boy? The

Athenaeum takes only its own, and we are not its own," Father says decisively.

"I might be," Tom contends.

Tom wants desperately to be accepted into the very finest of London society. Father thinks him foolish for it. I do hate it when they argue, and I don't want Tom to upset Father just now.

"Papa, I hear you shall come home soon," I say.

"Yes, so they tell me. Fit as a fiddle, your old man." He coughs.

"How nice that will be," Tom says without enthusiasm.

"Quite," Father agrees.

And with that we fall into silence. A flock of geese wander across the lawn as if they, too, have lost their way. A groundskeeper shoos them toward a pond in the distance. But there is no one to help us onto a new path, and so we sit, talking of nothing that matters and avoiding all mention of anything that does. At last, a moonfaced nurse with coppery hair going to gray approaches.

"Good day to you, Mr. Doyle. It's time for the waters, sir."

Father smiles in relief. "Miss Finster, like a ray of sunshine on a gloomy morning, you arrive and all is well."

Miss Finster grins as if her face will break. "A charmer, your father is."

"Well, off you go, then," Father says to us. "Wouldn't want to miss your train to London."

"True, true." Tom's already backing away. We've been here less than an hour. "We'll see you home in two weeks' time, Father."

"Quite right," Miss Finster says. "Though we'll be sorry to see him go."

"Yes, well," Tom says. He pushes an errant lock from his forehead but it only falls into his eyes again. There is no handshake or embrace. We smile and nod and leave each other as quickly as possible, relieved to be free of one another and the awkward silences. Yet I also feel ashamed at that sense of relief. I wonder if other families are the same. They seem so content to be together. They fit, like the parts of a puzzle already finished, the image clearly evident. But we are like those odd remaining pieces, the ones that can't be joined securely with a satisfying "Ah, that's it, then."

Father takes Miss Finster's arm like a proper gentleman. "Miss Finster, will you do me the honor?"

Miss Finster offers a schoolgirl laugh, though she is surely as old as Mrs. Nightwing. "Oh, Mr. Doyle. Go on!"

Arm in arm, they stroll toward the large white building. Father turns his head ever so slightly toward us. "I'll see you for Easter."

Yes, in two weeks, we'll be together again.

But I doubt he will really see me at all.

✶✶✶✶

I take Tom to task on the carriage ride to London. "Thomas, really, why must you bait Father as you do?"

"That's it. Defend him as you always do. The favorite."

"I'm not his favorite. He loves us equally." Saying it gives me a queer feeling in my stomach, though, like telling a lie.

"That's what they say, isn't it? Pity it isn't true," he says, bitterly. Suddenly, he brightens. "As it happens, he was wrong about the Athenaeum Club. I've been invited to dine there with Simon Middleton and Lord Denby."

At the mention of Simon's name, all breath leaves me. "How is Simon?" I ask.

"Handsome. Charming. Rich. In short, quite well." Tom gives me a little smile, and I can't help feeling he's rather enjoying himself at my expense.

Simon Middleton, one of England's most sought-after bachelors, is indeed all those things. He courted me quite fervently over Christmas and meant to marry me, but I refused him. And suddenly, I cannot remember why.

"It is premature to say," Tom continues, "but I believe old Denby will put me forth for membership. Despite your rather shoddy treatment of Simon, Gemma, I do know that his father remains a champion of mine. More so than Father."

"Did . . . Simon say that I had treated him shabbily?"

"No. He didn't mention you at all."

"How lovely it will be to see the Middletons again," I say, pretending his words haven't hurt me in the least. "I'm sure Simon must be happily squiring young ladies about town?" I give a little laugh meant to sound cavalier.

"Mmmm," Tom says. "I don't know."

"But they are in London currently?" My smile falters. *Come on, Thomas. Throw me a bone, you miserable cur of a brother.*

"They will be soon. They've a distant cousin from America who shall come to visit for the season, a Miss Lucy Fairchild. Worth a fortune, as I understand it." Tom smiles smugly. "Perhaps you could arrange an introduction for me. Or perhaps once I am a member in good standing of the Athenaeum, she shall ask to be introduced to me."

No. It is impossible to maintain a smile in my brother's presence. Monks haven't the sort of patience required.

"I don't see why you should care so much about the Athenaeum," I say irritably.

Tom chuckles in a most condescending way and I cannot help imagining him immersed in a large cauldron surrounded by hungry, fire-wielding cannibals. "You wouldn't, would you, Gemma? You don't wish to belong to anyone or anything at all."

"At least the members of the Hippocrates Society are men of science and medicine," I say, ignoring his slight. "They share your interests."

"They do not garner the respect that the Athenaeum Club does. That is where the real power lies. And I hear the men of Hippocrates may vote to allow women to join them in a lesser capacity." My brother snorts. "Women! In a gentlemen's club!"

"I like them already," I say.

He smirks. "You would."

CHAPTER SIX

THE LAST TIME I SAW OUR HOUSE IN BELGRAVIA, IT WAS cloaked in the starkness of winter. As our carriage winds through Hyde Park, we are greeted by the glorious sight of budding trees standing as proud as the royal guard. Daffodils show off their new yellow bonnets. London smiles.

Not so our housekeeper, Mrs. Jones. She greets me at the door in her black dress and white pinafore, a white doily of a cap on her head, and such a severe expression that I consider putting a glass to her mouth to see if there is still breath issuing from it.

"How was your journey, miss?" she asks without enthusiasm.

"Very pleasant, thank you."

"Very good, miss. I'll have your case brought to your room, then?"

"Yes, thank you."

We take such pains to be polite. We never say what we mean. For all it matters, we could greet each other and speak only of cheese—"How was your Limburger, miss?""Salty as a ripe Stinking Bishop, thank you.""Ah, very cheddar, miss. I'll have your Stilton brought to your Camembert, then."—and no one would likely notice.

"Your grandmother waits for you in the parlor, miss."

"Thank you." I cannot help myself. "I'll see myself into the Muenster."

"As you wish, miss."

And there we are, though it is a pity my wickedness has been wasted with no one to appreciate it but me.

"You're late," Grandmama announces the moment I open the doors to the parlor. I don't know why she's blaming me, as I was neither the driver nor the horse. She casts a disapproving eye over me from head to toe. "We've a tea to attend at Mrs. Sheridan's. You'll want to change, of course. And what has happened to your hair? Is this the fashion at Spence these days? It won't do. Stand still." Grandmama pulls my hair up so tightly that my eyes water. She sticks in three pins that nearly impale my skull. "Much improved. A lady must always be at her best."

She rings a bell and our housekeeper arrives like a phantom. "Yes, mum?"

"Mrs. Jones, Miss Doyle shall need assistance in dressing. Her gray wool, I should think. And another pair of gloves that do not look as if they're the charwoman's," she says, scowling at the smudges on my fingertips.

I've been home less than a minute, and already, I am under siege. I take in the dim parlor—the heavy burgundy velvet drapes, the dark green papered walls, the mahogany desk and bookcases, the Oriental rug, and the enormous fern in a heavy pot. "This room could do with a bit of light." *Hah.* If it's criticism she wants, two may play at that game.

Grandmama's face furrows into worry. "It is a fashionable room, is it not? Do you say that it is not fashionable?"

"I didn't say that. Only that it would be nice to let in the light."

Grandmama eyes the drapes as if considering. But it is short-lived and she once again regards me as a village's missing idiot. "The sun will only fade the settee. And now, if we have dispensed with matters of decorating, you would do well to dress. We leave at half past."

⌁⌁⌁⌁⌁

A silent maid welcomes us to Mrs. Sheridan's well-appointed library. The sight of so many books comforts me, which is more than I can say for the gray wool suit. It chafes and itches till I could scream. Mrs. Jones has laced me so tightly in my corset that if I dare take two sips of tea, one shall surely come out again. Five other girls have come with their mothers. I am horrified to find that I do not know any of them, though they seem to know each other. Even worse, not a one has been forced to wear drab wool. They look as fresh as spring, whilst I resemble the spinster aunt every girl dreads as chaperone. It is all I can do not to confide to the girl closest to me: "If I should die during tea—asphyxiated by my own corset—please do not let them bury me in such a hideous dress or I shall come back to haunt you."

I'm under no illusions that this is simply tea; it is a marketplace, and we girls are the wares. While the mothers talk, we sip our tea silently, our smiles mirroring theirs as if we are players in a pantomime. I must remember to speak only when spoken to, to echo the sentiments of others. We work in concert to maintain the clear, pretty surface of this life, never daring to make a splash.

With each question, each glance, we are being measured in the exacting scales of their minds, teetering in the balance between their expectations and their disappointments. This one laughs too frequently. That one's hair is coarse, her skin ruddy. That girl wears a dour expression; still another stirs her tea far too long, while one unfortunate girl daringly ventures that she finds the rain "romantic," and is told quite firmly that the rain is good only for the roses and for bringing on rheumatism. No doubt her mother will scold her mercilessly in the carriage and blame the misdeed squarely on the governess.

For a brief while, the women ask us questions: Are we looking forward to our debuts? Did we enjoy this opera or that play? As we give our slight answers, they smile, and I cannot read what is behind their expressions. Do they envy us our youth and beauty? Do they feel happiness and excitement for the lives that lie ahead of us? Or do they wish for another chance at their own lives? A different chance?

Soon the mothers tire of asking us questions. They fall into talk that does not concern us. During a tour of Mrs. Sheridan's gardens—of which she is exceedingly proud, though it is the gardener who has done all the work—we are left to our own devices, thank goodness. The trained masks melt away.

"Have you seen Lady Markham's tiara? Isn't it exquisite? I'd give anything to wear a tiara such as that, even for a moment."

"Speaking of Lady Markham, I suppose you have heard the gossip?" a girl named Annabelle says.

The others are immediately drawn in. "Annabelle, what is it? What has happened?"

Annabelle sighs heavily but there is a certain joy in it, as if she has been bottled up all this time, waiting for a chance to share her news. "I am burdened with a confidence I will disclose only if you make promises not to share it with anyone else."

"Oh, yes!" the girls promise, no doubt thinking of who shall be first to hear the unfortunate tale.

"I have heard that Lady Markham has had a change of heart and that she may not present Miss Worthington at court after all."

The girls put gloved hands to mouths but their glee shows like a slipped petticoat. They're glad for the gossip and doubly glad it's not about them. I don't know what to say. Should I tell them that Felicity and I are friends? Do they know?

The chorus begins: "Oh, dear. Poor Felicity." "What a scandal." "But she is so very cheeky." "Quite right. It is her own fault." "I do adore her, but . . ." "Indeed."

Annabelle cuts in. Clearly, she is the queen bee among them. "Her independence does not endear her to the ladies who matter. And then there is the question of her mother."

"Oh, what is it? I do hate my governess, for she never tells me a thing!" a girl with apple cheeks and a dainty mouth says.

Annabelle's eyes twinkle. "Three years ago, Mrs. Worthington went abroad whilst her husband, the admiral, was at sea. But everyone knows she ran off to Paris to be with her lover! If Admiral Worthington were not the hero he is and a favorite of Her Majesty's, Miss Worthington would have no place at all in decent society."

I know a great deal about the horrors the admiral has visited upon his daughter, how he went to her bedroom late at night as no father should. But I swore to keep that secret for Fee, and who would believe it even if the truth were told? People have a habit of inventing fictions they will believe wholeheartedly in order to ignore the truth they cannot accept.

"But there is more," Annabelle says.

"Tell! Tell!"

"I overheard Mother telling Mrs. Twitt that if Miss Worthington does not make her debut, her inheritance is forfeit. Her grandmother's will states most emphatically that she must make her debut 'as a lady in fine moral standing,' else the money shall go to the Foundling Hospital, and Felicity will be at the mercy of the admiral to chart her course."

Felicity wants nothing more than to have her freedom. But now she's in danger of losing that dream. I cannot keep the blood from rising in me. My cheeks must be crimson for all to see. If I could, I would box Annabelle's lovely ears. My corset's too tight, for I can scarcely breathe. My skin tingles; my head is light, and for a moment, it is as if I leave my body.

"Ow!" Annabelle cries, turning to the girl beside her. "Constance Lloyd! How dare you pinch me!"

Constance's mouth opens in a surprised O. "I didn't!"

"You most certainly did. I can feel the bruise rising on my arm!"

The other girls try to contain their glee as Constance and Annabelle engage in a war of martyrdom. The lightheadedness I felt a moment earlier has vanished, and I feel strangely fine, better than I have in ages.

"When I mentioned we might host an English garden party, Mrs. Sheridan gave me the queerest look. Do you suppose she thought it too ordinary? I felt it would make quite a nice party. Don't you?"

Grandmama has pestered me for the entire carriage ride home with such natter. She frets constantly over every possible slight or imagined judgment. Just once I wish she would live her life and not care so much about what others think.

Of course, I've my own fretting. How can I tell Felicity what I've heard without upsetting her? How does anyone talk sense to Felicity? It is like trying to tame a force of nature.

"I think an English garden party is quite lovely and appropriate. It isn't a Turkish ball, granted, but even Her Majesty finds such displays unseemly. Was it discussed among the young ladies? Did they find fault with it?"

"No, it was not discussed." I sigh, leaning my head against the side of the carriage. The London gas fog is settling in. The streets are murky, the people appearing like phantoms. I spy a young man with dark curls and a newsboy cap, and my heart leaps. I half lean out the window.

"Pardon me! You there! Sir!" I call.

"Gemma Doyle!" my grandmother gasps.

The young man turns. It's not Kartik. He offers the day's news. "Paper, miss?"

"No," I say, swallowing hard. "No, thank you." I settle back against the seat, determined not to look again and raise my hopes unnecessarily. *Where are you, Kartik?*

"That was most impolite," my grandmother tuts. Her eyes narrow with a new thought. "Did they find something wanting in you, Gemma, at the party? You didn't speak too freely or behave . . . strangely?"

I grew claws and bayed at the moon. I confessed that I eat the hearts of small children. I told them I like the French. Why is the fault always mine?

"We spoke of Mrs. Sheridan's flowers," I say evenly.

"Well, nothing wrong in that," my grandmother says, reassuring herself. "No, nothing at all."

⌇⌇⌇⌇⌇

By late evening of my last night in London, my misery has reached operatic proportions. Grandmama takes to her bed early, "exhausted" by the day's events. Tom is to dine at the Athenaeum at the behest of Lord Denby.

"When I return, I shall be a great man," he says, admiring himself in the mirror over the mantel. He has a new top hat, and it makes him look like a well-heeled scarecrow.

"I shall practice my genuflecting whilst you are away," I respond.

Tom turns to me with a sneer. "I'd send you to a nunnery, but even those saintly women haven't the patience for your petulance. But please don't see me out," he says, striding for the door with a spring in his step. "I shouldn't want to interrupt your sulking by the fireside."

"You needn't worry," I say, turning back to the fire with a sigh. "You shan't."

My season has not even begun and already I feel a failure. It's as if I've inherited a skin I cannot quite fit, and so I walk about constantly pulling and tugging, pinning and pruning, trying desperately to fill it out, hoping that no one will look at me struggling and say, "That one there—she's a fraud. Look how she doesn't suit at all."

If only I could get into the realms. Oh, what is happening there? Why can't I get in? What has become of the magic? Where are my visions? To think I once feared them. Now the power I cursed is the only thing I long for.

Not the only thing. But I've no power over Kartik, either.

I stare into the fire, watching the fat orange flames jumping about, demanding attention. Deep inside each one, a thin blue soul burns pure and hot, devouring every bit of tinder to keep the fire going.

The mantel clock ticks off the seconds; the steady sound lulls me into drowsiness. Sleep comes and I am lost to dreaming.

I'm enveloped by a thick mist. Before me is an enormous ash tree, its twisted arms reaching up toward a vanished sun. A voice calls to me.

Come to me. . . .

My pulse quickens, but I can see no one.

You're the only one who can save us, save the realms. You must come to me. . . .

"Can't get in," I murmur.

There is another way—a secret door. Trust in the magic. Let it lead you there.

"I have no magic anymore. . . ."

You're wrong. Your power is extraordinary. It builds within you and wants release. Unleash your power. That's what they fear, what you must not fear. I can help you, but you must come to me. Open the door. . . .

The scene shifts. I am inside the Caves of Sighs before the well of eternity. Below the icy surface of the water lies Miss Moore, her dark hair spreading out like Kali's. She floats beneath her glass prison, lovely as Ophelia, frightening as a storm cloud. I feel a shudder across the very marrow of my bones.

"You're dead," I gasp. "I killed you."

Her eyes snap open. "You're wrong, Gemma. I live."

I wake with a start to find myself still in the chair, the mantel clock showing half past eleven. I feel odd, feverish. Strands of hair hang limp by my mouth, and my blood pumps ferociously. I feel as if I've been visited by a ghost.

It was only a dream, Gemma. Let it alone. Felicity's right—Circe's dead, and if her blood is on your hands, you've nothing to feel shamed about. But I cannot stop shivering. And what of the other part of the dream? A door. What I wouldn't give for a way back into the realms, to the magic. I'd not be frightened of it this time. I'd cherish it.

Hot tears spring to my eyes. I'm useless. I can't enter the realms. I can't help my friends or my father. I can't find Kartik. I can't even be merry at a garden party. I've no place. I poke at the dying fire, but it falls to splinters. Seems I'm hopeless at that, as well. I toss the poker to the floor and bang my hand upon the mantel. I should like to drown in heat and banish the shivers.

My fingers tingle; my arms tremble. The same dizziness I felt earlier returns. I feel as if I might faint.

A sudden hot breath pushes through the mouth of the chimney. The fire blazes to life. With a loud shout, I pull my hand away and fall to the floor. At once, the fire sputters and dies.

I hold my hand in front of my face. Did I do that? My fingertips still tingle ever so slightly. I point them toward the quiet fireplace, but nothing happens. I close my eyes. "I command you to make a fire!" A blackened log splinters and falls to soot. Nothing.

Footsteps *tap-tap* nervously down the hall. Mrs. Jones hastens into the room. "Miss Gemma? What has happened?"

"The fire. It was out, and then it caught all of a sudden so that the whole of the fireplace was aflame."

Mrs. Jones takes the discarded poker to the last of the kindling. "It's out now, miss. Might be soot in the chimney. I'll call the sweep tomorrow first thing."

Tom has come home, and though the hour is late, I hadn't expected him until much later. He pours himself a tumbler of Father's scotch and settles into a chair.

Mrs. Jones casts a disapproving eye. "Good evening, sir. Will you be needing me?"

"No, thank you, Mrs. Jones. You may retire."

"Very good, sir. Miss."

Tom glances at me with contempt. "Isn't it past your bedtime?"

"How could I sleep knowing that the newest member of the Athenaeum Club would grace our home at any moment with his superior presence?" I bow with an excessive flourish and wait for Tom to return the jab. When he doesn't, I'm not entirely sure he's my brother. It isn't like him to let me have the last word without even a feeble attempt to take me down.

"Tom?"

He's slumped in his chair, his tie undone, his eyes red.

"They put Simpson through instead," he says quietly.

"I'm sorry," I say, and I am. I might find Tom's preoccupation with the Athenaeum Club silly, but it matters to him, and it was cruel of them not to have seen it. "Is there anything I can do?"

"Yes," he says, draining the last of his glass. "You can leave me be."

CHAPTER SEVEN

THOUGH I NEVER THOUGHT I'D SAY IT, I'M OVERJOYED TO see the dour, imposing lady that is Spence again. The three days I passed in London were torturous, what with Tom's sulking, Grandmama's constant fussing, and Father's absence. I do not know how I shall survive the season.

And there is that other matter: my troubling dream and the strange occurrence with the fireplace. The sudden flare of fire was only from stubborn soot inside the chimney—the sweep confirmed it. The dream is harder to dismiss, perhaps because I want to believe that there is a secret door into the realms, that the magic still lives inside me. But wishing won't make it true.

The chapel bell tolls, calling us to morning prayers. Dressed in our pristine white uniforms, our hair ribbons securely in place, we traipse the well-worn path up the hill to the old stone-and-beam chapel.

"How was your visit home?" Felicity asks, falling in beside me.

"Hideous," I say.

Felicity grins. "Well, it was an absolute misery here! Cecily insisted on playing charades, as if we are all still in nursery, and then, when Martha guessed hers straightaway, Cecily pouted. It was *Wuthering Heights*, and everyone knows that is her favorite book—it's no mystery."

I laugh at her tale, and for a second, I have the urge to tell her of my dream. But that will only bring up the subject of the realms again, so I think better of it. "It is nice to be back," I say instead.

Felicity's eyes widen in horror. "Are you ill, Gemma? Have you a fever? Honestly, I won't shed a single tear when it is time to say goodbye. I cannot wait to make my debut."

Annabelle's hateful gossip weighs heavily on my soul. "And Lady Markham is to present you, is she not?"

"Yes, as I must have a sponsor to put me forth," Fee says brusquely. "My father may be a naval hero, but my family hasn't the standing yours enjoys."

I ignore the swipe. The sun has blessed us with the first taste of the warm weather to come, and we turn our faces toward it like flowers.

"What sort of woman is Lady Markham?"

"She's one of Lady Denby's followers," Felicity scoffs.

I wince at the mention of Simon's mother. Lady Denby has no love for Felicity or for Mrs. Worthington.

"You know how that sort is, Gemma. They like to be flattered and led to believe that you revere their every word as if it has dropped from Zeus's tongue. 'Why, Lady Markham, I thank you for your good advice.' 'How clever you are, Lady Markham.' 'I shall take it to heart. How fortunate am I to have your counsel, Lady Markham.' They want to own you." Felicity stretches her arms overhead, reaching for the sky. "I shall leave that to my mother."

"And if Lady Markham were not to present you . . . what then?" I ask, my heart in my mouth.

Felicity's arms drop to her sides again. "I'd be done for. If I do not make my debut, my inheritance shall go to the Foundling Hospital, and I shall be at Father's mercy. But that won't happen." She frowns. "I say, you are quite keen on this subject. Have you heard something?"

"No," I say, hesitating.

"You're lying."

There's no getting around it. She'll badger me until I tell her the truth. "Very well. Yes. I heard a bit of gossip in London that Lady Markham was having second thoughts about presenting you to court . . . because of . . . because of your reputation. And I only thought, with so much at stake, perhaps it would be best if you were to . . . to . . . behave." The word is no more than a faint imprint.

Felicity narrows her eyes, but there is hurt in them. "Behave?"

"Just till after your season . . ."

Felicity sneers. "Shall I tremble at every scrap of nasty gossip? I've survived worse. Honestly, Gemma, since you've stopped taking us into the realms you've become a dull mouse of a girl. I hardly know you anymore."

"I only meant to warn you," I protest.

"I don't need warnings; I need a friend," she says. "If you wish to scold me like a schoolmarm, you might as well sit with Nightwing."

She flounces away, joining arms with Elizabeth, and the sun, which felt so warm, is no longer a comfort.

∿∿∿∿

I eschew Nightwing for Ann. The morning sun illuminates the musty chapel's stained-glass windows. It shows the coating of grime on the angels and lends a fierce brightness to the bizarre panel of a lone warrior angel beside a severed gorgon's head.

We bow our heads for prayer. We sing a hymn. And in the end, our French teacher, Mademoiselle LeFarge, reads a poem from William Blake.

> *And did those feet in ancient time*
> *Walk upon England's mountains green?*
> *And was the holy Lamb of God*
> *On England's pleasant pastures seen?*

Will this be my life forevermore? Careful tea parties and the quiet fear that I don't belong, that I'm a fraud? I held magic in my hands! I tasted freedom in a land where summer doesn't end. I outsmarted the Rakshana with a boy whose kiss I still feel somehow. Was it all for naught? I'd rather not have known any of it than have it snatched away after a taste.

With tears threatening, I fix my attention upon the stained glass and the odd mixture of dangerous angels and uncertain warriors to keep my composure. Mademoiselle LeFarge fills the chapel with Mr. Blake's lofty words.

> *And did the Countenance Divine*
> *Shine forth upon our clouded hills?*

And was Jerusalem builded here
Among these dark satanic mills?

Bring me my bow of burning gold!
Bring me my arrows of desire!

Several of the younger girls titter at *desire* and LeFarge must wait for silence before continuing.

Bring me my spear! O clouds unfold!
Bring me my chariot of fire!

I will not cease from mental fight
Nor shall my sword sleep in my hand
Till we have built Jerusalem
In England's green and pleasant land.

LeFarge leaves the pulpit and Mrs. Nightwing takes her place there. "Thank you, Miss LeFarge, for that. Most stirring. The poem reminds us that greatness lies even in the smallest of moments, in the humblest of hearts, and we shall, each of us, be called to greatness. Whether we shall rise to meet it or let it slip away is the challenge put before us all."

Her eyes sweep the room and seem to rest on every girl, bequeathing each of us with an unseen mantle. My earlier urge to giggle vanishes, and a heaviness settles over me like a late spring snow.

"April is nearly upon us; May beckons. And for some of our girls, the time will soon come to leave us."

Beside me, Ann rubs absently at the scars on her arm. I put my hands in hers.

"Every year, we host a small tea to honor our graduates. This year, we shall not."

A low rumble of shock reverberates in the small chapel. The girls lose their grins. Elizabeth looks as if she might cry. "Oh. Oh, no."

"She wouldn't dare," Cecily whispers, horrified. "Would she?"

"Quiet, quiet, please." Mrs. Nightwing's words echo. "It is my great pleasure to tell you that this year, we shall not host a tea but rather a ball."

A surge of excitement ripples through the girls from pew to pew. A ball!

"It is to be a masked ball, a jolly spectacle of costume, held on May Day for patrons and parents. No doubt you have already begun to dream of fairy wings and noble Indian princesses. Perhaps there will be among you a pirate or Nefertiti or a stately Queen Mab."

Another ripple of girlish exhilaration disturbs the calm of the chapel.

"I shall make a splendid Queen Mab," Felicity says. "Don't you think?"

Cecily's outraged. "Why, Felicity Worthington, that was to be my costume."

"Not anymore it isn't. I thought of it first."

"How could you have thought of it first when I did!"

"Ladies! Grace, strength, beauty!" Mrs. Nightwing shouts over the din, reminding us of the Spence motto as well as our manners. We settle like a flower garden after a sudden tempest of wind. "I've another surprise. As you know, our Miss McCleethy has been away these months attending to urgent personal matters. I am pleased to say that her obligations elsewhere are at an end, and she will be returning to us soon. I've a letter, which I shall read aloud." She clears her throat. "'Dear Ladies of Spence, I do hope this letter finds you well. Spring should be shining on our dear school. It must be a lovely sight, and I hope to enjoy it soon. Mrs. Nightwing has asked if I might permanently accept the position vacated by Miss Moore, and I am happy to say that I have accepted. It was not my intention to stay on at Spence, but it seems I am needed there, and I go wherever duty calls. It is my fervent hope to see you all by month's end. Until then, I wish you well with your studies and the best of luck with the porridge.'"

This is followed by laughter, as Spence's porridge is notoriously awful.

"'And for those leaving us soon to take their places in the world, I would ask them to remember their obligations as well as their dreams. Fondly, Your Miss McCleethy.'"

The gust has blown through: The girls fall into merry chatter again. Though I am excited too, I am not entirely at ease. I can't help feeling that this last bit is directed at me, an arrow flying straight from the hard bow of Miss McCleethy's desire to have the Order resume their place within the realms.

The last I saw of Claire Sahirah McCleethy was at Christmastime in London. She pretended to forge an alliance with the Rakshana and tried to force me to take her into the realms. Once I bound the magic to myself, she expected me to return the power to the Order, to join with them on their terms. When I refused, she warned me not to make enemies of them. And then she was gone. Mrs. Nightwing told the girls of Spence little about her absence. Now she's coming back, and I wonder what it bodes for me.

We pour out the chapel's ancient oak doors in twos and threes, talking breathlessly of what is to come.

"I am glad to hear Miss McCleethy's returning. That is welcome news, indeed," Cecily says.

"We should prepare a song or poem to welcome our Miss McCleethy home," Elizabeth trills. Her voice offends my ears at this hour.

Martha's joined the fray. "Oh, yes! I rather like Mr. Shakespeare's sonnets."

"I c-c-could sing for her," Ann offers. She's trailing just behind.

For a moment, no one speaks. "Oh, Elizabeth, you've a lovely voice. Why don't *you* sing for our Miss McCleethy?" Cecily coos, as if Ann never said a word. She reminds me of a bee, seemingly in the business of honey but with a rather nasty sting.

"Yes, do," Martha quickly agrees.

"Then it is settled. Martha and I shall read a sonnet. Elizabeth, you shall sing. Fee, perhaps you'd prepare with us?"

I wish Ann would defend herself, tell Cecily what a toad she is. But she doesn't. Instead, she slows her steps, falling farther behind.

"Ann," I say, holding out a hand. But she won't look at me, won't answer. She makes it clear that I'm one of them now. It's weeks yet until we part but she's already pushing me away.

Fine. Let her. I walk down the path to join the others. The trees wear their new greenery awkwardly still. Through the sparse leaves I spy the East Wing's progress. The turret is striking. I find I cannot help looking at it, as if it were a magnet pulling me in.

Loud shouts and threats erupt from the site and we rush to see what they are about. A group of men stand on the lawn, fists at the ready. When I draw closer, I see they're not the workers; they're Gypsy men. The Gypsies have returned! I search their faces, hoping to catch sight of Kartik. He's traveled with them before. But he's not among their number today, and my heart sinks.

The workers form a line behind their foreman, Mr. Miller. They outnumber the Gypsies two to one, but they keep their hammers close.

"Here now, what is all this fuss? Mr. Miller, why have your men stopped work?" Mrs. Nightwing demands.

"It's these Gypsies, missus," Mr. Miller sneers. "Causin' trouble."

A tall Gypsy with fair hair and a knowing smile steps forward. Ithal is his name. He is the Gypsy Felicity kissed behind the boathouse. Felicity sees him too. Her face goes pale. Hat in hand, he approaches Mrs. Nightwing. "We look for work. We are carpenters. We are building for many people."

"Shove off, mate," Mr. Miller says in a low, tight voice. "This is our job."

"We could work together." Ithal offers his hand. Mr. Miller doesn't take it.

"Oi. These are decent ladies. They don't need no dirty, thieving Gypsies here."

Mrs. Nightwing steps in. "We have had the Gypsies on our land for years. We've had no trouble from them."

Mr. Miller's eyes flash. "I can see yer a fine, charitable lady, mum. But if you show them kindness, they'll never leave. They should go back to their own country."

Ithal holds tight to his hat, bending the brim. "If we go back, they will kill us."

Mr. Miller smiles broadly. "See? Their own country don't

even want 'em. You don't want to hire them Gypsies, missus. They'll rob you blind." He lowers his voice. "And what with young ladies present, mum . . . What could happen, well, I shouldn't like to say."

I do not like Mr. Miller. His smile is an illusion. It does not match the venom of his words. Ithal says nothing in return, but I can see by the tight line of his jaw that he would like to.

Mrs. Nightwing straightens her spine as she does when she upbraids one of us. "Mr. Miller, I trust you'll finish this portion in time for our ball?"

"Aye, missus," Mr. Miller says, his eyes still on Ithal. "'Twas the rain what put us behind."

Mrs. Nightwing speaks to the Gypsies as she would to meddling children in need of bed. "I thank you for your concern, gentlemen. At present we have it well in hand."

I watch the Gypsies go, still hoping I'll see Kartik at any moment. Mrs. Nightwing is occupied with Mr. Miller and I seize my chance. Palming a penny, I traipse after the Gypsies.

"Pardon me, sir. I believe you may have dropped this," I say, offering the shiny coin.

The Gypsy knows I've invented the tale; I can see it in his suspicious smile. He looks to Ithal for guidance.

"It is not ours," Ithal says.

"It could be!" I blurt out.

The other man is intrigued. "For what?"

"Careful, friend," Ithal warns. "We are like dirt beneath their feet." He flicks his glance to Felicity, who does not even bother to see.

"I only wish to know if Mr. Kartik is among your company at present."

Ithal folds his arms across his chest. "Why do you want to know?"

"He had hoped for work as a driver. I happen to know of a family in need of such and thought I might inform him." I feel shamed by my lie.

"You see? Dirt." Ithal glares at me. "I have not seen Mr. Kartik for some months now. Perhaps he is already in the service of a fine family and cannot come to play anymore."

It's a slap of a comment, and I feel properly stung by it, but I'm more stung by the knowledge that no one has seen Kartik. I'm afraid something terrible has happened to him.

Mrs. Nightwing corrals the girls, and I hurry back into the fold. As I do, I hear Ithal talking to the other Gypsies. "Do not be tempted by English roses. Their beauty fades, but their thorns are forever."

"Miss Doyle! What were you doing with those men?" Mrs. Nightwing scolds.

"I'd a pebble in my boot. I only stopped to remove it," I lie.

"Scandalous," Cecily whispers. Her whispers could be heard by the dead.

Mrs. Nightwing takes hold of my arm. "Miss Doyle, with the others, if you please—" Her admonition is interrupted by a loud shout from one of the workers.

"Oi! There's somefin' down 'ere!"

Several of the men jump into the hole between the new turret and the old portion of the school. A lamp is called for and one is lowered. We follow Nightwing, crowding around the hole, hoping for a glimpse of whatever has been found.

The workers discard their shovels. They whisk dirt-stained hands back and forth, clearing the clumps of drying mud away.

There is indeed something beneath the ground—part of an old wall. The stone bears strange markings but they're too faint to see. Mr. Miller frowns. "What's that, now?"

"Could be a woine cellar," a man with a bushy mustache opines.

"Or a dungeon," another says, grinning. He smacks the boot of the smallest among them. "Oi, Charlie—be a good lad or it's into the 'ole wif you!" He makes a sudden grab for the young man's ankle, scaring him, and the men fall into rowdy laughter.

Mrs. Nightwing takes the lamp and holds it over the ancient stone. She examines it from above, pursing her lips, and then, just as quickly, gives the lamp back to Mr. Miller. "Likely it is a relic from the Druids or even the Romans. They say Hannibal himself may have led his troops through these parts."

"Ye might be right, missus. Looks to be a marker of sorts," the burly man says.

There is something strangely familiar about it all, like a dream I can't quite catch before it flies away forever. I can't keep from reaching fingers toward the relic. My breathing comes faster; my skin is warm. I want to touch it . . .

"Careful, miss!" Mr. Miller pushes me back as I topple forward.

The warmth leaves my hands, and I startle as if waking.

"Miss Doyle! You are entirely too close!" Mrs. Nightwing reprimands. "None of you girls should be here, and I do believe, in fact, that Mademoiselle LeFarge is waiting for quite a few of you."

"Yes, Mrs. Nightwing," we answer, but we don't leave.

"Should we clear it away, missus?" Mr. Miller asks, and again that queer feeling surges through me, though I cannot say why.

Mrs. Nightwing nods. The men strain to remove it. Again and again, they fall away, red-faced and gasping for breath. The biggest and strongest of them jumps into the hole and puts his full weight against it. He, too, steps aside. "Won't budge an inch," he says.

"Wot d'yer wanna do, missus?"

Mrs. Nightwing shakes her head. "It's been here this long. Just leave it be."

CHAPTER EIGHT

FELICITY'S NOT FORGIVEN ME YET FOR MY ADVICE ABOUT Lady Markham, so I find myself shut out of her tent in the great hall. It's not that she tells me I'm not welcome; she simply greets each of Cecily's dull tales with a jolly laugh and fawns over the simpering details of Elizabeth's latest trip to the dressmaker's, whilst every syllable I utter is met with complete disdain. Eventually, I take refuge in the kitchen.

I'm surprised to see Brigid leaving a bowl of milk on the hearth. Even more curious, she has affixed a crucifix to the wall beside the door, and small sprigs of leaves mark the windows.

I help myself to a hard crust of brown bread from the larder. "Brigid . . . ," I say then, and she jumps.

"By all the saints! Don't sneak up on your old Brigid like that," she says, putting a hand over her heart.

"What are you doing?" I nod toward the milk. "Is there a cat about?"

"No," she says, grabbing her basket of sewing. "And that's all I 'ave to say on the subject."

Brigid always has more to say on every subject. It's simply a matter of luring the gossip out of her.

"Please, Brigid. I won't tell a soul," I promise.

"Well . . ." She motions for me to sit with her by the fire. "It's for protection," she whispers. "The cross and rowan leaves on the windows as well."

"Protection from what?"

Brigid dips her needle into the fabric and pulls it through the other side. "The East Wing. Ain't right putting that cursed place back as it was."

"You mean because of the fire and the girls who died?"

Brigid cranes her neck to be sure we're not overhead. Her sewing sits idle in her lap. "Aye, that, but I always felt that there were somethin' not right about it."

"What do you mean?" I say, taking another bite of bread.

"You just get a knowin' in your very bones about such things." She fingers the cross she wears around her neck. "And one day, I heard Missus Nightwing askin' Missus Spence somethin' about the East Wing and Missus Spence, God rest her as an angel, tellin' 'er not to worry, that she would never let anything in, even if she 'ad to die first. Gives me a shudder jus' thinkin' abou' it."

Eugenia Spence giving her life to save everyone from the Winterlands creatures. The bread I've been chewing goes down hard.

Brigid looks through the windows at the dark woods beyond. "I wish they'd leave it be."

"But, Brigid, think how lovely it will look when it is complete and Spence is as she once was," I argue. "Wouldn't that be a fine tribute to Mrs. Spence?"

Brigid nods. "Aye, 'twould. But still . . ." She cups my chin in her hand. "You won't tell on your old Brigid 'bout the milk, will you?"

I shake my head. "Of course not."

"There's a good girl." She pats my cheek, and that, more than any good-luck charm, has the power to rid my soul of ghosts. "When you first came in your mourning weeds, I thought you the strangest thing. It's your green eyes—they put me in mind of that poor Mary Dowd 'oo died in the fire and her friend, Sarah. But you're nothin' like them. Nothin' at all."

"Thank you for the bread," I say, though it's turned to lead in my belly.

"You're welcome, luv. Best get back. You'll be missed." She looks again at the dark beyond. "Ain't right putting it back. I can feel it. Ain't right."

The all-seeing eyes of Eugenia Spence watch me climb the stairs to my room. Her white hair is arranged in the fashion of the day, with curls on her forehead and a mass of coiled hair at the back of her head. Her dress has a high collar and an elaborate ruffle running down both sides of the bright green bodice—no sedate gray or black for Eugenia Spence. And there at her neck is the crescent eye amulet that now hangs from my own, hidden beneath my gown.

My mother caused your death.

In my room, I take out my mother's diary and read again of Eugenia's heroism, of how she offered herself as a sacrifice in place of Sarah and my mother.

"I will have payment," the creature cried, grabbing fast to Sarah's arm.

Eugenia's mouth tightened. "We must hie to the Winterlands." We found ourselves in that land of ice and fire, of thick, barren trees and perpetual night. Eugenia stood tall.

"Sarah Rees-Toome, you will not be lost to the Winterlands. Come back with me. Come back."

The creature turned on her. "She has invited me. She must pay, or the balance of the realms is forfeit."

"I shall go in her place...."

"So be it. There is much we could do with one so powerful...."

Eugenia threw to me her amulet of the crescent eye. "Mary, run! Take Sarah with you through the door, and I shall close the realms!..."

The thing caused her to cry out in pain then. Her eyes were filled with a pleading that took my breath away, for I had never seen Eugenia frightened before. "The realms must stay closed until we can find our way again. Now—run!" she screamed ... and the last I saw of Eugenia, she was shouting the spell to close the realms, even as she was swallowed by the dark without a trace.

I close my mother's diary and lie on my back, staring at the ceiling and thinking of Eugenia Spence. If she hadn't thrown her amulet to my mother and closed the realms for good, there's no telling what sort of terrors might have been visited upon this world. In that one act, she saved us all, though it meant her destruction. And I wonder what became of her, what terrible fate befell the great Eugenia Spence because of my mother's sin, and if I could ever possibly be enough to atone for it.

꙳꙳꙳꙳

When my dreams find me, they are disquieting. A pretty lady in a lavender dress and hat races through London streets thick with fog. Her ginger hair falls loosely about her frightened face. She beckons me to follow, but I cannot keep pace; my feet are as heavy as lead and I can't see. The cobblestones are coated with paper adverts for a spectacle of some sort. I reach for one: *Dr. Theodore Van Ripple—Illusionist Extraordinaire!*

The fog clears, and I'm mounting the stairs of Spence, past the enormous portrait of Eugenia Spence. I climb until I find myself on the roof in my bedclothes. The wind rips through me. On the horizon, storm clouds gather. Down below, the men continue their work on the East Wing. Their hands are as quick as an owl's blink. The stone column rises higher. A shovel strikes the ground and will not go farther. It has hit something solid. The men look to me. "Would you like to open it, miss?"

The lady in the lavender dress opens her mouth. She's trying to tell me something, but there is no sound, only alarm in her eyes. Suddenly, everything moves very fast. I see a room lit by a single lamp. Words. A knife. The lady running. A body floating upon the water. I hear a voice like a whisper in my ear: "*Come to me. . . .*"

I wake with a start. I want to sleep again but I can't. Something's calling to me, pulling me downstairs and out to the lawn, where a full moon spreads its buttery light over the wooden skeleton of the East Wing. The turret rises into low-lying clouds. Its shadow reaches across the lawn and touches my bare toes. The grass is cold with dew.

Upon the roof, the gargoyles sleep. The ground seems to hum beneath my feet. And once again, I am drawn to the turret and the stone there. I step down into the hole. The framing of the East Wing looms above my head, and the night clouds move like lashes from an angry whip. The crescent eye glows, and in the faint light, I see an outline in the stone that matches the amulet's shape.

A tingling begins in my fingers. It travels through my body. Something inside me wants release. I can't control it, and I'm afraid of whatever it may be.

I put my hands to the stone. A surge of power pushes through me. The stone glows white-gold, and the world pitches. It is like looking at the negative of a photograph: Behind me is Spence; before me are the skeletal East Wing and, farther on, the woods. But if I turn my head, shimmering there is another image of something else that stands between. I blink, trying to clear the image.

And when I look again, I see the outline of a door.

"Gemma, why have you brought us out here in the middle of the night?" Felicity grouses, wiping sleep from her eyes.

"You'll see," I say, shining the light of a lamp over the back lawn.

She shivers in her thin nightgown. "We might at least have brought our cloaks."

Ann wraps her arms about her middle. Her teeth chatter. "I w-want to go b-b-back to b-bed. If Mrs. Nightwing should f-find us ..." She glances behind us for signs of our head-mistress.

"I promise you won't be disappointed. Now. Stand here." I position them beside the turret and place the lantern at their feet. The light washes them in an unearthly white.

"If this is some childish prank, I shall kill you," Felicity warns.

"It isn't." I stand on the ground above the old stone and close my eyes. The night air nips at my skin.

"Gemma, really," Felicity complains.

"Shush! I need to concentrate," I snap. Doubt whispers cruelly in my ear: *You can't do it. The power's left you.*

I won't listen. Not this time. Slowly, I let go of my fear. The ground vibrates beneath my feet. The land itself seems to call to me, pulling me under its spell. My fingers thrum with an energy that both frightens and excites. I open my eyes and put out my hand, searching for the hidden door. I don't see it so much as feel it. The sensation is one of exquisite longing and joy. A wound of desire that cannot be healed. It's whispering to me secrets I don't comprehend, languages I do not know. The wind howls. It whips up small tornados of dust.

The land shimmers. The faint outline of the door appears again.

"Blimey," Ann gasps.

Felicity reaches out tentatively. "You believe that leads to the realms?"

"On the night of the fire, the Winterlands creature came to take Sarah," I remind them. "And Eugenia Spence offered herself in Sarah's place. She threw her amulet—this amulet—to my mother and sealed the door into the realms. The East Wing burned. All traces of the door were gone."

"We don't know that this is the same door," Ann says, shivering. "It could lead anywhere. To the Winterlands, perhaps."

"I'm willing to take that chance," I say, embracing the glimmer of hope I've been offered.

"W-we c-c-could be trapped," Ann says.

"We're already trapped," Felicity says. "I want to find out

what has happened to Pip." She takes my arm. I grab the lantern.

"Ann?" I reach out, and she slips her cold fingers into mine, holding tightly. I take a deep breath, and we step forward. For a second, it feels as if we're falling, and then there is nothing but the dark. It smells musty and sweet.

"Gemma?" Ann's whisper.

"Yes?"

"What has happened to Felicity?"

"I'm here," Fee says. "Wherever that may be."

I swing the lamp in first and am able to see a few feet ahead. It's a long passageway. The lamplight falls on high arched ceilings of pale stone. Roots dangle through cracks here and there. In back of us, Spence sleeps, but it's as if that world lies behind glass, and we push on.

As we pass, the walls flicker with a faint glow, like hundreds of fireflies lighting the way ahead, while the path behind us shifts into darkness again. The passageway twists and turns in a confusing fashion.

Ann's jitters echo in the tunnel. "Don't get us lost, Gemma."

"Will you be quiet?" Felicity scolds. "Gemma, you'd best be right about this."

"Keep walking," I say.

We come to a wall.

"We're trapped," Ann says in a shaky voice. "I knew it would come to this."

"Oh, do stop it," Fee barks.

It has to be here. I won't give up. *Let the magic go, Gemma. Feel it. Unleash its power.* Something's calling to me. It's as if the stones themselves are waking. The outline of another door appears in the wall, fierce light bleeding around its corners. I give the door a shove. It swings open, accompanied by a flurry of dust, as if it has been sealed for ages, and we step into a meadow redolent of roses. The sky is a clear blue in one direction and the golden orange of sunset in the other. It's a place we know well but have not seen for some time.

"Gemma," Felicity murmurs. Her awe gives way to jubilation. "You've done it! We've made it back to the realms at last!"

CHAPTER NINE

"IT'S SO BEAUTIFUL!" FELICITY SHOUTS. SHE TWIRLS ABOUT, making herself so dizzy she falls down in the tall grass, but she's laughing as she does.

"Oh, it is like the most wondrous spring I've ever seen," Ann murmurs. And indeed, it is. Long velvet ropes of moss hang from the tops of trees like gossamer green curtains; branches blossom with pink and white flowers. A gentle breeze sweeps them onto our upturned cheeks and lips. They nestle in my hair, making it smell sweet as new rain. I rub a flower between my fingers, inhaling its scent; I have to be sure that it is real, that I am not dreaming.

"We're really here, aren't we?" I ask as Fee entwines herself in the moss as if it were ermine.

"Yes, we are," Fee assures me.

For the first time in months, hope flutters up through my soul: If I can do this, bring us into the realms, then all is not lost.

"This isn't the garden," Ann says. "Where are we?"

"I don't know," I say, looking about. Tall slabs of stone have been erected in a seemingly random pattern that puts me in mind of Stonehenge. Winding through them is a faint dirt path that reaches from the door to the realms beyond. The path is difficult to see, as if it hasn't been used in a very long time.

"There's a little trail here," I say. "We'll follow it."

As we walk away, the door fades into the rock.

"Gemma," Ann gasps. "It's gone!"

It's as if someone has tightened a string around my heart. I try to keep my wits about me. I take a step toward the rock, and the door glows once again.

"Oh, thank heavens," I say, letting my breath out in a whoosh, relieved.

"Come on," Felicity pleads. "I want to see the garden. I want . . ." She doesn't finish her sentence.

We follow the path through the stones. Despite being pock-marked with age and dirt, they boast an impressive array of friezes showing women of all sorts. Some are as young as we are; others are as old as the earth itself. Some are clearly warriors, with swords held aloft to the rays of the sun. One sits surrounded by children and fawns, her hair flowing in loose waves to the ground. Another, dressed in chain mail, wrestles a dragon. Priestesses. Queens. Mothers. Healers. It is as if the whole of womanhood is represented here.

Ann gawks at the woman with the dragon. "Who do you suppose they are?"

"Perhaps they were of the Order or older still," I say. I run my hand across a carving of three women on a barge. The one on the left is a young lady; the one on the right is a bit older; and in the center is a crone holding a lantern aloft, as though she's waiting for someone. The picture gives me a strange sensation in my belly, as if I've glimpsed the future. "They're remarkable, aren't they?"

"What's remarkable is that there isn't a single blasted corset among them," Felicity says with a giggle. "Oh, Gemma, let's do hurry. I can't wait much longer."

The path leads us through tall fields of wheat, past neat rows of olive trees and the grotto where the Runes of the Oracle once stood. At last we find ourselves in the garden we have come to think of as our own private fiefdom.

The moment we're on familiar ground, Felicity is running. "Pippa?" she calls. "Pippa! Pippa, it's me, Felicity! We've come back!" She searches every corner. "Where is she?"

I cannot bring myself to say what I'm thinking—that our dear friend Pippa is lost to us forever now. Either she has crossed the river to the land beyond or she has banded together with the Winterlands creatures and become our enemy.

I am waiting for the magic to spark inside me, but it doesn't behave as it has in the past. I am out of practice. *Right. Begin with something simple, Gemma.* I grab a handful of leaves and close my fingers over them.

I shut my eyes. My heart flutters a few beats faster, and then a sudden fever takes me. It is as if the whole of the world—all experience, past and present—flows through me as quickly as lightning. My blood pulses with new life. A rapturous smile spreads across my lips. And when I open my eyes, the leaves have turned to rubies in my palm.

"Ha! Look!" I shriek. I toss the gems into the air and they fall like red rain.

"Oh, it's been so long since we've played with magic." Ann gathers leaves in her hands and blows. The leaves fly on her breath, then drift in a slow spiral to her feet. She frowns. "I wanted them to become butterflies."

"Here, let me try." Felicity grabs a handful, but no matter how hard she tries, they become nothing new; they are only leaves. "Why can't I change them? What's happened to the magic? How were you able to make the rubies, Gemma?"

"I simply wished it, and there they were," I say.

"Gemma, you clever girl! You did bind the Temple magic to yourself after all!" Felicity says with a mix of awe and envy. "Every bit of it must live inside you now."

"I suppose that's true," I say, but I can't make myself believe it. I turn my hands palms up, palms down, staring at them as if I've never seen them before. They're the same dull, freckled hands I've always had, and yet . . .

"Do something else!" Felicity commands.

"Like what?" I ask.

"Turn that tree into a dragon—"

"Not a dragon!" Ann interrupts, wide-eyed.

"Or make the flowers into gentleman callers—"

"Yes, I like that," Ann says.

"Oh, honestly, Gemma! You've the whole of the Temple inside you. Do whatever you wish!"

"All right," I say. There's a small rock at my feet. "Hmmm, I'll, um, I'll just turn this into a . . . a . . ."

"Falcon!" Felicity shouts as Ann says, "Prince!"

I touch the rock, and for a moment, I feel as if we are one and the same; I'm part of the land. Something slimy bumps against my palm with a loud *ribbet*. The frog looks about with big eyes, as if shocked to discover that he is no longer a rock.

Ann grimaces. "I'd hoped for a prince."

"You could always kiss him," I offer, and Fee laughs.

Ann pulls up a daisy and plucks its petals one by one. "If you hold all the power, Gemma, what does that mean for us?"

Felicity stops laughing. "We'll have none of our own."

"Once we make an alliance with the other tribes in the realms and join hands, we'll share the magic—"

"Yes, but that could take months," Felicity argues. "What about now?"

Ann cradles the mangled daisy in her lap. She won't even look at me. A moment ago I was overjoyed. Now I feel terribly guilty that I have this power and my friends do not.

"If I am the Temple with all its magic," I say, haltingly, "then I should be able to give some to you as the Temple has always given it to us."

"I want to try," Felicity says. She puts a hand to my arm. Her craving warms the skin beneath my sleeve, and I want to shake it off. For if I give it to her, will I be left with less? Will she have more?

"Gemma?" Felicity says. Her eyes are so very hopeful, and I'm a rotten friend for thinking of denying her.

"Give me your hands," I say. Within seconds, we are joined. There's a sharp pull, almost an exquisite pain. It's as if we're the same person for a moment. I can hear echoes of her wishes inside my head. Freedom. Power. Pippa. Pippa is the strongest wish, and I feel Fee's ache for our missing friend like a deep wound. We break apart, and I have to steady myself against a tree for a second.

Fee sports a huge grin. "I feel it. I feel it!"

As I watch, a shimmering breastplate appears over her

nightclothes. Her hair hangs long and free. Strapped to her arm is a crossbow. On the other is a falcon. "Oh, if those dowagers could see me now!" She adopts an imperious tone. "I'm afraid, Lady Ramsbottom, that if you should sneer at me once more, I shall have to allow my falcon to eat you."

Ann looks at me hopefully.

"Here, give me your hands," I say.

A moment later, Ann holds her arms out in front of her as if she can't believe the miracle of her own skin. Tears stream down her face.

"I feel alive again," she says, laughing through them. "I was so dead inside, but now . . . Oh, don't you feel it?" she asks.

"Yes," I say, thrilled. "Yes!"

Ann gives herself a medieval gown of spun gold. She looks the part of a princess in a fairy tale.

"Ann, you're beautiful!" I call. I never want this night to end.

Felicity lets the falcon go. It soars higher and higher, making daring loops. It is free, and even the sky cannot stop it.

The river announces the arrival of something new. A great ship creaks upon the water. Along the bow is a massive fearsome creature with a green face, yellow eyes, and a head full of hissing snakes. The gorgon! I run to greet her, waving wildly.

"Gorgon!" I call. "Gorgon, it is I, Gemma! We've returned!"

"Greetings, Most High," she answers in her slithery, whisper-thick voice. Her eyes register neither surprise nor happiness. She nestles into the grassy shore and lowers her plank, allowing me to clamber on board. The ship's planks are a seaworn gray. Along the sides hang nets of silver and a tangle of ropes. The boat is large but dingy. Centuries ago, the once-proud warrior was joined to this ship as punishment for her part in a rebellion against the Order. She is free to leave it now, but she hasn't yet. "We had expected you sooner."

"I've not been able to enter the realms since I saw you last. I feared I'd never return. But we're here now, and oh, Gorgon, you're well? Of course you're well!" I'm overcome with happiness, for the magic has returned to me. I feel it setting my blood aflame. Yes, we've come back to the realms at last. We've come home.

I venture onto the bow, taking a perch very near Gorgon's giant green face. The snakes about her head slither back and forth, watching me, but they make no move to strike.

Gorgon's eyes narrow as she looks out to the horizon. "The realms have been strangely quiet these days. I've heard nothing from the Winterlands creatures."

"I should think that is good news."

"I wonder . . . ," Gorgon murmurs.

"And what of Pippa?" I ask, out of Fee and Ann's earshot. "Have you seen her anywhere?"

"No," Gorgon answers, and I don't know if I am relieved to hear it—or afraid. "I am ill at ease, Most High. I've not passed so many days without a single sign from those creatures."

The air is scented with blossoms. The river sings pleasantly, as always. The magic sparks in my veins with such sweet ferocity that it is impossible to imagine that anything shall ever be amiss again.

"Perhaps they've gone," I say. "Or crossed over at last."

The snakes rise and coil atop Gorgon's massive head, their pink tongues snapping into and out of their small cruel mouths. "I've seen no souls crossing the river."

"That doesn't mean they didn't go. And it's quite possible none needed assistance."

"Perhaps," Gorgon hisses, but the worry does not leave her face. "There are other matters at hand. Philon is asking after you. The forest folk have not forgotten your promise to form an alliance with them, to join hands at the Temple and share the magic. Shall I take you to them now?"

I've not been in the realms a half hour, and already I am burdened with obligations. "I think . . ." I look over at my friends scooping up handfuls of flowers and hurling them into the sky, where they fall in flakes of silver. "Not just yet."

Gorgon's yellow eyes stare through me. "You do not wish to part with the magic?"

I hop down and gaze at my reflection in the pleasant surface of the river. It stares back at me, waiting. Even it has expectations, it would seem. "Gorgon, I thought I'd lost everything. I've only just returned. I need to explore the realms and the magic, to sort out the best course," I say slowly, thinking out loud. "And I've need of it in my world, too. I should like to help my friends, to change our lives while we can."

"I see," Gorgon says, and I cannot read her feelings about the matter. The giant beast lowers her voice to a soft growl. "There are other concerns, Most High."

"What do you mean?"

"No person has ever held all the power. There must be a balance between chaos and order, dark and light. With the Temple magic bound to you, the realms are no longer in balance. The power could change you . . . and you could change the magic."

My happiness is evaporating. I drop a small pebble into the river. Ripples move across my reflection, distorting my face till I no longer recognize it. "But if I hold the power, there is no magic for anyone to take," I say, thinking aloud again as the idea forms in my mind. "The realms might be safe at last. And"—I watch Ann pull a leaf from a tree and turn it into a butterfly with one breath—"I wouldn't hold it for long."

"Is that a promise?" Gorgon hisses, her yellow eyes meeting mine.

"I promise."

Gorgon searches the horizon with an air of unease. "There is much we do not know about the Winterlands, Most High. It is best to make the alliance, and quickly."

This fear of Gorgon's is odd. I've not seen this side of her before.

"Tell Philon . . ." I stop. What can I tell Philon? That I need more time? That I'm not sure of anything just now except that I am happy to be in the realms—and I can't give up that happiness yet? "Tell him we'll discuss that matter."

"When?" Gorgon presses.

"Soon," I say.

"How soon?"

"When I return," I answer quickly, for I want to join my friends.

"I shall wait for you to return, Most High." And with that, she closes her haunting eyes and sleeps.

⌇⌇⌇⌇⌇

For hours we play, allowing the magic to flower fully within us till we feel that time itself is ours to hold. The hope that has been dormant in each of us blooms again, and we are giddy with the happiness that possibility brings. Felicity lazes in a swing she has fashioned from soft, leafy vines. She lets it cradle her and she drags her toes across the velvety grass.

"If only we could show the world the depth of our power . . ." Felicity trails off, smiling.

Ann picks a dandelion puff from the tall grass. "I should stand on the stage beside Lily Trimble."

I correct her. "Lily Trimble should beg to stand beside you!"

Ann brings her hands dramatically to her bosom. "'Fair is foul, and foul is fair!'"

"Bravo!" Felicity and I applaud.

"Oh, and I should be very, very beautiful. And wealthy! And I should marry an earl and have ten children!" Ann closes her eyes in a wish and blows hard on her dandelion, but the wind carries only part of the fluff away.

"What would you wish for, Gemma? What do you want?" Felicity asks.

What do I want? Why is that simple question—four little words—so impossible to answer? I would wish for things that cannot be: my mother alive again, my father well. Would I wish to be shorter, fairer, more lovable, less complicated? The answer, I fear, is yes. I would wish to be a child again, safe and warm, and yet I would also wish for something far more dangerous: a kiss from a certain Indian boy whom I have not seen since Christmas. I am a jumble of passions, misgivings, and wants. It seems that I am always in a state of wishing and rarely in a state of contentment.

They are waiting for my answer. "I should wish to perfect my curtsy so that I might not scandalize myself before Her Majesty."

"That will take magic," Ann says dryly.

"Thank you for your confidence. I do so appreciate it."

"I should bring Pip back," Felicity says.

Ann bites her lip. "Do you suppose she really is lost to the Winterlands, Gemma?"

I look out over the endless meadow. The flowers sway in a gentle breeze. "I don't know."

"She isn't," Felicity says, her cheeks reddening.

"That is where she was headed," I remind her gently.

The last time we saw our dear friend, she was already turning, becoming one of them. She wanted me to use the magic to bring her back to our world, but I couldn't. The creatures cannot come back. It is a rule I couldn't break, and Pippa hated me for it. Sometimes I believe Fee hates me for it too.

"I know Pip, I tell you. She would never leave me like that."

"Perhaps we'll see her soon," I say. But I'm not looking forward to it. If Pippa has truly become a Winterlands creature, she is no longer our friend. She is our enemy.

Felicity grabs her sword and sets off for the trees.

"Where are you going?" I shout.

"To find Pip. You may come or not."

We go, of course. Once Fee has set her mind on something, there's no talking sense into her. And I want to know the truth, though I hope we'll not see Pip. For her sake and ours, I hope she's already crossed over the river.

Felicity leads us through a flower-laden meadow. It smells of hyacinth and my father's pipe tobacco, fresh *dosa*, and my mother's skin-warmed rose water. I turn around, half expecting to see my mother behind me. But she isn't. She's gone, dead nearly a full year now. Sometimes I miss her so deeply it is as if I cannot breathe without feeling an ache lodged in my ribs. Other times I find that I've forgotten small things about her— the shape of her mouth or the sound of her laugh. I cannot conjure her memory. When that happens, I'm nearly in a panic to remember. I am afraid that if I cannot hold on to these memories exactly, I'll lose her forever.

We come to the poppy fields below the Caves of Sighs. The bright red flowers show us their dark hearts. Felicity picks one and places it behind her ear. High above us, the cliffs rise. The char pots belch their rainbow of smoke, hiding the very top, where the Untouchables guard the Temple and the well of eternity. It is the last place I saw Circe.

She's dead, Gemma. You killed her.

Yet I heard her voice in a dream, telling me she was still alive. I saw her face, ghostly white, in the well's depths.

"Gemma, what is the matter?" Ann asks.

I shake my head as if I can clear it of Circe's memory forever. "Nothing."

⁓⁓⁓⁓

We walk for some time, until the lush ripeness of the meadow gives way to thick copses of gnarled trees. The sky is gloomy here, as if it has been streaked with soot. There are no flowers, no bushes. In fact, there is no color at all, save for the brown of the brittle trees and the gray of the sky above them.

"Ugh," Felicity says. She lifts her boot and shows us the bottom. It is dark and mealy, like rotted fruit. When I look up, I see that the trees are laden with what seem to be clusters of berries. They hang flat and defeated on the branches.

"Oh, what has happened here?" Ann wonders aloud, pulling a rotting husk from a branch.

"I don't know," I say. "Let's change it back, shall we?"

We put our hands on a trunk. Color flows beneath its

withered bark. Leaves burst through the broken skin of the tree with a sound like the earth itself cracking open. Vines slither along the dusty ground. The shrunken fruits grow fat and purplish red; the branches sag under their succulence. The magic surges in me, and I feel as ripe and beautiful as the fruit.

I grab Ann, who yelps as I lead her about in a giddy waltz. I let go and take hold of Felicity, who, being Felicity, insists on leading. Soon we're all twirling round and round dizzyingly fast, my happiness fed by theirs.

Sudden thunder rumbles in the distance; the sky pulses red like an angry abrasion. I lose my hold on the others and we fly apart. Ann lands hard with an "oomph."

"Really, Gemma!"

"Did you see that?" I ask, running toward the path. "The sky turned all funny for a moment."

"Where?" Felicity searches the sky, which has settled into dusk again.

"That way," I say, leading them on.

We walk until we reach a long wall of brambles whose thorns are both sharp and plentiful.

"What now?" Ann asks.

Through the small gaps in the brambles, I see a strange mixture of green and rock, fog and twisted trees, much like the English moors in the Brontë sisters' eerie tales. And farther on, something rises from the mist.

"What is that?" I ask, squinting.

Felicity searches for a peephole. "This is hopeless. I can't see a thing. Let's find a way in."

She sets off running down the hard path, stopping here and there to test the strength of the bramble wall.

"Ahhh!" I pull my hand back. I've pricked my finger on one of the sharp points. My blood stains the tip. With an anguished sigh, the brambles unclasp. The long, thorny threads slither free of each other like snakes scattering. We fall back as a wide hole appears.

"What should we do now?" Ann whispers.

"We go inside," Felicity answers, and there is the hint of a dare in her smile.

We squeeze through the narrow opening and toward the barren forest. The air is noticeably cooler. It tickles our skin into gooseflesh. Thick vines twist along the ground, strangling the trunks of the trees, choking off much of what might grow here. A few valiant flowers poke their heads up here and there. They are few but large and beautiful—a deep purple with petals as fat as a man's fist. Everything is coated in a blue light that reminds me of dusk in winter. The land here has a peculiar feel. I am drawn to it, yet I want to run. It is like a warning, this land.

We reach the edge of the forest and are astonished at what we see. On a hill is a magnificent ruin of a castle. Its sides are overgrown with a pale, sickly moss and thick, ropelike vines gone tough with age. Tree roots have grown into the stones. They are like bony fingers twisting and turning about the castle, holding it tight in an unwelcome embrace. One limestone tower refuses to be taken, however. It rises majestically from the hill's grasping hands.

The ground near it is covered in a fine coating of frost. It is like a doll's castle under a shaking of powdery sugar. It is odd here. Hushed as a first snowfall.

"What is this place?" Ann asks.

"Let's have a look inside!" Felicity leaps forward, but I pull her back.

"Fee! We've no idea where we are or who lives there!"

"Exactly!" she says, as if I have missed the entire point of our excursion.

"Might I remind you of the Poppy Warriors?" I say, invoking the name of those gruesome knights who lured us to their cathedral in hopes of killing us and taking the magic for themselves. As we ran for our lives, they transformed into enormous black birds, chasing us out onto the water. We were lucky to escape them, and I shan't make the same mistake twice.

Ann shivers. "Gemma's right. Let's go back."

The stillness is broken by the rustling of leaves. A call comes from the forest; it puts a shiver up my spine.

Whoo-oot!

"What was that?" Ann whispers.

"An owl?" I say, my breath coming fast.

"No, I don't think so," Felicity says.

We huddle close. Felicity draws her sword. Magic swoops through me, battling my fear. There's movement to my right, a flash of white amidst the green. Just as quickly, something scurries through the thicket of trees on the left.

Whoo-oot. Whoo-oot.

It seems to be all around us. A sound here; a sound there. A streak of color darts past.

Whoo-oot. Whoo-oot.

Closer now. I hardly know which way to turn. The bushes are still. But someone's watching us. I can feel it.

"Sh-show yourselves," I say, my voice pale as a slice of moon.

She steps from behind a tree. Framed in the dusky purple of

night, she seems to glow. Her white gown's gone brown with dirt around the bottom; her skin is the color of the dead. In her matted hair, she wears a crown of flowers that have died and turned to weeds. But we know her all the same. She is the friend we buried months ago, the friend who would not cross the river, whom we thought lost to the Winterlands.

I say her name on a terrified whisper. "Pippa."

CHAPTER TEN

FELICITY'S EYES WIDEN. "PIP? IS IT YOU?"

Pippa rubs her hands up and down her arms as if trying to warm them. "Yes. It's me. It's your Pip." Not one of us dares to move. Tears streak Pip's pale cheeks. "Will you not embrace me? Do I mean so little to you now? Have you forgotten me so quickly?"

Felicity's sword clatters to the hard ground as she runs headlong to Pippa and wraps her arms about our lost friend. "I told them you wouldn't leave without telling me goodbye. I told them."

Pip looks at Ann. "Darling Ann, will you still welcome me as friend?"

"Of course," Ann says, reaching toward the small frail shell of her.

At last Pip comes to me. "Gemma." She gives me a sad little smile, biting her bottom lip nervously. Her teeth have grown sharper, and her eyes change back and forth from a beautiful violet to an unsettling milky blue with tiny pricks of black at the center. Her beauty has changed, but she is still mesmerizing. Her hair, always long and dark, is now a tangle of curls as untamed as the vines twisting round the castle. She catches me staring. Her laugh is quick and bitter. "Gemma, you look as if you'd seen a ghost."

"I thought you'd gone to the Winterlands," I say, uncertainly.

"I nearly did," she answers, shivering.

"But what happened?" Felicity asks.

Pippa calls out toward the forest. "It's all right! You can come out! It's safe. These are my friends."

A ragged group of girls emerge one by one from their hiding places behind the trees and the bushes. Two carry long sticks that look as if they could do damage. As the girls come closer, I see the singed tatters of their dresses, the horrific burns on their faces and arms. I know who they are—the factory-fire girls we met months ago. We last saw them marching toward the Winterlands, toward corruption. I am relieved to see that they did not meet their end there, but I cannot imagine how they escaped.

One of the stick holders—a big-boned lass with coarse skin and wounds running the length of her arms—takes a stand beside Pippa. I remember speaking to her in the realms before. Bessie Timmons. She's the sort I wouldn't want to be on the wrong side of.

She glances at us suspiciously. "Everfin' all righ', then?"

"Yes, Bessie. These are my friends, the ones I told you all about," Pippa says proudly.

"The ones wot took the Temple magic and lef' you 'ere?" Bessie snorts.

"But you see they came back." Beaming, Pippa puts her arm around Felicity.

Bessie doesn't like it one bit. "I wouldn't be too 'appy. They're not 'ere to stay."

Pippa wags a finger as a schoolmarm would. "Bessie, remember our motto: Grace, strength, beauty. A lady must be gracious when welcoming guests."

"Yes, Miss Pippa," Bessie says contritely.

"But, Pip . . . where have you been? I want to know everything!" Felicity says, embracing Pippa again.

I know I should embrace her as Fee and Ann have done, but I can see only those disturbing eyes and sharp teeth, and I am afraid.

"I shall tell you everything. But come inside. It's far too chilly out here." Pippa takes hold of Ann's and Felicity's hands, pulling them toward the castle. Grumbling, Bessie Timmons follows. The remaining girls fall into line, and I bring up the rear.

Pippa throws back the iron latch on the castle's warped wooden door. The weeds snake through the planks, plastering themselves to the front.

"Here we are," Pippa says, pushing open the door. "Home."

It seems as if it might have been a beautiful stronghold in its day, but now it is nothing more than ancient bricks with vines for mortar. The walls are slick with moss. It smells of damp and decay. Brittle daisies, dead on their stalks, peek up between broken flagstones. The only thing that seems to grow is belladonna. The poisonous purple flowers hang above our heads like little bells.

"This is where you've been . . ." I stop myself from saying *living*. "Where you've been all this time?"

"It's all that's left for me. A moldering castle for the Lady of Shalott." Pippa laughs, but it is hollow. She rubs her palms across the elaborate carvings etched into a hearth. The carvings are like saints' faces gone black with time. "But you can tell it was once magical and beautiful."

"What happened to it?" Ann asks.

Pippa glares at me. "It was forgotten."

Felicity pulls aside a threadbare tapestry, revealing a winding staircase. "Where does this lead?"

"To the tower," Pippa says, smiling wistfully. "It is my favorite place, for I can see for miles. I could even see you coming down the path. You looked so merry." Her smile falters but she quickly puts a new one in its place. "Shall I show you?"

We follow Pippa up and around the antiquated staircase. Cobwebs cling to rotting wooden rafters far above us. The silvery strands glint with moisture. Some unfortunate creature has met its end there. In the center of a web, its carcass lies trapped and rotting as a spider inches toward it.

I steady myself against the wall. The vines slither around my fingers. Startled, I leap back, slipping on the crumbling stone. Pippa reaches out and grabs my hand, pulling me to safety. "Hold still a moment," she says.

As we watch, amazed, the vines crisscross the stone like a conquering army. The walls groan with the strain, and I fear that the whole castle will fall down around us. Seconds later, it stops, but fresh tendrils have sprung up everywhere.

"What was that?" Felicity whispers.

"The land's swallowing it bit by bit every day," Pippa says sadly. "Soon, we'll need to find new lodgings, I suppose." She releases my hand. "Are you all right, Gemma?"

"Yes," I say. "Thank you."

"That's twice I've saved your life," she reminds me. "Do you remember the first time? The water nymphs nearly took you under, but I pulled you back," she says, and I feel the ledger book open between us.

Pip is right about the tower: it's magnificent. From the top, we can see beyond the way we've come—the Caves of Sighs, the olive trees that line the gardens, the blue sky and the orange sunset. We can also see beyond the Borderlands, where dark wintry clouds sit on their haunches on the horizon and an enormous wall stretches the length of the land.

"That is the way into the Winterlands," Pippa says, answering an unspoken question.

Lightning throbs against the roiling mass of black-and-gray clouds. For a moment, a plume of red snakes through the dark.

"We've seen that twice now. Do you know what it is?" I ask.

Pippa shakes her head. "Sometimes it happens. We should go downstairs. Wendy will be frightened, poor lamb."

"Who is Wendy?" Ann asks.

For the first time, Pip gives a true smile. Her eyes shift to violet, and I am reminded of the way she was, alive and beautiful, happy about new gloves or some romantic tale. "How terrible of me, for I've not introduced you properly to my new friends!"

Pippa leads us down and into a tapestry-lined room, which is as dismal as a tomb. There are no candles, no lamps, no fire in the enormous hearth. The factory girls have made themselves at home, however. Bessie stretches out on a divan, among the weeds that wrap around it. Her friend Mae sits on the floor, braiding the hair of another girl, whose name appears to be Mercy, for Mae keeps saying, "Mercy, sit still." Another girl, younger than the rest, sits in a corner, staring at nothing. I cannot keep from glancing at their wounds, their ghostly pale faces.

"What are you lookin' at, then?" Bessie snarls, catching me.

My cheeks burn red, and I'm glad for the cover of dusk. "I'm sorry. It's just that the last time I saw you all—"

"We thought you'd followed the girls in white to the Winterlands and were lost forever," Felicity interrupts.

"They were in the company of those ghouls," Pippa says, settling into a dilapidated throne.

"What happened?" Ann asks, breathless.

"That is the story I wished to tell you. By chance, I was on the same path, completely brokenhearted and filled with despair."

"Oh, Pip," Felicity says.

"There, there." Pip smiles. "It has a happy ending. You know how I love happy endings."

I swallow hard. I was the one who turned Pip away, who broke her heart so. I wish I could take it back.

"When I saw these poor lambs, I stopped feeling sorry for myself. I knew I had to do something or they would be lost. So I followed close behind. The moment they stopped to rest, and the girls in white went in search of berries, I took my chance. I told them what those hideous creatures were truly about. That they meant to lead them straight to those soul stealers, the trackers." She smiles at them as if they were her dear children. "I rescued them. I saved you, didn't I, my darlings?"

The girls join in a chorus of agreement. They gaze at Pippa in absolute adoration, as we all have from time to time.

"She's a saint. Saved us, she did," Mae says, wide-eyed. "'You mustn't follow them,' she said. 'They mean you 'arm. Come with me instead.'"

"She saved us sure as we're standing 'ere," Bessie says, concurring. "Didn't she, Wendy?"

A girl of about twelve nods. She sucks on the ends of her pigtails, making them into wet points. "The others weren't so lucky as us. They went on."

"And have you seen any of the Winterlands creatures since then?" I ask.

"Not for ages now," Mae says. "But Wendy has."

"You've seen them?" I ask.

Bessie gives a small snort of derision. "Wendy don't see nuffin'. Fire blinded 'er."

"But I hear things, sometimes," Wendy says, pulling the remnants of a ruined shawl about her. "Sounds like horses. And sometimes I 'ear somefin' makes my skin crawl."

"What is it?" I ask. "What do you hear?"

"A scream," she answers. "Faraway-like. And I 'ope it don't ever get no closer."

"Gotcha!" Bessie shouts, wrapping her meaty paws about Wendy's neck. Wendy screams, making us all jump.

Pippa is quite put out by the display. "Bessie, that is enough."

Bessie pulls away her hands. "You used to laugh at my tricks."

Pippa's eyes go blue-white. "Tonight, I don't find it amusing. It isn't ladylike." She turns to us, all smiles. "I'm teaching these girls to be ladies, just as if they were at Spence!" She claps as if she were Mrs. Nightwing herself. "Come now. A small demonstration for our guests."

The girls rise obediently, eager to please their mistress. Under Pip's direction, they show off their curtsies one by one. This is followed by a particularly amusing elocution lesson in which Pip works with Mae Sutter to change her thick East London accent. Mae struggles to put *h*s into her words where there are none, and Bessie teases her mercilessly.

"You ain't no lady, Mae. You ain't never gonna be a fine lady like Miss Pip."

"'Oo asked you?" Mae barks, and everyone laughs.

"Who asked you," Pippa corrects.

"'At's what I said," Mae asserts. "'Oo asked 'er?"

There is more laughter, especially from Ann, who seems happy not to be the girl getting taunted for once. Little by little, our awkwardness slips away, easing into a new closeness, until it feels as if we have never been apart. I've not seen Felicity like this in months. With Pip she's lighter, quicker to laugh than to challenge. And I feel a small pang of envy for the intimacy of their friendship.

"What are you thinking?" Felicity asks. I start to answer, but then I realize she's talking to Pip.

"I was thinking how different my life would have been had I done as my mother told me and married Mr. Bumble."

"Mr. Bartleby Bumble the barrister," Ann intones, pronouncing the *B*s hard.

The factory fire girls break into a fit of giggling. This is the only encouragement Ann needs to continue.

"This is my beloved, Mrs. Bumble," Ann says in perfect imitation of Mr. Bumble's plummy tones. "She wears a bright bauble bought from Barrington's Baubles."

We're lost to the giggles now. Ann can scarcely carry on for her own laughter. "Beware barristers bringing baubles! Better the berries than barristers!"

Felicity shrieks. "Oh, Ann!"

Ann giggles. "Bite bitter berries before becoming Bumble's beloved!"

Pippa's lips tremble. "Was it the better choice? I wonder." She buries her face in her hands and cries.

"Oh, Pip, darling. Don't cry." Felicity runs to soothe her—Felicity, who never offers kindness to anyone.

"Wh-what have I d-done?" Pip wails. Sobbing, she runs from the room.

Bessie Timmons gives us a hard look. She's a big girl and, I daresay, a bit of a brawler. She could give us a good pounding if she wished. "Miss Pippa's the kindest soul what ever lived. You best not make her cry again."

I can see from the set of her jaw that we have been warned.

Felicity goes to Pip and returns a moment later. "She wants to speak to you, Gemma."

I drift down a corridor thick with leaves and desiccated flowers.

"Gemma." I hear my name whispered from behind a tattered tapestry. I pull it back amidst a flurry of dust. Pippa motions for me to come in. Felicity is right on my heels, but Pip stops her.

"I must have a word with Gemma," she says.

"But . . . ," Felicity starts.

"Fee," Pippa scolds playfully.

"Oh, very well." Felicity turns on her heel, and Pip and I are alone in the grand room. An ornate marble altar sits at one end, and I surmise that this must have been the castle's chapel.

It seems a strange place for a private conversation. The emptiness of the room and its tall, arched ceilings make our words loop and echo. Pip sits upon the altar, her heels knocking gently against the moldy engravings there. Her smile vanishes, and in its place is an expression of utter anguish.

"Gemma, I can't bear this anymore. I want you to help me cross over."

I don't know what I expected her to say, but it wasn't this. "Pip, I've never actually helped anyone cross before—"

"Then I shall be the first."

"I don't know," I say, thinking of Felicity and Ann. "Perhaps we should discuss it—"

"I've given it thought. Please," she begs.

I know she should cross. And yet a part of me wants to hold on. "You're certain you're . . . ready to go?"

She nods. Only the two of us are in this room neglected by time and magic. It is as hopeless a place as one could find.

"Shall I get the others?" I ask.

"No!" she cries so sharply I fear that the chapel's old stones will break. "They'll try to stop me. Especially Felicity and Bessie. You can tell them goodbye for me. It was nice that we could be together one last time."

"Yes, it was." I swallow hard. My throat aches.

"Come back tomorrow alone. I'll meet you just beyond the bramble wall."

"If I help you cross now, Felicity will never forgive me," I say.

"She need never know. It will be our secret." Pip's eyes fill with new tears. "Please, Gemma. I'm ready. Won't you help me?"

She takes my hands, and though hers are as cold and white as chalk, they are still Pip's. "Yes," I say. "I'll help you."

CHAPTER ELEVEN

THE TROUBLE WITH MORNING IS THAT IT COMES WELL before noon.

Oh, to luxuriate in my bed for another hour. I've slept no more than two, and whilst I did, a family of squirrels must have taken up residence in my mouth, for I am sure there is a coating of fur upon my tongue. My tongue tastes of squirrel, if squirrel has a taste somewhere between days-old porridge and foul cheese.

"Gemma!" Ann pushes me. She's smartly turned out in her proper Spence uniform of white blouse, white skirt, and boots. *How did she manage that?* "You're late!"

I lie on my back. The morning light hurts my eyes, so I close them again. "Does your mouth taste of squirrel?"

She makes a face. "Squirrel? No, of course not."

"Woodchuck, then?"

"Will you get up?"

I rub my eyes and will my feet to the cold, unwelcoming floor. Even it is not ready to wake. I moan in protest.

"I've laid out your clothing for you." And so she has, just like a clever, good little girl. My skirt and blouse are stacked neatly across the foot of my bed. "I thought you'd rather find your stockings for yourself." She blushes as she says this. Poor Ann. How is it she can enjoy bloodthirsty tales of all manner of carnage yet nearly faint at the notion of bare shins? I step behind the dressing screen for modesty's sake—Ann's, that is—and dress quickly.

"Gemma, wasn't it so marvelous to be in the realms once again, to feel the magic?"

The night comes back to me—the discovery of the door, the joy of being there again, the magic. Yet my conversation with Gorgon about the alliance and my duties there has left a shroud upon my soul. So much is expected of me and so quickly. And I cannot shake the apprehension I feel about helping Pippa. I've not helped a soul, let alone a friend, cross the river before. And if I fail, I dare not guess at the outcome.

"Yes, marvelous," I say, fastening buttons.

"You don't seem very happy about it," Ann says.

I steady myself. At last we've regained entry into the realms. I can't allow worries about Philon and the forest folk to take this happiness from me. And as for helping Pippa, it isn't a choice, or something to discuss or debate with Felicity or Ann. It is the only honorable thing a friend can do. And now that the magic is back . . .

I step from behind the screen and take Ann's hands. "Perhaps there is a new beginning for us," I tell her. "Perhaps being a governess isn't your destiny at all."

Ann allows herself a miserly smile. "But, Gemma," she says, chewing nervously on her bottom lip, "I've only a little magic left. It's very weak. Have you . . . ?"

I can feel it inside me, a giddy wakefulness that has me attuned to everything, as if I've had several cups of strong black tea. I close my eyes, feeling what Ann does. Hope with an undercurrent of envy. I see her as she would like to see herself: beautiful, admired, singing on a stage bathed in gaslight.

A subtle change comes over Ann. I cannot say what exactly; I know only that I see her differently. Her nose, which is usually red and runny, is not. Her hair is shinier, and her eyes seem somehow bluer. Ann regards herself in the mirror. She smiles at what she sees.

"It's only the beginning," I promise.

Outside our room, girls rush for the stairs in a stampede, and I do wonder if we are ever able to get anywhere without running like bulls. Someone bangs on our door and pushes it open without waiting for a response. It's Martha.

"Here you are!" she trills. She tosses two frilly white nothings at Ann, who balks and throws them at me.

"What is this?" I ask, holding up a pair of what appear to be bloomers.

"For riding, of course!" Martha squeals. "Haven't you heard?"

"No, we haven't," I say, hoping my irritation is evident.

"There is to be no French instruction this morning. Inspector Kent has come and brought us bicycles! There are three of them. The inspector's waiting out front to teach us all! Bicycles! The darling!" Then she's off running down the hall.

"Have you ever ridden before?" Ann asks.

"Never," I say, eyeing the ridiculous bloomers and wondering which shall be more humiliating—the riding or the costume.

The other girls have gathered in front of Spence when Felicity and I arrive. We're outfitted in the latest fashion for bicycling—long bloomers, a blouse with leg-o'-mutton sleeves, and straw hats encircled with ribbon. The bloomers make me feel like a large duck. But at least I'm not as skittish as Elizabeth, who can barely walk for blushing.

She hides behind Cecily and Martha, shaking her head.

"Oh, I can't! They're immodest! Indecent!"

Felicity grabs her by the hand. "And absolutely necessary if you're to ride a bicycle. I find them a great improvement upon the uniform, I can tell you that."

Elizabeth shrieks and runs for cover again. *Dear God.* It is a wonder that she can even bathe herself without fainting at the immodesty of it all.

"Very well. Suit yourself," Felicity says. She's not shamed a bit, of course. "I cannot tell you how liberating it is to be without layers of skirts and petticoats. You are the witnesses to my solemn pledge: When I am free of these shackles and living in Paris on my inheritance, I shall never wear a dress again."

"Oh, Fee," Martha says, stricken. "How could you not want to wear those lovely gowns your mother has sent from France? Did I mention that my own gown is to be made by Lady Marble's atelier?"

"You didn't!" Cecily says.

They talk of dresses and gloves and stockings, buttons and baubles in such fevered, fawning detail I fear I shall go mad. The sounds of hammering and sawing drift out from the East Wing. The workmen glance at us, nudging each other, until Mr. Miller threatens to hold their pay.

"Ann, you look lovely this morning," Felicity says, and Ann

blooms at the compliment. Fee lowers her voice. "Wasn't last night perfection? To see Pip again—a weight has been lifted from me."

"Yes," I say, swallowing the lump in my throat. "It was good to see her again."

"And the magic," Ann whispers.

"Oh, the magic." Felicity beams. "I should like to have done everything I could think of with it, for I've none today."

"None at all?" Ann can barely hide her smile.

Felicity shakes her head. "Not a bit. Have you any?"

Ann looks at me.

"It seems to be coming to life again in me. I gifted Ann this morning, and I shall do the same for you," I say, holding her hands until I feel the magic spark between us.

"What are you three whispering about?" Martha asks, eyeing us suspiciously.

"Employing magic to better our lives," I answer. Felicity turns away, giggling quietly.

"You are rude and common, Gemma Doyle," Martha sniffs. "And you are wicked to encourage her, Felicity Worthington. And as for you, Ann Bradshaw—oh, why should I bother?"

Thank goodness, the three bicycles are brought round. We shall have to take turns. I've never seen a bicycle up close before. It's rather like a metal S with two wheels and a bar for steering. And the seat! It seems far too high to sit upon.

Inspector Kent greets us in his brown cotton coat and cap. He is Mademoiselle LeFarge's betrothed, a detective with Scotland Yard and a kind man as well. We are genuinely happy they shall be married come May. Mademoiselle LeFarge looks on from her spot on the grass, where she has laid out a blanket.

She wears a thick bonnet that frames her plump face, her merry eyes. Not so long ago, she pined for a lost love. But under Inspector Kent's kind attention, she has blossomed.

"The future Mrs. Kent is a picture of loveliness today, is she not?" the inspector says, making our French teacher blush.

"Do be careful no one is hurt, Mr. Kent," she says, dismissing his kindness.

"I shall afford your charges the utmost care, Mademoiselle LeFarge," he answers, and her face softens.

"I know you shall, Mr. Kent," she says, returning the compliment.

Inspector Kent's bushy mustache hides his smile, but we catch the twinkle in his eyes. "Now, ladies," he says, wheeling one of the bicycles toward us, "who would like to ride?"

Several of the younger girls bounce in excitement and beg to be chosen, but of course it's Felicity who marches forward and the question is answered. "I shall go first," she says.

"Very well. Have you ridden before?" he asks.

"Yes, at Falmore Hall," she answers, naming her family's estate in the country. She mounts the wobbling bicycle, and I fear she'll land in a heap upon the ground. But she gives the pedals a solid push and then she's off, wheeling effortlessly about the grass. We clap and cheer. Cecily is next. Inspector Kent runs beside her, keeping her aloft. When he threatens to let go, she throws her arms about his neck and screams. Martha doesn't fare much better. She falls over, and though she has injured nothing more than her pride, she refuses to remount. The workmen snicker, apparently amused to see us fine ladies so undone by such a simple piece of machinery, one they could fashion with their bare hands.

Felicity returns from her second go on the bicycle. Inspector Kent is helping Ann with her turn.

"Oh, Gemma," Felicity says, breathless and pink-cheeked. "You must have a ride! It's simply marvelous! Here, I'll help you."

She places my hands upon the unwieldy handlebars. My arms shake as I straddle the bicycle. It is the most awkward thing I have ever attempted.

"Now, sit," Felicity instructs.

I struggle to perch on the high seat and lose my balance, splaying out over the handlebars in a most unladylike fashion.

"Oh, Gemma!" Felicity laughs, doubled over.

I grab the handlebars with renewed determination. "Right. All I need is a proper push and I'll be off," I say with a sniff. "Steady the beast, if you please."

"Do you speak of the bicycle or of your behind?"

"Felicity!" I hiss.

She rolls her eyes. "Get on, then."

I swallow the lump in my throat and hoist myself onto the spectacularly uncomfortable seat. I grip the handlebars so tightly my knuckles ache. I lift one foot. The iron beast sways, and I put my foot down again quickly, my heart beating fast.

"You won't get far that way," Felicity scolds. "You have to let go."

"But how . . . ," I say, alarmed.

"Just. Let. Go."

With a solid push, Felicity launches me across the grass and down the slight hill, toward the dirt path. Time seems to stand still. I am terrified and exhilarated all at once.

"Pedal, Gemma!" Felicity screams. "Just keep pedaling!"

My feet push jerkily against the pedals, propelling me

forward, but the handlebars have a mind of their own. I cannot control them.

You will behave, bicycle!

A rush of power surges through my veins. Suddenly, the bicycle is very light. It's no trouble at all to keep it moving.

"Ha!" I shout in exultation. Magic! I am saved! I descend a small hill and come round the other side, the picture of Gibson Girl grace. The crowd on the lawn cheers. Cecily stares at me, openmouthed.

"There's a good girl!" Inspector Kent calls. "Like she was born to it!"

Felicity's mouth hangs open too. "Gemma!" she scolds, knowing my secret.

But I don't care. I am mad for bicycling! It is a most marvelous sport! The wind rips my hat from my head. It rolls down the hill, and three workmen run after it. Laughing, they fight amongst themselves over who will be the one to return it to me. This is freedom. I feel the turning of the wheels deep in my belly, as if we are one machine, and I cannot fall. It makes me bold. Picking up speed, I race up the hill and whoosh down the other side, toward the road, pushing harder and faster with each enchanted pedal stroke. The wheels leave the ground, and for one brief, glorious moment, I am airborne. My stomach tickles me from the inside. Laughing, I lift my hands from the handlebars, tempting fate and gravity.

"Gemma! Come back!" the girls yell, but it's their hard luck. I turn to offer them a cheery wave, watching as they grow smaller with distance.

When I face front again, there's someone in the road. I don't know where he's come from, but I'm headed straight for him.

"Look out!" I shout.

He ducks out of the way. I lose concentration. The beast is no longer within my control. It weaves frantically from side to side before pitching me to the grass.

"Let me help you." He offers his hand and I take it, standing on shaky legs. "Are you hurt?"

I'm scraped and bruised. I've a tear in my bloomers, and under it, where my stocking shows, is a stain of grass and blood.

"You might have been more careful, sir," I scold.

"You might have been looking out, Miss Doyle," he answers in a voice I know, though it has grown huskier.

My head snaps up, and I take in the sight of him: the long, dark curls peeking out from beneath a fisherman's cap. The rucksack on his back. He wears a pair of dusty trousers, suspenders, and a simple shirt, the sleeves rolled to his elbows. That is all familiar. But he's not the boy I left at Christmas. He has grown into a man these past months. His shoulders are broader, the planes of his face sharper. And there is something else changed about him that I cannot name. We stand facing each other, my hands tight on the handlebars, a thing of iron between us.

I choose my words as carefully as knives. "How good it is to see you again."

He offers me a small smile. "You've taken up bicycling, I see."

"Yes, much has happened these months," I snap.

Kartik's smile fades, and I am sorry for my uncivil tongue.

"You're angry."

"I'm not," I say with a harsh slap of a laugh.

"I don't blame you for it."

I swallow hard. "I wondered if the Rakshana had . . . if you were . . ."

"Dead?"

I nod.

"It would seem not." He lifts his head and I note the dark circles beneath his eyes.

"Are you well? Have you eaten?" I ask.

"Please don't worry on my account." He leans in and for one giddy moment I think he means to kiss me. "And the realms? What news of them? Have you returned the magic and formed the alliance? Are the realms secure?"

He only wants to know about the realms. My stomach's as heavy as if I'd swallowed lead. "I have it well in hand."

"And . . . have you seen my brother in your realms? Have you seen Amar?" he asks a bit desperately.

"No, I haven't," I say, softening. "So . . . you were not able to come sooner?"

He looks away. "I chose not to come."

"I—I don't understand," I say when I find words again.

His shoves his hands into his pockets. "I think it would be best if we parted ways. You have your path, and I have mine. It would seem that our fates are no longer intertwined."

I blink to keep the tears at bay. *Don't cry, for heaven's sake, Gemma.* "B-but you said you wished to be part of the alliance. To join hands with me—with us—"

"I've had a change of heart." He is so cold I wonder that he has a heart to change. What has happened?

"Gem-ma!" Felicity calls from beyond the hill. "It's Elizabeth's turn!"

"They're waiting for you. Here, I shall help you with that," he says, reaching for the bicycle.

I pull it away. "Thank you, but I don't require your help. It isn't your fate."

Pushing the bicycle ahead of me, I run quickly to the road so that he cannot see how deeply he has wounded me.

✧✦✧✦✧

I excuse myself from the bicycling under the pretense of tending to my knee. Mademoiselle LeFarge offers to help me, but I promise her I shall repair straight to Brigid and bandages. Instead, I slip through the woods toward the boathouse, where I can take refuge and nurse my deeper wounds in private. The small lake reflects the slow migration of pilgrim clouds.

"Carolina! Carolina!"

An old Gypsy woman, Mother Elena, searches the woods. She wears her silvery hair wrapped in a bright blue kerchief. Several necklaces hang to her chest. Every spring, when the Gypsies come around, Mother Elena is with them. It was her daughter, Carolina, whom my mother and Sarah led to the East Wing to sacrifice to the Winterlands. The loss of her beloved daughter was more than Mother Elena could bear; her mind frayed and now she is more a haunt than a woman. I've not seen her since the Gypsies returned this time. She hasn't ventured far from their camp, and I'm surprised to see how frail she is.

"Have you seen my little girl, my Carolina?" she asks.

"No," I say weakly.

"Carolina, love, do not play with me so," Mother Elena says, looking behind a large tree as if she were merely involved in a game of hide-and-seek. "Will you help me find her?"

"Yes," I say, though it makes my heart ache to join her folly.

"She's mischievous," Mother Elena says. "And a good hider. Carolina!"

"Carolina!" I call halfheartedly. I peek behind bushes and peer into the trees, pretending to look for a girl killed long ago.

"Keep looking," Mother Elena instructs.

"Yes," I lie, shame reddening my neck, "I'll do that."

The moment Mother Elena is out of sight, I steal into the boathouse, exhaling in relief. I shall wait here until the old woman goes back to the camp. Dust motes shimmer in the cracks of weak sunlight. I can hear the hammering of the workers and the hopeful call of a mother searching for the daughter who will not be found. I know what happened to little Carolina. I know that the child was murdered, nearly sacrificed to the Winterlands creatures twenty-five years ago. I know the horrible truth of that night, and I wish I didn't.

An oar propped haphazardly against a wall slides toward me. I feel the smooth weight of the wood in my hands as my body is seized by a sensation I have not had in months—that of a vision taking hold. Every muscle contracts. I squeeze the oar tightly as my eyelids flutter and the sound of my blood grows as loud as war drums in my ears. And then I am under, whooshing through light as if I alone am awake inside a dream. Images rush past and blend into one another as in a turning kaleidoscope. I see the lady in lavender writing furiously by lantern light, her hair plastered to her face with sweat. Sounds—a mournful cry. Shouts. Birds.

Another turn of the kaleidoscope, and I am on the streets of London. The lady motions to me to follow. The wind blows a handbill at my feet. Another leaflet for the illusionist Dr. Van Ripple. I pick it up, and I'm in a raucous music hall. A man with black hair and a neat goatee places an egg into a box and, as quick as a blink, he makes it disappear. The pretty lady who led me here takes the box away and returns to the stage, where the illusionist places her into a trance. He takes hold of a large slate, and with a piece of chalk in both hands, the lady writes upon it as if possessed: *We are betrayed. She is a deceiver. The Tree of All Souls lives. The key holds the truth.*

The crowd gasps and applauds, but I'm pulled out of the music hall. I'm on the streets again. The lady is just ahead, running over cobblestones slick with the damp, past rows of narrow, unlit houses. She runs for her life, her eyes wild with fear.

The rivermen shout to one another. With their long hooks they fish the cold, dead body of the lady from the river. She clutches one sheet of paper. Words scratch themselves onto the page: *You are the only one who can save us. . . .*

The vision leaves me like a train whooshing through my body, out and away. I come back to myself inside the musty boathouse just as the oar snaps in my hands. Trembling, I slump to the floor and place the broken pieces there. I'm unaccustomed now to a vision's force. I can't catch my breath.

I stumble from the boathouse, sucking in a great lungful of fresh, cool air. The sun works its magic, dispelling the last remnants of my vision. My breathing slows and my head settles.

The Tree of All Souls lives. You are the only one who can save us. The key holds the truth.

I've no idea what it means. My head aches, and it isn't helped by the steady syncopation of hammers drifting over the lawn.

Mother Elena startles me. She pulls her braid, listening to the hammering. "There is mischief here. I feel it. Do you feel it?"

"N-no," I say, staggering toward the school. Mother Elena falls in behind me. I walk faster. *Please, please go away. Leave me be.* We reach the clearing and the small hill. From here, the top of Spence rises majestically above the trees. The workmen are visible. Great panes of glass are hoisted on heavy ropes from the roof and fitted into place. Mother Elena gasps, her eyes wide with fear.

"They must not do this!"

She moves quickly toward Spence, yelling in a language I do not understand, but I can feel the alarm in her words.

"You do not know what you do!" Mother Elena screams to them, now in English.

Mr. Miller and his men have a small chuckle at the mad Gypsy woman and her fears. "Go on now and leave us to men's work!" they shout.

But Mother Elena is not swayed. She paces on the lawn, pointing an accusing finger at them. "It is an abomination— a curse!"

A worker yells a sudden warning. A pane of glass has gotten the better of its handlers. It twists on its rope, hovering precariously until it is guided into the hands of workers below. One man grabs for it and cuts his palm along the sharp edge. He cries out as the blood flows down his arm. A handkerchief is given. The bloody hand is wrapped.

"You see?" Mother Elena calls.

There's murder in Mr. Miller's eyes. He threatens her with a hammer till the other men pull him back. "You bloody Gypsies! You're the only curse I see!"

The shouts have drawn the Gypsy men to the lawn. Ithal stands protectively in front of Mother Elena. Kartik is there as well. Mr. Miller's men grab hammers and irons to stand with their foreman, and I fear there shall be a terrible row.

Someone has sent for Inspector Kent. He steps into the thin line of grass separating the Gypsies and the English workmen. "Here now, what's all the trouble?"

"Bloody Gypsies, mate," Mr. Miller spits.

Inspector Kent's eyes go steely. "I'm not your mate, sir. And you'll have a care around these ladies or I'll have you at the Yard." To Mother Elena, he says, "Best go back, m'um."

The Gypsies slowly turn but not before one of the workers— the man in the red-patched shirt—spits at them, and the insult lands on Ithal's cheek. He wipes it away but he can't erase his rage so easily. Anger burns in Kartik's eyes too, and when he glances at me, I feel as if I am the enemy.

Ithal speaks softly to Mother Elena in their native language. Her mouth tightens in fear as the men lead her away. "Cursed," she mutters, trembling. "Cursed."

CHAPTER TWELVE

DINNER IS A PERFECTLY FORGETTABLE AFFAIR OF FISH STEW that wants salt, and badly.

I've not stopped thinking of Kartik, his coldness. The last time I saw him in London, he pledged his loyalty. What could have happened to change his affections? Or is that the way of men—to pursue girls only to cast them aside? He seemed so haunted, so desperate about Amar, and I wish I knew what to say to comfort him, but I've not seen his brother, and perhaps that is comfort enough.

And then there is my vision. *The Tree of All Souls lives.* What tree? Where? Why is it important? *You are the only one who can save us.*

"Gemma, what are you brooding about?" Felicity taunts from her perch beside me. It wouldn't do for her to ask me discreetly.

"I—I'm not brooding." I slurp my soup, eliciting a scowl from Cecily.

"No. Of course not. You've merely forgotten how to smile. Shall I remind you? It's quite simple—see?" Fee beams charmingly. I grant her a strained smile that I'm certain makes me look as if I've a bad case of wind.

I chose not to come. Why can I not release that one small phrase from the cage of my thoughts?

"I must tell Pip that the soup is as awful as she remembers it," Felicity whispers, giggling.

Pip. One more weight to add, for tonight I am to return to her and help her cross the river to whatever lies beyond.

⌁⌁⌁⌁⌁

"Really, you *are* brooding, Gemma, and have been all afternoon," Felicity chides as we walk the well-worn path to the chapel for evening prayers. "And I think I know why. I saw you speaking to that Indian," she says, dismissing him in a word.

"Kartik, do you mean?" I say coolly.

Ann's ears prick up at this. "He's back?"

Blast. Now I've got both of them to badger me—Felicity with her snideness and Ann with her disturbing, eerie stare.

"Yes, that's the one. What has he said this time?" Felicity pantomimes a wild-eyed soothsayer. "Don't touch the magic! Don't go into the realms! The ghost of Jacob Marley will take your soul if you do. Stay home and darn your socks like a good, proper girl! Hmmm?"

"I see you've not lost your gift for the dramatic. Ann, don't let her take your talent so easily," I say, hoping to change the subject.

"He did, didn't he?" Fee presses.

"He simply came to say goodbye properly." I don't want to

tell them about Kartik. Fee is no friend of his, and if I told her the truth, she'd only gloat. It would be too mortifying to bear. "But if I am preoccupied, it is because I had a vision today—my first since Christmas."

Ann's eyes widen. Felicity yanks me to the side of the path, letting other girls pass us. "What was it?"

"A lady I've seen in my dreams before. She's a magician's assistant or a medium of some sort, for I see her with a Dr. Van Ripple, an illusionist. She writes on a slate as if in a trance—a very odd message."

"What?" Felicity prods.

Mrs. Nightwing and Mademoiselle LeFarge are coming up the path. They talk of whatever it is ladies talk about when they are not on display. They seem at ease, jovial. We try to stay a few steps ahead of them.

" 'We are betrayed. She is a deceiver. The Tree of All Souls lives. The key holds the truth.' "

Felicity has been hanging on my every word, but now she laughs. "A tree? Really, Gemma. Are you sure you didn't hit your head when you fell off the bicycle?"

I ignore her insult. "The images in my visions don't always tell a story that I can see. But I think the lady in the vision might be dead."

"Dead? Really?" Ann asks with a breathlessness that shows her love of the macabre. "Why do you say that?"

"Because I saw her pulled from the Thames, drowned."

"Drowned," she repeats, clearly relishing the inherent wicked excitement of it.

Up ahead, the chapel doors stand open. Candlelight brings a flickering drama to the windows, making them seem alive.

"What time are we meeting?" Felicity whispers as we reach the doors.

I turn away. "Not tonight. I'm far too weary from the bicycling. I need sleep."

"But, Gemma!" Felicity protests. "We have to go back! Pippa is expecting us."

"We'll go tomorrow night," I say, forcing a smile though I feel sick at the prospect of what I must do.

Felicity's eyes brim with tears. "We've finally found our way back, and you want to keep us from happiness."

"Fee . . . ," I start, but she turns her back, and I realize I shall have to allow them to hate me tonight though it is hard to bear.

The woods dance with the sudden brightness of lanterns. The Gypsies have come; Kartik is among them, and I can scarcely keep myself from trying to catch his eye, no matter how much I loathe myself for it.

"Here now, what's this? What is the matter?" Mrs. Nightwing demands. Sensing a fight, the girls pour out of the church and congregate at its doors, despite Mademoiselle LeFarge's entreaties for them to go inside. She might as well try rounding up chickens in the rain.

"We watch the woods," Ithal explains. He has a pistol stuck into his belt.

"Watch the woods for what, pray tell?" Nightwing bristles.

"Mother Elena does not like what she feels. I do not like what I see." He jerks his head toward the workmen's camp.

"There will be no trouble between you and Mr. Miller's men," Mrs. Nightwing says in a commanding tone. "Spence has always offered kindness to Mother Elena. But do not push me too far."

"We offer protection," Ithal asserts, but Mrs. Nightwing will not be swayed.

"We require no such protection, I assure you. Good night."

Kartik places a hand on Ithal's shoulder and speaks to him in Romani; Ithal nods. Not once does Kartik look at me. At last, Ithal motions to his men.

"We go," he says, and the Gypsies turn back toward the woods and their camp.

"Rubbish. Absolute madness. Protection! That is my duty, and I should think I am rather accomplished at it," Mrs. Nightwing grumbles. "To prayers, girls!"

Nightwing and LeFarge shoo us into the church. I take one last glance at the woods. The men have moved on, their lanterns burning small holes in the evening gloom. All except for one. Kartik is still there, hidden behind a tree, silently watching over us.

CHAPTER THIRTEEN

I CONSIDER NOT GOING. I WRESTLE WITH THE THOUGHT for the better part of an hour. I imagine Fee's and Ann's faces the next time we travel to the realms and Pippa is simply gone. I wonder how the factory fire girls will get on without her. I don't know for certain that this is the right course, but I've promised, and so I must go.

I wait until Ann's snoring deepens, and then I sneak down the stairs, hoping I'll not be caught by Brigid, Nightwing, Felicity, or anyone else. Under the shadow of the East Wing's skeleton, I put my hand to the secret door. It flares to life, and I steal into the realms by myself, running all the way.

Pippa is waiting by the bramble wall. "You came," she says, and I cannot tell whether there is relief or fear in her voice. Perhaps both.

"Yes."

"Fee will never know," Pippa says, as if reading my mind.

We take the path to the garden and the river. I am at a loss as to what I should do. Is there something I should say—a prayer or a spell? If so, I do not know it. So I close my eyes for a moment and say silently, *Please. Please help my friend Pippa.*

A small boat bobs on the river behind a tall bunch of marigolds. We wade through the marshy grass, and I pull it to us.

Pip picks a marigold and twirls it in her hands. "It's so beautiful here. I forget sometimes."

"We can go whenever you are ready," I say gently.

She tucks the posy behind her ear. "I'm ready now."

We settle ourselves in the rocking boat and push off from the shore. I have ridden to adventure, joy, and danger on this river, but never has my journey been tinged with such melancholy. This is goodbye forever, and though I feel it's right, it's still very hard to let her go. I keep seeing the Pip I knew before, the Pip who called me friend.

I steer toward the other side of the river, where the horizon glows the golden orange of sunset. It makes me feel sleep-drunk, as if I am napping in the sun. And then, suddenly, the boat stops. It will go no further.

"Why have we stopped?"

"I don't know," I say. I try to push off, to no avail.

"I thought you had the power to take souls across," Pippa says, sounding panicked.

"I've never done it before. You're the first. I don't think I can take you any further. I think you have to go the rest of the way on your own."

Pip's eyes widen. "No, I can't! I can't go in the water. Please, please don't make me."

"Yes, you can," I assure her, hoping my voice doesn't betray my nerves. "I'll help you. Here, grab hold of my arms."

I ease her into the water and let go. Her skirts billow out like lotus blossoms. "Goodbye, Gemma," she says, moving against the current. Watching her go is like seeing a part of myself vanish, and I have to clamp a hand over my mouth to keep from shouting, "Don't. Come back. Please." The light is swallowing her up. My cheeks are wet with tears. *Goodbye, Pip.*

With a sudden lurch, she slips below the water. Her hands thrash violently. She pops up, coughing up water, desperate for air.

"Gemma!" she screams, terrified. "Help me!"

Panic seizes me. Is that what is supposed to happen? But no, I've seen other souls cross without such anguish. "Pip!" I scream. I lean far over the boat. She grabs my hand and I pull her aboard.

"Go back," she says, coughing. "Go back!"

It isn't until we reach the shore safely and Pippa falls into the garden on her knees that she begins to breathe easily.

"What happened?" I say.

"I couldn't cross," she cries. "It wouldn't let me." Her eyes are wide with fear. "It wouldn't let me!"

"She cannot cross. It's too late." Gorgon slides into view.

Pippa grabs my arm, frantic. "What is . . . she . . . saying?"

"You ate the berries," Gorgon hisses. "Over time, they have worked their magic on you and claimed you for the realms. You are one of us now."

I think back to that horrible day when Pippa was left behind while we escaped. I remember the creature chasing her into the river. I remember later finding her, cold and pale, in the water. And I remember the fateful moment when she made her choice to stay by eating the berries. Why did I leave her? Why didn't I fight harder to save her?

Pippa rushes toward Gorgon and beats her with closed fists. The snakes roar to life, snapping and hissing. One nips Pip. She yelps and falls to the grass, cradling her hand. Her sobs come as hard as a choking rain.

"Do you mean . . . to tell me . . . that I shall have to stay here? Forever?"

Gorgon's yellow eyes betray no emotion. "Your lot is cast. You must adapt. Accept and live on."

"I can't!" Pippa wails. She chokes out words between sobs. "Gemma . . . you! You told me . . . I . . . had to cross!"

"I'm sorry. I thought—"

"Now . . . now you tell me I shall have to stay here . . . in the realms forever! All alone!"

Pippa is in a heap upon the ground. She rolls her forehead back and forth against the cool grass.

"You're not alone. You have Bessie and Mae and the others," I say, desperate to offer some hope, but even I can hear how hollow it sounds.

Her head whips up quickly; her eyes glitter with tears. "Yes, those horrid girls, with their hideous burns and coarse manners! What sort of friends are they? They were a way for me to pass the time—they'll never replace Fee and you and Ann. Please don't leave me here, Gemma. Take me back. Please, please, please . . ." She grabs fistfuls of grass in her tiny hands, crying as if her heart will break. I can scarcely hold back my own tears.

I sit beside her, try to stroke her hair. "There, there, Pip."

She pushes my hand away. "It's your fault!"

I've never felt so desperate, so awful. "Wh-what if you had magic to help you?" I blurt out between my own sobs.

Pip's tears slow. "Magic? Like we used to?"

"Yes, I—"

Gorgon cuts me off. "Most High. May I have a word?"

The ship's plank lowers to the ground with a soft creaking, and I climb on board and take my preferred seat near her face. "What is it?"

Gorgon whispers to me in that syrupy hiss of a voice. "I would warn you against hastiness, Most High."

"But I can't leave her here like this! She was one of us!"

"The girl has made her choice. Now she must accept the terms. She may choose the Winterlands, or she may choose another path. She need not fall."

I look over at Pip, who's tearing blades of grass neatly in two. Her skin is pale, but her cheeks are ruddy with grief. She seems a lost lamb.

"Pip has no talent for making decisions," I say, feeling more tears threaten.

"Then it is time to learn," Gorgon says.

She's behaving as if she were my mother, as Miss Moore and Miss McCleethy have. I've done with people telling me what to do. Tom and Grandmama and Mrs. Nightwing. So many who would lace me up tightly with their good intentions.

Gorgon is unbothered by my tears. "Sympathy can be a blessing and a curse. Be careful yours does not trap you. This is her battle, not yours."

"You are too hard by half. I don't wonder that you are the last of your kind," I say. I am sorry for it at once. But the damage is done. Something like pain moves across Gorgon's usually mysterious face. The snakes lie down softly, rubbing against her cheeks like children in need of soothing.

"It is not the way of things," she says.

"It wasn't the way of things. Everything is changing, and now that I have this power, I intend to make changes of my own," I snap.

Gorgon searches my face for what seems an eternity. At last, she closes her eyes, shutting me out. "Do what you will."

I have insulted her. I shall have to tend to that wound later. For now, I must help Pippa. She is sobbing, stretched out upon the shore, blades of grass strangled tight in her closed fists. She sits up with ferocity. "You'll go on, all of you. To dances and parties, marriage and children. You'll find happiness, and I shall be here forever, with no one but those horrid girls from the factory who've never even been to a tea."

She falls in on herself, rocking like a small child. I cannot bear her pain or my guilt for having brought her to the realms in the first place—and for not being able to help her now. I would do anything, say anything, to take this from her.

"Pip," I say, "shhh. Give me your hands."

"Wh-why?" she hiccups.

"Trust me."

Her hands are cold and wet but I hold fast. I feel the magic leave me in a fierce pull, as always. A few seconds of us joined. Her memories and emotions become mine to see, traveling as fast as scenery viewed from train windows. Young Pip at the piano, learning her scales dutifully. Pippa submitting to her mother's harsh brushing, her hair gleaming beneath each endured stroke. Pippa at Spence, looking to Felicity for guidance, to know when to laugh at a jest or cut someone deliberately. Her whole life she has done what was asked, without questioning. Her only rebellion was to eat that handful of berries, and it has stranded her here in a foreign, unpredictable world. I feel her joy, sadness, fear, pride, longing. Fee's face flashes, the light turning her golden. I feel Pip's aching fondness for our friend. Pippa wears a rapturous smile. She is changing before me, bathed in sparkles of white light.

"I remember . . . Oh, it's wonderful, this power! I shall change!"

She shuts her eyes tight and presses her lips together in furious determination. Slowly, her cheeks turn pink and her thick black ringlets return. Her smile is restored to its former glory. Only her eyes will not change. They waver between violet and that unsettling blue-white.

"How do I look?" she asks.

"Beautiful."

Pippa throws her arms about my neck, pulling me down. She's so like a child at times. But I suppose it is what we love about her.

"Oh, Gemma. You are a true friend. Thank you," she murmurs into my hair. "Dear me, I shall have to do something about this dress!" She laughs. Same old Pippa. And for once, I am glad of it.

"Did you ever imagine you'd be so very powerful, Gemma? Isn't it marvelous? Think, you can do whatever you wish."

"I suppose," I say, softening.

"It's your destiny! You were born for greatness!"

I should like to say that this statement brings a blush to my cheek and I quickly dismiss it as rubbish. But secretly, I treasure it. I am coming to realize that I should like to feel special. That I should like to make my mark upon the world. And that I don't want to have to apologize for it.

CHAPTER FOURTEEN

PIPPA AND I PART IN THE POPPY FIELDS. "I SHALL SEE YOU soon, dear friend. And don't worry—I shall keep our secret. I'll say that this change in me has happened of its own accord. A miracle."

"A miracle," I second, trying to push aside my misgivings. I can't gift Pippa forever.

She waves to me and blows a kiss before running back toward the Borderlands.

"*Gemma...*"

"Who said that?" I whirl around, but there is no one about.

I hear it again, like a faint cry on the wind. "*Gemma...*"

I crane my neck up toward the Caves of Sighs, where the Temple and the well of eternity lie. I have to know.

The climb to the top of the mountain is longer than I remembered. Dust clings to my legs. When I pass through the rainbow of colorful smoke, Asha, the Untouchables' leader, is there, waiting for me as if she knew I would come. A breeze blows aside her deep red sari, revealing her misshapen, blistered legs. I try not to stare at her or at any of the other Untouchables, the Hajin, as they are also known, but it is difficult. They have all been disfigured by disease. For this, they have been reviled within the realms and thought of as less than slaves.

Asha greets me as she always has: with a small bow, her palms pressed together as if in prayer. "Welcome, Lady Hope."

I return the gesture and am ushered inside the cave. Two of the Hajin carry bushels of bright red poppies gathered from the fields below. They sort through them, taking only the good, which they weigh on large scales before feeding them to the smoke pots. As I pass, the Untouchables welcome me warmly, offering flowers and smiles.

"Have you come to return the magic to the Temple?" Asha asks.

"Not just yet. But I shall," I assure her.

Asha bows, but I see from her lack of a smile that she does not believe me. "How may the Hajin be of help to you?"

"I should like to approach the well of eternity."

"You wish to face your fears?"

"There is something I must put to rest," I answer.

She shakes her head slowly. "Putting to rest is not so easy. You are free to enter."

A wall of water separates me from what lies within. I need only pass through it, and I will know for certain. My lips are dry with fear. I moisten them with my tongue, try to steady myself. Holding my breath, I push through the water's skin, and then I'm inside the sacred heart of the Temple.

The well of eternity sits in the center. Its deep waters make no sound. Heart hammering in my chest, I approach the well, until my fingers light upon the rough edge of it. I can scarcely draw a breath. My tongue catches against the roof of my mouth. I grip the edge of the well tightly and peer in. The water inside has turned to ice. My face is reflected in its smoky surface. I trace the outline of it there.

A woman's face presses against the surface, and I stumble back, gasping. Her features emerge from the murky deep of the well. The eyes and mouth are closed as in death. Her face is bleached of all color. Her hair floats on the water beneath the ice like the rays of a dark sun.

Circe's eyes snap open. "Gemma . . . you've come."

I back away further, shaking my head. My stomach lurches. I want to vomit. But fear keeps me from doing even that. "You . . . you're dead," I whisper. "I killed you."

"No. I live." Her voice is a strangled whisper. "When you bound the magic to yourself, you trapped me here. I shall die when the magic is returned."

"And I'm g-glad of it," I stammer, walking quickly toward the wall of water that separates this terrible room from the Caves of Sighs.

Circe's eerie voice echoes in the cave like the imagined murmurs of demons. "The Order is plotting against you. They plan to take back the realms without you."

"You're lying," I say, shivering.

"You forget, Gemma—I was one of them for a time. They'll do anything to have the power again. You can't trust them."

"You're the one I can't trust!"

"I did not kill Nell Hawkins," she says, naming the girl whose blood is on my hands.

"You gave me no choice!" But it's too late. She has found my wound and gouged it further.

"There is always a choice, Gemma. While there is time, I can teach you to harness your power, to make it obey you. Do you want it to lead you, or will you be its master?"

I approach the well cautiously. "My mother might have taught me in time. But she never got the chance. You killed her first."

"She killed herself."

"To keep her soul safe from you and that horrid Winterlands creature—that tracker! She did not wish to be corrupted! I'd have done the same."

"I wouldn't have. For a daughter such as you, I'd have fought with my very last breath. But Mary was never much of a fighter, not like you."

"You've no leave to speak of my mother," I snap.

I steal a quick glance, and for a second, I see in her face something of who she once was, a glimpse of my former teacher, Miss Moore. But then she speaks, and that chill runs up my spine.

"Gemma, you needn't worry about me. I would never harm you. But I might still help you. And all I ask in return is to have a taste of magic again—just once more before I die."

For a moment, her words sow doubt under my skin. But she is not to be trusted. It's only a ploy to get the power. She hasn't changed. "I'm leaving."

"There is a plan in motion. You cannot imagine what dangers you face. You cannot trust the Order. Only I can help you."

I was wrong to come. "You'll get nothing from me. You can rot in there for all I care."

She slips below the shadowy surface of the water, and the last thing I see before she disappears is one pale hand that seems as if it's reaching toward me.

"You'll come back to me," she whispers in a voice as cold as the icy water itself. "When there is no one else to trust, you will have to."

⌇⌇⌇⌇⌇

"Did you find what you sought, Lady Hope?" Asha asks as I return to the Cave of Sighs.

"Yes," I answer bitterly. "I know all I need to know."

Asha leads me down a corridor of faded frescoes and into a cave I remember. Carvings of lush-hipped women and sensual men adorn its walls. They draw me even though I blush at their nakedness. I spy something I've not noticed before. It is an engraving of two hands clasped in the center of a perfect circle. It is familiar to me though I cannot say why, like something glimpsed in a dream. The stones seem to speak to me: *This is a place of dreams for those who are willing to see. Place your hands inside the circle and dream.*

"Did you hear that?" I ask.

Asha smiles. "This is a special place. It was where the Order and the Rakshana would come as lovers."

The word brings another fiery blush that will not cool.

"They would place their hands together inside the circle so that they could walk in each other's dreams. It forged a bond that could not be broken. The circle represents love in eternity. For there is no beginning and no end. You see?"

"Yes," I say, letting my fingers trace the circle.

"They would come to test their devotion. If they could not

walk in each other's dreams, they were not destined to be lovers."

Asha leads me down the Temple's colorful corridor. I wait for her to ask me about the magic and the alliance, but she doesn't. "I do mean to form an alliance and bind the magic to us all," I explain without her prompting. "But there are matters I must attend to in my own world first."

Asha only smiles.

"I shall share it. You have my word."

She watches as I leave. "Of course, Lady Hope."

I make my way alone across the poppy fields and down a dusty lane hidden beneath the green lace canopy of willow trees. Their delicate leaves sweep against the ground with a comforting swish. I take a deep breath and try to clear my mind but find I can't. Circe's warnings have found a home there. I shouldn't have gone. I shan't make that mistake twice. And Pippa? Perhaps there is a reason she couldn't cross. Perhaps there is a chance to save her still. That thought makes my steps lighter. I've nearly reached the end of the lane when I hear the faint pounding of horses.

Through the willows' curtain of green, I spy a quick flash of white. One horse? Ten? Are there riders? How many? The leaves shift, and I no longer see anything. But I can hear the pounding getting closer. I lift my nightgown and run for all I'm worth, feeling the path hit hard against the soles of my feet. I slip between two trees and dart into the wheat field, parting the slapping stalks with my hands. Still I hear it. My heart beats its refrain: *Don't look behind you; don't stop; run, run, run.*

I'm nearly to the statue of the three-faced goddess that marks the ascent to the secret door. Gulping for breath, I turn the corner. Zigzag through the sentry stones, those watching women. Up ahead, the mossy hill gives no indication of a door. Behind me is the steady pounding of that unseen rider. I fling myself at the hill. *Open, open, open . . .*

The door appears and I push through, and the sound of horses fades. I race through the firefly glow of the passageway and out onto the lawn. The light settles and the door vanishes, as if it had never been there at all.

Atop Spence's roof, the gargoyles sit on their perches, keeping watch over everything. With their shadowy backs pressed against the moon's light, they seem almost alive, as if their wings might unfurl and fling them into flight.

The tingling starts in my hands, and before I can take my next breath, it's coursing through my blood with a power that brings me to my knees. The magic is strong. It surges like an animal that must run. I'm panicked; I shall be devoured by it if I don't let it free.

I stagger into the rose garden and run my hands over the sleeping buds. Where my fingers trail, the flowers burst into a symphony of color unlike anything I have ever seen—deep reds, fiery pinks, creamy white, and yellows as bright as summer sun. When I finish, spring has come to every rose. It has come to me, as well, for I feel magnificent—strong and alive. Color blooms inside me, a newfound joy.

"I did that," I say, examining my hands as if they were not my own. But they are. I brought forth roses in my world with them. And that is only the beginning. With this power, there is no telling what I can do to change what needs to be changed—for me, for Felicity, and for Ann. And once we have secured our futures, we'll forge an alliance in the realms.

The magic urges me toward the East Wing. I put my hand to the half-built turret and feel energy flowing through me, as if the land and I are one. The earth is suddenly illuminated. A series of lines appear in the ground like pathways on a map. One line leads far over the hills toward the workers' camp. Another meanders through the woods to the chapel. A third snakes off into the vicinity of the old caves, where we first ventured into the realms. But it shines most brightly where I stand. Time has slowed. Light bleeds around the edges of the secret door. I feel its pull. I place my other hand against it, and my body is seized by a rush of energy.

Images whip through my mind too quickly for me to grab hold; only threads remain: Eugenia's amulet tossed to my mother's hands, black sands flying past craggy mountains, a tree of stark beauty.

I'm released suddenly, and I fall to the ground. The night is still again, save for the fluttery beating of my heart.

Dawn raises its alarm of pink. Already it creeps over the treetops, bringing a new morning, and a new me.

ACT II

Noon

*You need chaos in your soul
to give birth to a dancing star.*
—FRIEDRICH NIETZSCHE

CHAPTER FIFTEEN

NOW THAT SPRING SEEMS TO BE MORE THAN A FICKLE suitor's promise, and the days are warming into a happy assurance that winter is on the run at last, Britain celebrates with a bounty of fairs. The morning after I've been to see Pippa, Nightwing and LeFarge herd us onto a train, and we chatter animatedly in the belly of the great steel dragon as it storms through the lush countryside, belching a long plume of thick black smoke that leaves cinders on our skirts and gloves. It takes some time for me to woo Felicity from her ill temper about last night, but I promise her we shall go into the realms tonight without fail, and all is forgiven. And once Felicity forgives me, Ann soon follows.

We disembark in a small town, and picnic baskets in tow, we amble along in the happy company of villagers, farmers, servants on holiday, excitable children, and men in search of work, coming at last to a large green, where the fair has been established.

The outdoor marketplace spreads over nearly a half mile. Each stall offers some new temptation—crusty loaves of bread, milk with the cream hard on top, delicate bonnets and shoes. We take it all in with longing, granting ourselves a taste of sharp cheddar or a peek into the looking glass when trying on a new scarf. Everyone has come in her Sunday best in the hopes of an afternoon's worth of dancing and merriment. Even Nightwing allows herself to observe the jolly spectacle of a cockfight.

In one corner, several men form a line to hire out as blacksmiths or sheepshearers. There is even a ship's captain who enlists young men as sailors, promising food and drink and the excitement of the sea. These bargains are struck with a signature, a handshake, and a penny given out as a token of the contract.

Others are here with the purpose of selecting livestock. They mill about the sheep and horse stalls, listening to the assurances of the traders.

"You won't find better, gentlemen. That I can promise!" a man in a leather apron and tall boots bellows to the two farmers inspecting his prized sheep. The farmers run their hands across the animal's flanks. It *baas* loudly in what I believe to be utter mortification.

"I shouldn't like that either," I say under my breath. "Terribly rude."

All in all, it's a noisy, happy affair, what with the animals and the people, the farmers' wives calling out: "The best cheese in England! Blackberry jam—sweet as a mother's kiss! A plump goose, perfect for your Easter supper!"

In the afternoon, we take our tea down by the riverbank,

where people have gathered to watch the boat races. Brigid has packed us a lovely luncheon of boiled eggs, brown bread and butter, raspberry jam, and currant tarts. Ann and I spread thick crusts of bread with generous slabs of butter and jam whilst Felicity grabs for the tarts.

"I've had a letter from Mother," Fee says, biting happily into the fruit.

"That doesn't usually put you in such a fine humor," I say.

"She doesn't often present me with such a grand opportunity," she answers, cryptically.

"Very well," I say. "Out with it."

"We are to see Lily Trimble in *Macbeth* at the Drury Lane Theatre."

"Lily Trimble!" Ann exclaims through a mouthful of bread. She swallows it in a lump, wincing. "You're awfully lucky."

Felicity licks her fingers clean. "I would take you, Ann, but Mother would never allow it."

"I understand," Ann says dully.

Mrs. Worthington has not forgotten Ann's fraud at Christmas while Ann was a guest in their home. It's no matter that we all had a hand in passing her off as a duke's daughter. In Mrs. Worthington's mind, Felicity and I are blameless, the victims of Ann's devious scheme. It is amazing what mothers will believe despite all evidence to the contrary—anything to save themselves.

"You couldn't go as yourself, Ann," I say. "But you could go as someone else."

She gives me an odd look.

"The magic," I whisper. "Don't you see? This will be our first chance to change our fortunes."

"Right under Mother's nose." Felicity grins. That temptation alone is enough to pull her in.

"What if it doesn't work?" Ann says.

"Shall we let that stop us from trying?" I protest.

Felicity puts out her hand. "I'm for it."

Ann adds hers, and I put mine on top. "To the future."

Excitement ripples through the crowd of fairgoers. The rowers are within sight. People crowd the banks to cheer them on. We scramble down beneath a bluff, where we can be closer to the river but hidden from Nightwing's view. Three boats battle for the lead with a trail of lesser rowers following in their wake. The men have rolled up their shirtsleeves to their elbows, and as they pull past us, we can see their brawny arms at work. Hands tight on the oars, they move as one, forward and back, forward and back, like a great engine of muscle and flesh. The movement is hypnotic and we are under its spell.

"Oh, they're quite strong, aren't they?" Ann says dreamily.

"Yes," I say. "Quite."

"Which would you marry?" Ann asks.

Kartik's face flashes in my mind, unbidden, and I shake my head to remove the thought before I feel melancholy. "I should have the one in the front," I say, nodding toward a handsome man with fair hair and a broad chest.

"Oh, he is lovely. Do you suppose he has a brother for me?" Ann says.

"Yes," I say. "And you shall honeymoon in Umbria."

Ann laughs. "He's rich, naturally."

"Naturally," I echo. Already the game has me in a lighter mood. *Take that, Kartik.*

"Which do you fancy, Felicity?" Ann asks.

Felicity barely considers them. "None."

"You've not even looked," Ann complains.

"As you wish." Felicity hops onto a rock. She crosses her arms and scrutinizes the men. "Hmmm, that one is balding. The fellows in the back are barely in whiskers. This one nearest us . . . dear me, are those ears or wings?"

My laugh is a harsh bark. Ann covers her mouth as she giggles.

"But the pièce de résistance is the one on the right," she says, pointing to a man with a round, doughy face and a large red nose. "He has a face to make a girl contemplate drowning."

"He's not as bad as all that," I say, giggling. It's a lie. For all the times men weigh us according to our beauty, we are none the better about it.

Felicity's eyes take on a sinister gleam. "Why, Gemma, how could I possibly stand between you and true love? He shall be your intended, I think."

"I think not!"

"Oh, yes, he shall," Felicity taunts in a singsong. "Think of all the grisly children you shall have—all with big, fat, red noses, just like his!"

"I can't bear your envy, Fee. You should have him. Please. I insist."

"Oh, no. No, I am not worthy of such loveliness. He must be yours."

"I'd die first."

"It would be the less painful course." Felicity jumps to her feet and waves her handkerchief. "Good afternoon!" she calls, bold as you please.

"Fee!" I squeal in embarrassment. But it is too late. We have their full attention now, and there is nowhere to run. The race forgotten, their boat floats on the river as they call out and wave to us young ladies under the bluff.

"You, sir," she says, pointing to the unfortunate fellow. "My dear friend here is far too modest to make a confession of her admiration for you. Therefore, I've no choice but to make a case on her behalf."

"Felicity!" I choke out. I dart behind the rock.

The poor fellow stands in the boat and I see, sadly, that he is as wide as his face—less a man, more a barrel in trousers. "I should like to make the lady's acquaintance, if she would be so kind as to show herself."

"Do you hear that, Gemma? The gentleman wishes to make your acquaintance." Felicity tugs on my arm in an attempt to get me to my feet.

"No!" I whisper, pulling back. This foolishness has gone far enough.

"I'm afraid she's rather shy, sir. Perhaps if you were to woo her."

He recites a sonnet that compares me to a summer day. "Thou art more lovely and more temperate," he intones. On that score, he is sadly misguided. "Tell me your name, fair lady!"

It is out of my mouth before I can stop myself: "Miss Felicity Worthington of Mayfair."

"Admiral Worthington's daughter?"

"The same!" I shout.

Now it is Felicity who pulls on my arm, begging me to stop. In their zeal to speak to us, two other fellows leap up, upsetting the boat's delicate balance. With a shout, they topple into the cold river, to the amusement of everyone.

Laughing like lunatics, we race away down the side of the bluff and take cover behind tall hedges. Our laughter is contagious: Each time the giggles subside, one of us begins anew, and it starts all over again. At last we lie on the grass, feeling the late-March breeze sweep over us as it carries along the merry shouts of the party in the distance.

"That was horrid of us, wasn't it?" Ann says, still giggling.

"But merry," I answer. Overhead the clouds are full and promising.

A note of worry creeps into Ann's voice. "Do you think God shall punish us for such wickedness?"

Felicity makes a diamond of her thumbs and forefingers. She holds them up to the sun as if she can catch it. "If God has nothing better to do than punish schoolgirls for a bit of tomfoolery, then I've no use for God."

"Felicity . . ." Ann starts to scold but stops. "And do you really think we can change the course of our lives with magic, Gemma?"

"We're going to try. Already I feel more alive. Awake. Don't you?"

Ann smiles. "When it's inside me, it's as if I can do anything."

"Anything," Felicity murmurs. She props herself up on her side, a beautiful S of a girl. "And what about Pip? What might we do for her?"

I think of Pippa in the water, thrashing about, unable to cross. "I don't know. I don't know if the magic can change *her* course. They say—"

"*They* say," Felicity snorts in derision. "*We* say. You hold all the magic now, Gemma. Surely we can make changes in the realms, as well. For Pippa, too."

I hear Gorgon's words in my head: *She need not fall.* A ladybug struggles on her back. I right her with a finger, and she toddles through the grass before getting stuck again.

"There's so little I know about the realms and the magic and the Order—only what people tell me. It is time we found out for ourselves what is possible and what is not," I say.

Felicity nods. "Well done."

We lie back in the grass and let the sun warm our winter-weary faces, which is a form of magic in itself.

"I wish it could be like this always," Ann says, sighing.

"Perhaps it can," I say.

We lie close together, holding hands, and watch the clouds, those happy ladies in their billowing skirts, as they dance and curtsy and become something else entirely.

❧❧❧❧

In the afternoon, the business in the marketplace has begun to dwindle, and several of the exhibitors have packed their goods. It's time for dancing and entertainment. Jugglers thrill children with gravity-defying acts. Men flirt with servant girls enjoying that rare day off from their labors. A troupe of mummers presents a pageant about Saint George. With their cork-reddened faces and tunics, they're a merry, boisterous sight. As it's near Easter, a morality play is staged at the far end of the green, near the hiring stalls. Nightwing takes us to see it, and we stand among the crowd, watching as a pilgrim makes his progress through his soul's darkest hours and on into morning.

From the corner of my eye, I spy Kartik at the ship captain's stall, and my stomach does a small flip.

"Felicity," I whisper, tugging on her sleeve. "I've just spied

Kartik. I must speak with him. If Nightwing or LeFarge looks for me, tell them I've gone to see the cockfights."

"But—"

"Please?"

Felicity nods. "Be quick about it."

Swift as a hare, I slip through the crowd, catching Kartik just as he shakes hands with the captain, sealing their bargain. My heart sinks.

"Excuse me, sir. Might I have a word?" I say.

My familiarity draws the consternation of a few farmers' wives, who must wonder what business a well-brought-up girl could have with an Indian.

I glance toward the captain. "Are you going to sea?"

He nods. "The HMS *Orlando*. It leaves from Bristol in six weeks' time, and I shall be on it."

"But . . . a sailor? You told me you didn't care for the sea," I say, a sudden lump forming in my throat at the memory of the first night we spoke in the chapel.

"If the sea is all there is, it will suffice." From his pocket Kartik takes a worn red bandana, the one we used as a silent communiqué before. I would place it in my bedroom window if I needed to speak with him, and he would tie it in the ivy nestled below if he needed me. He presses it to his neck.

"Kartik, what has happened?" I whisper. "When I left you in London, you pledged your loyalty to me and to the alliance."

"That person doesn't exist any longer," he answers, his eyes darkening.

"Has this anything to do with the Rakshana? What of all your talk of destiny and—"

"I no longer believe in destiny," Kartik says, his voice

shaking. "And if you recall, I am also not a member in good standing of the Rakshana. I am a man without a place, and the sea will suit me fine."

"Why do you not come with me into the realms?"

His voice is barely a whisper. "I'll not see the realms. Not ever."

"But why not?"

He won't look at me. "I have my reasons."

"Then tell me what they are."

"They are my reasons, and mine alone." He rips the bandana in two and places half in my hand. "Here, take it. Something to remember me by."

I stare at the crumpled ball of fabric. I should like to throw it at him and walk away in triumph. Instead, I clutch it tightly, hating myself for this weakness.

"You shall make a fine sailor," I say sharply.

⚓⚓⚓⚓

It is nearly sundown when we return to Spence, laden with parcels from the fair. Mr. Miller's men are quitting for the day. Dirty and damp with sweat, they load their tools onto a wagon and wash up in the buckets of water the scullery maid has left for them. Brigid offers them cool lemonade, and they drink it in greedy gulps. Mrs. Nightwing inspects the day's work with the foreman.

"Oi, Mr. Miller, sir," one of the men calls. "That old stone in the ground. It's broke clean in two."

Mr. Miller squats down to have a look. "Aye," he says, brushing his dirty hands against his strong thighs. "Can't say how it happened, though, thick and tough as it is." He turns to

• 152 •

Nightwing. "It ain't but an eyesore, missus. Should we take it out?"

"Very well," Mrs. Nightwing says, dismissing them with a wave of her hand.

The men grab shovels and picks and plunge them into the sodden earth around the stone. I hold my breath, wondering if the secret door will be revealed or if their efforts shall affect our ability to enter. But there's little I can do about it except hope. The men pry the pieces of stone loose and deposit them into the wagon.

"Might fetch a price somewhere," Miller muses.

Mother Elena staggers toward us from the woods. "You mustn't do this!" she cries, and I realize she's been hiding and watching. It gives me a shiver, though I can't say why, exactly. Mother Elena is mad; she's always saying strange things.

It's gotten to a few of the men, as well. They stop digging.

"Back to it, mates," Mr. Miller shouts. "And you, Gypsy— we've 'ad enough of your mumbo jumbo."

"Off you go, Mother," Brigid says, starting toward the old woman.

But Mother Elena doesn't wait. She backs away. "Two ways," she mutters. "Two ways. You'll bring the curse on us all."

CHAPTER SIXTEEN

WE DO NOT HAVE TO WAIT UNTIL AFTER MIDNIGHT TO make our escape from Spence. Everyone is so exhausted from the fair I can hear the snores resounding in the hallways. But the three of us are more awake than ever, giddy with anticipation. We gather in the great room. I try to make the door of light appear once more, but I cannot seem to summon it. I feel Fee's and Ann's eagerness turning to desperation, so I abandon that way for the other.

"Let's go," I say, leading the charge out onto the lawn.

The night is a living, breathing thing filled with possibility. The cloudless sky twinkles with thousands of stars that seem to urge us on. The moon sits fat and content.

I put out my hand and conjure the door in my mind. The energy of it makes my hand shake. The secret portal shimmers into view, as strong as before, and I let out my breath in relief.

"What are we waiting for?" Fee asks, grinning, and we race each other through the glowing passageway, laughing. We come out in the realms. Arm in arm, we take the trail that winds among the stones, sneaking about so that we're not seen, looking for any signs of trouble.

"Oh, Winterlands creatures," Felicity singsongs as we near the Borderlands. "Come out of your hiding places."

Ann shushes her. "I d-d-don't think we sh-should . . ."

"Can't you see they've gone? Or something has happened to them. When Gemma took the magic out of the Temple, perhaps that was the end of them."

"Then why hasn't Pip . . ." I let the words die on my tongue.

"Because she's not one of them," Felicity snaps.

When we come to the Borderlands, we step carefully through the thorn wall. Its snares are easier to escape this time, and we make it through without so much as a scratch.

Woo-oot! Woo-oot!

The call resonates in the blue-tinged forest. Bessie Timmons and Mae Sutter, sticks in hand, pop out from behind the trees, eliciting a yelp from Felicity.

"You needn't do that. It's only us," Felicity says.

"Can't be too careful," Bessie says.

"I don't care for how familiar they are," Felicity whispers to me. "Or how vulgar."

Pippa waves to us from the castle's tower. "Don't go away—I'm coming down!"

"Pip!" Felicity leads the charge to the castle's doors. Mercy opens them up and welcomes us inside. The castle seems a bit tidier than it was before. Some care has been taken. The floors swept, the fire lit. It is almost cozy. Even the vines do not seem quite so intimidating, their deadly nightshade flowers a pretty purple against the crumbling stone.

Pippa races into the room. "I saw you at the bramble wall! I counted the seconds until you reached us—two hundred thirty-two, to be exact!"

Pippa's dress is in tatters again, but the rest of her is still lovely. The magic seems to have lasted for her, which is curious, for when I have gifted Fee and Ann, it hasn't lasted longer than a few hours at best.

"You're absolutely radiant," Fee says, embracing her.

Pippa slides me a sly glance. "Yes! It must have been the joy of being reunited with my friends again, for I feel a different girl altogether. Oh, Gemma, will you help me with the kindling?"

"Of course," I say, ignoring Fee's curious stare.

Pip leads me behind the tapestry and into the old chapel.

"How are you?" I ask.

Her lips tremble. "How should I be? I am doomed to live here forever. To be this age forever while my friends grow older and forget about me."

"We shan't forget about you, Pip," I say, but it feels like a false balm.

Pippa puts her hand on my arm. "Gemma, it gave me hope to feel the magic once again. But now, it's slipping away." She gestures to her tattered dress. "Can you give me more? Something to keep my spirit bright while I try to make my peace with my fate? Please?"

"I—I can't do this forever," I say haltingly, afraid of what will happen, whichever course I take.

"I didn't ask you to do it forever." Pippa pulls a shriveled berry from a bowl and eats it, making a face. "And anyway, you were the one who offered. Please, Gemma. It means the world to me. If I must endure this place . . ."

She wipes away tears, and I feel the perfect louse of a friend. For all my talk of changing things, why do I hesitate with Pippa? If I could change her lot, wouldn't that prove it's a new world, a new hope, with no limits?

"Give me your hands," I say, and Pippa embraces me.

"I'll not forget it," she says, kissing my cheek. Then her brow furrows. "Can't you give me more this time, so that I might make it last?"

"I can't control how long it lasts," I explain. "I'm only just trying to understand it."

We hold hands, and once again, that thread connects us. I feel what she feels. I see her in a fine ball gown, dancing happily with her friends, twirling beneath Fee's arm, laughing all the while. Underneath, there's something else, though. Something unsettling, and I break the contact.

"There you are," I say, hoping she can't hear the nerves in it.

Pippa stretches her arms over her head and licks her lips, which are already getting pink. The change comes over her more quickly this time, and it's richer. Her eyes shine. "Am I beautiful?"

"You are the most beautiful girl of all," I say, and it is the truth.

"Oh, Gemma, thank you!" She embraces me again like a grateful child, and I melt under her charm.

"You're welcome, Pip."

Pippa flounces into the main hall, her eyes shining. "Darlings!"

Bessie rises as if Pip were her beloved sovereign. "Miss Pip. You look grand."

"I feel grand, Bessie. In fact, I am reborn. Look!" She puts her hands to Bessie's neck, and a beautiful cameo with a velvet ribbon looped through it hangs there suddenly.

"I don't believe it!" Bessie shouts.

"Yes, I have magic," Pippa says, glancing in my direction. "Gemma gave it to me. All the power of the realms rests with her now."

Felicity actually kisses my cheek. "I knew you'd do right by her," she whispers.

The girls have a million questions: Where is the magic from? How does it work? What can it do?

"I wish I knew more about it myself," I say, shaking my head. "Sometimes it's very powerful indeed. Other times, I can scarcely feel it. It doesn't seem to last long."

"Can you give it to us?" Mae asks, eyes bright, as if I can change their lot.

"I . . . I'd rather . . . ," I stammer. I don't want to give too much of it away, I find. What if my power should diminish? What if it meant I couldn't help us in our own world? The factory fire girls' eyes are on me.

Bessie Timmons snorts. "No, course she don't wanna share it wif the likes of us."

"That isn't true," I say, but in my heart, I know she's not entirely wrong. Why shouldn't they have magic too? Is it only because they worked in a factory? Because they speak with an accent different from my own?

"We're not ladies, like them, Bessie," little Wendy offers meekly. "We shouldn't expect it."

"Yes, we can't *all* expect it," Felicity adds as if speaking to a servant.

Pippa leaps up from the weed-choked floor. "I will gift you, Mae. Here, hold out your hands."

"Don't feel nuffin'," Mae says after a moment, and I'm glad that they cannot feel my relief. I like being the one who holds the magic.

Disappointment shows on Pip's face. "Well, it's only just come to me. If I could, my darling, I would gift you with it."

"I know you would, Miss Pip," Mae says, downhearted, and new shame takes me. Looking at the girls' terrible burns and sorry state, how can I possibly be so callous as to deny them a bit of happiness?

"Right. Let's have a jolly time now we're here, shall we?" I say, and I join hands with every one of them but Wendy, who insists she doesn't want to play. Soon we're all brimming with a shining power and even the walls cannot contain our jubilant cries. They creak and groan as the vines tighten their hold.

⌁⌁⌁⌁⌁

Felicity and Ann show the factory girls how to turn their ragged skirts into sumptuous silks with beads and embroidery like those from the finest shops in Paris.

Everyone is merry except for Wendy. She sits in a corner, hugging her knees to her chest.

I take a seat beside her on the cold, weedy floor. "What is the matter, Wendy?"

"I'm afraid," she says, holding tightly to her legs.

"Of what?"

"Of wantin' it too much, miss." She wipes her nose on her sleeve. "You said it don't last forever. But what if, once I go' a taste of it . . ." A tear slips down her dirty cheek. "What if I can't go back to how it was?"

"A teacher of mine once said that we can't go back; we can

only move forward," I say, parroting Miss Moore's words. Back when she was Miss Moore in my mind and not Circe. "You don't have to do it."

She nods. "Maybe I could 'ave just a little? Not too much?"

I give her only a little, and when I feel her pulling away, I stop.

"So, Wendy, what will it be first—a ball gown? Ruby earbobs? A prince?" I swallow hard and touch my fingers to her useless eyes. "Or . . . I might . . ."

She nods. "Yes, miss, if you please."

I cover her eyes and will the magic to its purpose. "Did it . . . ," I begin.

Wendy's mouth settles into a thin line. "Sorry, miss."

"You can't see?"

She shakes her head. "It was too much to hope for."

"Nothing's ever too much to hope for," I say, but my heart is heavy. It is the first limit to the magic: It cannot heal, it would seem. "Is there something else? Anything at all?"

"I'll show you," she says, taking my hands. Feeling her way, she leads me outside and around the castle to a small patch of grass bitten with frost. She kneels, pressing her palms to it. A perfect white rose snakes from the ground. Its petals are edged with a deep blood red.

She inhales deeply. A smile crosses her lips. "Is it there?"

"Yes," I say. "It's beautiful."

"Mum sold roses at the pub. I always liked the smell."

A sweet brown hare hops past, its nose wiggling at the ground.

"Wendy," I whisper. "Don't move."

I brush the frost from a patch of bitter herbs and offer them to the bunny. Curious, he hops closer, and I nestle him into my arms.

"Here, feel," I say, putting the rabbit near Wendy. She strokes his fur, and a smile lights her face. "What shall we call him?" I ask.

"No, you should name 'im," Wendy insists.

"Very well." I peer closely at his twitching nose. There's something noble and aloof about him. "Mr. Darcy, I should think."

"Mr. Darcy. I like it."

I fashion a cage for him of twigs and vines and a bit of magic and place the little fellow inside. Wendy holds fast to the cage as if it contains her dearest dreams.

⁂

Though it is hard to say goodbye, our night must come to an end, and we must return to our world. We embrace with promises of tomorrow, and Pippa and the others escort us as far as the bramble wall. We're on our way to the secret door when the ground begins to shake with the sound of horses.

"Let's go! Quickly!" I shout.

"What is it?" Ann asks, but we are already running and there is no time for replies.

"They're cutting us off," I call. "To the garden."

We run hard and fast with the riders in pursuit, but we're no match for them. By the time the river is in view, they've got us trapped.

"Use the magic," Felicity begs, but I'm so frightened I cannot gain control of it. It races through me till I'm on my knees.

Several magnificent centaurs step out from behind the lush

ferns. They are led by one named Creostus. He doesn't care for any mortal, and he especially doesn't care for me.

He crosses his muscular arms over his broad chest and eyes me with contempt. "Hello, Priestess. I believe you owe my people a visit."

"Yes. I had planned to do so," I lie.

Creostus leans close. His eyebrows are thick and his thin wisp of a beard comes to a point beneath a wide, cruel smile. He smells like earth and sweat. "Of course you did."

"All is in readiness, Most High. I shall take you to Philon now," Gorgon calls, slipping into view, and I know she's had a hand in this. She wants me to make the alliance no matter what.

"Yes, you see? We were on our way," I say, flashing Gorgon a glance, which she ignores. She lowers the plank for us, keeping her eyes on the centaur.

Creostus allows Felicity and Ann to pass but cuts me off. He puts his face near my ear, his voice a harsh purr that raises gooseflesh on my neck. "Betray us, Priestess, and you'll be sorry."

As I board, Felicity pulls me aside. "Must we go with that overgrown goat?"

I sigh. "What choice do we have?"

"What if they mean to make the alliance now, before we've really had a chance to change anything?" Ann asks, and I know it's her very existence she's speaking of.

"It is only a discussion," I tell them. "Nothing is decided yet. The magic is still ours for now."

"Very well," Felicity says. "But please, let's not stay long. And I won't sit near that Creostus. He's vile."

We sail the river, doing our best to ignore Creostus and his centaurs, who watch our every move as if we might jump ship. At last, Gorgon takes the familiar turn toward the home of the forest folk. A veil of shimmering water hides their island from view. The boat parts the curtain of it, and we pass through a fresh, cool mist that coats our skin with jeweled flecks, turning us into golden girls.

The haze lifts. The verdant shore of the forest folk slides into view, a thick green as inviting as a feather bed. As our massive ship anchors, several of the forest children stop their game and step forward to gape at the terrible wonder that is the gorgon. Gorgon is not charmed by their staring. She turns toward them and lets the snakes about her head stretch and hiss, their forked tongues quick whips of red among all the green. The children yelp and run for the cover of the trees.

"That wasn't very kind of you," I scold. I'm still angry that she's betrayed our presence to Philon.

"Miscreants," Gorgon says in her slithery voice. "No better than toads."

"They're only children."

"I am unbothered by the maternal instinct," she purrs. With that, the snakes settle into rest. The gorgon closes her eyes and speaks no more.

The floating lights that live in the forest beckon for us to follow. They lead us through tall trees that smell of Christmas morning. The spiciness makes my nose run. At last we reach the thatched-roof huts of the village. A woman the color of twilight plods past carrying buckets of glistening rainbow-hued water. She catches my eye, and quick as you please, she changes in appearance till I am staring at my own reflection.

"Gemma!" Ann cries.

"How did you do that?" I ask. It is odd to have two of me.

She smiles—my smile on another face!—and transforms once more, becoming an exact replica of Felicity, with the same full mouth and pale blond hair. Felicity is not amused. She picks up a rock and palms it.

"Stop that this instant or you'll be sorry."

The woman slides into her twilight self. With a sharp cackle, she hoists her glistening pails and walks away.

Philon greets us at the edge of the village. The creature is neither man nor woman but something in between, with a long, lean body and skin of dusky purple. Today Philon wears a coat of fat spring leaves. Their deep hue brings out the green in its wide, almond-shaped eyes.

"So you've come at last, Priestess. I had begun to think you'd forgotten us."

"I hadn't forgotten," I mumble.

"I am glad to hear it, for we would hate to think you'd prove no kinder to us than the Order priestesses who came before you," Philon says, exchanging glances with Creostus.

"I've come," I say.

"Let's not tarry here exchanging pleasantries," Creostus snarls.

We follow Philon's willowy, graceful form into the low thatched-roof hut where we first met. It is as I remember it: sumptuous pallets sit on a floor made of golden straw. The room holds four more centaurs and a half dozen forest folk. I do not see Asha or any of the Untouchables but perhaps they are on their way.

I take a seat on one of the pallets. "There was a woman who transformed into me before my eyes. How could she do that?"

"Ah. Neela." Philon pours a red liquid into a silver chalice. "She is a shape-shifter."

"Shape-shifter?" Ann repeats. She's having difficulty balancing on the pallet. She topples into me twice before finding a level spot in the middle.

"We had the ability to change into other forms. It served us well in your world. We could become any mortal's fantasy. Sometimes the mortals chose to follow us into this world, to become our playthings. It did not sit well with the Order and the Rakshana." Philon tells the tale with no apparent regret or remorse whatsoever.

"You stole mortals from our world," I say, horrified.

Philon sips from the chalice. "The mortals had a choice. They chose to come with us."

"You enchanted them!"

A smirk pulls at the corners of Philon's thin lips. "They chose to be enchanted."

Philon has been our ally, but I find this knowledge disturbing, and I wonder just whom I've made promises to.

"That power died out in many of us from lack of use. But it has remained in some, such as Neela."

As he says this, the twilight woman enters the tent. She looks from us to Philon and Creostus and says something to Philon in their language. Philon answers in kind, and with a suspicious glance in my direction, she takes her place beside Creostus. She places a hand on his back and rubs his soft fur.

Philon crosses the room in two long strides and settles into a large chair made of palm fronds. As we watch, the creature lights a long, slender reed and draws deeply from it until its eyes are soft and glassy.

"We must discuss the future of the realms, Priestess. We gave aid to you when you needed it. Now we expect payment."

"It is time to make the alliance," Creostus thunders. "We would go to the Temple and lay hands together. The magic will belong to each of us then, and we will govern ourselves as we see fit."

"But there are other considerations," I say, the knowledge that they took mortals for their own amusement burdening my mind.

"What considerations?" Philon asks, cocking an eyebrow.

"The Untouchables," I say. "Where are they? They should be here."

"The Untouchables," Neela spits. "Bah!"

Philon exhales and the room grows hazy. "I sent word. They did not come, as I knew they would not."

"Why?" I ask.

"They fear change," Philon answers. "They serve without question."

"They are cowards! They have always been slaves to the Order—diseased filth! I should rid the realms of them if I could," Creostus bellows.

"Creostus," Philon says, rebuking the centaur and offering him the pipe. He sneers and bats it away. Unperturbed, Philon smokes more, till the room is filled with a strong, spicy perfume that dizzies me. "There are many tribes within the realms, Priestess. You will never bring them all into accord."

"How do we know that you even told the Untouchables about this meeting?" Fee says accusingly.

Philon blows a stream of smoke into her face. She coughs, then raises her head for more.

"You have only my word," Philon answers.

Lean and restless, Creostus paces the length of the room. "Why should we share with those vermin the Untouchables? Filth of the Order. Diseased cowards. They deserve their lot."

Neela sits beside Philon and runs her fingers through the creature's silky hair. "Let her prove her loyalty to us. Tell her to take us to the Temple now."

"I won't join hands without speaking to Asha," I say. The smoke has loosened my tongue.

Creostus growls in anger. He kicks a table with his hoof, smashing it to pieces. "Another stalling tactic, Philon. When will you realize you cannot make bargains with these witches?"

"They will take the magic and keep us out," Neela hisses.

Creostus looks as if he would stomp us into dust. "We should be looking after ourselves!"

Neela glares at me. "She will betray us as the others did. How do we know she is not in league with the Order now?"

"*Nyim syatt!*" Philon's voice thunders in the hut till it shakes. All are cowed. Creostus lowers his head. Philon releases a great cloud of smoke and turns those catlike eyes to me. "You promised to share the power with us, Priestess. Do you revoke your word?"

"No, of course not," I say, but I am no longer certain. I fear I trusted too soon and promised too much. "I only ask for a little more time to better understand the realms and my duties."

Neela sneers. "She asks for time to plot against us."

Creostus takes a position near me. He is large and intimidating.

"I can offer a temporary share of the magic," I say, feeling that I must placate them. "A gift as a symbol of good faith."

"A gift?" Creostus snarls, bringing his face to mine. "That is not the same as to own! To be gifted is not to own! Would we beg for magic from you as we did from the Order?"

"I am not of the Order!" I say, trembling.

Philon's gaze is cool. "So you say. But it gets harder and harder to tell the difference."

"I . . . I meant only to help."

"We do not want your help," Neela spits. "We want our fair share. We want to govern ourselves at last."

Philon holds my gaze. "We would have more than a taste, Priestess. Do what you must. We shall give you time—"

Neela pounces. "But, Philon—"

"We shall give you time," Philon repeats, glaring hard at Neela. She slinks off to Creostus's side, glowering at us all. "But I will not find myself without and wanting this time, Priestess. I have a duty to my people. Soon, we shall meet again—as friends or as enemies."

~~~~~

"You certainly don't mean to join with those horrid creatures, do you?" Felicity asks as we make our way through the tall trees toward the shore and Gorgon.

"What can I do? I gave them my word." And now I'm sorry for it. My thoughts are as cloudy as the horizon, and my movements are slow. I breathe in the firm odor of the trees to rid my head of Philon's spicy smoke.

"Did they really spirit away mortals?" Ann asks. It's the sort of macabre fact she loves to collect.

"Horrible," Felicity says, yawning. "They don't deserve a share of the magic. They'll only misuse it."

I'm in a terrible spot. If I don't join hands with Philon, I make enemies of the forest folk and the tribes that support them. If I share the magic with them, they might prove untrustworthy.

"Gemma."

I've not heard that soft voice in a long time. My heart falls through the floor of me. Standing on the path in her blue gown is my mother. She opens her arms wide.

"Gemma, darling."

"Mother?" I whisper. "Is that you?"

She smiles brightly. The smile turns to a laugh. The form changes, shifts, becomes entirely new, and I'm staring at Neela. She giggles into her long, stemlike fingers.

"Gemma, dear." It is my mother's voice coming from that nasty little creature.

"Why did you do that?" I shout.

"Because I can," she says.

"Don't you dare do it again," I snap.

"Or what?" Neela taunts.

My fingers tingle with the itch of magic. In seconds, it rushes through me like a swollen river and my entire body shakes with its majestic force.

"Gemma!" Fee puts steadying arms around me. I can't hold it back. I must let it out. My hand lights on her shoulder, and the magic flows into Felicity with no warning, no control. Changes ripple through her: She's a queen, a Valkyrie, a warrior in chain mail. She falls onto all fours in the soft grass, gasping for breath.

"Fee! Are you all right?" I rush to her side but don't touch her. I'm afraid to.

"Yes," she manages to say in a thin voice as one last change comes over her and she is herself again.

I can hear Neela laughing behind me. "It's too much for you, Priestess. You're in over your head. Better to let someone more skilled wield it. I would be happy to relieve you of your burden."

"Fee," I say, ignoring Neela. "I'm sorry. I couldn't control it."

Ann helps Felicity to her feet. Felicity puts a hand to her stomach as if she has been punched. "So much change so fast," she says weakly. "I wasn't prepared."

"I am sorry," I say, and this time, I put Felicity's arm across my shoulder to steady her. Neela cackles as we stumble toward Gorgon.

"Priestess!" the creature calls out. When I turn, she wears my form. "Tell me: How will you fight when you cannot even see?"

⌇⌇⌇⌇

"How are you feeling now, Fee?" I ask as we wind through the earthen passageway with its faint heartbeat of light.

"Better. Look!" She transforms into a warrior maiden. Her armor gleams. "Shall I wear this as my new Spence uniform?"

"I think not."

We go through the door and onto the lawn. My senses are heightened. Someone is there. I put my finger to my lips for quiet.

"What is it?" Ann whispers.

I creep over to the East Wing. A figure slips away into the shadows, and dread fills me. We may have been seen.

"Whoever it was is gone now," I say. "But let's get to bed before we're well and truly caught."

CHAPTER SEVENTEEN

THE NEXT MORNING, AT A MOST DISAGREEABLE HOUR, Mrs. Nightwing summons the lot of us to the great hall. Girls stumble in with their uniforms poorly buttoned and their braids half plaited in haste. Many rub sleep from their eyes. But we don't dare yawn. Mrs. Nightwing would not ask us here this early for tea and kisses. There is an air of reproach; something terrible is at hand, and I fear that we *were* seen last night.

"I hope it's nothing to do with the masked ball in our honor." Elizabeth frets, and Cecily shushes her.

At five minutes past the hour, Mrs. Nightwing bustles into the room wearing a grim expression that puts the starch in our spines. She takes a position before us, her hands behind her back, her chin up, and her eyes as sharp as a fox's.

"A very serious offense has occurred, one that shall not be tolerated," our headmistress says. "Do you know of what I speak?"

We shake our heads, offer apprehensive nos. I am nearly ill with panic.

Mrs. Nightwing lets her imperious gaze fall upon us. "The stones of the East Wing have been violated," she says, enunciating each word. "They've been painted with strange markings—in blood."

The gasps catch from girl to girl like a brush fire. There is a sense of both horror and ecstasy: the East Wing! Blood! A secret crime! It will give us something to gossip about for a week at least.

"Quiet, please!" Mrs. Nightwing barks. "Has anyone any knowledge of this crime? If you shield another through your silence, you do her no service."

I think of last night, the figure in the dark. But I can't very well tell Mrs. Nightwing about it, else I'd have to explain what I was doing out of my bed.

"Will no one step forward?" Mrs. Nightwing presses. We are silent. "Very well. If there is no admission, all will be punished. You will spend the morning with pail and brush, scrubbing till the stones gleam again."

"Oh, but, Mrs. Nightwing," Martha cries above the hum of anguished murmurs, "must we really wash . . . blood?"

"I fear I shall faint," Elizabeth says, teary.

"You will do no such thing, Elizabeth Poole!" Mrs. Nightwing's frosty glare stops Elizabeth's tears straightaway. "The restoration of the East Wing is very important. We have waited years for it, and no one shall halt our progress. Don't we want Spence looking her best for our masked ball?"

"Yes, Mrs. Nightwing," we answer.

"Think what a proud moment it will be when you return

years from now, perhaps with your own daughters, and you can say 'I was there when these very stones were put in place.' Every day, Mr. Miller and his men toil to restore the East Wing. You might reflect upon that as you scrub."

⚡⚡⚡

" 'When you return with your own daughters,' " Felicity scoffs. "You can be sure I won't be coming back."

"Oh, I can't bear to touch it—blood!" Elizabeth wrinkles her nose. She looks ill.

Cecily scrubs in small circles. "I don't see why we should all be punished."

"My arms ache already," Martha grouses.

"Shhh," Felicity says. "Listen."

On the lawn, Mrs. Nightwing questions Brigid fiercely while Mr. Miller stands by, arms folded across his chest. "Did you do it, Brigid? I am only asking for an honest answer."

"No, missus, on my heart, I swear it weren't me."

"I won't have the girls frightened by hex marks and talk of fairies and the like."

"Yes, missus."

Mr. Miller scowls. "It's them Gyps. You can't trust 'em. The sooner you turn 'em out, the better we'll all sleep for it. I know you ladies have a delicate sensibility . . ."

"I can assure you, Mr. Miller, that there is nothing delicate about *my* sensibilities," Mrs. Nightwing snaps.

"All the same, m'um, say the word and me and my men will take care of the Gypsies for you."

Revulsion shows on our headmistress's face. "That will not be necessary, Mr. Miller. I am sure this little prank will not

· 174 ·

happen again." Mrs. Nightwing glares at us and we snap our heads down and scrub as hard as we can.

"Who *do* you suppose did this?" Felicity asks.

"I'll wager Mr. Miller has it right: It's the Gypsies. They're angry they haven't been given work," Cecily says.

"What can you expect from their sort?" Elizabeth echoes.

"It could be Brigid. You know how odd she is, with all her tales," Martha says.

"I can't imagine Brigid leaving her bed in the night to mark the stones. She complains about her back day in and day out," I remind them.

Cecily dips her brush in the pail of murky red water. "Suppose that's a ruse. What if she's really a witch?"

"She does know a lot about fairies and such," Martha says, wide-eyed.

It's becoming a game, this suspicion.

Felicity's eyes match Martha's. She leans close. "Come to think of it, didn't the bread taste just like the souls of children? I shall faint!" She puts a hand to her forehead.

"I'm quite serious, Felicity Worthington," Martha scolds.

"Oh, Martha, you're never serious," Felicity teases.

"But why mark the East Wing with blood?" I ask.

Cecily mulls it over. "For revenge. To frighten the workers."

"Or to raise evil spirits," Martha offers.

"What if it's the sign of a witch or . . . or the devil?" Elizabeth whispers.

"It could be for protection," Ann says, still scrubbing.

Elizabeth scoffs. "Protection? From what?"

"From evil," Ann replies.

Cecily narrows her eyes. "And how do you know this?"

Ann suddenly realizes she's walked into it. "I—I've read such things . . . in the B-Bible."

Something hard flashes in Cecily's eyes. "You did it, didn't you?"

Ann drops her brush into the pail and the water splashes her apron with muck. "N-no. I . . . I d-didn't."

"You can't bear our happiness, our talk of parties and teas, can you? And so you want to ruin it for us!"

"No. I d-don't." Ann retrieves her brush and resumes cleaning, but under her breath she mutters something.

Cecily turns Ann around to face her. "What did you say?"

"Stop it, Cecily," I say.

Ann's face is flushed. "N-nothing."

"What did you say? I should like to hear it."

"I should too," Martha says.

"Oh, Cecily, really. Do leave her alone, won't you?" Felicity says.

"I've a right to hear what is said behind my back," Cecily declares. "Go on, Ann Bradshaw. Repeat it. I demand that you tell me!"

"I s-said, you'll be sor-sorry someday," Ann whispers.

Cecily laughs. "I'll be sorry? And what, pray, will you do to me, Ann Bradshaw? What could you possibly ever do to me?"

Ann stares at the stones. She moves the brush up and down in the same spot.

"I thought not. In a month's time, you shall take your rightful place as a servant. That's all you were meant to be. It's high time you accepted that."

⋀⋁⋀⋁⋀⋁

Our work finished, we empty the disgusting water from the pails and trudge toward Spence, exhausted and filthy. Talk has turned to the masked ball and what costumes we shall wear. Cecily and Elizabeth want to be princesses. They'll have their pick of silks and satins from which to fashion pretty dresses. Fee insists she will go as a Valkyrie. I say I should like to go as Miss Austen's Elizabeth Bennet, but Felicity tells me it is the dullest costume in the history of costumes and no one should know who I was, besides.

"I should have told Cecily to jump in the lake," Ann mutters.

"Why didn't you?" I ask.

"What if she told Mrs. Nightwing I painted the stones? What if Mrs. Nightwing believed her?"

"What if, what if," Felicity says with an irritated sigh. "What if you stood up to her for once?"

"They hold all the power," Ann complains.

"Because you give it to them!"

Ann turns away from Felicity, wounded. "I wouldn't expect you to understand."

"No, you're right. I shan't ever understand your willingness to lie down and die," Felicity barks. "If you won't at least try to fight, I have no sympathy for you."

⌁⌁⌁

The day is as regimented as a soldier's. French is followed by music, which is followed by a joyless luncheon of boiled cod. The afternoon is taken up with dance. We learn the quadrille and the waltz. As it is wash day, we are sent to the laundry to give our linens and clothing to the washerwoman, along with a shilling for her work. We copy sentences from Mr. Dickens's

Nicholas Nickleby, perfecting our penmanship. Mrs. Nightwing strides between the neat rows of our desks, scrutinizing our form, criticizing the loops and the flourishes she feels fall short of the mark. If we have an inkblot upon the page—and with our leaky nibs and weary fingers, it is nearly impossible not to—then we must start the whole page over again. When she calls time, my eyes have begun to cross and my hand will surely never be rid of its ghastly cramp.

By the time the evening rolls around, we're exhausted. I've never been so grateful to see my bed. I pull the thin blanket up to my chin, and as my head dents the pillow, I fall into dreams as intricate as mazes.

The lady in lavender beckons to me from her cloak of London fog. I follow her into a bookseller's. She pulls books furiously from the shelves, searching until she finds the one she wants. She lays it open and begins to draw, covering the page in strange lines and markings that put me in mind of a map. She inks the page as quickly as possible, but we are interrupted by the sound of horses. The lady's eyes grow wide with fear. The window crackles with frost. Cold fog creeps around the cracks in the door. It blows open suddenly. A wretched monster in a tattered cape sniffs the air—a Winterlands tracker.

"The sacrifice . . . ," he growls.

I wake with a start to find I've pulled every one of my books from the shelf. They lie in a heap upon the floor.

Ann calls to me in a sleep-soaked voice. "Gemma, why are you making such a racket?"

"I . . . I had a nightmare. Sorry."

She rolls over and returns to her dreams. Heart still beating fast, I go about putting my books away. *A Study in Scarlet* has only a few bent pages but *Jane Eyre* has a wretched tear in it. I mourn the injury done to it as if I, myself, have been cut, and not Miss Eyre. Mr. Kipling's *The Jungle Book* is mangled. Miss Austen's *Pride and Prejudice* is wounded but still intact. In fact, the only book to escape without a scratch is *A History of Secret Societies,* and I suppose I should be grateful something has survived my midnight rampage.

I place them all neatly on the shelf, spines out, except for *Pride and Prejudice,* for I have need of the comfort of an old friend. Miss Austen keeps me company by lamplight until well into the morning, when I fall asleep dreaming only of Mr. Darcy, which is as good a dream as a girl may reasonably hope for.

CHAPTER EIGHTEEN

"I CAN'T BELIEVE THAT I, ANN BRADSHAW, SHALL SEE LILY Trimble perform her greatest role!"

"Yes, well, you will see her, but not as Ann Bradshaw," I say, bustling about my dressing table. I try the simple straw hat with a deep green ribbon. It does not make me into a beauty, but it is rather handsome. "I am sorry that you cannot go as yourself, Ann."

She nods, resigned. "It's no matter. I shall see her, and that is all I care about."

"Have you given thought to your illusion?" I ask.

"Oh, yes!" She beams.

"Very well, then. Let's give this a try, shall we?"

I take Ann's hands in mine. She's still got a bit of magic left inside her and it joins with what I'm giving her. Her joy over seeing her idol is contagious. I feel it traveling from my hand to hers and back again, an invisible thread connecting us.

"Go on, then. Make yourself into whomever you like," I say, smiling. "We'll wait for you."

"It will only take a moment!" she says, exulting. Her cheeks are already rosy. "I promise."

"This will end in misery, I've no doubt," Felicity grumbles when I go downstairs. She's fumbling with a bow at her neck. I put my hand over it, and it fluffs out, full and pretty.

"You're the one always saying the magic's no good unless we can make use of it here," I say.

"I didn't mean for little jaunts to the shows and new hats," she snaps.

"It means the world to Ann."

"I can't see how attending a matinee will change her life," Felicity grouses. "Instead of being a governess, she'll be a governess who has been to the theater."

"I don't know either. But it's a start," I say.

"Hello."

We turn at Ann's voice, but it isn't Ann who's standing on the stairs above us. It is someone else entirely—a Gibson Girl, roughly twenty years of age, with sumptuous dark curls, an upturned nose, and eyes the color of sapphires. There's no trace of our Ann in this creation. She wears a dress that could be on the cover of *La Mode Illustrée*. It's a peach silk confection with black moiré piping and a wide lace collar. The sleeves puff out at her shoulders but taper down the length of her arm. It is topped off by a hat of butterscotch velvet adorned with a single plume. A dainty parasol completes the ensemble.

She poses at the top of the stairs. "How do I look?"

"Simply perfect," Felicity answers, astonished. "I can't believe it!"

Ann regards me curiously. "Gemma?"

She's waiting for my response. It isn't that she's not lovely; she is. It's that she's no longer Ann. I look for the features I find so comforting in my friend—the pudgy face, the shy smile, and the wary eyes—and they are not there. Ann has been replaced by this strange creature I don't know.

"You don't like it," she says, biting her lip.

I smile. "It's only that you look so very different."

"That is the point," she says. She holds out her skirts and gives a small twirl. "And you're certain no one will be able to tell?"

"I cannot tell," I assure her.

Her face clouds. "And how long will the illusion hold?"

"I can't say," I answer. "Several hours at least. Perhaps even the whole day—certainly long enough for our purposes."

"I wish it could be forever," she says, touching a gloved hand to her new face.

Cecily prances through, all grins. She wears a beautiful pearl necklace with the daintiest cameo pendant. "Oh, Fee, come look! Isn't it absolutely gorgeous? Mother sent it. I shouldn't wear it before my debut but I can't resist. Oh, how do you do?" she says, seeing Ann for the first time.

Felicity jumps in. "Cecily, this is my cousin, Miss—"

"Nan Washbrad," Ann says coolly. Felicity and I nearly burst with laughter, for only we realize that that is an anagram of her name, Ann Bradshaw.

The spell is working well for Ann. Cecily seems absolutely enchanted with Felicity's "older cousin," as if she were speaking to a duchess.

"Will you be joining us for tea, Miss Washbrad?" she asks, breathlessly.

"I'm afraid I cannot. We're to see Miss Lily Trimble in *Macbeth*."

"I am a great admirer of Miss Trimble's," Cecily coos. *Liar.*

Ann is like a cat who has cornered the mouse. "What a lovely necklace." She runs a finger boldly over the pearls and frowns. "Oh, it's paste."

Horrified, Cecily brings her hand to her neck. "But they can't be!"

Ann gives her a look that is both pitying and contemptuous. "I am well versed in jewels, my dear, and I am so very sorry to inform you that your necklace is a forgery."

Cecily's face reddens, and I fear she will cry. She pulls the necklace off and examines it. "Oh, dear! Oh! I've shown everyone. They will think me a fool!"

"Or a fraud. Why, I heard a tale recently of a girl who passed herself off as nobility, and when her crime came to light, she was ruined. I should hate for such a fate to befall you," Ann says, a hardness creeping into her tone.

Panicked, Cecily cups the pearls in her hands, hiding them. "What shall I do? I shall be ruined!"

"There, there." Ann gently pats Cecily's shoulder. "You mustn't worry. I shall take the necklace for you. You may tell your mother it was lost."

Cecily bites her lip and gazes at the pearls. "But she'll be so angry."

"It is better than being thought the fool—or worse—isn't it?"

"Indeed," Cecily mumbles. "I thank you for your good advice." Reluctantly, she passes the necklace to Ann.

"I shall dispose of it for you, and you may be confident that no one shall ever know of it," Ann assures her.

"You are most kind, Miss Washbrad." Cecily wipes away tears.

"There is something in you that brings out this kindness," Ann purrs, and her smile is like the sun.

"That was a remarkable forgery," I say when we are alone. "How could you tell they were false? I could have sworn they were real pearls."

"They are real," Ann says, clasping the jewels around her own neck. "I am the remarkable forgery."

"Why, Ann Bradshaw!" Felicity exclaims. "You are brilliant!"

Ann beams. "Thank you."

We hold hands, relishing the moment as one. At last, Ann has bested the hideous Cecily Temple. The air feels lighter, as it does after a rain, and I am certain we are on our way to a happier future.

<hr />

Mademoiselle LeFarge lets us know that the carriage has arrived. We introduce "Nan" to her and hold our breath, waiting for her response. Will she see through the illusion?

"How do you do, Miss Washbrad?"

"V-v-very well, thank you," Ann answers in a faltering voice. I hold her hand tightly, for I fear that any lack of confidence might weaken the illusion she's created. She must believe it wholeheartedly.

"It's odd, but I can't help feeling we've met before. There is something so familiar about you, though I cannot put my finger on it," Mademoiselle LeFarge says.

I squeeze Ann's hand, strengthening our bond. *You are Nan Washbrad. Nan Washbrad. Nan Washbrad.*

"I am often m-mistaken for others. Once I was even taken for a poor mouse of a girl at a boarding school," Ann answers, and Felicity bursts out laughing.

"Forgive me," Fee says, collecting herself. "I've only just gotten a joke told me last week."

"Well, I am happy to make your acquaintance, Miss Washbrad," LeFarge says. "Shall we? The carriage awaits."

I let out the breath I've been holding. "That was a bit thick at the end, wasn't it?" I whisper as the coachman opens the carriage door.

Ann grins. "But she believed it! She didn't sense anything amiss. Our plan is working, Gemma."

"That it is," I say, patting her arm. "And it's only the beginning. But let's keep our heads about us."

"My, what a beautiful necklace," Mademoiselle LeFarge remarks. "Such exquisite pearls."

"Thank you," Ann says. "They were given to me by someone who did not properly appreciate their worth."

"What a pity," our teacher clucks.

⚘⚘⚘

The train ride to London is the most exciting yet. It is exhilarating to have such a powerful secret. I do feel a touch of remorse for tricking LeFarge, whom I like, but it was necessary. And I cannot deny that there is a thrill in knowing how easy it is to secure our freedom. Freedom—we'll have more of that. Curiously, I find that as I make use of the magic, I feel better—more alive and awake. Nearly giddy.

"What shall you do in London today, Mademoiselle LeFarge?" I ask.

"I've arrangements to make. For the wedding," she says with a happy sigh.

"You must tell us simply everything," Felicity insists, and we badger her with questions. Will she carry a fan? Will there be lace? A veil? Will she have orange blossoms embroidered on her dress for luck as Queen Victoria did?

"Oh, no, nothing so grand." She demurs, glancing down at her plump hands resting in her ample lap. "It will be a simple country wedding in the Spence chapel."

"Will you stay on at Spence?" Ann asks. "After you're married?"

"That rather depends on Mr. Kent," she answers, as if that settles it.

"Would you want to stay on?" Felicity presses.

"I should like a new life once I am married. In fact, the inspector has begun to ask my thoughts on his cases, to have a woman's perspective. I know it's out of the ordinary for a wife's duties, but I confess I find it quite thrilling."

"That is lovely," Ann says. She's smiling in that romantic way of hers, and I know that in her head she's conjured images of herself bustling about a kitchen, sending her husband off to work with a kiss. I try to imagine myself in such a life. Would I like it? Would I grow bored? Would it be a comfort or a curse?

My thoughts turn to Kartik—his lips, his hands, the way he once kissed me. In my mind I see myself running my fingers across those lips, feeling his hands at the nape of my neck. A warm ache settles below my belly. It ignites something deep inside me that I cannot name, and suddenly, it's as if I am inside a vision. Kartik and I stand in a garden. My hands are tattooed with henna, like an Indian bride's. He takes me into his arms and kisses me under a steady rain of falling petals. He gently lowers the edges of my sari, baring my shoulders, his lips trailing down my bare skin, and I sense that everything between us is about to change.

I come back to myself suddenly. My breathing is labored and I feel flushed from head to toe. No one seems to notice my discomfort, and I do my best to regain my composure.

"I shall never marry," Felicity announces with a wicked smile. "I shall live in Paris and become an artist's model."

She's trying to shock, and Mademoiselle LeFarge supplies the requisite admonishment—"Really, Miss Worthington"—but then she changes course.

"Have you no desire for a husband and children, Miss Worthington?" she asks plainly, as if on this train we have ridden from girls to young ladies who might be trusted to hold a different sort of conversation. It is nearly as powerful as the magic, this trust.

"No, I don't," Felicity says.

"And why not?" LeFarge presses.

"I . . . I wish to live for myself. I should never want to be trapped."

"One needn't be trapped. One's life can be made so rich by sharing burdens and joys."

"I've not seen it to be so," Fee mumbles.

Mademoiselle LeFarge nods, considering. "It takes the right sort of husband, I suppose, the sort who'll be a friend and not a master. A husband who will care for his wife with small, everyday kindnesses and trust her with his confidences. And a wife must be such a friend in return."

"I'd not make a good wife," Felicity says so softly it is nearly drowned out by the clacking of the train.

"What sorts of goodies will you shop for today?" Ann asks, abandoning the sophisticated Nan for a moment with a single girlish question.

"Oh, me, this and that. Nothing so nice as your necklace, I'm afraid."

Ann takes the pearls from her neck and holds them out. "I should like you to have this."

Mademoiselle LeFarge pushes them away. "Oh, no, you are far too kind."

"No," Ann says, blushing. "I'm not. You must have something borrowed, yes?"

"I couldn't possibly," Mademoiselle LeFarge insists.

I take Mademoiselle LeFarge's hand and imagine her in her wedding dress, the pearls at her neck. "Take them," I murmur, and my wish, borne on the wings of magic, travels quickly between us and nests inside her.

Mademoiselle LeFarge blinks. "You're certain?"

"Oh, yes. Nothing would make me happier." Ann smiles.

Mademoiselle LeFarge secures the clasp around her own neck. "How do they look?"

"Beautiful," we all say as one.

Ann, Felicity, and Mademoiselle LeFarge fall into easy conversation. I stare out the train's windows at the hills rolling by. I want to ask them if they know what *my* future holds: Will my father's health be restored and my family healed? Will I survive my debut? Can I prove myself within the realms and live up to expectations, especially my own?

"Can you tell me?" I whisper to the window, my warm breath making a foggy snowflake pattern upon the glass. It melts quickly away, as if I have never said a word. The train slows and the hills disappear behind billowing clouds of steam. The porter calls the station. We have arrived, and now our true test begins.

Mademoiselle LeFarge delivers us to Mrs. Worthington on the platform. With her fair hair and cool gray eyes, Mrs. Worthington is like her daughter, but finer. She lacks Felicity's bold, sensual features, and it gives her an air of fragile beauty. Every man takes note of her loveliness. As she walks, they turn their heads or hold her glance a second too long. I shall never have this sort of beauty, the sort that paves the way.

Mrs. Worthington greets us warmly. "What a nice day we shall have. And how lovely to see you again, darling Nan. Did you have a pleasant trip?"

"Oh, yes, quite pleasant," Ann answers. They fall into polite chatter. Felicity and I exchange glances.

"She really believes Ann is your cousin," I gloat quietly. "She didn't notice anything amiss!"

Felicity scoffs. "She wouldn't."

On the street, we pass an acquaintance of Mrs. Worthington's and she stops to chat. We stand idly by, not seen, not heard, not noticed. A few feet away, another group of women makes a bid for attention. The women wear sandwich board signs that announce a strike. *Beardon's Bonnets Factory Fire. Six Souls Murdered for Money. Justice Must Be Served—Fair Wages, Fair Treatment.* They call to passersby, imploring them to have a care for their cause. The well-heeled people on their way to the theater and the clubs turn away, their faces registering distaste.

A girl of about fifteen hurries over, a tin can in her hands. Her gloves are a farce. Ragged holes eat at the wool like a pox. Her knuckles peek through, red and raw. "Please, miss. Spare a copper for our cause?"

"What cause is it?" Ann asks.

"We work at Beardon's Bonnets Factory, miss, and a sorrier place there never was," she says. Dark half-moons shadow her eyes. "A fire took our friends, miss. A terrible fire. The factory doors was locked to keep us in. What chance did they have, miss?"

"Bessie Timmons and Mae Sutter," I whisper.

The girl's eyes widen. "Did you know them, miss?"

I shake my head quickly. "I . . . I must have read their names in the accounts."

"They was good girls, miss. We're striking so it won't happen again. We want fair wages and fair treatment. They shouldn't've died in vain."

"I'm sure that wherever your friends may be now, they would be proud of your efforts." I drop a shilling into her cup.

"Thank you, miss."

"Come along, girls." Mrs. Worthington clucks, ushering us on our way. "Why were you speaking to those unfortunate women?"

"They're striking," I answer. "Their friends were burned in a factory fire."

"How horrid. I don't like to hear such things." A gentleman passes, giving Mrs. Worthington a furtive glance. She responds with a satisfied smile. "They should have husbands to look after them."

"What if they don't?" Felicity asks, her voice harsh. "What if they are alone? What if they have children to feed and wood to buy for the fire? What if they have only themselves to rely upon? Or . . . or what if they have no wish to be married? Do they have no merit on their own?"

It is astonishing to see the fire in Felicity's eyes, though somehow I doubt this display is born of a reformer's zeal. I believe it is a way to goad her mother. Ann and I dare not enter this fray. We keep our eyes on the ground.

"Darling, there shall always be the poor. I don't very well see what I can do about it. I've my own obligations." Mrs. Worthington adjusts her fur stole until it sits high against her neck, soft armor for her soft world. "Come now. Let's not talk of such unpleasant business on such a beautiful spring day. Ah, a confectionary. Shall we go in and see what sweets there are for us? I know that girls enjoy their treats." She smiles conspiratorially. "I was a girl once, too."

Mrs. Worthington steps inside, and Felicity stares hard after her.

"You will always be a girl," she whispers bitterly.

CHAPTER NINETEEN

Mrs. Worthington takes forever to decide on her sweets, and we arrive at the Drury Lane with barely a moment to spare. The dusk particular to theaters descends, a romantic twilight that takes us away from our cares and makes the fantastic possible. The Drury Lane is known for its spectacle, and we are not to be disappointed. The enormous curtains part, revealing an extravagant set—a forest that appears as real as can be. In the center of the stage, three old witches tend a cauldron. Thunder crashes. This is only a man banging a large piece of copper, but it produces shivers anyway. The wizened crones speak to us:

> *"When shall we three meet again*
> *In thunder, lightning, or in rain?"*
> *"When the hurly-burly's done,*
> *When the battle's lost and won."*
> *"That will be ere the set of sun."*

"Where the place?"

"Upon the heath."

"There to meet with Macbeth."

"I come, Graymalkin!"

"Paddock calls: Anon!

Fair is foul, and foul is fair.

Hover through the fog and filthy air."

"Isn't this marvelous?" Ann whispers, delighted, and I'm glad for what we've done.

When Lily Trimble makes her entrance, the audience sits taller. Miss Trimble is a compelling creature with thick waves of auburn hair that cascade down the back of her purple cloak. Her voice is deep and honeyed. She struts and preens, plots and laments with such a fervor that it is almost impossible to believe she is not truly Lady Macbeth herself. When she walks in her sleep, crying with remorse for her evil deeds, she is riveting, and all the while, Ann sits on the edge of her seat, watching with keen attention. When the play comes to its end, and Lily Trimble takes her bow, Ann applauds more loudly than any other in attendance. I have never seen her quite so moved, so alive.

The lamps are brought to their full, dazzling light.

"Wasn't it marvelous?" Ann asks, beaming. "Her talent is extraordinary, for I actually *believed* her to be Lady Macbeth!"

Mrs. Worthington looks bored. "It isn't a pleasant play, is it? I so much preferred *The Importance of Being Earnest*. That was jolly."

"I'm sure the performances could not have been nearly so fine as the one we've just seen by Miss Trimble," Ann opines. "Oh, it was splendid! It was more than splendid. They shall have to invent the word to describe Lily Trimble, for none presently do her justice. I'd give anything to meet her. Anything."

As we fold into the crowd, Ann looks back longingly toward the stage, where a young man pushes a broom, erasing all traces of the performance that held her so in thrall.

I allow a man and his wife to separate us from Mrs. Worthington. "Ann, do you truly want to meet her?" I whisper.

She nods. "Desperately!"

"Then you shall."

Felicity pushes in, annoying a matron, who decries her rudeness with an "I say!"

"Gemma," Fee says, curiosity piqued. "What are you about?"

"We're taking Ann to meet Lily Trimble."

Mrs. Worthington cranes her neck over the exiting crowd, looking for us. She reminds me of a lost bird.

"Right, and how shall we rid ourselves of my mother?"

We need only a few moments of freedom. A distraction of sorts. I have to concentrate, but it is so difficult with the crowd bustling about me. Their thoughts invade mine till I can scarcely see.

"Gemma!" Fee whispers. She and Ann link their arms through mine.

I struggle to hold fast to my original intent. I repeat it silently as we near Mrs. Worthington: *You see a friend in the crowd. You must go to her. We shall be fine here alone.* I repeat it till even I believe it.

"Oh!" Mrs. Worthington suddenly exclaims. "Why, there is my dear friend Madame LaCroix from Paris! How could she come without writing me! Oh, she's getting away! Excuse me, I won't be but a moment."

Like a woman possessed, Mrs. Worthington presses into the crowd in search of her dear friend who is, no doubt, still in Paris as we stand there.

"What did you do?" Felicity asks with glee.

"I gave her a wee suggestion. Now, let's see about meeting Lily Trimble, shall we?"

<center>~~~~~~</center>

Behind the stage, it is another world entirely. A swarm of workers busy themselves with props and machinery. Burly men move long painted canvases to and fro. Several others hoist ropes whilst a man with a porkpie hat and a cigar clenched between his lips barks orders to them. We slip down a narrow corridor in search of Lily Trimble. The actor playing Banquo passes us in his dressing gown without the slightest bit of shame.

"Hello, my dears," he says, eyeing us up and down.

"We very much enjoyed your performance," Ann says earnestly.

"My next performance shall be in my dressing room. Perhaps you would like to attend? You are quite lovely."

"We are looking for Miss Trimble," Felicity says, narrowing her eyes.

The man's smile fades to a thin shadow. "To your left. Should you change your mind, I am on the right."

"The very cheek of some people," Felicity fumes, pulling us on.

"What do you mean?" Ann asks. Felicity is in full stride and we struggle to keep pace.

"He made an improper advance toward you, Ann."

"Toward me?" Ann asks, wide-eyed. A lightning-quick grin splits her face. "How wonderful!"

At last, we find Lily Trimble's door. We knock and await a response. A maid answers, her hands filled with costumes. I present my card. It is only a plain card from a shop, but that is no matter, for her eyes widen as she reads the illusion there.

"Begging your pardon, Your Grace," she says, giving a slight curtsy. "I'll be just a minute."

"What did you put on that card?" Felicity asks.

"Something that would gain us entrance."

The maid returns. "This way, if you please."

She ushers us into Lily Trimble's dressing room, which we take in at a glance: the damask chaise; the lamp with a red silk scarf thrown over the top; the dressing screen covered with a collection of silk robes and gowns and stockings sprawled in a shameless display; the vanity, where an array of creams and lotions sit next to a silver hairbrush and hand mirror.

"Miss Trimble, Misses Doyle, Worthington, and Washbrad to meet you," the maid says.

A familiar smoky voice comes from behind the screen. "Thank you, Tillie. And, darling, please, you must do something about that wig. It's like wearing a hornets' nest."

"Yes, miss," Tillie says, leaving us.

Lily Trimble emerges from behind the dressing screen in a deep blue velvet robe she secures about her waist with a gold tasseled tie. The long, flowing hair was only a wig; her true hair—a muted auburn—she wears in a simple braid. Ann is slack-jawed, awed to be in the presence of such a star. When Miss Trimble takes her hand, Ann curtsies as if greeting the Queen.

The actress's laugh is as thick as cigar smoke and just as intoxicating. "Well, this is a fancy reception, isn't it?" she quips with an American accent. "I must confess, I haven't met too many duchesses in my time. Which one of you is the Duchess of Doyle?"

Felicity offers me a naughty smile for my duplicity but there is something so very straightforward about Lily Trimble, I find it impossible to lie to her.

"I have a confession to make. None of us is a duchess, I'm afraid."

She arches a brow. "You don't say?"

"We are from the Spence Academy for Young Ladies."

She takes in our unchaperoned state. "My. A lady's education has changed rather dramatically since my time. Not that my time was so long ago."

"We think you are the most marvelous actress in the whole world, and we simply had to meet you!" Ann blurts out.

"And how many actresses have you seen?" Miss Trimble asks. She notes Ann's blush. "Mmmm, thought so." She sits before her dressing mirror and rubs cream over her face in practiced strokes.

"Our Ann, er, Nan is quite talented," I say in a rush.

"Is she?" Miss Trimble does not turn around.

"Oh, yes, she can sing beautifully," Felicity adds.

Ann looks at us in horror, and for a moment, the illusion flickers. I shake my head and smile at her. I see her close her eyes for a moment, and everything is as it was. Lily Trimble opens a silver case and pulls out a cigarette. The shock registers on our faces. We've never seen a woman smoke. It is terribly scandalous. She places the cigarette between her lips and lights it.

"And I suppose you'd like me to secure you a berth in the company?"

"Oh, I c-c-couldn't ask s-such a thing," Ann stammers, red-faced.

"In my experience, my dear, if you don't ask, you do not get."

Ann can barely force the words from her lips. "I should like . . . to try."

The actress appraises our friend through a stream of cigarette smoke. "You're certainly pretty enough to be on the stage. I was that pretty once."

She pulls her hair forward and grasps it tightly in one hand, brushing the long ends with the other.

"No one is as beautiful as you are, Miss Trimble."

Another smoky laugh escapes from Lily Trimble. "There, there, you're not auditioning for me, darling. You can keep a lid on the charm. And speaking of charm school, what would your mother have to say about all of this?"

Ann clears her throat softly. "I don't have a mum. I've no one."

Lily puffs thoughtfully on her cigarette. She blows a ring of smoke.

"The hand you hold the longest is your own." She glances at herself in the mirror, then holds Ann's gaze there. "Miss Washbrad, this life is not for the faint of heart. It is a vagabond's life. I have no husband, no children. But my life is my own. And there is the applause and the adoration. It helps to keep a girl warm at night."

"Yes. Thank you," Ann manages to say.

Lily regards her for a moment. She puffs on her cigarette. Her words push out in a stream of hazy smoke. "Are you quite certain this is what you want?"

"Oh, yes!" Ann chirps.

"A quick answer." She drums her fingers on her dressing table. "Quick answers often lead to quick regrets. No doubt you'll return to your charm school, meet a perfectly respectable man at a tea dance, and forget all about this."

"No, I shan't," Ann says, and there is something that cannot be ignored in her answer.

Lily nods. "Very well. I'll secure you an appointment with Mr. Katz."

"Mr. Katz?" Ann repeats.

Lily Trimble places her cigarette in a brass ashtray, where it smolders as she tends to her hair. "Yes. Mr. Katz. The proprietor of our company."

"Is he a Jew, then?" Ann asks.

In the mirror, Miss Trimble's eyes narrow. "Do you have an objection to Jews, Miss Washbrad?"

"N-n-no, miss. At least I don't think so, for I've never met one."

The actress's laughter comes fast and hard. Her face eases into a pleasant mask. "You'll have ample opportunity to get acquainted. You're speaking to one now."

"You're a Jewess?" Felicity blurts out. "But you don't look at all Jewish!"

Lily Trimble lifts a perfectly arched eyebrow and holds Felicity's gaze till my friend has to look away. I've rarely seen Fee so cowed. It is a moment of pure happiness, and I'm enjoying it immensely.

"Lilith Trotsky, of Orchard Street, New York, New York. It was suggested that Trimble would make a more suitable name for the stage—and for the well-bred patrons who come to see famous actresses," she remarks dryly.

"You're lying to them," Felicity says, challenging her.

Lily glares at her. "Everyone's trying to be someone else, Miss Worthless. Here I have the good fortune of being paid for it."

"It's Worthington," Felicity says, her teeth as tight as soldiers.

"Worthless, Worthington. Honestly, I can't tell the difference. You sort all look alike. Be an angel, Nannie, and hand me those stockings, will you?"

Ann, the girl who can scarcely say the word *stockings*, rushes to give Lily Trimble hers. She places them in the woman's hands with a reverence reserved for royalty and gods.

"Here you are, Miss Trimble," she says.

"Thank you, honey. You'd better be off now. I've got a suitor waiting for me. I'll send word to you regarding the appointment. Spence Academy, you say?"

"Yes, Miss Trimble."

"Very good. Until then, don't take any wooden nickels." Ann's brow furrows in confusion until Lily explains. "Look after yourself." She casts a withering glance at Felicity and me. "Somehow, I think you'll need to."

⌇⌇⌇⌇

Two gentlemen move a length of painted canvas past us as we scurry back to Felicity's mother. This close, it doesn't look at all like Birnam Wood, only blotches of color and brushstrokes. Ann hasn't stopped talking since we left Lily Trimble's dressing room.

"Wasn't she frightfully clever? 'Everyone's trying to be someone else.'" She parrots the words in Miss Trimble's broad American accent. I cannot decide if this habit will prove annoying or endearing.

"I found her common," Felicity sniffs. "And overly dramatic."

"She is an actress! It is her nature to be dramatic," Ann protests.

"I do hope it won't become yours. It would be unbearable," Felicity mocks. "Ann, you aren't in earnest about the stage, are you?"

"Why not?" Ann answers, a glumness creeping into her voice, her high spirits dampened.

"Because it isn't for decent girls. She's an actress." Felicity gives the word a sneer.

"What other choice have I? To be a governess for the rest of my days?"

"Of course not," I say, glaring at Felicity. For all her intentions, Felicity does not understand Ann's dilemma. She cannot see that Ann's life is a trap from which she cannot easily be sprung.

We've come to the foyer, which still boasts a small crowd. Up ahead, I see Mrs. Worthington looking about for us.

"And anyway, you've a bigger problem, Nannie," Fee says, deliberately using Miss Trimble's pet name for her. "You went wearing another girl's face—Nan Washbrad. She's the girl they expect to see, not Ann Bradshaw. How will you get past that?"

Ann's lips tremble. "I suppose they wouldn't want a girl like me—the true me—on their stage." Every bit of confidence she's mustered disappears, and the illusion of Nan Washbrad flickers.

"Ann," I warn.

It's no use. The full knowledge of what she's done, the complications of it, overwhelm her. The illusion is fading fast. She can't become Ann—not here, not now. It would prove disastrous.

"Ann, you're fading," I whisper urgently, pushing her behind a long velvet curtain.

Her eyes widen in horror. "Oh! Oh, no." Her hair shifts from a lustrous black to a dull, light brown. The gown she has fashioned fades to drab gray wool. We watch in horror as it begins with the sleeves and travels quickly up her arm to the bodice.

"If my mother sees you like this, we're as good as finished," Felicity snarls.

"Ann, you must change it back," I say, my heart beating fast.

"I can't! I can't see it in my mind!" She's too frightened. The magic will not respond. The dress reverts to its former self. Her hat vanishes. I must do something to stop it, and quickly. Without asking, I grab hold of her hands and force the magic on her, imagining Nan Washbrad standing before me once again.

"It's working," Ann whispers. What I've begun she completes, and within seconds, Nan is with us, her jaunty butterscotch hat securely on her head. "Thank you, Gemma," she says, trembling, as we step out from behind the curtain.

"There you are," Mrs. Worthington purrs. "I was afraid I'd lost you. It's very odd, for I was certain I saw Madame LaCroix, but when I reached the woman, she looked nothing at all like her. Shall we?"

✿✿✿✿✿

On the street, a man wearing a sandwich board passes out adverts for an exhibition at the Egyptian Hall. "Amazing and astounding! See the spectacle of all spectacles! Late of Paris, France—for a one-week engagement only at the Egyptian

Hall—the astonishing Wolfson brothers' famous magic-lantern show—moving pictures! Prepare to be amazed! Sights beyond your wildest dreams! Here you go, miss—wouldn't want to miss it."

He puts the leaflet into my hand. *The Wolfson Brothers present: The Rites of Spring. A Phantasmagoria.* "Yes, thank you," I say, folding it in my hand.

"Oh, no." Felicity stops suddenly.

"What is it?" I ask.

"Lady Denby and Lady Markham," she whispers, glancing up the street. I spy them in the afternoon crowd. Lady Denby, Simon Middleton's mother, is an imposing woman, both in form and in reputation. Today she wears one of her famous hats with a brim so broad it could blot out the sun, and she walks with the commanding stride of a naval hero. Lady Markham is as thin as a twig and struggles to keep pace with her friend. She nods as Lady Denby holds forth.

Ann gives a little gasp. It was Lady Denby who revealed Ann's charade at Christmas, largely to humiliate Mrs. Worthington. I hold my friend's arm to steady her. I won't risk another mishap with the magic.

"Lady Markham, Lady Denby," Mrs. Worthington says, all smiles. "How grand it is to see you. What a lovely surprise!"

"Yes. How nice." Lady Markham does not take Mrs. Worthington's hand. Instead, she looks to Simon's mother.

"Good afternoon, Mrs. Worthington," Lady Denby says without smiling.

"We've just come from the theater and were about to take tea. Would you care to join us?" Mrs. Worthington asks, blushing at the slight.

"Well . . . ," Lady Markham says, sparing a glance at Felicity.

"I'm afraid we cannot," Lady Denby answers for her. "My dear cousin, Miss Lucy Fairchild, has arrived from America, and I'm most anxious to introduce her to Lady Markham."

"Yes, of course." Mrs. Worthington's smile falters. Desperation creeps into her voice. "Lady Markham, I thought perhaps Felicity and I might pay a call at Easter, if you would be so good as to receive us."

Lady Markham fidgets, casts a glance toward her imperious friend again. "Yes, well, I am rather full of engagements, it would seem."

Lady Denby's thoughts intrude on my own: *This is what comes of not playing by the rules. Your daughter shall pay the price. No one will present her, and her inheritance shall be forfeit.*

I should like to slap Lady Denby. How could I have ever thought she was a good woman? She is petty and controlling, and I shan't let her ruin my friend's life.

I summon my courage and close my eyes, sending my intent to Lady Markham: *Felicity Worthington is the most wonderful girl in the world. You want to present—no, you'll insist upon presenting—her at court. And a lovely party in her honor is in order, I should think.*

"But I should like very much to receive you," Lady Markham says suddenly, brightening. "And how is our darling Felicity? Oh, what a beauty you are, my dear!"

Felicity looks as if a pile of books has fallen on her head. She smiles uncertainly. "I am well, thank you, Lady Markham."

"Of course you are. I shall expect you at Easter, and we shall speak of your debut—and a party!"

"Lady Markham, we must be on our way," Lady Denby says, her jaw tight.

"Good day," Lady Markham calls gaily. Lady Denby marches away, forcing her friend to catch up.

⌇⌇⌇⌇⌇

Everyone's in high spirits as we wait for our train back to Spence. A greatly relieved Mrs. Worthington chats pleasantly with Mademoiselle LeFarge, who clutches her few precious purchases, Cecily's purloined pearls shining at her neck.

"I should like to see that expression on Lady Denby's face forever in my mind," Felicity says.

"It was rather satisfying, wasn't it?" I agree.

"'Lady Markham, we must be on our way,'" Ann says, in perfect imitation of Lady Denby's pompous voice.

"Gemma, are you still holding on to that rubbish?" Fee points to the leaflet for the exhibition at the Egyptian Hall.

"Why, it isn't rubbish at all," I say with mock sincerity. "We have the Wolfson Brothers and their Phantasmagoria!"

Ann arches a brow. "Nothing compared to the realms, I daresay."

"But there is more!" I protest. In smaller script is a list of others who will exhibit at the hall, their names growing tinier in proportion to their importance. I read them one by one, making Ann and Felicity giggle.

And at the very bottom is Dr. Theodore Van Ripple, master illusionist.

CHAPTER TWENTY

FELICITY EXAMINES THE LEAFLET BY THE FIRELIGHT. "WE must get to the Egyptian Hall."

"How shall we do it?" Ann asks. She's no longer Nan, but some hint of magic remains, enough to keep a twinkle in her eyes. She's like a princess in a fairy tale who has been cursed to sleep and is finally awakening. "Gemma, will you make everyone at Spence fall asleep or leave an illusion of us behind so that no one notices our absence—or will you put the thought so firmly in Nightwing's head that she insists on attending and bringing us along?"

"I thought I would simply ask Mademoiselle LeFarge to take us. She loves this sort of exhibition."

"Oh," Ann says, clearly disappointed.

Felicity unwraps a toffee and plops it onto her tongue. "And you think this Dr. Van Ripple can tell us about the lady in your visions?"

"I hope so. I see her with him. Perhaps he knows something about this Tree of All Souls as well."

"Do you hear that?" Ann asks.

Horses, coming closer. It is nine o'clock. I can't imagine who would be calling at this hour.

"Mrs. Nightwing, it's a carriage!" one of the younger girls calls.

We push aside the draperies and peek out. The carriage approaches in the distance. The maids rush outside with their lanterns and form a line at the door. We girls beg to be let out as well, and Mrs. Nightwing relents.

The night's chilly breath tickles up my neck and finds my ear, whispering secrets only the wind knows. The dust rises on the path. The carriage draws to a stop, and the driver puts the steps to the door. The passenger emerges—a slender woman in a well-appointed blue-gray suit. She raises her head to take in the sight of the school, and I know her at once: dark, searching eyes under full brows; a small mouth set in a sharp face; and the stealthy grace of a panther. Miss Claire McCleethy has returned.

She greets our headmistress with a tight smile. "Good evening, Lillian. I am sorry for the late hour but the roads were muddy."

"It's no matter; now you're here," Mrs. Nightwing answers. The servants scurry about, Brigid barking orders and inviting the driver to come round the back to the kitchen for a repast. The younger girls rush toward Miss McCleethy to welcome her. I try to conceal myself, but as I'm tall, it's impossible for me to hide for long. Miss McCleethy's eyes find mine, and it's enough to make my heart beat more quickly.

"Ladies, I shall allow an additional hour that we might welcome our Miss McCleethy properly," Mrs. Nightwing announces to delighted cheers.

The fires in the great hall are stoked to blazing again. Biscuits and tea are brought round. We toast Miss McCleethy's return, and the girls regale her with tales of Spence and the coming London season and the costumes they shall wear for the masked ball. Miss McCleethy listens to it all without divulging anything about herself or her whereabouts these past three months.

At half past ten o'clock, Mrs. Nightwing announces that it is time for bed. Reluctantly, the girls soldier toward the staircase. I am nearly there when Miss McCleethy stops me.

"Miss Doyle, could you remain a moment?"

Felicity and Ann and I exchange furtive glances.

"Yes, Miss McCleethy." I swallow the lump rising in my throat and watch my friends climb the stairs to safety while I wait behind with the enemy.

Miss McCleethy and I perch on the velvet settee in the small parlor used to receive guests, listening to the ormolu clock on the mantel tick off the excruciating silence in seconds. Miss McCleethy turns her dark eyes to me, and I begin to perspire.

"How nice it is to be at Spence once again," she says.

"Yes. The gardens are lovely," I answer. It is like a game of lawn tennis in which neither of us returns the same ball.

Tick-tock, tick-tock, tick-tock.

"And you are excited to be having your season, I trust?"

"Yes, quite."

Tick. Tock. Tick.

"There is that other matter we must discuss. The matter of the realms."

Tock.

"Miss Doyle, I've begun the task of trying to find the last members of the Order. I do not know how many have survived or what powers remain, but it is my hope that soon we shall return the realms and our sisterhood to their former glory."

Tick-tock-tick-tock-tick-tock.

Miss McCleethy presses her lips into a semblance of a smile. "So you see, I've been trying to help you."

"You've been helping yourself," I correct.

"Is that so?" She turns that penetrating gaze on me. "You've had no trouble from the Rakshana, I trust?"

"No," I say, surprised.

"And did you not wonder why?"

"I . . ."

"It is because of me, Miss Doyle. I have kept them at bay through my own means, but I cannot keep them from you forever."

"How could you stop the Rakshana?"

"Do you think I would leave that to chance? We have our spies within their ranks, just as they have had theirs within ours," she says pointedly, and my stomach tightens at the memory of Kartik's last terrible mission for the Rakshana. The brotherhood ordered him to kill me. "I might remind you that your judgment has been hasty before."

"What do you want from me?" I snap.

"Miss Doyle. Gemma. You don't understand yet that I am your friend. I should like to help you—if you would allow it."

She places a gentle hand on my shoulder. I wish that small motherly gesture held no power over me, but it does. It is funny how you do not miss affection until it is given, but once it is, it can never be enough; you would drown in it if possible.

I blink against the sudden surprise of tears. "You told me not to make an enemy of you."

"I spoke rashly. I was disappointed that you did not come to us." Miss McCleethy takes my hands in hers. Her hands are bony and far too light and feel as if they are not accustomed to holding another's. "You have been able to do what no one before you has. You were able to open the realms again. You defeated Circe for us."

At Circe's name, my heartbeat quickens. I stare at a big brown spot on the floor where the wood is warped. "And what about my friends? What of Felicity and Ann?"

Miss McCleethy slides her hands from mine. She walks around the room, her fingers clasped behind her back, like a priest in thought. "If the realms haven't chosen them, there is nothing I can do about it. They are not destined for this life."

"But they are my friends," I say. "They've helped me. So have some of the tribes and creatures within the realms."

Miss McCleethy brushes an invisible speck of dirt from the mantel. "They cannot be a part of us. I am sorry."

"I can't turn my back on them."

"Your loyalty is commendable, Gemma. Truly it is. But it is misplaced. Do you suppose that if your roles were reversed and they were chosen for membership in the Order, the others would hesitate to abandon you?"

"They are my friends," I repeat.

"They are your friends because you have power. And I have seen how power changes everything." Miss McCleethy settles into the large wingback chair across from me. Her gaze bores into me. "Your mother fought bravely for our cause. You wouldn't want to sully her memory, to disappoint her, would you?"

"You've no leave to speak of my mother." My hair falls

into my face. I push it furiously behind my ear but it will not stay.

Miss McCleethy's voice is low and sure. "Haven't I? She was one of us—a sister of the Order. She died trying to protect you, Gemma. I would honor her memory by looking after you."

"She didn't want me to be part of your Order. That's why she kept me hidden in India."

Gently, Miss McCleethy secures the errant hair behind my ear, where it has the bad manners to obey her by staying put. "And yet, she asked your father to send you here should anything happen to her."

I've been so certain these past few days, but now my thoughts feel mud-soaked, and I cannot see the way clearly. What if they are right and I am wrong?

"What will you do, Gemma? How will you manage all on your own?"

"But you've not been inside in twenty-five years," I say, coming round again. "You are the one who doesn't know how it is now."

She stiffens. That motherly smile fades from her lips. "You'd be wise to listen to me, Miss Doyle. You may believe you can show largesse to these creatures, befriend them, join with them, but you are deceived. You've no idea what terrible acts they are capable of committing. They will betray you in the end. *We* are your friends, your family. There is only one way— our way—and it must be exercised with no exceptions."

The clock tsk-tsks in time. The brown spot in the wood seems to grow. I can feel Miss McCleethy's eyes upon me, daring me to look. Her voice softens once more to that motherly coo.

"Gemma, we've been protectors of the magic for generations. We understand its ways. Let us carry the burden. We shall bring you into the Order as one of our own. You'll take your rightful place."

"And if I refuse?"

Miss McCleethy's voice turns razor-sharp. "I can no longer protect you."

She means to frighten me. But I shan't give up so easily.

"Miss McCleethy, there is something I must confess," I say, still staring at the floor. "I cannot enter the realms. Not anymore."

"What do you mean?"

I force myself to meet her gaze. "I've tried, but the power has left me. I was afraid to tell you. I'm not who you thought me to be. I'm sorry."

"But I thought you'd bound the magic to yourself."

"I thought I had, too. But I was wrong. Or it wouldn't take in me after all."

"I see," she says.

For the longest moment of my life, McCleethy holds my gaze while I try desperately not to flinch, and the clock measures our unspoken hate in ticks and tocks. At last, she turns her attention to a small ceramic angel figurine perched near the edge of a side table.

"Miss Doyle, if you're lying, I'll know in time. Such power can't easily be hidden."

"I'm sorry to be such a disappointment," I say.

"Not half as sorry as I am."

She tries to move the angel back from the table's edge and nearly drops it. It wobbles precariously, then stops.

"May I go to bed now?" I ask, and she dismisses me with a wave of her hand.

~~~~~

"Gemma. Pssst!" It's Felicity. She and Ann have hidden in Ann's bed. She pops up like a jack-in-the-box in hair ribbons. "What happened? Did McCleethy bite you with her fangs?"

"In a manner of speaking," I say, pulling at my boots. I loosen the tiny loops from the hooks. "She wanted me to become one with the Order and follow their training."

"She wanted you to give them all your power, you mean," Felicity scoffs.

"Did she mention taking us into the Order?" Ann asks.

"No," I say, leaving my stockings on the floor in a heap. "She only wanted me."

Felicity's eyes narrow. "You told her no, then?" It is not so much a question as a demand.

"I told her I no longer held the power and that I couldn't enter the realms at all."

Felicity snorts in delight. "Well done, Gemma!"

"I don't think she believed me," I warn. "We shall have to be very careful."

"She'll be no match for us." Felicity bounds out of Ann's bed. "Till morning, *mes amies!*"

"*Mawah meenon ne le plus poohlala*," I say with an affected bow.

Felicity laughs. "What, pray tell, was that?"

"My French. I daresay it's improving."

Ann falls asleep within minutes, and I am left to stare at the cracks branching off left and right in the ceiling. What if Miss McCleethy is right? What if the realms don't choose my friends or the forest folk? Whom will they blame for that? Then again, Miss McCleethy tried to force me to take her into the realms once before. She'd say or do anything to return the realms to the Order.

So many decisions, so many responsibilities, and no clear path. Out my window, the woods are dark save for the firelight coming from the Gypsy camp. There is one matter I can put to rest tonight, and I will have answers about that, at least.

I creep down the stairs, taking care not to make a single sound. The doors to the great hall are ajar. A lamp still burns inside. I hear whispering voices, and I crouch low, listening.

"You're certain?"

"It's the only way. We can't leave it to chance. The risk is too great."

"You would place all your faith in this plan? We have no real proof—"

"Don't question me. I cannot do this without you."

"I am loyal. You know that I am."

"I do."

The door is opened, and I hide behind a tall potted fern. I watch Miss McCleethy and Mrs. Nightwing ascend the stairs, the candle flame casting their long shadows on the wall and ceiling till they seem to loom over everything. I wait until long after I hear the baize door click. When I am satisfied that they are gone, I fly on angel feet to the Gypsy camp.

I approach the camp stealthily, searching for the best way in. I wish I'd brought scraps to quiet the dogs. A twig breaks to my right, and suddenly, I'm yanked hard to the ground and the full weight of another pins me there.

"I shall scream," I gasp, but I've barely enough breath to speak.

"Miss Doyle!" Kartik lifts me from the ground. "What are you doing out here?"

"What are you . . . doing throwing me . . . about like a . . . highwayman?" I brush the leaves from my skirt and try to force air back into my lungs.

"I am sorry, but you shouldn't creep about the woods at night. It isn't safe."

"So I see," I reply.

"You've not answered my question. Why are you here?"

"I came to find you." My breath comes shakily but now it has little to do with being thrown to the ground. "I want answers, and I shan't leave until I have them."

"I've nothing to tell you," he says, turning away.

I fall in beside him. "I'm not leaving. I need your help. Wait—where are you going?"

"To feed the horses," he answers without stopping.

"But the Order has a secret plan!" I protest.

"That does not change the fact that the horses are hungry and must be fed. You may tell me along the way."

I match his stride. "Miss McCleethy returned this evening."

"She's here now?" Kartik cranes his neck toward Spence.

"Yes," I say. "But she's sleeping. We're safe."

"Not with that woman about," Kartik mumbles. "What did she tell you?"

"She wanted me to join the Order but I refused. And just now, I overheard her talking with Mrs. Nightwing. They mentioned a plan of some sort. She also said that she's kept the Rakshana from coming for me, but that if I don't join the Order, she won't protect me any longer." I steal a glance at him. "She has a spy within your ranks. Do you know anything about it?"

Kartik's pace doesn't slow. "They are not my ranks. I am no longer Rakshana."

"You've heard nothing, then?"

"The Rakshana think me a dead man, and I'd like to keep it that way."

I stop. "Why? What do you mean?"

"Some matters are best not discussed," he says, pushing on till I have to catch him.

We reach a small clearing where the horses are tethered. Kartik pulls an apple from his pocket and offers it to a dappled mare. "Here you are, Freya. Enjoy. This is Ithal's horse. She's a fine old girl," he says, stroking her nose gently. "Never a moment's trouble."

I fold my arms across my chest. "Is that what makes a fine girl, then? A lack of trouble?"

He shakes his head, a small smile starting. "No, that is what makes for good horses."

"What do you think of my story?" I stroke Freya's soft mane, and she allows it.

"Gemma . . ." He trails off. "You shouldn't tell me anything more about the realms. I am no longer privy to their secrets."

"But I—"

"Please," he says, and something in his eyes silences me.

"Very well. If you wish it."

"I do," he says, sounding relieved.

A hedgehog flees from the safety of a bush, startling me. It darts past us in a terrible hurry. Kartik nods toward the furry little thing. "Don't mind him. He's off to meet his lady friend."

"How can you be sure?"

"He has on his best hedgehog suit."

"Ah, I should have noticed," I say, happy to play this game—any game—with him. I put my hand on a tree's trunk and swing myself around it slowly, letting my body feel gravity's pull. "And why has he worn his best?"

"He's been away in London, you see, and now he has returned to her," Kartik continues.

"And what if she is angry with him for being away so long?"

Kartik circles just behind me. "She will forgive him."

"Will she?" I say pointedly.

"It is his hope that she will, for he didn't mean to upset her," Kartik answers, and I am no longer sure we speak of the hedgehog.

"And is he happy to see her again?"

"Yes," Kartik says. "He should like to stay longer, but he cannot."

The bark chafes against my hand. "Why is that?"

"He has his reasons, and he hopes his lady will understand them one day." Kartik has changed direction. He comes around the other side of the tree. We are face to face. A palm of moonglow reaches through the branches to caress his face.

"Oh," I say, heart beating fast.

"And what would the lady hedgehog say to that?" he asks. His voice is soft and low.

"She would say . . ." I swallow hard.

Kartik steps closer. "Yes?"

"She would say," I whisper, " 'If you please, I am not a hedgehog. I am a woodchuck.' "

A small sad smile plays at Kartik's lips.

"He is fortunate to have found so witty a lady friend," he

says, and I wish I could have the moment back again to play differently.

We offer more of the apple to Freya, who gobbles it greedily. Kartik strokes her mane and she softens under his touch, nuzzling him with his nose. Around us the night creatures have their say. We are surrounded by a symphony of crickets and frogs. Neither of us feels the need to speak, and I suppose that is one of the qualities I find comforting in Kartik. We can be alone together.

"Well, that's done," he says, wiping his hands on his trousers. "No more for you, Freya."

Yawning, Kartik stretches his arms overhead. His shirt comes untucked. It rises with his arms and a faint trail of dark hair is visible on the muscled plain of his stomach.

"Y-you seem tired," I stammer, grateful that he cannot see my red cheeks in the dark. "You should go to bed."

"No!" he says. "I thought I might walk by the lake, if you care to join me."

"Of course," I say, happy to be asked.

The lake laps lazily at the bank in a peaceful rhythm. An owl hoots in the distance. A light breeze blows my hair against my cheeks, tickling them. Kartik sits with his back against a tree. I settle near him.

"What did you mean when you said our fates were no longer intertwined?" I ask.

"I thought my fate was to be Rakshana. But I was wrong. Now I don't know what my destiny is. I don't even know if I believe in destiny."

As much as I've been infuriated by Kartik's arrogance, his sureness, I find I miss it now. It is hard to see him so lost.

We fall into silence again. His eyes flutter with sleep, but he fights it. "There's only one thing I must know and then I'll not ask again. Have you seen Amar?"

"No. I promise."

He seems relieved. "That is good. Good." His eyes close, and within seconds, he's asleep. I sit beside him, listening to his breathing, stealing secret glances at his beauty: long, dark eyelashes resting on high cheekbones; strong nose leading to full, slightly parted lips. They say a lady should not feel such desires, but how could a lady not? I should have to sleepwalk through my life not to feel the pull of those lips.

I reach out a tentative hand to touch them. Kartik startles awake violently, gasping for breath and frightened. I yelp, and he grabs hold of me and won't let go.

"Kartik!" I call, but he's fighting me. "Kartik, stop!"

He comes back to himself, releasing me. "I'm sorry. I have these dreams," he says, breathing heavily. "Such awful dreams."

"What sorts of dreams?" I still feel the imprint of his hands on my arms.

He rakes shaking fingers through his hair. "I see Amar on a white horse, but he's not as I remember him. He's like some horrible cursed creature. I try to run after him, but he's always just ahead. The mist thickens, and I lose him. When the mist parts, I'm in a cold, bleak land—a terrible, beautiful place. An army of lost souls comes out of the mist. They're looking to me, and I'm so very powerful. More powerful than I could have imagined."

He wipes an arm across his brow.

"And is that all?"

"I . . ." He steals a quick glance. "I see your face."

"Me? I'm there?"

He nods.

"Well . . . what happens next?"

He doesn't look at me. "You die."

Gooseflesh rises on my arms. "How?"

"I . . ." He stops. "I don't know."

The breeze coming off the lake gives me another shiver. "They're only dreams."

"I believe in dreams," he answers.

I take hold of his hands, not caring if it's too bold. "Kartik, why don't you come into the realms with me and look for Amar yourself? Then you would know for certain and perhaps the dreams would go away."

"But what if they're right?" He slips his hands from mine. "No. As soon as I have paid my debt to the Gypsies for their aid, I'll be on my way to Bristol and the HMS *Orlando*."

I stand. "So you won't even try to fight?" I say, swallowing the lump rising in my throat.

Kartik stares straight ahead. "Make the alliance without me, Gemma. You'll be fine on your own."

"I'm tired of being on my own."

Wiping away tears, I march into the woods. Just past the Gypsy camp, I see Mother Elena heaving a pail toward Spence.

"What are you doing?" I demand. I yank the pail away, and the dark liquid in it sloshes against the sides. "What is this?"

"The mark has to be made in blood," she says. "For protection."

"You're the one who painted the East Wing. Why?"

"Without protection, they'll come," she says.

"Who will come?"

"The damned." She grabs for the pail and I hold it out of her reach.

"I'll not spend another morning scrubbing," I say.

Mother Elena tightens her shawl about her. "Two ways! The seal is broken. Why would Eugenia allow it? She knows—she knows!"

The whole ghastly night rises in me like a battered dog who'll take no more taunting. "Eugenia Spence is dead. She's been dead for twenty-five years. You're not to do this again, Mother Elena, or I shall tell Mrs. Nightwing it was you, and you'll be banished from these woods forever. Do you want that?"

Her face crumples. "Have you seen my Carolina?"

"No," I say wearily.

"She's a good hider."

"She's not . . ." I trail off. It's no use talking sense to her. She's mad, and I feel if I stand here talking longer, I'll tip into madness myself. I empty the bucket into the grass and hand it back. "You mustn't do it again, Mother Elena."

"They'll come," she growls, and limps away, the empty pail clattering against her bangles like chimes.

It's noticeably colder on my return to Spence, and I curse myself for not bringing a wrap. Just one of the many foolish things I've done, such as trying to change Kartik's mind. Something flies close to my head and I yelp.

"*Caw! Caw!*" it cries, soaring ahead of me. Nothing but a bloody crow. It settles in the rose garden, pecking at the blooms.

"Shoo, shoo!" I flap at it with my skirts and it rises. Then I see a curious thing: A patch of frost has taken out several of the budding roses. They are stillborn on their stalks, half-formed and blue with cold.

"Caw! Caw!"

The crow perches on the East Wing turret, watching me. And then, before my astonished eyes, it flies over the spot that marks the secret entrance to the realms, and disappears.

CHAPTER TWENTY-ONE

BY THE FOLLOWING EVENING, OUR LAST AT SPENCE BEFORE Easter week, we are desperate to enter the realms again. I don't try to conjure the door of light on my own anymore; it's hardly worth the effort when I shall only be disappointed and we've another way in that never fails. Once we're certain our teachers are gone to bed, we run straight for the secret door by the East Wing and then on to the Borderlands. We no longer bother with the garden. It feels like child's play, somehow, a place where we turned pebbles into butterflies as girls do. Now we fancy the blue twilight of the Borderlands, with its musky flowers and the magnetic pull of the Winterlands. Each time we play, we find ourselves a toehold closer to that imposing wall that separates us from its unknown expanse.

Even the castle has grown less forbidding to us. The wealth of deadly nightshade blooming from its walls gives it color— like a Mayfair parlor covered in the most exotic paper. We burst through the castle's vine-twisted doors, shouting Pip's name, and she runs to us, squealing with delight.

"You're here at last! Ladies! Ladies, our fine party can begin!"

After the magic has joined us in blissful communion, we own the night. The party spills out of the castle into the blue-tinged forest. Laughing, we play hide-and-seek behind the fir trees and the berry bushes, running merrily across the tangled vines that crisscross the frosty ground. Ann begins to sing. Her voice is lovely but here in the realms it achieves a freedom it does not have in our world. She sings without apology, and the song is like wine, loosening our cares.

Bessie and the other factory girls cheer wildly for her—not with the polite, tempered applause of drawing rooms but with the boisterous, joyful whoops of the music hall. Bessie, Mae, and Mercy have clouded themselves in a glamour of gowns, jewels, and fancy shoes. They've never owned such finery before, and it does not matter that it is borrowed by magic; they believe, and the believing changes everything. We've the right to dream, and that, I suppose, is the magic's greatest power: the notion that we can pick possibility from the trees like ripe fruit. We are filled with hope. Alive with transformation. We can become.

"Am I a lady, then?" Mae asks, strutting in her new blue silks.

Bessie shoves her affectionately. "The Queen of Bloody Sheba!" She laughs hard and loud.

Mae shoves her back, a bit less gently. "'Oo are you, then? Prince Albert?"

"Oi!" Mercy chides. "Enuf! It's a happy occasion, ain't it?"

Felicity and Pip perform a comical waltz, pretending they are a Mr. Deadly Dull and a Miss Ninny Pants. In a ridiculously stuffy voice, Felicity prattles on about fox hunting—"The fox should be grateful to face our guns, for they are the finest guns in all of society trained on his lowly form. How lucky indeed!"—whilst Pippa bats her lashes and says only, "Why, Mr. Deadly Dull, if you say it's so, it *must* be so, for I'm sure I have no opinions of my own upon the subject!" It is rather like Punch and Judy come to life and we laugh till tears fall. Yet for all their silliness, they move beautifully. With exquisite grace, they anticipate each other's steps, sweeping round and round, Pip's gems winking in the dust.

Pippa prances about, grabbing each of us in turn for a dance. She sings a merry bit of doggerel. "Oh, I've a love, a true, true love, who waits upon yon shore . . ."

This makes Felicity laugh. "Oh, Pip!"

It's all the encouragement Pippa needs. Still singing, she pulls Fee into yet another dance. "And if my love won't be my love, then I will live no more . . ."

Indeed, Pip is charming at the moment; she's irresistible. I've not always liked her. She can annoy and delight in equal measure. But she saved these girls from a terrible fate. She saved them from the Winterlands, and she means to look after them. The old Pip would never have been able to look beyond her own troubles to help someone else, and that must count for something.

When at last we are exhausted, we sprawl on the cool forest floor. The fir trees stand guard. The jagged-leaved bushes offer a handful of tiny hard berries, no bigger than new peas. It smells like cloves and oranges and musk. Felicity lays her head in Pip's lap and Pip braids her hair into long, loose plaits. Bessie Timmons eyes them miserably. It is hard to be replaced in Pippa's affections.

Sparkling lights appear on the thick boughs of a fir.

"What's that?" Mae rushes to the tree and the lights fly away to another tree branch.

We follow them. Upon closer inspection, I see that they are not lights at all, but small fairylike creatures. They flit from branch to branch, and the tree swirls with movement.

"You have magic," they call. "We can feel it."

"Yes, what of it?" Felicity says, challenging them.

Two of the tiny creatures land on my palm. Their skin is as green as new grass. It glistens as if dew-kissed. They've hair like spun gold; it hangs in waves that tumble down their iridescent backs.

"You're the one—the one who holds the magic," they whisper, breaking into ecstatic smiles. "You're beautiful," they whisper sweetly. "Gift us with your magic."

Ann has come up behind me. "Oooh, may I see?" She leans close and one of the fairies spits in her face.

"Go away. You are not our beautiful one. Not our magical one."

"Stop that at once," I say.

Ann wipes the spit from her cheek. Her skin glistens where it has been. "I have magic, too."

"You ought to crush them with it," Felicity says.

The fairies moan and cling to my thumb and fingers. They stroke their faces against my skin like little pets. I reach out and touch one. Its skin is like a fish's. It leaves a wake of glittering scales on my fingers.

"What do you want, then?" Felicity demands. She flicks at one with her fingernail and it falls on its backside.

"Beautiful," the fairy creatures murmur again and again.

I know I'm not beautiful in the way that Pippa is, and I don't have Felicity's allure. But their words bathe me in new hope. I want to believe them, and that is enough to keep me listening. The larger fairy steps forward. She moves with a seductive grace, the way I have seen cobras dance for their masters: compliant yet able to strike at a moment's notice. I should like to hear them tell me that I am beautiful again. That they love me so very well. It is a curious thing: The more they say it, the more I feel a void opening inside me that I am desperate to fill.

The little creatures grab hold of me. "Oh, yes, lovely, lovely, our fair one is. We worship you. We would have some of you for our own, we love you so."

I put my hand to their heads. Their hair is as soft as corn silk. Eyes closed, body humming, I can feel the magic starting. But they are impatient. Their miniature hands grab greedily for my fingers. The scaly roughness of their skin is a surprise, and for a moment, I lose my concentration.

"No! Foolish mortal!" The voice hurts my ears. When I look down, they are staring at me with longing . . . and hatred, as if they would kill and eat me given the chance. Instinctively, I pull my hand back.

They jump for my fingers just out of reach. "Give it back! You were going to gift us!"

"I've changed my mind." I place them on a branch of the tree.

They turn their most brilliant shade of green yet. "We could never hope to be as grand as you, fair one. Love us, as we love you."

They smile and dance for me, but their words are not as intoxicating this time. I can hear the gritty hiss beneath their declarations.

"You love what I can do for you," I say, correcting them.

They giggle but there's no warmth in it. It reminds me of a dying man's cough. "Your power is nothing compared to that of the Tree of All Souls."

I turn quickly. "What did you say?"

They sigh in ecstasy. "One touch of it, and you will know true power—all your fears banished, all your desires granted."

I grab one in my fist. It struggles. Fear distorts its features into a terrible mask.

"Let me go, let me go!"

The other creature hops down and bites my thumb. I bat it away, and it somersaults through the air, grabbing hold of a branch to break its fall.

"I shall let you go in a moment! Stop struggling! I only want to know about this tree."

"I won't tell you anything."

"Squeeze it into juice," Felicity says, goading me.

The creature's mouth forms a terrified O. "Please . . . I'll tell you all. . . ."

Felicity gives a satisfied smile. "That is how you get what you need."

I cradle the creature in my palms. "What is the Tree of All Souls?"

The creature relaxes. "A place of very great magic deep within the Winterlands."

"But I thought the Temple was the only source of magic in the realms."

The creature's grin is like a death mask. It hops to a higher branch just out of reach.

"Wait . . . don't go," I call after it.

"If you would know more, you will have to travel to the

Winterlands and see for yourself. For how can you rule the realms if you've never even seen its stark beauty? How can you rule when you know only half the tale?"

"I know what I need to know about the Winterlands," I answer, but I'm not convinced. There is truth in the little beast's words.

"You know only what they have told you. Would you accept it as true without questioning it? Without seeing it for yourself? Have you never thought that they meant to keep you ignorant of its charms?"

"Go away!" Felicity blows hard. With a yelp, the creature falls, bouncing off branches till it lands on a fat leaf with an audible *oof*.

"You're a fool, a fool!" it gasps. "In the Winterlands, it shall be decided! You will know what true power is and tremble. . . ."

"What appalling little beasts. I'll show you how to tremble!" Felicity gives chase. The frightened things fly away through the trees.

"Go away! Leave us be, foolish mortals."

Little Wendy cowers, covering her ears. "There it is again, the screamin'."

Mr. Darcy hops wildly in his cage, and Wendy holds fast to it.

"Wendy, you stop that!" Mae scolds. "There ain't no screamin'."

"'Ere now, luv, take my hand," Mercy soothes, wrapping an arm around Wendy.

Far off over the Winterlands, a streak of red floods the gray sky. It burns for a moment, then disappears.

"Did you see it?" Ann asks.

"Let's get closer." Bessie runs through the tall reeds and cat-tails that stretch between the forest and the wall into the Winterlands. The heavy fog seeps into the Borderlands here, coating us in a fine shroud till we are like handprints in wet paint. We stop short of the enormous wall. On the other side of the gates, sharp mountaintops, black as onyx, rise above the fog. Ice and snow cling to them precariously. The sky churns gray, a constant storm. It spreads a tingle through me. It is forbidden; it is temptation.

"Can you feel it?" Mae asks. "Slips under your skin, don't it?"

Pippa steals in beside me and takes my hand. Felicity wraps an arm around Pip's waist, and Ann comes to take my other hand.

"Do you suppose there really is such a place of power inside the Winterlands?" Pippa asks.

The Tree of All Souls lives. That was what the mysterious lady wrote upon the slate. But no one has ever mentioned it to me before. I realize, once again, that there is very little I know about this strange world I am to help govern.

"It is so quiet. We've seen no Winterlands creatures at all since we've returned. What do you suppose is there now?" Ann asks.

Pippa leans her head against mine sweetly. "We should find out for ourselves."

CHAPTER TWENTY-TWO

THE MORNING BRINGS A FOYER FILLED WITH CASES AND trunks, girls going home for Easter week. They stand hugging goodbye as if they shall see each other never again rather than Friday next.

I have come down in my most sensible traveling dress—a brown tweed that will not show the train's smudges and soot. Ann has donned her drab traveling suit. Felicity, of course, will not be outdone. She wears a beautiful moiré silk dress in the perfect color of blue to complement her eyes. I shall look like a field mouse beside her.

The carriages that will take us to the train station are brought round. Groups of girls are paired with their chaperones. Spirits are high, but the true excitement is happening between Mrs. Nightwing and Mr. Miller.

"One of our men went missing last night," Mr. Miller says. "Young Tambley."

"Mr. Miller, how is it that I may keep watch over scores of schoolgirls yet you cannot keep watch over grown men?"

Brigid looks up from the back of a carriage, where she's instructing the footman on exactly how to secure our cases, much to his annoyance. "Whiskey! Devil whiskey!" she offers with a firm nod.

Mrs. Nightwing gives a sigh. "Brigid, if you please."

Mr. Miller shakes his head fervently. "It weren't whiskey, m'um. Tambley was on watch in the woods and up by the old graveyard, where we'd 'eard noises. Now 'e's gone." He hisses through gritted teeth. "It's them Gypsies, I tell ya."

"And the reason you were behind on the East Wing was the rain, as I recall. There is always some blame, some excuse." Mrs. Nightwing sniffs. "I'm sure your Mr. Tambley will show up. He is young, as you said, and the young tend to be rebellious."

"You might be right, m'um, but it ain't like Tambley not to show."

"Have faith, Mr. Miller. I'm sure he'll return."

Felicity and I embrace Ann. We're both to go to London, whilst Ann will spend the holiday with her horrid cousins in the country.

"Don't let those ghastly brats get the better of you," I tell Ann.

"It will be the longest week of my life," she says with a sigh.

"Mother will insist on paying calls so that we might ingratiate ourselves," Felicity says. "I'll be on display like some hideous china doll."

I look about, but Miss McCleethy is nowhere to be seen. "Here," I say, taking their hands. "A bit of courage to see you through."

Soon we all have magic running under our skin; it brings a

glow to our eyes, a flush to our cheeks. A crow flies past and with a loud cry settles on the turret, where one of Miller's men shoos it away. I'm reminded of the bird I saw the other night that vanished. Or did it? *It was late,* I tell myself, *and dark, and the two make for unreliable impressions.* And anyway, with the magic running high, I feel lovely just now, too lovely to worry.

Our carriage *clippity-clops* down the drive behind the others. I look back at Spence—at the men on the scaffolding mortaring stones into place, Mrs. Nightwing standing like a sentry at the front doors, Brigid helping girls on their way, the thick carpet of grass and the bright yellow of daffodils. The only threat is a band of rain clouds moving in. They puff out their cheeks and blow, sending shrieking girls after their hats. I laugh. The magic has me in its warm embrace, and I feel that no harm shall come to me. Even the dark clouds pressing against the silent gargoyles can't catch us.

Without warning, my blood gallops hard inside my veins till it is all I can hear—*thrum-thrum-thrum-thrum.* Outside, the world's merry-go-round gathers speed too. Storm clouds slither and stretch, dancing in the sky. I blink, the sound a cannon in my ears. The crow is in flight. Blink. It settles on the gargoyle's head. Blink. Sharp as a whip, the gargoyle's head twists round. My breath catches, and in that instant, the gargoyle's sharp teeth come down. My head feels light. My eyelids flutter, as frantic as the crow's wings.

"Gemma . . ." Felicity's voice carries as if underwater, and then it's clear as day. "Gemma! What is the matter?"

My blood settles into its normal cadence.

Felicity's wide-eyed. "Gemma, you fainted!"

"The gargoyle," I say, trembling. "It came alive."

The two other girls in the carriage regard me cautiously. The four of us crane our necks out the windows and peer up at the school's roof. It's quiet and still, nothing but stone. A fat raindrop hits me squarely in the eye.

"Ow," I say, sitting back. I wipe the rain from my face. "It seemed so real. Did I really faint?"

Felicity nods. Worry creases her forehead. "Gemma," she whispers. "The gargoyles are made of stone. Whatever you saw was some hallucination. There's nothing there, I promise you. Nothing."

"Nothing," I echo.

I chance a last look behind us, and it's an ordinary spring day before Easter, a patch of rain moving in from the east. Did I really see those things or did I only think so? Is this a new trick of the magic? My fingers shake in my lap. Without a word, Felicity places her hands over mine, silencing my fear.

⌇⌇⌇⌇⌇

It is said that Paris in springtime is a glory to behold, that it makes a man feel as if he shall never die. I should not know, for I have never been to Paris. But spring in London is a wholly different affair. The rain pitters and patters against the carriage's roof. The streets are choked equally with traffic and gas fog. Two young boys, crossing sweepers, have barely swept the muck and filth from the cobblestones so that a fashionable lady might pass when they are nearly run over by an omnibus whose driver curses them quite heatedly. The driver's curses are nothing compared to what the horses leave for them to clean away, and despite my misgivings about what I shall find in Belgravia, I am eternally grateful I am not a crossing sweeper.

By the time we reach the house, I'm bruised from the

carriage's incessant bumping and my skirts wear mud an inch thick. A parlor maid takes my boots at the door, saying nothing about the large hole in the toe of my right stocking.

Grandmama emerges from the parlor. "Good heavens! What on earth?" she exclaims at the sight of me.

"Spring in London," I explain, pushing a limp lock behind my ear.

She closes the parlor doors behind her and leads me to a quiet spot beside an enormous painting. Three Grecian goddesses dance in a grove by a hermitage whilst Pan plays his flute nearby, his little goat feet stepping merrily over clover. It is so ghastly as to take one's breath away and I cannot imagine what possessed her to purchase it, let alone display it proudly. "What is that?"

"The Three Graces," she tuts. "I am quite fond of it."

It is possibly the most appalling painting I've ever seen. "There is a goat-man dancing a jig."

Grandmama appraises it proudly. "He represents nature."

"He's wearing pantaloons."

"Really, Gemma," Grandmama growls. "I did not pull you aside to discuss art, of which it is apparent you know little. I wished to discuss your father."

"How is he?" I ask, the painting forgotten.

"Delicate. This is to be a peaceful trip. I'll have no outbursts, none of your peculiar habits, nothing to upset him. Do you understand?"

My peculiar habits. If she only knew. "Yes, of course."

⌁⌁⌁⌁

After I've exchanged my muddy dress for a clean one, I join the others in the drawing room.

"Ah, here is our Gemma now," Grandmama says.

Father rises from his chair by the fireplace. "Dear me, could this beautiful and elegant young lady be my daughter?" His voice is weaker, his eyes do not quite twinkle as they once did, and he is still very thin, but his mustache bends with a broad smile. When he holds out his arms, I run to him, his little girl again. Sudden tears threaten and I blink them back.

"Welcome home, Father."

His embrace is not as strong as it once was, but it is warm, and we shall fatten him up as soon as possible. Father's eyes soften. "You look more like her every day."

Tom sits sulking in a chair, taking tea and biscuits. "The tea has most likely gone cold by now, Gemma."

"You shouldn't have waited for me," I say, still holding on to my father.

"That is what I said," Tom complains.

Father offers me a chair. "You used to sit at my feet when you were a child. But as you are a child no more but a young lady, you shall have to sit properly."

Grandmama pours tea for us all, and despite Tom's grumbling, it is still hot. "We've been issued an invitation to dine at the Hippocrates Society in Chelsea this week, and Thomas has accepted."

Scowling, Tom drops two fat lumps of sugar into his tea.

"How nice," I say.

Father allows Grandmama to pour milk into his cup, turning it cloudy. "They're a fine bunch of fellows, Thomas—mark my words. Why, Dr. Hamilton himself is a member."

Tom bites into a biscuit. "Yes, old Dr. Hamilton."

"It's far more suited to your station than the Athenaeum," Father says. "It's for the best that nonsense is done with."

"It wasn't nonsense," Tom says sullenly.

"It was and you know it." Father coughs. It rattles in his chest.

"Is the tea too cold? Shall I see about more? Oh, where has that girl gone to?" Grandmama stands, then sits, then stands again until Father waves her off, and she takes her seat again. Her nervous fingers fold her napkin into neat tiny squares.

"You do look so like her," Father says again. His eyes are moist. "How did we get here? Where did it go wrong?"

"John, you're not yourself just now," Grandmama says. Her lips tremble.

Tom stares at the floor miserably.

"I would give my soul to forget," Father whispers through his tears.

He is broken, and the fault line runs through us all. I feel that my heart will break. It would take only a little magic to change the situation.

No, put that thought out of your mind, Gemma.

But why not? Why should I allow him his suffering when I might take it away? I cannot spend another wretched week in their company. I close my eyes and my body shakes with its secrets. Far away, I hear my grandmother call my name, confused, and then, time slows till they are a strange, frozen tableau: Father, his head in his hands; Grandmama stirring her worry into her tea; Tom with a scowl on his face that speaks to his discontent with us. I say my wishes aloud, touching them each in turn.

"Father, you shall forget your pain."

"Thomas, it is time for you to be less the boy and more the man."

"And, Grandmama, oh, do let's have a bit of fun, shall we?"

But the magic isn't finished with me yet. It finds my own

fierce longing for a family I once had but lost to tempests I could not control. For a moment, I see myself happy and carefree, running under blue Indian skies. My laugh echoes in my head. Oh, if I could, I would have that happiness back again. The power of that desire pulls me to my knees. It forces tears to my eyes. Yes, I should like to have that back again. I should like to feel safe. Protected. Loved. If magic can buy me that, then I will have it.

I take a deep breath and let it out shakily. "Now, let's begin again."

Time rushes forward. They raise their heads as if waking from a dream they are glad to be rid of.

"I say, what were we discussing?" Father asks.

Grandmama blinks her large eyes. "It is the strangest thing, for I can't remember. Ha! Ha, ha, ha! Dotty old me!"

Tom takes another biscuit. "Fantastic biscuits!"

"Thomas, how do you think our men will fare against Scotland today in the championship?"

"England shall be victorious, of course! Best cricket in the world."

"That's a good lad!"

"Father, I'm hardly a lad anymore."

"Right you are! You've been in long trousers some time now." Father laughs, and Tom joins him.

"The Gentlemen shall make Lord's proud," Tom adds. "Gregory's a good man."

Father strokes his mustache. "Gregory? A fine cricketer. Mind, he's no W. G. Grace. Seeing the Doctor play was thrilling. Nothing like it."

Father eats two biscuits, only stopping to cough once. Grandmama fills our cups to the brim.

"Oh, this room wants light! We must have light!" She does not call the housekeeper but ambles to the windows herself and throws open the heavy drapes. The rain has cleared. There's a hint of sun peeking through London's gray shroud like hope itself.

"Gemma?" Grandmama says. "My dear, what on earth is the matter? Why are you crying?"

"No reason." I smile through tears. "No reason at all."

᚛᚛᚛᚛᚛

It is one of the happiest evenings together I can remember. Father challenges us to a game of whist, and we play well into the evening. We place our wagers using walnuts, but as they are so delicious, we eat them sneakily, and soon, there is nothing left with which to make a bet, and we are forced to abandon our game. Grandmama settles herself at the piano and bids us sing along to a rousing round of novelty songs. Mrs. Jones brings us mugs of steaming chocolate, and even she is pulled to the piano to sing a chorus or two. As the evening winds down, Father lights the pipe I gave him for Christmas, and the smell conjures childhood memories that wrap themselves around me like a cocoon.

"If only your mother were here to share this fire with us," Father says, and I hold my breath, afraid this house of cards I've constructed shall fall in on itself. I'm not ready to let go of this happiness. I give him just a touch more.

"How odd," he says, his face brightening. "I had a remembrance of your mother, but it's left me now, and I can't get it back."

"Perhaps it's for the best," I say.

"Yes. Forgotten," he says. "Now, who would like a story?"

We all want one of Father's stories, for they are the most entertaining ever.

"I say, have I ever told you the one about the tiger . . . ," he begins, and we grin. We know it well; he has told it hundreds of times, but it hardly matters. We sit and listen and are enthralled anew, for good stories, it seems, never lose their magic.

CHAPTER TWENTY-THREE

EASTER SURPRISES US ALL WITH A GLORIOUS BLUE MORNING of such purity it makes the eyes ache. After a morning at church, we stroll amiably toward Ladies' Mile in Hyde Park. The streets become a sea of frilly white as parasols are opened to block the dim British sun. Weak as it is, it may still freckle, and our skins are to be as unblemished as our reputations. My skin is already covered in small brown spots, much to my grandmother's eternal dismay.

The ladies in their Easter finery strut like peacocks. Under cover of their parasols, they examine Lady Spendthrift's new fur-trimmed coat or Mrs. Fading Beauty's attempt at looking younger than her days, her corset pulled to straining. They pass sentence with no more than a glance or a pursing of the lips. The nannies and nurses follow the mothers and fathers, pushing prams, correcting children who get away from them.

Even in early bloom, the park is magnificent. Many ladies have placed their chairs on the grass so that they might chat and watch the horses. The path belongs to those eager to prove their skill in the saddle. Here and there, the horsewomen break free, showing a fierce competitive spirit. But then it is as if they remember themselves. They slow to a polite trot. That is a shame, for I should like to see them blazing a path through Hyde Park, their eyes alive with will, their mouths set in joyful, determined smiles.

I have the misfortune of walking with a wealthy merchant's daughter who must be mortally afraid of silence, for she never ceases talking. I give her the secret name Miss Chatterbox. "And then she danced with him for four dances! Can you imagine?"

"How scandalous," I answer without enthusiasm.

"Exactly so! Everyone knows that three is the limit," she answers, missing my point entirely.

"Steady. Here come the dowager soldiers," I warn.

We adopt a pose of demure innocence. A team of old ladies, powdered and puffed to the stiffness of meringue tarts, passes us with barely a nod. The crowd thins just a bit, and my heart nearly stops. Simon Middleton, resplendent in his white suit and boater hat, walks in our direction. I'd forgotten how handsome he is—tall, well formed, with brown hair and eyes the blue of clear seas. But it is the naughty twinkle in those eyes that makes a girl feel as if she has been undressed and has not cared to object. Strolling beside Simon is a lovely brunette. She is as small and dainty as the figurine on a music box. Her chaperone marches in time with her, the picture of respectability.

"Who is that girl with Simon Middleton?" I whisper.

Miss Chatterbox is overjoyed that I have joined her in

gossip. "Her name is Lucy Fairchild, and she is a distant cousin," she relates breathlessly. "American and very well-to-do. New money, naturally, but heaps of it, and her father has sent her in hopes she'll marry some poor second son and come home with a title to add luster to their wealth."

So this is Lucy Fairchild. My brother would throw himself on the tracks to gain her attention. Any man would. "She's beautiful."

"Isn't she absolute perfection?" Miss Chatterbox says wistfully.

I suppose I'd hoped to hear that I was mistaken—*"Why, I don't think she's as pretty as all that. She has a funny neck and her nose is oddly shaped."* But her beauty is confirmed, and why is it that her beauty casts such a long shadow over me that every bit of my light is extinguished?

Miss Chatterbox continues. "There are rumors of a betrothal."

"To whom?"

My companion giggles. "Oh, you! To Simon Middleton, of course. Wouldn't they make a lovely couple?"

An engagement. At Christmas Simon made the same pledge to me. But I turned him away. Now I wonder if I might have been too hasty in refusing him.

"But the betrothal is only a rumor," I say.

Miss Chatterbox glances about furtively, positioning her umbrella to hide us. "Well, I shouldn't repeat this, but I happen to know that the Middletons' fortunes have turned. They are in need of money. And Lucy Fairchild is exceedingly well off. I should expect they'll announce the engagement any day now. Oh, there is Miss Hemphill!" Chatterbox exclaims excitedly. Having spied someone far more important than I, she is off without so much as another word, for which, I suppose, my ears should be grateful.

While Grandmama prattles away with an old woman about gardens and rheumatism and the sorts of subjects that might very well be found printed in a primer under the heading What Old Women Must Talk About, I stand along Rotten Row, watching the horses and feeling sorry for myself.

"Happy Easter to you, Miss Doyle. You're looking well." Simon Middleton stands beside me. He is strong and shining and dimpled—and alone.

"Thank you. How lovely to see you," I say.

"And you."

I clear my throat. *Say something witty, Gemma. Something beyond the obvious, for heaven's sake.* "It's a lovely day, isn't it?"

Simon smirks. "Quite. Let's see . . . you look lovely. It's lovely to see one another. And, of course, the weather is quite lovely. I do believe we have encompassed the loveliness of all things lovely."

He has made me laugh. It is a talent of his. "How beastly a conversationalist I am."

"Not at all. In fact, I daresay you are . . . a lovely conversationalist."

Several horses streak past, and Simon greets them with a cheer.

"I hear congratulations may soon be in order." It is bold of me to say it.

Simon arches an eyebrow. His lips press into a wicked smile that makes him ever so attractive. "For what, pray tell?"

"They say your suit of Miss Fairchild is quite serious," I reply, looking down the dirt path to where Lucy Fairchild mounts her horse.

"It occurs to me that cricket is not the true sport in London," Simon says. "Gossip is."

"I shouldn't have repeated it. I am sorry."

"Don't be. Not on my account. I rather adore rudeness." The wicked smile is back. It works its magic, and I find I am lighter. "Actually, I do have my heart set on a new girl."

My stomach tightens. "Oh?"

"Yes. Her name is Bonnie. She's right over there." He points to a gleaming chestnut mare being led to the starting line. "Some say her teeth are too strong for her face, but I disagree."

"And think of what you shall save on a groundskeeper, for your grass shall be kept quite tidy by Bonnie," I say.

"Yes. Ours will be a happy union. Quite stable," he says, drawing a laugh from me.

"There is a matter I wanted to discuss with you, if I may," I say haltingly. "It concerns your mother."

"Indeed." He looks disappointed. "What has she done now?"

"It is about Miss Worthington."

"Ah, Felicity. What has *she* done now?"

"Lady Markham is to present her at court," I say, ignoring his jibe. "But your mother seems to object."

"My mother is not an admirer of Mrs. Worthington's, and their feud wasn't helped by your prank at Christmas with Miss Bradshaw. My mother felt her own reputation was injured by that."

"I am sorry. But Felicity must make her debut. Is there anything I can do to help her?"

Simon turns his wicked gaze to me, and a blush rises on my neck. "Leave well enough alone."

"I can't," I plead.

Simon nods, considering. "Then you shall have to secure Lady Markham's affections. Tell Felicity to charm the old bat and her son, Horace, as well. That should win the day—and her inheritance. Yes," he says, seeing my expression, "I know she must make her debut in order to claim her fortune. Everyone does. And there are plenty in London who'd rather see the brash Felicity Worthington under her father's control."

Down at the far end of Ladies' Mile, the horsewomen are at the line. They sit tall in their saddles, the picture of restraint and elegance, while their blindered horses snort and prance. They are ready to run, to show what they can do.

"It is good to see you, Gemma." Simon brushes my arm ever so slightly. "I have wondered how you were, if you still had the false-bottom box I gave you, and if you still kept your secrets locked inside it."

"I still have it," I say.

"The mysterious Gemma Doyle."

"And does Miss Fairchild possess secrets?" I ask.

He glances down the path, where Lucy Fairchild sits tall on her mount. "She is . . . untroubled."

Untroubled. Carefree. There is no dark lining to her soul.

The hand comes down. The horses are running. They kick up a dust storm along the path, but the dust cannot hide the naked ambition on the riders' faces, the ferociousness in their eyes. They mean to win. Lucy Fairchild's horse crosses the line first. Simon rushes to congratulate her. Fresh from battle, Lucy's face is dusty. Her eyes blaze. It doubles her beauty. But upon seeing Simon, she quickly sheds her fierceness; her expression settles into one of sweet shyness as she strokes her horse's neck gently. Simon offers to help her down, and though she could easily dismount on her own, she lets him. It is a pas de deux they seem to execute flawlessly.

"Congratulations," I say, offering my hand.

"Miss Doyle, may I present Miss Lucy Fairchild of Chicago, Illinois."

"How do you do?" I manage to say. I search her face for faults but find none. She's a true rose.

"Miss Doyle," she says sweetly. "How very nice it is to meet a friend of Simon's."

Simon. His Christian name. "You ride beautifully," I offer.

She bows her head. "You're too kind. I am only passable."

"Gemma!" I'm relieved to see Felicity coming our way. She's wearing a small velvet bonnet decorated with a cluster of silk flowers. It frames her face most agreeably.

"Here comes trouble," Simon mutters through his smile.

Felicity greets me warmly. "Happy Easter! Wasn't it an interminable sermon? Honestly, I can't see why we have to bother with church at all. Hello, Simon," she says, deliberately abandoning proper etiquette. "Jaunty hat. Did you take it from a bandstand?"

"Happy Easter, Miss Worthington. Tell me, when is Lady Markham to host a party in your honor, for I don't believe I've heard my mother mention it?"

Felicity's eyes blaze. "Soon, I'm sure."

"Of course," Simon says, smiling in triumph.

"Simon, I don't believe you've introduced me to your dear companion," Felicity purrs, turning the full glory of her charm on Lucy Fairchild.

"No, I didn't."

"Simon," Lucy whispers, mortified.

I step in. "Felicity, this is Miss Lucy Fairchild. Miss Fairchild, may I present Miss Felicity Worthington."

"How do you do?" Lucy offers her hand, and Felicity grasps it firmly.

"Miss Fairchild, how lovely to make your acquaintance. You simply must allow Miss Doyle and me to take proper care of you while you are in London. I'm sure Simon—Mr. Middleton— would want us to be true friends to you, wouldn't you, Simon?"

"That is very kind," Lucy Fairchild answers.

Felicity beams with her victory, and Simon gives a small nod in recognition of his defeat.

"Do be careful, Miss Fairchild. Accepting Miss Worthington's 'proper care' is not unlike lying down with lions."

Felicity laughs. "Oh, our Simon is such a wit, isn't he, Miss Fairchild?"

"We would love to stay and chat, but I'm afraid Mother is expecting us." Simon raises an eyebrow. "Best of luck with your efforts, Miss Doyle."

<hr/>

"What did he mean by that?" Felicity asks as we stroll in the park a clever distance behind our families. It's a beautiful day. Several children run after a wooden hoop they've set to rolling. Bright spring flowers waggle their petal finery at us.

"If you must know, I was soliciting Simon's help with his mother and Lady Markham. It doesn't help our cause to have you taunt him so."

Felicity looks as if I've said she should dine on maggots and chutney. "Court the Middletons' favor? I shan't. She's hateful, and he's a rake you've done well to be rid of."

"You want your inheritance, don't you? Your freedom?"

"My mother is the one who begs favor. I shan't bow to anyone but the Queen," Felicity says, twirling her parasol. She glares in Lady Denby's direction. "Really, Gemma, can't we cast a spell so that she wakes with a full mustache?"

"No. We can't."

"You don't still care for Simon. Tell me you don't."

"I don't," I say.

"You do still care! Oh, Gemma." Felicity shakes her head.

"What's done is done. I made my choice."

"You could have him back if you wished it."

I glance at Simon. He and Lucy make their rounds, smiling at all they greet. They seem content. Untroubled.

"I don't know what I wish," I say.

"Do you know what I wish?" Felicity asks, stopping to pick a daisy.

"What?"

"I wish Pip could be here." She plucks the daisy's petals one by one. "We were to see Paris in the summer. She would have loved it so."

"I'm sorry," I say.

Her face darkens. "Some things can't be changed about us, then, no matter how much we wish it."

I don't know what she means, but Fee doesn't give me time to ponder it. She pulls the last petal from the daisy with a cryptic smile.

"He loves me," she says.

A shadow falls over Felicity and me. Her father, Admiral Worthington, stands on the path, blocking the sun. He's a handsome man with a genial manner. If I didn't know better,

I'd be as charmed by him as everyone else is. He holds the hand of his ward, Polly, who is only seven.

"Felicity, will you look after our Polly for a spell? Her governess is undone by the heat and your mother is occupied at present."

"Yes, of course, Papa," Felicity says.

"That's my good girl. Careful of the sun," the admiral warns, and, dutifully, we raise our parasols.

"Come on, then," Felicity says to the child once her father is gone.

Polly walks two paces behind us, dragging her doll in the dirt. It was a Christmas gift, and already, it is bedraggled.

"What is your doll's name?" I ask, pretending for a moment that I am not completely useless with small children.

"She hasn't got one," Polly answers sullenly.

"No name?" I say. "Why not?"

Polly pulls the doll roughly over a rock. "Because she's a wicked girl."

"She doesn't seem so bad. What makes her wicked?"

"She tells lies about Uncle."

Felicity pales. She crouches low, covering the two of them with her umbrella. "Did you remember to do what I told you, Polly? To lock your door at night to keep the monsters out?"

"Yes. But the monsters still come in." Polly throws the doll to the ground and kicks it. "It's because she's so wicked."

Felicity lifts the doll and smooths the dirt from its face. "I had a doll like this once. And they said she was wicked, too. But she wasn't. She was a good and true doll. And so is yours, Polly."

The little girl's lips tremble. "But she lies."

"The world is a lie," Felicity whispers. "Not you and me."

She hands the child the doll, and Polly cradles it to her chest.

"Someday, I shall be a rich woman, Polly. I'll live in Paris without Papa and Mama, and you could come to live with me. Would you like that?"

The child nods and takes Felicity's hand, and they head up the path together, greeting people with defiant faces and fresh wounds.

CHAPTER TWENTY-FOUR

THE HIPPOCRATES SOCIETY IS HOUSED IN A CHARMING IF slightly worn building in Chelsea. The butler takes our coats and ushers us through a wide parlor—where several gentlemen sit smoking cigars, playing chess, and arguing politics—and into the largest library I have ever seen. An assortment of mismatched chairs fill out the corners. Several are grouped about the roaring fire as if there has just been a rousing debate there. The rugs are Persian and so old that they've worn through in spots. Every single bookcase is stuffed and seems it can hold no more. Medical texts; scientific studies; Greek, Latin, and classic volumes line the shelves. I should like to sit and read for weeks.

Dr. Hamilton greets us. He is a man of seventy with white hair gone to mere threads on top. "Ah, you're here. Good, good. Our man has prepared a marvelous feast. Let's not keep him waiting."

There are twelve of us at the table, a lively mix of doctors, writers, philosophers, and their wives. The conversation is spirited and fascinating. A bespectacled gentleman at the other end of the table argues vehemently with Dr. Hamilton.

"I tell you, Alfred, socialism is the way of the future! Imagine it! Economic and social equality among men. No more classes, perhaps the end to poverty. Complete social harmony. Utopia is at hand, gentlemen, and its name is socialism."

"Ah, Wells, best stick to writing fantastical novels, old boy. I did rather enjoy that time-travel story. Bit dotty at the end with the Eloi, though."

A man with ruddy cheeks and a broad belly speaks up. "Wells, perhaps you've confused us with the Fabian Society."

Everyone has a good chuckle at this. Some raise their glasses. "Hear, hear!" they say.

The man in the spectacles excuses himself. "I am only sorry that I must take my leave and cannot stay to argue the point with you. But I shall take up the cause when next we meet."

"Who was that gentleman?" I try to ask quietly.

"Mr. Herbert George Wells," the ruddy-cheeked man answers. "You may know him as H. G. Wells, the novelist. Good man. Solid mind. Wrong on socialism, though. Life without a queen? Without landowners but 'cooperative societies'? Anarchy, I say. Sheer madness. Ah, here is dessert."

A silent butler places a great crème soufflé before the man and he plunges his spoon into it with relish.

We discuss science and religion, books and medicine, the social season as well as politics. But it is Father who truly commands the table with his wit and tales of India.

"And then there is the story of the tiger, but I fear I have already held your attention far too long," Father says, that merry twinkle back in his eyes.

The guests will have their curiosity satisfied. "A tiger!" they cry. "Why, you must tell it."

Delighted, Father leans forward. His voice grows hushed. "We had taken a house in Lucknow for a month, hoping to escape the heat in Bombay."

"Lucknow!" a woolly-haired gentleman exclaims. "I do hope you didn't meet up with any mutinous Indian sepoys!"

The assembled break into arguments about the famous Indian uprising decades before.

"To think those savages murdered innocent British citizens, and after all we'd done for them!" One of the wives clucks.

"The fault was ours, dear lady. How could they ask Hindu and Moslem soldiers to bite cartridges greased with pig and cow fat when such a thing is abhorrent to their religious beliefs?" Dr. Hamilton argues.

"Come now, old chap, surely you're not justifying slaughter?" the woolly-haired man protests.

"Certainly not," Dr. Hamilton says. "But if we are to remain a great empire, we must have a greater understanding of the hearts and minds of others."

"I should like to hear Mr. Doyle's tale about the tiger," a woman in a tiara says, reminding us.

The guests are agreed, and Father continues his story. "Our Gemma was no more than six. She loved to play in the garden that bordered the trees whilst our housekeeper, Sarita, hung the wash and kept watch. That spring, the news spread from village to village: a Bengal tiger had been seen walking the villages, bold as you please. The daring fellow had destroyed a market in Delhi and scared the life out of a regiment there. There was a reward of one hundred pounds sterling offered for its capture. We never dreamed the tiger would reach us."

Every head is inclined toward Father and he basks in his audience's attention. "One day, as Sarita tended to the wash, Gemma played in the garden. She was a knight, you see, with a sword fashioned out of wood. Most formidable, she was, though I didn't quite know how formidable. As I sat in my study, I heard screaming from outside. I ran to see what the commotion was about. Sarita called to me, wide-eyed with fear, 'Oh, Mr. Doyle, look—over there!' The tiger had entered the garden and was making his way toward where our Gemma frolicked with her wooden sword. Beside me, our house servant, Raj, drew his blade so stealthily it seemed to simply appear in his hand by magic. But Sarita stayed his hand. 'If you run for him with your knife, you will provoke the tiger,' she advised. 'We must wait.'"

A hush has fallen over the table. The guests are enthralled with Father's story, and Father is delighted to have an audience. Playing the charming raconteur is what he does best.

"I must tell you that it was the longest moment of my life. No one dared move. No one dared draw a breath. And all the while, Gemma played on, taking no notice until the great cat was upon her. She stood and faced him. They stared at one another as if each wondered what to make of the other, as if they sensed a kindred spirit. At last, Gemma placed her sword upon the ground. 'Dear tiger,' she said. 'You may pass if you are peaceful.' The tiger looked at the sword and back at Gemma, and without a sound, it passed on, disappearing into the jungle."

The guests chuckle in relief. They congratulate my father on his tale told. I'm so very proud of him at this moment.

"And what of your wife, Mr. Doyle? Surely she heard the screaming?" one of the ladies asks.

My father's face falls a bit. "Fortunately, my dear wife was tending to the hospital's charity ward as she so often did."

"She must have been a pious and kind soul," the woman says sympathetically.

"Indeed. Not a bad word could be said about Mrs. Doyle. Every heart softened at her name. Every home welcomed her with open arms. Her reputation was above reproach."

"How lucky you are to have had such a mother," a lady to my right says.

"Yes," I say, forcing a smile. "Very lucky."

"She was tending to the sick," my father tells them. "Cholera had broken out, you see. 'Mr. Doyle,' she said, 'I cannot sit idly by while they suffer. I must go to them.' Every day she went, her prayer book in hand. She read to them, mopped their feverish brows, until she took ill herself."

It has the air of one of his well-told tales, but though those may be embellished, none of this is true. My mother was many things: strong yet vain, loving at times and ruthless at others. But she was not this confection—a self-sacrificing saint who looked after her family and the sick without question or complaint. I look at Father to see if anything betrays him, but no, he believes it, every word. He has made himself believe it.

"What a kind and noble soul," the woman in the tiara says, patting Grandmama's hand. "The very picture of a lady."

"Not a harsh word could be said about my mother," Tom says, neatly echoing Father.

Forget your pain. It was what I said when I took Father's hand in the drawing room yesterday, what I repeated again tonight. But I didn't mean this. I must be more careful. Yet what bothers me isn't the power of the magic or how, to a person, they've all accepted it as truth. No, what unsettles me most is how much I want to believe it too.

<hr />

The carriages are brought round, signaling the end of our evening. We congregate outside the club. Father, Tom, and Dr. Hamilton are deep in conversation. Grandmama has taken a tour of the club with some of the wives and hasn't returned yet. I've wandered down to see the garden when I'm pulled into the shadows.

"Luv'ly evenin', innit?"

The thug's hat is low on his forehead, but I know that voice as well as the angry red scar marring the side of his face. Mr. Fowlson, the Rakshana's loyal guard dog.

"Don't scream," he advises, taking my arm. "I just want a word on behalf of my employers."

"What do you want?"

"Awww, coy is it?" His smile turns to a hard scowl. "The magic. We know you've bound it to yourself. We want it."

"I gave it to the Order. They're in possession of it now."

"Now, now, you tellin' fibs again?" His breath smells of ale and cod.

"How do you know I'm not telling you the truth?"

"I know more than you fink, luv," he whispers.

The steel of his blade gleams in the chilly night. I look over at Father talking happily with Dr. Hamilton. He is very like the father I've missed. I would do nothing to upset that fragile peace.

"What do you want from me?"

"I've told you. We want the magic."

"And I've told you. I don't have it."

Fowlson rubs the flat of the blade along my arm, sending a dangerous tickle through my skin.

"'Ave it your way. You're not the only one wot can play games." He glances toward my father and Tom. "Good to see your father out and about. And your brother. I hear 'e wants to make a name for himself in the worst way. Old Tom. Good old Tom." Fowlson flicks a button from my glove with the point of his knife. "Maybe I should 'ave a lil chat wif 'im about wot his sister gets up to when 'e's not payin' attention. A word in his ear, and 'e could have you thrown in Bedlam."

"He wouldn't do that."

"Sure of it, are you?" Fowlson flicks another button from my glove. It skitters along the cobblestones. "Oi've seen girls 'oo won't buckle down given the old pick-and-mallet to the brain to cure their ills. 'Ow would you like spendin' your days in a room there, looking out at the world through a lil window?"

The magic flares inside me, and I use all my strength to keep it down. Fowlson mustn't know I have it. It isn't safe.

"Give the magic to me. I'll see it's taken care of proper."

"You'd use it for yourself, you mean."

"'Ow's our friend Kartik?"

"You should know more than I, for I've not seen him at all," I lie. "He proved as disreputable as the rest of you."

"Good ol' Kartik. When you see 'im next—if you should see 'im—tell 'im old Fowlson was askin' after 'im."

Kartik said the Rakshana assumed he was dead, but if Fowlson believes he is alive, then Kartik is in danger.

Suddenly, Fowlson sheaths his knife. "Looks like your carriage 'as arrived, miss. I'll be seein' you round. You can count on it."

He gives me a little shove from the shadows. Oblivious to what has just taken place, Tom motions to me. "Come along, Gemma."

The footman secures the steps.

"Yes, I'm coming," I answer. When I turn back, Fowlson has gone, disappeared into the night, as if he'd never been beside me at all.

CHAPTER TWENTY-FIVE

I WAKE TO SEE GRANDMAMA STANDING OVER MY BED, SMILing. "Wake up, Gemma! We're off to the shops today!"

I rub my eyes, for I must be dreaming. But no, she's still standing there. *Smiling.*

"We shall go to Castle and Sons to have a dress made. And then we shall take ourselves to Mrs. Dolling's Sweet Shoppe."

My grandmother wants to take me for an outing. It is fantastic! Mr. Fowlson's threat seems no more substantial than the fog to me now. Try to frighten me, will he? I hold all the magic of the realms, and neither the Order nor the Rakshana shall know it until I've accomplished what I must. After all, I've already worked a miracle with my own family, haven't I?

"Oh, I've not been to Mrs. Dolling's in ages. So many cakes!" Grandmama blinks. "Why have I not been? It's no matter. We shall go today and have whatever we wish and . . . Gemma! Why are you not dressed? We've so much to do!"

She does not need to ask again. I fly to gather my things,

grabbing my dress so quickly that the whole of my cupboard is
made a mess by my carelessness.

⌇⌇⌇⌇

Grandmama and I pass the most marvelous day together.
Rather than stern and fearful, she is jolly. She greets everyone—from the boy who wraps our cake to strangers in the
street—with a smile and a nod. She gives a pat on the head to
a shoeshine boy, who doesn't know at all what to make of such
a grandmotherly touch, as he is well past the age of eight.

"Oh, do look at those hats there, Gemma! The darling feathers! Should we see the milliner and be fitted for our own?" She
veers toward the door. I hold tightly to her arm.

"Perhaps another day, Grandmama."

Already the carriage was so laden with her purchases there
was barely room for us to sit. Grandmama sent our driver back
with an extra few shillings, insisting we'd take a hansom cab
back to Belgravia.

"Oh, this is glorious, isn't it? I can't think why we shouldn't
have done this sooner!" She pats my arm. "Good day!" she calls
cheerily to a milkman, who regards her warily, as if she were
someone's eccentric aunt let out of the attic. "Dear me, not terribly chatty, is he? I said, good day, sir!"

"Good day to you." The milkman gives a careful smile and a
tip of the hat but his eyes never lose their suspicion.

"Ah, much better." Grandmama smiles. "You see? They only
need a bit of encouragement to come out of their shells."

Castle and Sons, dressmakers, lies in Regent Street, and this
is where we have come to have a dress made for my debut. A
harried assistant, whose hair threatens to escape from its

· 261 ·

pinnings at any moment, carries out bolts of white silk for Grandmama to scrutinize. My measurements are taken. As the tape is crossed round my bosom, the seamstress shakes her head and gives me a sympathetic smile. My goodwill vanishes rapidly. We cannot all be Gibson Girls. When every single bit of me has been measured and recorded, I join Grandmama on a divan. Bins of buttons and lace, ribbon and feathers are hastily displayed for her, and just as quickly, Grandmama sends them back. I fear I shall have the plainest dress in all of London.

The shopgirl shows Grandmama the most exquisite dress I have ever seen. A small sigh escapes me. It has a corsage of silk roses along one shoulder and short, high sleeves adorned with bows. The skirt is embroidered with delicate rose beads, and the train—which appears to be miles long—is trimmed with a beautiful fluted ruffle. It is the gown of a princess, and I long to have one like it.

Grandmama runs a hand over the beaded silk. "What do you think, Gemma?" Grandmama has never asked my opinion on any matter ever.

"I think it is the loveliest dress I have ever seen," I answer.

"It is, isn't it? Yes, we shall have this one made."

I could kiss her.

"Thank you, Grandmama."

"Yes, well, I'm sure it will be far too dear," she grumbles. "But we are only girls once."

When we step out into the London murk, it is five o'clock, and already the sky is darkening and the streets are thick with gas fog that makes me cough. I don't care. I am a new girl who shall wear silk roses and carry a fan of ostrich feathers. And we shall buy cakes from the confectionary. Let the choking gas lamps do their worst!

At the corner, Grandmama and I cross the street, heading for Mrs. Dolling's Sweet Shoppe, and that is when the world goes topsy-turvy. My skin warms. A sweat breaks upon my brow. And the magic flows through my veins like a swollen river. I am flooded by thoughts, wounds, desires, secrets. Every private longing invades my soul.

"... the long days without end. He loved me once ..."

"... a beautiful home we'll make with a lovely garden in the front ..."

Can't think. Breathe. Make it stop. I ...

"... fancy a tumble with the likes of you ..."

My head turns but I can't tell which direction the offense comes from—there are too many to fight.

"... I shall offer my proposal this evening and be made the happiest of men ..."

"... my poor little baby laid to rest, and do they know I am dying inside, too ..."

"... a new dress with a bonnet to match ..."

Please stop. I can't. I can't breathe. I ...

Everything around me slows to a crawl. Beside me, Grandmama's foot hovers above the street midstep. On the curb, an organ-grinder moves the bellows of his instrument with excruciating slowness. One note takes an eternity, and matched to the slow toll of Big Ben's bells, the melody has the air of a funeral march. The wheels of wagons and carriages, the ladies and gentlemen, the liniment vendor hawking his miracle cure—they are like dreamy figures in a pantomime.

"Grandmama?" I say, but she cannot hear me.

I see quick movement from the corner of my eye. The lady in the lavender dress marches toward me; her eyes flash with anger. She grabs my wrist tightly, and my skin burns in her rough grasp.

"Wh-what do you want?" I say.

She thrusts out her arm, pulling up her sleeve to expose her flesh. Words etch themselves into her skin: *Why do you ignore me?*

The cold metal taste of fear lies on my tongue. "I'm not ignoring you, but I don't understand what—"

She pulls me hard into the street.

"Wait," I say, struggling. "Where are you taking me?"

She places her hands over my eyes, and I am joined to her in a vision. It's quick, too quick. The footlights of the music hall stage. The illusionist. The lady writing upon the slate: *The Tree of All Souls lives. The key holds the truth.* A woman in a tea shop. She turns her head and smiles. Miss McCleethy.

I hear the quick gallop of horses on cobblestone. The vision lady's head snaps up, and she looks about wildly. A black carriage drawn by four sleek horses breaks out of the London gloom and barrels swiftly down the street. Black curtains blow out its windows.

"Stop!" I scream, but the horses pick up speed. The carriage is nearly upon us. We shall be trampled.

"Let me go!" I scream, and the lady dissolves into leaves and blows away. The carriage passes through me as if I were made of air and disappears into the fog. The world snaps back into place, and I'm squarely in the road, between wagons and hansoms trying to navigate around me. A footman shouts at me to get out of the street.

Grandmama looks up, horrified. "Gemma Doyle! What are you doing?"

I stagger to her. "Did you not see it?" I gasp. "A carriage came out of nowhere and disappeared just as quickly."

Grandmama's dismay fights with the magic inside her. "Now we shan't have our sweets." She pouts.

"I tell you, I saw it," I mumble. I'm still searching the streets for signs of the carriage and the lady. They are nowhere to be seen, and I can't be certain I saw them at all. But one thing I am certain of: That was Miss McCleethy in the vision. Whoever this lady was, she knew my teacher.

ᴧᴧᴧᴧᴧ

Father rescues me from exile in my room, asking me to join him in the small study on the second floor. It is filled with his books and papers, his maps of distant places where he has traveled on various adventures. Only three photographs sit on his desk—a small daguerreotype of Mother on their wedding day, another of Thomas and me as children, and a grainy photograph of Father and an Indian man making camp on a hunting expedition, their faces grim and determined.

Father looks up from his birding journal, in which he has made a new entry. His fingers are stained with ink. "What is this I hear about carriage drivers gone amok in the streets of London?"

"I see Grandmama could not wait to share the news," I say, sullenly.

"She was quite concerned about you."

Do I tell him? What would he say if I did? "I was mistaken. In the fog, it was difficult to see."

"In the Himalayas, men have been known to lose their way when the clouds roll in. A man might find himself disoriented and see things that are not there."

I sit at Father's feet. I've not done this since I was a little girl, but I have need of comfort just now. He pats my shoulder gently as he tends to his journal.

"Was that photograph on your desk taken in the Himalayas?"

"No. It was a hunting expedition near Lucknow," he offers without further explanation.

I gaze at the photograph of my mother, searching for some of me in her face.

"What did you know about Mother before you married her?"

Father winks. "I knew she was foolish enough to say yes to my suit."

"Did you know her family? Or where she lived before?" I press.

"Her family died in a fire. That is what she said. She didn't wish to discuss so unpleasant a memory, and I never insisted."

That is the way of my family. We do not talk about the unpleasant. It does not exist. And if it pokes its ugly head out of its hole, we cover it quickly and walk away.

"She could have had secrets, then."

"Mmmm?"

"She could have had secrets."

Father packs tobacco into the bowl of his pipe. "All women have their secrets."

I keep my cheek against the comfort of his leg. "So it is possible that she could have led a secret life. Perhaps she was a circus clown. Or a pirate." I swallow hard. "Or a sorceress."

"Oh, I say, I rather like that one!" Father puffs on his pipe. The smoke lends the room a hazy sweetness.

"Yes," I continue, feeling bolder. "A sorceress who could enter a secret world. She had great power—so great that she passed it on to me, her only daughter."

Father cups my cheek. "She did, indeed."

My heart beats faster. I could tell him. I could tell him everything. "Father . . ."

Father coughs and coughs. "Blasted tobacco," he says, searching for his handkerchief.

Our housekeeper enters, bringing Father a brandy without having to be asked.

"Ah, Mrs. Jones," Father says, taking a soothing sip. "Like an angel of mercy, you appear."

"Would you care for your supper now, sir?" she asks.

Father did not dine with us this evening. He claimed not to be hungry. But he is so thin, I hope he'll take something.

"A bowl of soup will do nicely, I should think."

"Very good, sir. Miss Doyle, your grandmother asks that you keep her company in the sitting room."

"Thank you," I say, my heart falling. I don't want to face her yet.

Mrs. Jones leaves the room noiselessly, as servants do, as if even her skirts should not dare to make a sound lest they bring notice to the one wearing them.

Father looks up from his journal, his face ruddy from his coughing fit. "Gemma, was there something else you wanted to tell me, pet?"

I have a power, Father—an enormous power that I do not begin to understand. It is a blessing and a curse. And I fear if you knew it, I would never be your pet again.

"No, there was nothing," I say.

"Ah. Well. Off you go, then. Wouldn't want to keep your grandmama waiting tonight."

He bends his head in concentration over his birds, his maps, his notes on the constellations—things that can be observed and recorded and understood.

And when I leave the room, he scarcely takes notice.

⌇⌇⌇⌇⌇

Grandmama sits in her chair, her fingers busy with her needlework, while I try to make a house of cards.

"I was very upset with your behavior this afternoon, Gemma. What if you had been seen by someone we know? There is your reputation—and ours—to think of."

I drop a card onto the square I've built. "Isn't there more to be concerned about than what others think of us?"

"A woman's reputation is her worth," Grandmama explains.

"It's a small way to live." I drop a queen of hearts on top. The card walls shiver and collapse under the new weight.

"I don't know why I bother," she sniffs. Her stitching picks up new, furious speed. When she can't bring me to heel with scolding, she bends me into shape with guilt.

I try arranging the cards again, perfecting my balancing act.

"Stay," I whisper. I place the last card on top and wait.

"Is that all you have to occupy your time? Card houses?" Grandmama sneers.

I sigh, and the tiny gust of breath tears down my work. The cards flutter into a messy pile. I'm in no humor for this. The afternoon's events were upsetting enough, and if I cannot have comfort, I should like some peace. A little magic can remove her disappointment and my own.

"You'll forget everything that happened today after we left the dressmaker's shop, Grandmama. I am your beloved granddaughter, and we are happy, all of us . . . ," I intone.

Grandmama looks helplessly at the needlework in her lap. "I . . . I've forgotten my stitch."

"Here, I'll help you," I say, guiding her hands till she picks it up again.

"Ah, me. Thank you, Gemma. You are such a comfort to me. What would I do without you?"

Grandmama smiles, and I do my best to return it, though somewhere deep inside I wonder if I have traded one life of lies for another.

⁂

A terrible knocking has me awake and not at all happy about it. Rubbing sleep from my eyes, I creep downstairs. It's Tom who is making such a racket. He's returned in a lively mood; in fact, he enters the drawing room singing. It is an unnatural occurrence, like watching a dog ride a bicycle.

"Gemma!" he says happily. "You're awake!"

"Yes, well, it would prove difficult to sleep through this cacophony."

"I am sorry." He bows and comes up too quickly, stumbling into a small table and knocking over a vase of flowers. The water spills onto Grandmama's precious Persian carpet. Tom tries to rescue the vase but it only spins away from him.

"Tom, what are you doing?"

"This poor vessel is not well. It requires my care."

"It is not a patient," I say, taking it from him.

He shrugs. "It's still not well."

Tom flops into a chair and tries to muster what dignity he has left by arranging and rearranging his disheveled tie. The smell of spirits is quite strong on his breath.

"You're drunk," I whisper.

Tom holds up his finger like a solicitor addressing a witness. "That is a scur—shcurous—schurress . . . terrible thing to say."

"Scurrilous," I say, correcting him.

He nods. "Precisely."

I've been awakened by an idiot. I shall go back to bed and leave him to torment the servants and wither under their judging eyes come morning. Clearly, whatever magic I've given Tom has gone and he is back to his impossible self.

"Go on, ask me about my evening," he says, far too loudly.

"Tom, mind your voice," I whisper.

Tom wags his head. "Exactly so, exactly so. Quiet as a church mouse, that's me. Now. Ask." He folds his arms, nearly clocking himself in the face.

"Very well," I say. "How was your evening?"

"I've done it, Gem. Proved myself. For I have been asked to join a very exclusive club." *Exclusive* comes out sounding more like "ex-cuusif." Seeing my puzzled face, he frowns. "You could offer congratulations, you know."

"Is it the Athenaeum, then? I thought . . ."

His face darkens. "Oh. That." He waves it away with his hand. "They don't take chaps like me. Haven't you heard? Not good enough." The liquor has only added to his bitterness. "No. This is different. Like the Knights Templar. Men of crusades! Men of action!" He gestures broadly, nearly taking out the vase again. I rescue it quickly.

"Men of clumsiness is more like it," I grumble. "Very well, you've intrigued me. What is this saintly club?"

"No. I can't tell. Not yet. For now, it will remain a private matter," Tom says, putting his finger to his lips and scraping his nose. "A secret."

"That is why you are discussing it openly with me, no doubt."

"You mock me!"

"Yes, and I shouldn't, for it is far too easy."

"You don't believe a club would choose me?" His eyelids waver and his head nods a bit. He'll be out in a moment. "Why, just this evening . . ."

"Just this evening," I prompt.

". . . gave me a token. A mark of dish . . . dishtinction . . . They said it would protect me from . . . unwanted . . . influence . . ."

"From what?" I ask, but it's no use. Tom snores in the chair. Sighing, I take the blanket from the settee and place it over his legs. I pull it up to his chin, and my blood goes cold. There on his lapel is a familiar pin—the skull-and-sword insignia of the Rakshana.

"Tom," I say, shaking him. "Tom, where did you get this?"

He turns slightly in the chair, his eyes still closed. "I told you, I've been called to membership in a gentlemen's club. At last, I shall make Father proud and prove . . . myself . . . a man . . ."

"Tom, you mustn't trust them," I whisper, holding fast to his hand. I try to join our thoughts with my power, but the spirits he has drunk begin to work on me. I pull away, light-headed and reeling.

Fowlson has made good on his promise. Bile rises in my

throat, and a new fear washes over me. I've been caught in his endgame: If I tell Tom my secret, he'll think me mad. If I employ the magic, the Rakshana will know I still have it, and they'll come for me before I've had a chance to do what I must.

For the time being, I can't trust my brother. He is one of them.

〰〰〰

The next morning, Tom delivers me to the railway station, where I am to meet a Mrs. Chaunce, an elderly acquaintance of Grandmama's, who will travel as far as Spence for a small fee. Tom's the worse for wear this morning. He's not a drinker, and the pallor of his face shows it. He's in a foul humor and it serves him right.

Tom continues to check his pocket watch, complaining bitterly. "Where is she? Women. Never on time."

"Tom, this club you've pledged to . . . ," I start, but just then Mrs. Chaunce arrives, and Tom cannot hand me over fast enough.

"Cheerio, Gemma. Pleasant trip."

After a brief round of pleasantries, Mrs. Chaunce, who, thank goodness, has as little interest in me as I have in her, sees to the luggage. She offers the porter one penny for his trouble. He looks at it with disdain, and I rummage in my purse to find two more. Mrs. Chaunce is not a very good chaperone, for I've lost her already, but I spy her boarding the train and hurry to catch up.

"Did you drop this, miss?"

I turn to see Mr. Fowlson behind me holding a lady's

handkerchief. It isn't mine but it's no matter; it is merely a means for talking to me.

"Stay away from my brother or—"

"Or what, luv?"

"I shall go to the authorities."

He laughs. "And say what? That yer brother 'as joined a gentlemen's club and you don't approve? Why, I'll be in Newgate before mornin'!"

I lower my voice to a hiss. "Leave him alone or I . . . I . . ."

His smile is replaced by a flinty stare. "You'll what? Use your power on me? But you don't have it anymore, right, luv?"

The magic rears up inside me like horses ready to run, and it takes every bit of my strength to tether it. I mustn't let it loose; not now.

Mrs. Chaunce calls to me from an open window, coughing through the steam. "Miss Doyle! Miss Doyle! Do hurry!"

"Nice bloke, your brother. Wants to be respected in the worst way. And that's a lot to work wif. Ambition's a good match against magic. Safe journeys, Miss Doyle. I'm sure I'll see you soon."

I settle into my compartment with Mrs. Chaunce, and the train is under way. Fowlson's threat is fresh in my mind, and I wish I had someone with whom to share it. The train is filled with people eager to reach their destinations or happy to be leaving others. They chatter with one another; mothers offer children small bits of food to keep them content; fathers look on admiringly; ladies traveling together watch the scenery roll by with excited smiles. I can't hold back the magic anymore, and I feel the constant press of their thoughts till I fear I shall go mad. I try to stop it, but it proves too difficult with so much going on around me, so I do the only thing I know how to: I make a wish that I could hear nothing. Soon, though life pulses on around me, I'm alone in a cocoon of quiet.

And I wonder, what good is this power if it only makes me feel more alone?

ACT III

Dusk

Absolute power corrupts absolutely.
—LORD ACTON

CHAPTER TWENTY-SIX

Two days later
SPENCE ACADEMY

THE RAIN HAS BEEN AT US AGAIN. FOR TWO DAYS IT HAS kept us captive, soaking the woods and turning the lawn to a muddy mess. It lashes my bedroom window as I finally remove the soggy red bandana I posted there upon my return from London, and hide it under my pillow again, out of sight. Kartik has always come before, but not this time. At first, I'd feared he'd gone on to Bristol and the *Orlando* without bothering to say goodbye. But just yesterday, I saw him from my window. He noted the red cloth and left it behind without a second glance.

Since then, I've begun three different letters to him.

> *My Dear Kartik,*
>   *I am afraid I must end our acquaintance. I am*
> *enclosing the bandana. Please use it to dry your tears—*

that is, if you have any to shed, for I have begun to wonder.

Fondly,
Gemma

Dear Kartik,
   I am terribly upset to hear that you have gone blind. You must have, for surely if you had sight you would have seen the red bandana I affixed to my bedroom window, and understood it to be an urgent correspondence. I wish you to know that, though you are sightless as Mr. Rochester, I remain your friend and shall make every effort to visit you in your hermitage.

With greatest sympathies,
Gemma Doyle

Mr. Kartik.
   You are a wretched excuse for a friend. When I have become a great lady, I will pass you on the street without so much as a nod. If you are half so kind to the Orlando, *it shall surely sink.*

Regretfully,
Miss Doyle

My hand hovers over the page once again, searching for words to match my heart, but I find only these: *Dear Kartik . . . Why?* I tear it into tiny pieces and feed it to the flame of my candle, watching the creeping black curl the edges of my hurt into something dark and smoky falling to ash.

⌁⌁⌁⌁

Ann and Felicity have both returned at last, and we are together again in the great hall. Felicity tells us about visiting Lady Markham whilst Ann recounts the horrors of Lottie and Carrie. But my thoughts are elsewhere; my troubles with Kartik, Fowlson, and Tom have put me in a dark humor.

"And then Lady Markham introduced her son, Horace, who is as dull as a water pitcher. Actually, I'm sure a more pleasant conversation could be had with a water pitcher."

Ann laughs. "Was it as bad as all that?"

"Indeed it was. But I smiled sweetly and tried not to cross my eyes and the day was won. I believe I have secured Lady Markham's affections and her sponsorship."

"Do you know what Charlotte said to me?" Ann says. "'When you are my governess I shall do as I please. And if you don't do as I say, I shall tell Mother I saw you touching her jewels. Then she'll turn you out on the street with no character.'"

Even Felicity is appalled. "She's a bad seed! We should hang her from her toes. Aren't you glad you won't be her governess after all?"

"Only if I secure that appointment with Mr. Katz," Ann says, chewing a fingernail. "I do hope my letter arrives soon."

"I'm certain it will," Felicity says, yawning.

"Gemma, how was *your* holiday?" Ann asks.

"I had a visit from Fowlson," I say. "He means to blackmail me into giving up the magic to the Rakshana by recruiting my brother, Tom, into the brotherhood. I'm afraid of what they might do to him in order to reach me."

"The Rakshana!" Ann exclaims.

"Why don't you turn Fowlson into a giant bullfrog or wish him deep into the jungles of Calcutta?" Felicity harrumphs.

"Don't you see? The moment I tip my hand that I've got the realms magic, they'll take it from me. I can't let them know."

"What will you do?" Ann asks.

"There is something else. When I was in London, I had another vision—and I saw Miss McCleethy in this one." I tell them about the lady and the ghostly carriage. Firelight shadows writhe on the curtains of Felicity's tent like demons.

"McCleethy," Ann says, shivering. "But what does it mean?"

"Yes, what's the good of a messenger you can't understand?" Felicity complains. "Why, just once, can't one of these haunts simply say, 'Hello, Gemma, frightfully sorry to bother you, but I thought you might like to know that Mrs. X is the one to watch out for—she'll eat your heart. Cheerio!'"

I roll my eyes. "Most helpful. Thank you. I'm afraid my visions don't work quite that way. It's up to me to assign the meaning. Not that I've a clue. But there is someone who might. We must attend the exhibition at the Egyptian Hall and find this Dr. Van Ripple. I shall get to work on LeFarge as soon as possible."

"Agreed," Ann and Felicity chime.

"I want to show you something." Felicity opens a box and peels back layers of tissue. Inside is a truly exquisite cape—midnight blue velvet with white fur trim round the collar and silk ribbons for ties.

"Oh," Ann gasps. "How lucky you are."

Felicity holds the cape at a distance. "Father wants to take little Polly on a trip. I objected, and he bought me this."

"Why should you object?" Ann asks, still eyeing it.

Fee and I exchange a glance neither of us is eager to hold. We both know what it means for the admiral to take his young ward on a trip. The horror of it silences me.

"I'm giving it to Pip," Fee says, folding it carefully into its box.

Ann's mouth opens in shock. "Won't your mother be angry?"

"Let her be," Felicity says, her lips pressed into a hard line. "I shall say it was ruined by the washerwoman. She'll be angry and say I am careless with my things. I shall tell her she is careless with hers as well."

The box is stored beneath Felicity's chair. "But what of tonight? Gemma, the realms?"

They look to me hopefully.

"Yes. The realms." I pull back a section of the tent, and we spy on Miss McCleethy. She sits with Nightwing and LeFarge, sharing tea and good spirits. Nightwing steals peeks at the clock, and I know she is itching for her evening sherry. At least we may be assured she'll sleep through our adventures. But McCleethy is a different matter. She's waiting for me to make a mistake, to prove I have the magic, and I'm doubly suspicious of her now after my vision.

"Blasted McCleethy," Felicity snarls. "She's going to ruin everything."

Ann nibbles her bottom lip, thinking. "What if we were to put a spell on her? We could make her so sleepy that she must go to bed for days."

Felicity snorts. "Are you mad? She'll probably come for our skins—while we still inhabit them!"

"No," I say. "The slightest hint of magic used against her and she'll know. We can't chance it just now. She mustn't suspect a thing. I'm afraid we'll simply have to wait until she's safely asleep before we go into the realms."

"She doesn't look at all sleepy," Ann laments.

I spy Mademoiselle LeFarge getting up from her chair.

"Keep the wolves at bay," I say, rising as well.

I catch our teacher in the library, where she searches for a book among the many on the shelves.

"*Bonsoir, Mademoiselle LeFarge,*" I manage to say. "*Er, comment allez-vous?*"

She corrects my pronunciation without looking up. "*Como tallay-voo.*"

"Yes, I shall make more of an effort."

"I should be happy, Miss Doyle, if you would make an effort at all."

I smile like a buffoon. "Yes. Quite right." Our little talk has gotten off to a grand start. Perhaps I could mangle another language or insult her dress or, heaven forbid, sing. "It's a lovely evening, isn't it?"

"It's raining," she notes.

"Yes, so it is. But we need rain, yes? It makes the flowers grow so nicely and . . ."

Mademoiselle LeFarge's knowing stare stops me. "Out with it, then. What is it you really want, Miss Doyle?"

I see that betrothal to Inspector Kent has sharpened LeFarge's own skills of detection.

"I thought perhaps you might take us to this exhibition."

I unfold the slip of paper for the exhibition at the Egyptian Hall and hand it to her. She brings it to the lamp. "A magic-lantern show? Tomorrow afternoon!"

"It promises to be extraordinary! And I know how dearly you love this sort of spectacle!"

"That I do. . . ." With a sigh, she folds the paper. "But it is hardly edifying."

"Oh, but—"

"I'm afraid the answer is no, Miss Doyle. In another month's time, you'll be in London for your season and may go to see whatever you wish. And I should think your time might be better spent perfecting your curtsy. After all, you will face your sovereign. It is the most important moment of your life."

"I hope not," I mutter.

She gives me a kind smile along with the advert, and I curse my luck. How will we get to the Egyptian Hall and Dr. Van Ripple now?

I could *make* her do what I want. No, that's horrible. But how else will we find Dr. Van Ripple? Right, only this once and never again.

"Dear Mademoiselle LeFarge," I say, taking her hands.

"Miss Doyle? What—"

She is silenced by magic.

"You want to take Felicity, Ann, and me to the Egyptian Hall tomorrow afternoon. You're desperate to take us. It will be . . . edifying. I promise," I intone.

There's a knock, and I break the contact with LeFarge just in time to see Miss McCleethy at the door.

"Gemma, you should be in bed," Miss McCleethy says.

"Y-yes, I was j-just going," I stammer. My hands shake. The magic has been stirred inside me now, and it wants out. I try desperately to keep it under control.

Mademoiselle LeFarge brandishes the leaflet above her head like a letter from a beloved suitor. "Isn't this marvelous? A magic-lantern show at the Egyptian Hall tomorrow. I shall ask Mrs. Nightwing's permission to take the girls. It promises to be most edifying."

"A magic-lantern show?" Miss McCleethy laughs. "I hardly think—"

"See for yourself—the Wolfson brothers!" She shoves the advert at Miss McCleethy. "Miss Doyle brought it to my attention, and I am very glad she did. I shall speak to Mrs. Nightwing straightaway. Do excuse me."

McCleethy and I are left alone.

"I'll go on to bed."

"Just a moment," she says as I try to slip past her. "Are you ill, Miss Doyle?"

"N-no," I croak. I don't dare look at her. Can she tell? Can she read it in my face? Smell it on me like a perfume?

"This is rather sudden. I wonder how she came to be so excited about this."

"Mademoiselle LeFarge l-loves that sort of thing." I barely manage to say it. Sweat beads on my forehead. The magic wants out. I shall go mad trying to rein it in.

For the longest moment of my life, neither of us says a word. At last, McCleethy breaks the silence. "Very well. If it is so 'edifying' perhaps I shall come, too."

Bloody hell.

Finally released from McCleethy's stare, I stagger to my room, nearly retching from the power I've held back. I throw open the window and crouch on the sill, letting the soft rain pelt my upturned face, but it's no use. The magic's calling me.

Fly, it bids.

I stand on the narrow sill, holding tightly to the frame, my body bowing out. And then I let go. My arms transform into the shiny blue-black wings of a raven, and I'm soaring high above Spence. It is exhilarating. I could live inside this power forever.

I loop past the workers' camp; the men play cards and box.

Far down the road, a troupe of mummers wander, drunk, passing a whiskey bottle among them. I dart over to the Gypsy camp, where Ithal keeps watch and Mother Elena sleeps fitfully in her tent, mumbling a name that is lost to dreams.

There's a light in the boathouse, and I know who's there. I land, as softly as snow, and shake off my raven form. Through the grimy window, I see him with his lantern and his book. Will I have what I want?

I push through the door, and Kartik takes in the sight of me—face flushed, hair a ruin. "Gemma? What has happened?"

"You're dreaming," I say, and his eyelids flutter under my persuasion. When he opens his eyes again, he is in that twilight land between waking and sleep.

"Why didn't you come to me?" I ask.

His voice is faraway. "I'm a danger to you."

"Well, I am tired of the safe. Kiss me," I say. I take a step forward. "Please."

He is across the floor in two strides, and the force of his kiss steals my breath. His hands are in my hair, my head bent back, his lips on my throat, everywhere at once.

It's only magic, not real. *No, don't think about that. Think only of the kiss.* There is only this. Only this. Kiss.

His tongue slips inside my mouth—a surprise—and I pull away, frightened. But he draws me to him in another kiss, hungrier this time. He makes small explorations with the tip of his tongue. His hand slides down the length of my torso and back up; he cups my breast and moans. I can scarcely catch my breath. I no longer feel in control of this power or my emotions.

"S-stop!" I say. He releases me, and it is all I can do not to pull him back. "Sleep now."

He settles to the floor and closes his eyes.

"Only pleasant dreams," I say.

I slip from the boathouse, my fingers touching my kiss-swollen lips. And despite all the power I hold, I cannot possibly keep a satisfied grin from blooming there.

⊰⊱⊰⊱⊰⊱

When we reach the Borderlands, the factory girls call out their familiar *Whoo-oot*. We answer in kind, and they appear, like magic, from the trees and brush. Mae's and Bessie's skirts are stained with dark red streaks.

"Got us a pheasant," Bessie says, catching me looking. "'Magine that?" She smiles and her teeth are sharp.

"You've come back!" Pippa exclaims. She's pinned up her skirts to the waist, forming a pouch that sags with a harvest of berries. She embraces each of us, and when she reaches me, she whispers sweetly, "Join me in the chapel."

"Pip, I've got a present for you," Felicity says, holding up the box.

"And I can't wait to see it. I'll just be a moment!"

Felicity's face falls as Pip spirits me away to the crumbling abbey, humming a merry tune. Once we're safely behind the rotting tapestry, she empties her berries into a large bowl and grabs my hands. "All right, I'm ready for the magic."

I pull away. "And hello to you, too, Pip."

"Gemma," she says, putting her arms round my waist. "You do know how very much I love you, don't you?"

"Is it me or the magic you love?"

Hurt, Pippa takes refuge on the altar, tearing marigolds from the floor by their stalks and tossing them aside. "You wouldn't deny me some measure of happiness, would you, Gemma? I shall be trapped here an eternity with no one but those coarse, common girls as my companions."

"Pippa," I say gently. "I want your happiness, truly I do. But someday soon, I'll have to return the magic to the Temple and form an alliance to oversee its safety. I won't always have it at my fingertips like this. Have you given any thought to how you will spend the rest of your days?"

Tears pool in her eyes. "Can't I join your alliance?"

"I don't know," I say. "You're not—" I bite the word off before it comes out of my mouth.

"Alive? A member of a tribe?" A fat tear rolls down her cheek. "I don't belong to your world and I don't belong to theirs. I'm not a part of the Winterlands, either. I don't belong anywhere, do I?"

It's as if she's pierced me straight through, for how often have I felt that way myself?

Pip buries her head in her hands. "You don't know how it is for me, Gemma. How I count the hours until the three of you return."

"It is the same for us," I assure her. For when we are together, everything seems possible, and there is no end in sight. We will simply go on like this forever, dancing and singing and running through the forest laughing. That alone is enough to make me take her hands and share the power with her.

"Here," I say. I stretch out my arms and she comes running.

⚹⚹⚹

"Pip, I've a present for you!" Felicity says again when we return. She unfurls the fur-trimmed cape.

"Oh," Pip sighs, cuddling it. "It's extraordinary! Darling Fee!" She gives Felicity a sweet kiss on the cheek, and Felicity smiles as if she were the happiest girl in the world.

Bessie Timmons muscles between them. She holds the cape up, examining it. "Don't seem so special."

"Now, Bessie," Pip scolds, snatching it from her hands. "That won't do. A lady must say something kind or not speak at all."

Bessie leans against a marble column whose many cracks are threaded with weeds. "Guess I'll keep it shut, then."

Pippa lifts her hair and allows Felicity to secure the cape's ribbons around her slender neck, and she preens and prances about in it.

Ann and the factory girls take over the altar. She tells them about *Macbeth*. She makes it sound like a ghost story, which I suppose it is.

"I ain't never been to no real theater," Mae Sutter says when Ann finishes.

"We shall have our own here," Pippa promises. She settles into the throne as if born to it.

Felicity finds an old drape. Under her touch it becomes a cape just like the one she's given Pip. It's lovely, but when she settles beside Pip, the illusion shows. It cannot compare to the real one. "Our Ann is to have an audience with Lily Trimble."

"Go on!" Mae laughs.

"I am," Ann says. "In the West End."

"Back there," Mercy says with a mixture of admiration and jealousy. "Remember them chips we could get on Wednesdays, Wendy?"

"Aye. Greasy."

"Drippin' with grease and pipin' hot!" Mercy's smile fades. "I miss it."

"Oi, not me." Bessie Timmons jumps up from her spot by the fire and pushes to the front. "Nuttin' but misery. Work from dark to dark. And nuttin' waitin' for yer at home, neither, 'cept yer mum with too many moufs to feed and no' enuf to go round."

Mercy keeps her eyes on her boots. "Wasn't all bad. M'sister Gracie was right sweet. And I 'ad grand dreams." Tears come, and she sniffles, wiping her nose.

Bessie crouches low and brings her snarl to the girl's face. "A bellyache and stiff fingers from the cold is wot you 'ad, Mercy Paxton. Don't go cryin' fer it."

Mae steps in. "We've got ever'thin' here, Mercy. Don't you see?"

"Mercy, come to me," Pippa commands. The girl struggles up from the floor and walks shyly to her. Pippa cups the girl's face in her palm, smiling at her. "Mercy, that's all done now, so let's dry our tears. We're here, and it shall be everything we ever dreamed it could be. You'll see."

The girl rubs her nose on her sleeve, and with that one movement, her youth shows. She's no more than thirteen. It's terrible to think of her working in that factory from sunup till sundown.

"Who wants to go on a merry adventure, then?" Pippa asks.

The girls erupt in enthusiastic cries. Even Mercy manages a smile.

"What sort of adventure?" Ann asks.

Pippa giggles. "You'll have to trust me. Now, close your eyes and follow me. There shall be no peeking!"

With Pip at the lead, we're pulled along holding hands, a paper chain of girls. We're out of the castle. I can feel the cool of the Borderlands on my skin.

"Open!" Pip commands.

Before us is an enormous hedge, well over eight feet tall. At one end I spy an entrance.

Ann breaks into a grin. "It's a maze!"

"Yes," Pip says, clapping. "Isn't it splendid? Who's game?"

"I am," Bessie Timmons says. She runs around the corner, disappearing into the maze's belly.

"And me." Mae runs after her.

"I love a good hide-and-seek. Find me, Fee!" With that, Pippa pulls up her skirts, and Felicity, giggling, gives chase. I'm the last in. I don't know how the others could have gotten away from me so fast. I turn corner after corner, but all I see is a maddening flutter of color and then nothing. The hedge walls are the most unusual I've ever seen, made of tightly woven clover and small black flowers, and I swear they shift so that when I look behind me, the passage has changed. The isolation sends my mind into strange corners, and I quicken my steps.

"Ann!" I cry.

"Over here!" she shouts back. The sound comes from everywhere at once, so I cannot be at all certain where to go next. I hear whispering. Is it coming from up ahead?

When I go round the edge, there are Felicity and Pippa standing close, foreheads touching, hands clasped. They murmur in private conference, and I can hear only a word here, a phrase there.

". . . there's a way . . ."

". . . but how . . ."

". . . we could . . . together . . . you see?"

". . . Pip . . ."

". . . promise me . . ."

". . . promise . . ."

I step on a downed branch. It breaks with a loud crack. At once, they drop hands and charm me with too-quick smiles.

"You oughtn't sneak up like that, Gemma," Fee scolds, but her hand is at her heart, and her face is flushed.

Pippa jumps in, all smiles. "Fee was teaching me how to curtsy for the Queen. It's hideously difficult, but she can do it brilliantly, can't you, Fee?"

On cue, Felicity drops to the ground, her arms holding her skirt, her head low. Those cool eyes dart a glance upward at me.

"You were discussing the curtsy," I repeat dumbly.

"Yes." Pippa's smile is a lie.

"It's no matter. You needn't tell me," I say, turning.

"Gemma, you're being silly!" Felicity calls after me. "It was the curtsy we were speaking of!"

I hear them whispering behind my back as I walk away. Fine. Let them have their secrets. I twist and turn through the maze. The magic swirls and eddies inside me. I could eat the world, devour it whole. I need to run. To hit. To wound and heal in equal measure.

I *need*, and it is more than I can bear.

On nimble feet, I fly into the forest. Where my hands touch, something new is born. Strange flowers as tall as men. A flock of butterflies with shiny yellow wings edged in black. Dark purple fruit, fat and heavy on the branch. I squeeze one hard in my hand and the juice turns to maggots. I throw it quickly away from me; the disgusting creatures burrow into the earth, and the earth responds with a crop of wildflowers.

Lights blink in the trees, and a fairy creature appears. "Such power," she says, marveling.

My head is light; I'm swollen with magic. Suddenly, I want only to get rid of it. "Here," I say, laying my hand upon her head. It's as cold as snow where we touch, and I glimpse a vast darkness before I pull away.

The creature turns loops, trailing sparkles. "Ahhh, I know you now," she purrs, and trails a finger across my heart.

I shake my head. "No one knows me."

The creature circles me slowly till I feel dizzy. "There is a place where you *will* be known. Loved." Her cold breath whispers in my ear. "Wanted. You need only to follow."

She flies deep into the fog banks that obscure the Winterlands, and I give chase, letting the mist swallow me till my friends' laughter is a faint memory of sound. I'm farther in than I've ever been. Slimy vines slither across my bare feet like serpents come aground; I hold still, calming my breath.

The fairy creature hovers near my shoulder. Her eyes are black jewels. "Listen," she whispers.

Close in my ear, I hear a voice from the Winterlands, as soft as a mother's goodnight kiss: "Tell us your fears and your desires. . . ."

Something deep inside me wants to answer. Such longing, as if I've found a piece of myself I never knew was missing till now.

The voice comes again: "This is where you belong, where your destiny lies. There is nothing to fear. . . ."

The fairy's lips turn up in a smile. "Do you hear it?"

I nod, but I can't speak. The pull is strong. I want only to go, to join with whatever waits on the other side.

"I could show you the way to the Tree of All Souls," the thing with the bright golden wings says. "And then you would know true power. You'd never be lonely again."

The vines caress my ankles; one slithers up my leg. The mist parts; the gate to the Winterlands beckons. I take a step toward it.

The little creature shoos me on with her spindly fingers. "That's it. Go on."

"Gemma!" My name drifts through the mist, and I take a step back.

"Don't listen! Go on!" the fairy hisses, but my friends call out again, and this time I hear something else—horses riding hard and fast.

I turn away from the Winterlands and the fairy creature, running till the fog thins and I'm back near the castle. The girls spill out of the maze. "What is it? What's happening?" Ann shouts. She's got Wendy by the arm.

"Over there!" Felicity shouts, and we run to the bramble wall.

Coming quickly up the path is a band of centaurs, Creostus in the lead. They slow at the sight of us.

Creostus points to me. "Priestess! You're coming with me."

"She isn't going anywhere with the likes of you," Felicity says, standing to my right like a soldier.

The centaur paces on his strong legs. "She is called by Philon. She must account for herself."

"We shall accompany you, Gemma," Ann vows.

"But we were having such fun." Pippa pouts.

"Shall we come?" Felicity asks, but she doesn't let go of Pip's hand.

I think of the two of them whispering behind my back, sharing secrets, leaving me out. Well, perhaps I'd like a secret of my own.

"No. I'll go alone," I say, and duck through the brambles to the other side.

"Yes, Gemma will sort it all out, won't you?" Pippa says, dragging Felicity toward the maze again.

Creostus eyes Wendy hungrily. "I should like to take *you* with me and make you my queen. Have you ever ridden on a centaur's back?"

Mae pulls Wendy away. "'Ave a care, sir. We are ladies."

"Yes, I know. Ladies. My favorite sort."

"Creostus, if you've done with your suit of Miss Wendy, I shall accompany you to Philon," I interrupt, wondering what is so urgent that Philon has sent for me.

Creostus's booming laugh leaves gooseflesh upon my arms. He paces close to me. "Jealous, Priestess? Do you wish to compete for my affections? I should like to see that."

"I'm sure you would. But you will die first and so let us journey to Philon, if you please."

"She worships me," he says with a wink, and I have the urge to put a bonnet on his head and paint him dancing to the pipes to hang on a fashionable lady's wall.

"Creostus, do we ride or not?"

He brushes my body with his. "Desperate to be alone with me, are you?"

"I shall turn you into a ladybug. See if I won't."

With seemingly no effort at all, Creostus swoops me up

onto his back. As we ride toward the forest, I clutch his waist for dear life. Whatever the reason for this visit, it can't be good. Down below in the river, I see that Gorgon steams ahead, keeping pace with us.

No, this isn't good at all.

CHAPTER TWENTY-SEVEN

THERE IS A DIFFERENT AIR TO THE FOREST TODAY. THE creatures do not loll about. The children do not play their games. Instead, they are hard at work. Some whittle wood into sharp points. Others test crude crossbows. A hail of arrows screams over my head, making me duck. They find their targets in the soft bark of distant trees. Gorgon slides to the shore, and I run to her.

"Gorgon, what is the matter?"

"I cannot say, Most High. But there is trouble."

Philon strides toward us in a magnificent coat of twigs and leaves with a high collar and sleeves that end in points near the tips of those long fingers. The catlike eyes narrow at the sight of me.

"You have betrayed us, Priestess."

"What do you mean? Betrayed you? How?"

The forest folk gather around Philon. Some carry spears. Neela hops onto Creostus's back, her lips curled in disgust.

"You have been seen at the Temple in secret talks with the Hajin," Philon says, accusing me.

"I haven't!" I protest.

Philon and Creostus share a glance. Is Philon tricking me? Is this a ruse or a test of some sort?

"Do you deny that you have paid visits to the Temple?"

I've been to see Circe, but I cannot tell them that.

"I have been to the Temple," I say carefully. "That is where we shall join hands in alliance, is it not?"

Neela climbs onto a stump and crouches down. As she talks, her hair shimmers from blue to black and back again. "She will join with them and betray us for the Order! They will build the runes once again!" she shouts. "While we toil here, the filthy Hajin reign over the poppy fields and we are forced to bargain for their crop."

Discontent ripples through the assembly.

Neela smirks. "While Philon has us wait, the Hajin will enter into secret alliance with the Order. It will give them all the power. Things will be as they always have been, and once again, it is the forest folk who will suffer."

"*Nyim syatt!*" Philon thunders, but the forest folk's leader is drowned out by the loud arguing of the tribe. They shout, "What of our share?" and "Let us not be taken again!"

"How long before they come for our land? Before they take the little power we do have?" a centaur demands angrily.

Neela returns to Creostus's back. "I say we fight! Let us force this priestess to join hands now."

Philon prepares the leaf pipe. Those long, dusky fingers press the crumbled red petals down into the mouth of it. "What do you say to these charges, Priestess?"

"I gave you my word that I would honor your tribe, and I shall keep my promise."

Neela appeals to the crowd. "Do you hear how smoothly she lies?"

"I am not lying!" I shout.

Creostus takes a stand behind me, blocking the path to escape. "I told you she could not be trusted, Philon. She's one of them, and they will never part with the magic willingly. The Order." Creostus sneers. He paces as he speaks, as if addressing his soldiers. "I remember when the Order punished my family. They stripped us of everything. Our fathers were banished to the Winterlands. The cold was too much for our kind. Those who did not die from the elements were taken by the creatures there. They were tortured and worse. A generation of centaurs was lost. We will not allow that to happen again. Never again."

The centaurs beat their hooves against the ground and roar.

"They took my father from me. I will take two of their people for my honor."

"Honor," Gorgon hisses from the lagoon. "What do you know of it?"

Creostus sidles up to the giant beast at the head of the ship. "More than one who would be their lackey. Have you told her how you betrayed your own people?"

"That is enough talk," Gorgon growls.

"Philon, if the Hajin plot against us with the Order, we should strike while we still can, before they take everything from us," Neela argues.

"The Hajin are peaceful," I protest.

"They are traitors and cowards." Neela nestles close to Philon. She takes a puff from the pipe and blows it into the creature's mouth. "Why should those filthy diseased have all the poppies, Philon? Why should we need to barter for them?"

"It has been their right since the rebellion," Philon answers.

"Because they sided with the Order. Now they plot against us! The Order will take what is ours and give it to the Untouchables! We will be left with nothing!"

"Do you have so little faith in me, Neela?" Philon's eyes narrow.

"You do not see clearly. You have too much faith in the girl. A battle for the realms has begun. They mean to destroy us. We must strike to defend ourselves."

"They did not strike us first."

Creostus bellows, "Have you forgotten what they did to us?"

More angry shouting erupts in the crowd, each fear more terrible than the last, till they're frenzied. "They will take our land! They will kill our children! We must strike!"

An arrow splits the air above my head and skitters across the ground behind me.

"*Nyim!*" Philon thunders. "We are not at war with the Hajin or the Order. Yet. As for you, Priestess, I will give you the benefit of the doubt. For now. But you must prove good faith to me."

"How?"

Philon's gaze is inscrutable. "I require an act of good faith. You said you could gift others with the magic. Very well. I accept. Gift me so that I might hold magic of my own."

I did say that, but now I am not so sure that I should have. "What will you do with it?" I ask.

Philon regards me coolly. "I do not ask what you do with yours."

When I make no move, Creostus crosses his arms and smirks. "She hesitates. What further proof do you need?"

"The magic does not last for long," I say, stalling. "What help will it be to you?"

"Because you put some enchantment upon it!" Creostus spits.

"No! I have no control over it."

"We shall see." Philon's eyes are glassy. "Will you gift us? Or is it war?"

The forest folk wait for my answer. I'm not at all sure this is the best course, but what choice do I have? If I don't give them any, it's war. If I do, there's no telling how they might use the power.

But no one says I have to give them much.

I join hands briefly with Philon, and when I break away, the creature regards me with those cool eyes. "And is that all, Priestess?"

"I told you I have no control over it," I say.

Philon shakes my hand but whispers in my ear. "That is your first lie. Do not let there be a second."

As I leave, Neela shouts after me. "You witches cannot be trusted! Soon, we will no longer live in your shadow!"

⚮⚮⚮⚮

Gorgon steers a course back to the garden. I perch beside her neck, listening to the gentle rhythm of the water sluicing against the ship's enormous sides. Gorgon has said nothing since we left the forest.

"Gorgon, what was Creostus speaking about earlier?"

"It is nothing. Creostus knew me as a warrior."

"But why do you choose to stay here in this prison?"

Gorgon's voice deepens. "I have my reasons."

I know this tone. It means the conversation will go nowhere. But I am not in a stopping humor. I wish to know more. "But you could be free—"

"No," she says bitterly. "I will never be truly free. I do not deserve it."

"Of course you do!"

The snakes nestle about her face, making it hard to see her eyes. "I am many things, Most High, not all of them noble."

One of the snakes slithers close to me. Its thin pink tongue flicks against my skin. Instinctively, I pull my hand back, but its dangerous kiss lingers.

"We should not be speaking of the past but of the future of the realms."

I sigh. "The tribes can't even agree amongst themselves. How will they form an alliance when they are constantly fighting?"

"It is true they have fought always. But they may still be joined in a common cause. Discord need not be an impediment. Differences can bring strength."

"I don't see how. It makes my head hurt to hear them." I stretch my arms and feel the river spray on my face, cool and sweet. "Oh, why can't there be peace like this moment always?"

Gorgon glances sideways at me. The line of her mouth tightens. "Peace is not happenstance. It is a living fire that must be fed constantly. It must be tended with vigilance, else it dies out."

"Why has this power come to me, Gorgon? I can scarcely govern myself. At times, I feel as if I could dance through the halls with happiness, and then, just as suddenly, my thoughts are dark and lost and frightening."

"The question is not why, Most High. The question is what. What will you do with this power?"

We've come to a narrow strait bordered by mossy rocks. The water shines with iridescent scales. A school of water nymphs emerges from under the current. They're exotic creatures, half mermaid, with bald heads, webbed fingers, and eyes that show the depths of the oceans. Their song is so lovely it can bewitch any mortal, and once they have you in thrall, they take your skin.

I've had one encounter with those ladies and barely lived to tell it; I shan't chance another.

"Gorgon," I warn, moving to the nets that hang from the side of the ship.

"Yes, I see them," Gorgon says.

But the nymphs make no move toward us. Instead, they dive under again, and I see the bow of their silvery backs as they swim away.

"That's odd," I say, watching them go.

"All is strange these days, Most High," Gorgon answers, cryptic as ever.

I settle again at Gorgon's neck. We're nearing the Borderlands. The air is hazier here, and in the distance the sky is the color of lead.

"Gorgon, what do you know about the Winterlands?"

"Very little, and yet it is too much."

"Do you know of something called the Tree of All Souls?"

Gorgon startles; the snakes hiss at the sudden movement.

"Where did you hear that name?" Gorgon asks.

"You do know of it! I want to know. Tell me!" I command, but Gorgon's as still as stone. "Gorgon, you were once bound to tell only truth to the Order!"

Her lips pull back in a snarl. "Only moments ago, you reminded me of my freedom."

"Please?"

She takes in a deep breath, lets it out slowly. "It is only a myth passed down through the generations."

"Which states . . . ?" I prompt.

"It is said that hidden within the Winterlands is a place of enormous power, a tree which holds great magic much like that of the Temple."

"But if that's so," I argue, "why haven't the Winterlands creatures made use of it to take over the realms?"

"Perhaps they cannot retrieve its power. Perhaps they were stopped by the seal of the runes or the Temple." Gorgon slides her yellow eyes toward me. "Or perhaps it does not exist at all. For none that I know have seen it."

"But what if it *does* exist? Shouldn't we venture into the Winterlands and find out for ourselves?"

"No," Gorgon hisses, "it's forbidden."

"It *was* forbidden! But I hold all the magic now."

"That is what worries me."

We've reached the Borderlands. A light snow has begun to fall. Torches have been lit. They cast an eerie glow over the scene.

"You must forget about the Winterlands. No good can come of it."

"How would you know? You've never seen it," I say bitterly. "No one has."

"None who can be trusted," Gorgon answers, and at once, I think of Circe.

"Gemma!" Felicity yells from the shore. She's in her chain mail, and Pippa wears her beautiful cape and they both shine like borrowed jewels.

Gorgon lowers the plank for me. "Most High, the sooner you can make the alliance and share the magic, the better."

She stares intently at the sky toward the Winterlands.

"What are you looking for?" I ask.

The snakes move restlessly. Gorgon's placid face darkens. "Trouble."

∿∿∿∿

"Hooray! Our Gemma has returned," Pippa says, half dragging me into the forest, where the girls have set up a game of croquet. They take turns with their mallets. Ann lounges on a blanket of silver threads. She plucks them like a harp and beautiful music drifts over to us. Wendy sits stroking Mr. Darcy's fuzzy head.

"How were the horrid forest folk?" Felicity asks as she prepares to take her shot.

"Angry. Impatient. They think I will betray them," I say, settling next to Wendy and Ann.

"Well, they will just have to wait until we're ready, won't they?" Felicity knocks her ball cleanly through the hoop.

"Bessie, when you were with the three girls in white on your way to the Winterlands, did they mention the Tree of All Souls?" I ask.

Bessie shakes her head. "They wasn't the chatty sort."

"And you've still not seen any Winterlands creatures?" I ask them all.

"Not a one," Pippa says.

I want to be comforted by this, but a small voice deep inside reminds me that Pippa and the girls are still here, and beneath that glamour they wear, their cheeks are pale, their teeth sharp.

Yet they are not like those horrible trackers, those hideous wraiths that steal souls. But what are they? *She need not fall.* That was what Gorgon said. Is there a way around it? Do I want there to be? If I gave this power to McCleethy and the Order tonight, I'd not have to worry about it; it would be their decision to make, not mine. And they'd banish Pip to the Winterlands, for sure. No, the choice is mine to make. I've got to see this through.

"What are you brooding about now, Gemma?" Felicity asks.

I shake my head, clearing it of the night's heaviness. "Nothing. Here, let me have a try."

I take the mallet and knock it against the ball, and the ball rolls far out into the Winterlands fog.

<hr/>

Our visit over, we travel the now familiar path back to the secret door and step into the long, ill-lit corridor. It feels odd to me, though, as if someone else might be inside with us.

"Do you hear anything?" I whisper.

"No," Felicity says.

It's a faint rustling, like leaves. Or wings. We've gone no more than a few feet when I hear it again. I turn quickly and catch a slight glimmering like a firefly. It is there just long enough for me to make out wings, a tooth. And just like that it's gone.

"I know you're in here," I say. "I saw you."

Fee and Ann peer into the dark.

"I don't see a thing," Felicity says with a shrug.

"I saw something," I say, whirling about. "I swear that I did."

"Right! Show yourself!" Felicity demands. Only the dark answers. "Gemma, there's nothing there, I tell you. Let's move on."

"Yes. All right," I agree.

Felicity sings the bit of doggerel she learned from Pippa, and Ann joins in. "Oh, I've a love, a true, true love . . ."

I chance one last look behind me. Tucked away under a rafter is the fairy creature from the Borderlands, teeth bared in an ugly sneer. The creature gleams as brightly as a burning coal, then quickly fades to black.

CHAPTER TWENTY-EIGHT

THE EGYPTIAN HALL IN PICCADILLY IS A MAGNIFICENT building. From the front, it looks as if we are about to walk into an ancient tomb resurrected from the sands of the Nile itself. The entrance is adorned by giant statues of Isis and Osiris. A large placard above advertises the Wolfson brothers' exhibit, at three and eight o'clock. There is another for the Dudley Gallery, where many an artist has exhibited his work.

Inside, it seems a perfect replica of those far-off temples. There is a great room supported by rows of columns fashioned in the Egyptian style, complete with hieroglyphs. I should not be surprised to see Cleopatra walking among us.

We've received our souvenir program for tonight's spectacle. The Wolfson brothers appear on either side of the cover, and in the center are drawings of a strange metal box on three legs, a levitating table, a fearsome specter, and a skeleton kicking his bony head about. The first page promises an evening we'll not soon forget.

The Wolfson Brothers Present:
THE RITES OF SPRING
A Phantasmagoria Conjuring Spirits Before Your Very Eyes!

"How exciting!" Mademoiselle LeFarge exclaims. "I'm so grateful Mrs. Nightwing allowed us to come. I hear it isn't at all like looking at photographs. The pictures move as if they were real as you and I!"

"I should like to see that," Ann says.

"Soon, we shall," Miss McCleethy grumbles, fanning through her own program with little interest.

Felicity holds fast to my arm. "How shall we find Dr. Van Ripple with her here?" she asks irritably.

"I don't know—yet," I answer.

Several exhibitors have taken the opportunity to promote themselves within the hall. They have set up tables—some elaborate, some small—to show their wares. They call to us like barkers, and we are not certain where to look first.

"I'd have them all before the magistrate on Bow Street," Inspector Kent mutters, mentioning London's famous court.

"Oh, Mr. Kent," Mademoiselle LeFarge chides.

"Mr. Kent, sir. I hear congratulations are in order." A policeman offers his hand to the inspector, who introduces his soon-to-be wife. Now is the perfect time to slip away—if I can distract McCleethy. If I make use of the magic, will she truly know it? If I cast an illusion, will she see through it? Do I dare chance it?

"Gemma, what shall we do?" Felicity whispers.

"I'm thinking," I whisper back.

McCleethy eyes us suspiciously. "What are you girls whispering about back there?"

"We'd like to see the exhibits," I say. "May we?"

"Certainly. I should like to see them as well."

"Well done," Felicity growls. "She'll not leave our sides."

"I said I was thinking, didn't I?"

"I've seen many exhibitions here," an older woman says to her companion. "When I was a girl, my father brought me to see the famous Tom Thumb. He stood no taller than my waist, and I was but a child."

"Tom Thumb!" Ann exclaims. "How marvelous!"

"This hall has housed many an extraordinary exhibition," McCleethy lectures. "In 1816, Napoleon's carriage was on display, and later, the wonders of the tomb of Seti the First were shown."

"Oh, what else?" Ann draws McCleethy into a conversation like a clever girl, and I've a moment to think. What would draw McCleethy from our sides? A raging lion with canines bared? No, they'd probably greet each other as fellow predators. Blast! What would threaten the unthreatenable McCleethy?

My lips twist into a wicked grin. An old friend, that's what we need. I start to summon my power, and stop. What if I am too overcome by the magic? It is so unpredictable. And she said she would know if I employed it.

There is only one way to find out, I suppose.

I draw in a deep breath and try to calm myself. The voices of McCleethy and my friends, the calls of the exhibitors, and the noise of the crowd fade to murmurs. My fingers itch, and the tingling travels the length of my arms toward my heart. *Steady, Gemma. Set your mind to your purpose.* Within seconds, Fowlson appears in the crowd, for I've conjured him—or the illusion of him, at least.

"Miss McCleethy, it would seem you are wanted," I say quietly, nodding toward the imaginary Fowlson.

Shock registers on McCleethy's face as the horrible man crooks a finger to beckon her. I do my best to remain impassive. *Breathe in, breathe out.* Simplest thing in the world, really.

"How dare he . . ." Miss McCleethy glowers. "Ladies, I'm afraid I shall have to take you back to Mademoiselle LeFarge for a moment."

"Miss McCleethy, can't we wait here? Please? We won't move at all," Felicity pleads.

"Fowlson" makes his way toward the back of the hall. "Yes, yes, all right, but behave yourselves," McCleethy snaps. "I won't be a moment."

"What just happened?" Felicity asks as our teacher hurries away.

My smile is as big as life as I tell them what I've done. "Now we know McCleethy is a liar. She can't tell when I've drawn on the magic, for I just did, and she didn't suspect a thing."

"I knew it!" Felicity exults.

"Right, look about, eyes sharp," I command. "Dr. Van Ripple is a tall, thin man with dark hair and a neatly trimmed goatee."

Watched by the eyes of indifferent gods, we wander the hall, searching for the man I've seen in my visions, the one I hope can shed light on the curious messages I've received.

"Would you care to see the Book of the Dead?" a red-nosed gentleman asks. His wife sits behind him, arranging books on a table. The book in his hands has an engraving of a god with a jackal's head.

"Book of the Dead?" Ann asks. Her face lights up at the mere mention.

Smelling a mark, the man opens the book, flipping through its pages so quickly that we see snow. "The Book of the Dead. With this sacred tome, the ancient Egyptians mummified their dead and prepared them for the afterlife. Some say they could even call the dead from their graves."

Felicity's brow furrows. "Does it mention gorgons or water nymphs? Does it say how to defeat the creatures of the Winterlands?"

The man laughs uncomfortably. "Course not, miss."

"Well, then it isn't much use, is it?"

A man in a turban offers to tell our fortunes for two shillings.

"Wouldn't you like to know your fortune, Gemma?" Ann asks, and I know she'd like me to loan her the money for it. "After all, what if he tells you that you will marry a handsome stranger?"

"What if he tells me I shall die alone surrounded by many cats and a collection of ceramic dolls? That isn't our purpose here," I remind her as she purses her lips.

Felicity hurries to us. "You must see this!"

We scurry to a corner where a burly man with a walrus mustache has a small booth. A handful of ladies gather there. "Step up, don't be shy," the man calls merrily. "Mr. Brinley Smith, photographer, at your service." Photographs. I cannot understand in the least why Felicity should find this exciting or why she'd squander valuable time on it.

"What I have here will astound you. For in this box is proof that life continues after death." I daresay we know a good deal more about the subject than dear Mr. Smith. He opens a box of photographs and offers one to the lady in front for inspection. We peer over her shoulder as best we can. It isn't much, just a picture of a man at his desk, writing a letter. But when I look again, I see something else. Beside the man is a ghostly presence in white, a woman as sheer as lace.

"These are true spirit photographs, ladies. See the spirit world come to life before your very eyes. Herewith lies irrefutable proof of ghosts among us, of life after death!"

"Oh, may I see?" a lady to our right asks.

"See it? Why, madam, for a mere ten pee, you can own it. Amaze your friends and family! I took this very photograph at a séance in Bristol." He lowers his voice to a charged whisper. "What I saw there changed my life—spirits, among us!"

The ladies gasp and whisper. One pulls out her coin purse. "I should like proof, if you please."

"Any one you like, madam, plenty to go round."

I nudge my friends. "We've no time for this. We've got to—"

A commanding voice breaks through from behind us. "Do not believe his claims, dear ladies. This is nothing more than optical trickery at work."

An elegant gentleman with a thicket of black hair, streaked through with silver, and a neatly trimmed goatee steps forward. There are deep wrinkles around his eyes and mouth, and he leans upon a walking stick, but though he is an older man than I've seen in my visions, there is no doubt he is the man we seek: Dr. Theodore Van Ripple.

"That's him," I whisper to Ann and Fee.

The doctor hobbles closer. "This ghostly image is no more a spirit than you or I. It is simply an ordinary photograph soaked too long in a photographer's bath. A trick, you see?"

"Do you call me a liar, sir?" Mr. Smith sniffs.

The man bows. "You'll forgive me, sir, but I cannot allow such kind, good-hearted ladies to be taken in by untruths."

Mr. Smith can smell doubt robbing him of a sale. "Ladies, I assure you, I saw these spirits with my own eyes! Here is proof, I tell you!"

But it is too late. The lady in front has walked away, shaking her head. Others come to take her place. They still want to believe.

Felicity pushes her way toward Dr. Van Ripple. "Is that true, sir?"

"Oh, yes. Quite. I am familiar with a great many illusions. I deal in the world of smoke and mirrors myself. I am a magician by trade. In fact, I performed this evening. For a few moments," he adds bitterly. "But I shall perform a special show for you."

He reaches into his pocket and produces a deck of cards. "Here. I shall show you. Take a card. Any card you wish. You may reveal it to your dear friends but do not show the card to me."

I crane my neck, but I don't see McCleethy yet, so I select a card—the ace of spades—and reveal it to Ann and Felicity before tucking it into my palm out of sight. Dr. Van Ripple passes the deck to Mr. Smith.

"Would you do me the favor of shuffling these cards, dear sir?"

With great irritation, Mr. Smith rearranges the deck. He hands it back to Dr. Van Ripple, who shuffles the cards again and again, making polite chatter the entire time like a born showman. At last, he places his white-gloved hand upon the deck and pronounces, "You hold the ace of spades, dear lady. Do you not?"

Astonished, I show him the ace. "How ever did you do it?"

His eyes twinkle. "The rules of magic, my dear, are best not discussed. For once we understand the illusion, we no longer believe in it."

"He's marked the cards," Mr. Smith huffs, indignant. "Sheer fakery."

Dr. Van Ripple tips his hat and produces a frog from inside it. The frog hops onto the shoulder of a very startled Mr. Smith.

"Ahh, slimy beast!" The photographer nearly topples his own table trying to get away. The crowd laughs.

"Dear me," Dr. Van Ripple says. "Perhaps we should stand elsewhere."

The doctor hobbles ahead, leading us past other exhibitions: A painted Turk's head pushes fortunes out of its mechanical mouth; a snake dancer balances a giant serpent across her shoulders, undulating slowly as the beast coils and slithers; a man holding a stuffed bird trumpets the wonders of a traveling museum of natural history. I even spy Madame Romanoff, otherwise known as Sally Carny of Bow's Bells, conducting a séance. I once took this false spiritualist to the realms by accident. We lock eyes and Sally abruptly ends her reading.

Dr. Van Ripple pauses before a statue of Osiris to mop his brow with a handkerchief. "Our Mr. Smith was nothing more than a faux-tographer, it would seem."

"Your card trick was most impressive!" Ann says.

"You are too kind. Allow me to present myself properly. I am Dr. Theodore Van Ripple, master illusionist, scholar, and gentleman, at your service."

"How do you do? I am Gemma Dowd," I say, giving my

mother's maiden name. Ann holds fast to "Nan Washbrad" whilst Felicity becomes "Miss Anthrope."

"Dr. Van Ripple, I do recall hearing of you," I begin. "I believe my mother attended one of your shows."

His eyes sparkle with interest. "Ah! Here, in London? Or was it perhaps in Vienna or Paris? I have played for both princes and the populace."

"It was here in London, I am sure," I offer. "Yes, she said it was a most marvelous spectacle. She was amazed by your talents."

The doctor positively glows with the adulation. "Splendid! Splendid! Tell me, which illusion did she prefer—the disappearing doll or the glass of ruby smoke?"

"Ah . . . yes, em, I think she rather fancied both."

"They are my specialties. How marvelous!" He cranes, searching the crowd. "And is your dear mother with you here tonight?"

"I'm afraid not," I say. "I do remember that she said there was one illusion which thrilled her beyond all the others. It was one in which a beautiful lady was placed into a trance and instructed to write upon a slate."

Dr. Van Ripple regards me warily. His voice has a chill in it. "The illusion you speak of belonged to my assistant. She was a medium of sorts. I no longer perform that trick—not since her tragic disappearance three years ago."

"She disappeared during the performance?" Ann gasps.

"Dear me, no," Dr. Van Ripple replies. He fluffs his collar, and I imagine that in his day he was quite the dandy.

"What happened to her?" I prod.

"My associates suggested she ran away with a sailor or

perhaps joined a circus." He shakes his head. "But I think otherwise, for she claimed she was being hunted by dark forces. I am quite certain she was murdered."

"Murdered!" we say as one. Dr. Van Ripple is not one to lose an audience of any sort, even for a tale so unseemly as this one promises to be.

"Indeed. She was a woman of many secrets, and, I am sorry to say, she proved quite untrustworthy. She came to me when she was but a girl of twenty, and I knew very little of her life other than that she was an orphan who had lived away at school for a time."

"She didn't speak of her past?" I ask.

"She could not, dear lady, for she was a mute. She had a remarkable talent for drawing and transcendental writing." The doctor takes a bit of snuff from an enameled box and sneezes into a handkerchief.

"What is transcendental writing?" Ann asks.

"The medium goes into a trance, and whilst communing with the spirits, she receives messages from beyond which are communicated through writing. We turned a tidy profit. . . ." He coughs. "That is, we aided those poor grieving souls desperate to speak with loved ones who had passed on to the spirit realm.

"Then one day, she came to the theater quite merry. When I asked her why she was so happy, she wrote upon the slate—for that was how we spoke to one another—that her dear sister had visited her, and they had a plan to 'restore what has been too long lost.' I did not know what she meant, nor did she explain. I was rather astonished at the mention of a sister, as I knew of no family she had. It seems the lady in question was a cherished friend from her school days. When I asked if I might meet her sister, she was evasive, callous.

"'That would not be possible,' she wrote, smiling. She was one for small cruelties, and I was quite certain she felt her dear friend to be far above my station.

"Soon after, she changed. One day, I found her in the shop among our many tricks and properties, holding fast to her slate. 'My sister has deceived us,' she wrote. 'She is a monster. Such a wicked, wicked plan.' When I asked her what could have caused her such distress, she wrote that she had had a vision—'a most terrible vision of what should come to pass, for what I took as fair is foul and all shall be lost.'"

"Did she tell you what she saw in the vision?" I press.

"I'm afraid not." The doctor's brow furrows. "I should say that she had an unfortunate habit—a fondness for cocaine. She could not be without it. I believe it began to destroy her, body and soul."

I think of my father, and my stomach tightens at the memory of finding him in the opium den.

"But cocaine is perfectly harmless," Ann says. "It is in many tonics and lozenges."

Dr. Van Ripple's smile is strained. "So they say, but I think otherwise, my dear. For I saw how it ruined the girl so that she no longer knew what was truth and what illusion. She was suspicious in the extreme, seeing haunts in the shadows. She insisted that she was the only one who might stop this terrible plan, and she wrote long into the night on a secret tome which she said was of the utmost importance. Once, I surprised her as she worked past midnight in the studio, the candle burned nearly to the last of its wick. She startled and covered the pages quickly. She would not show it to me. I suspected her of divulging the secrets of my magic. I dismissed her, and that was all I saw of her for many months, until one spring day three years ago. Just after I'd dined, she knocked upon my door.

"I scarcely recognized her, so shocking was her appearance. Her eyes were those of the doomed. She'd not slept or taken food in some time. And her behavior was most odd. She asked for paper and pen, and I provided them. 'I am wicked,' she wrote. Naturally I thought her unsettled in mind and implored her to stay. But she insisted that dark forces were at work. 'They will keep me from revealing the truth,' she wrote. 'I must act quickly before I am found.'"

"What forces did she speak of?" Ann presses.

The doctor stretches his long fingers over the top of his walking stick, preening like a rooster. "It seems we shall never know. The lady left my home—and vanished."

"What became of the pages she wrote?" I ask.

He takes a deep breath. "I cannot say. Perhaps that terrible secret she feared died along with her. Or perhaps, even now, some diabolical plan is at work, and we are at its mercy." The doctor smiles like a kind uncle. He offers his card. "For your mother. She might have need of a magician to entertain her guests some evening?" I take the card; he closes his hands over mine. "Open them."

When I do, they are empty. The card is gone. "How did you—"

He pulls the card from behind my ear and places it triumphantly in my palm. "Ah, there it was! Such mischievous calling cards I have, I'm afraid." Dr. Van Ripple pats his pockets and frowns. "Oh, dear. Oh, my."

"What is the matter?" Felicity asks.

"I seem to have misplaced my wallet. I do hate to impose, but might you lend an old man a few shillings? I give you my word as a gentleman that I shall repay you in full on the morrow—"

"There you are! Really, girls, you had me quite worried," Mademoiselle LeFarge announces, hastening straight for us with a fuming McCleethy behind her. I do hope the magic lantern show is a wonder, for this may be my last night on earth.

Dr. Van Ripple's smile is kind. "Fear not, dear lady. Your daughters are well in hand and safe from the riffraff, I assure you."

"These young ladies are not my daughters, sir. They are my charges," Mademoiselle LeFarge splutters. "You had me quite worried indeed, girls."

"Trouble, my dear?" Inspector Kent takes a stand beside Mademoiselle LeFarge. He gives the doctor the penetrating stare he has perfected as a policeman, and the magician blanches.

"Well, I shall be off, then," Dr. Van Ripple says quickly.

"Hold a moment. I know that face—Bob Sharpe. It's been a while, but I see the years haven't changed *everything* about you, sir." Inspector Kent stares hard at Dr. Van Ripple. "You weren't attempting to extort money from these young ladies, were you?"

"Inspector, you do wound me," Dr. Van Ripple says. "I merely watched over them like a mother hen."

The inspector folds his arms and looms over Dr. Van Ripple. "Like a fox guarding the hens, you mean. Mr. Sharpe, I trust that you have no desire to return to prison, and that I'll not see you again this evening?"

"As it happens, I have a previous engagement."

Miss McCleethy's stare nearly stops my blood. "I am sorry, Mademoiselle LeFarge. I was gone but a moment," she says.

"Ladies," Mademoiselle LeFarge chides, "if you ever wish to leave the confines of Spence again—"

"Spence, you say? Spence Academy for Young Ladies?" Dr. Van Ripple asks.

Mademoiselle LeFarge nods. "The very same, sir."

Dr. Van Ripple gives us a little push. "Yes, well, wouldn't want to miss the show. Best to take your seats now. A good evening to you all. Inspector." And with that, the old man hobbles away, as fast as he can.

LeFarge shakes her head. "What an odd fellow."

"Dr. Theodore Van Ripple, né Bob Sharpe. Magician, thief, fraud. Did he tell you ladies a fantastic tale, then claim he could not find his wallet?" the inspector inquires.

We nod sheepishly.

"He told us of a vanishing lady. His assistant," Ann says. "He believed her to be murdered."

Miss McCleethy frowns. "I think that's quite enough."

"Yes, I assure you Dr. Van Ripple is a conjurer of tales and cannot be trusted," Inspector Kent says. "Now, shall we see the miracle of moving pictures?"

It would seem that Dr. Van Ripple is nothing but a con. I can't understand why my visions have led me to this aging magician with a vivid imagination and a coat as shabby as his reputation. And to think I've chanced magic on it.

"Did you find your acquaintance, Miss McCleethy?" Felicity asks, and I should like to kick her for it.

"I did, indeed," she says. "At first, I thought my eyes deceived me, for he disappeared in the crowd, but happily, I found him again."

I'm confused. How could she have met up with Fowlson when he was nothing more substantial than ether? Is she lying? Or is Fowlson really here among us?

~~~~

We're led to our seats, which have been arranged so that we face the wall. A strange instrument is wheeled in and placed in the center aisle—a box perched upon metal legs, much like a camera, but larger. One of the Wolfson brothers, in full tails and top hat, stands before us, rubbing his white-gloved hands together in anticipation.

"Ladies and gentlemen, I welcome you to the Egyptian Hall, where in this hour, you shall witness an amazing spectacle of spirits, ghosts, and hobgoblins conjured before your very eyes!

"The Wolfson brothers, masters of the magic lantern, shall astonish and astound you with our feats of illusion—or are they illusion after all? For some would swear that these spirits walk among us, and that this machine powered by gas and light is but an instrument for their release into our world. But I shall leave that to your discretion. It is my duty to advise you that in Paris alone, no fewer than fourteen ladies fainted within the first several minutes, and one gentleman's hair turned white as snow from sheer terror!"

Gasps and excited whispers roll through the audience, to the manager's delight.

"Why, even the great Maskelyne and Cooke, those renowned illusionists and our gracious hosts here at this famed house of mystery, found the spectacle thrilling beyond all imagining.

Therefore, it is my solemn duty to ask any here who may be weak of heart or otherwise unsound in mind or body to please leave now, as the management cannot be held accountable."

Three ladies and a gentleman are ushered from the hall. It heightens the excitement.

"Very well. I cannot say what shall happen this afternoon, whether the spirits will prove kind—or angry. I bid you all welcome . . . and good luck."

The lights are dimmed until the hall is nearly black. In the center aisle, the iron machine hums and hisses to life. It casts an image upon the far wall—a sweet-faced girl standing in a meadow. As we watch, she bends to pick a flower and brings it to her nose. She moves! Oh, the wonder of it. Delighted, the audience breaks into applause.

Ann squeezes my hand. "She seems so real—as if she were here now."

Another image comes, one of a regiment on horseback. The horses prance, their legs moving up and down. We see an angel hovering over the bed of a peaceful sleeping child. Each image is more spectacular than the one before it, and in the dim gaslight, every face gazes straight ahead in awe.

The wall flickers with new light. A woman, chalky pale, appears in her nightgown, sleepwalking. Slowly, she transforms—the arms lose their flesh; the face becomes a death mask—until standing before us is a skeletal creature. Now there are gasps of a different sort. And then the skeleton seems to move closer to us.

Small cries of fear pierce the dark. Someone shouts, "My sister! She's fainted! Oh, do stop the show!"

Inspector Kent leans in toward us. "Not to worry, ladies. All part of the act." And I confess I'm grateful for his aside.

"Spirits!" Mr. Wolfson calls. "Leave us now!"

The ghostly specters stretch across the wall, their faces shifting from benevolent to grisly.

"Please, do not leave your seats! I'm afraid I must inform you that the spirits will no longer listen to the Wolfson brothers! They do not obey our commands! Be on your guard, for I cannot say what shall come next!"

The air is thick with excitement and fear. And then, quickly, the apparition shifts. It grows smaller until it is nothing more than a sweet-faced child offering a flower. Relieved laughter fills the hall.

"Gracious me." Mademoiselle LeFarge chuckles. And that's when I notice that Miss McCleethy's chair is empty. Surely, McCleethy isn't frightened by a magic-lantern show; she isn't frightened of anything.

I spy her hurrying out of the gallery.

"Gemma," Felicity whispers. "Where are you off to?"

"The ladies' dressing room, if anyone should ask."

McCleethy slips into a long room and behind a curtain that hides a winding staircase. I take a deep breath and trail her at a safe distance. When I reach the bottom, I fear I have lost her. But soon, I hear her footsteps. Taking great pains to be as quiet as possible, I follow. We seem to be in a tunnel under the hall, for I still hear the hustle and bustle above us.

Miss McCleethy goes into a large dimly lit room that houses all sorts of exhibitions—statues, exotic costumes, magic apparatus, a placard for the Wolfson brothers with the word *scoundrels* painted across it. I secrete myself behind a bust of some Egyptian goddess sporting a lion's head.

McCleethy is arguing with someone in the shadows. "You lied

to me. I don't take kindly to liars. This is not a game we're play-ing! I saved your life. You're in my debt. Or have you forgotten?"

I can't hear the answer, nor can I see more without revealing myself.

"I must know everything from now on," McCleethy commands. "I don't think I need remind you that they would kill you where you stand if they knew you were here with me. If you mean to save them, you must follow me. It's the only way."

She pushes her hair into place and fiddles with the brooch at her collar until it's straight. "For twenty-five years, I've been de-voted to the cause. I do not mean to lose to the Rakshana or a sixteen-year-old girl. Go on, then, before you're seen."

The figure in the dark retreats. I shrink behind the giant statue, and Miss McCleethy hurries back the way she came. I wait until I no longer hear the echo of her footsteps, and then I return to the hall, where the audience delights in the merry image of a jumping dog and a clown juggling balls.

I steal a quick glance at McCleethy. The triumph I felt ear-lier at deceiving her has been replaced by wariness. To whom could she have been talking? Was it Fowlson? Is he her spy within the Rakshana? *You lied to me*, she said. Lied about what? And whom did they mean to save?

At last, Mr. Wolfson shuts down the lamp that fuels the magic lantern. The room burns with light once again, and the ghostly apparitions vanish from the walls. But the haunts in-side me won't leave so easily.

"I thank you for your kind attention, ladies and gentlemen!" Mr. Wolfson's voice booms out. "These images are enchant-ments of a sort, but they are illusions—dreams born of gas and light. Our good hosts, Maskelyne and Cooke, have made it their work to expose the fraudulent among us. I would advise you to be on guard against all forms of trickery and deceit disguised as truth. We shall play again at eight o'clock this evening and tomorrow again at three and eight. We bid you good evening, all!"

We're ushered from the hall in a crushing sea of excited people making their last-minute purchases. I try to keep a safe distance from McCleethy, holding fast to my friends' arms.

"Where did you go, Gemma?" Felicity asks.

"I followed McCleethy. She had a secret meeting with someone."

"Who?" Ann asks.

I look behind me, but McCleethy is deep in conversation with LeFarge and Inspector Kent. "I couldn't see who it was. Perhaps it was someone from the Rakshana or the Order," I say, and tell them all I know.

The streets are a madhouse of people and carriages, gloom and bustle. The program has promised carriages at five o'clock but there are far too many people for so few carriages, and we shall be forced to wait an eternity.

"Right," Inspector Kent says. "Let's see what the law can do."

He marches purposefully toward the man corralling the cabs.

"I am sorry to abandon you like this, Mademoiselle LeFarge," Miss McCleethy says. "Are you certain you'll be fine on your own with the girls?"

"Of course," Mademoiselle LeFarge says, patting Miss McCleethy's hands.

"Miss McCleethy, are you leaving us?" Felicity pries.

"Yes, I've a dinner engagement with a friend this evening," our teacher answers.

"What friend is that?" Fee says, abandoning all propriety.

"Now then, Miss Worthington, it's none of your affair, is it?" Mademoiselle LeFarge reprimands, and Fee falls quiet. Miss McCleethy does not grant us an answer to the impertinent question.

"I trust you'll give Mademoiselle LeFarge no trouble, ladies," she says. "I shall see you on the morrow."

"I didn't know Miss McCleethy had any friends," Ann mutters once McCleethy has taken her leave of us.

Nor did I, but Miss McCleethy has been full of surprises tonight.

The London fog envelops us in its murkiness. Figures emerge at first like ghosts, like something that belongs to the mist, before taking on form—top hats, coats, bonnets. It is an effect as thrilling as anything conjured by the Wolfson brothers' magic lantern.

Ann, Felicity, and LeFarge are distracted by the sight of a Mr. Pinkney—the Human Calliope—as he mimics the sound of the instrument with his mouth while also banging a drum.

Dr. Van Ripple emerges from the fog, hobbling quickly on his cane. He collides with a gentleman. "I do beg your pardon, sir. It's this leg and the damp."

"No harm done," the gentleman says. As he helps to right Dr. Van Ripple, I see the magician reach into the man's pocket and relieve him of his gold watch.

Master illusionist, indeed. Master pickpocket would be more like it.

"Pardon me, pardon me," he says, shooing the ladies and gentlemen in their finery out of his way. I block his path. He locks eyes with me, startled.

"Did you enjoy the show, my dear?"

"Which show would that be, sir?" I say sweetly. "The Wolfson brothers'? Or the one I just witnessed in which you relieved a man of his pocket watch?"

"An honest mistake," Dr. Van Ripple says, his eyes wide with fear.

"I shan't tell," I assure him. "But I expect something in return. When Miss LeFarge mentioned Spence, you paled at the name. Why?"

"Really, I must be going. . . ."

"Shall I call for the constable?"

Dr. Van Ripple glowers. "My assistant attended the Spence Academy."

"She was a Spence girl?"

"So she said."

I search his face. "How do I know you're telling me the truth?"

He puts his hand over his heart. "On my reputation as a gentleman—"

I stop him. "I believe your reputation as a gentleman is very much in question, sir."

He holds my gaze. "On my reputation as a magician, then. I promise you this is the truth."

Our carriages have arrived. "Come along, girls!" Mademoiselle LeFarge calls.

"Best not keep them waiting," he says, pocketing the stolen watch.

Can I trust the word of a thief?

"Dr. Van Ripple," I start, but he waves me off with his cane. "Please, sir, I only wish to know her name, nothing more, and I shall leave you in peace. I promise."

Seeing I will not surrender, he sighs. "Very well. It was Mina. Miss Wilhelmina Wyatt."

<hr/>

Mina, Miss Wilhelmina Wyatt, author of *A History of Secret Societies* and the lady in my visions, was a Spence girl, and one of her sisters betrayed her.

The moment Mademoiselle LeFarge falls asleep in the carriage, we break into low chatter.

"Wilhelmina Wyatt! To think that we have her book—and its dangerous secrets—in our possession!" Ann blurts out.

"But we've read the book," I say. "What could we have possibly missed? There is nothing dangerous there."

"Unless it is the danger of putting one to sleep." Felicity yawns.

"We did discover some truth about the Order," Ann says, defending herself. "Without the book, Gemma, you'd never have discovered the true identity of Circe," she reminds us, and she's right. For that was how we discovered that the Order often hid their identities by use of anagrams, and that Hester Asa Moore, the name of our trusted mentor, was an anagram for Sarah Rees-Toome.

Felicity drums her fingers on the seat. "There is something that has always troubled me about that book. What purpose could Miss McCleethy have had in purchasing it? If she's a member of the Order, why should she need a book about the Order?"

At Christmastime, we followed Miss McCleethy to the Golden Dawn bookseller's in the Strand. She purchased the book, so we did the same, but until now, I've thought it one of her peculiarities. I've not thought there could be a deeper, and perhaps much darker, reason for her wanting it.

"I saw McCleethy's face briefly in one of my visions," I remind them. "She could be the sister Dr. Van Ripple mentioned."

"Yes, though you said you only saw her face," Felicity adds. "You didn't see them together."

Outside our windows, the still-bare branches scrape against the carriage. The night has claws, but we escape, bumping along until Spence comes into view once more. With its lamps still ablaze, the sprawling estate glows brightly in the sooty night. Only the East Wing is dark. The clouds shift; the moon shows her face. Atop the roof, the leering gargoyles perch, the high arches of their wings formidable shadows against the moon's light. The stone beasts seem taut and ready. And for a moment, I remember that chilling hallucination in the carriage that day with Felicity—the creature's open mouth, the glint of sharp teeth coming down, the thin stream of blood— and I have to look away.

"Well, I still say if there were some grand secret within the book we'd have discovered it by now," I insist.

Ann peers out at the vast expanse of stars. "Perhaps we didn't know where to look."

⭒⭒⭒⭒⭒

An hour later, we're in Felicity's room, crowded around our copy of *A History of Secret Societies*, trying to read it by faint candlelight.

"Look for anything that makes mention of this Tree of All

Souls," I instruct. "Perhaps we missed it the first time round because it held no meaning for us before."

We read page after frustratingly oblique page until the words begin to blind us. We take turns reading aloud. There are entries on the Druids, the Gnostics, witchcraft, and paganism, a few illustrations that add nothing. We read again about the Order and the Rakshana and find no new facts of interest. There is not a single word about a Tree of All Souls.

We turn the page and there's an illustration of a tower. I keep reading.

"'Glastonbury Tor. Stonehenge. Iona in the Hebrides. The Great Pyramids and the Great Sphinx of Giza. These are all thought to be imbued with magic derived from the alignment of the earth and the stars,'" I read with a yawn. "'Sacred points within the earth are indicated by various markers, which include churches, cemeteries, stone circles, the wood, and castles, to name but a few. For the great priestesses, the venerable Druids, the noble pagans believed that here the spirits walked—'"

"Gemma, there's nothing more there," Felicity grouses. She hangs her head and arms over the end of her bed like a bored child. "Can we please go on to the realms? Pip's waiting."

"The book is five hundred pages long," Ann agrees. "We'll be here all night, and I want to play with magic."

"You're right," I say, closing the book. "To the realms."

CHAPTER TWENTY-NINE

NOW THAT MISS MCCLEETHY HAS RETURNED TO US, SHE wastes no time in making her presence felt. She cracks her whip at every opportunity. There is a right way and a wrong way to do things, and the right way, it would seem, is always the McCleethy way. Despite her will of iron, she is a great one for taking walks, and as the days grow greener, we are grateful for these sojourns from the stuffy halls of Spence.

"I believe we shall sketch outdoors today," she announces. As it's a rather lovely day, this news is greeted with enthusiasm. We don bonnets to protect our fair complexions from the threat of freckles, though it is, of course, a moot point for me. I remember beautiful, hot days in India, running barefoot over cracked ground, the sun tattooing a reminder of those days in small brown patches, as if the gods threw a handful of sand across my cheeks and nose while my skin was wet.

"The sun has blessed you," Sarita used to say. "Look how he has left his kisses on your face for all to see and be jealous."

"The sun loves you more," I said, rubbing my hands over her dry arms, the color of an aged wine gourd, and she laughed.

But this is not India, and we are not prized for our freckles here. The sun is not allowed to show his love.

Miss McCleethy marches us through muddy grass that makes a ruin of our boots.

"Where are we going?" Elizabeth grumbles behind us.

"Miss McCleethy, will it be much farther?" Cecily asks.

"The walk shall do you good, Miss Temple. I'll hear no more complaining," Miss McCleethy answers.

"I wasn't complaining," Cecily sputters, but not one of us shall join her cause. If there were a championship held for whiners, she would hold the trophy easily.

Miss McCleethy leads us through the woods, past the lake with its mirror image of the gray sky, and down a narrow, crooked road we've not seen before. It winds for some time before coming to a hill. A small graveyard is visible at the hill's summit, and that is where Miss McCleethy takes us. She spreads out a cloth between the headstones and settles our picnic basket upon it.

Elizabeth holds her cloak fast to her. "Why have we come to such a dreadful place, Miss McCleethy?"

"To remind us that life is short, Miss Poole," Miss McCleethy says, catching my eye ever so briefly. "It is also a lovely spot for a picnic. Who would care for cake and lemonade?"

With a flourish she opens the basket and the smell of Brigid's heavenly apple cake drifts from its depths. Thick slices of it are offered all around. Lemonade is poured. We sketch and eat in lazy fashion. Miss McCleethy sips her lemonade. She gazes out at the expanse of rolling green hills, the clusters of trees like tufts of unruly hair on a balding man's head. "There is something quite special about this land."

"It's lovely," Ann agrees.

"Bit muddy," Cecily grumbles through a mouthful of cake. "Not as pretty as Brighton." I imagine her polishing that whining trophy.

Ann pipes up. "Brigid said that Jesus himself may have walked these hills with his cousin, Joseph of Arimathea, and that the Gnostics were also drawn to this place."

"What are Gnostics?" Elizabeth titters.

"A mystical sect of early Christians, more pagan than Christian, really," Miss McCleethy answers. "I've heard that story, too, Miss Bradshaw. Many Britons believe that Camelot itself may have been erected in this region, and that Merlin chose the spot because the land held such enchantment within it."

"How could the land be enchanted?" Felicity asks. Her mouth is far too full, and McCleethy gives her a hard look.

"Miss Worthington, we are not savages, if you please," she chides, handing Felicity a napkin. "Many of the ancients did believe that there were sites that held extraordinary power. That is why they worshipped there."

"Does that mean that if I stand in the center of Stonehenge, I could become as powerful as King Arthur?" Cecily asks with a laugh.

"No, I rather think it was not meant to be given to everyone indiscriminately but governed carefully by those who know best," she says, pointedly. "For when we read about magic in fairy stories or tales of myth, we read time and again that it is subject to strict laws, else chaos follows. Look out there. What do you see?" Miss McCleethy waves her hand toward the green horizon.

"Hills," Ann offers. "Roads."

"Flowers and shrubs," Cecily adds. She looks to Miss McCleethy as if there might be a prize for the right answer.

"What we can see is proof. Proof that man can conquer nature, that chaos can be turned back. You see evidence of the importance of order, of law. For conquer chaos we must. And if we see it in ourselves, we must root it out and replace it with steadfast discipline."

Can we really conquer chaos so easily? If that were so, I should be able to prune the pandemonium of my own soul into something neat and tidy rather than this maze of wants and needs and misgivings that has me forever feeling as if I cannot fit into the landscape of things.

"But aren't many gardens beautiful because they are imperfect?" I say, glancing at McCleethy. "Aren't the strange, new flowers that arise by mistake or misadventure as pleasing as the well-tended and planned?"

Elizabeth purses her lips. "Are we speaking of art?"

Miss McCleethy smiles broadly. "Ah, a perfect segue to the topic at hand. Look at the art of the masters and you will see that their work has been created according to strict rules: Here we have line and light and a color scheme." She holds my gaze as if she has me in checkmate. "Art cannot be created without order."

"What of the Impressionists in Paris, then? It is not ordered so much as felt with the brush, it seems," Felicity says, eating cake with her fingers.

"There are always rebels and radicals, I suppose," McCleethy allows. "Those who live on the fringes of society. But what do they contribute to the society itself? They reap its rewards without experiencing its costs. No. I submit that the loyal, hardworking citizens who push aside their own selfish desires for the good of the whole are the backbone of the world. What if we all decided to run off and live freely without thought or care for society's rules? Our civilization would crumble. There is a joy in duty and a security in knowing one's place. This is the English way. It is the only way."

"Quite so, Miss McCleethy," Cecily says. But really, what would I expect from her?

I know that is to be the end of the discussion, but I can't let it go. "But without the rebels and radicals, there would be no change, no one to push back. There would be no progress."

Miss McCleethy shakes her head thoughtfully. "True progress can only happen when there is safety first."

"What if safety . . . is only an illusion?" I say, thinking aloud. "What if there is no such thing?"

"Then we fall." Miss McCleethy squeezes what's left of her cake, and it falls to bits. "Chaos."

I take a small bite of my cake. "What if that is only the beginning of something new? What if, once we let go, we are freed?"

"Would you take that chance, Miss Doyle?" Miss McCleethy holds my gaze till I'm forced to look away.

"What *are* we talking about?" Elizabeth clucks.

"Miss McCleethy, the ground is so hard. Couldn't we return to Spence now?" Martha complains.

"Yes, very well. Miss Worthington, I leave you in charge. Girls, follow her lead." Miss McCleethy places the crumbles of cake into a napkin and ties it up neatly. "Order. That is the key. Miss Doyle, I'll need your help to gather our things."

Felicity and I exchange glances. She draws her finger across her throat like a blade, and I make a note to tell her later how very witty I find her. Miss McCleethy takes a bouquet of wildflowers and bids me follow her farther into the graveyard. It is a steep climb to the very top of the hill. The wind blows hard here. It pulls tendrils of her hair free so that they whip wildly about her face, lessening its severity. From here I can see the girls tripping through the trees in a merry line, Ann bringing up the rear. In the distance, Spence rises from the land as if it were a part of it, as if it has always existed, like the trees or the hedgerows or the distant Thames.

Miss McCleethy lays the flowers at the base of a simple headstone. Eugenia Spence, Beloved Sister. May 6, 1812–June 21, 1871.

"I did not know there was a gravestone for Mrs. Spence."

"It is how she would have wanted to be remembered— simply, without ceremony."

"What was she like?" I ask.

"Eugenia? She had a quick mind and a skilled grasp of the magic. In her time, she was the most powerful of the Order. Kind but firm. She believed that the rules must be followed without exception, for to deviate in any way was to court disaster. This school was her life's work. I learned a great deal from her. She was my mentor. I loved her dearly."

She wipes her hands free of dirt and pulls on her gloves.

"I am sorry for your loss," I say. "I'm sorry that my mother . . ."

Miss McCleethy buttons her cape with quick fingers. "Chaos killed her, Miss Doyle. Two girls stepping outside the rules took our beloved teacher away. Remember that."

I swallow my shame, but my red cheeks do not go unnoticed.

"I am sorry," she says. "That was too hard of me. I confess that when I discovered it was Mary's daughter who was the key to the realms, I was disappointed. That the one whose misadventure led to Eugenia's death could have birthed our salvation . . ." She shakes her head. "It seemed fate had played a cruel joke."

"I am not so bad as all that," I protest.

"It is one thing to prepare for greatness. It is another entirely to have it thrust upon you. I feared your mother's blood would lead you to make perilous choices . . ." She looks toward Spence, where the men hammer away, fleshing out the ruined East Wing. "And you've still not been able to enter the realms or recover the Temple's magic?"

"I'm afraid not." I study Eugenia Spence's headstone, hoping Miss McCleethy doesn't notice the lie bringing a blush to my cheek.

"I wonder why I have such trouble believing that," she says.

"And is there no other way of entering the realms?" I ask, changing the subject.

"None that I know of," Miss McCleethy says. She passes a hand over my hair, securing one of my wayward curls behind my ear. "We shall have to be patient. I'm sure your powers will return."

"Unless the realms haven't chosen me to continue," I remind her.

She smirks. "I rather doubt that, Miss Doyle. Come, let's gather our things."

She leads the way back to our picnic spot, and I follow.

I free the curl she's tucked so neatly; it hangs wild and loose. "Miss McCleethy, *if* the magic were to spark inside me . . . and *if* I were able to enter the realms again . . . would the Order join with the tribes of the realms in an alliance?"

Her eyes flash. "Do you mean join with those who have been committed to our destruction for centuries?"

"But if things have changed—"

"No, Miss Doyle. Some things will never change. We have been persecuted for our beliefs and our power both in the realms and out. We will not cede it so easily. Our mission is to bind the magic to the Temple, to rebuild the runes, and return the realms to the way they were before this terrible tragedy destroyed our security."

"Were they ever truly secure? Doesn't seem it."

"Of course they were. And they might be again if we go back to the way it was."

"But we can't go back. We can only go forward," I say, surprised to hear Miss Moore's words coming out of my mouth.

Miss McCleethy lets out a rueful laugh. "How could it have come to this? Your mother nearly destroyed us, and now you've come along to nail the coffin shut. Help me with this basket, please."

When I hand her the lemonade glass, we collide, and the glass fractures into pieces too small to put back together.

"I'm sorry," I say, gathering them into a pile.

"You make a mess of the simplest things, Miss Doyle. Leave me. I'll see to it myself."

I stomp away, weaving dangerously through the aged tombstones bearing inscriptions to those who are beloved only once they are gone.

A mutiny is in progress at the East Wing when I return. Felicity runs to me and pulls me into the cluster of girls watching it unfold from the safety of the trees. The men have abandoned the building. They stand together, hats on, arms folded across their chests, while Mr. Miller barks orders, his face red.

"I'm the foreman here, and I say we've a job to finish or there's no pay for the lot of you! Now, back to work!"

The men shuffle their feet. They fidget with their hats. One spits in the grass. A tall man with the build of a boxer steps forward. He glances anxiously at his mates.

"Don't feel right, sir."

Mr. Miller cups his hand to his ear and frowns. "What's that?"

"Me and the men been talkin'. Sumfin' don't feel right 'bout this place."

"What don't feel right is not having pay in your pocket!" Mr. Miller shouts.

"Where's Tambley gone to, then? And Johnny goin' off last night, not comin' back this mornin'?" another man shouts. He seems more frightened than angry. "They joos up and gone wifout a word and you don' fink what there's a bit o' the strange about it?"

"It's talk like this what probably scared 'em off. And good riddance to them. Cowards. If you ask me, we need to clear the woods of them filthy Gyps. I wouldn't be surprised if they've got a hand in this. Comin' into our country and takin' a proper Englishman's job? Will you let them put their curses on us without a fight?"

"Your men drink. That is their curse." Ithal swaggers down the hill trailing a dozen Gypsies in his wake, as well as Kartik. My heart beats a little faster. The Gypsies are far outnumbered by Miller's men.

Miller staggers up the hill at a run. He takes a swing at Ithal, who dodges and weaves like an expert boxer. The two men fall into fighting with both sides egging them on. Ithal catches Mr. Miller hard on the jaw. He reels from it. Kartik keeps his hand near the dagger in his boot.

"Here now! Stop this fuss!" Brigid yells.

The whole of the school empties to see the men fighting. New blows are thrown. Everyone has a hand in it now.

"How is it none of yer lot is missing?" one of Mr. Miller's men shouts.

"That is not proof," Ithal says, dodging a fist.

"Proof enuf for me!" another man growls. He jumps onto Ithal's back, tearing at his shirt like an animal. Kartik pulls him off. The man grabs for him, and quick as a flash, Kartik's leg swings under the man, robbing him of his balance. The lawn erupts into chaos.

"Isn't this exciting?" Felicity says, eyes flashing.

Mrs. Nightwing has come. She strides across the lawn like Queen Victoria reprimanding her guard. "This will not do, Mr. Miller! This will not do at all!"

Mother Elena stumbles into the clearing. She calls to the men to stop. She's weak and leans against a tree for support. "It is this place! It took my Carolina! Call for Eugenia—ask her to stop this."

"Mad as a hatter," someone mutters.

There's a break in the melee. Kartik steps forward. He has a fresh cut on his lower lip. "If we join forces we'd have a better chance at catching whoever it is causing trouble. We could stand guard while you sleep—"

"Let the likes of you stand watch? We'd wake to have our pockets emptied and our throats cut!" a worker shouts.

There is more yelling; accusations are thrown, and another fight threatens to break out.

Mrs. Nightwing marches into the fray. "Gentlemen! The proposal is a sound one. The Gypsies will stand watch in the evenings so that your men might rest easy."

"I won't let them watch us," Mr. Miller says.

"But we will watch," Ithal says. "For our own protection."

"Such a fuss." Mrs. Nightwing tuts. "Girls! Why are you standing there with your mouths open like geese? To the schoolroom with you at once."

I pass Kartik, keeping my eyes squarely on the other girls. *Don't look at him, Gemma. He did not answer your call. Keep walking.*

I manage to reach the doors of Spence before I allow myself a fleeting glance behind me, and there is Kartik watching me go.

<center>~~~~~</center>

"Letters! Letters!" Brigid comes through with the week's post, which she has brought from the village. Our studying forgotten, we girls clamor around her, hands reaching for some word from home. The younger ones cry and sniffle over their mothers' letters, so homesick are they. But we older girls are eager for gossip.

"Aha!" Felicity holds out an invitation in triumph. "Feast your eyes."

"'You are cordially invited to a Turkish ball in honor of Miss

Felicity Worthington at the home of Lord and Lady Markham, eight o'clock in the evening,'" I read aloud. "Oh, Felicity, how marvelous."

She clutches it to her chest. "I can nearly taste my freedom. What have you got, Gemma?"

I peer at the return address. "A letter from my grandmother," I say, sticking it inside my book.

Felicity raises an eyebrow. "Why don't you open it?"

"I shall. Later," I say, glancing at Ann. Every one of us has a letter except for her. Every time the post is delivered, it is a misery for her to come away with nothing, no caring soul to write and say she is missed.

Brigid holds a letter up to the light, scowling. "Oh, that man 'as lost 'is wits. This one isn't ours. Miss Nan Washbrad. No Nan Washbrad 'ere."

Ann nearly leaps for the envelope. "May I see it?"

Brigid holds it away from her. "Now, now. It's for Missus Nightwing to decide what to do wi' it."

We watch, helpless, as Brigid shuffles Miss Trimble's long-awaited letter into Nightwing's correspondence and places them neatly into the pocket of her apron.

"It must be from Mr. Katz. We have to get that back," Ann says desperately.

"Ann, where does Brigid put Nightwing's letters?" I ask.

"On her desk," Ann says, swallowing hard. "Upstairs."

⊹⊹⊹⊹⊹

We are forced by circumstances to wait until evening prayers before we are able to try for Ann's letter. Whilst the other girls gather their shawls and prayer books, we steal away and let ourselves into Nightwing's office. It's old and starched-looking and, much like the bustle at the back of Nightwing's dress, terribly out of fashion.

"Let's be quick about it," I say.

We open drawers, poking about for any sign of Ann's letter. I open a small wardrobe and peer inside. The shelves are lined with books: *When Love Is True*, by Miss Mabel Collins. *I Have Lived and Loved*, by a Mrs. Forrester. *The Stronger Passion. Trixie's Honor. Blind Elsie's Crime. A Glorious Gallop. Won By Waiting.*

"You'll not believe what I just found," I say, giggling. "Romance novels! Can you imagine?"

"Gemma, really," Felicity chides from her lookout post at the door. "We've more important matters at hand."

Shamed, I go to close the wardrobe when I notice a letter, but its postmark is from 1893. It is far too old to be Ann's letter. Still, the script is oddly familiar. I turn it over, and there's a broken wax seal with the impression of the crescent eye, so I slide the letter free of the envelope. There is no salutation of any kind.

> *You've ignored my warnings. If you persist in your plan, I shall expose you . . .*

"I found it!" Ann exults.

Felicity's voice is panicked. "Someone's coming up the stairs!" she calls.

Hurriedly, I put everything back as it was and close the cabinet doors. Ann grabs her letter and we walk quickly down the hallway.

At the baize door, Brigid greets us with a scowl. "You know you're not allowed 'ere!"

"We thought we heard a noise," Felicity lies smoothly.

"Yes, we were terribly frightened," Ann adds.

Brigid glances down the hall with both suspicion and trepidation. "I'll call for Mrs. Nightwing, then, and—"

"No!" we all say as one.

"No need for that," I say. "It was nothing but a hedgehog that had gotten in."

Brigid blanches. "Hedgehog? I'll get my broom! He'll not run amok in my 'ouse!"

"That's the spirit, Brigid!" I call after her. "I think it was a French hedgehog!"

"A French hedgehog?" Felicity repeats with a bemused expression.

"*Oui,*" I say.

Ann clutches the letter to her chest. "We've got what we came for. Come on. I want to know my fate."

A sliver of day remains as we hurry to the chapel, but the sun is falling below the horizon fast.

"What does it say?" Felicity tries to steal a peek at Ann's letter but she won't relinquish it just yet.

"Ann!" Fee and I protest.

"All right, all right." Ann passes it to us, and we grab it greedily from her hands. "Read it aloud. I should like to know that I'm not dreaming!"

" 'My Dear Miss Washbrad,' " Fee and I begin in unison. Eyes shut, lips in a grin, Ann mouths every word. " 'I hope this letter finds you well. I have spoken to Mr. Katz and he is disposed to offer you an appointment with him on Monday next, at two o'clock in the afternoon. I advise you not to be late, my dear, as nothing puts Mr. Katz in a darker mood than a lack of punctuality. I have recommended your talent. Your beauty speaks for itself.

"'Yours Affectionately, Lily Trimble.'"

"Oh, Ann, that's wonderful," I say, handing back the letter, which she tucks into her dress next to her heart.

"Yes, yes, it is, isn't it?" Ann's joy transforms her. She walks taller for this token of hope.

Holding hands, we race for the chapel as the day slips free from its moorings and sinks below the land, leaving behind a fiery wake of pink.

<hr />

One of the younger girls reads from the large Bible at the pulpit. She is a small thing, no more than ten, and she has a pronounced lisp, which threatens to turn our prayers into giggles at any moment.

"'And the therpent thaid unto the woman, Ye thall not thurely die . . .'"

"Gemma," Ann whispers. "I cannot possibly keep my appointment with Mr. Katz."

"What do you mean?" I murmur from behind my Bible.

A sudden cloud passes over her face, extinguishing her earlier joy. "He thinks that I am Nan Washbrad."

"It's only a name. Lily Trimble changed hers."

Cecily shushes me and I do my very best to show I'm ignoring her.

"But what she said—'Your beauty speaks for itself.' Don't you see? I am not that girl. It's one thing to create an illusion, but how—how do you live it forever?"

"'For God doth know that in the day ye eat thereof, then

your eyeth thall be opened, and ye thall be ath godth, knowing good and evil.'"

"We thall be ath godth," Felicity mimics, and there is a sudden round of coughing in our pew to cover our snickers.

Miss McCleethy cranes her head and narrows her eyes at us. We raise our Bibles as if we were a school of missionaries. My gaze travels to Mrs. Nightwing. She sits straight, eyes ahead, her expression as inscrutable as the Sphinx's.

My thoughts turn to the letter hidden in her wardrobe. What warnings could Mrs. Nightwing have ignored? What plan?

Suddenly, the words in my Bible blur, and the world once again slows to stillness. At the lectern, the girl's tortured recitation has stopped. The room is stifling; my skin crawls with sweat.

"Ann? Felicity?" I call, but they belong to that other time.

A syrupy hiss echoes in the chapel.

"F-Fee," I whisper, but she can't hear me. The hiss comes again, stronger. To the right. I turn slowly, my heartbeat gaining speed. My eyes travel the impossible distance from the floor to the stained-glass window with the angel and the gorgon's head.

"Oh, God . . ."

Panic has me scrambling backward, but the motionless girls block my path, so I can only gaze in horror as the window comes alive. Like a moment from the Wolfson brothers' magic-lantern show, the angel walks toward me with the severed gorgon's head held aloft. And then the thing opens its eyes and speaks.

"Beware the birth of May," it hisses.

With a loud yelp, I fall back, and the world comes to its full speed again. I've collided with Ann, who has bumped into Felicity, and so on, like a row of dominoes.

"Gemma!" Ann says, and I realize I'm holding fast to her.

"S-sorry," I say, wiping the sweat from my brow.

"Ugh. Here." Felicity hands me a handkerchief.

The pump organ's blast of missed notes calls us to sing, and I hope its garish tones can mask the frantic beating of my heart. Hymnals are lifted and girlish voices rise without question of a bulwark ever failing. My lips move but I cannot sing. I'm trembling and drenched in a cold sweat.

Don't look. But I must, I must. . . .

I slide my eyes ever so carefully to the right, where moments ago an angel's bloody trophy hissed a warning I don't understand. But now the angel's face is peaceful. The gorgon's head sleeps. It's only a picture in a window, nothing more than colored glass.

⌇⌇⌇⌇

My blood will not settle, so I sit, alone, and read the letter from home I put away earlier. It is the usual twaddle from Grandmama, with mention of this party and that social call and all the latest gossip, but I've no head for it at present. I am surprised to read that Simon Middleton asked after me, and for a moment, my gloom is dispelled, and then I hate myself for allowing my thoughts to be turned so easily by a man; and just as quickly, I forget to hate myself and read the sentence three times over.

Just behind Grandmama's letter is a note from Tom.

Dear Gemma, Lady of Pointed Tongue, he writes. *I am writing* this under duress, as Grandmama will not grant me peace until I do. Very well, I shall meet my obligation as a brother. I trust you are well. I, myself, am simply superb, never better. My gentlemen's club has expressed a very keen interest in me, and I've been told I shall face a rigorous initiation into their sacred rites before the season commences. They've even been so kind as to ask after you with all manner of questions, though I can't imagine why. I've told them exactly how disagreeable you can be. So you see that you and Father are wrong about me after all, and I shall try to be kind and acknowledge you on the street with a nod and a smile when I am a peer. And now, my duty finished, I leave you. Fondly as is possible given your unsuitable temperament, Thomas.

I crumple the note and throw it into the fire. I desperately need advice—about my brother, the Order, Wilhelmina Wyatt, the realms, and this magic inside me that both astounds and frightens. There is only one person I can turn to who might hold the answers to all my questions. And I shall go to her.

CHAPTER THIRTY

AT THE BRAMBLE WALL, I LEAVE MY FRIENDS. ANN PUTS her face close to the barbs that separate us. "Aren't you coming?"

"Yes, later. There is a matter I must attend to."

Felicity is suspicious. "What is it?"

I sigh dramatically. "I must speak to Asha about a matter between the Untouchables and the forest folk. A dispute."

"Sounds terribly dull," Felicity says. "Best of luck."

Arm in arm, they hurry toward the castle, which juts up from its nest of vines like a bony mirage.

The smudge pots that line the dusty road to the Temple belch their colorful smoke. Usually, the scent is of the sweetest incense, but today, there's a different smell, something sharp and unpleasant. The Hajin seem agitated. It is as if they await a promised storm.

"Lady Hope," Asha says with a bow.

"I must approach the well of eternity," I say, heading for it without stopping.

Asha keeps pace with me through the maze of corridors. "Lady Hope, my people are afraid. The forest folk accuse us of collaborating secretly with the Order—"

"And have you?" I query.

"Surely you do not believe it also?"

I don't know what I believe anymore. The Order has some plan, and I intend to have answers about that when I leave. We've reached the Caves of Sighs. "Asha, I need to be alone."

She bows again, shielding her eyes. "As you wish, Lady Hope."

Circe's body floats beneath the glasslike surface of the well. She seems weightless, yet I feel her presence so heavily I can scarcely breathe.

"So you've come back after all."

I need your help. Try as I might, I cannot choke out those words.

"Something is at hand, and I want to know what it is!"

Her voice is like a dying woman's. "You understand . . . the price . . . for my counsel?"

I swallow hard. Once this has begun, there is no turning back. And if I give her magic as she wants, who is to say that she can't cause me harm? "Yes. I understand."

"And you would give it . . . of your own free will?"

"What choice do I have?" I retort, and then I laugh bitterly, knowing full well what her response shall be. "Yes, I know, there is always a choice. Very well. I choose to give you what you want in exchange for what I need."

"Of your own free will . . ."

"Yes, I give it of my own free will!" I snap.

"Then come to me," she whispers, no more loudly than the rustling of silk.

I approach the well, where her body presses against the seal of water like a phantom. It takes every bit of strength I have to look into those staring eyes.

"Listen closely, Gemma," she says in her slow, hoarse whisper. "Do exactly as I say, else you will kill me and know nothing."

"I'm listening," I say.

"Put your hand on the surface of the well and bestow it with life—"

"But I thought it would kill—"

"Just until the seal breaks and the water clears."

My fingers linger on the edge of the well. *Go on, then, Gemma. Get it over with.* Slowly, I lower my trembling hands to the surface and rest them there. It is like a sheet of ice that melts at my touch. The water clears and Circe rises till her face is nearly breaking the surface.

"Good, good," she whispers. "Now, place your palm over my heart and give me a small bit of magic—but only a small token. I am weak and cannot take more."

My hand sinks into those waters until it is flush against the soggy fabric of Circe's bodice, and I stifle a scream.

"Now," she sighs.

Soon, the magic travels between us, an invisible thread. I feel nothing of her thoughts, only my own reflected to me.

"There," I say, pulling quickly away.

Miss Moore rises until she's floating peacefully on the surface. Her cheeks and lips show the palest hint of pink. Those unseeing eyes blink for the first time. Her voice gains strength.

"Thank you, Gemma," she murmurs.

"I've done what you asked. Now I'll have my answers."

"Of course."

I circle the well as I talk, not wanting to look at her. "What did you mean when you said the Order was plotting against me? How can I stop the Rakshana? What should I know about the realms, about the Winterlands creatures, and this magic? And Pippa. What do you know of—"

"So many questions," she murmurs. "And yet, the answer is very straightforward. If you want to defend yourself against the Order and the Rakshana, you'd be best served to look inside yourself first, Gemma."

"What do you mean?" I approach the well with caution.

"Learn to master yourself—to understand both your fears and your desires. That's the key to the magic. Then, no one shall have any hold over you. Remember"—she takes a deep, wheezing breath—"the magic . . . is a living thing, joined to whomever it touches and changed by them as well."

I pace the room, careful to avoid looking at her. "I am nearly seventeen. I should think I know myself."

"You must come to know everything—even your darkest corners. Especially those."

"Perhaps I have no dark corners."

A thin rasp of a laugh comes from the well. "If that were true, I should be out there and you would be in here."

I start to answer but no words come.

"You must know what the magic will cost you."

"Cost me?" I repeat.

"Everything has its price." She takes another shuddering breath. "I've not spoken so much . . . in ages. I must rest now."

I hurry to the well, where she floats, her eyes closing. "Wait! But what about Tom and the Rakshana and Pippa and the Winterlands? I have more questions! You said you would help me!"

"And so I did," she answers, drifting into the well's depths. "Search those dark corners, Gemma. Before you find yourself caught there."

I can't believe I've given so much and gotten so little in return. I should never have thought to trust Circe in the first place.

"I won't be back until the day I return the magic to the Temple—the day you die," I say, storming from the room.

When I emerge from behind the curtain, Asha is there. She sits upon a small mat with her legs crossed, shelling bright orange peas into a bowl. Behind her, several Hajin sort through bushels of poppies, selecting only the brightest blooms, discarding the rest.

Asha gestures to me. "Might I have a word, Lady Hope?"

I sit beside her on the mat, but I can scarcely keep still. I'm far too agitated by my conversation with Circe, and angrier with myself for having trusted her.

"I have considered your offer," Asha says. "I believe it best the Hajin not join your alliance."

"Not join? But why?"

Asha's fingers work diligently at separating the pea from its useless husk. "We do not wish to become involved in such a struggle. It is not our way."

"But, Asha, with a share of the magic, your people could become a power in the realms. You could change your lot. You could cure—"

I bite the words off, afraid I will offend her. The Hajin cast a curious glance at me. Asha nods to them, and bowing, they take their leave.

"Back in the dark time, we were persecuted. Treated as slaves. Murdered for sport," Asha explains. "And then the Order came and made us safe. Since the talk of an alliance, that safety has been in question. Our people have been taunted in the fields and beyond. A Hajin was whipped at the river by centaurs. And just last night, a crop of poppies was stolen—only a small basket, but it is enough."

I ball my hands into fists. "That will not stand! I shall speak to Philon at once!"

Asha shakes her head. "No. We shall withdraw. Here, away from all, we are safe."

I look about at the rugged caves where they have lived in exile for centuries. "But you are forced to live in these caves. How is that safety?"

Asha smooths her sari over her blistered legs. "It is best not to question."

"Would you make that decision for the rest of your people?"

She drops the peas into a bowl with a hard clatter. "They should not know everything. It will only bring discontent."

"For whom?" I ask.

"It is for the best," she says as if it's a mantra.

One of the Hajin approaches. Her face is limned with worry. "It is not a good harvest, Asha," she says in apology. "We have lost many flowers to frost and blight."

Asha frowns. "Frost?"

The Untouchable opens her blistered hand to reveal a poppy withered and blue with cold. "They do not survive."

"Here," I say. I put my hand to it and new poppies spring out, fat and red. "That is what you could do if you wanted."

The girl looks hopefully to Asha, who shakes her head.

"That way does not last," Asha answers. She plucks the first blossom from the Hajin girl's hand and throws it into the rubbish pile.

∼∼∼∼

I take the path through the willows again. The majestic branches fan out over my head, and I walk through the cocoon of them, lost in thought. What plan does the Order have for me? Could they have killed Wilhelmina Wyatt to silence her, and if so, what secret did she hold that was worth murdering for? How can I help govern the realms when the very people who would form my alliance do not trust one another?

Even the promise of seeing Pip and the others in the Borderlands doesn't soothe me just now. They will not want to hear of my troubles. They'll want to dance. To play merry games. To make ball gowns from thin air and capes from threadbare tapestries. And when Felicity and Pippa are together, it is as if the rest of us do not exist. Their friendship is exclusive. I am envious of their closeness, and I hate myself for it. I cannot decide which is worse—the envy or the small, petty way it makes me feel inside.

A little dust storm kicks up along the road. It is followed by a galloping sound. My heart quickens. It's gaining fast and I cannot possibly outrun it this time. I try to squeeze between the willows but there is not enough room. Magic. But what? Cloak myself. What, what, what? Can't think. Illusion. An illusion. But what? *Look about, Gemma. What is here?* Road. Sky. Dust. Willow. A willow tree!

He's getting closer.

Let go of the fear. Let go. Let go. I feel the magic working within me, and I can only hope it has obeyed. When I look at my hands, they appear as branches. I've done it. I've masked myself.

The rider slows to a trot and then stops altogether. I can scarcely breathe for my fear. It's Amar. He wears a cape of animal skins—the animals' eyes still move within it—and a helmet made of human skulls. His eyes are black holes, and I bite back a scream. *Don't lose your purpose, Gemma. Calm, calm . . .*

The horse is an unearthly thing with eyes like Pip's have been at times. It snorts and bares its teeth while Amar searches the path.

"I know you are here," he calls. "I smell your power. Your innocence."

My heart beats faster than I am certain it can bear. A crow flies from tree to tree, and I fear it shall find me out. It flies instead to Amar and settles on his shoulder.

"The time nears. Beware the birth of May."

He kicks the horse's flanks and rides off in a cloud of dust.

I stay hidden for a full count of one hundred, and then I run hard and fast for the Borderlands.

I want to tell them about Circe, but I'm afraid. How can I possibly confess that she is still alive? That I've gone to her for counsel? That I've given her magic? I'm ill when I think of what I've done, of the risk I've taken. And for what? Rubbish. Admonitions to search my dark corners, as if she weren't the most evil soul I've ever met.

Once I reach the castle and see my friends laughing and playing a game of catch, I'm cheered considerably. It was a mistake seeing Circe, and one I'll not make again. I won't go back until it is time to return the magic and make the alliance, the day she'll be gone from our world forever.

CHAPTER THIRTY-ONE

WE WAKE TO A GLORIOUS SUNDAY MORNING FULL OF color and dappled with a soft light that blurs the landscape into the sort of palette that might please Mr. Monet. After a hideously dull sermon, compliments of the half-dead Reverend Waite, Mrs. Nightwing offers a reward for our saintly endurance by asking our help in preparing for Spence's masked ball. We are turned out of doors in our artists' smocks with paintbrushes in the pockets. On the back lawn, long stretches of canvas have been spread out on tables. Pots of paint hold down the corners. Miss McCleethy directs us to paint pastoral scenes befitting a paradise so that we may employ them as scenery for our masked ball performances. The only scene that comes to my mind is the ridiculous frolicking Pan in pantaloons from my grandmother's home in London. I refuse to copy that monstrosity, though the prospect of outfitting him in a corset is rather tempting.

Felicity is hard at work. Her brush dips from pot to pot, and when I see the castle emerge, I smile and add the craggy mountains of the Winterlands behind it. Miss McCleethy walks between the tables, her hands behind her back. She makes improvements with her paintbrush, correcting a bush here, a flower there. It is quite annoying and I have the thought of painting a mustache on Miss McCleethy.

"What is this?" Miss McCleethy frowns at our picture of the Borderlands in progress.

"A fairy tale," Felicity answers. She adds touches of purple berries to a tree.

"Fairy tales are rather treacherous. How does this one end?"

Felicity's smile is a challenge. "Happily ever after."

"It's a bit dreary." Miss McCleethy grabs a paintbrush and dabs a bright pinkish orange over the churning gray of my distant Winterlands sky. It doesn't improve it; it only makes it into a muddy mess with a false dash of color.

"That helps," she says. "Carry on."

"Monster," Felicity mutters under her breath. "Promise you won't give her a drop of magic, Gemma."

"I shouldn't share with her if my life depended upon it," I vow.

<hr />

In the afternoon, the Gypsy women come bearing baskets of jams and other sweets. We slather jam on bread, not caring about our paint-smeared fingers. Miss McCleethy asks if one of the Gypsies might be hired to chop firewood, and a short while later, Kartik comes, and the heat rises in my face. He removes his coat, rolls his shirtsleeves to his elbows, and takes the ax to a tree.

Miss McCleethy leaves us so that she might inquire after the East Wing's progress, and I sneak over to where Kartik is working. His shirt is damp and clings to him. I offer him water. He glances toward McCleethy, who pays not a whit of attention to us. Satisfied, he gulps the water and wipes the back of his hand across his forehead.

"Thank you," he says, smiling in a curious way.

"What is so amusing?" I ask.

"I'm reminded of the oddest dream I had." He rubs his thumb across his lower lip.

The blush begins at my toenails and whooshes up to my face. "Well," I say, fumbling with the water bucket. "It was only a dream."

"If you remember, I believe in dreams," he says, gazing at me in such a way that I find I must look elsewhere to keep from kissing him again.

"I . . . I need to speak to you about an urgent matter," I say. "Mr. Fowlson paid me a visit in London. We'd been invited to dinner at the Hippocrates Society. He was waiting outside."

Kartik pulls the ax from its resting place in the tree stump. His jaw tightens. "What did he want?"

"The magic. I told him I'd given it to the Order, but he didn't believe me. He threatened trouble, and when Thomas returned home the next evening, he told me he'd been asked to join an exclusive gentlemen's club. There on his lapel was the pin of the Rakshana."

"That would not be given idly. He is being courted," Kartik says.

"I must meet with the Rakshana," I say. "Can you arrange it?"

"No." He brings the ax down with new determination.

"They could hurt my brother!"

"He's his own man."

"How can you be so hard? You had a brother."

"Once." He swings the ax again, and the log is cleaved in two.

"Please . . . ," I say.

Kartik glances again at the East Wing, then nods toward the laundry house. "Not here. In there."

I wait inside the laundry. There are no washerwomen today; the old wood-and-stone room is empty. Impatiently, I pace, past the stove where the flatirons are lined up to be heated. I step around the big copper tubs and bang my knuckles against the ribbed washboards lying inside, flit past the hooks holding the possers—those long sticks with flared ends for pushing the clothes about. I give the mangle's wheel a churn. I know it works wonders on the wet clothes, squeezing every bit of water from them as they pass through its long rollers. How I wish I could pass my sodden thoughts through the machine, releasing the heaviness weighing me down.

At last Kartik comes. He stands so close I can smell the grass and sweat on him. "You don't know what the Rakshana can do," he warns.

"All the more reason for me to keep them from Tom!"

"No! You must stay away from Fowlson and the Rakshana. Gemma, look at me."

When I won't, Kartik takes my face in his hand and forces me to look him in the eye. "If your brother continues on this foolish path, he must be lost to you. I will not take you to the Rakshana."

Angry tears threaten. I blink them back. "I have seen Amar. In the realms."

It's as if I've punched him. "When? Where?" He loosens his hold, and I move a safe distance to the washtub.

"The realms."

"Tell me everything. I must know!" He advances but I keep the washtub between us.

"First, you help me. Arrange a meeting for me with the Rakshana, and I'll help you find Amar."

"That is blackmail."

"Yes. I've learned much from you."

He bangs the wall with his fist, shaking the washboard hanging there and rattling me as well. His moods are as black as my own at times and his temper just as mercurial.

"I will need some time," he says evenly. "When I've arranged it, I'll tie my scarf in the ivy beneath your window."

"I understand. Thank you."

He does not so much as nod. "Once our business is concluded, I'm leaving. We will not see each other again."

He pushes through the laundry doors, and soon I hear him hacking the tree into kindling. I wait a few minutes. It is long enough to let his words settle into my belly like molten lead, hardening every part of me.

"Gemma, where have you been?" Elizabeth asks when I come round to the tables.

"A lady need not announce her need for the privy, need she?" I say, deliberately shocking her.

"Oh! Of course not." And she doesn't say another word to me, which is fine.

McCleethy was right—I do make a mess of everything. I dip my brush into the garish yellow and paint a big happy sun in the center of her muddy pink sky. If it's sunny skies they want, then let me oblige them.

Ann sidles up to me. "I've just overheard Miss McCleethy and Mr. Miller," she says, breathless. "Another of the men has gone missing. The inspector's been called to look into it. What do you suppose has happened to them?"

"I'm sure I don't know," I grouse. I steal a look at Kartik, who chops at the remains of the tree, obliterating it.

A gust of wind knocks over the purple paint. It splatters across the canvas, marring the scene of the Borderlands castle.

"Bad luck, Gemma," Ann says. "Now you'll have to start over."

⁓⁓⁓⁓⁓

In the evening, Inspector Kent pays his visit, and though he makes a fuss over our paintings drying by the fires, we know that this is far from a social call. With three men gone, it must be seen to. He brushes the mud from his boots, having spoken already to Miller's men and the Gypsies. He makes discreet inquiries among the younger girls, turning it into a sort of game to see if any of them have heard or seen some clue, however small. At last it is our turn, and we are ushered into the small parlor with its cozy furnishings and warm fire. Brigid has brought the inspector a cup of tea.

The inspector's eyes have always had a merry twinkle in them, but now he's on official business for the Yard, those eyes seem to look through me and find my sins. I swallow hard and take my seat. The inspector chats merrily with us about our day, the parties we shall attend shortly, Spence's impending masked ball. It is meant to disarm us, but it seems only to increase my apprehension.

He takes out a small notebook. He wets his thumb and uses it to flip through pages until he has the one he wants. "Ah, here we are. Now. Ladies. Have you heard anything unusual—sounds late at night? Have you noted anything amiss? Anything suspicious?"

"N-n-nothing," Ann stammers. She bites her cuticle until Felicity takes hold of her hand, no doubt squeezing it tight enough to cut off the flow of blood in her arm.

"We are asleep, Inspector. How could we possibly know what goes on with Mr. Miller's men?" Felicity says.

The inspector's pencil hovers over the page. His eyes flick from Ann's face to the sudden hand-holding. He smiles warmly. "The smallest detail might be the biggest of clues. No need for shyness."

"Have you any suspects?" I ask.

Inspector Kent holds my gaze for a second longer than is comfortable. "No. But that gives credence to my theory that these men, under the bottle's spell, wandered away from the camp to sleep it off and then, fearing the foreman's wrath, decided to leave altogether. Or perhaps it is an effort to bring suspicion on the Gypsies."

"Perhaps it is the Gypsies," Felicity adds quickly. I should like to kick her.

"That would be convenient," the inspector says, stirring milk into his tea. "Too convenient, perhaps, though I did see that one of theirs was missing this evening."

Kartik. He's gone already.

"Well, the truth shall come to light. It always does." Inspector Kent sips his tea. "Aye, that's what's right with the world. A good cup of tea."

✣✣✣✣✣

When we return to the realms, I'm ill at ease. The trouble with my brother, my visit with Circe, and the fight with Kartik all weigh heavily on me. But the others are merry and ready for a grand party. Felicity takes Pippa's hands in hers, and they twirl about on the thick carpet of vines. They laugh like the old friends they are. I envy them. Soon, the others join in the dance. Mae and Mercy take Wendy's hands and lead her about. Even Mr. Darcy hops in his cage as if he should like to take a partner. Only I stand apart. And secretly, I fear it shall always be this way, me alone, belonging to no one, no tribe, always standing just outside the party. I try to push the thought away, but it has already spoken truth to my soul. The sadness of my independence sinks deep into my blood. It rushes through my veins with a fierce, pulsing refrain: *You are alone, alone, alone.*

Felicity whispers in Pip's ear. They close their eyes, and Pip calls out, "Gemma! For you!"

There is a tap on my shoulder from behind. I turn to see Kartik dressed in a black cloak, and my heart leaps for a moment. He could be Kartik, but he isn't. The others laugh at Pip's little joke. I'm not amused. I put my hand on his shoulder, drawing on my own magic, and he becomes a doddering old pirate with a peg leg.

"That one," I say, pointing to Pippa. "She desires a dance. Off with you."

It is a very happy party, everyone laughing, singing, and dancing, so they don't notice when I slip away and walk to the river, where I find Gorgon returning from her travels.

"Gorgon!" I call, for I've missed her more than I realized.

She pulls to the shore and lowers the plank for me, and I

climb aboard, happy to see the twisting snakes that flick their tongues at me.

"Most High. You are missing the party, it would seem," Gorgon says, nodding toward the castle.

"I tired of it." I stretch out and lie on my back, looking up at the few pricks of light peeking through the clouds. "Have you ever felt as if you were utterly alone in the world?" I ask softly.

Gorgon's voice is tinged with quiet sadness. "I am the last of my kind."

High-pitched laughter escapes from the castle as if from another world. Beyond the watery blue-ink sky of the Borderlands, the deep gray clouds of the Winterlands rumble with distant thunder.

"You never did tell me that story," I remind her.

She takes a heavy breath. "Are you certain you would hear it?"

"Yes," I answer.

"Then sit close and I will tell it."

I do as she asks, taking a perch right beside her enormous green face.

"This was many generations ago," she says, briefly closing her eyes. "All feared the Winterlands creatures and the chaos they brought, and so, when the Order's power began to rise, we welcomed it. The Order brought the tribes together, and for a time, the tribes flourished, the gardens blossomed; in your world men were influenced, history was made. But still the Winterlands creatures rode, drawing more souls to their side. The Order sought to stop the threat by taking greater control.

"There were small concessions at first. Certain freedoms were denied, for our own good, we were told. Our own powers atrophied from lack of use. And the Order grew stronger."

I interrupt. "I'm confused. I thought the Order was good, that the magic was good."

"Power changes everything till it is difficult to say who are the heroes and who the villains," she replies. "And magic itself is neither good nor bad; it is intent that makes it either."

The castle hums with music and laughter. The light shining from the windows does not quite reach us. Gorgon and I sit in our pool of shadows.

"The discontent festered," Gorgon continues after a pause. "There was a rebellion, every tribe fighting for its own survival without a care for the others. In the end, the Order won the day, but not without cost. They no longer allowed the tribes to draw magic from the runes. The creatures in your world were stranded there. And my people . . ." She trails off, her eyes closed tightly as if she is in pain. Long minutes pass with nothing but the music drifting from the castle.

"Your people were lost in the battle," I say, because I can stand the silence from her no more.

Gorgon's eyes are downcast. "No," she says in a voice sadder than I have ever heard. "Some remained."

"But . . . where are they? Where did they go?"

Gorgon lowers her great head, and the snakes hang like willow branches. "The Order meant to make an example of me."

"Yes, I know. And so they imprisoned you in the ship and bound you to only tell truth to them."

"True. But that was later, as punishment for my sin."

A weight settles into my stomach, pulling it down. Gorgon has never told me this, and I am not certain I want to know it now.

"I was a great warrior then. A leader of my people. And proud." She spits the word. "I would not have us living as slaves.

We were a warrior race, and death was the honorable choice. Yet my people agreed to the priestesses' terms of surrender. That was not our code. I was shamed by their choice, and my rage became my righteousness." Her head lolls back as if her face seeks a sun that is not there.

"What happened?"

Restless in their sleep, the snakes of her hair slither over one another. "While the Order slept, I employed the very charms I had used against so many of my enemies. I enthralled my people, held them in a trance. I turned them to stone, and one by one, they fell to my sword. I killed them all, no quarter given. Not even to the children.

"My crime was discovered. As I was the last of the gorgons, the witches would not execute me. Instead, they bound me to this ship. In the end I lost my freedom, my people, and my hope."

Gorgon opens her yellow eyes, and I turn my head, afraid to look upon her face now that I know the truth.

"But you've changed," I whisper. "Haven't you?"

"It is the scorpion's nature to sting. Just because he has no opportunity doesn't mean that he cannot." The snakes wake, crying, and she soothes them to sleep with a gentle rock of her head. "As long as I remain on this ship, I shall be safe. That is my curse and my salvation."

She turns her yellow eyes toward me, and though I do not mean to, I avert my own.

"I see my tale has changed your opinion of me after all," she says with a touch of sadness.

"That isn't true," I protest, but it sounds false.

"You should return to the party. They are your friends, and

it seems merry enough." She lowers the creaking plank and I scramble over it and into the light dusting of snow at the shore.

"I will not see you for a while, Most High," Gorgon says.

"Why? Where are you going?"

From the corner of my eye, I see her arching her majestic head toward the sky over the Winterlands. "Far down the river, farther than I have yet gone. If something is at hand, I'll not be caught unawares. You must guard yourself."

"Yes, I know. I hold all the magic," I answer.

"No," she corrects. "You must guard yourself because we would not lose you."

CHAPTER THIRTY-TWO

THE FOLLOWING MORNING, JUST AFTER BREAKFAST, ANN and I sneak into the laundry.

"I could hardly sleep for thinking about our adventure today," she says. "This afternoon, I might very well change my fate."

I've spent the better part of the past few days perfecting our plan for today's jaunt to the theater. Fee has forged a letter from her "cousin" Nan Washbrad asking if we might accompany her to London for the day, and Mrs. Nightwing has allowed it.

"Do you think this will work?" Ann asks, biting her lip.

"That rather depends on you. Are you ready?" I ask.

Ann breaks into an enormous grin. "Absolutely!"

"Right. Let's begin."

We work in tandem, the magic flowing between us. I can feel Ann's excitement, her nerves, her unbridled joy. It makes me feel a bit drunk, and I can't keep from giggling. When I open my eyes, she's in flux. She cycles through physical changes like a girl trying on different gowns. At last, she settles into the appearance she sought, and Nan Washbrad is back. She twirls about in her new dress, an indigo satin trimmed in lace at the collar and along the hem. A jeweled pin sits at her throat. Her hair has darkened to the color of ebony. It's piled high upon her head like a very grand lady's.

"Oh, how nice to be Nan again. How do I look?" she asks, patting her cheeks, examining her hands, her dress.

"Like someone who should be on the stage," I answer. "Now, let's see if we can put your thespian talents to the test."

Moments later, Nan Washbrad makes her entrance and is shown to the parlor, where Mrs. Nightwing chats amiably with her, not knowing that her fashionable guest is really Ann Bradshaw, poor scholarship student. Felicity and I can barely contain our wicked glee.

"That was marvelous," Felicity says, giggling, as we wait for our train. "She never suspected. Not once. You've fooled Mrs. Nightwing, Ann. If that doesn't give you confidence for facing Mr. Katz, nothing will."

✺✺✺✺✺

"What time is it?" Ann asks for possibly the twentieth time since we left Victoria Station and set off for our appointment.

"It is five minutes later than the last time you asked," I grouse.

"I can't be late. Miss Trimble's letter was quite firm on that point."

"You shan't be late, for here we are in the Strand. You see? There is the Gaiety." Felicity points to the great bowed front of the famous music hall.

A trio of beautiful young ladies exits the theater. In their hats adorned with eye-catching plumes, their long black gloves, and fashionable dresses replete with corsages of flowers, they are impossible to ignore.

"Oh, it's the Gaiety Girls!" Ann exclaims. "They are the most beautiful chorus girls in the world, aren't they?"

Indeed, men admire their beauty as they walk, but unlike Mrs. Worthington, they do not seem to live only for that recognition. They have their own work and the money to show for it; when they take to the street, it is as if the world is theirs.

"Someday, people shall say, 'Why, look, there goes the great Ann Bradshaw! What a marvel she is!'" I tell her.

Ann adjusts and readjusts the pin at her neck. "Only if I am not late to my appointment."

Address in hand, we travel the Strand in search of our destination. At last we find the unremarkable door, and our knock is met by a lanky young man in trousers and suspenders, no waistcoat, and a bowler hat. He's got a cigarette clenched between his teeth. He eyes us warily.

"Can I help you?" he asks with an American accent.

"Y-yes, I've an appointment with M-Mr. Katz." Ann produces the letter. The young man reads it over and swings the door open. "Right on time. He'll like that." He lowers his voice. "Mr. Katz'll dock your pay for bein' late. Charlie Smalls, by the way. Pleasure."

Charlie Smalls has a gap-toothed grin that makes his narrow face come alive. It's the sort of smile you can't help returning, and I'm glad he's the first to welcome us.

"Are you an actor?" Ann asks.

He shakes his head. "Composer. Well, hope to be. For the present I'm the accompanist." The smile is back, broad and warm. "Nervous?"

Ann nods.

"Don't be. Here. I'll show you around. Welcome to the Taj Mahal," he jokes, gesturing to the modest room. In one corner is a piano. Several chairs have been placed facing the piano. Curtains hang to suggest a stage. It's a bit dark, the only source of light being one small window that affords us a view of the horses' legs and the carriage wheels in the street. Dust motes dance in the weak light, making me sneeze.

"Gesundheit!" a wiry man with a thin mustache says as he barrels into the room. He wears a simple black suit, and his pocket watch is in his hand. "Charlie? Where the devil's that note from George?"

"Mr. Shaw, sir? On your desk."

"Right. Swell."

Charlie clears his throat. "Young lady to see you, sir. Miss Nan Washbrad."

The clock strikes two, and Mr. Katz puts away his watch. "Terrific. Right on the nose. Great to meet you, Miss Washbrad. Lily said you were a looker. Let's see if she's right about your talent, too." Mr. Katz shakes my hand till my whole arm vibrates. "And who are these charming ladies?"

"Her sisters," I say, breaking free.

"Sisters, my foot. They're her school chums, Marcus. And I'd keep an eye on my wallet, if I were you." Lily Trimble sweeps into the room in an emerald green dress that hugs her every substantial curve. A fur-trimmed capelet hangs fetchingly about her shoulders. She drops into what looks like the most comfortable chair in the room. "Don't get too nervous, Nannie. This isn't Henry Irving."

"Henry Irving," Mr. Katz grumbles at the mention of the great actor-manager of the Lyceum. For there is no person of the theater more esteemed; Queen Victoria even knighted him. "That old snob may have helped to change the profession, but I'll take it where it's headed. Vaudeville. Dancing girls and popular entertainment—that's what the people want, and I'm the man who's gonna give it to 'em."

"Could we save the speeches for later, Marcus?" Lily says, taking a small mirror from her handbag.

"Right. Charlie?" Mr. Katz bellows.

Charlie takes a seat at the piano. "What're you singing, Miss Washbrad?"

"Um, ah . . ." I fear that Ann's nerves will play havoc with her illusion and her singing.

Go on, I mouth. I give her a big smile, and she smiles back, rather maniacally.

Felicity leaps up. "She'll be singing 'After the Ball'!"

Lily Trimble looks into her mirror, powders her nose. "See what I mean, Marcus? Miss Washbrad may not need your services as manager—not with these two at her heel."

"Ladies, you're going to have to pipe down if you want to stay in this room," Mr. Katz says.

"How vulgar," Felicity whispers, but she sits.

" 'After the Ball'?" Charlie asks Ann, who nods. "What key, then?"

"Em, I—I . . . C?" Ann manages to say.

I feel I might faint from nerves. I have to bite my handkerchief to keep from making a sound.

Charlie plucks the waltzing tune from the keys. He plays four bars and looks to Ann. She's too terrified to jump in, so he gives her another measure as a help, but still she hesitates.

"No time like the present, Miss Washbrad," Mr. Katz calls out.

"Marcus," Lily Trimble says, shushing him.

Ann is as rigid as Big Ben. Her chest rises and falls with each shallow breath. *Come on, Annie. Show them what you can do.* It's too much. I can't even look. Just when I think I shall die from this torture, Ann's voice floats above the jangling keys and the cigar smoke. It's delicate at first, but then it begins to build. Felicity and I sit forward, watching her. Soon, her voice fills the room, sweet and clear and enchanting. This is no trick of magic; this is Ann's magnificence, her soul married to sound, and we are under its spell.

She holds the last note for all she's worth, and when she finishes, Mr. Katz stands and puts his hat on. Does he mean to leave? Did he like it? Hate it? His meaty hands come together in a clear, loud clap.

"That was terrific! Just terrific!" he shouts.

Lily Trimble raises an eyebrow. "The kid's not half bad, is she?"

"Well done," Charlie says.

"You're too kind." Ann demurs, blushing.

Charlie puts his hand to his heart. "On my life, you were terrific. Like an angel! When I compose my musical, I'll have to write you a song." Charlie plinks about on the keys, and a merry tune starts to come to life.

"All right, Charlie, all right. Flirt on your own time. I need Miss Washbrad to read for me."

Ann is given a passage from *The Shop Girl*, and she is every bit as good as Miss Ellaline Terriss. Better, in fact. It is obvious that everyone in the room is impressed by Ann's talents, and I feel a mix of fierce pride and envy at her success here.

"I will write that musical," Charlie whispers to Ann. "And you'll be in it. That's the voice I want."

Mr. Katz extends his hand and helps Ann from her spot beside the piano. "Miss Washbrad, how would you like to become the newest star in the Katz and Trimble Repertory Company?"

"I . . . Nothing could make me happier, Mr. Katz!" Ann exclaims. I've never seen her so full of joy. Not even in the realms. "If you're certain you wish to take me on."

Mr. Katz laughs. "My dear, I'd be a fool not to. You're a very pretty girl."

Ann's smile fades. "But that isn't everything. . . ."

Mr. Katz chuckles. "Well, it certainly doesn't hurt. People like to hear a nice voice, my dear, but they like to see where that voice comes from, too. And when it comes from a beauty, they'll pay more for a ticket. Right, Lily?"

"I don't rouge my cheeks for nothing," Lily Trimble says on a sigh.

"But—what about my talent?" Ann bites her lip, and it only enhances her loveliness.

"Of course, of course," Mr. Katz says, but he hasn't stopped gazing at her. "Now, let's see to your contract."

✦✦✦✦✦

When we emerge from the darkened hole of Mr. Katz's office, the world seems a different place, full of excitement and hope.

The mud and dirt flecking the hems of our dresses is *our* mud and dirt—proof that we've been here and done what we set out to do.

"We should toast your success! I knew you'd do it," Felicity squeals.

"You didn't even want her to audition," I remind her. I shouldn't, but her smugness compels me.

"I believe that Charlie Smalls is smitten with you," Felicity singsongs.

Ann keeps her eyes trained on the ground. "Smitten with Nan Washbrad, you mean."

"You mustn't say that. It's a glorious day." Felicity turns to a hapless shopkeeper sweeping his walk. "Excuse me, sir, did you know you are in the presence of the new Mrs. Kendal?" she says, mentioning the name of the celebrated actress. The man regards her as he would an escaped lunatic.

"Felicity!" Ann says, laughing. She pulls Fee away, but the man gives Ann a little bow, and it makes her smile.

Big Ben strikes the hour. "Oh," Ann says, wilting. "We'd best go back. I don't want this day to end."

"Let's not end it just yet, then," Felicity says.

We repair to a tea shop to celebrate. Over glasses of tickly ginger ale, we toast Ann, and Fee and I tell her again and again how absolutely brilliant she was. At a table nearby, four suffragists sit discussing a demonstration before the House of Commons. With their banners worn proudly and their *Votes for Women* posters at their feet, they are a sight to behold. They speak to one another with passion and zeal. Some of the ladies in the shop look on in disapproval. Still others approach shyly, taking a leaflet or asking questions. One pulls up a chair to join them. They make room, welcoming her, and I see that Ann is not the only woman who means to change today.

✕✕✕✕

When we return to Spence, I search for Kartik's bandana in the ivy under my window, but it isn't there, and I hope that he'll return with news soon.

"Have you seen Ann?" Felicity asks when I step into the great hall. "She disappeared after dinner. I thought we were to play cards."

"I haven't," I answer. "But I'll go and have a look, shall I?"

Felicity nods. "I'll be in my tent."

Ann isn't to be found in any of her usual haunts—our room, the library, the kitchen. I know of only one other place, and that is where I find her—sitting alone on the third-floor terrace that overlooks the lawn and the woods beyond.

"Care for some company?" I ask.

She gestures to the empty spot on the railing. From here I have a perfect view of the half-completed turret and the skeletal East Wing. I wonder if my mother and her friend Sarah ever experienced the sort of happiness we did today. I wonder what they might have changed if they'd had the chance.

A gentle breeze blows. Far off I can see the lights of the Gypsy camp. Kartik. No, I shan't think about him just now.

"I thought you'd be packing for your trip to the world's stages," I say.

"We shan't leave until next week."

"It will be here before you know it. What's that?" I point to the sealed envelope in her lap.

"Oh," Ann says, fiddling with it. "I can't seem to post it. It's a letter to my cousins, informing them of my decision. Was I really all right today?"

"You were magnificent," I tell her. "Your voice enchanted them."

Ann stares out at the lawn. "They only wanted to hear me because they liked what they saw first. And don't go lying to me and saying that we're judged on our character, because that's rubbish." She laughs but there's no mirth in it. "Beauty is power, and my life would be far easier if I were as beautiful as Nan Washbrad."

Ann *is* lovely, but not in the way that matters to her. She's not a beauty. It is the careful knowing of her over time that makes her handsome. But that's not what she wants to hear. And even if I did say she was beautiful, even if I meant it, would she believe it?

"Yes. It's easier if you're beautiful," I say. "The rest of us have to try harder."

She smooths out the letter in her lap, and I fear that I've wounded her with my honesty.

I squeeze her hand. "You've done it, Ann. You've changed your life. I'll say it to anyone who will listen: Ann Bradshaw is the bravest girl I know."

"Gemma, how will I explain to them? Either I keep up this illusion forever or I find a way to make them believe in Ann Bradshaw."

"We'll sort it out. We need only enough magic to convince them they hired Ann in the first place. You'll do the rest with your talent. That's your magic." But I know how she feels. It's getting harder to imagine giving this up. I want to hold tightly to it and never let go.

"It was a good day, wasn't it?" A small smile dispels the worry on Ann's face.

"And better days to come."

Ann turns the letter over in her hands. "Guess I'd best get it over with."

I present my arm like a courtier. "It isn't every day I'm privileged to escort a star of the stage."

"Thank you, Lady Doyle," she says as if entering stage right for her bow. She walks straight up to Brigid and offers the letter with a hasty "Brigid, will you post this for me tomorrow?"

"Course I will," Brigid says, tucking it into her apron pocket.

"There, now that's done," I say.

"Yes. Done."

"Come on, then. Fee wants to play cards, and I'm determined she'll not whip us at it as she always does."

Buoyed by Ann's success, the three of us sit up playing hand after hand, wagering wishes like shillings—"I'll see your dream of becoming princess of the Ottoman Empire and I'll raise you one journey into Bombay riding on an elephant's back!" Ann wins most rounds, and not even Fee minds. She swears it's further proof that Ann has changed her luck at last, and that nothing is beyond us now.

CHAPTER THIRTY-THREE

SEVERAL DAYS PASS, AND STILL THERE IS NO SIGN OF Kartik's red scarf. I worry that he's met with misadventure. I worry that when he returns, I will not be able to help him with Amar. I worry that he will not return at all but will travel on to Bristol and the *Orlando*.

Such worry has put me in an ill humor. Already we have suffered the ignominy of walking backward as we shall do when presented to Her Majesty at Saint James's Palace. I stumbled twice, and I cannot imagine how I shall manage with the long train of my gown thrown over my left arm, my head bowed toward my sovereign. It makes my stomach hurt to think of it.

Mrs. Nightwing has settled us at the dining room table. At each of our places is a daunting array of silver. Soupspoons. Oyster forks. Fish knives. Fish forks. Butter knives. Dessert spoons. I half expect to see a whaling harpoon and perhaps, in case we find it all too overwhelming and wish to die with honor, the seppuku sword of Japanese legend.

Mrs. Nightwing drones on. I find it difficult to pay attention, and only catch every few sentences. "The fish course . . . the bones, pushed to the side of the plate . . . buttermilk, by the by, preserves the softness of a lady's hands . . ."

The vision steals over me quickly. One moment, I am listening to Mrs. Nightwing's voice, and the next, time stands still. Mrs. Nightwing is frozen at Elizabeth's side. Felicity's eyes are trained on the ceiling in an expression of utter boredom. Cecily and Martha, too, are suspended in time.

Wilhelmina Wyatt stands in the open doorway wearing a grim expression.

"Miss Wyatt?" I call. Leaving my frozen companions, I chase after her.

She stands at the top of the first flight of stairs, but when I reach the landing, she steps through the portrait of Eugenia Spence and vanishes like a ghost.

"Miss Wyatt?" I whisper. I am suddenly alone. The very bones of the school seem to murmur to me. I cover my ears but it does not stop the ghastly whispers, the muffled cackles, the hissing. The peacock paper on the walls comes alive, the eyes blinking.

Wilhelmina's spidery handwriting emerges on the portrait of Eugenia Spence: *The Tree of All Souls. The Tree of All Souls. The Tree of All Souls.* It fills the whole of the painting. The whispers grow louder. I put my hand to the painting, and it's as if I fall straight through it and into another time and place.

I'm in the great hall, but it's changed. I see what must surely be Miss Moore as a girl, the brooding concentration in her face. A girl with startling green eyes smiles at her, and I gasp as I recognize my own mother.

"Mama?" I call, but she does not hear me. It is as if I'm not really here.

An older woman with white hair and blue eyes sits with them, and I know her, too. Eugenia Spence. The face that seems so intimidating in her portrait is kind here. Bright and ruddy with life.

A girl brings her an apple, and Mrs. Spence smiles. "Why, thank you, Hazel. I shall relish it, I'm sure. Or should I cut it up with a share for all?"

"No, no," the girls protest. "It is for you. For your birthday!"

"Very well, then. Thank you. I do so love apples."

A small girl in the back raises her hand shyly.

"Yes, Mina?" Mrs. Spence calls.

Now I see traces of the woman in the girl's face. Little Wilhelmina Wyatt trudges toward her teacher and presents her with a gift of her own, a drawing.

"What is this?" Mrs. Spence's smile fades as she examines the drawing. It is a perfect representation of the enormous tree I've seen in my dreams. "How did you come to draw this, Mina?"

Wilhelmina hangs her head in shame and misery.

"Come now. You must tell me. Lying is a sin and speaks badly to a girl's character."

I hear the scrape of the chalk as Wilhelmina writes upon the slate, the words taking shape slowly: *The Tree of All Souls.*

Hurriedly, Mrs. Spence takes the chalk from the girl's fingers. "That's quite enough, Mina."

"What is the Tree of All Souls?" a girl asks.

"A myth," Eugenia Spence answers, cleaning the slate with a rag.

"It's in the Winterlands, isn't it?" Sarah asks. Her eyes glimmer with mischief. "Is it very powerful? Won't you tell us, please?"

"All you need to know at present lies within the pages of your Latin book, Sarah Rees-Toome," Mrs. Spence scolds in a teasing way.

She throws the drawing into the fire, and tears fall from little Mina's eyes. The other girls snicker at her crying. Mrs. Spence lifts the girl's chin with her finger. "You may draw me another picture, hmmm? Perhaps a nice meadow or a drawing of Spence. Now, dry your tears. And you must promise to be a good girl and not listen to voices you shouldn't, for anyone can be corrupted, Mina."

The scene shifts, and I see Wilhelmina slipping a jeweled dagger from a drawer into her pocket. Her body changes with the years until the womanly Wilhelmina stands before me again, the dagger in hand. Her face is twisted in fury. She raises the dagger.

"No!" I scream. I put up my hand to block the blow.

I'm still shouting when I come back to myself in the dining room. Everyone's gawking at me, horrified. Pain. In my hand. Rivulets of blood trickle down my palm and onto the damask tablecloth. The knife at my plate. I've gripped it so tightly I've cut my hand.

"Miss Doyle!" Mrs. Nightwing gasps. She rushes me to the kitchen, where Brigid keeps the gauze and salve.

"Let's 'ave a look," Brigid says. She rinses my hand, and it stings. "Not too deep, thank goodness. More a scratch 'n' a scare than anythin' else. I'll fix it right up."

"How did it happen, Miss Doyle?" Mrs. Nightwing asks.

"I—I don't know," I answer truthfully.

She holds my gaze a moment past what is comfortable. "Well, I trust you'll pay closer attention in the future."

⌁⌁⌁⌁

Felicity and Ann are waiting for me in my room. Felicity has taken over my bed and helped herself to *Pride and Prejudice*. Seeing me, she tosses the book aside like one of her suitors.

"Have a care with that, if you please." I rescue the poor book, soothing its ruffled pages, and put it back to bed on the shelf.

"What the devil happened?" Felicity asks.

"I had a very strong vision," I say. I tell them what Wilhelmina Wyatt showed me, the scene in the schoolroom. "I believe she's trying to tell me that the Tree of All Souls *does* exist. I think she needs us to find it. The time has come for us to go into the Winterlands."

Felicity sits forward. Some fire has been lit within her. "When?"

"As soon as possible," I answer. "Tonight."

⌁⌁⌁⌁

The woods are patrolled by one of Mr. Miller's men. We see him with his pistol, walking back and forth. He's as jumpy as a cat.

"How will we get to the door without being seen?" Ann asks.

I concentrate, and suddenly, there's a haunt of a woman in the woods. The man quakes at the ghostly sight of her. "Wh-who's there?" Shaking, he directs the pistol at her. She ducks behind a tree and comes out farther on.

"Y-you'll answer to m-my foreman," the man says. He

follows at a careful distance as she leads him toward the graveyard, where she will disappear, leaving him scratching his head at the mystery of it all. But we'll be inside the realms by then.

"Come on," I say, dashing for the secret door.

Felicity lifts her skirts, grinning. "Oh, I do like this."

The tall stone slabs with their watchful women greet us on the other side. But they can't give me the answer I seek. Only one person can, much as I'm loath to admit it.

"You go on to the castle. I'll join you shortly," I say.

"What do you mean? Where are you going?" Ann asks.

"I shall ask Asha if she has protections to offer us," I explain, feeling awful for the lie.

"We'll accompany you," Felicity says.

"No! That is, you should prepare Pippa and the other girls. Gather everyone."

Felicity nods. "Right. Hurry back."

"I shall," I say, and that, at least, is true.

I run through the dusty corridors of the Temple and head straight for the well of eternity. Circe is waiting, floating below the surface, a pale thing raised from the deep and forced into the light.

"Has the time of my demise come so soon?" she asks in a voice stronger than before.

I can barely control my anger. "Why didn't you tell me that you knew Wilhelmina Wyatt?"

"You didn't ask."

"You could have told me!"

"As I said, everything has its price." She lets her breath out in a sigh.

"For all I know, you were the one who killed her," I say, inching closer to the well.

"Is that why you've come back? To question me about an old school chum?"

"No," I say. I hate myself for coming, but she's been to the Winterlands before. My mother's diary chronicles it. She's the only one I can ask. "I need for you to tell me about the Winterlands."

A note of wariness creeps into her voice. "Why?"

"We're going in," I say. "I want to see it for myself."

She's quiet for a long time. "You're not ready for the Winterlands."

"I am," I declare.

"Have you searched your dark corners yet?"

I run my fingers along the polished stones of the well. "I don't know what you mean."

"That is how you can be snared."

"I'm tired of your riddles," I snap. "Either you will tell me about the Winterlands or you won't."

"Very well," she says after a moment. "Approach."

Once again, I put my hand to the well, where I can feel the power still lingering in the stones, and then I place it on her heart. Somehow it's easier to do this time; my need to know about the Winterlands and my desire to find out about the Tree of All Souls are stronger than my apprehension. For a few seconds, she glows with the power. A hint of a smile touches her pinkening lips. With this second gift, she's become even lovelier and more vibrant—more like the teacher I loved, Miss Moore. Seeing that face startles me. I wipe my wet hand on my nightgown as if I could rid it of all traces of her.

"Now, I've given you the magic you asked for. The Winterlands, please."

Circe's voice whispers in the cave. "At the gate, you will be asked questions. You must answer them truthfully, or you'll not enter."

"What sort of questions? Are they difficult?"

"For some," she answers. "Once inside, follow the river. Make no bargains, no promises. You cannot always trust what you see and hear, for it is a land of both enchantment and deceit, and you will need to discern which is which."

"Is there anything else?" I ask, for it's not much to go on.

"Yes," she says. "Don't go. You're not prepared for it."

"I'll not make the same mistakes you did; that's for certain," I snap. "Tell me one thing more: Does the Tree of All Souls exist?"

"I hope you will return and tell me," she says at last.

A rippling sound comes from the well, like the smallest of movements. But that's impossible—she's trapped. I look back, and Circe is as still as death.

"Gemma?" Circe calls.

"Yes?"

"Why does Wilhelmina want you to go into the Winterlands?"

"Because," I say, and stop, for I've not asked myself that question until now, and it fills me with doubt.

There it is again—a slight rustling in the water. The walls of the cave trickle with moisture and I think that must be the sound I hear.

"Do be careful, Gemma."

Pippa and the others wait for me in the blue forest. The berries have ripened on the trees. Half-filled baskets of them are everywhere. The front of Pip's dress, stained with juice, looks like a butcher's apron.

"Did she offer us any protection?" Ann asks when I catch up to them.

"What?" I ask, confused.

"Asha," she explains.

I see Circe's pale face in my mind. "No. No protection. We'll do our best."

Pippa claps in delight. "Splendid! A true adventure at last. The Borderlands have grown dull. I should call them the Boredomlands!"

I look toward the Winterlands' churning sky and the gate that separates us from it.

"What about those terrible creatures, miss?" It's Wendy. She holds tight to Mercy's skirts.

Pippa loops her arm through Felicity's. "We shall band together. We're clever girls, after all."

"It is the only way to be certain," Ann says.

"I'm not leaving until I know whether the Tree of All Souls exists," I say.

A small light blinks in the trees, growing as it descends. It's the fairylike creature with the golden wings.

"You wish to see the Winterlands?" she whispers huskily.

"What business is it of yours?" Felicity demands.

"I would light the way," she purrs.

Mae Sutter shoos the creature away. "Go on! Leave us be."

Undaunted, the creature flits from branch to branch and lands on my shoulder. "The Winterlands are not easily traveled. One who knows the way could prove helpful."

Circe's words come back to me: *Make no bargains*.

"I'll give you nothing for it," I say.

The creature's lip curls into a sneer. "Not even a drop of magic when you've got so much?"

"Not even a drop," I answer.

The fairy gnashes her teeth. "I shall take you anyway. Perhaps someday you'll reward my service. Leave that one behind. She'll prove a nuisance," she says, flicking a wing at Wendy's cheek. Wendy gasps and puts a hand there. The fairy cackles.

"Stop it!" I snap, and she falls back.

"I don't want to be no trouble," Wendy mumbles, hanging her head.

I take Wendy's hand. "She does what we do."

The fairy scowls. "Too dangerous."

"Wendy, you stay 'ere," Bessie commands.

"I want to go," she says. "I want to know where that screamin' comes from."

"She'll only slow us down," Pippa argues, as if the girl isn't standing right there.

"We go all of us together or not at all," I say firmly. "Now, I must confer with my companions. Shoo! Away with you."

The creature beats her shiny wings, hovering. There's hatred in her eyes as she zips a few feet away, keeping watch.

I take in the sight of us. We're a motley band—factory girls in their new finery, Bessie holding fast to a long stick, Pippa in her queenly cape, Ann and I in our nightgowns, and Fee with a layer of chain mail over hers, sword at the ready.

"We don't know if that overgrown firefly out there can be trusted, so let's be on our guard," I say. "Memorize the way, for we may have to get out again on our own. Are we ready?"

Felicity pats her sword. "Quite."

"I grow weary, mortal girl," Golden Wings complains. "This way!"

We leave the safety of the blue forest and cross the vine-covered plain of the Borderlands. In the distance, the high, jagged gate into the Winterlands rises like a warning through the fog. We cannot see what lies beyond it save for the twisting, steel gray ropes of clouds. I carry a torch I've fashioned from sticks and magic. It casts a deep pool of light. The fairy sits on my shoulder. The tiny claws of her feet and hands dig into my nightgown, and I hope the thin fabric will keep them from scratching my flesh to ribbons.

The wall that separates the Borderlands from the Winterlands is a fearsome construction. It stretches as tall as the dome on Saint Paul's Cathedral and runs in either direction as far as the eye can see. In the gloom, it appears to glow.

I put my hand to the tall pilings. They are smooth.

"Bones," the fairy whispers.

I lift the torch. The light catches the outline of a large bone, a leg perhaps. I recoil from it. The bones have been fastened with ropes of hair. Red flowering vines have threaded their way between the bones to look like startling wounds. It is a macabre sight. The fairy snickers at my distress.

"For one so powerful, you are easily frightened."

"How do we get in?" Mercy asks. Her face is cradled in deep blue shadow.

The winged creature darts in front of me. "The gate is near. You must feel for it."

We place our hands against the bones and matted hair, feeling for a way in. It makes my stomach churn, and I've a mind to turn back at once.

"I've found it!" Pippa calls.

We crowd around her. The gate has a latch fashioned from a rib cage. The sharp points of the ribs are joined so that it is impossible to tell where one side ends and the other begins. Most disturbing of all, there is a heart that beats behind it. The faint *thump-thump* of it reverberates in my stomach.

"What is that?" Ann gasps.

"The way in," the creature replies. She flutters near the beating heart and back again. "Answer it true," she warns. "Else it will not allow you to pass."

"Do you wish to enter the Winterlands?"

The voice is silk-soft, and I cannot be certain I've heard it at all.

"Did you hear that?" I ask.

The girls nod. The heart shines a deep purplish red, like a wound festering. The voice comes again.

"Do you wish to enter the Winterlands?"

The heart is speaking to us.

"Yes," Pippa answers. "How may we enter?"

"Tell us your secrets," it whispers. "Tell us your heart's greatest desire—and its greatest fear."

"That's all?" Bessie Timmons scoffs.

"That is everything," the fairy creature says.

Bessie steps up. "My greatest desire is to be a lady. And I'm afraid of fire."

A huge gust of cold wind blows out from the Winterlands. The bones clatter in the wind. The heart's pace quickens and it burns brightly in the gloom. The rib cage splits apart. A giant door swings open.

"You may pass," the heart says to Bessie. Bessie steps through, and the gate slams behind her.

"That wasn't so difficult," Felicity says. She takes her turn at the gate. "My desire is to be powerful and free."

"And your fear?" the heart prompts.

Felicity pauses. "Being trapped."

"Not entirely true," the heart answers. "You have another fear, greater than the rest. A fear wrapped in desire; a desire wrapped in fear. Will you say it?"

Felicity pales noticeably. "I'm sure I don't know what you mean," she answers.

"You must answer truthfully!" the fairy hisses.

The heart speaks again. "Shall I name your fear?"

Felicity falters a little, and I do not know what could frighten her so.

"You fear the truth of who you are. You fear that they will find out."

"Very well. You've said it; now let me pass," Felicity commands. The door swings open again.

The others take their turns. They confess their longings and fears one by one: to marry a prince, being alone, a loving home with flowers along the walk, the dark, a never-ending banquet, hunger. Pippa admits that she fears losing her beauty. When she states her desire, she looks straight at me. "I should like to go back." And the door opens wide.

Ann is so ashamed she whispers till the gate asks her to speak more loudly.

"Everything. I fear everything," she says, and the heart sighs.

"You may pass," it says.

At last it is my turn. The heart thumps in anticipation. My own beats just as fiercely.

"And you? What is your greatest fear?"

Circe warned that I must answer honestly, but I don't know what to say. I fear that my father will not heal. I fear that Kartik doesn't care for me, and I fear equally that he does. That I am not beautiful, not wanted, not lovable. I fear that I will lose this magic I've come to cherish, that I will be only ordinary. I fear so much I cannot choose.

"Go on! Out with it!" The flittery creature places her hands on her waist in impatience and bares her teeth at me.

Felicity puts her pale face to the bones on the other side. "Gemma, come on. Just say something!"

"What is your fear?" the gate asks again. A cold wind blows from the other side, chilling me. The clouds churn and boil, gray and black.

"I fear the Winterlands," I say carefully. "I fear what I will find there."

The gate's cold breath pushes out in a long, satisfied sigh, as if it smells my fear and loves it.

"And your wish?"

I do not answer straightaway. The bitter wind slaps my cheeks, makes my nose run. The heart of the Winterlands is impatient.

"Your wish," it hisses on.

"I . . . I don't know."

"Gemma!" Felicity pleads from the other side.

The fairy zips around my head till I'm dizzy. She digs her claws into my shoulder. "Tell! Tell!"

I bat her away and she snarls at me.

"I don't know! I don't know what I want, but I wish I did. And that is the truest answer I can give."

The heart beats more quickly. The gate rattles and moans. I

am afraid I have angered it. I shrink back. But the gate creaks open, the bones banging in the harsh wind.

Felicity grins at me and reaches out her hand. "Let's go before it changes its mind!"

My foot hovers near the entrance, then comes down on the rocky ground of the other side. I'm inside the Winterlands. There are no flowers here. No green trees. It is black sand and hard rock, much of it covered in snow and ice. The wind shrieks and howls across the tops of the cliffs and nips at my cheeks. Great handprints of dark clouds move on the horizon. Small puffs of steam rise to meet them, creating a billowing mist that casts everything in a thin wash of gray. There is a feeling to this place, a deep loneliness that I recognize in myself.

"This way!" The fairy bids us follow her toward the craggy mountains, pockmarked with ice, that guard the horizon.

Our feet leave faint traces in the black sand as we walk.

"What a melancholy land," Ann says.

It is barren and mournful, but it does have a strange, hypnotic beauty.

There isn't another soul for miles that we can see. It's eerie, like a town that has been emptied. For a moment, I think I see pale creatures watching us from a distance. But when I shine the torch, they are gone, a mirage of the mist and the cold.

I can hear the sounds of water. A narrow gorge cuts through the cliffs and a river runs straight through it. Keep to the river, Circe said, but this seems to be certain death. The current is fierce, and the pathway on either side of it looks no wider than our feet.

"Is there another way?" I ask the fairy.

"None that I know of," she answers.

"I thought you said you were a guide," Felicity mutters.

"I do not know all, mortal girl," Golden Wings snaps.

We tread lightly on the rocks, careful not to slip on the patches of glassy ice that show our pale faces like ghost mirrors. I take Wendy's hand and help her through.

"Look!" Ann shouts. "Over there."

A magnificent vessel floats through the mist and drifts to the black sand of the shore. The boat is long and narrow with oars sticking out of holes in the sides. It reminds me of a Viking ship.

"We are saved!" Pippa shouts. She hikes up her skirts and rushes for the boat. The factory girls follow. I grab Felicity by the arm.

"Wait a moment. Where did that boat come from? Where does it go?" I ask the fairy.

"If you want to know, you will have to take the risk," she answers, showing sharp teeth.

"Come on, Gemma," Felicity pleads, watching Pippa and the others get ahead.

"We'll be fine," Ann agrees, taking the torch from me, ready to run.

"Might be treacherous for the sightless one." The fairy lifts a lock of Wendy's hair and puts it to her nose, inhaling, then gives it a lick. "Leave her behind. I'll look after her."

Wendy holds fast to my arm.

"I most certainly will not," I say.

The fairy flutters near my mouth. "She'll only slow your passage."

"I've had enough of you, I think." I blow hard and the green shining beastie tumbles through the air. She curses me as I lift my gown and run for the boat, pulling Wendy quickly behind me.

"Right," I say, stepping into the pitching craft. "We're on our own now. Let's keep our wits about us. There could be traps. There could be trackers—or worse."

"But what about your power, miss?" Mae asks.

Felicity takes a seat and tucks her sword between her feet. "Precisely. We'll serve notice if they're foolish enough to trouble us."

"We don't know that I'm a match for them," I warn. "We know nothing about the Winterlands at all, really. The magic isn't always within my control, and I don't want to have to employ it unless there's no other choice."

I look about at the solemn faces of my friends, and I suddenly feel small. I wish there were someone else to carry this burden. The passage ahead is impossible to see clearly; the mist sits heavily on the water, and I hope we're not sailing into a terrible mistake.

"Ready, then?" Bessie calls. She's got one foot on the boat and the other on the narrow ledge.

Ann hands the torch to me again. I secure it near the front of the boat to light our way.

"Cast us off, if you please, Bessie," I answer.

She gives us a sharp shove, and the boat drifts out into the river, away from any safe harbor. We scramble to places at the oars. Pippa stands at the bow and peers through the mist. Felicity, Wendy, and I work the same oar, grunting with the effort. The water's weight makes it heavy to move but soon we ride upon the river. The mist thins, and we marvel at the great masses of glistening rock that rise on either side of us like the enormous weathered hands of a forgotten god.

The only color in this bleak landscape comes from the primitive paintings that stretch along the inside of the cliffs. The boat passes pictures of terrifying specters, their cloaks spread out to show the souls they've devoured. Water nymphs tearing the skin from a victim chained to a rock. The Poppy Warriors in their tattered knights' tunics and rusty chain mail. Black birds circling over battlefields. Amar's likeness stares out from the rock—the white horse and the ghastly helmet—and I wish I'd not glimpsed it. There is so much drawn here, an entire history, that I cannot possibly absorb it all. But one image does catch my eye; it shows a woman standing before a mighty tree, her arms stretched out in welcome. The mist thickens again and I can see no more.

"There's something ahead!" Pippa calls. "Slow your pace!"

"I'm not . . . a sailor . . . or a . . . pirate," Ann pants between strokes.

We turn on our planks to see what it could be. A vast rock formation fronts the gorge. It has two holes at the top and a wide hole at the bottom, like a screaming face.

"Aim for the mouth!" Pip calls over the rush of water.

With a whoosh, the boat hits a sudden drop, and we're pushed along by a faster current. Mercy screams as a wave of water crashes over the side of the boat. There's little we can do against the fierce tide. The boat rocks and turns round till we're dizzy.

"We'll be dashed!" Pippa shouts. "Steady!"

"We have to row into it!" Felicity shrieks.

"You're mad! We've got to stop—" I say.

Water splashes into me. It smells of sulphur.

"I'm an admiral's daughter, and I say we need to row into it!" Felicity barks as if she were a commander.

"We're getting closer!" Pippa calls. "Do something!"

"You heard Felicity—row into it!" I shout. "All your strength now. Don't hold back!"

We heave with all our might, and I am surprised by the strength in our arms and hearts. We match strokes, and soon, we're able to right ourselves and head for the gorge's tall, slender mouth. Four hard strokes and we're through. The river calms, carrying us deep down into the Winterlands.

We shout in exultation of our victory over the river, and as there is no one to tell us to temper our outburst, the cheer echoes for a full minute.

"Oh, look!" Pippa calls.

Colored light streams through the sorrowful sky. Gloomy clouds have given way to swirls of purple and indigo, pink and gold. And there are stars! Several of them shoot through the heavens and fall away. It is vast. I feel small and insignificant and yet larger than I have ever felt before.

"It's beautiful," I say.

Pippa throws out her arms. "To think we might have missed this."

"We're not back yet," I warn.

Water nymphs undulate beneath the river's surface, the soft, round arcs of their silvery backs peeking through like a reflection of the starry sky above.

"Oh, wot's that, then? Mermaids?" Mae asks, peering into the water's depths for a better glimpse.

Ann pulls her away from the boat's edge. "You don't want to know."

"But they're so beau'iful!" Mae stretches a hand toward the water.

"Do you know how they stay so pretty? They take your skin and bathe in it," Ann announces.

"Blimey!" With a horrified expression, Mae snaps her hand back and gets to her rowing.

The river rounds a bend. Fog rolls in again, as thick and white as clouds. The boat comes to rest beside a patch of frozen shore.

"Can you see anything?" Pippa asks, cupping a hand over her eyes and peering through the brume.

"Nuffin'," Bessie answers. She holds fast to her stick.

"Anything could be out there, waiting," Ann says quietly.

The boat will go no farther. It seems to have decided the destination for us. A plank lowers and we scramble off. The ship drifts back into the blanket of fog and is gone.

"Wot we gonna do now?" Mae asks. "'Ow we gonna get back?"

Bessie gives her a quick slap on the arm. "Shut it! We're goin' on."

The fog is heaviest here; the landscape intrudes like a phantom. We walk through a barren forest with trees like stunted ghosts. Gnarled branches pierce the mist here and there. It's quiet. Not a sound penetrates except for the ragged cadence of our breathing.

Something brushes against my shoulder, making me gasp. I turn round, seeing nothing. It comes again. Above me. I look up to see a bare foot swaying.

"Oh, God," I gasp.

A woman's body hangs from a branch. Sharp twigs wrap themselves around her neck, securing her to the tree. Her skin has turned the graying brown of the bark, and her fingernails are curved and yellowed. Her eyes are closed, and I'm grateful for it.

But she's not the only one. Now I see them in the mist, all around us. Bodies hang from the trees like ghastly fruit. An unholy harvest.

"G-Gemma," Ann whispers. Her eyes are wide and I can sense the scream that she's holding back, that we all hold back.

Pippa looks at the bodies with a combination of revulsion and sorrow. "I'm not like that. I'm not," she says, starting to cry.

Felicity draws Pip away. "Of course you're not."

"I want to go back. Back to Spence. To life. I can't be here anymore. I can't!" Pippa's on the verge of hysteria. Fee strokes her hair, tries to comfort her with private murmurings.

"This is where them ghouls would've taken us if not for Miss Pippa," Bessie says. With a sharp pull, she rips a bit of filthy fabric free of a corpse's hem, wraps it around her stick, and hands the stick to Ann. "You light it so we can see. I don' like fire."

Ann pulls matches from inside her dress. She strikes four to no avail. "They must've gotten wet on the boat."

Bessie is adamant. "I'm not goin' through there wif no torch." I lay my hand on the stick and put the magic to its purpose. The torch flares to life.

I am repulsed, and yet I have to know, so I reach toward the swinging arms of one of the bodies. I touch the cold, hard hand, and in my fright, a bit of magic escapes. The body jerks, and I jump back.

"Gemma . . . ," Ann gasps.

A fierce wind shakes the bodies in the trees, rattling them like leaves. Their eyes snap open, black as pitch and ringed in blood. A dreadful chorus of high-pitched shrieks and moans and low, angry growls of suddenly wakened beasts rises in the forest, clamors in our ears. Underneath it all, I hear a terrible refrain scratching itself into my soul: *"Sacrifice, sacrifice, sacrifice . . ."*

"Gemma, what did you do?" Ann wails.

"Turn back!" I shout.

We've gone no more than a few steps when the path disappears under our feet.

"Which way?" Mercy shrieks, running in circles.

Wendy stumbles forward, feeling the empty space with frantic arms. "Don't leave me, Mercy!"

"I don't know!" I shout. Circe said to stay to the river, but she said nothing about this. Either she lied or she doesn't know. Either way, we're alone, without aid.

Suddenly, a voice drifts through the din, calm and clear. "This way. Quickly . . ."

A path of light appears in the frozen grass and ice.

"Come on! This way!" I call. Brandishing the torch, I hurry through the trees, following the thin ribbon of light. Bodies kick and grab at us, and it is all I can do not to scream. A man reaches for Pippa, and Felicity's sword is swift. His severed hand flies, and he howls in outrage.

I would howl myself but it's as if I have been struck dumb with fear.

"Go!" I croak, finding a small sliver of voice at last. I push my friends on and run after, staring only at their backs, not daring to look left or right at the hideous things that swing from the trees.

At last we reach the edge of the gruesome woods. The din quiets to a gasp and then to nothing, as if they have all drifted back into the same sleep.

We take stock for a moment, leaning on each other, sucking cold air into our lungs.

"What were those things?" Pippa manages to say between breaths.

"Don't know." I wheeze. "Might have been the dead. Souls lured here before."

Mercy shakes her head. "Weren't like us. Didn' 'ave no souls left. Least I 'ope not."

Bessie points ahead. " 'Ow will we get through that, then?"

Blocking the way is a wall of black rock and ice as tall as it is wide. There's no going around it as far as I can tell.

The wind whispers again. "Look closer. . . ."

At the base of the enormous cliff is a tunnel hung with blood-streaked rags.

"Follow . . . ," the wind urges.

"Did you hear that?" I ask to be sure.

Felicity nods. "It said to follow."

"Follow it where?" Ann peers doubtfully into the dark tunnel.

No one charges ahead. No one will be the first to push aside the foul rags and step into that narrow crevasse.

"We've come this far," Pippa says. "Would you stop now? Mae? Bessie?"

Mae pulls back. Bessie shifts from one foot to the other.

"Bit dark, innit?" Mae says.

"I think we should turn back," Wendy whispers. "Mr. Darcy will be hungry."

"Will you shut it about that bunny?" Bessie barks. She nods at me. "Was your idea, wuddn't it? Findin' this tree? You're the one wot's supposed to lead."

The fetid wind blows the rags toward us. The tunnel is like a starless night. There's no telling what could be waiting for us in there, and we've already experienced one hideous surprise. But Bessie's right. I should go first.

"Right," I say. "We go on. Stay close behind me. If I give the word, run back hard as you can."

Wendy has found her way back to me and still clings to my sleeve. "Is it terrible dark, miss?"

It is funny that she should be afraid of the dark when she cannot see it, but I suppose that is the sort of fear one feels deep in the soul.

"Don't worry, Wendy. I shall go first. Mercy will lead you in, won't you?"

Mercy nods and takes Wendy's hand. "Aye. Hold tight to me, luv."

My heart hammers against my chest. I take a step inside. The tunnel is narrow. I can't stand to my full height, and have to move stooped. "Watch your heads," I call back. My hands feel their way. The walls are cold and wet, and for a moment, I fear I am in the mouth of some giant beast, and then I'm shivering all over and near to screaming.

"Gemma?" Fee's voice. In the pitch-darkness I cannot tell where she is. She sounds miles away, and yet, I know she can't be.

"Y-yes," I manage to say. "Keep coming."

I pray we'll be through it quickly, but the tunnel seems to go on forever. I hear a faint murmur under the rock. It sounds like a snake hissing, all *ss*, though I swear I hear *sacrifice* and, once, *save us*. I can't hear the footfalls of my friends anymore, and I'm in a panic, when at last a dim shaft of light falls. There is an opening in sight. Relief floods through me as I tumble through the slender gap, followed by my friends.

Pip wipes at the muck on her sleeves. "Horrid tunnel. I felt the hot breath of some foul thing on my neck."

"That was me," Ann confesses.

"Where are we?" Felicity asks.

We've come out on a windswept heath surrounded by a circle of stony peaks. A light snow falls. The flakes cling to our lashes and hair. Wendy turns her face up to it as if it's a blessing.

"Oh, that's nice," she murmurs.

Dark, heavy clouds sit above the cliffs. Sharp veins of light pulse against them, and thunder sounds. Through the thin veil of snow, I see it: An ancient, weathered ash tree, as thick as ten men and as tall as a house, rises majestically from a small patch of green grass. Its many branches stretch out every which way. It is commanding; I cannot look away. And I know that this is the tree in my dreams. This is what Wilhelmina Wyatt wanted me to find.

"The Tree of All Souls," I say in awe. "We've found it."

The snow pelts my face, but I don't care. The magic hums sweetly inside me as if called. The sound wraps itself around my every sinew; it pulses in my blood with a new refrain I cannot yet sing but long to.

"You have come at last," it murmurs, as softly as a mother's lullaby. "Come to me. You need only to touch and you will see. . . ."

Shards of lightning cut the sky around us. The power of this place is strong, and I want to be part of it. My friends feel it too. I can see it in their faces. We put our hands to the ancient bark. It is rough against my palms. My heartbeat quickens. I shake with this new power. Overcome, I fall.

She is before me, bathed in a gentle light, and I know her at a glance. The white hair. Blue eyes. The colorful dress. The world falls away until there is nothing but the two of us burning brightly in the wilderness.

Just Eugenia Spence and me.

CHAPTER THIRTY-FOUR

"I'VE WAITED SUCH A LONG TIME FOR YOU," SHE SAYS. "I nearly gave up hope."

"Mrs. Spence?" I say when I find my voice at last.

"Yes. And you are Gemma, Mary's daughter." She smiles. "You are the one I'd hoped for—the only one who can save us and the realms."

"Me? How—"

"I will tell you everything, but our time together is brief. There is only so long I can appear to you in this form. Will you walk with me?"

When I look confused, she reaches out a pale hand. "Take my hand. Walk with me. I will show you."

My hand inches toward hers and grazes the cold tips of her fingers. She takes hold with a firm grip. We're bathed in a brilliant white light. It burns away, and she and I stand together on the windswept plain. The snow, the lightning, my friends— that all exists outside of where I am now. Eugenia is more substantial here. Her cheeks are flushed; the color warms the blue of her eyes.

"I thought you were"—I swallow hard—"dead."

"Not entirely," she says sadly.

"The night of the fire," I say. "What happened after you sealed the door?"

She steeples her hands as if praying. "I was taken by that foul beast here, to the Winterlands. All the creatures had come to see the exalted Eugenia Spence, high priestess of the Order, now a lowly captive of the Winterlands. They meant to break me, to corrupt me and use me to their wicked ends," she says, her eyes flashing. "But my power was greater than they knew. I resisted, and as punishment, they imprisoned me inside the Tree of All Souls."

"What is the Tree?" I ask.

She smiles. "The only spot within this forsaken land that also belongs to the realms, to the Order."

"But how?"

"If you would understand the present, you must come to know the past." She waves her hand in a wide arc, and the scenery changes. Before us, like the image in a pantomime, is a land newly born.

"Long before we slithered, pink and mewling, into this world, the realms existed. The magic was; it came from the land itself and it returned to the land, a never-ending cycle. All was in balance. There was only one inviolable rule: The dead who passed through this world could not remain here. They had to cross or become corrupted.

"But some of the dead could not relinquish their hold on the past. Afraid, angry, they ran, taking refuge in the most desolate part of the realms—the Winterlands. But it did not kill their longing for what they could not have. They wanted to return, and for that they would need the realms' magic. Soon, the wanting turned to coveting. They would have it at all costs. You know of the rebellion and what happened here in the Winterlands, I trust?"

"The Winterlands creatures captured several initiates of the Order and sacrificed them here. The first blood sacrifice," I answer.

"Yes, but that is not all of the story. You must see." Eugenia moves her hands over my eyes. When I open them, I see the young priestesses, no older than I, cowering before a band of ghastly creatures. One priestess has escaped; she hides behind a rock, watching.

"This dagger is rich in magic," one of the frightened priestesses says, offering the jeweled piece. "It can be shaped to any purpose you would give it. Take it in exchange for our freedom."

The Winterlands wraith snarls at her. "You mean to placate us with this?" He grabs the dagger away. "If it is powerful, then let us put its gifts to work for us now!"

The creatures surround the cowering priestesses. The hideous wraith raises the dagger and it descends again and again, until all that can be seen of the girls is one blood-smeared hand reaching toward the sky, and then, even that falls.

Where their blood spills, the ground cracks open. A mighty tree rises, as barren and twisted as the creatures' hearts—and full of magic. The creatures bow before it.

"At last, we have power of our own," the wraith says.

"It is the sacrifice that made it so," another hisses.

"What has been forged in blood demands blood. We will offer it souls in payment, and twist its power to our needs," the wraith announces.

"But there was one saving grace," Eugenia whispers, waving her hand again, and now I see the young priestess still behind the rock. While the creatures revel in their new power, she steals the dagger and runs quickly to the Order. She tells the tale, and the high priestesses listen, their faces grim. The runes are constructed, the veil between the worlds is closed, and the dagger passes from priestess to priestess through the generations.

"The Order protected the dagger from all harm. And we did not dare speak of the tree for fear someone might be tempted. Soon, its existence passed into myth." Eugenia wipes away the image with a wave of her hand. "I was the last guardian of the dagger, but I don't know what has become of it."

"I've seen it in my visions, with one of your former students, Miss Wilhelmina Wyatt!" I blurt out.

"Mina appears in your visions?" Eugenia asks. Worry limns her face. "What does she show you?"

I shake my head. "I cannot make sense of most of it. But I've seen the dagger in her possession."

Eugenia nods, thinking. "She was always attracted to it, to the darkness. I hope she is to be trusted. . . ." Her gaze is steely. "You must find the dagger. It is imperative."

"Why?"

Now we are on a mountaintop. The wind licks at us. It threatens to turn my hair into a lion's mane. Far below in the valley, I see my friends, as small as birds.

"I suspect that a rebellion brews once again—that old alliances are being forged between the tribes of the realms and the Winterlands creatures," Eugenia says. "And that one of our own has made a wicked pact in exchange for power. I didn't believe it possible before, and that naïveté cost me dearly," she says, and I feel shamed for what my mother and Circe did. I want to tell her about Circe, but I cannot bring myself to do it.

"But I thought the Winterlands creatures were gone," I say instead.

"They are here somewhere, make no mistake. They have a fearsome warrior to lead them—a former brother of the Rakshana."

"Amar," I gasp.

"His power is great. But so is yours." She cups my chin in her cold hand. On the horizon, the inky sky pulses with strange, beautiful lights again. "You must be careful, Gemma. If the Order has been corrupted in some fashion, they could use your power against you."

Electricity wounds the sky, leaving momentary scars of light upon my eyes seconds after. "How so?"

"They could make you see what they wish you to see. It will be as if you are mad. You must be vigilant at all times. Trust no one. Be on your guard. For if you fall, we are lost forever."

My heart's beating has begun to match the storm's frenzy. "What should I do?"

Light pulses again, and I see the hard determination in Eugenia's eyes. "Without the dagger, they cannot bind my power to the tree. You must find it and bring it to me in the Winterlands."

"What will you do with it?"

"What I must to make things right and restore peace," she says, taking my hand. Suddenly, we stand at the edge of a lake where the mist clears. A ferry carrying three women emerges. An old woman with a timeworn face pushes the barge along the placid water with a long pole. Another woman, young and beautiful, raises a lamp to guide their passage. A third woman stands holding a cornucopia. They move along, taking no notice of us.

"Those women—I've seen their likenesses on the stones that guard the secret door. Who are they?"

"They have been called by many names—the Moirai, Parcae, Wyrd, Fates, the Norn, and the Badb. We have always known them as the Three. When a priestess's death is imminent, she walks through the mists of time and is met at the crossing by the Three, where she is granted a final request and a choice."

"A choice," I repeat, not understanding at all.

"She may choose to travel on their barge to a world of beauty and honor. When she has crossed safely, her likeness will appear in the immortal stones as testament."

"So all of those women depicted on the stones . . ."

She smiles and it is as if the sun shines only on me. "Were once priestesses like you and me."

"You said she had a choice. But why would she not choose to go on to such a place?"

"She may feel that some important duty has been left unfinished. If she refuses, she returns to this life to complete the task, but she forgoes glory."

The crone guides the ferry farther out on the lake. The mist rushes in to hide them.

Eugenia watches until they're gone. "I should like to be freed, to take, at last, my place in that land beyond and on the stones that sing our history." She strokes my face as lovingly as a mother. "Will you bring me the dagger?"

The fog envelops us. "Yes," I answer, and we are once again before the Tree of All Souls. I stare up at its majesty—the three strong branches, the thousands of smaller twigs twisting out and around, the faint veins underneath the tree's skin. My friends still stand with their hands to it, looks of awe on their faces. It's as if they are listening to voices I cannot hear, and I feel apart and alone.

"What is happening to my friends?" I ask.

"It is the magic of the tree. It shows them the secrets within their hearts," Eugenia answers. "I must go now, Gemma."

"No, please. I need to know—"

"You mustn't come back until you have the dagger. Only then will we be safe."

"Don't go!" I call. I try to grab hold but she's as inconsequential as air. She vanishes into the tree. It absorbs her. The tree throbs; the veins pump its blood faster.

"Would you see?" the tree calls in a strangled whisper.

Around me, my friends have already glimpsed whatever wonders lie inside, and I am weary of standing apart.

"Yes," I answer, defiant. "I would."

"Then look inside," it murmurs.

I press my palms against the rough bark of the trunk and am lost.

Images dance around me like the fractured pieces in a kaleidoscope. In one sliver of the prism, Mae sits at a table crowded with an opulent feast. As she finishes each dish, another arrives to take its place. Beneath the table, lean dogs sit, panting and hopeful. They fight each other for scraps, tearing into each other's flesh till they are bloody, but Mae takes no notice. She will never be hungry again.

I see Bessie in a fine gown made completely of gold and jewels, an ermine cape resting upon her shoulders. She walks past the rows of bedraggled, dirty women sewing in the factory where she lost her life, until she reaches the owner, a fat man with a cigar in his mouth. She slaps him hard, again and again, until he cowers at her feet, no better than an animal. Ann is bathed in the glow of footlights. She bows to her audience, drinking in their thunderous applause. Wendy has a small cottage with a rose garden. She waters the buds and they flower into magnificent blossoms of red and pink. Mercy rides in a fine man's carriage. I see Felicity dancing with Pippa in the castle, the two of them laughing as if at a joke only they are privy to, and then I see Pippa sitting on the throne, eyes blazing.

Beside me, Pippa wears a rapturous smile. "Yes," she says to no one I can see. "Chosen, chosen . . ."

"Look closer," the tree whispers, and my eyelids flutter. Everything I lace tightly to myself is loosed.

I open a pair of doors and I'm back in India. It must not yet be summer, for Father and Mother sit drinking their tea out of doors. Father reads aloud from *Punch*, and it makes Mother laugh. Tom is a blur of a boy as he runs past with two small wooden knights locked in fierce battle in his hands, that one impossible lock of hair falling across his eyes. Sarita scolds him for nearly upending Father's old urn. And I am there. I am there under a long ribbon of bright blue sky, not a cloud to be seen. Father and Mother smile upon seeing me, and I feel a part of them all; not separate and alone. I am loved.

"Come to me, Gemma," Mother calls. Her arms open wide to receive me, and I start to run, for I feel that if I can reach her, all will be well; I need to catch the moment and hold it tightly. But the more I run, the farther away she gets. And then I am in the cold, dark parlor of my grandmother's house. Father in his study, Tom on his way out, Grandmama with her calls to pay; none of us seeing the others. All of us alone, a few odd beads strung together by sadness, by habit, by duty. A tear trickles slowly down my cheek. This power's truth is like a poison I cannot spit out.

Small pale creatures crawl from under the rocks and stones. They touch the hem of my gown and stroke my arms. "This is where you belong, where you are needed, special," they say. "Love us as we love you."

I turn my head, and there is Kartik, bare-chested, walking toward me. I take his face into my hands, kissing him hard and recklessly. I want to crawl inside his skin. This magic is nothing like the magic we have played with before. It is raw and urgent, with no facade to hide behind. This is what they don't want us to feel, to know.

"Kiss me," I whisper.

He presses me against the tree; his lips are on mine. Our hands are everywhere. I want to lose myself to this magic. No body. No self. No concerns. Never to be hurt again.

The Tree of All Souls speaks inside me. "And would you have more?"

For a moment, the Temple magic fights within me. I see myself standing before the tree while Kartik screams my name, and I feel as if I'm struggling to wake from a laudanum dream.

"Yes," someone answers, and it isn't me. I struggle to see who has answered so, but the tree's branches hold me fast. It holds me like a mother and coos as softly.

"Sleep, sleep, sleep . . ."

I fall through the floors of myself, waiting for someone to catch me, but no one does, so I just keep falling into a dark that never ends.

Later—I cannot say when, for time has lost all meaning—I hear a voice telling us it is time to go. I am suddenly aware of the cold. My teeth chatter. There is frost on my friends' eyelashes. Without a word, we turn from the tree and stumble back the way we came. We pass the bodies hanging from the trees like ghoulish chimes, their entreaties whispered on the wind: *"Help us. . . ."*

✳✳✳✳✳

The rest of the journey out of the Winterlands is a dream of which I remember little. My arms are scratched, and I cannot recall how they have come to be this way. My lips are bruised, and I wet them with my tongue, feeling small cracks in the skin. When we step across the mist-shrouded threshold of the Borderlands, I ache with a desire to turn back. The strange twilight beauty of the Borderlands no longer excites. I can feel it in the others as well, can see it in their backward glances. We step over the vines that slither from the Winterlands. They stretch their arms, reaching closer and closer to the castle.

Bessie speaks as if in a daze. "It's like it knew me. *Really* knew me. I saw m'self and I were a proper lady—not pretend, but respected."

"No fear," Felicity murmurs, stretching her arms overhead. "No lies."

Pippa twirls around, faster and faster, till she falls down laughing. "It all makes sense now. I understand everything."

Gorgon is waiting for us in the river. I try to avoid her, but she sees me slipping behind a tall wall of flowers.

"Most High, I have been looking for you."

"Well, you have found me, it seems."

Her eyes narrow, and I wonder if she can smell the forbidden on my skin like another's sweat. The other girls run wild. They wear a new fierceness that brings a gleam to their eyes and a flush to their cheeks. Felicity laughs and it sounds like a call to arms. I want to go to them, to relive our experience in the Winterlands, not suffer under the watchful eye of Gorgon.

"What is it?" I call.

"Come closer," that syrupy voice demands.

I stand on the grass a good ten feet from where Gorgon sits on the river. She turns her head and takes in the sight of me—hair a ruin, arms scratched, skirt torn. The snakes dance hypnotically. "You have been, I see," Gorgon says.

"And what if I have?" I answer, defiant. "I had to see for myself, Gorgon. How could I possibly govern without knowing? The Tree of All Souls exists, and its power is immense!"

The snakes round her face writhe and hiss. "Promise me you will not return to that place until you have made the alliance. Most High, your power—"

"Is that all I am—the magic? No one sees who I am. They see what they want to see, what I can do for them. Who I am, how I feel doesn't matter a bloody bit!" I've started to cry, which I hate. I turn my head away till the tears subside, and when I face Gorgon again, I am a different girl, one who will not be told what to do or where to go.

"You may go now, Gorgon. Our conversation has ended."

For once the proud warrior seems unsure, and I'm glad of it. "Most High . . ."

"Our conversation has ended," I repeat. "If I want to speak with you, I shall find you."

On the grass, a merry game has sprung up. Felicity pushes Bessie, who pushes back harder.

"Ye can't best me," Bessie taunts. Her eyes glimmer.

Felicity's laugh is brittle as weeds. "I already have, or hadn't you noticed?"

Howling like banshees and laughing, they lock arms and struggle to see who shall remain standing while Pippa cheers them on. I run with speed and force, knocking them down like pins and bloodying my lip. And no one laughs more than I do as the hard, metallic taste fills my mouth and the blood spills over my dress like a merciless rain.

CHAPTER THIRTY-FIVE

Though our masked ball is weeks away yet, Mrs. Nightwing is adamant that we girls should prepare some sort of entertainment for our guests.

"It would be a tribute to them to show what fine young ladies you've become—and how talented," she says, though I suspect our little trained-monkey performances have far more to do with proving the talents of our headmistress.

We've been assigned our various parts: Cecily, Martha, and Elizabeth are to perform a ballet. Felicity will play a minuet. As I have no talent in singing, dancing, French, or an instrument of any kind, I ask Mrs. Nightwing if I might read a poem, and she agrees, apparently relieved that there is something I can do that does not involve animal husbandry or cymbals played between the knees. There is only the matter of my choosing a poem and not tripping over my words. Sadly, Ann is not allowed to sing for our guests. Our scheme at Christmas has cost her this, for Mrs. Nightwing can't afford to upset her patrons, and by now, they all know of the scandal.

Ann bears the injustice stoically, and I'll relish the day she tells them all she's off to tread the boards as a member of Mr. Katz's company under the tutelage of Miss Lily Trimble herself.

Felicity sits at the piano, playing a minuet. "It's but a small party, really, no grander than a garden tea. It's only the costumes that give it flair," she grouses. "It's nothing compared to the ball Lady Markham's hosting for me in two weeks. Did I tell you she's to have fire-breathers?"

"I believe you might have, once or twice." *Or twelve times.* I comb through a book of poems given to me by Mrs. Nightwing. They're so treacly they make my teeth ache. I should never get through a one of them with a straight face.

"This one about the light bearer isn't too awful," Ann offers.

I grimace. "Is that the one in which Florence Nightingale appears on the battlefield like an angel, or is it the poem that likens Admiral Nelson to a Greek god?"

Felicity leaves the piano and joins us on the floor. "I can't stop thinking about last night. It was the most exciting time yet in the realms."

"You mean the Winterlands," Ann whispers. "And you really saw Eugenia Spence there, Gemma?"

"She didn't appear to us," Felicity sniffs, and I fear it shall become a competition.

"I told you everything," I say, defending myself. "Do you realize that we can save her and the realms?"

Felicity purses her lips. "*You* can, you mean."

"*We* can," I say, correcting her. "But first, we must find the dagger Wilhelmina took, and I've no idea where to look."

"Perhaps it's here at Spence," Ann suggests.

"We don't even know that Wilhelmina is trustworthy. After all, she stole it, didn't she?" Felicity muses.

"I think she made a mistake and now she means to redeem herself by leading me to it," I say.

"But why take it in the first place?" Felicity presses.

"You're supposed to practice your performances!" Cecily chides, hands on her hips.

"They are helping me to select a poem," I answer with as much disdain as is possible.

The doors swing open, and I fear that Mrs. Nightwing has come to reproach us for not working harder. Instead, she calls for Ann.

"Miss Bradshaw. Will you come with me, please?"

Head down, Ann follows her out, and I can't imagine what sort of trouble she could be in.

"At last," Cecily says, gloating.

"Cecily, what do you know?" Felicity asks.

Cecily twirls in a pirouette. "Her cousins have arrived from the country to take her away. Brigid is upstairs now packing her case."

"But they can't!" I cry as Felicity and I exchange horrified looks.

"They decided it was time. *High* time, if you ask me."

"Well, we didn't!" I snap.

Cecily's mouth opens in an outraged O just as Miss McCleethy makes her appearance, and I curse my timing. "Miss McCleethy, will you allow Miss Doyle to speak to me so appallingly?"

Miss McCleethy levels her gaze at me. "Miss Doyle? Is an apology called for?"

"Do forgive me, dear Cecily." My smile is as false as a street vendor's remedies.

Cecily's hands fly to her hips again. "Miss McCleethy!"

I rush to Miss McCleethy's side. "Is it true? Have Ann's cousins come for her?"

"Yes," she answers.

"But they can't do that!" I protest. "She doesn't want to go with them! She's not meant to be a governess. She—"

Something resembling true concern shows in Miss McCleethy's hard face. "It was Miss Bradshaw herself who arranged for it."

It's as if Miss McCleethy's words are spoken underwater. I can scarcely make sense of them, and a cold dread tightens in my stomach.

I run for the stairs and take them two at a time, Felicity calling my name and Miss McCleethy demanding order. When I reach our room, completely out of breath, Ann is sitting on her bed wearing her drab brown traveling suit and modest wool hat. She makes a neat pile of her halfpenny papers and the fashion magazine Felicity handed down. The program for *Macbeth* sits on top. Brigid tucks the last of Ann's clothes into her suitcase.

"Brigid," I pant. "Could I have a moment with Ann?"

"All righ' then," Brigid says, sniffling. "Close the case proper. And don't forget your gloves, dearie." Our housekeeper bustles past me, dabbing at her moist eyes with a handkerchief. It's just Ann and me.

"Tell me it's a lie," I say.

Ann closes her case and sets it on the floor at her feet. "I left you the halfpenny papers. Something to remember me by."

"You can't go with them. You've a position in Mr. Katz's company waiting for you. The world's stages!"

Anguish shows on Ann's face. "No. That was for Nan Washbrad, whose beauty speaks for itself, not Ann Bradshaw. The girl they want doesn't exist. Not really."

I throw her case onto the bed, open it up, and start unpacking it. "Then we'll find a way. We'll make it work with the magic."

Ann puts her hand on mine, stopping me. "Don't you see, Gemma? It would never work. Not forever. I can't be who they want me to be."

"Then be someone else. Be yourself!"

"Not good enough." She twists her gloves in her hands, crumpling them into a ball and straightening them out again. "That's why I sent the letter asking them to come for me."

I think back to the night of Ann's audition and the letter in her hands, the one she had so much trouble posting. She never meant to go with Lily Trimble and Mr. Katz. I sink onto her bed; her case rests between us. She puts her things back in and latches it shut.

"Tell me, then, what was all that trouble for?" I bite the words off.

"I'm sorry, Gemma." She tries to touch me but I shrink away. "If I leave now, I can remember that day as it was. I can always believe that I could have done it. But if I take that chance—if I go to them as myself and fail . . . I couldn't bear it."

Felicity bursts through the door and blocks it. "Don't you worry, Ann. I won't let them take you."

Ann pulls on her gloves and grabs the handle of her case. "Step aside, please."

Fee opens her mouth in protest. "But—"

"Let her go, Fee." I want to kick Ann—for not trying. For giving up on herself and on us.

Ann's face falls into a well-trained mask that betrays no emotion. She might use that talent to thrill audiences from the world's stages. Instead, she will use it to ease into the lives of her cousins so seamlessly that it will be as if she has never existed at all. And I see now that she might have made a good magician as well as an actress, for she knows how to make herself disappear.

Suitcase in hand, Ann marches down the stairs for the last time. Her shoulders are straight and her back is stiff but her eyes are blank. She's even begun to walk like a governess. Down the hall, I can hear the phonograph playing, McCleethy putting the girls through their careful paces.

Mrs. Wharton waits at the bottom of the stairs with Mrs. Nightwing and Brigid. Mrs. Wharton wears a confection of a dress—beaded and feathered and overwrought. "Ah, here's our Annie now. I was just telling Mrs. Nightwing how fond I know you'll become of our house in the country. Mr. Wharton and I have named it Balmoral Spring, as Balmoral is so dear to Her Majesty."

"What a ridiculous name for a country house," Felicity mutters. "Have they never spent a spring at Balmoral? It makes one long for English winters."

Mrs. Wharton chatters on about the nuisance of maintaining a country estate in the proper style and how her days are made a ruin by constantly keeping after the servants. Brigid gives Ann a handkerchief though she's the one who could use one.

"No shame in service," she says, cupping Ann's chin tenderly. "You remember your old Brigid."

"Goodbye, Ann," Felicity says. "It won't be the same without you."

Ann turns to me. I know she's waiting for some hint of kindness—a kiss, an embrace, even a smile. But I can't muster any of it.

"You'll make a fine governess." My words are like a slap.

"I know," she answers, a slap of her own.

The girls crowd the foyer. They sniffle and make a fuss as they never did while Ann was here and it might have mattered. I can't bear it, so I slink off to the great hall and peek out from behind the drapes as Ann and her sudden admirers step outside.

A footman secures Ann's case and, after tending to Mrs. Wharton, he helps Ann into the carriage. She pokes her head out the window, holding fast to her one good hat. I could rush after her, give her a kiss on the cheek, send her off with a fond farewell. I could. It would mean the world to her. But I can't make my feet move. *Just say a proper goodbye, Gemma. That's all.*

The reins are snapped. The horses kick up dust. The carriage jolts as it makes the turn around the drive and toward the road. It grows smaller and smaller till it's nothing more than a dark speck moving away.

"Goodbye," I whisper at last, when it no longer matters and there is no one to hear it but the window.

CHAPTER THIRTY-SIX

ABSENCE IS A CURIOUS THING. WHEN FRIENDS ARE ABSENT, they seem to loom ever larger, till the lack of them is all one can feel. Now that Ann has left, the room is too big. Try as I might, I cannot fill the space that remains. I find I miss the snoring that pestered me so; I miss her gloomy character and silly, romantic notions and macabre fascinations. A half dozen times during the day, I think of some small observation I should like to share with her—an aside about Cecily or a complaint about the porridge that might make them both more bearable—only to realize that she isn't here to enjoy it. There's a moment of profound sadness that can be dispelled only by summoning my anger.

She chose to leave, I remind myself as I put the needle to my embroidery, sing hymns, and practice my curtsy for the Queen. But if the fault is hers, why do I take it to heart? Why does her failure also feel like my own?

I am glad when Miss McCleethy, acting as games mistress,

calls us outdoors to play at sports. Several girls amuse themselves with lawn tennis. Some intrepid souls take up fencing, with Felicity leading the charge, a fierce gleam in her eye. A small group campaigns for cricket, "just like the boys' schools!", but as we have no bats or balls, it's a moot point, and grumbling, they are forced to settle for croquet.

I am for hockey. Running about the lawn, stick at the ready, cradling the ball down the field, passing it successfully to a teammate, shouting without restriction, all the while with the wind in my face and the sun on my back, is most invigorating. I should like a bit of hockey to clear my mind and sharpen my senses, to make me forget my loss. I find I should like to hit something with a stick.

Miss McCleethy calls to us from the lawn without restraint. "That will never do! Your chum needs an assist, Miss Temple—look sharp! You must work together, ladies, toward a common goal! Remember: Grace, strength, beauty!"

She may speak to the others, for I've done with assisting. I tried helping Ann, to no avail. When the ball is in play again, Cecily and I race for it at the same time. My blasted skirt tangles in my legs a bit—oh, what I wouldn't do for the freedom of trousers just now—and Cecily gains the advantage. She may be closer but I don't yield. I want it. More importantly, I don't want her to have it, else she'll be smug for a week.

"I'm for it!" I call.

"No, no—I have it!" she shouts.

Our sticks lock, and she gives mine a smack with hers. One of our opponents, a thick girl with ginger hair, seizes the moment. She reaches between us and steals the ball, setting up a most brilliant play.

"I told you I had it, Miss Doyle," Cecily says with a tight smile.

"Clearly, you didn't," I reply with a false smile of my own.

"It was mine."

"You're wrong!" I insist.

Miss McCleethy strides onto the field and separates us. "Ladies! This is hardly a demonstration of proper sportsmanship. Enough, or I shall give you both poor conduct marks."

Glowering, I return to form. I should like to show Cecily—show them all—what I can do. No sooner have I thought it than the magic rears inside me with new force, and the ball is all I can see. I'm as bold as Richard the Lion-Hearted as I race down the field, outwitting my opponents. This time, the play will be mine.

Cecily is quick, though. She's nearly to the ball. "I have—"

I run hard, knocking Cecily down. She sprawls on the grass and begins to wail. Miss McCleethy comes at a clip.

"M-Miss M-McCleethy!" she blubbers. "She deliberately charged me!"

"I did not!" I protest, but my red cheeks show the lie for what it is.

"You did so!" Cecily wails.

"You're being babyish," I say, putting the blame back on her shoulders.

"All right, that's enough. Miss Temple, part of sportsmanship is keeping a stiff upper lip." Cecily's mouth opens and I gloat. "And you, Miss Doyle, are far too hot, it seems. Cool your temper off the field, please."

"But I—"

"Your recklessness might cause an even graver injury, Miss

Doyle," Miss McCleethy says, and I know she isn't speaking solely of the game.

My cheeks burn. The other girls snicker. "I am not reckless."

"I'll have no further argument. Off the field until you have regained your composure."

Mortified and angry, I walk past the smirking schoolgirls and the chuckling workers and straight into the school, not caring that I'm demonstrating the most appalling lack of sportsmanship.

Bloody McCleethy. If she knew what I know—that Eugenia Spence is alive in the Winterlands and trusts me and not her—she might not speak to me that way. Right, I've more important matters at hand. I crawl into Felicity's tent, where I've left our copy of *A History of Secret Societies*, and, lounging on the settee in the great room, proceed to read it anew, hoping for some clue to the hiding place of the dagger. With a sigh, I resign myself to combing through it page by page, though 502 pages is so many to wade through, and I curse authors who write such lengthy books when a few neat pages of prose would do.

First is a title page. Next is a poem. "The Rose of Battle," by Mr. William Butler Yeats.

"'Rose of all Roses, Rose of all the World!'" I read aloud. "'You, too, have come where the dim tides are hurled / Upon the wharves of sorrow, and heard ring / The bell that calls us on; the sweet far thing.'"

It seems a fine poem, from what I can tell, as it doesn't make my teeth ache, and I decide it shall be the poem I'll recite at our masked ball.

Opposite that page is one of the illustrations that grace the book. I must have glanced at it a half dozen times without really seeing it—a simple ink drawing of a room with a table and a single lantern, a painting of boats hanging on the wall. With growing excitement, I realize it is rather like the room I've seen in my visions. Could it be the same one? And if so, where is it? Here at Spence? And could this be where Wilhelmina Wyatt took the dagger? I run my fingers over the inscription beneath it: *The Key Holds the Truth.*

Quickly, I flip through the pages, searching for other illustrations. I locate the tower again, and I wonder, could it be the East Wing as it once stood? Flip again, and there's a drawing of a leering gargoyle above the inscription *Guardians of the Night.* Another drawing shows a merry magician, much like Dr. Van Ripple, placing an egg inside a box, and the next panel shows the egg vanished. It is entitled The Hidden Object.

The drawings don't correspond with the text, from what I can tell. It's as if they exist as their own entity, a form of code. But for what? For whom?

Miss McCleethy enters, fuming. "Miss Doyle, I'll not tolerate such an appalling lack of discipline and sportsmanship. If you don't care to play the game, you may sit on the field and cheer your schoolmates."

"They are not my mates," I say, turning a page.

"They might be, if you weren't so desperately in love with being all alone in the world."

It's a shame Miss McCleethy did not take up riflery, for she's an excellent shot.

"I tired of the game," I lie.

"No, you tired of the rules. That would seem to be a habit of yours."

I turn another page.

Miss McCleethy steps forward. "What are you reading that is so captivating you feel it necessary to ignore me?"

"*A History of Secret Societies* by Miss Wilhelmina Wyatt." I glare at her. "Do you know it?"

Her face drains of color. "No. I can't say I do."

"And yet you purchased a copy from the Golden Dawn bookseller's at Christmastime."

"Have you been spying on me, Miss Doyle?"

"Why not? You spy on me."

"I look after you, Miss Doyle," she says, correcting me, and I hate her for this lie most of all.

"I know you knew Wilhelmina Wyatt," I say.

Miss McCleethy rips off her gloves and drops them onto a table. "Shall I tell you what I know of Wilhelmina Wyatt? She was a disgrace to the Order and to the memory of Eugenia Spence. She was a liar. A thief. A filthy addict. I tried to help her, and then"—she taps the book with her finger—"she wrote these lies to expose us—all for money. Anything for money. Did you know that she tried to blackmail us with the book so that we might abandon our plan to raise funds for the restoration of the East Wing?"

"Why would she do that?"

"Because she was spiteful and without a shred of honor. And her book, Miss Doyle, is no more than twaddle. No, it's more dangerous than that, for it contains perfidies, corruptions of truth written by a traitor and peddled to the highest bidder."

She closes the book with a loud crack and, snatching it from my grasp, marches straight for the kitchen. I run after her, catching up just as she opens the oven door.

"What are you doing?" I say, aghast.

"Giving it a proper burial."

"Wait—"

Before I can stop her, Miss McCleethy throws *A History of Secret Societies* into the oven and shuts the door. For a second, I'm tempted to tell her what I know—that I have seen Eugenia Spence, and that this book may save her—but Eugenia told me I should be careful, and for all I know, McCleethy is the one who cannot be trusted. I can only stand by whilst our best hope burns.

"That cost us four shillings," I croak.

"Let that be a lesson to you to spend your money more wisely in the future." Miss McCleethy sighs. "Really, Miss Doyle, you do try my patience."

I might tell her that is a common sentiment where I am concerned but it seems ill-advised. Something new pricks at me.

"You said 'was,'" I say, thinking.

"What?"

"You said Wilhemina *was* an addict and a liar, a traitor. Do you think she might be dead?" I say, testing.

Miss McCleethy's face pales. "I don't know whether she lives or not, but I cannot imagine, given her state, that she's still alive. Such a life takes a toll," she says, seeming flustered. "In the future, if you wish to know about the Order, you need only ask me."

"So that you can tell me what you want me to hear?" I say, challenging her.

"Miss Doyle, you only hear what you want to believe, whether it's true or not. That has nothing whatsoever to do with me." She rubs the sides of her head. "Now, go and join the others. You are dismissed."

I storm out of the kitchen, cursing Miss McCleethy under my breath. The girls pour in from the lawn. They're flushed and smell a bit ripe, but they're giddy with the excitement that running about in games of spirited rivalry brings. We rarely are allowed to give free rein to our competitive natures, though they live in us just as strongly as they do in men. Cecily turns her chin up at the sight of me. She and her clan give me withering looks, which, I suppose, they think the height of insult. I put my hand to my heart mockingly and gasp, and, freshly offended, they march off whispering about me anew.

Upon seeing me, Felicity crouches like a master swordsman, cutting swoops into the air with her fencing foil. "Villain! You shall answer to the King for your treachery!"

Delicately, I push the long, thin blade aside. "Might I have a word, d'Artagnan?"

She bows low. "Lead the way, Cardinal Richelieu."

We steal into the small sitting room downstairs. It's where Pippa famously spurned her intended, Mr. Bumble, before being claimed by the realms forever. The loss of Pippa is one more I feel acutely today.

"What the devil did you do to Cecily?" Felicity plops into a chair and dangles her legs over the arm in a most unladylike way. "She's telling everyone who'll listen that you should be hanged at dawn."

"If it would keep me from hearing her voice ever again, I'd happily submit to the noose. But that isn't what I need to tell you. I had another look through Wilhelmina Wyatt's book. We missed something the first go-round. The drawings. I think they're clues."

Felicity makes a face. "To what?"

I sigh. "I don't know. But one of them seemed as if it might have been the East Wing tower. And in the very front of the book was a room that I keep seeing in my visions."

"Do you think that room was once part of the East Wing, then?" Fee asks.

"Oh," I say, deflating. "I'd not thought of that. If so, it's long gone."

"Well, let's have a look," Felicity says.

"We can't. Miss McCleethy threw it in the oven," I explain.

Felicity's mouth opens in outrage. "That cost us four shillings."

"Yes, I know."

"And tonight's meal shall taste strangely of book." She sticks the tip of her foil into the floor and scrapes a small F there.

"There's something not right about it," I say, pacing the room and nibbling my fingernails, a habit I should stop, and will. Tomorrow. "I don't trust McCleethy. She's hiding something for certain. Do you know what she said to me? She referred to Wilhelmina Wyatt in the past tense. What if McCleethy knows Wilhelmina is dead? And if she does, *how* does she know it?"

"Dr. Van Ripple said Wilhelmina was betrayed by a friend," Felicity adds. "Could it have been McCleethy?"

I chew my nail, shredding it to ribbons. It hurts, and I am instantly sorry I've done it. "We must speak with Dr. Van Ripple again. He may know something more. He may know where the dagger is hidden. Are you for it?"

A wicked grin spreads across Felicity's mouth. She touches her foil to my shoulders as if knighting me. "All for one and one for all." Her expression changes suddenly. "Why do you think she did it?"

"McCleethy or Miss Wyatt?" I ask.

"Ann." She leans on the hilt of her foil. "Freedom was within her grasp. Why turn away from it?"

"Perhaps it was one thing to yearn for it and another to hold it."

"That's ridiculous." With a scoff, she sprawls across the chair again, one foot on the floor, the other leg hanging over the arm.

"I don't know, then," I say with no small irritation.

"I'll not turn my back on happiness. I can promise you that." She jabs at the air with her foil. "Gemma?"

"Yes?" I say with a heavy sigh.

"What will happen to Pip? When I was one with the tree, I saw . . ."

"Saw what?"

"I saw her alive and happy. I saw the two of us in Paris, the Seine glittering like a dream. And she was laughing, as she did before. How could I see that if . . . Do you think it could be true? That she could come back?"

She rolls her head toward me, and I can see the hope in her eyes. I want to tell her yes, but something deep inside me says no. I don't think it could ever be this way.

"I think there are some laws that cannot be broken," I say as gently as I can, "no matter how much we wish they could be."

Felicity draws in the air with her blade. "You think, or you know?"

"I know if it were possible, I should bring my mother back tomorrow."

"Why don't you, then?"

"Because," I say, searching for the right words. "I know she's gone. Just as I know that time when we were all together in India is gone, and I shan't get it back."

"But if the magic is changing—if everything is changing,

then perhaps . . ." She trails off, and I don't try to correct her. Sometimes the power in a *perhaps* is enough to sustain us, and I shan't be the one to take it from her.

I can hear Brigid's off-key warbling in the hall, and it gives me an idea. "Fee, if one wanted to know about a certain inhabitant of a house, a former schoolgirl perhaps, where would one turn for the most trustworthy account?"

Smiling, Fee bends the foil in her hands. "Why, I should think the servants would have that sort of knowledge."

I throw open the door and peek my head out. "Brigid, might we have a word?"

She scowls. "Wot you doin' in there? Emily's cleaned it just yesterday. I won't 'ave it set to ruin."

"Of course not," I say, biting my lip in a fashion I hope passes for wistful. "It's only that Felicity and I are heartbroken now that Ann's gone. We know you loved her, too. Will you sit with us for a moment?"

I'm a bit ashamed of twisting Brigid's sympathies this way—even more so when it works. "Oh, luv. I miss 'er, too. She'll be fine, though. Just like 'er old Brigid." She barrels past, giving me a warm pat on the shoulder, and I couldn't possibly feel more deplorable.

"'Ere now. Sit proper, miss," Brigid scolds, seeing Felicity. Felicity slides both of her feet to the floor with a loud stomp, and with a glance I beseech her to behave.

Brigid runs a finger over the mantel and scowls. "That won't do."

"Brigid," I begin, "do you remember a girl who attended Spence—"

"Lots of girls 'ave attended Spence," she interrupts. "Can't remember them all."

"Yes, well, this one was here back when Mrs. Spence was still alive, before the fire."

"Oh, so long ago." She tuts, wiping the mantel with the edge of her apron.

Felicity clears her throat and glares at me. I suppose she thinks she's helping.

"This girl was a mute. Wilhelmina Wyatt."

Brigid whirls around, a funny expression on her face. "Blimey, now wot you want to know about that one fer?"

"It was Ann who knew of her. Had a book written by her. And I—we—just wondered what sort of person she was." I finish with a smile that can only be described as feeble.

"Well, it were a long time ago," Brigid repeats. She dusts a small Oriental vase with her apron. "But I remember 'er. Miss Wil'mina Wyatt. Mrs. Spence said she was special, in 'er way, that she saw wot most of us don't. 'She can see into the dark,' she said. Well, I didn't pretend to know wot that meant. The girl couldn't even speak, bless her soul. But she were always with 'er little book, writing and drawing. That's 'ow she spoke."

Just as Dr. Van Ripple told us.

"How did she come to be here? She had no family, I know," I say.

Brigid's brow furrows. "Bless me, she did, too."

"I thought—"

"Wilhelmina Wyatt was Missus Spence's own blood. Mina was 'er niece."

"Her niece?" I repeat, for I wonder why Eugenia didn't tell me this.

"Came to us after 'er mother died, bless 'er soul. I remember the day Missus Spence went to town to fetch 'er. Lil Mina 'ad been put on a boat by 'erself and was found near the Customs

'Ouse. Poor thing. Must've been terrifyin'. And things weren't much better 'ere." Brigid returns the vase and gets to work on the first of a pair of candlesticks.

"What do you mean?" Felicity asks.

"Some o' the girls picked on 'er. They pulled on 'er braids to see if she would talk."

"Did she have friends at all?"

Brigid frowns. "That awful Sarah Rees-Toome would sometimes sit with 'er. I'd 'ear 'er askin' Mina if she really could see into the dark, and wot it was like in that place, and Mrs. Spence took Sarah to task for that and forbade them from playin' together."

"Did Miss Wyatt have haunts that were special to her—hiding places, perhaps?" Felicity presses.

Brigid thinks for a moment. "She liked to sit out on the lawn and draw the gargoyles. I'd see 'er wif her book, lookin' up at 'em and smilin', like they were 'avin' a tea party of their own."

I recall my strange hallucination as I left for London at Easter. The gargoyle with the crow in its mouth. It gives me a shiver to think of Wilhelmina smiling at those hideous stone watchers. Guardians of the Night, indeed.

Brigid slows her dusting. "I do recall Missus Spence frettin' over Mina later on. The girl had taken to drawin' dreadful things, and Missus Spence said she were afraid Mina were under a bad influence. That's what she said. And then the fire happened shortly after, and those two girls and Missus Spence gone wif it, God rest 'em." With a sigh, she returns the candlestick and takes the other.

"But what happened to Wilhelmina? Why did she leave?"

Brigid licks her thumb and works at a smudge on the silver.

"After the fire, she were actin' peculiar—'cause of the grief, if you ask me, but no one did."

Felicity quickly intervenes. "Yes, I'm sure you're right, Brigid," she says, rolling her eyes at me. "What happened next?"

"Well," Brigid continues, "Mina started scarin' the other girls with 'er odd behavior. Writin' and drawin' those wicked things in 'er book. Missus Nightwing told 'er, relation or no relation to the missus, if she didn' stop, she'd turn 'er out. But before she could, Mina left in the middle of the night, takin' somefin' valuable wif 'er."

"What was it?" Felicity jumps in.

"I don' 'ear ever' fin', Miss Pesterpants," Brigid chides.

I mouth *Miss Pesterpants* to Felicity, who looks as if she could cheerfully strangle me.

"Wotever it was," Brigid continues, "Missus Nightwing were very cross about it. I've never seen 'er so angry." Brigid puts the candlestick back just so. "There. That's better. I'll 'ave to 'ave a word with that Emily. And you best get to prayers, before Missus Nightwing turns *you* out and me righ' after."

⌁⌁⌁⌁⌁

"What do you think it all means?" Felicity asks as we fall in with the other girls. They gather their prayer books and straighten their skirts. They crowd around too-small mirrors, pretending to tidy their hair when really they're only gazing at themselves, looking for hopeful signs of budding beauty.

"I don't know," I say with a sigh. "Is Wilhelmina trustworthy or not?"

"She does appear in your visions, so it means something," Felicity says.

"Yes, but so did the girls in white, and they were fiends who would have led me astray," I remind her. The very girls who meant to lure Bessie and her friends into the Winterlands for who knows what purpose also came to me in my visions, giving me a measure of truth and lies. In the end, they led us straight into the clutches of the gruesome Poppy Warriors.

"So what is Miss Wyatt?" Felicity asks. "The lady or the tiger?"

I shake my head. "I honestly can't say. But she took the dagger—that's for certain—and that's what we need to find."

CHAPTER THIRTY-SEVEN

OUR TRIP TO THE REALMS ISN'T AS MERRY WITHOUT ANN. Even the magic can't lighten the mood. The factory girls take her departure particularly hard. "Our lot got no chance," Mae grumbles to Bessie.

"You must make your own chances," Felicity retorts.

Bessie gives her a hard look. "Wot would you know of it?"

"Let's not fight. I want to dance and play with magic. Gemma?" Pippa gives me a knowing look.

With a sigh, I tread the familiar path to the chapel and Pip follows. This time when we join together in the magic, the draw on me is hard. It's as if I fall into her deeply. I'm part of her sadness, her envy, her bitterness—things I'd rather not see. When I break away, I'm tired. The magic itches beneath my skin like insects crawling.

But Pip sparkles once again. She nestles into my side and wraps her arms about my waist like a little girl. "It's wonderful to feel special, even for just a few hours, isn't it?"

"Yes," I say.

"If I were you, I should never give up this power but keep it always."

"Sometimes I wish I could."

Pippa bites her lip, and I know she's worried.

"What is it?" I ask.

She picks berries from a bowl and moves them between her fingers. "Gemma, I don't think you should give quite as much magic to Bessie and the others this time."

"Why not?"

"They're factory workers," she says on a sigh. "They're not accustomed to having such power. Bessie's gotten quite full of herself."

"I hardly think that's—"

"She wanted to go into the Winterlands again. Without you," Pip admits.

"She did?"

Pip takes my arm. We step carefully over the groaning vines slithering across the floor. "It's better if I have more, don't you think? That way they have someone to look up to, someone to guide them. They're such children, really. And I can keep them safe for you."

That's a laugh coming from Pip, but the news about Bessie sounds an alarm inside me. "Yes, all right. I'll give them less," I agree.

Pip kisses my forehead. She drops the berries she's been playing with into her mouth, one, two, three.

"Should you be eating those?" I ask.

Pippa's eyes flash. "What does it matter now? The damage has been done."

She drops the fourth into her mouth and wipes the juice

from her lips with the back of her hand. Then she pushes the tapestry aside with a "Greetings, my darlings!" just like a queen greeting her subjects.

✦✦✦✦✦

As promised, I give the factory girls sufficient magic to allow them the appearance of clear skin and fine dresses but not enough to create true change. They have no real power this time, only borrowed illusion.

"Don't seem to work so good tonight," Bessie grumbles. "Why's that?"

I swallow the lump in my throat, but Pippa is cool as can be. "That's the way of the realms, Bessie. It only takes in some. Isn't that right, Gemma?"

"That is what I've been told," I say, appraising Bessie to see if she will give anything away, but all I see is her disappointment.

"Maybe it's 'cause we're not the proper station," Mercy says.

"Ain't no stations here. That's wot I like about it. And besides, it always took in Miss Ann, and she ain't no better 'n' us," Bessie says.

"Bessie, that's quite enough," Pippa clucks, and Bessie skulks off to sit at the hearth. She feeds small flowers to the fire, watching them spark and burn. "Come now, let's not pout. I want to dance!"

I'm in no humor for a dance just now, and I can't find it within me to pretend. Instead, I go for a walk. The cool air is refreshing; the dusky sky feels sheltering. I push on through the billowing mist, letting my yearning pull me. I want to put my hands on the Tree of All Souls once more, to be joined to it as if we are one being.

The gate opens without a word this time. It has what it wants from me. My feet sink into the black sand. The air, cold and gritty, presses itself against me; I put out my tongue, tasting it. I follow the roar of the river. A dinghy waits, so I step into it and head toward the heart of the Winterlands. I know not to fight the tide this time, and my little boat sails easily over the rapids, but the path is unfamiliar. It's not the same one we traveled last time, and panic blooms in me. Where am I? How did I get so lost?

There's a splash beside the boat, and a water nymph strokes the side of it. She gestures with her head at a cave to the right; then she swims toward it, knifing into and out of the water like a serpent.

Right. I shan't let her get the best of me. If necessary, I'll employ the magic. Comforted by that thought, I turn the boat and paddle after her, drifting into the hollowed-out rock. Stalactites hang over my head, great daggers of ice. The cave is bordered by two strips of rocky land that must vanish under the tide, for I see the high-water marks upon the cave's walls. High above on each side is a ledge.

The water nymph's webbed hand caresses my ankle. With a gasp, I shake it loose. Her colored scales remain on my skin in a jeweled handprint.

"You'll not take my skin without a fight," I warn, and my words echo in the cave's emptiness.

The nymph slinks away, dipping below the surface of the water until only her glistening black eyes and water-slicked bald head are visible, and a new wariness steals over me. On the ledge, there is movement. The faces of ghastly, pale creatures squeeze out of the cracks in the rocks like moths' heads. They have no eyes, but they sniff, crawling closer to the edge.

My heart's a fist. Silently, I turn the boat around and am paddling back toward the mouth of the cave when the opening disappears. That can't be. I hear a snort and the clip-clop of hooves, and Amar sidles into view on his magnificent white steed. He travels over the narrow land on the side of the cave until he is even with me in my boat. My breath catches. Up close he has the same full lips and proud carriage as Kartik. But his eyes are black swirls ringed in red. They hold me fast, and I can't look away, can't scream, can't run.

Use the magic, the magic, my heart pleads. But it will not catch spark. I'm too afraid.

"I know you've seen the priestess. What did she tell you?" Amar asks. His teeth are jagged points.

"You'll never know," I manage to say.

Amar's eyes waver, and for just a moment, they are as brown as Kartik's. "Tell my brother to remember his heart in all things. That is where his honor and his destiny will be found. Tell him."

And then, quickly, they revert to that terrifying black abyss circled in red. "We'll have you yet. Beware the birth of May."

My breath comes out in quick white puffs, my fear joined with the cold.

"Let me out!" I scream.

Suddenly, the mouth of the cave is visible again, and I paddle for it with all my might, leaving Amar and those pale, blind creatures far behind. The tree is forgotten. I want only to return safely to the Borderlands.

I stagger into the blue forest, breathing hard, and am

relieved to see the lights of the castle bleeding out its windows, dispelling the gloom. I'm also relieved to hear my friends' laughter, for I should like to join it now.

There's a small rumble of thunder, and when I look behind me at the Winterlands sky, it is drenched in red.

CHAPTER THIRTY-EIGHT

It is a tedious sort of day at Spence. We spend the whole of our French lesson conjugating verbs. Frankly, I do not care whether it is *I have dined on snails* or *I shall dine on snails,* as I do not intend ever to allow a snail past my lips and so the entire lesson is moot. We repeat the steps of the quadrille until I could perform them in my sleep; we practice our sums so that we might manage the household books someday and be assets to our husbands. Under Miss McCleethy's direction, we sketch one another in profile; Elizabeth protests that I've given her a nose as big as a house when, in truth, I've been far too kind. But when it comes to art, everyone is a critic, and there you have it.

When the teachers are not around, the girls fall into excited chatter about their approaching debuts. They've stacks of invitations—those tempting promises of romance, elaborate feasts, and new gowns engraved in neat script upon fine cream-colored cards. I should be thinking of my own debut.

But I'm far too distracted. That time seems to exist in another world, and I cannot see my way clear to it just now.

Rather than take tea with the others and listen to talk of this party or that ball, I excuse myself on the pretense of practicing my curtsy, and comb the school's nooks and crannies, hoping I might find the dagger Wilhelmina Wyatt stole or additional clues to its whereabouts. Unfortunately, I discover nothing but dust, empty drawers, and overstuffed cupboards, and the rather unfortunate surprise of an unwrapped toffee gone to goo, which even after three soapings still coats my fingers in a nasty stickiness. I'm at a loss, especially now that Miss Wyatt won't show herself to me in visions or dreams. It's as if she's toying with me, and I recall Dr. Van Ripple's comment about her enjoying her little cruelties. It casts doubts on her trustworthiness.

I'm just about to give up and return to the others when I spy Kartik's bandana in the ivy. I reach down and pluck it free. There's a note attached: *I've arranged it. Meet me in the laundry. Midnight. Bring five pounds. Dress sensibly.*

Tonight. I shall have to thank him for giving me such short notice. Still, it is arranged, and if I can speak with a representative of the Rakshana about saving my brother, I'll go whenever called.

Felicity's not happy about my plans. She expects another visit to the realms, and she's sure Pip won't forgive her absence—but she understands that I must help Tom. She even offers me the use of her fencing foil in case I need to stab anyone. I assure her that won't be necessary, and I hope I am correct in this assumption.

Just before midnight, I ready myself for my meeting with

Kartik in the laundry. He has said to dress sensibly, and as we will travel through London's streets at night, I decide there is only one possible solution.

With the magic at hand, I give myself trousers, a shirt, a waistcoat, and a coat. I shorten my hair and am astonished to see myself like this—all eyes and freckles. I make a good boy, perhaps a prettier one than I am a girl. A cloth cap completes the illusion.

The laundry house is dark when I enter. I don't see or hear a thing, and I wonder if Kartik has come after all.

"You're late," he says, stepping out from behind a beam.

"It is good to see you as well," I snap.

"The note distinctly said midnight. If we're to make London in time, we must leave now. Have you the money?"

I hold up my coin purse and give it a jingle. "Five pounds, as requested. Why do I need it?"

"Information is costly," he answers. He takes in the sight of my trousers. "Sensible." His gaze travels up. He turns away. "Button your coat."

My bosom swells slightly under the shirt. That part of me has not been disguised. Embarrassed, I button the coat.

"Here," Kartik says, wrapping his scarf around my neck. The ends hang down, obscuring the front of me.

He leads me to the hitching post where Freya waits. Kartik pats her nose, soothing her. He swings into the saddle and offers his hand, then pulls me up behind him. We take off with a start. I put my arms around his waist and he does not object.

We ride for what seems an eternity—my backside aches—and at last the lights of London glimmer in the distance. Just short of the city, we dismount, and Kartik leaves Freya hitched to a tree with assurances to her that we will return. He feeds her a carrot and we join the pulse of London nightlife. The streets are not as quiet as I would think. It is as if the city itself has sneaked out of doors while its counterpart, the ordinary day city, sleeps. This is a different London, a London more daring and unknown.

Kartik secures a cab and raps on the roof to signal the driver. With Kartik sitting beside me, the cab feels quite close. His hands rest rigidly on his thighs. I push myself into the corner.

"Where are we to meet?"

"Near Tower Bridge."

The night is smeared with hazy light. Kartik is close enough to touch. His shirt is open at the neck, exposing the curve of his throat, the delicate hollow there. The cab feels warm. My head is as light as down. I require some distraction before I go mad.

"How did you arrange the meeting?"

"There are channels."

Kartik offers no further comment, and I ask no more questions. The cab falls into silence again save for the horses' quick clip-clop shuddering through me. Kartik's knee falls against mine. I wait for him to move it, but he doesn't. My hands tremble in my lap. From the corner of my eye, I see him looking out at the streets. I do the same, but I cannot say that I notice the scenery. I am aware only of the warmth of his knee. It seems impossible that so small a collection of bones and sinew could produce such a thrilling effect.

The driver stops short, and Kartik and I alight on the streets just below the Tower Bridge. The bridge has been in operation for only two years, and it is a sight to behold. Two large towers rise like medieval buttresses. A walkway is suspended between them high over the Thames. The bridge lifts to allow the passage of the ships that come into port—and there are many. The pools of the Thames are crowded with them.

An old beggar woman sits in the damp muck on the walk. She shakes a beaten tin with one penny in it. "Please, sir, spare a copper."

Kartik places a sovereign in the lady's cup, and I know that it's likely all he has.

"Why did you do that?" I ask.

He kicks a rock on the ground, balancing it nimbly between his feet like a ball. "She needed it."

Father says it isn't good to give money to beggars. They'll only spend it unwisely on drink or other pleasures. "She might buy ale with it."

He shrugs. "Then she'll have ale. It isn't the pound that matters; it's the hope." He kicks the rock in a high arc. It skitters down some stone steps. "I know what it's like to fight for things that others take for granted."

We've reached the pools, which are crowded with vessels of every type, from small dinghies to large ships. I cannot see how they make their way in and out, as the ships are crowded so closely together that one could easily step from the bow of this ship to that one without getting wet at all. They line the wharves and docks waiting to unload and receive their cargo.

Small steps lead down to the bank. I wait for Kartik to offer me the aid of his arm. Instead, he starts down without me, his hands bunched in his coat pockets.

"What's keeping you?" he asks.

"Nothing," I say, taking the stairs at a fairly quick clip.

Kartik rolls his face heavenward. "Why do ladies refuse to

say when they are angry? Is it a skill they teach you? It's terribly confusing."

I stop and face him in the weak blue light. "If you must know, you might have offered me your arm at the top."

He shrugs. "Why? You have two of your own."

I struggle to keep my composure. "It is customary for a gentleman to help a lady down the steps."

He smirks. "I'm no gentleman. And tonight, you're no lady."

I try to protest but find I cannot, and we follow the Thames without another word. The great river laps against its banks with a rhythmic sloshing. It rises and falls and rises again, as if it, too, should like to be free for a night. I hear voices coming from below.

"This way," Kartik says, running toward them. The voices grow louder. The accents are hard and rough. The mud thickens as the fog lifts. In the water are perhaps a dozen people of all sorts—from old women to dirty-faced children.

One of the old women sings a seafaring song, stopping only for the violent coughing fits that rack her body. Her dress is little more than rags. She is so caked in mud she folds into the murk like a shadow. As she sings, she dips a shallow pan into the Thames and brings it up. With quick fingers, she picks through the pan while shaking it, searching for what, I'm sure I don't know.

"Mud larks," Kartik explains. "They sift through the Thames for whatever they can find of value to sell or keep—rags, bones, a bit of tin or coal from a passing ship. If they're lucky, they might find the purse of a sailor who met with a bad end—that is, if the riverman's hook hasn't found him first."

I make a face. "But to wade into the Thames . . ."

Kartik shrugs. "It's far better than being a tosher, I can tell you that."

"What, pray, is a tosher?"

"Much like a mud lark, but they scour the sewers for their finds."

"What a wretched existence."

Kartik takes on a hard tone. "It is a means to live. Life isn't always fair."

The comment is meant to sting and it does. We fall into quiet.

"You're the one always speaking of fate and destiny. How do you explain their lot, then? Is it their fate to suffer so?"

Kartik shoves his hands into his pockets. "Suffering isn't destiny. Nor is ignorance."

A woman's voice cuts through the fog. "Wot's the rivah give you tonigh'?"

"Luv, I go' apples 'n' stuffin'!" another shouts back.

They fall into loud gales of laughter.

"They've found apples and stuffing here?" I ask.

Kartik grins. "It's Cockney rhyme. The last word is a rhyme for the word they mean. 'I've got apples 'n' stuffing' really means 'I got nothing,' or, as she'd say, 'I got nuffin'.'"

"Oi! Kartik!" One of the urchins stumbles up from the filth and muck of the river. "Been waitin' on you, mate."

"We were delayed, Toby." He apologizes to the mud-coated boy with a bow.

Toby nears, and so does his smell. It is a horrible mixture of stagnant river water, rubbish, and worse. I dare not think about what lives in his ragged clothes. My stomach lurches and I find I have to breathe through my mouth so as not to swoon.

"How is the treasure hunting?" Kartik asks. He thinks he's clever but he's got his hand at his chin. His fingers cover his nose.

"No' grand, but no' bad, neither." Toby holds out his palm. In it is an odd collection—a small lump of coal, two hairpins, a tooth, a shilling. Every bit of it is coated in filth. He smiles widely, revealing a lack of teeth. "That will buy a pint of ale." Toby views me suspiciously. "'At a lady in gent's trousers?" I'm certain the horror shows on my face.

Kartik raises an eyebrow. "Can't fool everyone."

Toby jingles the loot in his hand. "She's no beauty, mate, but she looks clean. 'Ow much?"

I do not understand straightaway, but when I do, a fierce rage overtakes me.

"Why, I—"

Kartik wraps his hand over my fist and stays it. "Sorry, mate. She's with me," he says.

Toby shrugs and adjusts his grimy cap. "Meant no 'arm."

Big Ben announces the hour. The great chime cuts through the fog and I feel it in my belly.

"Let's take a walk, eh?" Toby says.

"The cheek of it," I grumble.

She's no beauty, mate. He thought me no better than a prostitute, and yet, why is it that this statement is the one that pierces me through?

A young boy steps from the shadows. He has sores on his lips and great hollows under his eyes. His voice hasn't yet changed—he can't be more than ten—but there's an empty sound to it already, as if no one is left inside him. "Lookin' for comp'ny, guv? Tuppence."

Kartik shakes his head, and the boy fades back, waiting anxiously for the next passerby.

"There are others here who will take what he offers," Kartik tells me.

Toby leads us to a wharf stacked with empty crates, and the greasy light of only one lamp. "This is a good spot," he says.

Kartik looks about. "No escape route. You could be cornered easily here."

"By wot?" Toby asks. "Ships ever'where."

"And the men on them are drunk or sleeping. Or the very sort we need to watch out for," Kartik warns.

"You fink I'm daft?" Toby says, challenging him.

"Kartik," I warn.

"Fine." Kartik relents. "Gemma, the money."

I give him the small purse with five pounds inside. It's all the money I've got, and I'm loath to part with it. He hands it to Toby, who opens it, counts the coins, and packs it into his pocket.

"Now," Kartik says, "what did you discover about Mr. Doyle?"

I look from Kartik to Toby and back again. "He's the one we've come to meet?"

"Toby makes himself useful as an errand boy sometimes. He knows how to barter knowledge for money."

Toby smiles as big as life. "I can find out anyfin'. On my life."

"But this meeting was to be with the Rakshana," I protest. I want my money back.

"First, we gather information, so that we know where to strike," Kartik explains. "If we called a meeting, they'd have us caught for sure. I was one of them. I know."

"Very well," I grumble.

Out on the Thames, the boats sway with the current. There's something soothing and familiar about it.

"They're pullin' 'im in, all righ'. Got a 'nitiation planned for 'im and ever' fin'," Toby says. "Don' know 'ow much they've told 'im, though."

"And is Fowlson the one who brought him in?" Kartik asks.

Toby shakes his head. "Fowlson's 'is minder. Somebody at the top asked for it. A gen'leman." He points to the sky. "High up."

"Do you know who?"

"Naw. Tha's all I know."

"I want to find this gentleman," I insist.

"Fowlson reports to 'im. 'E's the one 'oo knows."

Footfalls echo in the fog behind us. They're joined by a jaunty whistle that makes my blood run cold. Kartik's eyes narrow. "Toby."

The filthy boy offers a shrug and a sad smile as he backs away. "Sorry, mate. 'E give me *six* pounds, and m'mum's dreadful sick."

"Well, well, well, what 'ave we 'ere? Back from the dead, brother?" A pair of black boots shine under the lamp's light. Mr. Fowlson emerges from the shadows, flanked by a large man. Coming up the other side of the wharf are two of Fowlson's hooligans. Behind us is the Thames. They've got us cornered.

Kartik pushes me behind him.

Fowlson smirks. "Protecting your lady love?"

"What lady?" Kartik says.

Fowlson laughs. "She may be done up in trousers and coat, but it's the eyes. They don't lie."

"Give me your word as a brother that you'll leave her alone," Kartik says, but I can see the fear pulsing at his throat.

Fowlson's lips curl with hate. "You left the fold, brother. There's no honor between us no more. I don't haf to promise you nuffin'." Fowlson pulls a knife from his pocket. He flicks it open and the blade gleams in the weak gaslight.

I scour the banks of the Thames, looking for anyone who might hear my screams and offer aid. But the fog is rolling in thicker. And who would come rather than scatter at such a ruckus? Magic. I can conjure it if need be, but then he'll know for certain that I've been lying about no longer having it.

One of the ruffians tosses Fowlson an apple, which he catches neatly in one hand. He plunges the knife into it and separates the skin from the meat in long curls that drop at his feet.

Swallowing hard, I step forward. "I would like for you to leave my brother alone."

Fowlson gives me a vicious grin. "Would you, now?"

"Yes," I say, wishing my voice had more steel in it. "Please."

"Well, then. That depends on you, Miss Doyle. You've got sumfin' wot belongs to us."

"What is that?" I find my voice despite my fear.

"Awww, coy, are you?" His grin tightens to a grimace. "The magic."

He moves forward, and Kartik and I step back. We're close to the Thames.

"I've told you—I no longer have it."

Kartik's eyes shift left and right, and I hope he's finding us an escape route.

"You're lying," Fowlson snarls.

"How do you know she's lying?" Kartik asks.

His smile is grim. "She's talking."

"The Rakshana is supposed to protect the realms and the magic, not steal it." I need to stall for time.

"That's the way it used to be, mate. Things are changing. The witches 'ad their day."

Fowlson puts his knife into his mouth and pulls off an apple slice with his teeth. We're trapped here. There's nowhere to go but into the Thames.

"The way I see it, I take you bof in, I'm a hero." He points his knife at Kartik. "You're a traitor to the brotherhood, and you"—he shifts the blade toward me—"you 'ave the answer to all our problems."

"Can you jump?" Kartik whispers to me. He flicks a glance toward the boat anchored behind us. I nod.

"Wot're you luvbirds whisp'rin 'bout?" Fowlson asks.

"On three," Kartik whispers. "One, two—"

I'm too frightened to wait. I leap on the count of two, dragging him down with me, and we fall to the bow of the ship below with a thud that shudders through my entire body.

"I said three." Kartik gasps as if his lungs are broken.

"S-sorry." I wheeze.

Fowlson shouts at us from the wharf, and I see him readying to jump.

"Let's go." Kartik yanks me up, and we hobble to the stern, where the boat abuts another, smaller vessel behind it. There's a small gap between them, but in the dark with the Thames lapping below, it seems a mile. The boat shifts, making it even more precarious.

"Jump!" Kartik calls. He leaps across the divide, dragging me along with him. "What the devil!" a surprised sailor shouts as we careen into his boat.

"Surprise inspection!" Kartik calls, and we're off and running again.

Another jump and we're on the embankment. We race over the slick ground at breakneck speed, trying not to tumble. Fowlson and his thugs are close behind. There's an opening under the street. A sewer.

"This way!" Kartik shouts, and his words echo. The sewer is so malodorous I want to vomit. I press the back of my hand to my nose.

"I don't think I can," I say, gagging.

"It's a way out."

We creep into the foul, stinking hole. The walls trickle with moisture. A wash of filth floods the bottom of the tunnel. It seeps into my boots and coats my stockings and I have to fight the bile rising in my throat. The tunnel is alive with movement. Fat black rats scurry on their tiny legs, squeezing suddenly out of small breaks in the walls. Their squeaking cries raise gooseflesh on my arms. My very skin crawls. One bold fellow pokes a nose out near my face and I scream. Kartik clamps a hand over my mouth.

"Shhh," he whispers, and even that echoes in the fetid sewer.

We stand, huddled together in the moist, foul tunnel, listening. There are a constant drip and the hideous scuttle of the rats' claws. And something else.

"'Ello, mates. We know you're in there."

Kartik keeps moving, but up ahead, the sewer darkens, and it fills me with dread. I can't go on.

"Just close your eyes. I'll lead you," he whispers. He comes beside me and wraps his arm around my waist.

I stand firm. "No. I can't. I'm—"

"Gotcha!" Quick as a wink, Fowlson's men are on us. They

grab Kartik, bending his arm behind his back till he grimaces in pain.

"Now I'm quite put out," Fowlson says, walking slowly toward us.

"I gave it to the Order," I blurt out. "You're right—I lied to you before. But just this morning I met with Miss McCleethy. She prevailed upon me to see her wisdom. I joined hands with her in the realms. The Order truly does have the power now. I swear it!"

Fowlson's expression softens. He looks worried, confused. "This mornin'?"

"Yes," I lie.

Fowlson's so close I can smell the apple on him, see his jaw tighten with new anger. "If that's true, there's nuffin' to keep me from cuttin' Kartik here and now." He presses the blade to Kartik's throat. "Poor Brother Kartik. Shall I tell you wha' 'appened to 'im, miss?"

Kartik struggles against the knife. "We pulled 'im in. Do you know 'ow long a man can last under our scrutiny?" Fowlson puts his mouth so close to my ear I can feel the heat of his breath. "I've broken souls in less than a day. But our Kartik, 'e wouldn't bend. Wouldn't tell us wot 'e knows about you and the realms. 'Ow long was it, Kartik? Five days? Six? I lost count. But in the end, 'e broke like I knew 'e would."

"I'll kill you," Kartik gasps, the knife to his throat.

Fowlson laughs. "Is that your achin' heel, mate? Don't want 'er to know?" Fowlson has caught the scent of Kartik's fear and he wants blood. He presses the knife hard to Kartik's throat, but his words to me are harder. "'E went bloomin' mad in the end. Started seein' Amar in 'is 'ead. Old Amar 'ad a message for him: 'You'll be the death of 'er, brother.' An' whatever 'e saw next must 'ave been awful indeed, because 'e screamed and screamed till 'e didn't 'ave no screams left and there weren't nuffin' but air comin'. And that's when I knew I'd broken 'im after all." Fowlson's angry grin spreads. "But I can see why 'e wouldn't want to tell you that story."

Kartik's eyes are moist. He seems broken again, and I should like to kill Fowlson for what he did. I won't let Kartik be hurt again. Not while, I can stop it.

"It's Achilles'," I say.

Fowlson's knife falters for a moment. "Wot?"

"Achilles' heel, not aching heel, you bloody stupid fool."

His eyes go wide as he laughs. "Oh, that's a pretty mouf you've got, luv. When I finish wif 'im, I'll cut it wide open."

"No, I think not." Quickly as a hare, I've got my hand on his arm. Power rushes through me like the Thames itself. Fierce light fills the tunnel, catching the look of frightened surprise on Fowlson's face as we're joined, his thoughts pulsing through mine.

His bully rage and cruelty run through my veins for only a second. They are replaced by a fleeting memory—a small boy, a dark kitchen, a pot of water, and a large scowling woman, her lips tight in a sneer. I don't know what it means, but I feel the child's dread. Indeed, my stomach tightens in fear. It is gone in an instant, and now the magic is fully alive in me.

"Yes," I say. "I lied. And now, I shall have to ask you to remain here, Mr. Fowlson."

I harness the magic to shape what's in his mind and in the goons' minds as well. *You cannot follow.* I don't say it, but the effect is the same. Mr. Fowlson is surprised to find that his legs will not obey his commands. They are frozen in place. The knife falls from his fingers; his hands hang limply at his sides, and Kartik is freed. Fowlson's hooligans can only look to each other as if they might discover an explanation. Try as they might, they cannot move.

"Wot are you doing to me, you witch!" Fowlson screeches.

"You brought this on yourself, Mr. Fowlson," I reply. "You are to leave my brother alone."

Fowlson strains to free himself. "Turn me loose, or I'll tear you apart!"

"That's quite enough. Promise me."

He grins, and his defiance infuriates me. "The only thing I'll promise you is this: I don't care about any of it now. It's you and me. I'll come for you, you little witch. You'll beg for mercy."

The magic sours inside me. I can't quite feel myself anymore. I feel only a rage so fierce it blinds. I want to hurt him, to bend him to my will. I want him to know who has the power here. *You'll be sorry. . . .*

Fowlson's eyes open wide with a new fear. Slowly, he falls, his face lowering ever closer to the watery muck on the floor of the sewer. He cannot speak; my rage won't allow it. My eyelids flutter. Kartik speaks reason to me but I do not want to hear it; I want only to bathe in retribution.

Something darts across my soul. The boy in the kitchen. The angry woman rolls up her sleeves. The little boy cringes before her terrible rage. *You miserable bastard,* she curses, *I'll show you respect. I'll tear you apart.* She plunges his head into the pot of water and holds it while the boy thrashes. *You'll beg for mercy!* The boy comes up gasping and she plunges him under once more. I feel his fear as he comes up, again and again. He is near to collapsing, and for a moment, he considers it, considers flooding his lungs with that water to make her happy, to make her right. But he cannot do it. He fails. She pulls his head up an inch, and he manages to sputter one word: *mercy.* She hits him hard and her ring cuts his cheek. He curls up in the corner, pressing his hand to the deep cut, but he doesn't dare call out. Tomorrow he will try harder. Tomorrow she will love him. Tomorrow he will not hate her so very much.

It's as if I've been hit. The magic wavers; I stumble, slamming my palms against the wet wall to stop my fall. Fowlson's face is an inch from the filthy water. *Stop,* I tell myself. *Stop.* The magic settles inside me, dogs circling down to sleep. My head aches and my hands shake.

Fowlson springs up, gasping and trembling.

"I'm sorry," I say, my voice raw. "Your mother . . . she hurt you. She gave you that scar."

Fowlson struggles to speak. "You shut it about my mother! She were a saint!"

"No," I whisper. "She was a monster. She hated you."

"You shut it!" he screams, spittle forming at the corners of his mouth.

"I didn't mean to do it," I protest. "Believe me."

"You'll be sorry for that, luv." He turns to Kartik. "I 'ope you learned a lot during your days wif us, brother. You'll be needin' it."

Fowlson swings at me, though I am out of reach. He needs to do it; it's all he has left. "I'll crush you, you bitch!"

I should slap him for it, but I won't. I can see only that little boy in the corner of the kitchen.

"The magic won't last long. An hour, maybe two at most. And once you're free, you're not to come after us, Mr. Fowlson, or I shall unleash my powers again."

Kartik takes my hand and leads me out of the sewer. We leave Fowlson, swinging and cursing at the dark, behind us.

⚡⚡⚡⚡

Walking along the dirty Thames is a relief. The river air that seemed so foul an hour ago is sweet compared to the suffocating odor in the sewer. The wracking coughs and the tuneless songs of the mud larks float through the fog like phantoms. A sudden shout cuts the mist. Someone has found a lump of coal, and the news is greeted with excitement and a great thrashing of water as every one of the mud larks rushes to find the sweet spot. But it turns out to be nothing more than a rock. I hear the heavy plink as it's tossed back into the Thames riverbed, that graveyard of hope.

"I need to sit," I say.

We wander down by the wharves and rest for a moment, looking out at the boats bobbing on the river.

"Are you all right?" I ask after a long silence.

He shrugs. "You heard what he said. And think less of me for it."

"That's not true," I say. "Amar said . . ." I stop, thinking of my recent encounter with Kartik's brother in the Winterlands. But I'm not ready to disclose that just yet. "In your dream, he said you'd be the death of me. Is that why you've kept your distance?"

He doesn't answer straightaway. "Yes, that is part of it."

"What is the other part?"

Kartik's face clouds. "I . . . it's nothing."

"Is that why you didn't want to become part of the alliance?" I ask.

He nods. "If I don't enter the realms, the dream can't come true. I can't hurt you."

"You said ignorance wasn't destiny," I remind him. "If you don't go into the realms, you'll only not have been in the realms. Besides, there are hundreds of other ways to do me in here, if you wish. You could pitch me in the Thames. Shoot me in a duel."

"Hang you with the entrails of a large animal," he says, joining in, a smile forming.

"Abandon me to Mrs. Nightwing forever so that I might be pecked to death."

"Ah, that's cruel, even for me." Kartik shakes his head, laughing.

"You find my imminent death so amusing?" I tease.

"No. It isn't that. You bested Fowlson," he says, grinning madly now. "It was . . . extraordinary."

"I thought you found my power frightening."

"I did. I do. A bit," he admits. "But, Gemma, you could change the world."

"That should take far more than my power," I say.

"True. But change needn't happen all at once. It can be small gestures. Moments. Do you understand?" He's looking at me differently now, though I cannot say how. I only know I need to look away.

The ships' masts press against the fog, letting us know they're here. In the distance there's a foghorn. Some vessel is slipping out farther toward the sea.

"Such a mournful sound. So lonely," I say, hugging my knees to my chest. "Do you ever feel that way?"

"Lonely?"

I search for the words. "Restless. As if you haven't really met yourself yet. As if you'd passed yourself once in the fog, and your heart leapt—"Ah! There I am! I've been missing that piece!" But it happens too fast, and then that part of you disappears into the fog again. And you spend the rest of your days looking for it."

He nods, and I think he's appeasing me. I feel stupid for having said it. It's sentimental and true, and I've revealed a part of myself I shouldn't have.

"Do you know what I think?" Kartik says at last.

"What?"

"Sometimes, I think you can glimpse it in another."

And with that, he leans forward as I do. We meet in a kiss that is not borrowed but shared. His hand cups the back of my neck. My hands find his face. I pull him closer. The kiss deepens. The hand at my neck slides down my back, drawing me into his chest.

Noises come from the docks. We fly apart, but I want more. Kartik grins. His lips look slightly swollen from our kissing, and I wonder if mine do as well.

"I shall be arrested," he says, nodding toward my trousers and noting my boyish appearance.

Big Ben's commanding chime reminds us that the hour is late.

"We'd best go," Kartik says. "That enchantment won't last forever, and I shouldn't like to be standing here when Fowlson and his men are free."

"Indeed."

We pass by the pools, where the mud larks sift. And for only a few seconds, I let the magic loose again.

"Oi! By all the saints!" a boy cries from the river.

"Gone off the dock?" an old woman calls. The mud larks break into cackles.

"'S not a rock!" he shouts. He races out of the fog, cradling something in his palm. Curiosity gets the better of the others. They crowd about trying to see. In his palm is a smattering of rubies. "We're rich, mates! It's a hot bath and a full belly for every one of us!"

Kartik eyes me suspiciously. "That was a strange stroke of good fortune."

"Yes, it was."

"I don't suppose that was your doing."

"I'm sure I don't know what you mean," I say.

And that is how change happens. One gesture. One person. One moment at a time.

⌁⌁⌁⌁

Freya takes us toward Spence. The new moon offers us little help, but the horse knows the way and there's not much for us to do but ride and rest after the adventure of our evening.

"Gemma," Kartik says after a long while, "I have upheld my end of the bargain. Now you must tell me what you know of Amar."

"He spoke to me. He said I should give you a message."

"What was it?"

"He said to tell you to remember your heart in all things, that it is where your honor and your destiny will be found. Does it mean anything to you?"

"It is something he would say from time to time—that the eye could be misled, but that the heart was true."

"Some part of your brother remains, then."

"It would have been better if it hadn't."

We settle into quiet again. The road smooths. I'm so tired my head nods against Kartik's shoulder.

"I'm sorry," I say, yawning.

"It's all right," he answers softly, and my head eases against his back again. My eyes are heavy. I could sleep for days. We pass the graveyard on our left. Crows perch on the headstones, and just before my eyes shut, I think I see a faint glimmer. The crows disappear into it, and everything on the hill goes dark and still as death.

CHAPTER THIRTY-NINE

THE MORNING BREAKS WITH A FUROR. LOUD SHOUTING comes from the lawn. There is trouble, and trouble draws us in as a carnival barker would. When I open my window and stick my head out, I count at least a dozen others poking from other windows, including Felicity's. It is so early that Miss McCleethy is still in her dressing gown, a cap upon her head. Mrs. Nightwing wears her customary dark dress with that preposterous bustle at the back. I've no doubt she sleeps in it. For all I know, she was born in full corsetry.

Mr. Miller has Mother Elena's arm in one hand; in the other is her bloody pail.

"We found the vandal, and jus' like I said, it's one of them!" he shouts.

"Here now, Mr. Miller. Unhand her at once," Mrs. Nightwing commands.

"You won't be so quick to say that, m'um, when you hear what she done. She's the one wot painted the hex marks. And who knows what else besides."

Mother Elena's face is gaunt. Her dress has grown bigger on her. "I try to protect us!"

The Gypsies stream over the lawn from the camp, drawn by the clamor. Kartik hurries behind, pulling up his suspenders, his shirt half undone, and warmth pools in my stomach.

One of the Gypsy women steps forward. "She is not well."

Mr. Miller doesn't let go of Mother Elena's arm. "No one's goin' anywhere till them Gyps tell me where to find Tambley and Johnny."

"We did not take them." Ithal marches down the lawn, pushing up his sleeves as if he would fight. He takes hold of Mother Elena's other arm.

Mr. Miller tugs hard on the old woman, making her stumble. "What sort of people travel round all the time?" he shouts. "People what can't be trusted, that's who! No better than jungle savages! I'll ask you again: Where's my men?"

"That is quite enough!" Mrs. Nightwing bellows at full headmistress volume, and the field goes silent. "Mr. Miller, Mother Elena is not well, and it would be best to allow her people to care for her. When she is well enough to travel, I will expect to see no more of her." She faces Ithal. "The Gypsies will no longer be welcome on our land. As for you, Mr. Miller, you've work to tend to, haven't you?"

"I'll 'ave my men 'fore you leave," Mr. Miller grumbles to Ithal. "Or I'll 'ave one of yours for it."

Later in the day, Mrs. Nightwing relents and has us help Brigid prepare a basket of food and medicine for Mother Elena as an act of charity.

"Mother Elena has been here as long as I have," our headmistress says, packing a jar of plum preserves neatly into the basket. "I remember when Ithal was a boy. I hate to think of them gone."

Brigid pats Nightwing's shoulder and she stiffens under the sympathy. "Still, it won't do to forgive the vandalism."

"Poor old madwoman," Brigid says. "She looks worn as my handkerchief."

Regret shows itself briefly on our headmistress's face. She tucks in an extra tin of lozenges. "There now. Will someone volunteer to take this to—"

"I will!" I blurt out, and loop my arm through the basket before anyone else can take it.

The sky threatens rain. Clouds gather in angry clumps, ready to unleash their fury. I hurry through the woods to the Gypsy camp, holding tightly to the basket. The Gypsy women are not happy to see me. They fold their arms and eye me suspiciously.

"I've come with food and medicine for Mother Elena," I explain.

"We do not want your food," an older woman with gold coins woven into her long braid says. "It is *marime*—unclean."

"I only want to help," I say.

Kartik speaks to the women in Romani. The conversation is heated—I hear the word *gadje* used bitterly—and occasionally, they glance back at me, scowls on their faces. But at last, the woman with the long braid agrees to let me see Mother Elena, and I scurry off to Mother Elena's wagon and pull the bell attached to a nail.

"Come," she calls in a weak voice.

The wagon smells of garlic. Several heads of it sit on a table by a mortar and pestle. The wagon's sides are lined with shelves housing various tinctures and herbs in glass jars. Small metal charms live there as well, and I'm surprised to see a small statue of Kali tucked between two bottles, though I have heard that the Gypsies came from India long, long ago. I run my fingers over the figure—the four arms, the long tongue, the demon's head in one hand, and the bloody sword in another.

"What do you look at?" Mother Elena calls. I see her face through a large bottle, her features distorted by the glass.

"You have a talisman of Kali," I answer.

"The Terrible Mother."

"The goddess of destruction."

"The destruction of ignorance," Mother Elena says, correcting me. "She is the one to help us walk through the fire of knowledge, to know our darkness that we should not fear it but should be freed, for there is both chaos and order within us. Come where I can see you."

She sits in her bed, shuffling a deck of worn tarot cards absently. Her breathing is heavy. "Why have you come?"

"I've brought food and medicine from Mrs. Nightwing. But they tell me you will not eat it."

"I am an old woman. I will do as I please." She nods for me to open the basket. I present the cheese. She sniffs and makes a terrible face. I put it away at once and take out the bread, which she nods to. She tears off small bits with her craggy hands.

"I try to warn them," she says suddenly.

"What is it you tried to warn them about?"

Her hand wanders to her hair, which wants a good brushing. "Carolina died in the fire."

"I know," I say, swallowing against the raw tickle at the back of my throat. "It was a long time ago."

"No. What's past is never past. It is not finished," she mumbles. She chokes on the bread and I pour her a glass of water and help her take small sips until the spasm subsides. "What opens one way can be opened the other," she whispers as she rubs the talisman that hangs from her neck.

"What do you mean?"

The dogs bark. I hear Kartik soothing them, and one of the Gypsy women chiding him for petting them.

"One of them brings the dead to us."

A chill works its way up my spine. "One of them brings the dead?" I repeat. "Who?"

Mother Elena doesn't answer. She turns over a tarot card. It has a picture of a tall tower struck by lightning. Flames leap from the windows, and two hapless people fall to the rocks below.

I put my fingers to the terrible card as if I could stop it.

"Destruction and death," Mother Elena explains. "Change and truth."

The tent flaps open suddenly, making me jump. The Gypsy woman with the long dark braid eyes me with suspicion. She asks Mother Elena a question sharply in her native tongue. Mother Elena answers. The woman holds open the curtain to the tent.

"Enough. She is not well. You must go now. Take the basket with you."

Shamefaced, I reach for the basket and Mother Elena grips my arm. "The door must remain closed. Tell them."

"Yes, I'll tell them," I say, and walk quickly out of the wagon.

I nod to Kartik on my way past him. He falls into step behind me with the dogs until we are far enough from the camp and Spence not to be seen by anyone.

"What did Mother Elena have to say?" he asks. The dogs sniff at the ground. They're restless. Low thunder rumbles far off. The air has the coppery smell of rain, and the wind has picked up. It blows my hair wild.

"She believes the East Wing is cursed, that it will bring the dead. That someone wants them to come."

"Who?" he asks.

"I don't know. I don't understand what she's saying."

"She's very ill," Kartik explains. "She's heard an owl calling in the night; that's a harbinger of death. She may not live till summer."

"I am sorry to hear it," I say.

One of the dogs puts its paws to my skirts and stretches up for a pat. I scratch it gently behind the ears and it licks my hand. Kartik strokes the dog's fur, and our fingers touch for a moment. A current passes through me.

"I had a new dream last night," he says, looking about for others. When he's sure we can't be seen, he moves closer and kisses my forehead, my eyelids, and, at last, my mouth. "I was in a garden. White blossoms fell from the trees. It was the most beautiful place I'd ever seen."

"You've described the realms," I say, trying to talk though his lips are on mine. "And was I in this dream?"

"Yes," he says, offering no further explanation, only a trail of kisses down my neck, which makes me a bit dizzy.

"Was it awful?" I manage to ask, for suddenly I'm afraid of what it could have been.

He shakes his head slowly, and a wicked smile steals over him. "I may have to see these realms for myself."

The thunder grows closer; small streaks of light crackle in the sky. Fat drops of rain spatter through the trees and hit my face. Kartik laughs and wipes the wet from my cheeks with the back of his hand.

"Best go indoors."

By the time I reach the top of the clearing, the rain's coming down with a fury, but I don't care. I'm grinning like an idiot. I throw my arms out and raise my face to greet its wet kisses. *Hello, rain! Happy spring to you!* I step hard in a fresh puddle and laugh as the muck spatters the front of my dress.

Mr. Miller's men aren't so happy. They hurry on their coats and hats, their shoulders bunched up against their ears to keep the bruising wind away from their work-damp necks. They gather tools and shout to one another over the din.

"It's not so bad, really," I say, as if they can hear me. "You should come have a splash in it. Do you good to—"

It comes over me so suddenly I can scarcely draw a breath. One moment, I see the turret and the men, and the next, it's sliding sideways. I'm in a tunnel, being pulled fast. And then I am inside the vision.

I'm in a small room. Strong smell. Makes me gag. Birds shriek. Wilhelmina Wyatt writes on the walls, a woman possessed. The light's too dim. And what I see jerks about like a windup toy. Words: *Sacrifice. Lies. Monster. The birth of May.*

The scene shifts and I see little Mina with Sarah Rees-Toome. "What do you see in the dark, Mina? Show me."

I see Mina on the back lawn of Spence smiling up at the gargoyles. And then I see her drawing a perfect likeness of the East Wing, drawing the lines I have seen stretching across the earth. The scene is washed away, and now Wilhelmina writes a letter, the words etched with angry strokes: *You've ignored my warnings. . . . I shall expose you. . . .*

"Miss? Miss?" My eyes flutter open for the briefest of

moments to see Mr. Miller's men crowded around me on the lawn, and then I'm in the dim room again. Wilhelmina sits on the floor, the dagger in her hands. The dagger! She takes out a small leather roll, which she unties to reveal a syringe and vials. Carefully, she wraps the dagger in the leather pouch. So that's where it is! All I need do is—

Wilhelmina rolls up her sleeve, exposing her arm. She taps fingers against the veins at the bend of her elbow. She plunges the syringe into it and lets go, and I feel a whoosh inside me.

"Miss!" someone calls.

I come to on the back lawn in the soaking rain. My heart beats wildly out of time. My teeth grind. A strange exhilaration takes hold.

"She's smilin', so she must be awl righ'," one of the men says.

I feel very odd. The cocaine. I've been joined to Wilhelmina Wyatt. I feel what she does. But how? The magic. It's changing. Changing what I see and feel.

The men wrap my arms across their shoulders and half drag, half carry me to Brigid's kitchen.

"Mary, Mother of God, wot's happened?" Brigid asks. She sits me in a chair by the fire and shoos the men off.

"Found 'er in the woods, 'avin' a fit, like," a man says.

A fit. Like Pippa. Yes, that's it. I had a fit. I laugh, even though I sense that it's not right for me to be laughing.

"She awl righ'?" another asks, backing away.

"G'won, then. Back to your men's work. Leave this to us women." Brigid clucks, and I can see on their faces they're relieved to be out of it. The kitchen. The laughing. The fit. The mysteries only women know.

A quilt is draped across my shoulders. The kettle's put on. I hear the match struck, the oven lit.

"You're fidgety as a cat," Brigid chides.

Mrs. Nightwing has been summoned. She comes close and I instinctively back away. The letter in the vision: *I saw it in her wardrobe.* Was Wilhelmina trying to warn me about Nightwing?

"Here now, what's this fuss about?" my headmistress asks.

"Nothing," I snarl.

She tries to put a hand to my forehead. I move out of her reach.

"Hold still, Miss Doyle, if you please," she commands, and it sounds wicked.

"I only want Brigid's help," I say.

"Do you?" Nightwing's eyes narrow. "Brigid is not headmistress at Spence Academy. I am."

She pours a foul liquid into a spoon. "Open, please."

When I won't, Brigid forces my lips apart and the thick oil oozes down my throat till I nearly retch. "You've poisoned me!" I say, wiping a hand across my lips.

"'S only cod-liver oil," Brigid coos, but I don't take my eyes off Mrs. Nightwing.

"I will expose you," I say aloud.

Mrs. Nightwing whirls around. "What did you say?"

"I will expose you," I repeat.

The momentary surprise in Nightwing's expression settles into calm. "I think Miss Doyle should spend the day in bed until she is feeling more herself, Brigid."

Though I am ordered to bed, I cannot sleep. It's as if someone has let ants loose in my skin. By the afternoon, my muscles ache and my head pounds, but I no longer feel seized by Wilhelmina's habit. I've not enjoyed this vision, and I'm afraid of having another.

Mrs. Nightwing herself brings me tea on a tray. "How are you feeling?"

"Better." The smell of buttered toast meets my nose, and I realize how hungry I am.

"Sugar?" she asks, the spoon hovering near the bowl.

"Please. Three—two spoonfuls, if you please."

"You may have the three if you wish it," she says.

"Yes. Three, then. Thank you," I say, swallowing bites of toast faster than is mannerly. Mrs. Nightwing looks about my room and at last takes a seat, perching on the edge of it as if it holds tacks.

"What did you mean by that remark earlier?" she asks. Her gaze is penetrating. My toast is suddenly a thick lump going down.

"What remark?" I ask.

"You don't recall what you said?"

"I'm afraid I don't recall anything," I lie.

She holds my gaze a moment longer, then offers milk for the tea, and I accept.

"Did Mother Elena say why she painted the hex marks?" she asks, changing the subject.

"She believes it will protect us," I say carefully. "She believes someone is trying to bring back the dead."

My headmistress betrays no emotion. "Mother Elena isn't well," she says, dismissing it.

I spoon preserves onto my toast. "Mrs. Nightwing, why are you rebuilding the East Wing?"

Mrs. Nightwing pours herself a cup of tea, no milk or sugar to sweeten it. "I'm afraid I don't know what you mean."

"It's been twenty-five years since the fire," I say. "Why now?"

Mrs. Nightwing picks a fluff of lint from her skirt and smooths the fabric flat. "It has taken us years to secure the funds, else we'd have done it sooner. It is my hope that the restoration of the East Wing will rub the cobwebs from our reputation and give us a new measure of esteem." She sips her tea and makes a face, but though it's clearly too bitter, she does not reach for the sugar bowl. "Every year, I lose girls to newer schools such as Miss Pennington's. Spence is seen as a debutante grown old; her fortunes dwindle. This school has been my life's work. I must do everything within my power to see that it continues.

"Miss Doyle?" Mrs. Nightwing's penetrating gaze is back. I force a pleasant expression. "I did not mean to speak so freely, but I feel you can be trusted, Miss Doyle. You have endured your share of hardship. It seasons one, builds character." She offers me a miserly smile.

"And do you also trust Miss McCleethy?" I hold fast to my teacup, avoiding her eyes.

"What a question. Of course I do," she answers.

"As a sister, would you say?" I press.

"As a friend and a colleague," Mrs. Nightwing replies.

Despite the tea, my throat feels dry. "And what of Wilhelmina Wyatt? Did you trust her?"

This time, I do chance a look at my headmistress. Her lips press into a line. "Where did you hear that name?"

"She was a Spence girl, was she not? Mrs. Spence's niece?"

"She was," Mrs. Nightwing says, tight-lipped. I'll not pry information from her so easily.

"Why does she not come round?" I say, feigning innocence. "As one of Spence's proud daughters."

"She was not one of its proud daughters but one of its disappointments, I'm afraid," my headmistress sniffs. "She tried to stop us from restoring the East Wing."

"But why would she do that?"

Mrs. Nightwing folds her napkin neatly and lays it on the tray. "I cannot say. After all, it was at her suggestion that we undertook the restoration in the first place."

"Miss Wyatt's suggestion?" I say, confused.

"Yes." Mrs. Nightwing sips her tea. "And she took something that belonged to me."

"Belonged to you?" I say. "What was it?"

"A relic entrusted to my care. A valuable piece. More tea?" Mrs. Nightwing raises the teapot.

"Was it a dagger?" I push.

My headmistress blanches. "Miss Doyle, I have come to offer tea, not be interrogated. Do you care for more tea or not?"

"No, thank you," I say, placing my cup on the tray.

"Very well, then," she says, gathering everything. "Rest. I'm sure you'll be right as rain come morning, Miss Doyle."

And with that, Mrs. Nightwing takes the tray away, leaving me with more questions than answers as always.

⚬⚬⚬⚬⚬

I'm too restless to sleep. I'm fearful of my dreams and deathly afraid that I shall have another vision. And as I've had nothing but toast, I'm famished. I shall eat the bed linens.

Cupping the flame of my candle, I tiptoe through Spence's cold, hush-dark corridors and down to the kitchen. Brigid's odd collection of talismans is still there. The rowan leaves on the windows, the cross on the wall. I hope she hasn't left all the food for the pixies. I rummage about in the larder and discover an apple that is only slightly bruised. I gobble it down in giant bites. I've just begun to work on a wedge of cheese when I hear voices. I snuff my candle and creep down the hall. Weak light leaks out through the slight crack in the great room's doors.

Someone's coming down the stairs. I duck into the shadows underneath and tremble in the darkness, wondering who could be about at this hour. Miss McCleethy descends in her dressing gown, carrying a candle. Her hair falls loose about her shoulders. I flatten myself against the wall till I fear my spine will break.

She slips into the room, leaving the door slightly ajar.

"Let myself in." A man's voice.

"So I see," McCleethy answers.

"She abed, wif dreams of sugar plums?"

"Yes."

"Sure 'bout that?" the man scoffs. "She paid me a lil visit down by the Thames the other nigh'. She and Brother Kartik."

Fowlson!

"She's been lyin' to you, Sahirah. She's got the magic, awl righ'. I felt the jab o' its boot in my face." Fowlson stands; I can see his shadow on the wall.

"Don't you think I know she has it?" Miss McCleethy answers, steel in her voice. "We'll get it from her. Patience."

"She's dangerous, Sahirah. Reckless. She'll bring us to ruin," Folwson insists.

Miss McCleethy's shadow presses close to Fowlson's. "She's only a girl."

"You underestimate 'er," he answers, but his voice has softened.

Their shadows move closer. "Once we build the tower of the East Wing, the secret door will be illuminated for us. And then we'll have possession of the realms and the magic once more."

"And then?" Fowlson asks.

"Then . . ."

Fowlson's shadow head dips toward Miss McCleethy. Their faces meet and blend into one shadow on the wall. My stomach tightens with hate for them both.

"You're a bit mad, Sahirah," Fowlson says.

"You used to like that quality in me," Miss McCleethy purrs.

"Din't say I don't still."

Their voices fade to sighs and murmurs I feel in my belly, and I blush.

"I need this, Sahirah," Fowlson says softly. "If I'm the only one o' 'em allowed in wif you and the Order, I'll be able to name my price. They'll cawl me a great man for it. I don' wanna be their strong arm forever. I want to sit a' the table proper wif power o' my own."

"And you shall. I promise. Leave it to me," Miss McCleethy answers.

"Brother Kartik is a problem. 'E tried to cawl a meetin'. What if m'lord knew I'd let Kartik go 'stead of killin' 'im like they asked me to do?"

"Your employer will never know. But I need Kartik just now."

I hold my breath. What if they mean to harm him? I've got to get to him, to warn—

"He and I have our agreement," Miss McCleethy continues. "He can't forget it was I who bargained for his life with you, I who sheltered him in London for those months until he was well. Now he is in my debt, and he will answer to me."

"'E was s'posed to spy on the girl, tell us ever' fin' 'e 'eard and saw, not sneak behind our backs."

"I'll speak to him," Miss McCleethy vows.

The weight of their words has me sinking slowly down the wall. Miss McCleethy at the Egyptian Hall. The figure in the shadows. It was Kartik. She sent him to spy—on me. Bile, hot and acidic, claws up my throat.

"It'll take more 'n words. Let me take the strap to 'im again. That's 'ow you get fings done, Sahirah."

"That's how *you* get things done," Miss McCleethy says. "I shall stick with my methods."

"You're sure she don't suspect nuffin'?"

Miss McCleethy's voice is as sure as always. "Not a thing."

There's the scraping of boots on the floor. I sit numbly in the dark as Miss McCleethy shows Fowlson to the door and treads the stairs to her bed. I sit awhile longer, unable to move. And when I feel my legs again, I march straight to the boat-house, where I know I will find him.

I'm not disappointed; he's there, reading Homer by lantern light.

"Gemma!" he calls, but his smile fades when he sees my expression. "What is wrong?"

"You lied to me—and don't try to deny it! I *know*!" I say. "You're working for *them*!"

He doesn't try to feign innocence or offer an excuse to save himself, as I knew he wouldn't.

"How did you find out?" he asks.

"That is hardly the point, is it?" I snarl. "That's the other part you didn't want to tell me when we were sitting on the wharf? Just before you . . ."

Kissed me.

"Yes," he says.

"And so, you were spying for them and kissing me?"

"I didn't want to work for them," he argues. "I wanted to kiss you."

"Should I swoon now?"

"I didn't tell Miss McCleethy anything. That's why I kept pushing you away—so I'd have nothing to confess. I know you're very angry with me, Gemma. I understand but—"

"Do you?" The magic sparks in my belly. I could make this all go away, but it wouldn't. Not really. Not for good. I'd still know. I use every bit of my concentration to push the magic down, and it coils inside me, a sleeping snake. "Just tell me why."

He sits on the floor, resting his arms on his bent knees. "Amar was all I had in this world. He was a good man, Gemma. A good brother. To think of him trapped in the Winterlands, damned for eternity . . ." He trails off. "And then I had that terrible vision when Fowlson"—he swallows—"tortured me. He would have killed me, and at that moment, I wouldn't have minded. It was Miss McCleethy who stopped it. She told me that with her help, I could save Amar. That I could save you. But she needed to know what you were about. She knew you wouldn't tell her."

"For good reason," I spit.

"I thought I could save you both," he says.

"I don't need saving! I needed to trust you!"

"I'm sorry," he says simply. "People make mistakes, Gemma.

We take the wrong action for the right reasons, and the right action for the wrong reasons. If you like, I'll go to McCleethy tomorrow and tell her she has no more hold over me."

"She'll send Fowlson," I remind him.

He shrugs. "Let him come."

"There's no need to go to McCleethy," I say, pulling a loose thread till my hem unravels further. "Then she'll know that I know. And anyway, I'll not be telling you my secrets again. And you're wrong. Amar wasn't all you had in this world," I say, blinking up at the wooden rafters of the boathouse. "You didn't have any faith in me."

He nods, accepting the blow, and then he is ready with his own. "I wonder if you allow yourself to have faith in anyone."

Circe's words return to me: *You'll come back to me when there is no one else to trust.*

"I'm going. I shan't be back." I bolt for the door and push through it with all my strength, letting it slap against the side of the boathouse.

Kartik comes after me, and takes hold of my hand. "Gemma," he says, "you're not the only lost soul in this world."

It's tempting to keep holding fast to his hand, but I can't. "You're wrong about that." I slide my fingers free of his and ball them into a fist at my stomach and run for the secret door.

I pass Neela, Creostus, and two other centaurs in the poppy fields on the way to the Temple. They've a bushel of poppies, and they argue with the Hajin over the price.

"Off to make bargains with the Hajin?" Neela sneers.

"What I do is none of your concern," I snap back.

"You promised us a share," she says, shifting into a perfect replica of me and back again.

"I'll give it when I choose," I say. "*If* I choose. For how do I know you're not in alliance with the Winterlands creatures?"

Neela's lips curl back in a snarl. "You accuse us?"

When I don't answer, Creostus steps forward. "You're just like the others."

"Go away," I say, but I'm the one who leaves, traveling up the mountain to the well of eternity.

I put my hands on the well and stare straight into Circe's placid face.

"I want to know everything you can tell me about the Order, the Rakshana. Leave nothing out," I say. "And then I want you to tell me how to be the master of this magic."

"What has happened?" she asks.

"You were right. They're plotting against me. All of them. I won't let them take the power away from me."

"I am glad to hear it."

I perch on the edge of the well, drawing my knees to my chest. The hem of my skirt floats out on the water, reminding me of funeral flowers set upon the Ganges. "I'm ready," I say, more to myself than to her.

"I must know something first. The last time I saw you, you were headed for the Winterlands. Tell me, did you find the Tree of All Souls?"

"Yes."

"And was it as powerful as the Temple?"

"Yes," I tell her. "Its magic is different. But extraordinary."

"What did it show you?" she asks, and a small sigh echoes in the cave.

"Eugenia Spence. She's alive," I answer.

Circe is so quiet I think *she* has died.

"What did she want?" she asks at last.

"She wants me to find something for her. A dagger."

There is a moment's pause. "And have you found it?"

"I've answered enough of your questions. You shall answer mine," I snap. "Teach me."

"It will cost you more magic," she murmurs.

"Yes, I'll pay it. Why do you want it?" I add. "What can you possibly do with it if you can't leave the well?"

Her voice floats up from the depths. "What do you care? This is a chess match, Gemma. Do you want to win or not?"

"I do."

"Then listen closely. . . ."

I sit for hours at Circe's side, listening until I understand, until I stop fearing my strength, until something deep within me is unleashed. And when I leave the Temple, I am no longer afraid of the power that lives inside me. I worship it. I will close the borders of myself and defend them without mercy.

I walk through the willows, and I hear Amar's horse galloping fast behind me. I don't run. I stand and face him. He draws close; his horse's icy breath cools my face.

"I'll not be frightened away," I tell him.

"The birth of May, mortal girl. That is what you should fear," he answers, and rides away in a cloud of dust.

Crows alight in the willows. I move by them like a queen passing her subjects, and they flutter their dark wings and caw at me. Their cries swell, shaking the trees like the cries of the damned.

ACT IV

Midnight

By the pricking of my thumbs,
Something wicked this way comes.
—MACBETH

CHAPTER FORTY

IN MAY, THE ANNUAL EXHIBITION AT THE ROYAL ACADEMY of Arts will signal the traditional start of the London season. Parliament will commence, and hordes of families will begin their assault on our fair city for parties and teas, concerts, derbies, and entertainments of all sorts. But the unofficial start of these festivities is Lady Markham's ball in honor of Felicity's debut. For the occasion, Lady Markham has let a magnificent hall in the West End, which has been outfitted lavishly in a style that would do justice to a sultan. It is an unspoken sport, holding these parties, and each hostess is in fierce competition with the others to host the most gilded, lavish affair of all. Lady Markham means to set the bar quite high.

Enormous palm trees line the sides of the hall's ballroom. Tables have been set with white linens and silver that glitters like a pirate's treasure. An orchestra plays discreetly behind a tall, red screen painted with Chinese dragons. And all sorts of entertainments are provided: A turbaned fire-breather with a face painted as blue as Krishna's blows a fat orange plume of flame from his pursed lips, and the guests gasp in delight. Three entwined ladies of Siam in beaded gowns and slippered feet perform a slow, elaborate dance. They seem to be one body with many slithering arms. Gentlemen gather around the dancers, mesmerized by their sinewy charms.

"How vulgar," my chaperone, Mrs. Tuttle, says. Grandmama has paid a pretty price for her services this evening, and I am finding Mrs. Tuttle to be the worst sort of chaperone one could hope for—punctual, sharp, and overly attentive.

"I rather like them," I say. "In fact, I think I shall learn to dance just like that. Perhaps tonight."

"You'll do nothing of the kind, Miss Doyle," she says as if that settles the matter, when it settles nothing.

"I shall do as I like, Mrs. Tuttle," I say sweetly. Discreetly, I wave my hand at her skirts and they whoosh up, exposing her petticoats and pantalets.

With a gasp, she pushes down the front of her dress, and the back rises. "Oh, dear!" She reaches behind her and the front billows again. "Gracious! It . . . I . . . Will you excuse me, please?"

Mrs. Tuttle rushes for the ladies' dressing room, holding fast to her mischievous skirts.

"I eagerly await your return," I murmur after her.

"Gemma!"

Felicity's here with a chaperone, a tall reed of a lady with a beak of a nose. "Isn't it marvelous? Have you seen the fire-breather? I'm so glad my party shall be the talk of the season. I don't possibly see how anyone can compete with this!"

"It's wonderful, Fee. Truly, it is."

"At least my inheritance is secure now," she whispers. "Father and Lady Markham have become fast friends this evening. She's even been civil to my mother."

She takes my arm and we promenade, her chaperone—a Frenchwoman named Madame Lumière—three paces behind us.

"Mother insisted on paying for a chaperone tonight," Felicity whispers. "She believes it will make us look more important."

As we walk, the men survey us as if we're lands that might be won, either by agreement or in battle. The room buzzes with talk of the hunt and Parliament, horses and estates, but their eyes never stray too far from us. There are bargains to be struck, seeds to be planted. And I wonder, if women were not daughters and wives, mothers and young ladies, prospects or spinsters, if we were not seen through the eyes of others, would we exist at all?

"We might pass the time with cake," Madame Lumière suggests.

I do not want to *pass* the time. I want to grab hold of it and leave my mark upon the world.

"Oh, poor Madame Lumière. Do have some. Miss Doyle and I shall wait here for your return," Felicity says, giving one of her brightest smiles. Madame Lumière promises to return *tout de suite*. The moment she is out of our sight, we walk quickly away so that we might explore the wonders of the ball unfettered.

"Have you anyone lovely to dance with?" I ask, noting Felicity's dance card.

"They're all horrors! Old Mr. Carrington, who smells of whiskey. An American who actually asked if my family owned any land. And several more suitors, not a one of whom I would save from drowning, much less consent to marry. And there's

Horace, of course." Felicity growls low. "He follows me about like a mournful puppy."

"You've thoroughly bewitched him," I say, laughing.

"Simon said to be charming, and so I have charmed my way through every appointment with Lady Markham and her son, but I don't think I can bear much more of his attention."

"You'd best prepare, for here he comes now."

I nod toward the crowd of three hundred people, where Horace Markham pushes his way toward us, raising his hand like a man trying to secure a hansom. He's tall and slender, aged twenty-three, according to Felicity. His face is boyish and given to frequent blushing. I can tell at a glance from the way he carries himself—slightly stooped forward, a little embarrassed—that he hasn't the courage or, frankly, the devil it would take to keep pace with Felicity.

"Oh, dear," I say under my breath.

"Indeed," Felicity shoots back.

"Miss Worthington," Horace says, out of breath. A curly lock breaks free and sticks to the sheen on his high forehead. "Here we are again, it would seem."

"Yes, so it would." Fee glances up at Horace through downcast eyes. A coy smile plays at her lips. It's no wonder the poor boy is besotted.

"I believe the polka is next. Would you care to join me for it?" he asks, and it sounds like begging.

"Mr. Markham, that's very kind, but we've already had so many dances that I am afraid of what people will say," Fee says, playing proper, and it is all I can do not to laugh.

"Let them talk." Horace straightens his waistcoat as if preparing for a duel to defend his family's honor.

"Gracious," I mutter.

Felicity's sidelong glance says, *You've no idea.* Lady Denby sits at a table eating cake. She looks on with disapproval and it doesn't escape Felicity's notice.

"How very brave you are, Mr. Markham," Fee says, allowing Horace to squire her right past Lady Denby to the dance floor.

"I don't suppose there is still room on your dance card for one more?"

I turn to see Simon Middleton smiling at me. With his white tie and tails and that wicked twinkle in his eyes, he is ever so handsome.

"I was to dance with a Mr. Whitford." I demur.

Simon nods. "Ah, old man Whitford. Not only does he walk with the aid of a cane, but his memory is rather faulty. Chances are he's forgotten you, I'm sorry to say, and if he hasn't, we could have our dance and be back here again before he's hobbled to your side."

I laugh, glad for his delicious wit. "In that case, I accept."

We glide into the swell of dancers, brushing past Tom, who is intent on charming his dance partner: "Dr. Smith and I cured the poor man of his delusions, though I daresay it was my insight into the case that started it all. . . ."

"Was it really?" she says, drinking his story in, and it is all I can do not to give Tom the ears of a rabbit.

Mrs. Tuttle has returned from the ladies' dressing room. She holds two glasses of lemonade. She sees me dancing with Simon, a look of pure horror on her face, for it is her duty to see that every gentleman who might court me passes muster. She holds the keys to the gate. But she has been relieved of duty whether she knows it or not. *No, Mrs. Tuttle. You want to*

stay there. *I am fine here in Simon's arms. I need no tending. Please,
enjoy your lemonade.* Blinking and confused, Mrs. Tuttle turns
around and drinks from both glasses of lemonade.

"I say, your chaperone is a bit wobbly. Is she a drinking
woman?" Simon asks.

"Only lemonade," I answer.

Simon gives me a flirtatious smile. "I daresay there is something changed in you."

"Is there?"

"Mmmm. I cannot say what it is. Miss Doyle and her secrets." He appraises my form with a sweeping glance that is far
too bold and, I must confess, very thrilling. "But you are quite
lovely this evening."

"Is your Miss Fairchild here tonight?"

"She is indeed," he answers, and I do not need the power of
the realms to feel the warmth in his answer.

I'm filled with a sudden regret for having refused him. He is
handsome and merry. He thought me beautiful. What if I do
not find anyone like him ever again?

What if I could have him again?

"Miss Fairchild is an American. I suppose she'll want to go
home as soon as the season is over," I say, leaning in just a bit
closer to Simon.

"Perhaps so, though she claims to find England agreeable."
Simon's hand presses a bit more firmly at the base of my spine.
"And what are your plans, Miss Doyle? Have you set your
sights on anyone special?"

I think of Kartik and turn that thought out of my mind before it can taint my mood. "None."

Simon's thumb moves ever so slightly against my dress. My

back tingles where it touches. "That is welcome news," he purrs.

The dance ends, and I excuse myself for the ladies' dressing room so that I might allow the flush on my cheeks to cool. Ladies' maids stand at the ready, but I've no need. Where my hair has gone limp, I put it to rights with a wave of my hand. I decide I don't care for the gloves I've donned, so, away from prying eyes, I give myself a different pair. I smile at my handiwork.

"Good evening, Miss Doyle." I turn to see Lucy Fairchild beside me.

"Miss Fairchild," I say.

She smiles at me with great warmth. "It's a splendid ball, isn't it? How happy you must be for your friend Miss Worthington."

"Yes," I say, smiling back. "I am."

"I watched you dance. You are very graceful," she says, and I blush, thinking of Simon's hand at my back, the way I leaned into him.

"Thank you," I say. "Though my grace is very much in question, and I'm sure Si—Mr. Middleton much prefers dancing with you."

We smile uncomfortably at one another in the mirror. She pinches her cheeks for color though there's no need. She's lovely.

"Well . . . ," I say, rising to go.

"Yes. Do enjoy the ball," Lucy Fairchild says with sincerity.

"And you as well."

A gong sounds and the guests are called to the ballroom. Lord Markham staggers to the center of the floor. He's had a bit to drink, and the red of his nose shows it.

"Ladies and gentlemen, our esteemed guests," Lord Markham says, slurring his words a bit, "my dear wife has arranged a most stirring entertainment for this evening. The Whirling Dervishes of Konya have come to us as refugees from the Ottoman Empire, which has of late been the site of an unspeakable massacre of the Armenian people by the Sultan's army. Such atrocities cannot stand! We must—"

Throats are cleared. Women fan themselves. Lady Markham looks at her husband beseechingly, that he might talk no more of politics, and he nods, cowed.

"I present to you the Dervishes of Konya."

Eight men in very tall hats take the floor. The gleaming of the crystal chandeliers makes the white of their long, priestly robes shine. The music is hypnotic. The dancers bow to one another and slowly they begin their revolutions. The music swells, the tempo rises, and the dancers' long skirts float out like bells.

The music speeds along with a passion that stirs my blood. The dervishes turn in ecstasy, their palms raised toward heaven as if they could hold God briefly on their fingers but only if they do not stop turning.

The guests watch in awe, caught up in the frenzy of the Dervishes' spinning. To my right, I see Mr. Fowlson dressed in servant garb, a tray in his hand. He's not watching the dancers; he's watching my brother. Seconds later, he exits the room. I'll not let him go tonight. I intend to shadow his every move. He'll let my brother be or feel my wrath.

He walks upstairs and knocks on the door to the gentlemen's parlor. I dart behind an enormous potted fern to spy. A moment later, Lord Denby appears.

"Yes, Fowlson?"

"'E's watchin' the dance, sir," Fowlson reports. "I'm keepin' my eye on 'im, jus' like you asked."

Lord Denby pats Fowlson's shoulder. "Good man."

"I wondered, sir, if I might 'ave a word."

Lord Denby loses his smile. "It's not really the time or the place, old chap."

"Yes, sir, forgive me, but it never seems to be, and I was wondrin' when I migh' advance in the Rakshana like we talked about. I 'ave some thoughts. . . ."

Lord Denby sticks his cigar into his mouth. "All in good time."

"Just as you say, sir," Fowlson answers, his head down.

"We need more fine soldiers like you, Mr. Fowlson," Lord Denby crows. "Now, do keep to your duties, won't you?"

"Yes, sir," Fowlson says. He turns on his heel and strides back to the ballroom, where he might keep watch over my brother.

Lord Denby is of the Rakshana. The full weight of it hits my stomach like a fist. All this time. I've been in his home. I've kissed his son. Simon. Anger, hot and unforgiving, rises in me. He will answer for this, for my brother.

I don't bother to knock. I open the door and step into the parlor, where only the men sit, smoking their pipes and cigars. The hard glint of their eyes makes it clear that I am a trespasser here. Swallowing hard, I march through the clusters of silently outraged men and straight up to Lord Denby. He puts on a false smile.

"Why, Miss Doyle! I'm afraid this is a room for gentlemen only. If you're lost, perhaps I could escort—"

"Lord Denby, I must speak with you," I whisper.

"I'm afraid I'm wanted at the tables, my dear," he answers.

You're wanted under my boot, you miserable cur. I force a smile that is pure sugar and lower my voice. "It is rather urgent. I'm sure these kind gentlemen will wait. Or should I see if Mr. Fowlson is more receptive to my request?"

"Gentlemen," he says, turning to the men in his circle, "do spare me a moment. You know how ladies can be when they are insistent." The gentlemen chuckle at my expense, and it is all I can do not to inflict a painful rash on every one of them.

Lord Denby ushers me through a door into a private library. Ordinarily, I would be comforted by the sight of so many lovely books, but I'm far too angry for comfort tonight, and I suspect the books are rather like the people here—unread and purely decorative.

Lord Denby takes a seat in an overstuffed leather chair beside a chess table and blows out a stream of heavy smoke that makes me cough. "You wished to speak with me, Miss Doyle?"

"I know who you are, Lord Denby. I know you are of the Rakshana, and I know you're courting my brother."

He turns his attention to the chessboard, moving pieces for himself and an imaginary opponent. "What of it?"

"I want you to leave my brother alone, please."

"My dear, I'm afraid that is quite out of my hands."

"Who ranks higher than you? Tell me and I shall go to—"

"The Rakshana's ranks are filled by some of the most important and influential men in the world—heads of state and captains of industry. But that isn't what I meant. I meant that the decision rests in *your* hands, dear lady," he says through a puff of smoke. His hand hovers over a piece for a split second before attacking and capturing a pawn in his way and moving swiftly across the board. "You only need to give us the magic and control of the realms, and your brother will be quite safe, I assure you. In fact, he'll be a great man, a peer, even. He'll be well looked after. You *all* shall. Why, I'm sure Lady Denby would host a ball for your debut that would put all the others to shame. The Queen herself would attend."

"Do you think I've come to discuss parties? That I'm a child who can be won over with a new pony? Have you no honor, sir?" I take a deep breath. "The Rakshana was meant to protect the realms and the Order. It was a venerable profession. Now you're fighting against us. You would bully me and try to corrupt my brother. What have you become?"

Lord Denby knocks off his imaginary opponent's rook and moves his bishop into position. "The times have changed, Miss Doyle. Gone are the days when a nobleman served as patron to all who worked his land. The Rakshana must change, as well—become less the chivalrous handshake of brotherhood and more the profitable fist of industry. Can you imagine how great our reach would be if we were to have power such as yours at our control? Think like an Englishwoman, Miss Doyle! What could this power do for the empire, for the future sons of England?"

"You're forgetting: We are not all English, and we are not all men," I say, insinuating myself into his chess game. I move a pawn forward, taking his bishop unawares. "What of Amar and Kartik and others like them? What of my sex—or of men of Mr. Fowlson's station? Will any of us sit at your table?"

"Some rule; others are meant to be subjects." His knight takes my queen, putting my king in danger. "What do you say, Miss Doyle? Your whole future could be arranged to your liking. Everything you could possibly want. Your pick of beaux—my son, perhaps."

An icy cold presses its thumbs against my ribs. "Did you arrange for Simon and me to meet? Was that all part of your plan?"

"Let us call it a happy coincidence." Lord Denby attacks my king. "Checkmate, my dear. It's time I returned to the tables and you to the dance." He stamps out the last of his cigar. Its cloying smoke lingers as he strides to the door. "Do consider our offer. It is the last time it will be presented. I am sure you'll do what is in our best interests—and yours."

I want to throw his fading cigar after him. I want to cry. I press my fingers to my eyes to keep the tears at bay. I've been so dreadfully stupid to underestimate the Rakshana's reach—and to trust Simon Middleton. He never cared for me. He played me like a pawn, and I took the fall willingly.

Well, I won't be unguarded anymore.

"Miss Doyle!" Mrs. Tuttle scurries toward me with a scowl when I reach the ballroom. "Miss Doyle, you mustn't run off like that again. It isn't proper. It is my duty to see to it that you are right at all times—"

"Oh, do shut it," I growl.

Before she can object, I weave my spell. "You're thirsty, Mrs. Tuttle. Thirstier than you've ever been in your life. Do try the lemonade and leave me in peace."

"I should like some lemonade now," she says, putting a fluttering hand to her throat. "Dear me, I'm parched. I must have something to drink."

I leave her and watch the ball from behind a pillar. I'm alone, full of magic and hate, the two twinning into a new force.

Nearby, Lady Denby gossips with Lady Markham and several other important women.

"I have grown very fond of her in these few weeks, as if she were my own daughter," Lady Denby crows.

"She will make a most suitable match for him," another lady agrees.

Lady Denby nods. "Simon has not always shown good judgment in such matters. And we have been misled before. But Miss Fairchild is the best sort of young lady—well-bred, agreeable, without flaw, and of good standing."

An ample matron, beaded and bejeweled within an inch of her life, hides behind her fan. "Lady Markham, have you decided on the other matter, of young Miss Worthington?"

"I have," she sniffs. "I've spoken to the admiral tonight, and he is agreed: Miss Worthington shall come to stay with me, where I might shepherd her season; her mother will not have a say in the matter."

Lady Denby pats Lady Markham's hand. "That is as it should be. Mrs. Worthington must pay for her disgrace, and her daughter is far too bold and tempestuous a creature. You'll take the girl under your wing and mold her into the sort of lady acceptable to all."

"Indeed," Lady Markham says. "I feel it is my duty, as her mother has failed in that regard." The women cast glances toward Mrs. Worthington, who dances with a man half her age. "And let's not forget the young Miss Worthington's substantial inheritance. If brought to heel, she would make a valuable wife for any man."

"Perhaps your Horace," Lady Denby coos.

"Perhaps," Lady Markham says.

I imagine Felicity a cosseted debutante in Lady Markham's parlor instead of a free spirit in a Paris garret, as she desires. She'll be pitied and powerless, the very qualities she hates most. It will never happen; I'll see to it if I must.

"Ah, here is our Miss Fairchild now," Lady Denby announces.

Simon delivers Miss Fairchild to his mother, and she fawns over the girl while he attends to her in a courtly fashion. I burn with a terrible longing. For as much as I claim to hate them, I envy the way in which they all seem to fit one another so perfectly, the ease of their careful little lives. Cecily was right: Some people don't belong. And I am one of them.

Demon beasts. That's what they are. Ann's words come back to me: *But they are the ones who rule.* Not tonight, they shan't, for the power of the realms flames within me, and I'll not temper it. *Don't go up against me, mates. I will win.* And I want to win. I want to win at something.

I close my eyes, and when I open them, Simon has broken away from his mother, Miss Fairchild, and all the acolytes. He strides toward me with a hungry look and extends his gloved hand, palm up, though it feels as tense as a fist. His jaw is determined, his voice raw as he says, simply, "Dance with me, Gemma."

He has called me by my first name, and it sends a shock through those near enough to hear it. Mrs. Tuttle looks as if she might drop her lemonade. For a moment, I do not know what to say. I should feel remorse. Instead, a terrible satisfaction flows through, exciting me. I have won. And winning, however cheaply bought, is thrilling.

"Dance with me, Gemma," Simon says again, more loudly

and insistently. It gains the attention of the other guests. Many of the dancers have slowed, watching the scene. There is whispering. Lady Denby's mouth has fallen open in disbelief.

Lord Denby has taken notice now. His eyes meet mine, and there's no mistaking my intent. *Corrupt my brother, will you? I'll see you in hell first, sir.*

The smile I give Simon is like a fallen angel's. He seizes my wrist tightly, and half drags me to the dance floor. He's making a spectacle of himself. Roughly, he pulls me into waltzing position. The music begins anew, and Simon and I twirl around the floor. There is a heat between us that does not go unnoticed by the others. With each push of his hand against the small of my back, it feels as if Simon wants to eat me alive. I have brought about this affection in him. Let everyone see how powerful I am. Let them think me a beauty, nakedly desired by an important gentleman. And let Lord and Lady Denby be disgraced in the bargain. I cannot keep the satisfied smile from my lips. I am in command and it is intoxicating. On the edge of the dance floor, Lord Denby watches, fuming. He was wrong to doubt me.

An older gentleman taps Simon on the shoulder to signal his intention to break in, but Simon pulls me closer. We dance on, gathering more and more attention, and when it is enough—when *I* decide it's enough and the point has been made—I bring it to an end. *Time to stop, Simon. Say good night, sweet prince.*

Blinking, Simon comes back to himself, utterly perplexed to find me in his arms.

"Thank you for the dance, Mr. Middleton," I say, stepping away.

A faint confused smile appears on his lips. "It was my pleasure." At once, he searches for Lucy in the crowd.

Gossip spreads like contagion. I'm whispered about, glared at from behind fans as I leave the floor.

The magic crashes over me in a wave. I'm suffocating with it. It comes off me like a sickness, infecting all who come into contact with me, liberating their hidden desires. A gentleman gives me a helpful arm, and in that gesture he is seized. He turns to the older gentleman sitting near.

"What did you say to me earlier, Thompson? You'll answer for that."

The older man's mouth tightens. "Fenton, have you gone mad?"

"Is it madness to say that I will not be blackmailed for my debts to you any longer? You do not own me." He lays a hand on old Thompson, and just like that, the magic spreads.

The old man rises to his feet. "Here now, chap, I daresay if it weren't for my charity, your standing would be a shambles and your family in the workhouse."

Quiet, quiet, I think. *Forget. To your brandy and cigars.* They take up their glasses again. What has been said is forgotten, but the bitter rancor remains, and they eye each other warily.

I careen into a spinster chaperone with her charge, and I feel the pain in her heart. The aching desire she has for her married employer, a Mr. Beadle.

"He does not know," she says in a sudden rush. "I must tell him. I must confess my fondest affections for him at once." And it is all I can do to grab hold of her hands until the feeling is replaced by the one I put in its stead.

"Shall we have cake?" she says to her confused charge. "I have a sudden need for cake."

A prickly sweat rises upon my brow. The magic burns in my veins.

Lord Denby sidles up to me. His face is florid; his eyes burn. "You're playing a very dangerous game, Miss Doyle."

"Have you not heard, sir? I am a very dangerous girl."

"You've no idea what we can do to you," he says evenly, but his eyes flash.

I whisper low in his ear. "No, sir. You've no idea what *I* can do to *you*."

Fear shows itself briefly in his eyes, and I know I have won this round.

"Let my brother be or face the consequences," I warn.

"Thank heavens I've found you!" Felicity trills. "Good evening, Lord Denby. Would you mind awfully if I borrowed Miss Doyle?"

Lord Denby is all smiles. "Not in the slightest, my dear."

"Where have you been? You must save me," Felicity insists, linking her arm tightly through mine.

"From what?"

"Horace Markham," she says with a laugh. I glance over her shoulder and see Horace looking after her. He holds fast to her fan as if it were Felicity herself. "The way he moons over me," she says, making a face. "Hideous."

I laugh, happy to be in Fee's world, where everything from a lovesick suitor to the choosing of a hat is ripe for drama. "You shouldn't be so charming," I tease.

"Well," she says, tossing her head, "I can't help that, now, can I?"

Felicity and I take refuge on a terrace overlooking the street. The drivers have gathered in a huddle, keeping one another company. One tells a joke, and I can see by the way the others lean in that it is naughty. They fall into laughter but quickly disperse at the sight of one of the guests. Hats are donned, spines are stiffened as Lucy Fairchild walks toward her carriage. Simon keeps pace, but Lucy's chaperone shuts him out. The driver helps the women into the carriage and it pulls away from the curb, leaving Simon behind.

"How delicious!" Felicity exclaims. "Scandal! At my ball—and not involving *moi*. Astonishing!"

"Yes, it is rather astonishing that there are events which have nothing at all to do with you, isn't it?" I quip.

Felicity puts her hands on her hips, a wicked smile on her lips. "I was to offer you lemonade, but now, I shall only satisfy myself. You may watch me enjoy it and suffer."

She saunters off and I let the cool night air wash over me. Down below, Lord Denby consoles his son. They exchange words I cannot hear. Lord Denby prevails, and he and Simon return to the ball.

As they pass, Lord Denby sees me on the terrace. He stares daggers at me, and I put my fingers to my mouth and blow him a kiss.

⌁⌁⌁⌁

I spend the day after the ball, Sunday, with my family before returning to Spence. The seamstress has come to fit my gown to me and make minor adjustments. I stand before the mirror in my half-finished gown whilst she takes in a pinch here, adds a ruffle there. Grandmama hovers nearby, barking instructions to the woman, fretting over every little detail. I pay her no mind, for the girl staring back at me from the mirror is starting to become her own woman. I can't say exactly what it is; it's not something that can be named. I only know that she's there, emerging from me like a sculpture from marble, and I'm most anxious to meet her.

"You look like your mother. I'm sure she would have wanted to be here for this," Grandmama says, and the moment is ruined utterly. Whatever was struggling from the marble of me is gone.

You'll not mention my mother again, I think, closing my eyes. *Tell me how beautiful I look. Tell me how happy we are. Tell me I shall be someone, and there's nothing but blue-sky days ahead.*

When I open my eyes, Grandmama smiles at my reflection. "Dear me, aren't you a vision in that dress?"

"The picture of loveliness," the seamstress chimes in.

There. That's so much better.

✦✦✦✦

"Grandmama tells me you'll be the loveliest girl in London for your debut," Father says when I join him in his study. He's sorting through drawers as if looking for something.

"Can I be of help?" I ask.

"Hmmm? Oh. No, pet," he answers, distracted. "Just cleaning out a few things. I must ask you something unpleasant, however."

"What is it?" I take a seat and Father does the same.

"I heard Simon Middleton was far too familiar with you last night at the ball." Father's eyes flash.

"He wasn't," I say, attempting a laugh.

"I hear that Miss Fairchild refuses to admit him," he adds, and I feel a twinge of remorse, which I push away.

"Perhaps Miss Fairchild wasn't a proper match."

"Still . . ." Father trails off into a coughing fit. His face is red, and he wheezes for a full minute before settling into easier breathing. "London air. Too much soot."

"Yes," I say, uneasily. He looks tired. Unwell. And suddenly, I've the urge to be with him, to sit beside him like a child and let him pat my head.

"You say Simon Middleton has nothing to answer for?" Father presses.

"No, nothing," I say, and mean it.

"Well, then." Father nods. He turns back to his search, and I know I've been dismissed.

"Father, shall we play a game of chess?"

He riffles through papers and looks behind books. "I've no mind for chess just now. Why don't you see if your grandmother wants to go for a walk?"

"I could help you look for whatever it is you've lost. I could—"

He waves me away. "No, pet. I'm in need of my solitude."

"But I shall leave tomorrow," I complain. "And then it shall be my season. And then . . ."

"Now, let's not have tears, shall we?" Father chides. He opens a drawer, and I see the brown bottle lying there. I know at once it's laudanum. My heart sinks.

I take his hand, and I can feel his sadness intruding. "We'll get rid of it, then, won't we?" I say aloud.

Before Father can answer, I feed him happiness like an opiate, till the furrows of his brow smooth and he's smiling.

"Ah, here's what I was looking for. Gemma, pet, would you put this in the rubbish?" he asks.

Tears prick at my eyes. "Yes, Father. Of course. Straightaway."

I kiss him on the cheek and he wraps his arms around me, and for the first time ever, I let go before he does.

At supper, Tom is like an expectant father whose nerves have the better of him. His leg jiggles so throughout the meal that my teeth rattle from it, and once, he kicks me quite by accident.

"Will you settle yourself, please?" I ask, rubbing my shin.

Father looks up from his supper. "Thomas, what is the matter?"

My brother moves his food about his plate, not eating any of it. "I was to have gone to my gentlemen's club this evening, but I've had no word from them."

"None at all?" I ask, savoring the victory along with my potatoes.

"It's as if I no longer exist," Tom grumbles.

"That isn't very sporting," Father says between bites of his quail, and I'm glad to see him eating.

"Yes, very bad form." Grandmama tuts.

"Perhaps you should go to the Hippocrates tonight," I suggest. "You know you've a standing invitation to join them."

"An excellent idea," Father agrees.

Tom pushes his peas to the side of his plate. "Perhaps I will," he says. "If only to get out for a bit."

I'm so cheered by this news that I eat two pieces of cake for dessert. When Grandmama frets that such an appetite will mean bringing back the seamstress, I laugh, and once I put the idea into her head, she laughs, too, and soon, we're all laughing while the servants look on as if we're barking mad. But I don't care. I have what I want. I have it, and it will not be taken from me. Not by Lord Denby or anyone.

CHAPTER FORTY-ONE

DR. VAN RIPPLE'S CALLING CARD LISTS AN ADDRESS IN a shabby little district that reminds me of a comfortable chair in need of an upholsterer. The row houses are not particularly well kept. They have no aspirations beyond providing lodging to their inhabitants.

"Charming," Felicity says as we make our way down a narrow, poorly lit street.

"It got you out of the house, didn't it?" I say. Children run past us. They play in the dark, their mothers too tired to care.

"Well, my mother still believes that I'm there, sitting at the piano. That was an impressive trick, Gemma. Tell me, do your powers detect Dr. Van Ripple's lodging house yet?"

"For that we only require our eyes and direction," I reply.

We pass a pub that spills out working folk. Some are stooped with age; others can't be older than eleven or twelve. Mothers cradle babes to their bosoms. A man stands on a crate just outside the pub. He speaks with vigor and conviction, holding his audience in thrall.

"Should we work for the sweater fourteen hours a day for a pittance? We should do like the match girls done at Bryant and May, and our brothers on the docks!"

There are mumbles of encouragement and of dissent.

"They'll starve 'oos," a man with hollows under his cheeks shouts. "We'll 'ave nuffin'."

"We already 'ave nuffin'—it's the only fing I don't want more of!" a lady calls and everyone laughs.

"A strike! Support our sisters o' the Beardon factory. Take courage from their stand, brothers and sisters. Fair pay, fair hours, a fair London!"

A cheer goes up. The crowd applauds. It draws the attention of a constable.

"Here now," he says. "What's this about?"

The man steps off the crate, holding out his hat. "Evenin', guv'nah. We're collectin' for the poor. Spare us a copper?"

"I'll spare you a room for the night—in Newgate."

"Can't throw us in jail for assemblin'," the man says.

"The law can do what it bloody well likes!" the constable says, waving his nightstick. He disperses the crowd but he cannot disband their convictions; the people talk in excited whispers still.

"'Ere now," a lady holding a baby chides. "You sum o' them fancy ladies come slummin'?"

"Certainly not," Felicity replies, sounding every bit like the sort who would hire a carriage with friends to gawk at the poor.

"Well, you can clear off. We won't be your entertainment fo' th'evening. No' for the likes of you."

"Have a care—"

I take Fee's arm. "Not a word."

We turn the corner and there it is. We've invented a tale to gain entry, but the tired landlady knows not to ask questions of her lodgers' lady callers, lest she discover her suspicions are ugly truths. She knocks twice on the magician's door and wearily announces us.

Dr. Van Ripple's eyes widen in surprise. He wears a worn-out dressing robe over his trousers. "Come in, come in. Dear me, I wasn't expecting callers this evening."

He closes the door and bids us have a seat. An enormous board in a gilded frame looms in the corner. It shows a painting of a much younger Dr. Van Ripple in a turban. His fingers point toward a dazed woman who would appear to be under his spell. The board reads *Doctor Theodore Van Ripple, Master Illusionist! Feats of magic that must be seen to be believed!*

On one wall hangs a portrait of an older woman with dark hair and eyes like Dr. Van Ripple's. Beside the portrait is a hair wreath, made to honor the dead, the hair cut and framed as a reminder of the loved one. This one is a coiled braid of faded gray and brown.

"My mother," he says, catching me staring. "Even the best illusionist cannot cheat death."

Dr. Van Ripple offers us a seat on a shabby settee covered in an old paisley shawl. I sit on something hard—a book, *The Picture of Dorian Gray* by Oscar Wilde.

"Ah, so that is where it went! I'd been wondering," Dr. Van Ripple exclaims, seizing it.

Felicity makes a face. "Mr. Wilde was tried for indecency. Papa says he is a thoroughly immoral man."

"It is Queensberry and men like him who are 'indecent,'" Dr. Van Ripple says, referring to the man who brought the charges against Mr. Wilde.

"Why do you say such, sir?" Felicity presses.

Dr. Van Ripple bends the flower in his buttonhole toward his nose and inhales deeply. "True affection and love have a purity which shall always prevail over bigotry."

"We have not come here to speak of Mr. Wilde's misfortunes," Felicity says hastily, and far too rudely, but Dr. Van Ripple shows no sign of being affronted by her brashness.

"Indeed. To what do I owe this unexpected visit?"

"We have need of your services," I say.

"Ah. I am sorry to disappoint you. But I am recently retired as an illusionist. I've nothing to offer but old tricks from an old man. That is not what the people want these days. They want vulgar thrills," he grouses. "Like this Houdini chap, escaping from chains and boxes. It is cheap, music hall entertainment. In my day, I played the best theaters, from Vienna to St. Petersburg, from Paris to New York. But now, the days of magic are ending, I fear. The new power in the world is industry. Industry and greed." He takes a deep breath and lets it out in a sigh. "But you did not come to listen to tales of the glory days of an old magician, my dears. And so I would bid you a good night."

"We would pay, of course," I say.

Dr. Van Ripple's eyes glimmer with interest. "Ah. Yes. Well. I could, perhaps, be convinced to aid ladies in need for a modest sum."

"How modest?" Felicity asks.

"Miss Worthington," I say through a forced smile. "I am quite sure Dr. Van Ripple will treat us fairly. We should hate to offend."

"No offense taken," the old man says. "Now, how might an

old magician be of assistance to two such lovely young ladies?" he asks, all smiles.

"We wondered if you might tell us more about Wilhelmina Wyatt," I say.

Dr. Van Ripple frowns. "I don't see how I can be of help in that regard."

"I'm sure you can be of great help," I say sweetly. I hold up my coin purse, and Dr. Van Ripple's lips curl into a smile once more.

We agree upon a fee, and though it is more than I wished to pay, it is the only way the bargain shall be struck. Dr. Van Ripple pockets the coins at once. I half expect him to test their worth between his teeth.

"Did Miss Wyatt have a dagger in her possession?" Felicity blurts out, much to my chagrin.

"Not that I recall. And certainly one would recall such a weapon." Dr. Van Ripple strokes his beard, thinking.

"Does the phrase 'The key holds the truth' mean anything to you?" I ask.

Dr. Van Ripple purses his lips, thinks some more. "I'm afraid not."

"Did she ever make mention of a key—any key that was special to her?" Felicity presses.

"No, no," the doctor answers.

"Did she leave anything behind?" I ask, but my hopes are fading fast.

"A few of her dresses remained at the hall, and those I sold. I kept only one of her possessions—the slate."

"Might we see it?" I plead.

Dr. Van Ripple rifles through a cupboard and comes back

with the slate I've seen in my dreams and visions, and my excitement grows. The slate is of a good size, perhaps a foot tall by a foot wide, and it rests upon a wooden base. My fingers trace over the board, feeling the marks grooved into it from use.

"May we purchase this from you?" I ask, emboldened.

He shakes his head. "Dear me. It has such sentimental value that I couldn't possibly—"

"How much?" Felicity interrupts.

"Perhaps five pounds?" he suggests.

"Five pounds!" Felicity gasps.

"Four?" he counters.

It doesn't matter whether it's four or five; we haven't got it. Or do we? I wave my hand over my coin purse. I know I shall hate myself for this later, but that is later.

"Here you are, sir," I say, opening my purse and counting out four pounds to Fee's astonishment. She takes the slate from the magician.

"Dr. Van Ripple," I say, "you said that Wilhelmina had been in contact with a sister, a friend, whom she no longer trusted. Are you certain you can't recall her name?"

He shakes his head. "As I said, I was never introduced. The lady never came round, and as far as I know, she did not attend our shows. I only know that Wilhelmina feared her, and Mina did not fear much."

A cold shiver speeds up my spine.

"Thank you for your time, Dr. Van Ripple," I say, and he sees us out. At the door, he reaches behind Felicity's ear and produces a perfect red rose, which he hands to her. "I understand they are Mr. Wilde's favorite."

"I will not have it, then," Felicity says rudely.

"Judge not, lest ye be judged, my dear," Dr. Van Ripple says with a sad smile, and Fee's cheeks burn.

"However did you do that?" I ask him, for I find the trick merry even if Fee doesn't.

"In truth, it is the simplest act in the world. The trick works because you wish it to. You must remember, my dear lady, the most important rule of any successful illusion: First, the people must want to believe in it."

<center>~~~~~~</center>

"I cannot believe he asked five pounds for this." Felicity clucks as we cloak ourselves in the gloom of London's streets again.

"Well, let's hope he spends it quickly before it disappears," I say.

Under the narrow glow of a streetlamp, we examine the slate, turning it this way and that, but there's nothing unusual about it that we can see.

"Perhaps words will etch themselves as we watch," Felicity says.

It's ridiculous, but we watch it anyway. Absolutely nothing happens.

I sigh. "We've bought ourselves a useless slate."

"But it's a clean slate," Felicity quips, and I can't even be troubled to give her a roll of my eyes.

On our way to the London underground, we pass the striking ladies from Beardon's Bonnets Factory. Their faces are long; they lean into one another, resting their protest signs against their skirts whilst passersby pay no attention to their plight or, at the worst, heckle them, calling them the most appalling names.

"Spare a copper for our cause?" the girl with the coin cup asks, her voice weary.

"I can spare more than that," I say. I reach into my purse and give her what real coins I have, and then I press my hand to hers and whisper, "Don't give up," watching the magic spark in her eyes.

"The tragedy of the Beardon's Bonnet Factory!" she shouts, a fire catching. "Six souls murdered for profit! Will you let it stand, sir? Will you look away, m'um?"

Her sisters-in-arms raise their placards again. "Fair wages, fair treatment!" they call. "Justice!"

Their voices swell into a chorus that thunders through the dark London streets until it can no longer be ignored.

CHAPTER FORTY-TWO

WE'VE ONLY JUST ARRIVED BACK AT SPENCE AND PUT OUR suitcases in our rooms when Mrs. Nightwing comes brandishing an invitation. "There is to be a birthday party in honor of Miss Bradshaw's cousin Mr. Wharton at Balmoral Spring," Mrs. Nightwing says, rolling the estate's name on her tongue as if it were wine gone to vinegar.

"No doubt they think we can do them some favor in society," Felicity mutters for my ears only.

"The party is tomorrow noon, though the invitation only arrived two days ago," Mrs. Nightwing says, and I hear her add under her breath, "Ghastly manners.

"I know you have missed Miss Bradshaw's company," she continues. "Would you care to attend?"

"Oh, yes, please!" Felicity exclaims.

"Very well. You must be dressed and ready to leave first thing in the morning," she says, and we promise to do so.

In the evening, Felicity sits with the other girls, basking in the praise they heap upon her ball. "And did you adore the Dervishes?" she asks, eyes bright.

"Very nice. And for such a long program it wasn't too tiring," Cecily says, managing to put a slap in the compliment as is her skill.

"Mother will only allow me a tea," Elizabeth says, pouting. "I'll not be remembered at all."

I leave them and sequester myself in my room to examine Wilhelmina Wyatt's slate. I turn it over in my hands, scrutinize the tiny nicks as if I might read its history of words there. I put my ear to it in hopes it might whisper its secrets. I even summon a bit of magic, instructing it to reveal all, as if I, myself, were Dr. Van Ripple. But whatever secrets Miss Wyatt's slate may hold remain locked tightly inside.

"The key holds the truth," I say to myself. "The key to what?"

Nothing, as far as I can see. I abandon the slate beside my bed and cross to the window, gazing at the woods beyond, toward the Gypsy camp. I wonder what Kartik is doing now, if he is still tortured by dreams of Amar, of me.

There's a light below. I spy Kartik with his lantern, looking up at my window. My heart gives a little leap, and I have to remind it not to beat faster for a man who can't be trusted. I close the drapes, turn down my own lamp, and crawl into bed. Then I shut my eyes tight and tell myself I am not to get back up and go to the window, no matter how much I'd like to.

~~~~~

I can't say what it is that wakes me. A sound? A bad dream? I know only that I am awake with my heart beating a bit faster. I blink, adjusting to the dark. I hear a noise. It's not inside the room; it's above me. The roof groans over my head as if something very heavy were moving about. A long shadow crosses my wall, and I'm up.

Now I hear something else in the hall: a faint scuffling like the rustle of dead leaves. I open the door a crack, but there's nothing there. I hear it again; it's coming from below. I tiptoe down the corridor and around the stairs, following the sound. When I reach the great hall, I stop. From deep inside the vast room, the noise is stronger. Scratching. Whispers. Moans.

Don't look, Gemma. Pass it by.

I peek through the keyhole. Moonlight falls across the room in windowpane blocks. I search each small box of light for movement. A slight shift catches my eye. Something is moving in the dark. I snuff the candle and wait, my knees weak with fear. I count silently—*one, two, three*—ticking off the seconds. But there is nothing. *Thirty, thirty-one, thirty-two . . .*

Whispers come again. Soft and chilling as rats' claws on stone. I press my eye to the keyhole again and my heart bangs against my ribs.

The column. It's moving.

The creatures molded to it slowly reveal themselves in raised fists and the faint fluttering of reanimated wings. Gasping and gurgling, they squirm and push against the thinning membrane of stone like things ready to be born. I cannot scream, though I want to. A nymph breaks free of the ooze with a snap. She shakes the vestiges of the column from her body and glides through the air. I gasp. She cocks her head, hearing.

Quick as wind she's at the keyhole. Her eyes are as large as a doe's. "You can't stop us," she whispers. "The land is awakened and we with it. And soon will come the day when your blood is spilled and we rule forever. The sacrifice!"

"Here now, wot are you about, miss?"

I fall back against something with a shout and turn to see Brigid staring at me, her hands on her hips, her nightcap on her head. "You should be in bed!" she says.

"I h-heard a n-noise," I stammer, gulping down my fear.

Brigid frowns and flings open the doors. She lights the lamp nearest us. The room is hushed. Nothing is amiss. But I hear those beastly scratches. Feel them under my skin.

"Don't you hear that?" I ask, and my voice is desperate.

Brigid frowns. "'Ear what?"

"The column. It was alive. I saw it."

Brigid's face shows worry. "Now, now. You're not tryin' to scare your old Brigid, are you?"

"I saw it," I say again.

"I'll get awl the lights on, then."

Brigid scurries for the matches.

Scratching. Above my head. Like hell's messengers. Slide my eyes up, and there she is—the nymph, flattened against the ceiling, a wicked smile on her lips.

"Up there!" I scream.

Brigid turns up the lamp and the nymph is gone. She puts a hand to her chest. "Mary, Mother of God. You frightened the life out of me! Let's 'ave a look at that column."

We inch closer. I want to run. Brigid peers at it, and I half expect something to pull her in. "Well, it's right queer, like ever'thin' in this place, but it's no' alive. Jus' ugly."

She pats the column, and it's solid. Or is it? For I think I see an empty space in the marble that wasn't there before.

"Did you have the cabbage?" Brigid asks, turning down the lamps.

"What?" I say.

"Cabbage for dinner. It can give you wind somethin' terrible and then you've got the most 'orrible dreams, too. No more cabbage, if you want m'advice."

She turns down the last lamp, and the room is cast in shadows again. Brigid closes the door and locks it. As we travel the stairs, she speaks to me of what foods and drink make for pleasant sleep, but I'm not really listening to her. My ears are tuned to the dark below us, where I hear that soft scratching and the faintest of cackles.

CHAPTER FORTY-THREE

TRUE TO HER WORD, THE NEXT MORNING MRS. Nightwing has us traveling the five miles to Balmoral Spring. As the carriage bounces over muddy roads, I find I'm eager to see Ann again, and I'm hopeful that she will accept an apology for my beastly behavior at her departure.

At last we arrive. Balmoral Spring is a nightmare of a country estate purchased by the sort who have new fortunes, old ambitions, and an appalling lack of taste in all regards. I wonder whether there is a servant left in the whole of England, for footmen stand at the ready for our carriages, and butlers and maids of all stripes line the walk and bustle about the grounds, tending to every need.

I whisper to Fee, "Do you see Ann?"

"Not yet," she answers, searching the throngs. "What on earth is *that?*"

She nods toward an enormous marble fountain that features Mr. Wharton as Zeus and Mrs. Wharton as Hera. The rays of a bronzed sun shine behind them. Water trickles from Mr. Wharton's mouth in a rather unfortunate stream, as if he were spitting.

"How absolutely appalling!" Felicity says, clapping in delight. "What other wonders await us?"

Mrs. Nightwing takes in the spectacle of the fountain, the lawns, the ceramic cherubim posed near groomed shrubbery, the newly constructed bandstand. "Merciful heavens," she mutters.

Mrs. Wharton's laugh can be heard above the din. We have come in simple summer-weight dresses, straw hats perched upon our heads, but she wears an elaborately beaded blue gown more appropriate for a ball. Diamonds drip from her neck, though it is afternoon. And her hat is a continent unto itself. One quick turn of her head and she nearly takes out a contingent of servants.

"How wonderful you could come," she says, welcoming us. "Do try the caviar—it has come all the way from France!"

I do not recognize Ann at first. In her stiff gown, her hair pulled back severely, she does not resemble the girl who left us several weeks ago. She is one of those gray phantoms haunting the edges of every party, not quite family, not quite servant, not a guest—something in between acknowledged by none. And when our eyes meet, she does not hold the gaze. Little Charlotte tugs hard on Ann's dress.

"Annie, I want to play in the rose garden," she whines.

"You broke the roses last time, Lottie, and I was called to account for it," Ann says quietly.

"Oh, Miss Bradshaw," Ann's cousin calls to her, "let her play in the roses. She loves them so."

"She does not handle them with care," Ann answers.

"It is your duty to see that she does," Mrs. Wharton tells her.

"Yes, Mrs. Wharton," Ann answers dully, and Charlotte smiles in triumph. I can only imagine what other horrors Ann endures.

Felicity and I follow them at a safe distance. Ann tries desperately to keep up with the abominable children. Carrie, who is all of four, has her fingers in her nose nearly every moment, only taking them out to examine her disgusting finds. But Charlotte is far worse. When no one looks, she yanks the roses off their stalks so that their full blooms dangle sadly on broken necks. Ann's admonishments fall on deaf ears. The moment her back is turned, Charlotte continues her carnage.

"Ann!" we call. Ann sees us but pretends she hasn't.

"Ann, please don't ignore us," I beg.

"I hoped you wouldn't come," she says.

"Ann—" I begin.

"I've made a mess of it, haven't I?" she whispers. "Carrie!" she calls. "You mustn't eat what is in your nose. It isn't done."

Felicity scowls. "Ugh. I shall never have children." Carrie offers her the hideous pearl on her finger. "No, thank you. What a horrid little beast. How do you stand it?"

Ann wipes away a quick tear. "I've made my bed . . . ," she starts, but doesn't finish.

"Unmake it," Felicity urges.

"How?" Ann dabs at her other eye.

"You could run away," Felicity suggests. "Or pretend to have some ghastly disease—or you could make yourself so odious that not even the most terrible children would want you for governess."

"Gemma?" Ann looks to me, beseeching.

I've not given up my wounds so easily. "I offered you my help before," I remind her. "Do you really want it this time?"

"Yes," she says, and I can see from the set of her jaw that she means it.

"What are you discussing?" Charlotte demands, trying to break into our tidy cluster.

"A big monster who eats too-curious little girls and swallows their bones whole," Felicity hisses back. Ann lets out a strangled laugh.

"I shall tell my mother on you."

Felicity bends till she's level with the child's face. "Do your worst."

Charlotte flinches first. With a glance at Ann, she runs to her mother, wailing. "Mummy, Annie's friend told me a monster would eat me!"

"I'm done for," Ann sighs.

"All the more reason to put our plan into effect," I say.

⁂

After Mrs. Wharton has thoroughly taken Ann to task for Charlotte's tantrum—in full view of the discomfited guests—she orders Ann back to her duties. We trail just behind them as Charlotte murders the roses. I bend down and say sweetly, "You mustn't break the roses, Lottie."

She stares at me with hateful eyes. "You're not my mother."

"That's true," I continue. "But if you don't stop, I shall be forced to *tell* your mother."

"Then I shall say it was Annie who broke the rose."

To demonstrate her power, she throws a rose at my feet. How delightful. What a pleasant child.

"Here we go," I whisper in Ann's ear.

"Lottie, you mustn't hurt the roses," Ann says as sweetly as possible. "Or the roses might hurt you."

"That's silly." She breaks another.

She has moved to a third when Ann says, quite firmly, "Don't say I didn't warn you." She waves her hand over the roses, summoning the magic I've bequeathed her. Charlotte's eyes widen as the decapitated blooms fly free of their broken stems. They rise in a sparkling red spiral. It's a lovely effect and would most likely make a point all on its own, but it is important to impress the little beast thoroughly. The roses fly quickly toward her and hover for only a second above her astonished face before they descend in full attack, the thorns pricking her arms, her hands, her legs, and her backside several times. Charlotte screams and runs for her mother. The roses lie back down. I can see the girl pulling on her mother's arm while rubbing her sore bottom. Within seconds, a whimpering Charlotte drags her mother to us. Several guests follow to see what the commotion is about.

"Tell her!" Charlotte cries. "Tell her what the roses did! What you made them do!"

We give Mrs. Wharton our most innocent smiles, but Ann's is the biggest.

"Why, Lottie, what do you mean, dear?" Ann asks, all concern and worry.

Charlotte is having none of it. "She made the roses fly! She made them hurt me! She made the roses fly! She did!"

"My goodness, how did I do that?" Ann chides gently.

"You're a witch! And you are, too. And you!"

The guests chuckle at this, but Mrs. Wharton is chagrined. "Charlotte! Such an imagination. You know how Papa feels about fibbing."

"It isn't a fib, Mama! They did it! They did!"

Ann closes her eyes, spinning one last charm. "Oh, dear," she says, examining Charlotte's face. "What are those spots?"

Indeed, small red bumps appear on the child's face, though they are nothing more than an illusion.

"Why, it's pox," a gentleman says.

"Oh. Oh, dear," Mrs. Wharton says. A ripple of concern passes through the guests. No one wants to be near, and though Mrs. Wharton fights to hold on to her perfect party, she's losing her grip. Already, wives are tugging on husbands' sleeves, making their excuses to leave.

And then it begins to rain, though Ann, Felicity, and I can take no credit for that event. The brass band stops playing. The carriages are brought round. The guests scatter, and the children are ushered to the nursery by Mr. Wharton. We are left blissfully alone.

"Oh, I should like to relive that moment again and again," Ann says as we take cover under a pergola draped in grapevine.

"Witches!" Felicity says in imitation of Charlotte, and we snicker behind our hands.

"Still," Ann says, a note of concern creeping into her voice, "she is only a child."

"No," I say. "She is a demon cleverly disguised in a pinafore. And her mother deserves her utterly."

Ann considers that. "True. But what if her mother believes her?"

Felicity tears a blade of grass in two. "No one listens to children, even when they speak the truth," she says bitterly.

꧁꧂

The doctor arrives and makes his diagnosis: chicken pox. As Ann has never had it, he orders her away from the children and the house for three weeks. Mrs. Nightwing agrees to host Ann until she can safely return, and we have our friend packed and in our carriage within minutes.

Mrs. Wharton objects strenuously to Ann's leaving.

"Couldn't she stay on?" she says as Ann's case is secured to our carriage.

"Indeed she cannot," the doctor insists. "It would be very serious if she were to contract the pox."

"But how will I manage?" Mrs. Wharton pleads.

"Come now, Mrs. Wharton," Mr. Wharton says. "We've a nurse, and our Annie will be with us again in three weeks' time. Won't you, Miss Bradshaw?"

"You'll hardly notice I'm gone," Ann answers, and I do believe she rather enjoys saying it.

CHAPTER FORTY-FOUR

ANN'S RETURN TO SPENCE IS GREETED WITH CHEERS FROM the younger girls, who clamor for her attention. Now that she's been "away," they find her exciting and exotic. No matter that it has only been a few weeks and only to a country house, there is an air of the lady about her to them. Brigid promises a toffee pudding for all in celebration, and by the time we settle in the tent next to the fire in the evening, it's as if we've never been apart and Ann's journey has been but a bad dream.

Only Cecily, Elizabeth, and Martha keep their distance, but Ann doesn't seem to mind. We tell Ann about everything— our visit to Dr. Van Ripple, the slate, my discovery of McCleethy and Fowlson's plan to take back the power. Kartik. That part plunges me into melancholy. The only thing I don't confess is my association with Circe, for I know they'd not understand it. I scarcely do myself.

"So," Ann says, reviewing, "we know that Wilhelmina was betrayed by someone she trusted, someone she knew from her days at Spence."

Felicity bites into a chocolate. "Correct."

"Both Eugenia Spence and Mother Elena feel that someone is in league with the Winterlands creatures, and Mother Elena fears that this association will bring the dead to us."

"Doing very well, carry on," I say, stealing a chocolate for myself.

"The tribes of the realms might also be joining with the Winterlands creatures in rebellion."

We nod.

"In order to free Eugenia and bring peace to the Winterlands, we must find the dagger, which Wilhelmina Wyatt stole from Spence. And Wilhelmina, who was an addict and a thief and a generally disreputable person, might be trying to guide us to its location through Gemma's visions. Or it's quite possible she could be leading us to a very bad end."

"Indeed." Felicity licks her fingers.

"Miss McCleethy and, it stands to reason, Mrs. Nightwing know about the secret door into the realms but believe that they can only unlock it by rebuilding the tower. Eugenia confirms that this is so. Yet, Wilhelmina didn't want them to rebuild the East Wing." Ann stops. "Why?"

Felicity and I shrug.

"She's on Gemma's side?" Felicity offers as if that makes perfect sense.

"Then there is the matter of the phrase 'The key holds the truth,'" Ann continues. "The key to what? What truth?"

"Dr. Van Ripple said there was no key—or dagger—that he knew of," I say again. "And the slate tells no tales; it's only an ordinary slate."

Ann takes a chocolate. She pushes it around in her mouth,

thinking. "Why did Wilhelmina take the dagger in the first place?"

For a moment, the tent holds nothing but the sound of the three of us drumming our fingers to separate rhythms.

"She knew that the dagger in the wrong hands would bring chaos," I offer. "She didn't trust McCleethy or Nightwing with it."

"But they worship the memory of Mrs. Spence. She's like a saint to them," Ann argues. "What reason would they have for harming her?"

"Unless they never really did care for her. Sometimes people pretend to have affection for you when they don't," I add bitterly, thinking of Kartik.

We peer through the tent's crack at the two of them deep in conversation. Brigid brings Mrs. Nightwing her sherry on a silver tray.

"I don't see how we can possibly solve this mystery tonight," Felicity complains.

We are disturbed by a loud knocking at the door. Brigid comes to Mrs. Nightwing. "Pardon, m'um, but there's a troupe o' mummers outside. They say they've a jolly pageant to present, if you'd be so kind as to admit them."

Mrs. Nightwing whips off her spectacles. "Mummers? Certainly not. You may turn them away, Brigid."

"Yes, m'um."

Mrs. Nightwing has scarcely put on her spectacles again when the girls besiege her, begging her to reconsider.

"Oh, please!" they cry. "Please!"

Our headmistress is resolute. "They're not to be trusted. When I was a girl, they were likely to be run out of town. Beggars at best, thieves and more at worst."

"What's worse than beggars and thieves?" Elizabeth asks.

Mrs. Nightwing's lips tighten. "Never you mind."

This sends every girl to the windows to peer out into the dark, hopeful of a glimpse of these forbidden men. Danger calls and we answer too eagerly, our noses pressed to the glass. The mummers are not turned away so easily, it would seem. They've set their lanterns upon the grass and have commenced with their performance. We open the windows and stick our heads out.

"We bid you good evening, gentle ladies!" one of the mummers calls. He juggles several apples at once, taking a bite out of one each time it comes round, till his mouth is filled. We laugh at such sport.

"Please, Mrs. Nightwing," we beg.

At last she relents. "Very well," she says with a deep sigh. "Brigid! Keep close watch over the silver and let no one inside!"

We push out onto the lawn. Fireflies wink to us with their shining tails. The air is calm and pleasant and we're thrilled to have a show. For all Mrs. Nightwing's hand-wringing, the mummers are more clowns than criminals. Their faces have been blackened with burned cork, and their costumes are well-worn, as if they have been walking England's roads for weeks. The tall man in the middle wears a tunic with the emblem of Saint George upon it. Another man wears Oriental dress, like a Turk. Yet another looks like a physician of sorts. I see the feet of two others beneath the costume of a dragon.

The leader of the troupe steps forward. He's a tall, gangly fellow with hair that wants cutting. His face has the sharp planes of the thin and hungry. He wears a top hat that has seen better days, and his tunic is graying. In his hand is a wooden sword. He speaks with the rolled *r*s and airs of a music hall actor.

"What story shall we tell to enthrall you, my fair damsels? Do you wish a tale of sweet love? Or a tale of adventure and possible death?"

Excited gasps trickle through our motley crew of girls. Someone calls for love, but she is shouted down.

"Adventure and death!" we cry. The romantic girl pouts but there it is. Death is infinitely more thrilling.

"Perhaps the tale of Saint George conquering the dragon, then? A princess fair on the brink of sacrifice? Will she live? Will she die? Tonight, we shall introduce to you a hero, a doctor, Doubt, the Turkish knight, and of course, a dragon. But first, we require a princess. Is there one among you who would be our doomed maiden fair?"

Immediately the girls beg to be chosen. They wave their hands and clamor for attention while the mummer appraises us while slowly striding up and down.

"You there, my Titian-haired lady." It takes me a moment to realize that the mummer points to me. By virtue of being the tallest and having the reddest hair, I've stood out. "Would you honor us by being our maiden fair?"

"I . . ."

"Oh, go on with you," Felicity says, giving me a push forward.

"Ah, thank you, fair maiden." He places a crown upon my head. "Our princess!"

The girls are disappointed. They clap halfheartedly.

"Let us begin our tale in a most bucolic city-state where a golden river runs. But what is this? Alas! A dragon has built its nest there!"

The men in the dragon costume move forward, growling and snarling. They hold a pennant to suggest fire.

"The citizens, living in mortal terror, can no longer draw water from the river, so frightened are they of the hideous beast. And so, they devise a desperate plan—they sacrifice a princess to the dragon to satisfy his hunger—a daily sacrifice!"

The younger girls gasp. There are a few girlish screeches. Felicity calls out, "Bad luck, Gemma!" and the older girls fall into laughter. Even Miss McCleethy and Mademoiselle LeFarge chuckle at this. I am well loved. How fortunate. The dragon's incinerating breath grows more appealing by the second.

The mummer doesn't care for having his show corrupted in such a fashion. He uses his most commanding voice. It thunders in the dusky air in a way that brings goosebumps to my arms. "The fair princess screams for salvation!" He points to me, waiting. I answer his patience with a perplexed expression.

"Scream," he whispers.

"Aaaah." It is the most anemic scream in the history of screaming.

The mummer's irritation shows beneath his bearded smile. "You are a maiden fair on the precipice of death! The fearsome dragon's flaming breath mere inches from your red-gold curls! You shall burn like tinder! Scream! Scream for your life!"

It seems a simple request, and yet, I'm far too mortified by it all to utter a sound. The crowd waits restlessly. I might remind them that I did not volunteer for this role. A soul-splitting screech rings out, loud and true. It sends shivers running through me. It's Ann. Hand to forehead, she screams, playing the part like Lily Trimble herself.

The mummers cheer. "Ah, there is our princess!"

They bring forth Ann and place the crown upon her head. I

am ushered back to the other girls with nary a thank-you for my efforts.

"I wasn't as bad as all that," I grumble when I am by Felicity's side.

Fee pats my arm. The pat says, *Indeed you were.*

I cannot remain churlish for long, for Ann is magnificent. Watching her, I forget that she is Ann. She truly is a princess in danger of being devoured. With the mummers securing her wrists, she thrashes and begs for mercy. She screams as the paper dragon draws near.

"Will no one save this lady? Will she face death?" the mummer pleads with glee.

An injured bugle is blown. It sounds less a call to arms than a dying cow. Saint George arrives in his plumed helmet.

"Ah! But who is this? Be he friend or be he foe? Can anyone tell me true?"

"'Tis Saint George!" a girl cries out.

The mummer pretends not to have heard. "I pray you, who is it?"

"Saint George!" we yell merrily.

"And be he hero . . . or villain?"

"Hero!" For who would dare name the patron saint of England as anything but a hero?

"Oh, who will save me?" Ann cries mournfully. She really is quite good, but the mummer does not care to be upstaged. He places a firm hand round her arm.

"The princess, so overcome by terror, faints dead away," he says pointedly.

Annoyance shows itself in Ann's sideways glance, but as requested, and with a dramatic sigh, she closes her eyes and allows her body to go limp in the paper chains. Saint George faces the dragon.

"But what is this? Our hero hesitates. Doubt hath found a path to his heart."

A mummer whose face is painted with two different expressions—a smile and a frown—sidles up to the actor playing Saint George. "The maid cannot be saved. Why sacrifice yourself for her?"

We greet this with a chorus of boos.

The actor with the painted face turns the smile side toward us. "This is how it has always been, the sacrifice of a maiden to soothe the beast. Would you dare to challenge it?"

"Doubt troubles our fair hero," the tall mummer booms. "He will need assistance from such fair and good ladies as are assembled here to find his heart and win the day. Will you cheer him on?"

"Yes!" we shout.

Saint George pretends to deliberate as the paper dragon weaves nearer to Ann with a feeble growl. We give another loud cheer, and he draws his sword with purpose. A fierce battle ensues. The dragon is defeated, but Saint George is injured. Clutching his side, he falls to the ground and we go silent.

"What is this?" the mummer says, wide-eyed. "Our hero has been dealt a blow! Is there a doctor?" Nothing happens, and the mummer, clearly irritated, repeats, "I say, is there a doctor?"

"That's me." The three-toothed mummer beside us remembers his part. He rushes forward, holding his hat on his head, a glass vial raised high in his other hand. "I am the good doctah. And I've a magic potion that shall restore him to his former health. But for its magic to spark, every one of us must believe—believe and take hold."

With great solemnity, the good doctor passes the glass vial from girl to girl and asks her to add her wish to it. The vial is rushed to the fallen Saint George and put to his lips. He springs to his feet to our roaring approval.

"Our hero has recovered! Your magic hath restored his former vigor! And now, to the princess fair."

Saint George rushes to Ann's side. He seems ready to kiss her cheek, but a loud throat-clearing from Mrs. Nightwing changes his mind. He gives a peck to her hand instead.

"The princess is saved!"

Ann comes alive with a smile. Again we cheer. The mummers in charge of the paper dragon pop up and join with Ann and Saint George, moving so that it appears as if the brave knight and the fair maiden ride the beast. They wave happily. The dragon meows, making us laugh. It is a very happy ending, which, I suppose, is what we expected. The mummers bow and we clap for them. The lead mummer places his cap upon the ground, inviting us to make a donation, "no matter how small." We toss our coins, much to Mrs. Nightwing's dismay.

"Yes, yes," she says, shepherding us toward Spence. "Let's not catch a chill."

"Ann, you were wonderful," I say as she joins us. Her cheeks are pink, her eyes clear. Her moment of glory becomes her.

"When the dragon was beside me, I felt real fear! It was thrilling. I could perform every night of my life and never tire of it." She shakes her head. "If I could sing for Mr. Katz now, I'd do it, and I'd not throw it away. But it's too late. They've gone."

A few of the younger girls trot by to congratulate Ann and

tell her she made a perfect princess. Ann basks in their praise, smiling shyly at each compliment.

Suddenly, my ears are filled with a growing hiss that sounds like a gas lamp being turned to its brightest flame. The breath is torn from me. It feels as if someone is pulling on every part of my body. Everything goes topsy-turvy. Time slows. I see the girls moving so very slowly, their hair ribbons defying gravity as they turn their heads by infinitesimal degrees. The sounds of their laughter are low and hollow. Ann's mouth twists with words too slow for me to decipher. I alone seem to move at ordinary speed. It's as if I'm the only one truly alive.

I turn toward the trees and feel a chill in my soul. The mummers haven't slowed at all. As they walk into the woods, they appear to grow fainter till they are nothing more than outlines. Before my astonished eyes, they transform into crows and fly away, their dark wings stirring trouble into the calm sky. The tremendous pull is gone but I feel drained, as if I've run for miles.

Ann's mouth spits out its words now. "... I dare say, don't you agree? Gemma? You've a queer expression."

I grip Ann's arm too tightly and she winces. "Gemma!"

"Did you see that?" I gasp.

"See what?"

"The mummers ... they ... they were there and then ... they turned into birds and flew away."

Hurt burns in Ann's eyes. "I didn't ask them to choose me over you."

"What? No, that isn't it at all!" I speak more softly. "I'm telling you, one moment, the mummers were there, and the next, they'd changed into birds—just like—" I go cold all over. "Just like the Poppy Warriors."

Ann peers into the dark. The mummers' lamp weaves through the trees, growing smaller with the distance. "Do birds carry lanterns?"

"But I—" I cannot finish. I'm no longer certain of what I saw.

"Ann Bradshaw! How could you not have told us how brilliant you are?" Elizabeth exclaims. She and Martha draw Ann into an eddy of girlish fawning, and Ann goes happily with the current.

I stand alone on the lawn, searching for some sign that I did not imagine what I saw. But the woods are quiet. Eugenia's voice echoes in my head: *They could make you see what they wish you to see. It will be as if you are mad.* I turn to see Mrs. Nightwing and Miss McCleethy chattering. Cool prickles of sweat break out on my brow and I wipe them away.

No. I won't listen to what they say. I am not their pawn, and I am not insane.

"The dark plays tricks, Gemma," I say to comfort myself. "It was nothing. Nothing, nothing, nothing."

I repeat the word with every step until I convince myself it is true.

⌁⌁⌁⌁⌁

"Isn't this wonderful? Just like old times," Ann says as we ready for bed.

"Yes," I say, running a brush through my hair. My hands still shake, and I'm glad Ann is back in her bed this evening.

"Gemma," she says, taking note of my trembling, "I don't know what you thought you saw in the woods, but there was nothing there. You must have imagined it."

"Yes, you're right," I say.

And that is what frightens me most.

CHAPTER FORTY-FIVE

WHEN IT IS TIME TO WAKE, I DO NOT WELCOME IT. MORE than a lack of sleep has me uncomfortable. I do not feel well. My body aches, and my thoughts are sluggish. It's as if I have run hard and fast for so long that every step now is an effort. My edges blur into everything else—other people's humors and emotions, the painful sunlight, the myriad sensations— until I cannot tell where the world begins and I leave off.

But the others at Spence are alive with the excitement the masked ball brings. The girls cannot resist flitting about in their costumes for a trial. They prance before the mirrors that are already too crowded, jockeying for their moment to see themselves as princesses and fairies with ornate masks festooned with feathers and beads. All that can be seen are their eyes and mouths. Some of the younger girls growl at each other, their hands bent into claws. They swipe and jab like wild tigers.

Mrs. Nightwing enters, clapping her hands. "Ladies, let our rehearsal commence."

The other teachers corral the younger girls, separating the tigers from the fairies. They have them sit on the floor whilst Mrs. Nightwing oversees our performances with the charm and largesse of a prison warden: "Miss Eaton, are you playing the piano or murdering it?" "Ladies, your curtsies must be as snowflakes falling to earth. Softly, softly! Miss Fensmore, that is not a snowflake but an avalanche." "Miss Whitford, sing out, if you please. The floor may hear your song quite well, but it is only the floor and cannot applaud it."

When Mrs. Nightwing calls me to recite my poem, my stomach churns. I do not relish standing before them all, being the center of attention. I shall never remember the words. The girls look at me with expectation, with boredom, with pity. Mrs. Nightwing clears her throat, and it is like a gun firing the start of a race. I am off and running.

"'Rose of all Roses, Rose of all the World—'"

Mrs. Nightwing interrupts me. "Gracious, Miss Doyle! Is this the derby or the recitation of a poem?" Tittering trickles through the girls. Some of the little tigers giggle behind their hands.

I start again, trying my best to temper my voice and rhythm, though my heart thumps with such force I can draw only the shallowest of breaths. "*Turn if you may from battles never done, /* I call, as they go by me one by one. / *Danger no refuge holds, and war no peace, /* For him who hears love sing and never cease.'"

The word *love* has the younger girls giggling again, and I have to wait while Miss McCleethy upbraids them for their rudeness and threatens not to allow them cake if they do not behave. Mrs. Nightwing nods for me to continue.

"'Rose of all Roses, Rose of all the World! / You, too, have come where the dim tides are hurled / Upon the wharves of sorrow, and heard ring / The bell that calls us on; the sweet far thing...." I swallow once, twice. They look at me with such expectation, and I feel that no matter what I do, I shall disappoint. "Um ... 'Beauty grown, beauty grown sad ...'" My eyes are itchy with tears I want to shed for no reason that I can name.

"Miss Doyle?" Mrs. Nightwing calls. "Do you intend to add a dramatic pause? Or have you gone into a catatonic state?"

"N-no. I only forgot my place," I murmur. *Don't cry, Gemma. For heaven's sake, not here.* "'Beauty grown sad with its eternity / Made you of us, and of the dim grey sea. / Our long ships loose thought-woven sails and wait, / For God has bid them share an equal fate; / And when at last, defeated in His wars, / They have gone down under the same white stars, / We shall no longer hear the little cry / Of our sad hearts, that may not live or die.'"

There is halfhearted applause as I leave my spot. Head raised, Mrs. Nightwing glares at me through the bottom of her spectacles. "That wants work, Miss Doyle. I had rather hoped for more."

Everyone seems to hope for more from me. I am a thoroughly disappointing girl all around. I shall wear a scarlet *D* upon my bosom for all to see so that they will know not to raise their expectations.

"Yes, Mrs. Nightwing," I say, and the tears threaten again, for underneath it all, I should like to please her, if it's possible.

"Yes, well," Mrs. Nightwing says, softening. "Do practice, will you? Miss Temple, Miss Hawthorne, and Miss Poole, I believe we are ready for your ballet."

"You shall be proud of us, indeed, Mrs. Nightwing," Cecily trills. "For we have rehearsed ever so much."

"I am relieved to hear it," our headmistress replies.

Blasted Cecily. Always so very superior. Does she ever have bloodstained dreams? Does her sort ever worry about anything at all? Living in her precious cocoon where no trouble may intrude.

Cecily floats across the floor with absolute grace. Her arms arch over her head as if they would shield her from all harm. I cannot help it: I hate her smugness and sureness. I wish I could have what she does, and now I hate myself for that.

Before I can stop it, the magic roars through me. And before I can call it back Cecily slips out of her graceful pirouette. She falls hard, her ankle twisting painfully underneath her as she hits the floor with a loud bang.

Everyone gasps. Cecily's hands fly to her bleeding mouth and her swelling ankle as if she cannot decide which hurts more. She bursts into tears.

"Good heavens!" Mrs. Nightwing exclaims. Every girl scurries to her side save for me. I stand watching, the magic still weighting my limbs. A tea towel is offered for Cecily's lip. She sobs while Mrs. Nightwing offers cold comfort by telling her she shouldn't make such a fuss.

My skin still itches with the magic. I rub my arms as if I could make it go away. I'm overcome with the shouts, the gasps, the confusion, and below that—far below—I hear the raw scratchings of wings. Something glows in the corner, near the draperies. I move closer. It's the nymph I saw the other night, the one who broke free of the column. She hides inside a fold in the velvet.

"How . . . how did you get here?" I ask.

"Am I here? Do you see me? Or is it only your mind that says I am here?"

She flits above my head. I make a grab for her but come away with only air.

"Funny. What you did to that mortal." She giggles. "I like it."

"It wasn't amusing," I say. "It was awful."

"You made her fall with your magic. You're very powerful."

"I didn't mean to make her fall!"

"Miss Doyle? To whom are you speaking?" Mademoiselle LeFarge asks. I've drawn attention away from Cecily. They're watching me now.

I look back but there's nothing. Only a drapery. "I . . . I . . ."

Across the room, Miss McCleethy looks from me to Cecily and back again, an expression of alarm stealing slowly over her.

"You did it, didn't you?" Cecily sobs. There is real fear in her eyes. "I don't know how she did it, Mrs. Nightwing, but she did! She's a wicked girl!"

"Wicked." The nymph cackles in my ear.

"You be quiet!" I shout at it.

"Miss Doyle?" Mademoiselle LeFarge says. "Who . . ."

I do not give an answer, and I do not wait for permission. I run from the room, down the stairs, and out the door, not caring that I shall earn one hundred bad-conduct marks for it and be made to scrub the floors forevermore. I run by the startled workers trying to erase the East Wing's past with fresh white limestone. I run till I reach the lake, where I fall into the grass. I lie curled on my side, gasping for breath, and watch the lake through long blades of grass that welcome my tears.

A shy brown mare saunters out from the cover of the trees.

She puts her nose to the water but does not drink. She wanders closer and we watch each other warily, two lost things.

When she nears me, I see that it's Freya. There's a saddle on her strong back, and I wonder, if she was to be ridden, where is the rider?

"Hello, you," I say. She snorts and lowers her head, restless. I stroke her nose and she allows it. "Come on," I say, grabbing hold of her reins. "Let's take you back home."

The Gypsies are not usually happy to see me, but today, they blanch at my approach. The women put their hands to their mouths as if they would stop what words might leap out. One of them calls for Kartik.

"Freya, you naughty girl! We were worried about you," he says, putting his head to the horse's nose.

"I found her down by the lake," I say coolly.

Kartik strokes Freya's nose. "Where have you been, Freya? Where's Ithal? Did you see him, Miss Doyle?"

"No," I say. "She was alone. Lost." A kindred spirit.

Kartik nods gravely. He takes Freya to her post and brings her oats, which she gobbles up. "Ithal went riding last night and did not return."

Mother Elena speaks to the others in their language. The Gypsy men shift uncomfortably. A small cry goes up among the women.

"What are they saying?" I whisper to Kartik.

"They say he might be a spirit now. Mother Elena insists they must burn everything of his so that he will not come back to haunt them."

"And do you think he's dead?" I ask.

Kartik shrugs. "Miller's men said they'd get their justice. We will search for him. But if he doesn't return, the Gypsies will burn every trace of him."

"I'm sure he'll turn up," I say, and head for the lake again.

Kartik follows me. "I tied the bandana into the ivy three days ago. I waited for you."

"I'm not coming," I say.

"Will you punish me forever?"

I stop, face him.

"I need to talk to you," he says. There are dark circles under his eyes. "I'm having the dreams again. I'm in a desolate place. There's a tree, tall as ten men, frightening and majestic. I see Amar and a great army of the dead. I'm fighting them as if my very soul depended upon it."

"Stop. I don't want to hear any more," I say, because I'm tired. *I'm half sick of shadows*, I think, remembering the poem Miss Moore taught us so many months ago, "The Lady of Shalott."

"You're there," he says quietly.

"I am?"

He nods. "You're right beside me. We're fighting together."

"I'm beside you?" I repeat.

"Yes," he says.

The sun catches his face in such a way that I can see the tiny golden flecks in his eyes. He's so earnest, and for a second, I should like to lay down my arms and kiss him.

"Then you've nothing to worry about," I say, turning from him. "For that is most assuredly a dream."

⊹⊹⊹⊹⊹

To say that Mrs. Nightwing is displeased with me is to say that Marie Antoinette received a small neck scratch. Our headmistress allots me thirty conduct marks, and in penance, I am to do her bidding for a week. She begins by having me tidy up the library, which is not the torture she imagines, for any time spent in the company of books cheers my soul. That is, when my soul can be cheered.

McCleethy enters my room without knocking and settles herself in the only chair. "You didn't come to dinner," she says.

"I'm not well." I pull the blanket to my chin as if that might shield me from her prying.

"Whom were you talking to in the ballroom?"

"No one," I say, not meeting her eyes. "I was rehearsing."

"You said you didn't mean to make her fall."

She waits for me to answer. I lie upon my back and stare at a spot on the ceiling where the paint peels.

"Miss Temple's ankle is injured. She will not perform her ballet. It's a pity. She was quite good. Miss Doyle, you might do me the courtesy of looking at me when I am speaking to you."

I lie on my side and look straight through her as if she were made of glass.

"You can stop pretending, Gemma. I know you have the magic still. Did you cause her fall? I am not here to punish you. But I must know the truth."

Again I am sorely tempted to tell her everything. It might be a relief. But I know McCleethy. She lures. She entices. She says she wants the truth when what she really wants is to be proven right, to tell me where I am wrong. And I can't trust her. I can't trust anyone. I'll not fail Eugenia.

I turn back to my fascination with the tear in the ceiling. I want to pick at the wound in the plaster. Rip it down to the boards and start over. Paint it another color. Make it a different ceiling entirely.

"She fell," I say, my voice hollow.

McCleethy's dark gaze is upon me, weighing, judging. "An accident, then?"

I swallow hard. "An accident."

I close my eyes and feign sleep. And after what seems an impossibly long time, I hear the scrape of the chair against the floor, signaling Miss McCleethy's departure. Her footsteps are heavy with disappointment.

<hr/>

I do sleep. It is fretful, with dreams of running over both black sand and fresh grass. No matter where I run, what I want is just out of reach. I wake to Felicity's and Ann's faces hovering mere inches from mine. It gives me a start.

"It's time for the realms," Felicity says. Anticipation burns in her eyes. "It's been ages, hasn't it, Ann?"

"Feels as if it has," Ann agrees.

"Very well. Give me a moment."

"What were you dreaming about?" Ann asks.

"I don't recall. Why?"

"You're crying," she says.

I put my fingers to my damp cheeks.

Felicity throws my cloak to me. "If we don't leave soon, I shall lose my mind."

I secure my cloak and place my finger and my tears deep into my pocket, where it's as if they do not exist at all.

CHAPTER FORTY-SIX

THE MOMENT WE STEP INTO THE BORDERLANDS, IT FEELS different. Everything seems to have fallen into disarray. The vines are ankle-deep. Crows have settled into the highest parts of the fir trees like inkblots. As we travel to the castle, they follow us, hopping from branch to branch.

"It's as if they're watching us," Ann whispers.

The factory girls do not greet us with their familiar cry.

"Where are they? Where's Pip?" Felicity says, quickening her steps.

The castle is deserted. And just like the grounds outside, it is overgrown and ill tended. The flowers have gone brittle, and worms slither along their purple husks. I step in a mealy patch and pull up my boot in disgust.

We wander through the vine-covered rooms, calling the girls' names, but no one responds. I hear a faint rustling from behind a tapestry. I pull it aside, and there's Wendy, her face dirty and tear-streaked. Her fingers are blue.

"Wendy? What has happened? Why are you hiding?"

"It's that screamin', miss." She sniffles. "Used to be a lit'le. I 'ear it all the time these days."

Felicity checks behind the other tapestries in the room on the chance it's all a game of hide-and-seek. "Allee-allee-all free! Pip? Pippa Cross!" She drops into the throne with a pout. "Where is everyone?"

"It's as if they've vanished." Ann opens a door but there's nothing but vines inside.

Wendy shivers. "Sometimes I wake up and it feels like I'm the only soul 'ere."

She flutters her blue-stained fingers to a basket of the berries Pip has gathered, the berries that have cursed our friend to her existence here. I note the blue stains on her mouth as well.

"Wendy, have you been eating the berries?" I ask.

Her face shows fear. "It's all there was, miss, and I was so hungry."

"Don't fret," I say, because there is nothing else that can be done.

"I'm going to the tower for a lookout," Fee says, and I hear her feet making quick work of those crumbling stairs.

"I'm afraid, miss," Wendy says, fresh tears falling.

"Now, now." I pat her shoulder. "We're here. It will be all right. And what of Mr. Darcy? Where is your twitchy friend?"

Wendy's lips quiver. "Bessie said 'e gnawed through his cage and got out. Been callin' for 'im but 'e won't come."

"Don't cry. Let's see if we can scare him up. Mr. Darcy," I call. "You've been a very naughty bunny."

I search anywhere a mischievous rabbit might hide—in the berry baskets, under the moldy carpets, behind doors. I spy the cage sitting upon the altar in the chapel. There's no sign of the twigs having been nibbled through; they're right as rain. But the cage door is open.

"Looking for your friends?" The fairy glows brightly in the gloom of a corner. "Perhaps they have gone back to the Winterlands."

Felicity bounds into the room at precisely that moment. "Pippa wouldn't go without me."

"Do you know for certain?" the winged thing asks.

"Yes, I do," Fee says, but her face darkens, and she glances quickly toward the Winterlands.

"Someone comes," the fairy says. Quick as a snap, she flits out of the castle. Felicity, Ann, and I chase after her into the forest. On the other side of the bramble wall, a cloud of dust moves toward us. It is the centaurs riding fast. They pull up short, not daring to cross into the Borderlands.

One of the centaurs shouts to me through the thorns. "Philon has called for you, Priestess."

"Why? What has happened?"

"It's Creostus. He's been murdered."

᭙᭙᭙

Beneath the olive trees in the grotto where the Runes of the Order once stood, Creostus's body lies sprawled, his arms stretched out on either side. His eyes are open but unseeing. In one hand he clutches a perfect poppy. It mirrors the bloody wound in his chest. Creostus and I were not friends—his temper was far too great—but he was so very alive. It is hard to see him dead.

"What do you know of this, Priestess?" Philon asks.

I can scarcely look away from Creostus's blank eyes. "I knew nothing of it until a few moments ago."

"Liar." Neela hops onto a rock. "You know who is responsible." She transforms herself into Asha—the orange sari, the blistered legs, the dark eyes.

"You think it is the Hajin," I say.

"You know it is! Creostus had ridden to bargain for poppies. The foul tribe had cheated him of a full bushel. Now we find him here with a poppy in his hand. Who else could be responsible? The filthy Hajin, helped by the Order!"

Neela's voice chokes with emotion. She strokes Creostus's face lovingly. Crying, she lowers herself to his chest, stretching out across his lifeless form.

Gorgon speaks from the river. "The Order can be hard, but they have never killed. And you forget that they have no entry into the realms at present. They have no power here."

Neela glares at me. "And yet I saw the priestess on her way to the Temple, alone."

"Neela speaks the truth, for we were with her. We saw the priestess, too," a centaur adds.

"You're lying!" Felicity shouts, coming to my defense, but my cheeks redden, and it does not go unnoticed by Philon.

"Is this true, Priestess?"

I'm done for. If I tell them what I know, they will accuse me of disloyalty. If I lie and they discover it for themselves later, it will be much worse.

"I did go to the Temple alone," I say. "But it was not to see the Hajin. I saw another. Circe."

"Gemma . . . ," Ann whispers.

Philon's eyes widen. "The deceiver? She is dead. Killed by your hand."

"No," I say. "She is still alive. Imprisoned in the well of eternity. I needed to see her, to ask her about the Winterlands and—"

A ripple moves through the crowd. They press closer. Felicity stares at me in horror.

Neela is up, her voice slicked with fury, her mouth twisted in a deranged smile. "I told you, Philon! I told you she could not be trusted! That she would betray us as the others did. But you would not listen. And now, now Creostus is dead. He is dead. . . ." She buries her face in her hands.

"So this one of the Order is housed in the Temple. With the Hajin," Philon says.

"No. That's not quite how it is. And she isn't of the Order. They would have nothing to do with her—"

"But you would?" a centaur growls.

Neela addresses the crowd. There are no tears in her eyes. "Would you take the word of one who has lied? You see that even her own friends did not know of her deception. The Order priestess and the deceiver have conspired with the Hajin to take the power! Perhaps Creostus knew too much, and this is why he was murdered! Philon! Will you not demand justice?"

The centaurs, the forest folk, the Gorgon—all turn their faces toward Philon, who closes those catlike eyes and breathes deeply. When the eyes open again, there is something hard and determined in them, and I am afraid.

"I have given you the benefit of the doubt, Priestess. I have defended you to my people. And in return, you have given us nothing. Now I will side with my people, and we will do whatever is necessary to protect ourselves. *Nyim nyatt e volaret.*"

The centaurs lift their fallen brother above their heads, then carry his dead body on their shoulders.

"Philon, please . . . ," I start.

The creature turns its back to me. One by one, like doors slamming, the forest folk turn as well, shunning me. Only Neela acknowledges my presence. As she follows her people from the grotto, she turns back and spits in my face.

Felicity takes me roughly aside. "You've been talking to Circe?"

"I needed answers. I needed to know about the Winterlands," I say. "She was the only one who could tell me what I—what we—needed to know."

"We?" Felicity looks daggers at me. Ann takes her hand. "Circe doesn't offer anything without a price. What did you give her?" Felicity demands.

When I do not answer, Ann does. "Magic."

Felicity's laugh is brutal. "You didn't. Tell me you didn't, Gemma."

"I needed answers! She got us safely through the Winterlands, didn't she?" I say, only then realizing how paltry a defense it is.

"She likely killed Wilhelmina Wyatt herself! Did you consider that?" Fee barks, and a terrible coldness snakes through me. I told Circe about Eugenia, about the tree. What if . . .

"It wasn't like that," I say, less sure.

"You're a fool," Felicity scoffs.

I give her a shove. "You know so very much about how to run things; maybe you should be the one to hold all the magic!"

"I wish I were the one," she growls through gritted teeth. "I'd make an alliance with Pip and my friends, not consort with the enemy."

"Certain of Pip, are you? Where is she, then?"

Felicity's slap is hard and sudden. I feel the sting to my toes. She's cut my lip. I taste the blood with my tongue, and I'm flooded with magic. At once, Felicity's hand is on her sword, and I fling it away like a toy.

"I'm not the enemy," she says quietly.

My body trembles. It takes every bit of strength I have to push the magic down. It leaves me with a sick, shaking sensation, as if I haven't slept for days. Fee and I stand facing each other, neither of us willing to apologize. My stomach lurches. I turn and vomit into a bush. Felicity marches ahead on the path to the Borderlands.

"You shouldn't have said that about Pip," Ann chides, offering me her handkerchief.

I push it away. "You shouldn't tell me what to do."

Ann's wounded expression is only momentary. Her well-trained mask settles over her true feelings. I've won the round, but I hate myself for it.

"I believe I shall walk with Fee," she says. Head down, she runs to Felicity, leaving me behind.

CHAPTER FORTY-SEVEN

PIPPA AND THE GIRLS ARE IN THE CASTLE'S OLD CHAPEL when we return. They've a basket of plump berries, which Pippa sorts through, dropping the fruit into a chalice she's found. The girls seem more worn than usual. Their hair is terribly matted, and if I catch them in a certain slant of light, their complexions are a mottled yellow, like fruit gone bad.

Pippa hums a merry tune. Seeing our long faces, she stops. "What is the matter? What has happened?"

Felicity gives me a hard look but neither she nor Ann confesses what I've done. My head aches now, and I have to keep my hands tucked under my armpits to quiet the shaking.

"Creostus has been killed," I say tersely.

"Oh, is that all?" she says. She returns to her berry picking. Mae and Bessie don't even look up. Their indifference is enraging.

"The forest folk have shunned me."

Pippa shrugs. "They don't matter. Not really."

"I might have thought that once, but I was wrong. I do need them."

"Those horrid creatures? You said they used to come into our world and take playthings. Horrid!" Pippa removes a mealy berry with her fingertips and drops it onto a cloth with the other discarded fruit.

"Yes, it's wrong. And I might not like it. I might tell them I don't. But Philon has never lied to me. When I needed help, the creature was an ally. All they asked was to have a voice, to share in their own governance, and I have failed them." I take a steadying breath, and the magic settles a bit.

"Well," Pippa says, dusting off her skirts, "I still don't see why you need them when you have us. Bessie, darling, will you put these aside?"

Bessie takes the basket of fruit. She looks longingly at it. "How come them folk turned their backs on you, eh?"

The room feels close. Felicity and Ann avoid my eyes.

"They believe the Untouchables and I had something to do with Creostus's murder."

"That's queer, innit?" Bessie stares at me. "How come they fink that?"

"Gemma's been having secret talks with Circe," Felicity announces.

"Oh, Gemma," Pippa scolds. Her violet eyes flash, and in that moment they lose their color and become the milky blue-white of the Winterlands. The stare sends a chill down my spine.

"'Oo's Circe?" Mae asks.

"The worst sort of villain," Pippa explains. "She tried to kill Gemma. She would do anything to possess the magic of the Temple and rule the realms. She can't be trusted." Pippa glares at me. "And those who consort with her cannot be trusted either. For there is nothing worse than a deceiver who would betray her friends."

"I didn't betray anyone!" I shout, and the power I've silenced rumbles in me again, till I am forced to sit.

Felicity moves in beside Pippa, her arms folded. "Where were you earlier?" she asks in a low voice.

Pippa shrugs her off. "Gathering berries."

"We looked for you in the forest." Felicity presses.

"Not everywhere, it would seem."

Bessie steps to Pippa's side. She towers over Felicity by a good head. "Trouble, Miss Pippa?"

Pippa doesn't rush to say *Now, now, Bessie, don't be silly, all is well*. She lets the threat dangle for a moment, relishing the power in it. "No, thank you, Bessie." Hands on her hips, she turns to Fee. "I might ask where you've been, but I suppose you've been busy with your life. Out there."

"Pip . . ." Felicity tries to lace her fingers in Pippa's but Pip won't have it. She pulls away. "I brought you a gift," Fee says, hopefully. She offers Pip a slim package wrapped in brown paper.

Pippa's eyes light up as she opens it. For there are three ostrich feathers.

"So that you might have your coming out," Felicity says softly.

"Oh. Oh, they are exquisite!" Pippa throws her arms around Felicity, who smiles at last. Bessie lumbers across the room with the basket of berries, nearly knocking over poor Mercy.

"Oh, do help me secure them," Pip says.

Felicity fastens them to Pip's hair at the back with the stem of a weed stolen from the altar.

"How do I look?" Pippa asks.

"Beautiful," Felicity answers hoarsely.

"Oh, how enchanting! That is what we need to lift our spirits—a merry party. And every girl here shall make her debut. It will be a most magnificent ball—the grandest ever! Mae? Mercy? Who's with me? Bessie, you'll play, won't you?"

The girls jump with excitement. Mae rips nightshade from the wall and tucks it behind her ear. A worm drops to the floor with a plop, and I cannot say whether it fell from the flower or her ear.

"Gemma?" Pip extends her hand. "Will you join our debut ball?"

Creostus's death has cast a long shadow across my soul. For the first moment in a very long time, I do not care for a party. I do not want to forget my troubles or attempt to fill the holes deep inside us with fleeting illusions.

"I'm afraid I'm not in a festive mood. You'll have to have your party without me."

I expect an argument. Pouts and tears and begging for me to turn the castle into the Taj Mahal, our skirts into Parisian gowns. Instead, Pippa smiles brightly.

"Oh, Gemma, darling, you rest. I shall do it all."

She closes her eyes and reaches her arms forcefully to the castle's ancient rafters. An ecstatic smile spreads across her lips. Her body trembles, and the castle begins its transformation. The grime clears from the windows till they gleam. The vines recede, clearing enough floor for dancing. Mold vanishes from the walls and the ceiling, and in its place is a dark purple carpet of berries and belladonna.

Awestruck, Ann turns round, taking in the whole of the chapel. "How did you do that?"

"It seems the magic is changing. Gemma isn't the only one with the power," Pippa answers.

"That's extraordinary," Felicity says, and there's a hint of sadness in her voice. "Can you gift it to others as Gemma can?"

Pippa reaches into a tangle of berries and selects the biggest, which she eats. "No. At least not yet. But when I am able, you can be certain I will share it without delay. Now, we must prepare for our debuts!"

"Pippa," I say, more harshly than I mean to, "might I have a word with you?"

Pip gives the other girls a playful pout and rolls her eyes, and they laugh at my expense. "I shan't be but a moment," she says. "You might practice your curtsies while I'm away."

Pip and I travel the winding staircase. A mouse has been caught in the spider's web. It lies trapped in a shiny cocoon of silk, barely moving, knowing its fate. We reach the top of the stairs and I can feel the chill in the air. In the distance, the shadows of the Winterlands beckon. But I do not feel its siren song so strongly tonight. The sight of Creostus lying on the ground is fresh in my mind.

Pippa stands at the window. Silhouetted by the swirling gloom of the Winterlands, an enigmatic half smile on her lips, she is even more beautiful than usual.

"I must say, Gemma, you don't seem very happy for me."

"I'm only confused. How did this power come to you? It's been days since I—"

"This has nothing to do with you," she says, and I hear hatred in her voice. "The magic has taken root in me. I can't explain why it is. But you might be happy. You should be. Now you're not so alone."

Should. That word, so like a corset, meant to bend us to the proper shape. Pippa leans out the window arch and stretches her arms wide, letting the wind howling off the Winterlands mountains hold her up.

"Oh, that is jolly!" She giggles.

"Pip, come in," I say, worried.

Her eyes turn milky white. "Why? Nothing shall happen to me. I'm immortal."

She steps away from the window. Her hair is a tangle of curls. "Gemma, I want you to know that while I do not approve of your consorting with Circe, I am prepared to forgive you."

"You . . . forgive me?" I say slowly.

"Yes. For I've been reborn and I see everything so clearly. There will be changes made around here." She smiles and kisses my cheek, and it makes my skin tingle.

"Pip, what are you saying?"

Those eyes of hers shimmer like a mirage—violet, blue-white, violet, blue-white—till I cannot be sure what is true and what is only a false hope in the desert.

"I've had a vision of my own. There will be a new day of empire within the realms. Those who are not with us are against us. And then there is the matter of those who, in truth, are not fit for our new day: the diseased and the poor. The ones who shall never really amount to anything." Her face hardens. "Degenerates."

Pippa slips her arm through mine, and I have the urge to shake it off and run. "I confess I don't know what to do about poor Wendy," she says with a sigh. "She's become quite a burden."

My voice is a whisper. "What do you mean?"

Pip purses her berry-stained lips. "She hears screaming when there is nothing at all to hear. None of us hears a thing. I've told her to stop. I even slapped her for it."

"You hit Wendy?"

There's a hard determination in Pippa's voice. "She frightens the other girls, and then no one wants to play. There is no screaming; she's only being contrary."

"Just because you don't hear it doesn't mean it isn't there."

Pip's face eases into one of her childlike smiles. "Oh, Gemma. When will you go with me into the Winterlands again? Isn't it such fun? To travel the gorge on the ship. To run up the heath and let the Tree of All Souls whisper to us of who we really are, what we could truly become."

"You sound as if you have been going without us."

That strange half smile is back. "Of course not. I wouldn't go without you."

A chilly gust howls through the tower's windows. A terrible thought crawls its way into my mind.

"What happened to Mr. Darcy?" I ask in a whisper, and am surprised by how fast and fluttery my heartbeat is.

Pip holds my gaze for a long moment. "He was only a rabbit. Not to be missed."

Merry laughter floats up the stairs from the floor below. Someone shouts, "Come on, Pip!" and Pippa grins.

"My subjects await."

She starts down the stairs, only turning back when she doesn't hear me just behind her. "Aren't you coming?"

"No," I say. "I don't feel much like dancing."

Pip's eyes turn the color of the Winterlands. "Pity."

When I leave the tower, they are in the chapel. Felicity and

Pip sit upon the thrones like royalty. Pippa holds a stick like a scepter in one hand, and she's wearing the cape Felicity gave her a few weeks ago. It seems like years since that happy time. Ann secures Mercy's train. Mae pulls on her long gloves; Bessie snaps her ivory fan shut. Only Wendy is alone, clutching Mr. Darcy's empty cage.

"Now you'll finally have your chance to become true ladies, and no one will tell you you're not equal to the finest of them," Pippa calls.

The girls' eyes shine. Pip wears her ostrich feathers proudly, like the debutante she will not get to be in our world.

"Miss Bessie Timmons!" Fee calls, and the walls groan. Under the illusion, the vines continue their creeping assault.

One by one, the girls glide solemnly toward Pip. They curtsy low before her, and she nods sternly and bids them rise. As they back away, their faces are bright, exultant. They believe with all their hearts that they have become ladies.

And in Pip's disquieting eyes, I see that she believes without reservation that she is queen.

⌁⌁⌁⌁

I run through the dusty corridors of the Temple, brushing past a startled Asha, and head straight for the well of eternity. Circe floats there as she has every time I've been.

Every time. I've not realized how much I've come.

"Creostus the centaur has been murdered," I say. "Did you have anything to do with it?"

"How could I manage it from in here?" she says, and it doesn't soothe me.

"I need to know what is happening," I say, a little out of

breath. The air is damp and warm. It makes my lungs ache. "You promised me answers."

"No. I promised to help you understand your power in exchange for magic."

"Yes, the magic! Why do you want it? How do I know you haven't been using it to orchestrate trouble? You could have left the well, for all I know. You could have murdered Creostus. You could be in league with the Winterlands creatures."

The full force of what I have done rises inside me. With a grunt, I kick the side of the well and a small bit of stone crumbles under my boot.

Circe's voice is steely. "You needn't torture the well. It hasn't done anything to you. What's the trouble? Is it Eugenia?"

"N-no," I stammer. I'll not tell her anything else about Mrs. Spence. That was a mistake. I palm the bit of rock and turn it between my fingers. "It's Pip. She has magic of her own. I haven't gifted her for days now but perhaps there are remnants of it—"

"Stop lying to yourself. You know how she has it. She's made a pact in the Winterlands."

The truth sinks into me by degrees. "There was a pet rabbit one of the girls had," I say softly. "Pip said it went missing."

"Next time it will not be a bunny," Circe warns. "But what of our illustrious Eugenia? The Tree of All Souls? Have you found the dagger yet?"

"Not yet, but I will," I say. "Why did you hate her so much?"

"Because," she says with difficulty. "She would not look into her own darkness, so how could she possibly understand the hearts of others? I suppose the centaur's death means there will be no alliance."

"I suppose not," I say, only now realizing the trouble ahead. I made a promise I didn't keep. Now I have enemies. "And you swear you had nothing to do with Creostus's murder?" I ask again, passing the pebble through my fingers.

"How could I?" she answers.

When I emerge from behind the water, Asha is waiting for me. She bows quickly.

"Lady Hope, I would speak with you," she says urgently.

"What is it?"

Asha guides me into a room where the Hajin sit on pallets, stringing beads. Red smoke belches from the many copper pots. "Is it true one of the centaurs was murdered and they blame the Hajin?"

"Yes," I say. "He was found with a poppy clutched in his hand."

"But we had nothing to do with his murder." She rubs her thumb against her palm like a worry stone. "We wanted no part of these politics. We only wish to be left alone, to live in safety—"

"There is no bloody safety!" I shout. "When will you realize that? Do your people even know that I offered them a share of the magic and that you refused it on their behalf?"

The Hajin look up from their poppies.

"Asha, is this true?" a girl asks.

"It is not our path, our destiny. We do not extend beyond our tribe," Asha says calmly. "You know this."

"But we could have a voice at last," a Hajin man says assertively.

The smoke has thinned. Asha stands at the pot, revealed. "And would you use that share of magic to change who we are?

Here we have accepted our afflictions. We have found solace in each other. What if suddenly we had the power to remove all flaws? Would you find beauty in each other still? At least now we are one caste."

The Hajin weigh her words. Some resume their work, pulling their garments across their misshapen legs to hide them.

"It is how it has always been. We will accept the legacy of our ancestors," Asha says, smiling, and in her smile I do not see warmth or wisdom; I see fear.

"You're afraid of losing your hold on them," I say coolly.

"I? I have no power."

"Don't you? If you keep them from the magic, they will never know what their lives could be."

"They will remain protected," Asha insists.

"No," I say. "Only untested."

One of the Hajin stands uncertainly, holding tightly to her skirts. "We should have a voice, Asha. It is time."

A spark of anger flashes in Asha's eyes. "We have lived this way always. We shall go on living this way."

The girl sits, but she does not bow as is customary. In her eyes are the twin gods of doubt and desire. When her skirt falls open, showing her scarred and blistered legs, she does not rush to cover them.

I shake my head. "Change is coming, Asha. Whether you're ready for it or not."

⚬⚬⚬⚬⚬

My mind is a jumble as I march toward the Borderlands. Who could have murdered Creostus and why? Is Circe telling me the truth? Did Pippa make a bargain with the Winterlands creatures for her magic, and if so, how powerful is she? How will I get Fee to see this? She'll rightly claim that I'm one to talk, for I've been having meetings with a murderess. And still I haven't deciphered Miss Wyatt's cryptic messages. Oh, I'm a bloody fool.

No. There's still a chance to put things right. Eugenia. I'll find the dagger and save her. I'll put the realms and the Winterlands to rights, and then . . . and then? I'll worry about then another time.

At the turn toward the bramble wall, I note something strange. The fruit of the trees we restored our first day back in the realms has withered to mealy husks. And all the flowers have turned a brittle blue, as if they've been strangled upon their stalks. Every last bloom is dead.

I hurry to the bramble wall and tread the path through the blue forest to the castle.

Whoo-oot. The sound is near. Bessie steps out, her stick at the ready.

"Step aside, please, Bessie. I don't mean you any harm. You know that."

"You couldn't do me no 'arm if you wanted," she says, towering over me.

I shout Pip's name and Felicity's and Ann's, too.

"See? They don' wan' you no more," Bessie snarls.

The castle door swings open and Felicity barrels out, trailed by Ann, Pip, and the others.

"Gemma! What is it?" Felicity calls.

"Bessie wouldn't let me pass," I say.

Pippa gives Bessie a playful pout. "Is that true, Bessie?"

"Don' know where she's been," Bessie offers in explanation.

Pippa twirls a marigold in her fingers. "It's true, Gemma. If you don't want to be questioned, you shouldn't run off by yourself."

"Yes," I say, my apprehension growing. I fear her now, and I wonder if she can sense it in me. "It's time to go back to Spence."

"But I'm not ready to go back," Felicity complains.

"Then don't go. Stay here with me," Pippa says as if proposing a holiday, and Felicity's face floods with happiness.

"We can't get back without Gemma," Ann says bitterly.

"Tomorrow," Felicity says softly.

"Tomorrow." Pip gives Fee a gentle kiss on the cheek and strides back to the castle, the factory girls behind her like ladies-in-waiting. No one offers to help Wendy.

Wendy feels her way until she finds purchase in my sleeve. "Miss? Can't you take me with you?"

"I'm sorry, Wendy. I can't bring you back into my world," I say, helping her toward the castle.

"I'm afraid, miss. I don't like it 'ere. The castle's so still at night without Mr. Darcy to keep close. When I call, nobody answers—"

"Wendy!" It's Bessie come back for her. She stands like a warrior, her stick tall at her side. "Come on, then. Miss Pippa's waitin'." She lets Wendy stumble toward her and moves out of the way just as the girl closes in. "Missed me!" She laughs, and then she leads the girl roughly toward the castle.

<hr />

"Where did you disappear to, Gemma? Off to see Circe?" Felicity goads. She trails her fingers along the corridor that leads to our secret door.

"Yes," I say, because I'm tired of lying.

"You're a fine one, aren't you? You don't trust Pip but you'll trust that . . . that thing who murdered your mother!"

"You wouldn't understand," I say, pushing through the shimmering light of the secret door to the East Wing.

Felicity pulls me round to face her. "Of course I wouldn't. For I'm only your friend who cares about you."

"Would you care about me if I didn't have magic?" I ask.

"That is like asking 'Would you like me if I weren't myself?' The magic is a part of you, and you are my friend," she says. Her answer brings tears to my eyes, and I feel awful for the way I treated her earlier, for not trusting her, for what I shall have to tell her about Pip.

"Oh, no!" Ann says suddenly. She pats her shoulders. "My shawl! It must have fallen."

Without thinking, she puts her hand out, and the world is flooded with light as the door opens for her.

"Ann, how did you do that?" Felicity asks, wide-eyed.

"I don't know," she answers. "I just wanted to get in and . . . there it was."

"Stand aside," Felicity orders. This time, Felicity puts her hand to the door, a look of fierce concentration on her face. Again, the portal into the realms opens wide. She grins as if it were Christmas morning. "Do you realize what this means? Gemma isn't the only way into the realms! Anyone can open that door. We may come and go as we please!"

They hop up and down in their excitement.

"I'll just get your shawl for you, will I?" I say.

Ann laughs. "I can get it for myself." She opens the door and comes out with her shawl, happy as can be. "Isn't it marvelous?"

Go on, Gemma. Say 'Yes, it's wonderful that you don't need me so much.'

"It's late," I say. "We should be in."

I hear them behind me, giggling and giddy. I keep walking toward Spence, hoping they will follow, knowing they might not.

CHAPTER FORTY-EIGHT

THE WHOLE OF THE DAY, I CANNOT REST EASILY IN MY skin. Creostus has been murdered. I am no longer trusted by the forest folk, and I cannot say I blame them for their suspicion of me, for what have I done to earn their trust? I see specters and shadows that aren't there. Wilhelmina has vanished as in one of her magic tricks. And the magic and the realms are changing: The door will open without my aid now, and Pippa . . .

Pip. The magic has taken root in her. It's building. And every time I try to talk myself out of my growing fear of her, I remember Mr. Darcy.

The key holds the truth. I wish I had the key, for my head spins so, and I'm desperately in need of truth.

There is one error I might put to rights. When our tasks are completed at day's end, I go in search of Cecily. I find her in the library. Brigid has propped her up on a chaise, her ankle resting upon a pillow. She's in a thoroughly disagreeable mood now she cannot participate in the masked ball—not that I can blame her. And she isn't happy to see me. When I approach, she lifts her *La Mode Illustrée* so that I am face to face with an illustration of an elegant woman modeling the most fashionable frock.

"I've brought *Pride and Prejudice*. I thought perhaps I could read to you," I offer.

Cecily thumbs through the pages of beautiful gowns. "I've been doing my own reading for many years now."

"How is your ankle?" I ask, taking the chair beside the chaise.

"It hurts. I shall not perform my ballet. I shall not even be able to dance. My evening is ruined," she says, sniffling.

"I thought perhaps you might recite Mr. Yeats's poem in my stead."

Cecily's eyes narrow. "Why?"

"Well, you are an excellent reader, far better than I and—"

"No, why are you offering? Have you a troubled conscience, Miss Doyle?" Cecily's glare is quite penetrating, and I realize I have not given her powers of observation sufficient acknowledgment.

"It is a fair offer," I say.

"Let me see it," she says after a moment, and I hand over the poem. She begins her recitation at once, and when I leave her, she rehearses with such whispered ferocity from her sickbed that I know she shall be the star of the ball.

Heaven help us.

Ann stops me in the hall. In her hands is a copy of *The Era Almanack*, which lists adverts for performers of all sorts as well as management companies and theaters.

"Gemma, look." She shows me an advert for the Gaiety Theatre.

THE MERRY MAIDENS

A new and original musical entertainment to be performed in July.

Composed by Mr. Charles Smalls.

Young ladies of sound form and good

voice should make an appointment with Mr. Smalls for Wednesday,

the twenty-ninth of April, between the hours of noon and three o'clock.

Some dancing.

"You remember Charlie Smalls, the accompanist? He liked my voice," she says, and bites her lip. "If I could get in to see him . . ."

"The twenty-ninth. That's tomorrow," I say.

"I know I shouldn't ask," she says. "But I promise I shan't fail this time."

I nod. "All right. We'll manage. I don't know how, but we will."

᛭᛭᛭

Just after supper, Inspector Kent comes to call on Mademoiselle LeFarge. Their wedding is only weeks away. In the great room, the inspector regales us with tales of Scotland Yard's derring-do. We want to know about Jack the Ripper, but he politely declines to discuss it. All the while, Mademoiselle LeFarge sits near, proud that he will be hers.

"Do tell us another!" we plead.

"Now, I fear I shall haunt your sleep if I tell you this one," he says, smiling wickedly. That is all it takes for us to fall into desperate pleas for more and fervent promises that we shall not wake in the night crying for help.

Inspector Kent takes a sip of his tea. "This tale concerns a troupe of mummers who seem to have gone missing not too far from these parts."

"Gracious," Mademoiselle LeFarge says. "We had a visit from some mummers recently."

"Against my better judgment," Mrs. Nightwing grumbles.

"It's a strange little story. Apparently, these chaps were due to rendezvous with others of their profession in Dorset, but they never showed. Meanwhile, we've reports of them spotted in various villages, like phantoms. And in their wake, there have been rumors of missing persons."

The girls delight in the story, especially when Inspector Kent waggles his eyebrows at them.

But every hair on my neck is at attention. "Were they ghosts?"

Inspector Kent's booming laugh rings out. The other girls giggle, too, thinking me foolish.

"In my twenty years with the Yard I have seen all manner of skullduggery but never have I seen a ghost. I shall tell you what I think. I believe these mummers, being of dubious station in life, owed money to these chaps in Dorset. That's why they've not showed. And as for reports of missing persons, well, in every village there is someone who needs a means of escape from his present circumstances."

"What sort of circumstances?" Cecily presses.

"Never you mind about that." Mademoiselle LeFarge tuts, leaving us to wonder about it all the more.

The inspector chuckles. "With your curiosity, you should all work for me."

"Ladies cannot become detectives," Martha says. "They haven't the constitutions for it."

"Tommyrot!" the inspector answers, slapping his thigh. "My dear mother reared four boys, and it was woe unto any one of us who tried to fool her. She could have been a chief inspector, such were her talents. Someday there shall be women at Scotland Yard. Mark my words."

"Oh, Mr. Kent." Mademoiselle LeFarge chortles. "No more of this or these girls won't sleep tonight. Let us talk of the wedding, shall we?"

"As you say, Mademoiselle LeFarge, as you say," he answers.

"I thought perhaps you girls could help us decide which hymns we might sing." She frowns. "Oh, dear. I've forgotten to bring a hymnal from the chapel. And there I was reminding myself all day long."

"I shall get it," Inspector Kent says, putting down his teacup.

Mrs. Nightwing stops him. "No. I'll send Miss Doyle for it. She's a few days of penance left, by my ledger. It will do her good. Miss Poole, you will accompany her."

Bloody Nightwing.

Elizabeth follows me out to the lawn. She jumps at every sound. "What was that?" she gasps. A frog hops over her foot and she yelps and grabs hold of my arm.

"It's only a frog, Elizabeth. You'd think it a dragon the way you're carrying on," I grumble.

We've gone no more than a few feet when Elizabeth gasps and nearly climbs up me.

"What is it now?" I say, pushing her off.

"I don't know," she says, her eyes tearing. "It's so dark! I hate the dark! I always have. It frightens me."

"Well, I can't help you with that," I grouse, and she starts to cry. "Very well," I say with a heavy sigh. "Go hide in the kitchen. I'll fetch the hymnal and come back for you."

She nods and runs for the safety of the kitchen without so much as a thank-you. I hurry toward the chapel, my lamp leading the way. Night animals are tuning up their orchestra of chirps and croaks. It is not comforting this evening but a reminder that many things live in the dark. The dogs at the Gypsy camp start a chorus of barking that trails off into restless whimpering. It makes my nerves jangle.

Right. I shan't tarry. The hymnal's what I've come for, and I intend to be quick about it. The chapel's ancient oak door is heavy. I pull hard and it creaks open a sliver to allow me passage. Inside it's murky and silent. Anything could be waiting. My heartbeat quickens. I prop open the door with a rock and proceed.

The inky blue of late dusk surges against the stained-glass windows, casting patterns on the floor. My lamp sends shards of light through them. I find no hymnals at the back, so I'm forced to make my way down the center aisle, away from the doors and quick escape. I swing my lamp over the pews from side to side until at last I spy what I'm after in the middle of one. A sudden gust of wind bangs the door shut, and I drop the hymnal and hear it slide under the pew.

Blast.

Heart beating even faster now, I crouch on the floor, feeling for the book until I have it. A voice, hard as fingernails rapping on metal, sounds in the dark.

"Stay. . . ."

I whip around so quickly the flame wobbles in the lamp. "Who's there?"

The chapel is still, save for the wind that gusts against the now closed door. Hurriedly, I grab the hymnal and scurry up the aisle, breathing hard.

"You must not go. . . ."

I turn myself around in a mad whirl. My lamp casts angry shadows on the walls.

"I know you're here. Show yourself!"

"The woods be not safe now."

The windows buckle and shift. The stained-glass images move. They're alive.

"We would keep you safe, Chosen One. . . ."

The voice comes from the odd window panel, the one of the angel in armor brandishing a bloody sword in one hand and a severed gorgon's head in the other. At least, I have always taken the icon to be an angel; now, in the deepening dark, I am no longer certain of anything. The angel grows taller inside its glass prison. Its body bows the front of the window, and its face looms like the moon.

"They are in the woods. . . ."

"You're not real," I say aloud. The gorgon's head drips blood onto the chapel's floor. I hear it hit in sickening drops, as steady as rain. Bile rises in my throat. I breathe through my nose, swallowing it in burning gulps.

"If you be sacrificed in the Winterlands, the magic falls to them, and all is lost. Do not leave the chapel!"

It's too late. Abandoning my lamp and the hymnal, I bolt for the door. I throw my body against it and it flies open. Night's army has come with a vengeance. I can barely see my way, and I curse myself for leaving the lamp. The dogs have not ceased their barking.

I rush down the path, taking very little care. A tree slaps me in the face and I look round. I gasp for breath. Something is moving in the trees. Two men step out from behind a large fir, and I scream. It takes me a moment to recognize them—Tambley and Johnny, Mr. Miller's missing men.

"You frightened me to death," I sputter. My heart thumps as quickly as a rabbit's.

"Sorry, miss," Johnny says, his voice calm.

"We didn't mean no 'arm," young Tambley adds. There is something odd about them. They seem as inconsequential as dust, two shimmers of men, and when they step forward into a stream of moonlight, I could swear I see their bones glowing beneath their skin.

"You've given us all quite a scare," I say, moving back. "They said you'd gone."

"Gone?" Johnny repeats without seeming to understand.

The trees shake with the fluttering of birds' wings. Several crows perch on the branches, watching silently. A grim voice inside speaks its fear to me: *Hide, Gemma.*

"You should report to Mr. Miller straightaway. He's worried about you."

My hand strays out, searching for the trunk of a tree. A sound comes from my right. I slide my eyes toward the sound and there is Johnny. He was before me a second ago. How could he possibly . . . ?

Tambley points a finger at me. His bones seem to shine under the surface of his skin, which is as pallid as a fish at the bottom of a pond.

"We're back now," he says. "For you."

The birds raise a clamor with their chilling caws. Johnny's hand grips my cape. I slip the clasp and let the cape drop in his fingers. I waste no time. I turn and scramble for the path. I run hard and fast the way I have just come, for they block the way to Spence. The wind rises behind me, bringing the sounds of cackles and whispers, rat scratchings, and the flapping of wings. The crows' cries are like the screeches of hell. For all I know, I am screaming with them.

The chapel wavers before me, shaking along with my ragged breath. Whatever is behind me is gaining fast, and now I hear horses as well, horses that seem suddenly to have come out of thin air. I slam hard into the chapel doors. I tug but they will not open. The dirt of the path whirls and eddies around me.

Dogs. I hear dogs barking, and they are near. And just like that, the dirt on the path settles. The sound of horses and birds fades to a throb and then nothing. Torches flicker and smoke in the woods. The Gypsies have come—some on horseback, some on foot.

"Gemma!" Kartik's voice.

"I saw . . . I saw . . ." I put a hand to my stomach. I cannot talk. Can't breathe.

"Here," he says, taking my arm to steady me. "What did you see?"

Several gulps of air and my voice returns. "Men . . . in the woods. Miller's men—the ones who disappeared."

"You're certain?" Kartik asks.

"Yes."

Immediately the Gypsies fan out. The dogs sniff the ground, confused.

"Mrs. Nightwing sent me to the chapel for a hymnal," I explain.

"Alone?" Kartik's eyebrows arch.

I nod. "In the chapel . . . the windows came alive," I whisper. "They warned me not to go into the woods!"

"The windows warned you," Kartik repeats slowly, and I am aware that I sound mad. For all I know, I am.

"The angel, the one with the gorgon's head . . . it came alive, warned me. 'The woods be not safe.' And that's not all. He said something about a sacrifice—'If you be sacrificed in the Winterlands, the magic falls to them, and all is lost.'"

Kartik chews his lips, thinking. "Are you certain it wasn't a vision?"

"I don't think it was. And then, on the path, I saw those men, and they seemed like specters. They said they had come for me."

A sudden, startled cry rings out from the Gypsy camp. It's followed by more shouts.

"Stay here!" Kartik instructs.

There isn't a prayer that I will stay here alone. I'm right on his heels. With each footfall, the angel's voice rumbles through me: *The woods be not safe.* The camp is in chaos—screams, curses, men's shouts. There are no spirits here. It is Mr. Miller and his men. They pull the women from the tents and ransack the wagons, stuffing their pockets with whatever they find. When the women try to protect what is theirs, Mr. Miller's men threaten them with torches. One woman rushes a slightly built thug, beating him with her fists until she is struck across the face by another.

The dogs are loosed. They attack one of the men, knocking him to the ground, where he screams and cowers. Daggers are drawn.

"Inspector Kent has come to call at Spence. I'll run for him," I say, but when I think of the unquiet woods, where ghostly figures seem to wait, my feet are like lead. I hesitate, and in that moment, Mr. Miller raises his pistol and fires two shots into the air. "Right. Who wants lead in his belly? I want to know where my missing men are."

He takes aim at one of the Gypsy men. There is no time for the inspector. Something must be done at once.

"Stop!" I shout.

Mr. Miller cups his hand over his brow, peering into the dark. "Who said that?"

"I did," I say, stepping forward.

Mr. Miller breaks into a huge grin and a big cackle. "You? Aren't you one of them Spence girls? What ya gonna do, then? Pour me tea?"

"Inspector Kent of Scotland Yard has called upon us this evening," I say, hoping I sound much surer of myself than I feel. My insides have gone to jelly. "If you do not leave at once, I shall send for him. In fact, he may very well be on his way now."

"You're not going anywhere." Miller nods and two of his men come for me. Kartik steps between us. He gets off a solid punch to each of them, but another joins the fray. He is outnumbered. He is hit hard across the mouth, his lip bloodied.

"Stop!" I growl.

Mr. Miller's feral grin returns. "I told Missus Nightwing them dirty Gypsies would sully her girls. Guess I was right."

I hate him for that. I wish I could show him how much, and at once, the magic eats through me with a terrible velocity. I am inside Mr. Miller's head, an unwelcome guest.

I know what you fear, Mr. Miller, what you desire.

Mr. Miller whips around wildly. "Who said that? Which one of you?"

These woods know your secrets, Mr. Miller. I know them, too. You like to hurt things. You like it very much.

"Show yourself!" Mr. Miller's voice is raw with fear.

You drowned a kitten once. It struggled and scratched for its tiny life, and you squeezed harder. You squeezed till it hung limp in your hands.

"Don't you hear that?" Mr. Miller screams at his men. They regard him as one would a madman, for they hear nothing.

Retribution rumbles over my soul. I make the wind gather force. It rattles the leaves, and Mr. Miller sets off running, his men chasing after, all thoughts of revenge abandoned for now. The magic calms, and I fall to my knees, gasping. The Gypsies regard me warily, as if I were something to be feared.

"It is you who brings the curse," Mother Elena says.

"No," I say, but I'm not sure I believe it.

Immediately, the women set about cleansing the camp of the wickedness we foreigners have brought. They pour out water from all the pitchers. I see some of the women placing small bits of bread in their pockets, which Brigid has told us wards off bad luck.

Kartik offers me his hand, and I take it. "The men you saw in the woods—now you see they were not specters but flesh and blood. They had come seeking revenge on the Gypsies."

I want to believe him. I would do anything to have it all explained away with easy assurances, like those from a governess patting a fretting child's head. "And the windows?"

"A vision. A most unusual one. You said yourself that things are changing." He combs his fingers through his thick curls, which I know he does when he is thinking. I find I've missed that. I've missed him.

"Kartik . . . ," I start.

Lanterns appear in the trees. Inspector Kent has come with Nightwing, McCleethy and two of our stableboys. Elizabeth trails behind. They call my name and it sounds foreign, the name of a girl who played happy games with her friends inside the realms weeks ago. I no longer remember that girl. I have become someone else, and I am not quite sure she is sane.

"I'm here!" I call, because I would be found.

Nightwing's face displays a mixture of relief and fury. Now that she has found me safe, she looks as if she would kill me for the trouble I've caused.

"Miss Doyle, it was most ungracious of you to run off and abandon Miss Poole," Mrs. Nightwing reprimands. Elizabeth slinks behind her.

I open my mouth to protest but it isn't worth it.

"We heard shots!" the inspector says, taking charge. Just now he is not the twinkly-eyed man who sips tea by our fire. He is a hardened man of the law. It's astonishing that men can inhabit their two selves so easily.

"Miller's men came to hurt the Gypsies," I say, and Kartik explains what has happened.

"I shall have a word with Mr. Miller," Inspector Kent says gravely. "He will answer for this. And you say you saw his missing men in the woods?"

"Yes," I whisper.

"Will you see if they have Ithal in their camp?" Kartik asks. "He is still missing."

"Missing? Since when? Why wasn't I told of this?" the inspector demands.

Kartik's jaw tightens. "No one cares about one missing Gypsy."

"Rubbish!" the inspector growls. "I shall see to it immediately. I'll search the camp from top to bottom, if necessary. Mr. Miller has a great deal to answer for, indeed."

Mrs. Nightwing and Inspector Kent lead us through the woods. It no longer feels as if this place belongs to us girls for our games and wanderings. It feels as if it is being claimed by someone else.

"Mrs. Nightwing was sick with worry. She never would have allowed you to go to the chapel had she thought there was the slightest danger," Miss McCleethy tells me, but I'm not listening. I don't trust either of them.

A slice of moon peeks out from behind the clouds for a moment, illuminating Spence's roof. My steps slow. There's something odd about it, though I cannot quite place it. I see the spires, the bricks, the jumble of angles, the gargoyles. An enormous shadowy outline of wings stretches out against the moon's brief light. The stone beast is standing tall.

It's *moving*.

"Miss Doyle?" Miss McCleethy looks from me to the roof and back again. "Is something the matter?"

They could make you see what they wish you to see. It will be as if you are mad. Eugenia warned me, didn't she?

"No, nothing's the matter," I answer, but my hands shake, and now I hear Neela's words in my head: *How will you fight, when you cannot even see?*

CHAPTER FORTY-NINE

"HOW ARE YOU FEELING TODAY, GEMMA?" ANN ASKS. SHE'S sitting on the edge of her bed, an excited smile on her lips. She has on her gloves and her best dress, one of Felicity's cast-offs let out on the sides by Brigid.

"Tired," I say, rubbing my aching head. "Why are you dressed like that?"

"Today's the day," she says. "Don't you remember? Charlie Smalls? The Gaiety? Between noon and three o'clock?"

"Oh, no!" I say, for with all that's happened, I'd forgotten.

"We'll still go, won't we?" she asks.

In truth, I'd rather not draw on the magic today, not after last night. Not with my mind so tenuous. But there is Ann. She is my friend. She means to take command of her life, and I should like to believe she will this time. But to do that, she will need my help—and I will need hers.

I throw back the covers. "Go and fetch Felicity. This will take all of us."

We devise our plan together. We direct our efforts toward Brigid. I make her believe that both Ann and I are taken ill with the monthly curse and must not be disturbed. She will repeat this story throughout the afternoon, for I've put it in her head quite thoroughly. And of course, Felicity embellishes the tale, as she is wont to do, until everyone at Spence fears to venture anywhere near our door. But it takes time to accomplish this, and once we catch the train to London and secure a hansom to Piccadilly, we are a full hour late. We huff and puff on our way to the theater, but when we arrive, Charlie Smalls is just leaving. In his company is another man.

"Oh, no," Ann gasps. "What shall I do?"

For a second, I am tempted to influence the clock, pave the way and make it all fine, but I think better of it. This is Ann's show. Let her run it.

"Do what you must," I say.

"Mr. Smalls!" she calls out.

Charlie Smalls squints at us. He looks from Ann to me, and finally, there's a glimmer of recognition. "Miss Washbrad's chum, isn't it?"

"Yes, that's right," I say. "And this is my friend Miss Bradshaw."

They tip their hats. "What ever happened to Miss Washbrad? Mr. Katz and Miss Trimble waited but she never showed."

Ann's cheeks redden. "She ran off."

He nods, grinning. "Got married, then? Miss Trimble said that's what happened. Guess she was right."

"I read about your composition in the *Era*," Ann says. "Miss Doyle says you are very talented."

His face brightens further. "Exciting, isn't it? My first musical entertainment, bowing at the Gaiety come July. *The Merry Maidens*."

"I am a performer," Ann says so quietly it is hard to hear her over the rumble of the wagons and horses on the street. "I should like to sing for you."

Charlie's partner looks Ann over. He nudges Charlie. "Not much to look at."

"It's *Merry Maidens*, Tony, not *Gorgeous Girls*," Charlie whispers back, and I fear that Ann will take offense and call it all off.

"It's true I'm not a Gaiety Girl," Ann says. "But I can sing whatever you like. And read, too!"

"Don't mind him. He didn't mean no harm, miss," Charlie says. "Look at me, with these big ears and long snout." He pulls at his nose.

"Call was for noon to three," Tony says, checking his watch. "It's after four, nearly half past."

"I am sorry," Ann says. "We couldn't secure a cab and—"

"The other girls made it on time," Tony says. "We're off to the pub. Good day to you."

"Sorry, miss," Charlie says, tipping his hat. "I hope you'll come to the show."

"Yes, thank you," Ann says, her head low. As they brush past, Ann's features settle into that emotionless mask, and I know that's it. She's done. It's Balmoral Spring and little Charlotte's tantrums and Carrie's nose picking. And I can't help it: I'm angry.

"Mr. Smalls!" Ann shouts, startling me. She turns and runs after him. "I'll sing for you here! Right now!"

Charlie's eyes widen. He breaks into a grin. "On the street?"

"No time like the present, Mr. Smalls," Ann rejoins.

He laughs. "Now you sound like Mr. Katz."

"She's a nutter. The pub, mate," Tony says, pulling on Charlie's sleeve.

But Charlie folds his arms. "All right, then, Miss . . . I'm sorry, I've forgotten your name!"

"Bradshaw," Ann says crisply.

"All right, Miss Bradshaw." He gestures to the curious passersby. "Your audience awaits. Let's hear it."

A small crowd gathers to see the spectacle of the young lady singing for her supper for the two impresarios on a street in the West End. I feel a blush forming on my cheek, and I cannot imagine how Ann will manage to get out a single note. But sing she does, as I've never heard her before.

The sound that pours out of her is as pure as anything I've ever heard, but it has a fresh strength. There's a bit of grit under the notes and it's married to heart. Now the song tells a story. There's a new Ann Bradshaw singing, and when she finishes, the crowd responds with whistles and cheers—honey to any budding showman.

Charlie Smalls breaks into a huge grin. "It's funny, 'cause you sound a lot like Miss Washbrad—only better! Tony, I think we've found ourselves one of our merry maidens!"

Even the surly Tony nods in approval. "Rehearsals commence the end of May, the twenty-fifth, at the Gaiety, two o'clock—and that's two o'clock sharp!"

"I won't be late," Ann promises.

"You won't run off and get married on me like Miss Washbrad, will you?" Charlie teases.

"Not on your life," Ann says, smiling, and she's more beautiful than ten Nan Washbrads.

CHAPTER FIFTY

THE WHOLE OF SPENCE IS ENGAGED IN PREPARATIONS FOR our masked ball tomorrow evening. A fleet of maids has been employed to buff the old girl as if she herself were readying for the marriage market. Carpets are dragged to the back lawn, where they are beaten of every speck of dirt. Floors are scrubbed and waxed to a high shine. Grates are cleaned. Nooks and crannies are dusted. Nightwing bustles about as if we were expecting Her Majesty to come rather than a small coterie of parents and patrons.

She sends us out of doors—for fear we might breathe and somehow sully the pristine rooms of Spence—which suits everyone fine, as it's a particularly lovely day. We set up camp along the mossy bank beside the river. We are allowed to take off our boots and stockings and run barefoot over the cool grass, and that alone is heaven.

A rough-hewn maypole has been erected on a gentle slope farther on. The younger girls run giggling around it, crossing this way and that, their flower crowns perched precariously on their shining heads. They are scolded by the older, more serious girls, who are quite keen on producing a perfect plait. They weave in and out, over and under each other, until the pole wears a colorful gown of ribbon.

Felicity, Ann, and I walk through the grass to a bluff overlooking the river, a smaller cousin of the mighty Thames. Mrs. Nightwing would do well to turn the maids loose here, for the river wears a coat of moss and new leaves. Ann and I dip our feet into the cold water whilst Felicity gathers posies. Her dress is stained with pollen.

"I'm marked, I'm afraid." She sinks next to us. "Violet?" she says, offering a flower.

Ann waves away the delicate bloom. "If I should wear that, they'll think I intend not to marry. That is what it means to wear violets."

Unbowed, Felicity places the violet in her white-blond hair, where it shines like a beacon.

"Now that Mrs. Nightwing will allow me to attend the ball, I must have a costume," Ann says. "I rather thought I'd go as Lady Macbeth."

"Mmmm," I murmur, casting backward glances at the girls playing round the maypole, then beyond, toward the camp. But I've not seen Kartik since the night of the men in the woods.

Felicity dangles a violet over my forehead like a spider, and I scream, which pleases her beyond measure.

"Don't," I warn.

"Very well, Your Ladyship Brooding St. Petulant," she says. "What are you thinking about so intently?"

"I was wondering why Wilhelmina hasn't shown me where to find the dagger or the key that holds the truth. I'm wondering what she meant to warn me about."

"*If* she meant to warn you," Felicity argues. "Perhaps it was a trick, and you were wise enough to avoid it."

"Perhaps," I say. "But what of Eugenia?"

"Are you certain you really saw her?" Ann asks. "For none of us did, and we were there with you."

And I wonder if I imagined that, too. If I can even discern truth from illusion anymore. But, no, I saw her—I *felt* her. She was real, and the danger she sensed was real, but for the life of me, I cannot put the pieces together.

"And McCleethy and Nightwing?" I ask.

Felicity kicks her feet, making little splashes. "You know that they're rebuilding the East Wing to take advantage of the secret door. But that's all you know for certain. It will take ages to restore, and they've no inkling that we're already making use of it. And by the time they do know, we'll have already made the alliance and it shall be too late."

"You're forgetting that the Hajin won't join us and the forest folk hate me," I say.

Fee's eyes flash. "They had their chance. Why don't we make the alliance, just the four of us—you, me, Ann, and Pippa?"

"About Pip . . . ," I say warily.

Felicity's face darkens. "What is it?"

"Aren't you alarmed by the changes in her?"

"You mean her power," Fee says, correcting me.

"I think she's been going to the Winterlands," I continue. "I think she sacrificed Wendy's rabbit. Perhaps she's made other sacrifices as well."

Felicity crushes the violet between her fingers. "Shall I tell you what I think? I think you don't like that she has power now. Or that Ann and I can enter the realms without you. I saw your face when the door opened for us!"

"I was only surprised . . . ," I start, but the lie dies on my tongue.

"And anyway, you're the one acting strangely, Gemma. Cavorting with Circe. Seeing things that aren't there. You're the one who's not right!" She gives the water one final splash and the droplets arc neatly over the river and land back on me.

"I—I just think it best if we go into the realms together," I say. "For now."

Felicity looks me straight in the eyes. "You're no longer in charge."

"Come on, Gemma," Ann entreats. "Let's have a go round the maypole. Leave it for now."

She takes Felicity's hand and they run for the maypole. They weave in and out, laughing, and I wish I could forget everything and join them. But I can't. I can only hope that I will sort this out in time. I make my way past the lake and up the hill to the old cemetery. The jutting headstones welcome me, for I am suitably grave.

I lay one of Felicity's violets at Eugenia Spence's stone. *Beloved sister.* "I don't suppose you know where to find the dagger," I say to the slab. The wind answers by blowing the posy away. "Thought not."

"Talking to headstones?" It's Kartik. He carries a small lunch in a pail. A shaft of sunlight halos his face and for a moment I am taken with how beautiful he is—and how truly happy I am to see him. "You only need worry if they answer," he says. "I'll go if—"

"No, stay," I say. "I'd like that."

He sits on a grave whose markings are nearly gone with time and nods toward the maids beating carpets in a fury. "There is a masked ball, I hear."

"Yes, tomorrow," I say. "I shall go as Joan of Arc."

"Fitting." Kartik examines an apple, pushing at a bruise with his thumb. "I assume there will be many gentlemen in attendance. English gentlemen."

"I'm sure there will be many people in attendance," I answer carefully.

He bites into the fruit. I pull a leaf from a tree and tear it into small strips. The awkward silence stretches.

"I'm sorry," I say at last.

"You needn't apologize. I lied to you."

I perch near him. The distance between us isn't much and yet it feels vast.

"Come to the ball," I say softly.

Kartik laughs. "You're joking."

"No, not at all. It is a masked ball. Who shall know?"

Kartik pulls back his sleeve, revealing the warm brown of his skin. "And no one shall notice this, I suppose? An Indian amongst the English?" He bites into his apple with a hard crunch.

"An Indian prince," I say. "And you shall have an invitation. I shall give you one."

"If I cannot go as myself, I shall not go," he says.

"You may think on it. If you have a change of heart, place the cloth in its spot, and I shall meet you tomorrow in the laundry at half past six."

Kartik squints up at the sun. He shakes his head. "That is your world, not mine."

"What if . . ." I swallow hard. "What if I should like you in my world?"

Kartik bites into his apple again, looks out at the rolling hills of the peaceful countryside. "I don't believe I belong there."

"Neither do I," I say, laughing, but two tears escape, and I have to grab them quickly with my fingers. The magic tingles in them, a temptation: You could make him stay.

I will it into silence.

"Then come into the realms with me," I say instead. "We could look for Amar together. We—"

"No. I don't want to know what Amar has become. I want to remember him as he was before." He puts the apple back into his lunch pail. "I've given it much thought these past few days, and I think it best for me to travel on to the *Orlando*. There's nothing for me here."

"Kartik . . . ," I start, but what can I say, after all? "You must do what you feel is best."

"I'll remember you in India," he says. "I'll offer a prayer for your family at the Ganges."

"Thank you." There's a lump in my throat that will not go away.

He gatheres his pail. "Good day, Miss Doyle."

"Good day, Kartik."

He shakes my hand and walks down the hill. I'm alone in the cemetery.

"This is what it's come to," I say, pressing the backs of my hands to my eyes. "Only the dead want my company."

My knees are the first to go. The force of my vision is so violent, I sink to the ground, clutching my stomach. My muscles are taut. The sky seems to tear in two; the clouds are limned in red.

God. Can't breathe. Can't . . .

Wilhelmina Wyatt stands among the headstones, her face contorted with fury. She grabs hold of my hair and drags me toward the graves. I kick and fight, but she's strong. When we reach Eugenia Spence's grave, she gives me a hard shove, and I fall, watching in horror as the ground closes over me.

"No, no, no!" I scrabble at the sides of the grave with my fingernails, crying, desperate. "Let me out!"

The earth falls away, and I am standing on the heath in the Winterlands before the Tree of All Souls. I see Eugenia's frightened eyes. "Save us . . . ," she pleads.

I kick for all I'm worth. The grave collapses, and I cover my eyes as the dirt rains down on me.

It is silent. I hear . . . girls playing. Laughter. I take down my hands and open one eye. I'm on my back in the cemetery. The breeze brings the sounds of a croquet game on the back lawn. There is dirt on my boots and my skirts where I've been writhing. Wilhelmina is gone. I am alone. Eugenia Spence's grave is whole. The violet I dropped is there, and all I can do is sob—out of fright and frustration.

On rubbery legs, I weave through the gravestones. The crows descend like black raindrops. They light on the headstones. I put my hands to my ears to silence their hideous caws but they crawl under my skin like a poison.

I stagger down the hill and sit, crying softly, hugging my knees to my chest. If I hadn't kicked my way out of that grave . . .

Or was I even there?

No, I felt her pull my hair, felt myself fall, the dirt closing in. And then, it was as if it had never happened. Wilhelmina Wyatt frightens me.

She could see into the dark. That was what Eugenia said about her once. But what if she is part of the darkness? What if she's working with the creatures?

And I no longer know if she means to help me or kill me.

I watch the girls running around the maypole. Tomorrow they'll don their costumes and flit about it like pixies without a care in the world at our May Day masked ball. A little tickle of cold starts in my stomach and whooshes out to the rest of me.

Tomorrow. May Day. May first. The "birth" of May.

Beware the birth of May.

I cannot get warm. Whatever Eugenia feared, what Miss Wyatt meant to warn me about, will happen tomorrow, and I've no idea what it is or how to stop it. When I see Miss McCleethy and Mrs. Nightwing bent toward each other in conference, I shake. In their every glance, every laugh, every touch, I see danger.

All around me, the girls prance about, drunk on excitement, oblivious to my fear. The little ones play in their costumes whilst Brigid scolds them and insists they'll dirty their pretty dresses and then where will they be? They nod solemnly and promptly ignore her.

"Why don't you come join us, luv?" Brigid calls, seeing my long face.

I shake my head. "No, thank you. I'm not good company just now."

Mrs. Nightwing glances at me, brow slightly furrowed, and my skin itches. I can't stay here. I decide to take refuge in Fee's tent. I'm surprised to see her sitting there, all alone. Her lips tremble.

"Fee?" I say.

She wipes her tears with unforgiving hands. "Well, I've done it now," she says with a laugh that's too hard. "I've charmed them, all right."

"What do you mean?"

She holds up a letter. "It's from Mother. Lady Markham has agreed to sponsor me—if I will marry her Horace."

"She can't do that."

"She can," Felicity says, wiping away more tears. "She means to mold me into the proper wife; it will be a feather in her cap if she does. She's told Father that it might be a way for them to find favor in society again. And of course, there's the money."

"But it's *your* inheritance. . . ." I trail off.

"Don't you see? Once I am married, my inheritance belongs to my husband! There will be no garret in Paris. My future has been decided for me." She's as small and lifeless as a porcelain doll.

"I'm sorry," I say, though it is far too little.

Felicity takes both my hands in hers. My bones ache from her grip. "Gemma, you see how it is. They've planned our entire lives, from what we shall wear to whom we shall marry and where we shall live. It's one lump of sugar in your tea whether you like it or not and you'd best smile even if you're dying deep inside. We're like pretty horses, and just as on horses, they mean to put blinders on us so we can't look left or right but only straight ahead where they would lead." Felicity puts her forehead to mine, holds my hands between hers in a prayer. "Please, please, please, Gemma, let's not die inside before we have to."

"What can I do?"

"Promise me we might hold on to this magic a bit longer, until I can secure my future—just until our debut," she pleads.

"That is weeks away yet," I answer. "And I must make amends with the forest folk. We should make the alliance."

"Gemma, this is the rest of my life," she begs, her tears turning to anger.

Two giggling girls streak past the tent in a blur of ribbon and lace. They twirl furiously in their princess gowns, picking up speed, laughing madly. It's no matter that the dresses are only a night's borrowed finery. They believe, and the belief changes everything.

I put my palms to Felicity's in promise. "I'll try."

⌁⌁⌁

I sit on my bed trying to make sense of everything, but I can't, and May first will soon be here. As a distraction, I tidy up my few possessions, arranging them neatly in my cupboard: the ivory elephant all the way from India, my mother's diary, Kartik's red bandana, Simon's false-bottom box. I should toss that out. I open the secret chamber, and it's as empty as I feel inside. *A place to keep all your secrets*, he told me. It will take a box larger than this for my secrets. I leave it on Ann's bed as a gift and resume my straightening. I stack my books in one corner. Gloves and handkerchiefs. Wilhelmina Wyatt's slate, mute as its owner. What to do with that? Useless. And heavy. That thick wooden base weighing it down . . . Suddenly, I realize how stupid I've been.

The illustration in the book—it told me where to look all along. The Hidden Object. Wilhelmina Wyatt was a magician's assistant, with a knowledge of sleight of hand. If she'd wanted to hide something . . .

I feel around the edges of the slate until my fingernail finds a small latch in the wood. I press it down, and the board loosens. When I slide it out of the way, there's the leather roll I've seen in my visions. My fingers shake as I slip the ties loose and peel back the ends.

And there inside is a slim dagger with a jeweled hilt.

CHAPTER FIFTY-ONE

May 1

THE SUN HAS TAKEN ITS BOW, AND DUSK DESCENDS. THE air is warm; birds give a last concert before sleep. All in all, it is the perfect night for Spence's masked ball, but I shall not rest easy until the night passes.

Lanterns have been set out on the lawn and far down the road to light the way. A long black line of carriages snakes toward us and around the drive. Our families arrive. Servants help Marie Antoinette and Sir Walter Raleigh, Napoleon and Queen Elizabeth from their coaches. All sorts of colorful characters drift over the lawn. With their masked faces, they lend the festivities a fantastical air. Music fills the ballroom. It floats from the open windows and into the woods. Girls streak by in layers of lace and tulle. I'm enjoying none of it.

I'd hoped Kartik would surprise me tonight. But there has been no signal, so I take my lantern to the front lawn to wait for my own family to arrive. I see Father first. He is a raja with a jeweled turban. Grandmama, who lives in terror of enjoying herself, has worn one of her gowns, but she has added a Harlequin mask on a stick. Tom wears a jester's hat, which is far more appropriate than he knows.

"Ah, here is our Gemma now," Father says, taking in the sight of my tunic and boots—and the jeweled dagger at my waist. "But soft, she is not our Gemma at all but a leader of men! A saint for the ages!"

"It's Gemma of Arc," Tom sneers.

"And the fool," I counter.

"I am a jester. It is not the same at all," he sniffs. "I do hope there is supper."

Father has one of his coughing fits.

"Are you well enough, Papa?"

"Fit as a fiddle." He wheezes. His face is red and sweaty. "Just haven't quite got used to this country air."

"Dr. Hamilton said it would do you good." Grandmama tuts.

"The doctor was called for?"

Father pats my hand. "Now, now, pet. Nothing to worry about. All well and good. Let's see what fine entertainment is in store tonight."

A parlor maid holds a serving bowl offering ornate masks—birds, animals, imps, and Harlequins. They turn the smiles worn beneath them into threatening leers.

Felicity is a Valkyrie, her shining blond hair flowing over a dress of silver complete with wings. Her mother has come as Little Bo Peep; her father wears his naval uniform and a fox mask. The Markhams have come as well, much to Mrs. Nightwing's delight and Felicity's misery. Each time Horace, in his Lord Fauntleroy blues, draws near, she looks as if she could strangle him, which only makes him want her the more.

I wish I could go to her, to dance and turn the magic loose as we've done before. But a refrain beats inside me: *Beware the birth of May.* And I can't say what this night will bring.

Mrs. Nightwing is eager to show the assembly why Spence has its reputation for grace, strength, and beauty, as our motto promises. She has come as Florence Nightingale, her hero. It would prove amusing if I didn't distrust her so.

"Ladies and gentlemen, I thank you deeply for your attendance this evening. Since its inception, Spence has enjoyed a reputation as an institution where girls become the finest of young ladies. But for many years, our great school has borne the painful reminder of a terrible tragedy. I speak of the East Wing and the fire that claimed it along with the lives of two of our girls and of our beloved founder, Eugenia Spence. But in her honor, we have resurrected the East Wing, and your generous donations shall make it possible to see to its refurbishment. I humbly thank you.

"And now, without further ado, I should like to present a program by our shining jewels. These jewels of which I speak are not diamonds or rubies but the kind and noble girls of Spence."

Mrs. Nightwing dabs quickly at her eyes and takes her seat. Several of the younger girls—princesses and fairies all—perform a dance, enchanting the guests with their easy innocence.

A man sidles up next to me. His mask hides his face, but I'd know that voice anywhere.

"Nice evenin' for a party, innit?"

"What are you doing here?" I demand, my heartbeat quickening.

"I was invited, luv." He grins like a devil.

I snarl low in his ear. "If you do anything to me or my family or my friends, if you make any move at all, I shall employ the magic against you in such a way that you'll never threaten anyone ever again."

Fowlson's grin is quick and wide. "That's the spirit, luv." He puts his mouth dangerously close to my neck. "But don't fret, Miss Doyle. I'm not 'ere tonight for you. Is your friend Kartik 'ere? If not, it's no worries—I'll find 'im, I'm sure."

Kartik.

I turn and run from the room as the little girls curtsy politely, like the adorable dolls they are, and the guests applaud them. I'm out of breath by the time I reach Kartik in the boathouse. "Fowlson is here. I believe he's come for you," I gasp. "To hurt you."

He doesn't seem alarmed, doesn't make a move.

"Did you hear what I said?"

"Yes," he says, closing his book. "*The Odyssey*. I've finished it, if you'd care to read it."

I grab hold of his arm. "We have to hide you. I could turn you into someone else or—"

"I'll not go into hiding again," he says. "And I'm not concerned about Mr. Fowlson."

"You're not?"

He places the book on a high ledge by the window. "I've changed my mind. I need to know if Amar . . . I need to know. Do you understand?"

"You're ready to see the realms," I say.

"I don't know that I'm ready," he says, with a small scoffing laugh. "But I would go. I would see them."

I offer him my hand. "Trust me."

Kartik laces his fingers in mine. "Show me."

"We must be careful," I say. With everyone watching the performance, the lawn is empty and silent. But I wouldn't want to draw any attention. We crouch and run low across the grass until we reach the turret of the East Wing. I put my hand out. The air crackles. The door shimmers into view. Kartik's face shows true awe.

"That is extraordinary," he whispers.

"That is nothing," I say. I grip his hand and lead him through the corridor, and when we go through the door, he is a man transformed.

"Welcome to the realms," I say.

CHAPTER FIFTY-TWO

I SHOW HIM THE GARDEN FIRST, BECAUSE THAT IS WHERE I first came to know this world and because it is so beautiful I want to share it with him. Kartik spins around, his head leaned back. White blossoms rain down, coating his hair and eyelashes like snow. He opens his palms to accept them.

"This is the garden," I say almost proudly. "There is the river. Over there is the grotto where the Runes of the Oracle once stood. This is where the Order ruled, where the Rakshana once ruled with them."

"I feel as if I'm in a dream." Kartik strides to the river and moves his hand over the singing waters. Eddies of silver, gold, and pink spring to the surface where he has touched it.

"Look at this," I say. I blow on blades of grass and they become a flutter of butterfly wings. One lands on Kartik's outstretched hand before flying away. I've never seen Kartik so happy, so carefree. He finds the hammock I wove weeks ago and falls into it, listening to the sweet murmuring of its threads. He rolls the sleeves of his shirt to a point above his elbows, and though it is immodest, I cannot keep myself from stealing quick glances at his exposed arms.

"Would you care to sit?" He offers the narrow strip beside him.

"No, thank you," I manage to say. "There is so much else to see."

⌁⌁⌁⌁⌁

I lead him through the poppy fields below the Temple, pointing to the high cliffs that rise above us. Etched into the sides are the sensual carvings of half-dressed women that brought a blush to my cheek the first time I saw them. From the corner of my eye, I watch Kartik, wondering if he will find them scandalous.

"They remind me of India," he says.

"Yes, exactly so," I say, hoping my voice does not betray me.

Kartik's gaze dips to my neck and shyly down.

"I should show you the Caves of Sighs," I say, my voice slightly hoarse.

I lead him through the narrow passage in the earth, up the mountain pass, among the pots that belch their colorful smoke, and to the top. The Hajin bow to us, and Kartik returns the gesture with respect.

"These are the Caves of Sighs," I say. We pass the engraving of the two hands clasped inside a circle. Kartik stops before it.

"I know this. It's Rakshana."

"It belongs also to the Order," I say.

"Do you know what it means?" he asks, moving closer to it.

I nod, blushing. "It is the symbol for love."

· 610 ·

He smiles. "Yes, I remember now. The hands inside a circle. You see? The hands are protected by the circle, the symbol of eternity."

"Eternity?"

"Because there is no telling where it begins or ends, nor does it matter."

He traces the pattern with his fingers.

I clear my throat faintly. "They say you can see each other's dreams if you place your hands inside the circle."

"Is that so?" He lets his palm rest just outside it.

"Yes," I say.

Wind blows through the caves and they sigh. The stones speak. *This is a place of dreams for those who are willing to see. Place your hands inside the circle and dream.*

I put my hands inside the circle and wait. He doesn't look at me and he doesn't move. He will not do it. I know him. My heart sinks with the knowledge.

He shifts his hand inside, near my own. Our fingers and thumbs reach toward each other but do not quite touch, our hands two countries separated by the narrowest of oceans. And then his fingers nudge mine. The stones fade away. A bright white light forces me to close my eyes. My body falls away and I am inside a dream.

∿∿∿∿

My arms shine with golden bangles that catch the light. My hands and feet have been painted in ornate patterns, like a bride's. I wear a sari the deep purple of an orchid. When I move, the folds of the fabric change color, glistening from orange to red, from indigo to silver.

A celebration is taking place. Girls in bright yellow saris dance barefoot on a blanket of lotus blossoms. Smiling warmly, they dip their hands into large clay bowls, scooping up rose petals, which they throw high into the air. The colorful rain falls slowly, the petals settling in my hair and on my bare arms. The scent reminds me of my mother, but I am not sad. It is too joyful a day.

The girls clear a path for me. They run, tossing flowers until the way ahead is a fluttering spectacle of red and white. I follow them toward blue sky. I am at the mouth of a mighty stone temple as ancient as days. Above me, Shiva, the god of destruction and rebirth, sits meditating, his third eye seeing all. Below me are perhaps one hundred steps. I take my first step and everything vanishes—the temple, the girls, the flowers, everything. I am alone on desert sand, the only blot of color for miles. There is nothing in any direction but sky. Hours feel like seconds; seconds are hours, for time is a dream.

A warm wind rushes past, the grains of sand brushing gently at my cheeks. And then I see him. He's no more than a speck coming toward me from the distance, but I know it's him, and suddenly, he's before me. He rides a painted horse, and his clothes are black and fine. A garland hangs from his neck. In the center of his forehead is a red mark made with turmeric, like an Indian bridegroom's.

"Hello," he says. He smiles, and it is brighter than the sun. He reaches down; I take his hand; and the world falls away again. We stand in a garden made fragrant by lotus blossoms as large as beds.

"Where are we?" I ask. My voice sounds strange in my ears.

"We're here," he says, as if that answers everything, and in a sense, it does.

He takes his knife and draws a ring around me in the dirt.

"What are you doing?" I ask.

"This circle symbolizes the joining of our souls," he answers. He circles me seven times, stepping into the enclosure on the seventh. We stand facing each other. He presses his palms to mine.

I do not know if I am dreaming.

He slips his hand behind my neck, pulling me gently toward him. His hands twine in my hair and he rubs the strands between his fingers like a fine silk he longs to purchase. And then his mouth is on mine, hungry, searching, overpowering.

This is a new world, and I will travel it.

I don't know what I should like him to say: *I love you. You are beautiful. Never leave me.* It seems I hear all of this and yet he says only one word, my name, and I realize I have never heard him say it this way before: as if I am known. The skin of his chest is smooth under the weight of my fingers. When my lips brush against the hollow of his throat, he makes a sound that is a bit like a sigh and a growl.

"Gemma . . ."

His lips are on me in a fever of kissing. My mouth. My jaw. My neck. The insides of my arms. He places his hands at the small of my back and kisses my stomach through the rough fabric of my dress, sending sparks through my veins. He lifts my hair and warms the back of my neck with his mouth, trailing kisses down my spine while his hands cup my breasts gently. The laces of my corset are loosened. I'm able to breathe him in now. Kartik has shed his shirt. I don't recall when it happened, and for some reason, I forget to be shamed by it. I only note his beauty: the smooth brown of his skin, the breadth of his shoulders, the muscles of his arms, so very different from my own. The rose-strewn ground is soft and yielding under my body. Kartik presses against me, and I feel as if I could sink right through the giving earth. Instead, I push against him, feeling warm, till I think I could die from it.

"Are you certain . . . ?"

For once, I do not feel apart. I kiss him again, letting my tongue explore the warmth just inside his lips. Kartik's eyes flutter, and then he opens them wide, with a look I cannot describe, as if he has just glimpsed something precious that he thought lost. He pulls me tightly to him. My hands grip his shoulders. Our mouths and bodies speak for us in a new language as the trees shake loose a rain of petals that stick to our slickness like skins we will wear forever. And just like that, I am changed.

✦✦✦✦✦

When I open my eyes, I am back in the Caves of Sighs. My fingers just graze Kartik's on the stone. My breathing is heavy. Did he see what I saw? Did we dream the same dream? I dare not look at him. I feel his finger, as light as rain, beneath my chin. He turns my face to his.

"Did you dream?" I whisper.

"Yes," he answers, and kisses me.

For the longest time we sit in the Caves of Sighs, talking of nothing and yet saying everything.

"I understand why my brothers in the Rakshana wanted to hold fast to such a place," he says. He strokes the underside of my arm with his fingers. "It would be hard to leave it, I think."

My throat is tight. Could we stay here? Would he stay if I asked him?

"Thank you for bringing me," he says.

"You're welcome," I answer. "I've something else to share with you."

I press our palms together. Our fingers tingle where they touch. His eyelids flicker and then they open wide in understanding of the magical gift I've given him.

Reluctantly, I take my hand away. "You can do anything."

"Anything," he repeats.

I nod.

"Well, then."

He closes the small distance between us and puts his lips against mine. They are soft but the kiss is firm. He puts his hand sweetly on the back of my neck and pulls my face to him with the other. He kisses me again, harder this time, but it's just as lovely. His lips are so necessary that I cannot imagine how I can live without tasting them always. Perhaps this is how girls fall—not in some crime of enchantment at the hands of a wicked ne'er-do-well, a grand before and after in which they are innocent victims who have no say in the matter. Perhaps they simply are kissed and want to kiss back. Perhaps they even kiss first. And why should they not?

I count the kisses—*one, two, three, eight*. Quickly, I pull away to catch my breath and my bearings. "But . . . you could have whatever you wished."

"Exactly," he says, nuzzling my neck.

"But," I say, "you could turn stones to rubies or ride in a fine gentleman's carriage."

Kartik puts his hands on either side of my face. "To each his own magic," he says, and kisses me again.

CHAPTER FIFTY-THREE

WHEN WE EMERGE FROM THE CAVES, ASHA IS THERE.

"Lady Hope, the gorgon is below. She would speak with you. She says it is urgent."

"Gorgon?" Kartik says, eyes wide. His hand moves instinctively to his knife.

"You won't have need of that," I say. "The worst she shall do is vex you to death. Then you may wish it to end your own misery."

Gorgon waits on the river. Kartik gasps at the sight of her fearsome green face and yellow eyes, the many snakes wriggling round her head like the rays of some forgotten sun god.

"Gorgon! You've returned," I say, beaming. I have missed her, I find.

"I am sorry, Most High. You asked me not to seek you out, but it is of the utmost importance."

My cheeks turn pink. "I was wrong. I spoke too harshly. May I present Kartik, late of the Rakshana."

"Greetings," Gorgon says.

"Greetings," Kartik replies, his eyes still wide, his hand still on his knife.

Gorgon's slithery voice is tinged with apprehension. "I have been to the Winterlands through a route my people once knew ages ago. I would show you what I have seen."

"Take us," I say, and we climb aboard.

I sit at the base of Gorgon's thick neck, avoiding the snakes that hiss and writhe about her head. They venture too close at times, reminding me that even the most trusted of our allies have the power to maim. Kartik steers well clear of them. He stares at the strange, forbidding world ahead, for we are passing into the Winterlands. Green fog rolls in. The ship slips quietly down a narrow channel and into a cave. We pass under icy stalactites as long as a sea serpent's teeth, and I recognize this place.

"I have seen Amar here," I tell Kartik, and his face becomes grim.

"Here," Gorgon says, slowing to a halt. "Just over there."

She lowers the plank, and I wade through the few inches of stagnant water to the side of the cave, where something has washed up. It's the water nymph who led me to Amar. Her lifeless eyes stare up at nothing.

"What has happened to her?" I ask. "Is it an illness?"

"Look closer," Gorgon says.

I don't want to touch her, but I do. Her skin is cold. Scales come off in my hands. They're matted with dried blood. She has a wound—a deep red line at her neck.

"And you suspect the Winterlands creatures?" I ask.

Gorgon's voice pulses in the cave. "This is greater than the Winterlands creatures. It is beyond my knowing."

I close the nymph's dull eyes so that she appears only to sleep.

"What would you have me do, Most High?" Gorgon asks.

"You're asking me?"

"If you would lead, yes."

If I would lead. Standing in this forsaken cave with the water nymph's cold body so near and my friends so far, I must make a decision.

"I want to see more. I want to know. Can we travel farther?"

"As you wish."

"You do not have to accompany me," I say to Kartik. "I could return you to the camp first."

"I will come," he says. He checks the dagger in his boot.

"Most High," Gorgon says. There is worry in her voice. "We have come this far without being detected. But I would not go farther without some protection. It might be wise to call upon your powers to aid us."

"Agreed," I say. "But I shall need to gift you, so that we might work our purpose together—"

"No," Gorgon interrupts. "I would not hold the magic even for a moment."

"I need you, Gorgon," I say. "It requires all of us together."

"I must not be freed," Gorgon says. "As long as you understand this."

"I understand," I say. "We shall decide on an illusion and concentrate on only that one goal. Agreed?"

Kartik nods.

"Agreed," Gorgon hisses.

I board the ship. I place one hand on Gorgon's thick, scaly neck and the other on Kartik's arm. The magic stretches between the three of us. I feel as if it is a wave I sit upon and I am not sucked under by it. We are united by purpose and we share the burden equally. I imagine the Viking ship we rode in the Winterlands—the tall sails, the oars. I imagine Kartik and myself as phantoms in tattered cloaks. Our hearts beat in rhythm. When I open my eyes, we have accomplished our task. Kartik and I appear as wraiths. Gorgon is like a statue, her snakes as still as marble.

"Gorgon?" I ask warily.

"I am well, Most High. You have done well."

"*We* have done well," I say, and the satisfaction is no less for sharing it. "Let's see what the Winterlands may be hiding."

⌁⌁⌁⌁⌁

Gorgon guides us along the river where it winds through a canyon of black rock. Gray-green brume rises from the water. It thins as we move along, and as it does, I can see more of this strange land than I've seen before. Ragged flags marked with red stick up from the tops of the craggy mountains. They snap in the brisk wind, and it sounds like rifles firing. Hollows have been carved into the black rock. Gorgon glides close to one. Skulls are stacked dozens high. My heart gallops faster and faster. I want to turn back, but I must know what is happening.

A school of silver fish floats upon the water, dead.

"Perhaps it is nothing," I say, uncertain.

"Perhaps," she hisses. "And perhaps it is something very wrong indeed. I fear some terrible magic is at work."

A crow circles overhead, a thick black thumbprint in the sky.

"Follow it," I say to Gorgon.

A roaring fills my ears. We've come to a canyon where majestic falls border us on both sides. The water churns and we are buffeted. Kartik and I hold fast to each other and to Gorgon. Sharp rocks poke above the water and I am afraid we shall be dashed upon them, but Gorgon steers us clear, and we pass safely out of the canyon and into a shallow tidal pool glazed with ice. It is littered with bones and the carcasses of small dead animals. The cold wind cannot blow away the smell of death and decay. Small fires burn around the periphery. Smoke billows from them, thick and harsh, and I feel the burn of it in the back of my throat. A mix of ash and snow drifts down. It sticks to my skin. In the distance, an arch in the cliffs yields to the black sands of the plains.

Gorgon edges closer, and I could choke on my fear. For there behind the fires is an army of Winterlands creatures—skeletal trackers in tattered black robes, Poppy Warriors, pale creatures with skin like chalk and eyes ringed in black. So many creatures. I had not realized. This appears to be their camp, shielded as it is by the cliffs. They sit with the dead, who appear dazed and unseeing.

"Stop!" a creature to my left says, and I feel Kartik's hand hovering near his dagger. The creature is as gray as death. He pulls back rotting lips to reveal yellow nubs of teeth. His eyelids are lined in red, but his eyes are the milky blue of Pippa's. "Have you come for the ritual?"

Kartik nods. I pray our illusion will hold.

Six trackers emerge at the arch. "Follow!" the hideous beasts call. The creatures rise, and the dead shuffle behind as if sleepwalking. With a last glance at Gorgon's stony face, Kartik and I join the others.

The trackers thunder over the plains and we follow. The

ground crunches like shells beneath my feet. I think I see a leg bone poking up through the grit and quickly look away. *Calm, Gemma. Calm. Keep the illusion.*

We come to a narrow pass. Pale, skinless creatures emerge from behind the rocks and from crevices, blinking against the dim light of the churning gray sky. The creature beside us snarls and gnashes his teeth at one of the pale things, which slips back under the rock until all I can see are its blinking eyes.

The crows circle overhead, crying. They lead us out of the chasm and my pulse quickens, for we are on the heath. And there before us is the Tree of All Souls.

The Winterlands creatures gather on the plains. Kartik squeezes my hand, and I can feel his terror joined to mine. Three of the dead are brought forth—a woman and two men. Beside me, Kartik draws a short breath. Just behind the creatures, on a magnificent steed, is Amar.

"The more we sacrifice, the greater our power grows," he thunders as the dead are made to kneel before the Tree of All Souls.

"Do you give yourselves willingly to the greater glory? Will you be sacrificed for our cause?" Amar asks them.

"We will," they answer numbly.

"These souls are ready," Kartik's brother says.

The vines move like whips, wrapping around the necks of the victims, pulling them up into the tree's expanse like puppets. Amar draws a sword from a sheath at his side. He rides out, then turns, running hard for the dead like a knight in a joust.

On the heath, the Winterlands creatures watch; some cower while others chant their approval: *"Sacrifice, sacrifice, sacrifice . . ."*

As we watch in horror, Amar's sword comes down on the dead. Kartik starts, and I hold fast to his arm. Their blood drips, and the roots accept it greedily. With a terrible scream, the souls of the victims are drawn into the enormous ash tree. Before our eyes, it grows even taller. Its mighty boughs stretch out in every direction like giant claws. The sky bleeds red.

Amar and the trackers place their hands to the tree's twisted trunk, drinking in what power there is, while the army of creatures looks on.

"One day, you, too, shall feed," a tracker shouts. "After the sacrifice."

The creatures nod. "Yes, one day," they answer, believing it without question.

"Our cause is just!" another one of the trackers shouts. His robes open to reveal the howling spirits within.

"Freedom is within our reach at last," Amar thunders. "She has set the plan in motion. All pieces come together. When she gives the word, we will sacrifice their great priestess and both worlds—the realms and the mortals'—will fall to us."

The creatures shout and raise their fists in imagined victory.

One of the trackers sniffs the air. "Something is amiss," he howls. "I feel the living among us!"

Snarling and shrieking, the creatures turn on each other, pointing accusing fingers. One of the beasts jumps on the back of another with shouts of "Traitor!" before sinking his teeth into the other's neck. The trackers try to take control but it is hard for them to be heard above the din.

"Kartik," I whisper, "we must leave."

He still stares at his cursed brother, his eyes wet. I do not wait for his response. Quickly, I pull him away from the crowd and the terrible sight of what his brother has become. We slip carefully through the crowd, narrowly avoiding the punches thrown. As we come to the chasm through the rock, I hear Amar shouting for order amidst the chaos. The sky screams. Another soul has been sacrificed, and the creatures unite, cheering.

More skinless creatures slither from the rocks. They grab at our ankles with hands as slick and fast as fish, making me scream. It echoes for a moment, and I fear it shall be heard by the others. I kick at the thing's hand. It slinks back into its hiding place, and I pull Kartik as quickly as I can toward the boat.

"Gorgon, we must leave with the utmost haste," I say.

"As you wish, Most High." She steers a course out of the Winterlands. I tell her what we have seen, though as a kindness, I do not mention Amar's part in it. The churning sky eases into the indifferent dusk of the Borderlands, then into the bright blue near the Caves of Sighs, and into the orange sunset of the garden.

Kartik has not spoken a word the entire voyage. He has sat on deck, his knees drawn to his chest, his head buried in his hands. I do not know what to say. I would have spared him that.

"She," I say, shaking my head. "She set the plan in motion."

"What is it?" Gorgon asks.

An anger I've never known rises in me. "Circe. She made a pact with the creatures long ago, and she wanted me to think that was in the past. She's never stopped trying to take back the power. I won't be her pawn any longer."

"What would you bid me do, Most High?"

"Ride to Philon and the forest folk. Tell them what has

happened and that I would join hands with them tonight. I will return with my friends, and we will meet at the Temple. Offer to the Untouchables again as well. They may still be swayed."

"As you wish."

"Gorgon," I call.

"Yes, Most High?"

I do not know how to ask what I want to know. "If I share the magic, if we join hands, will that end it?"

Gorgon shakes her head slowly. "I cannot say. These are strange days. Nothing is as it was before. All rules are forfeit, and no one knows what will happen."

<hr>

I lead Kartik over the path by the Borderlands and through the corridor. We step through the secret door onto the lawn of Spence. From the open windows above, I can hear applause and murmuring. Nightwing announcing Miss Cecily Temple's recitation of "The Rose of Battle."

Everything is familiar and yet nothing seems as it was. Kartik won't look at me, and I wish we could go back to that moment in the Caves of Sighs when we put our hands to the stones.

"That creature feeding souls to the tree. That was my brother."

"I'm very sorry." I reach out my fingers but he will not be touched. "Kartik."

"I've failed him. I've failed—"

He brushes past me and breaks into a run.

CHAPTER FIFTY-FOUR

I'M TREMBLING AS I RETURN TO THE MASKED BALL. A MAN in a Harlequin mask brushes past, startling me.

"Terribly sorry," he says, giving me a smile that seems demonic beneath that hideous mask.

I slip back into the ballroom, where the girls perform their recital. I see Felicity sitting with Ann in her Lady Macbeth costume. "I must speak with you both at once," I whisper, and they hurry after me to the library. Ann flips idly through a halfpenny paper: *Mabel: A Girl of Newbury School*. I've no doubt it follows the same story as all the others: A poor but decent girl is subjected to the cruel taunts of her school chums, only to be saved by a rich relative. And then all the petty schoolgirls are right sorry they've teased her so. But Mabel (or Annabelle or Dorothy—they are all the same) forgives them sweetly, never thinking a bad thought about anyone, and everyone has learned a valuable lesson in the end.

I should like to throw that rubbish on the fire.

"All right, Gemma. Out with it," Felicity commands. "We're missing the party."

"The Winterlands creatures are not dying out. They have an army, thousands strong," I say, words tumbling out of me as from a patient at Bedlam. "They've been sacrificing souls to the tree to gather their power, but they're waiting for something. For someone." I take a breath. "I believe it's Circe."

"Now you believe it," Felicity says.

I ignore her jab. "We must go into the realms, return the dagger to Eugenia, and make the alliance—"

"You mean give back the magic?" Ann asks.

"It isn't ours. It's only borrowed—"

Felicity interrupts. "But what about Pip? We must tell her!"

"Fee," I start, "we can't. If she is one of them—"

"She's not! You just said it was Circe." Felicity's eyes narrow. "How did you come to know this, Gemma?"

Too late I realize my folly. "I went into the realms. To see."

"Alone?" Felicity presses.

"No. With Kartik."

Ann glares at me. "You took him in without telling us?"

"I needed to show him—"

"The realms belong to us, not him!" Felicity insists. "Only yesterday you said we shouldn't go into the realms without one another. Now you've done it!"

"Yes, and I'm sorry, but this was another matter," I argue, though even I can hear how weak it is.

"You lied!" Felicity shouts.

"Listen to me, please! Will you listen to me for one moment? I've asked Gorgon to gather the Hajin and the forest folk at the

Temple so that we might share the magic with them. We must go tonight. Don't you see?"

"I see that you don't care what your friends think. What they want." In her costume, Felicity is every bit the warrior maiden. Her eyes sparkle with hurt. "Pip warned me this might happen."

"What do you mean? What did she say?" I ask.

"Why should I tell you? Perhaps you can ask Kartik. You share more confidences with him than you do with your friends."

"I'm here with you now, aren't I?" I say, my anger sparking.

"She said you wouldn't like sharing the magic. That you never meant to, not the way she would," Felicity says.

"That isn't true." But I cannot deny how much I have relished having something others did not.

Felicity takes Ann's hand. "It's no matter," Felicity says, pulling Ann toward the door. "You forget that we may do as we please. We may enter the realms when we wish. With or without you."

⌁⌁⌁⌁⌁

I pass through the rooms as if in a fever. The ballroom blooms with merry dancers. But I am not in the mood for dancing. In my mind, I see those horrid creatures, Amar leading the dead to sacrifice. I see the pain in Kartik's eyes. I wonder where he has gone and when he will come back. If he will come back.

People crowd the floor for a dance with intricate steps, but they follow them without mishap, and I am envious. For there are no steps for me to follow on this journey; I must find my own way. I cannot be part of this gaudy convocation of princesses and fairies, jesters and imps, specters and illusions. I am so very tired of illusions. I need someone to listen, to help me.

Father. I could tell him everything. The time has come for truth. I hurry through room after room, searching for him. Fowlson lurks in a corner. He sneers at me. "Joan of Arc. She came to a bad end, didn't she?"

"You could come to a bad end now," I whisper fiercely, and press on. At last, I see my father holding court with Mrs. Nightwing, Tom . . . and Lord Denby. I march straight up to the snake.

"What are you doing here?" I demand.

"Gemma Doyle!" Father barks. "You will apologize."

"I will not. He's a monster, Father!"

Tom's face reddens. He looks as if he could kill me. But Lord Denby only laughs. "This is what comes of empowering women, old chap. They become dangerous."

I spirit Father away to the parlor and close the door. Father settles himself into a chair. From his pocket he removes the pipe I gave him for Christmas and a small pouch of tobacco. "I am very disappointed in you, Gemma."

Disappointed. That word, like a knife to the heart. "Yes, Father. I'm sorry, but it truly is urgent. It's something you must know about me. About Mother." My pulse quickens. The words catch in my throat and burn there. I could swallow them like a bitter pill as I have done so many times before. It would be easier. But I cannot. They come back up, and I choke on them as they do.

"What if I told you that Mother was not who she appeared to be? What if I told you that her true name was

Mary Dowd, and that she was a member of a secret society of sorceresses?"

"I would say it was not a very good joke," he says darkly, packing tobacco into the bowl of his pipe.

I shake my head. "It is not a joke. It's true. Mother attended Spence years before me. She caused the fire that burned Spence's East Wing. She was a member of a society of magical women called the Order. They trained at Spence. She could enter a world beyond this one called the realms. It is a beautiful place, Father. But also frightening at times. She was part of the magic there. And I have the same magic running through my veins. And that is why they want to kill me—to take my magic."

Father's smile fades. "Gemma, this tale is not amusing."

I can't stop. It is as if every truth I have ever held secret inside me must come out. "She wasn't killed by accident. She knew that man in India, Amar. He was her protector. They died trying to protect me from a murderous sorceress named Circe."

Father's gaze is hard, and it frightens me, but I don't stop. I can't. Not now. "I saw her there, in the realms, after she died. I talked to her! She was worried about you. She said—"

"That is quite enough!" Father's words are quiet but coiled, a whip at the ready.

"But it's true," I say, choking back tears. "She did not visit charity wards in hospitals or tend to the sick! She never did, Papa, and you know it."

"It is how I wish to remember her."

"But doesn't it matter that it isn't really how she was? Didn't you ever wonder why you knew nothing of her past? Why she was so mysterious? Did you not ask?"

He rises and walks toward the door. "This conversation has come to an end. You will apologize to Lord Denby for your rudeness, Gemma."

Like a child, I run to keep up with him. "Lord Denby is a part of this. He's of the Rakshana and he means to recruit Tom in order to take my magic from me. He—"

"Gemma," he warns.

"But, Papa," I say, my voice strangled by the sob I dare not let out. "Isn't it better to speak the truth, to know—"

"I do not want to know!" he bellows, and I am silenced.

He doesn't want to know. About Mother or Tom or me. Or himself.

"Gemma, pet, let's forget this nonsense and return to the party, shall we?" He coughs hard into his handkerchief. He can't seem to draw a clear breath. But the spasm subsides; the red in his face fades like a sunset.

I cannot answer. It is as if a cold, hard weight has been placed upon my chest. Everyone thinks my father such a charming man. If only I wanted charm and nothing deeper, I should be a happy girl. I want to hate him for his easy charm. I want to but I can't, because he is all I have. And if I have to, I will *make* him see.

"Father."

Before he can object, I take hold of his arm and we are joined. His eyes widen. He tries to pull from my grasp. He can't stay with me—not even for this one moment. And this small knowledge hits the deepest wound within me hard.

"You will see, Father. You'll know the truth even if I have to force you to see it."

The more he fights it, the more magic I have to employ. I

show him everything, feeling him tremble in my grasp, hearing the small cries of denial. Soon I am aware of him as well. His secrets. His vanities. His fears. His life flits past my mind, a thick ribbon unspooling. And I am the one who should like to look away. But I can't. There's too much magic at work. I am no longer in control. We're recklessly joined. I am aware of the small scrap of paper in his pocket, an address in East London where he will find the opium he craves. It has begun again. I feel his struggle turning to resolve. He will do it, and the cycle will begin again.

Despair, shiny and jagged, rakes across me. I swallow hard and will myself not to feel. Not to care. But I can't. I know that the magic can't heal, but that doesn't stop me from trying. I will take this longing from him, and then I will cure Tom of his attraction to the Rakshana, and we will be as happy as we were before.

Father gives another small cry, and suddenly, I feel nothing from him. My hand is cold where it touches his. I break the contact, and Father falls to the floor, unmoving. His eyes are open; his mouth is twisted. His breathing is strangled.

"Father!" I shout, but he's beyond me. What have I done?

I run for Mrs. Nightwing and Tom.

"It's Father," I blurt out. "He's in the parlor."

With me leading the way, we hurry back. Tom and my headmistress move Father to a chair. His breath is still raspy, and there is bloody spittle on his bottom lip. His eyes stare straight at me, accusing.

"What the devil happened?" Tom asks.

I can't answer. I want to cry, but I'm too horrified. Lord Denby appears. "Can I be of assistance?"

"Stay away from my father!" I shout. The magic roars to life again, and it takes all my strength to silence it.

"Gemma!" Tom reprimands me.

"She's overcome by grief. Perhaps we should help the young lady to her room," Lord Denby suggests, reaching for my arm.

"No! Don't touch me!"

"Miss Doyle . . . ," Mrs. Nightwing starts, but I don't stay to hear the end of it. I run fast for the secret door, and as I stagger through the passageway, I could swear I see the Borderlands fairy there, but I can't stop. Magic leaks from my pores. My legs shake, but I make it all the way up the mountain and to the well of eternity and Circe.

"Asha, have the forest folk come?"

"I have not seen them," she answers. "Are you well, Lady Hope?"

No. I am not well. I am diseased with hate. "Stand by. I may have need of you."

"As you wish, Lady Hope."

Face your fears. That's what the well is for. I'm ready. And after tonight, I'll have nothing more to fear.

The room is warm. Close. And the floor is wet. Water trickles from tiny cracks in the well.

"Circe," I call.

"Hello, Gemma," she answers, and my name echoes in the cave.

"I know you've made a pact with the Winterlands creatures. You were in league with them all along. But now I have the dagger, and I'll set things right."

It's quiet save for the trickling of the water.

"Do you deny you wanted my power?"

"I've never denied that," she says, and there is nothing of the careful whisper to her voice now. "You say you have the dagger?"

"I do, and I'll return it to Eugenia, and all your plotting will be for nothing," I say. "Wilhelmina Wyatt tried to warn me. The two of you were close—Brigid told me. And Wilhelmina told Dr. Van Ripple that her sister had betrayed her—'A monster.' I can think of no one that description fits more. She trusted you," I say, fighting the magic inside me. "As my mother did. As I did for a time. But not anymore."

"And what will you do now?"

"What I should have done already," I say. "The forest folk are coming to make the alliance along with the Hajin. We will lay hands together at the well. I'll return the magic and bind it. And you will die."

A rippling sound, clear and strong, comes from the well. Movement. One of the stones pushes out of the well, and water splashes out in a stream. It is followed by another and another, and then, like some leviathan of the deep, Circe rises from the well, pink and alive.

"How—"

"I am part of this world now, Gemma. Like your friend Pippa."

"But you were trapped. . . ." I trail off.

"I had you give the magic to the well first, so that I could draw from it. I used it to loosen the stones. But really, the die was cast the first time you gifted me—when you gave it to me of your own will. That was all I required to be free."

I tuck the dagger into the sheath at my waist, safely out of sight. "Then why didn't you do this earlier?"

"I needed more magic," she says, stepping over the broken wall. "And I am patient. It is a reward for having lived through a great deal of disappointment."

I take a step back.

"I'd had higher hopes for you, Gemma. You're in over your head. I shall see this Tree of All Souls for myself."

"I won't let you," I say, the magic building inside. "I've lost enough tonight."

With everything I have in me, I call up the magic, and then Circe flies back, landing in a heap on the floor.

She crawls to her feet, panting. "Nicely done."

I wave my arm over the stones of the well and send them shooting toward her. She stops them inches from her face and they drop to the floor in shards.

"Your power is impressive, Gemma. How much I would have enjoyed a true friendship with you," she says as we circle one another.

"You're not capable of true friendship," I snap. I reach for a shard, and it becomes a snake under Circe's touch. I drop it fast.

"Don't just react, Gemma. Think. The Order was right about that, at least."

"Don't tell me what to do!" I turn Circe's snake into a whip that gashes her across the back.

She cries out in pain, and her eyes go steely. "I see you've searched those dark corners after all."

"You should know. You put them there."

"No, I only helped you to see them," she says, but then I'm forcing her to her knees under the magic's heel.

"Gemma." I hear Kartik's voice, and when I turn, he's there on the floor. His face is bloodied.

Abandoning Circe, I run to him. "Did she do this? How did—"

He starts to laugh. "Careful."

Before my eyes he vanishes, an illusion. I turn and Circe unleashes her power, pinning me to the wall. "I've searched your dark corners, too, Gemma."

I try to fight back, but when the magic comes, it is out of my control. It bends back on me, and I cannot see clearly. My father stands beside Circe, his eyes staring straight ahead, the laudanum bottle clutched in his hand. I see Felicity and Pippa and Ann dancing in a circle without me. Tom under Lord Denby's sway. I close my eyes to clear the visions, but the night has been too much. My body shakes. I can't even call out for Asha. I can do nothing but hang in Circe's grip.

"This is not a battle you can win, Gemma. It belongs to me. I'm going to the Winterlands to finish what I started. But I will remember you to Eugenia Spence."

"I'll kill you," I whisper. Once more I try to call the magic, and once more my head swims with visions. Circe draws the dagger from its sheath, and for a moment, I know she will kill me with it. "Thank you for this," she whispers.

Circe lets me go and I fall to the floor, shaking. She crouches beside me, and her eyes are warm, her smile sad. "There are times when I wish I could go back and change the course of my life. Make different choices. If I had, perhaps you and I would have met as wholly different people in another life." She strokes my hair softly and I am unable to shy away from her touch. I cannot say whether it's the magic or my need at work. "But the past cannot be changed, and we carry our choices with us, forward, into the unknown. We can only move on. Do you remember that I told you that at Spence? It seems forever ago, doesn't it?"

In the corners of the cave, I still see my father and the others. They look on with disapproval. They break into bits that become a nest of snakes.

"I should be careful with the magic, if I were you, Gemma. For you and I have shared it. It has changed—the realms have changed—and there is no telling what you might conjure now." Circe kisses me sweetly on the cheek. "Goodbye, dear Gemma. Don't be foolish and come after me. It won't end well."

She waves her hand over me, and I'm plunged into cold darkness. I vaguely feel myself staggering past Asha and into the poppy fields, my body on fire and my mind not my own. Everything I see is like a pantomime shadow made upon a wall. Amar on his white horse, a line of wraiths behind him with their capes of screaming souls. I lurch away from that image only to fall into Simon's arms. "Dance with me, Gemma," he insists, and I'm twirled till I'm dizzy and desperate to be let go. I struggle free, and there is Pippa holding the dead rabbit in her hands, blood smeared on her mouth.

At the stones near the secret door, I watch in horror as every last one of those honored women disappears, and the empty monuments are overgrown with weeds. I return to the party, swaying into the masked revelers. I don't feel right. There's too much magic.

"I hear your thoughts," I whisper to the guests, and their masks cannot hide their confusion, their disdain.

A crow flies through the open window, and as quick as a blink, it transforms into the tall mummer who entertained us on the lawn. I blink and see the kohled eyes and the flower-inked flesh of a Poppy Warrior. He grins at me, vanishing into the crowd.

I run desperately after him, spilling one woman's punch on her dress. "Sorry," I mumble. I see him. Chain mail. Tunic. A mask of black feathers. He takes the arm of a lady and leads her away from the ballroom and into the great room, where I lose them both. They are not among the fairies, imps, and birds of prey assembled here.

The column pulses with life. One of the beasties trapped there breaks free and lights upon Cecily's shoulder. I see her eyes flutter as the thing licks her neck.

"Get away!" I shout, charging her.

"You're the most appalling girl!" Cecily huffs.

Up on the ceiling, the shiny winged creature puts a finger to her lips. I blink twice, but she is still there.

"It's not real! None of it! She's done this to me!" I hear my laugh—a great big witch's cackle—and it terrifies me. I reach for the dagger and remember that it is gone.

"She took it," I say.

"Shhh," the fairy says, and warmth floods through me. I feel as though I have drunk honeyed wine. My head is heavy. The guests' words are long velvet strings of sound too plush to hear. I am attuned only to the scratchy whispers of the tiny creatures. Their voices are as sharp as flint against stone, each word a spark.

"Sacrifice, sacrifice, sacrifice . . ."

"Leave me alone!" I shout, and the revelers stare at this girl who has lost her mind.

"'Eard you're 'avin' a bit o' trouble tonight, miss," Fowlson says. My brother, Lord Denby, Grandmama, McCleethy and Nightwing, Brigid—they are all with him, worry in their faces. Or hatred. It is so hard to tell just now.

"I'm fine," I protest.

Wasn't I warned? *She is a deceiver. Wilhelmina feared her—and she didn't fear much. Beware the birth of May.*

Brigid puts a hand to my forehead. "Poor dear, burning up."

"Where's Father?" I say, wild.

"Not to worry, my dear." Lord Denby's mouth moves beneath his fox mask. "My carriage has been brought round. Your brother and I shall see him safely to London, where Dr. Hamilton will see to him at once."

"Straight to bed." Mrs. Nightwing tuts. There's real worry in her eyes, and I wish I could tell her everything.

Fowlson takes hold of one side of me while Brigid takes the other, leading me toward the stairs. Lord Denby puts his arm around my brother like the father Tom has always wanted.

Run, Tom, I think, but the words die inside my head.

I drag my feet, so Fowlson carries me. Down below, I see the Poppy Warrior leading his lady fair out toward the woods. Brigid undresses me, puts me under the covers like a child. I'm given a glass of something that warms my insides and makes me drowsy. I cannot make words.

I stumble to the open window. The air is warm and fragrant with spring, and I breathe it in deeply as if it alone has the power to help me. I see more of those dark birds.

Something white flashes in the trees, and I think I see Pippa on the lawn, moving toward Spence as she did in life. She's as pale as a sliver of moon, as elusive as truth. No, she's not there. *Please help me,* I pray, even though I don't believe in a white-bearded God who delivers justice to the unrighteous and mercy to the deserving. I have seen the wicked go unpunished, the suffering given more suffering to bear. And if such a God does exist, I do not believe that I shall merit his attention. But for just this one moment, as I see my dead friend floating across Spence's lawn like a fallen star, I wish I could believe in such comforts, for I am frightened.

My head burns. I burrow into my covers and close my eyes tightly, listening to my heart beating a warning in my blood. I fight back the only way I can. I tell myself it's not real.

You're not real, Pippa Cross. I do not see you; therefore, you are not here. Yes. Good. Very good. If that is illusion, it will do for to-night.

Eyes still closed, I singsong, "I don't see you. . . ." This makes me giggle, and the giggle terrifies me anew. *Stop, Gemma, before you go mad.*

Or am I already there?

·᚜᚜᚜·

Sleep's curtain is raised, and a pageant of dreams parades upon the stage. Wilhelmina Wyatt running her hands over the slate. My father laughing and happy and my father on the floor, his eyes accusing me. Philon's people readying their weapons. The Temple burning. Kartik's kiss. Pippa's blue-white eyes. An army thundering over the black sand and bone of the Winterlands. I climb the stairs and stand before the portrait of Eugenia Spence. The vines of the Winterlands circle more tightly around the throats and bodies of those lost souls readied for sacrifice. Their faces are gray. And I see Circe marching through them toward the Tree of All Souls.

I wake to a sound. Something is in the room with me. The nymph glows in the corner. She has caught a mouse, which she gently swings from hand to hand, catching it each time.

"Troubled?" Her laughter is like the splintering of bones. "Everything is set in motion. You cannot stop it. The day of sacrifice comes."

"Hush!"

Her whisper wraps around me in a spiral. She dangles the mouse by its tail. Its tiny claws splay out in fear. It tries to climb up itself. "So long, we've waited so long, so long. Now she will be free, and so will we all. For that was the bargain made long ago. One soul in exchange for the other."

I cover my ears. "Stop!"

"As you wish," she says. She opens her mouth and bites down hard on the mouse's neck.

I wake with a start, my forehead damp. My nightgown clings to me as if I've broken a fever. I let my eyes adjust to the deep dark, and when my room takes shape, I know I'm really awake this time. The rain is splattering against my window, and my body aches. I'm as weak as a new kitten. I don't hear Ann's snoring.

"Ann?" I call. She's not in her bed, and I know in my heart that she has gone into the realms with Felicity.

I have to go after them. I stumble down the stairs and into

the kitchen, heading for the lawn and the door. A sharp rap at the window makes me jump. It is too dark to see who is there, and in truth, I am afraid to look. The rapping comes again. The window has fogged. I put my hands to the pane and peer into the night. Ithal puts his face to the pane, startling me. Ithal! I run to open the kitchen door. He stands on the threshold in the pouring rain.

"Ithal! Where have you been?" He looks grim. "What is the matter?"

"It is Kartik. They have taken him. You must save him."

"Who has taken him?"

"There is no time. We must go now."

I think of Ann and Felicity inside the realms. "I have to—"

He hands me a strip of soggy fabric from Kartik's cloak. It has been branded with the Rakshana insignia. Fowlson.

"Take me," I say, for if I can get to Kartik, he can help me with my friends.

I follow Ithal through the rain to where Freya waits. My legs are weak, and I stumble once or twice. Ithal's eyes are so ringed in shadow they seem hollow.

"Where have you been?" I ask again. "Mother Elena has been terribly worried."

"The men came for me."

"Miller's men? You must tell Inspector Kent! He will not let it stand," I say, helping myself onto Freya's back.

"Later. We must go to him now."

He swings himself onto the horse, behind me, and I feel the coldness of him at my back. With a small kick to the horse's flanks, we are off. Rain lashes my cheeks and soaks my hair as we gallop into the woods, turning left at the lake. The horse stops suddenly, spooked. She whinnies loudly, pacing before the edge of the water, sensing something.

"Freya, *kele!*" Ithal commands.

The horse will not go on. Instead, she pats her right hoof on the ground and sniffs at the water's edge, as if searching for something she has lost.

The Gypsy gives a sharp tug on the reins, and Freya turns away, picking up speed until she is in a full gallop that makes my heart pound in rhythm with the strike of her hooves against the road. I can feel the night's breath on my neck. Only small flashes of lightning brighten the path ahead of us.

We turn off at the graveyard. The sky's an angry throb of light and sound. Freya weaves between the headstones. Her hooves catch in the mud, and she pitches me dangerously close to the sharp edge of one. I scream and cling to Ithal's shirt as he rights her, guiding the horse onto a grassy path, which she takes at a more cautious clip.

"Where are we going?" I shout.

The storm is coming down heavier than before. It blinds me and I have to tuck my head to keep the water from my eyes. Ithal answers, but I can't hear over the pounding of the rain.

"What did you say?" I ask.

It sounds like humming or praying. No, he's chanting. Words fly past as fast as rain on wind, filling me with an icy dread.

"A sacrifice, a sacrifice, a sacrifice . . ."

The piece of cloth turns to snakes in my hand. I scream and the snakes turn to ashes. Just ahead, mounds of earth sit on either side of an open grave. Ithal steers Freya straight for it, gathering speed. I jab him with my elbows, but he doesn't stop. With all my might, I pitch myself from the horse's back. I land hard against the wet earth just as Freya screams and tumbles into the open grave. I do not hear her hit bottom.

I struggle to my feet, feeling my muscles pinch as I do. My legs will bear my weight, but they ache, and my shoulder and left arm are in agony. Trembling, I peer around the headstone, and the ground is as solid as can be.

I choke back a sobbing laugh, and will myself to wake again in my bed, but I don't. "You'll wake soon, Gemma," I tell myself as I hobble through the dark graveyard. "Just sing something to help you through. I had a l-lass in Lincoln-sh-shire, sold mussels from a pail . . ."

I pass a headstone. Beloved Wife. "S-sold m-mussels f-from a-a . . ."

Thunder breaks. It makes my teeth chatter. "F-from a p-p-pail . . ."

Something blocks my path. A flash of lightning splits the sky, illuminating Ithal. Where his eyes should be, there are two deep black pits.

"Sacrifice . . . ," he says.

I cannot move, cannot think. My legs are frozen in fear. I try to summon the magic, but I'm exhausted and afraid, and it will not come. A voice booms inside my head: *Run. Run, Gemma.*

Fast as I can, I bolt away from him, running through a labyrinth of headstones as the sky explodes in thunder. Out of the corner of my eye, I see Ithal vanish behind a marble angel and reappear on the other side. He is gaining ground. My night-gown is sodden. It slaps against my already weak legs, slowing my gait with its weight. I pull frantically at it, hoisting it to my knees to run faster. Ithal moves steadily behind me. By the time I reach the lake, each breath feels like a razor's edge slicing through my lungs.

At last, I see it: Rising above the trees is the silhouette of Spence with its ornate, twisted spires. There's something odd about it. I can't say what. All I can do is run. Strong moonlight pushes the clouds apart.

The roof is empty. The gargoyles are gone. They are gone, and I feel the earth slipping from beneath me. Ithal is coming faster, closing the gap between us, and I stumble on. My lungs feel as if they will explode.

Something lands behind me, as hard as stone striking the earth. Every part of me goes cold with fear. I should turn to look, but I can't. Can't breathe. Scratching sounds. Like claws on stone. A low growl comes from whatever is behind me. *Don't turn, Gemma. It isn't real if you don't turn. Close your eyes. Count to ten. One. Two. Three.* The moon is full. A shadow rises tall, much taller than my own on the path. And then the enor-mous wings unfold.

My head is as light as a balloon. A faint threatens. "Lass . . . in, in . . . L-L-Lincolnshire . . . mussels . . . a p-pail . . ."

A loud screech pierces the night. The gargoyle takes flight and lands before me on the path with a tremendous thud, cut-ting off any hope of escape. I sink to my knees at the sight of the enormous stone bird-beast towering above me. Its face is a hideous living mask, the mouth stretched into a gruesome smile, the fangs as long as my leg. Its claws are terrifyingly sharp. A scream dies in my throat. The beast screeches as its claws come around me, closing firmly about my waist. Blackness steals over me.

"Hold fast," the gargoyle commands in a gravelly voice, snapping me back to fear. He tucks me in close to his body, and we take flight. I hold tightly to those frightening claws. It takes me a moment to fully realize what is happening. The gargoyle doesn't wish me harm. He means to protect me. The sky is alive with winged beasts. They screech and growl. The sounds reverberate in my ears but I don't dare let go to cover them. The rush of air is cool against my sodden gown and wet skin. I shiver as we pass over the tops of trees and land gently on Spence's roof.

"Do not look," he advises.

But I cannot look away. Below, the other gargoyles have cornered Ithal. They reach down and pluck him from the ground, flying toward the lake.

"What will they do?" I ask.

"What they must." He does not elaborate, and I dare not question him further.

"Wh-who are you?"

"I am one of the guardians of the night," he says, and I am reminded of Wilhelmina's drawing. "We protected your kind for centuries when the veil between worlds had no seal. Now the seal is broken. The land is enchanted again. But I fear we cannot keep you safe from what has begun."

The sky blackens with wings. Overhead, the gargoyles circle, casting me in shadows. They swoop low and land as lightly as angels upon the roof. A gargoyle with the nose of a dragon approaches.

"It is done," he growls. "He has been returned to the dead."

The gargoyle who saved me nods. "This is not the last we shall see of them. They will come again and stronger."

A ribbon of pink shows in the eastern sky. The other gargoyles take their familiar perches on the edge of the roof. As I watch, they return to stone.

"I am dreaming," I whisper. "This is all a dream."

The head gargoyle spreads his wings till all his darkness surrounds me. His voice is as deep as time. "Yes, you have been sleeping. But now is the time to wake."

***

I open my eyes. My ceiling takes shape. I can hear Ann's gentle snoring. I'm in my room, as I should be. It is past dawn but barely so. I sit up, and my body aches with the effort. A great clamor rises in the woods. Hardly dressed, girls push out of their doors to see what has happened. In the early morning mist, the Gypsies gather at the lake with their lanterns. A cry of grief rises from them.

Now I see. Ithal lies in the water facedown, drowned. That was why Freya stopped beside the lake, why she seemed so upset. She knew that her master was dead, and the thing on her back was undead, a hellish messenger from the Winterlands sent to take me to them.

No. No, that did not happen. I imagined it all. Or dreamed it. A dead man did not come to spirit me away. I did not fly in a gargoyle's grip.

I look up for confirmation. The gargoyles sit on the roof's edge, silent and unseeing. I turn my head this way and that, but they do not change. *Of course not. They are stone, silly girl.* I chuckle. This gets the attention of the crowd, for I am laughing while they pull a dead man from the lake.

Kartik is there, right as rain, not a mark on him. He looks at me with concern.

The men cover Ithal with a jacket.

"You must build the fire," Mother Elena says. "Burn him. Burn everything."

CHAPTER FIFTY-FIVE

IT IS ASTONISHING THAT WITH A MAN DROWNED IN THE woods, my behavior at the ball should become the talk of Spence, but it has. At breakfast, girls hush as I walk past; they track me with their eyes, like vultures waiting for carrion. I sit with the older girls, and they fall silent. It's as if I were Death himself, scythe at the ready.

I hear the girls whispering to each other. "Ask her."

"No, you!"

Cecily clears her throat. "How are you feeling, Gemma?" she asks with pretend sympathy. "I heard you had a terrible fever."

I spoon porridge into my mouth.

"Is that true?" Martha presses.

"No," I say. "I was overcome by too much magic. And by the lies and secrets that make up this place as surely as the stones and mortar."

Their mouths open in shock, and uncomfortable giggling follows. Fee and Ann look on with alarm. I'm no longer hungry. I push away from the table and walk out of the dining room. Mrs. Nightwing glances up, but she doesn't try to stop me. It's as if she knows I'm a lost cause.

<hr/>

Felicity and Ann come to visit in the afternoon. Their curiosity about my madness has won out over their anger. Felicity pulls a sack of toffees from her pocket.

"Here. I thought you might need these."

I let them sit on the bed, untouched. "You went into the realms last night, didn't you?"

Ann's eyes widen. It is a wonder that she could make so fine an actress yet be so terrible a liar.

"Yes," Felicity says, and I'm grateful for her honesty. "We danced and Ann sang and it was such a merry time that I didn't care if we never came back. It is like paradise there."

"You can't live in paradise all the time," I say.

Felicity pockets the toffees. "You can't keep us from the realms," she says, rising.

"Things have changed. Circe has the dagger," I say, and I tell them everything I remember from last night. "I can't hold the magic by myself anymore. We need to make the alliance and go after Circe."

Felicity's face clouds. "You promised we wouldn't give the magic back until after our debuts. You promised to help me."

"You might come away with enough magic of your own—"

"And I might not! I'll be trapped! Please, Gemma," Felicity begs.

"I'm sorry," I say, swallowing hard. "It can't be helped."

Felicity's passion cools, and I find her calm much more

frightening than her anger. "You don't hold all the magic anymore, Gemma," she reminds me. "Pip has power, too, and it's growing stronger. And if *you* won't help me, I know *she* will."

"Fee . . . ," I croak, but she won't listen. She's already out the door, Ann at her heels.

<hr />

The afternoon is a suddenly chilly one, as if winter has one last gasp before summer takes hold. Inspector Kent has come to see about Ithal's death. His men comb the woods for evidence of foul play, though they find none. Phantoms leave no trail. Mr. Miller is taken from a pub and brought round for an inquiry, though he protests his innocence, insisting there are ghosts in the woods of Spence.

Kartik has left his calling card—the red cloth—nestled in the ivy outside my window along with a note: *Meet me in the chapel.*

I slip inside the empty chapel and stare at the angel with the gorgon's head. "I'm not afraid of you anymore. I understand you meant to protect me."

A deep voice answers. "Go forth and conquer."

I jump. Kartik shows himself from behind the pulpit. "Forgive me," he says with a sheepish smile. "I didn't mean to frighten you."

He looks as if he hasn't slept in days. We're quite the pair with our long faces and shadowed eyes. He runs a finger across the back of a pew. "Do you remember the first time I surprised you here?"

"Indeed. You frightened me, telling me to close my mind to

the visions. I should have listened. I was the wrong girl for all of this."

He leans against the end of the pew, his arms folded across his chest. "No, you're not."

"You don't know what I've done, else you wouldn't say that."

"Why don't you tell me?"

It seems to take forever for the words to travel through the wreckage inside me. But they do come, and I don't spare myself. I tell him everything, and he listens. I'm afraid he'll hate me for it, but when I've finished he only nods.

"Say something," I whisper. "Please."

"The warning was for the birth of May. Now we know what it meant, I suppose," he says, thinking already, and I smile a little because I know this means he's heard, and we have moved on. "We'll go after her."

"Yes, but if I so much as dip a toe into the magic, I fear I'll be joined to Circe, to the Winterlands. That I'll go mad as I felt last night."

"All the more reason to stop her. Perhaps she hasn't bound Eugenia's power to the tree just yet. We might still save the realms," he says.

"We?"

"I'm not running away again. That is not my destiny."

He slips his hand under my chin and tilts it up, and I kiss him first.

"I thought you stopped believing in destiny," I remind him.

"I haven't stopped believing in you."

I smile in spite of everything. I need his belief just now. "Do you think . . ." I stop.

"What?" he murmurs into my hair. His lips are warm.

"Do you think, if we were to stay in the realms, that we could be together?"

"This is the world we live in, Gemma, for better or for worse. Make of it what you can," he says, and I pull him to me.

⊰⊱⊰⊱⊰⊱

After the weeks of excited preparation for the masked ball, Spence is rather like a balloon that has lost all its air. Down come the decorations. Costumes are packed away in tissue and camphor, though some of the younger girls refuse to give theirs up just yet. They want to be princesses and fairies for as long as they can.

Others, ready for the next party, badger Mademoiselle LeFarge for details of her upcoming wedding.

"Will you wear diamonds?" Elizabeth asks.

Mademoiselle LeFarge blushes. "Oh, dear me, no. Too precious. Though I was given a most beautiful pearl necklace to wear."

"Will you honeymoon in Italy? Or Spain?" Martha asks.

"We will take a modest trip to Brighton," Mademoiselle LeFarge says, and the girls are deeply disappointed.

Brigid taps my shoulder. "Missus Nightwing is calling for you, miss," she says sympathetically, and I am afraid to ask what has provoked her kindness.

"Yes, thank you," I say, following her beyond the baize door to our headmistress's solid, staid sanctuary. The only spot of color is on a corner table, where wildflowers spill over the boundaries of a vase, dropping petals without care.

Mrs. Nightwing motions to a chair. "How are you feeling today, Miss Doyle?"

"More myself," I say.

She rearranges the letter opener and the inkwell, and my heart picks up speed. "What is it? What has happened?"

"You've a cable from your brother," she says, handing it to me.

FATHER VERY ILL STOP WILL MEET YOUR TRAIN AT
VICTORIA STOP TOM

I blink back tears. I shouldn't have pushed as I did at the masked ball. He wasn't ready for truth, and I forced it on him, and now I fear I have delivered an injury from which he cannot fully recover.

"It's my fault," I say, dropping the note on her desk.

"Poppycock!" Nightwing barks, and it is what I needed—a bracing wind at my back. "I shall have Brigid help you with your things. Mr. Gus will drive you to the train station first thing in the morning."

"Thank you," I murmur.

"My thoughts are with you, Miss Doyle." And I think she means it.

On the long walk to my room, Ann runs up to me, out of breath.

"What is it?" I can see the alarm on her face.

"It's Felicity," she gasps. "I tried to reason with her. She wouldn't listen."

"What do you mean?"

"She went into the realms. She's gone to be with Pip," she says, wide-eyed. "Forever."

CHAPTER FIFTY-SIX

WE STAND BESIDE THE HALF-FORMED EAST WING. FIRE-
flies blink in the trees, and I have to look twice to be certain
they are only those harmless insects. The passageway into the
realms feels colder to me, and I hurry my steps. The moment
we step through the door in the hill, I can feel that something's
not right. Everything's a bit gray, as if the London fog has
rolled in.

"What is that smell?" Ann asks.

"Smoke," I answer.

In the distance, a large black plume of smoke scars the sky. It
is rising from the mountain that houses the Temple and the
Caves of Sighs, where the Hajin live.

"Gemma?" Ann says, her eyes wide.

"Come on!" I shout.

We race to the poppy fields. Ash rains down, coating our
skin in a fine layer of silver-gray soot. Coughing, we fight our
way up the mountain. The path bleeds with crushed poppies.

Ann nearly stumbles over the body of an Untouchable. There are more. Their charred corpses line the path to the smoldering Temple. Asha stumbles from the smoking wreckage.

"Lady Hope..."

She sags against me, and I rush her to a rock where the air is not so heavy with ash.

"Asha! Asha, who has done this?" I sputter.

She collapses, coughing. Her scorched orange sari settles around her like the singed plumage of a magnificent bird.

"Asha!" I shout. "Tell me."

She looks into my eyes. Her face is streaked with black. "It...it was the forest folk."

Gorgon calls from the river below. Ann and I take Asha to the ship and bring her water, which she drinks like a woman whose thirst will never be slaked. I shake with anger. I cannot believe that Philon and the forest folk would do such a thing. I thought them to be peaceful. Perhaps the Order was right after all and the magic cannot be shared.

"Tell me what happened," I say.

"They came as we slept. They swarmed the mountain. There was no way out. One of them held a torch to the Temple. 'This is for Creostus,' it said. And the Temple burned."

"This was retaliation?"

She nods, wiping her face with the moistened edge of her sari. "I told them we had no part in the slaughter of the centaur. But they did not believe me. The decision was in their eyes already. They came for war, and they would not be stopped."

She puts her trembling fingers to her lips as the Temple burns. Where the flames fall on the poppy fields, beautiful curls of red smoke rise. "We have never questioned. It is not our way."

I put my arm around her shoulders. "Your way needs to change, Asha. It is time to question everything."

⌁⌁⌁⌁

We form several lines with the Hajin, passing buckets of water till we douse what we can of the flames.

"Why do you not cure this malady with magic?" a Hajin boy asks.

"It isn't a good course just now, I'm afraid," I say, looking at the ruined, smoldering Temple.

"But the magic will fix everything, won't it?" He presses, and I can see how desperately he wants to believe, how much he wants me to sweep my hand over his broken home and make it whole. I wish I could.

I shake my head and pass the water down the line. "It can only do so much. The rest is up to us."

Gorgon ferries us through the golden veil to the island home of the forest folk. They flank the shore in an ominous line, their newly fashioned spears and crossbows at the ready. Gorgon keeps us a safe distance from the shore—close enough that I can be heard but far enough that we can retreat. Philon glides to the water's edge. The creature's leaf coat has taken on tinges of orange, gold, and red. The high collar blazes about Philon's slender neck.

"You are not welcome here, Priestess," Philon shouts.

"I have just come from the Temple. You burned it!"

Philon stands imperiously. "So it is."

"Why?" I ask, because I can think of no truer question.

"They took one of our own! Would you deny us justice?"

"And so you took twenty of theirs? How is this justice?"

Asha stands feebly. She clutches the ship's railing. "We did not kill the centaur."

"So you say," Philon thunders. "Then who did?"

"Look within for the answer," Asha replies cryptically.

Neela throws a rock at us. It lands in the water, spraying the side of the ship. "We'll have no more of your lies! Be gone!"

She throws another and it narrowly misses me, landing on the deck. On impulse, I grab the rock, feeling its weight in my hand.

Asha stays my arm. "Retaliation is a dog chasing its tail."

There is wisdom in what she says, but I want to throw the rock, and it takes every bit of strength to hold it firmly in my palm.

"Philon, did you stop to consider this: How will we join hands in an alliance now that you have burned the Temple?"

A ripple passes through the assembled folk. And for a moment, I see a hint of doubt in Philon's cool eyes. "The time for alliances is past. Let the magic take its own course now. We shall see who stands in the end."

"But I need your help! The Winterlands creatures are plotting against us! Circe has gone to them—"

"More lies!" Neela shouts, and the forest folk turn away.

"Come, Most High," Gorgon says. "We have done all there is to do here." She steers us away from the shore, but it is not until we are well past the golden veil that I am able to loosen my grip on the rock. I drop it into the river, where it makes not a single sound.

Ann takes my arm. Her face is grim. "We must find Felicity."

We find Pippa and the girls in the castle, drinking wine and playing. Dusky light coats the chapel in a pretty gloom. Bessie pulls the wings from a dragonfly, and she and Mae laugh as it hops about on the floor, desperate to fly away. Pippa sits on the throne, eating berries from a golden chalice till her lips are a deep shade of blue. Platters and goblets are stacked high with the fruit.

"Where is Fee?" I ask. "Have you seen her?"

"I'm here." Felicity waltzes in, outfitted in her warrior chain mail, her cheeks rosy and her eyes bright. "What do you want?"

"Fee, you can't stay here," I say.

She takes a seat beside Pip. "Why not?"

"The realms are falling to chaos. The tribes are at war, the Temple's been razed, and Circe has gone to the Winterlands to join with the creatures."

"Nothing has touched us here," Pip says, gesturing to the chapel walls. "Now, shall we have another ball this evening?"

"Pippa," I say, incredulous. "We can't have a party."

Pippa's laughter is light and girlish. "Let the creatures have at each other. They're no match for me."

She lowers a berry onto her tongue and licks her fingers.

"That's right," Bessie agrees. "Miss Pippa will serve notice."

She and Mae gaze at Pippa with a fierce devotion, and I want to knock Pippa from her throne.

"Did you tell them how you came to be here? Why you can't cross?"

Pippa's eyes flash. "Oh, Gemma, really." She shares a grin

with the factory girls. It turns to a round of giggling that makes my skin crawl.

"She asked me to help her cross the river, but she couldn't go on. Because she stayed too long here. Because she ate the berries," I say. I knock over a chalice; the fat purplish berries spill across the floor and are swallowed by the vines.

"You meant to cross? Without telling me?" Felicity says softly.

Pippa ignores Fee's hurt. She fixes those wavering eyes on me. "What does it matter now? For I was saved for a higher purpose."

I look around at the girls' adoring faces. Wendy isn't among them.

"Where's Wendy?" I demand. In Mercy's eyes, I see a flicker of fear.

"She ran away," Pippa answers coolly.

Next time it will not be a bunny.

"Will you tell me she bit through her cage, too?"

Pippa shrugs. "If it will amuse you."

"Tell me where she is!" I bang my hand on the altar.

Pippa puts her hands to her hips, a taunting pose. "Or what?"

Felicity steps in. "Pippa, stop."

"Are you on her side now?" Pippa demands.

"There are no sides," Ann says. "Are there?"

"There are now," Pippa answers, and my blood pumps a little faster.

"She took Wendy to the Win'erlands," Mercy says quickly.

Bessie hits her hard across the mouth, knocking her to the floor. "'At's a bloody lie, Mercy Paxton. Take it back!"

"No one likes a traitor, Mercy," Pippa scolds.

The girl cowers on the floor. The castle groans. The vines are blighted, diseased. When they move, they seem to calcify. One, heavy as stone, creeps over my foot, and my foot is nearly trapped under it. I yank it free.

"Pippa," I say, "what have you done?"

"What you wouldn't. Poor Gemma, always so afraid of her power. Well, not me."

"Pip, you didn't make a bargain with those creatures."

"What if I did?"

Felicity shakes her head. "You didn't."

Pippa strokes her face gently. "It was such a small thing they asked. A sacrifice no one would miss. I offered that silly bunny—that's all. You see what we've been given in return!" She opens her arms wide but all I see is a moldering castle corrupted by weeds.

"Tell me that you didn't take her to the Winterlands, that I'm wrong for thinking it," I plead.

"I shall tell you whatever you'd like to hear," she says, gorging on berries.

"Tell me the truth!"

Pip's eyes flash. Her teeth are blue-black with juice. "She. Was. A. Burden."

Felicity clutches her stomach. "Oh, God."

"No, Fee, you'll see. It's going to be so wonderful." Pippa grins coquettishly at the others. "Shall I tell you what the tree promised? What I saw there after my sacrifice? I saw the Order's time ending and something new being born," she says, her voice tinged with wonder. "Their days have passed. Our time is at hand."

The girls move close and sit at her feet, lost in the pull of her sureness. Her features are a mesmerizing amalgam of before and after. The delicate cheekbones, the long tangle of black curls, the dainty nose are still there. But every now and then, her eyes waver between a deep violet and an alarming blue-white circled by black rings. It is a new, savage beauty, and I cannot look away.

"I heard the voice whisper sweetly in my head: *So special you are. You are chosen. I will exalt you.*"

She smiles brightly with a giggle. Cold fear slithers in my belly.

"I am the chosen one. *I* am the way. To follow me, you must be as I am."

With two fingers, Felicity turns Pip's face gently to hers. "Pip, what are you saying?"

Pippa wrenches free of Felicity's touch and marches purposefully to Bessie. She offers the chalice of berries. "Would you follow me, Bessie?"

"Yes, miss," Bessie answers hoarsely. She opens her mouth obediently.

With her eyes on Felicity, Pippa places the berry on Bessie's waiting tongue. Horrified, Felicity runs for her and grabs her hand, knocking the berry free. Pippa pushes her, and Felicity shoves back hard. Pip's face crumples for a moment, her eyes roll back in her head, and a high keening escapes her, like a laugh gone wrong. Her limbs jerk as she falls to the ground, her body swept into a dance of beautiful violence.

"Pippa!" Felicity calls. "Pippa!"

Bessie and the others back away, frightened. At last, the fit subsides; Pippa's clawlike hands go limp, and she lies upon the ground, a misshapen stick. Slowly, Pip sits up, her breathing labored. A bit of drool runs from her mouth; there is dirt in her hair and along her dress where she has fallen. Felicity cradles her.

"Wh-what has happened?" Pippa whimpers. She tries to stand and stumbles, her legs as weak as a newborn colt's.

"Shhh, it was a fit," Felicity says softly. She guides Pip to the altar and helps her sit.

Pip's lips tremble. "No. Not here. Not now."

She reaches toward Bessie, offering the berry once more, but Bessie shrinks from her touch. The factory girls stand apart from her. Fear shows on their faces.

"No!" Pip wails. "I am special! Chosen! You will not leave me!"

She throws out her hands, and we're surrounded by a wall of fire. The heat of it blows me back several steps. This is no magic-lantern show, no illusionist's trick meant to frighten and entertain. This is real. Whatever power Pippa has inside seems to have grown with her seizure into something new and terrible.

The girls fall back even more, the flames shadowing the terror and awe in their widening eyes. A strange smile lights Bessie's broad face, a cross between ecstasy and fear. She falls to her knees in devotion. "Oh, miss, you've been touched by the hand of God!"

Mae prostrates herself as well. "I knew it when you saved us from those ghouls."

Even Mercy falls to her knees, swayed by the might of Pippa's power.

"We saw it! We all did! A miracle it was. A right sign!" Bessie exclaims with the passion of the converted.

"A right sign of what?" I ask.

"It's proof that she's chosen, like she said." Tears stream down Mae's face. She believes she has witnessed a miracle, and I cannot tell her otherwise.

Felicity keeps a tight grip on Pip's arm. "It was a fit. You have to tell them."

I witnessed one of Pip's fits when she was alive. It was frightening in its fury, but nothing like this.

Pippa stretches her arms wide. "I will lead you to glory. Who will follow?"

"You must tell them the truth!" Felicity hisses.

"Shut yer mouth," Mae warns, and in her eyes I see a devotion that would kill.

"Don't order me about!" Pippa snaps. "Everyone's forever ordering me about."

Felicity looks as if she's been hit hard. Pip twists out of her grip and walks among the factory girls, who reach up to touch her. She graces them with a soft laying of hands and they cry out in happiness, eager for a blessing. Pippa glances at us, tears in her eyes, her smile the picture of innocence.

"It was meant to be. It was all preordained! That is why I could not cross," she says. "How else to explain why the magic has grown in me?"

"Pip," I begin, but I do not finish. For what if she is right after all?

"You had a fit," Fee says, shaking her head.

"It was a vision, like Gemma's!" Pippa shouts.

Felicity slaps Pippa, and Pip turns on her with the ferocity of a cornered animal. "You'll be sorry for that."

The factory girls are on Felicity, Ann, and me, holding our

arms behind our backs till we are forced to bend. I could try for the magic. I could. I try to summon it, and see Circe in my head, and then I'm gasping for air, terrified and woozy.

"I felt that, Gemma!" Pippa shouts. "Don't try again."

"Unbelievers." Bessie spits and it lands as an ugly spot on Fee's cheek.

They pull us outside, holding us tightly, and Pip unleashes her fury in a new ring of fire. It makes my eyes burn and sting.

If Pippa has crowned herself queen, Bessie has surely made herself second-in-command. "Mistress Pippa, we'll do wha'ever you ask of us. Just a word and it's done."

"My whole life I've been ordered about. Now I shall give the orders."

I've never seen Felicity so wounded. "Not me," she says. "I never ordered you about."

"Oh, Fee." The old Pippa surfaces for just a moment, hopeful and childlike. She pulls Felicity to her. Something I cannot name passes between them, and then Pip's lips are on Fee's in a deep kiss, as if they feed on one another, their fingers entwined in each other's hair. And suddenly, I understand what I must have always known about them—the private talks, the close embraces, the tenderness of their friendship. A blush spreads up my neck at the thought. How could I not have seen it before?

Felicity breaks away, her cheeks inflamed, but the fierce passion of that kiss lingers. Pip grabs her arm. "Why do you always go? You are always leaving me."

"I'm not," Felicity says. Her voice is raw with smoke.

"Don't you see? Here we can be free to do as we wish."

Felicity's lips tremble. "But I cannot stay."

"Yes, you can. You know how."

Felicity shakes her head. "I can't. Not that way."

Pippa speaks in low, measured tones. "You said you loved me. Why will you not eat the berries and stay with me?"

"I do," Felicity whispers. "But—"

"You do what?" Pippa demands. "Why will you not say it?"

"I . . . do," Felicity says with terrible difficulty.

Pip lets go Felicity's arm. Her eyes fill with angry tears. "The time has come to make a choice, Fee. Either you are with me or against me."

Pippa opens her hand. The berries sit waiting, fat and ripe. I can scarcely breathe. Felicity's face shows her torment—her affection and her pride locked in fierce battle. She stares at the berries for a long moment, neither accepting nor declining them, and I come to realize that the silence is her answer. She will not trade one trap for another.

Pippa's eyes brim with tears. She closes her hand over the berries, squeezing so tightly that the blue-black juice runs over her knuckles and onto the ground, and I fear what she will do to us now.

"Let them go. We do not need unbelievers in our midst," she says at last. She parts the flames for us. "Go on, then. Leave."

The only way out is through the fire, and there is no promise that she will not burn us to cinders as we pass. Swallowing hard, I lead Ann and Felicity through the passage in the flames.

Pippa sings loudly, ferociously. "Oh, I've a love, a true, true love, and my true love lies waiting . . ."

It was a simple, merry tune once, but now it chills me. It is a desperate song. One by one, the girls join in, their voices gaining power until Fee's sobs have been completely drowned by them. I do not dare to glance back until we are through the bramble wall on the path to the garden, and Pippa and her followers, set against the flames, seem like white-hot coals going to ash.

CHAPTER FIFTY-SEVEN

FELICITY WILL NOT SPEAK TO EITHER OF US. THE MOMENT we return to Spence, she stumbles up the stairs, holding the banister as if it were the only thing tying her to the earth. Ann and I do not speak of what has happened. The night feels heavy and hard and no words can lighten it. Only when Ann has joined Cecily for needlework do I make my way to Felicity's room. I find her lying on her bed, so still I fear she is dead.

"Why did you come?" Her voice is a shadow of itself. "Did you come to see the degenerate?" She turns to me, her face slick with tears. In her hand she clutches Pippa's glove. "I can see it in your eyes, Gemma. Go on—say it. I'm a degenerate, then. My affections are unnatural."

My mouth opens, but I can find no words.

"Say it! Tell me what you long to say, what everyone suspects!"

"I never suspected it. Truly."

Her breathing is labored. Her nose runs. Strands of hair are caught in the moisture and stick to her cheeks. She will not look at me again. "But now you know, and you despise me."

Do I? No. What I feel is confused. I have questions I do not yet know how to ask: Has she always been this way? Does she feel this same affection for me? I have undressed before her. She has seen me. And I have seen her, have noted her beauty. Do I harbor these secret feelings for Felicity? Am I just as she is? How would I know if I were?

Felicity splays across the bed, choking on her tears. Her body shudders with sobs. I reach out a nervous hand and touch her, letting my palm rest on her back. I should say something, but I am at a loss. So I say the only words that come to mind.

"You will love again, Fee."

Felicity's face is pressed to her pillow, but she rolls her head back and forth. "No. No, I won't. Not like this."

"Shhh—"

"Never like this." She is lost to her sobbing now. It comes over her in violent waves. There's nothing to do but let her be lost. At last, the tide recedes. She lies beside me, limp and damp, wholly spent. Long shadows of evening creep up the walls, inching closer. Gradually, they reach fully across us, holding us in the stillness that only night can bring. In the hazy gloom of dusk, we are silhouettes of ourselves, reduced to our very essence. I lie down beside her. She takes my fingers in her moist palm. She holds and I do not break away, and that is something after all. We lie there, tethered to each other by the fragile promise of our fingers while the night grows bolder. Unafraid, it opens its mouth and swallows us whole.

CHAPTER FIFTY-EIGHT

THE TRAIN STEAMS ACROSS THE COUNTRYSIDE TOWARD London. I've left the cloth in the ivy, along with a note for Kartik explaining about my father and promising I will return as soon as I can. I've left notes for Felicity and Ann as well. Heartsick, I pass from carriage to train to carriage until at last our street is in view.

The house in Belgravia is gloomy and quiet. Dr. Hamilton is in attendance. He and Tom stand in hushed conference in the foyer while Grandmama and I sit in the parlor, staring into a fire we do not need. The house is already uncomfortably warm, but Grandmama insists. In her hand, Father's handkerchief bursts open like an angry flower. There on the field of pristine white is a small red stain of blood.

Tom enters silently, his shoulders slumped. He closes the door behind him, and the silence is more than I can bear.

"Tom?" I say.

He sits by the fire. "Consumption. Months now."

"Months?" I ask.

"Yes," Tom says.

It wasn't my doing. It is the drink and the laudanum and the opium and that bloody refusal to live. That selfish grief. I thought I could change it with magic, but I can't. People will be who they are, and there is not enough magic in any world to change that.

Grandmama folds Father's handkerchief over and over, making neat squares that hide the stain. "That infernal climate in India."

"It isn't the climate. Let's not pretend," I say. Tom glares a warning.

Grandmama prattles on. "I told him he should return to England. India's no place for an Englishman. Far too hot . . ."

I'm out of my chair. "It isn't the bloody weather!"

I've shocked them into silence. I should stop. Apologize for my outburst. Make amends. Blame the climate. But I cannot. Something in me has given way and it cannot be put back again. "Did you know that he had returned to the laudanum? That he couldn't give it up? That our good intentions were not nearly so powerful as his will to die?"

"Gemma, please," Tom snaps.

"No, Thomas. Is this the life you want for me? To be like you? To wear blinders and talk of nothing that matters and drink weak tea with other people who would do anything to hide the truth, especially from themselves? Well, I won't do it! And I won't lie for you anymore."

Grandmama presses her thumb across the white plain of the folded handkerchief, forcing it to lie down. She is suddenly small and frail. I'm ashamed to have treated her so shabbily and more ashamed that I hate her for her frailty. As I storm from the room, I hear her voice, faint and unsure. "It's the climate."

Tom catches me on the stairs and pulls me into the library. Father's books stare down at us from their shelves. "Gemma, that was unkind."

My blood has settled and my anger is now tamed by remorse, but I'll not give Thomas the satisfaction of knowing it. I take a book from Father's shelves, and perching in a rather uncomfortable wooden chair, I open to its title page. *The Inferno* by Dante Alighieri.

"Father's health isn't the sole reason I sent for you. Your behavior at the ball was . . ." He trails off. "Frightening."

You've no idea, Tom. I turn the page, feigning passionate interest.

"Since the moment we arrived in England, you've been rebellious and difficult. It only takes one infraction, one whiff of scandal, to ruin your reputation and your chances forever."

Anger surges past the constraints of shame. "My reputation," I say coolly. "Is that all I am?"

"A woman's reputation is her worth, Gemma."

I flip a page hard and it tears slightly. "It's wrong."

Tom lifts the stopper from a crystal decanter and pours a splash into a tumbler. "It is the way it is. You may hate me for saying so, but there is the truth. Do you not remember that this is how our mother died? She would still be here and Father would be well and none of this would ever have happened if she had simply lived according to the time-trusted codes of society."

"Perhaps it proved impossible. Perhaps she could not fit within so tight a corset."

Perhaps I am the same.

"One does not have to like the rules, Gemma. But one does need to adhere to them. That is what makes civilization. Do you think that I agree with every rule at Bethlem Hospital or with every decision made by my superiors? Do you think I would not rather do as I please?" He takes a sip of the spirits, making a grimace as he swallows. "I had no control over Mother, but I do over you. I won't allow you to follow the same path."

"You won't allow it?" I scoff. "I don't see that you've a say in my life."

"You're wrong on that score. With Father ill, it falls to me to be your guardian, and I intend to take my position very seriously indeed."

A new fear takes root in me. All this time, I've been worried about what the Order, the Rakshana, and the creatures of the Winterlands could do to me. I'd forgotten the very real dangers I face here, in my own world.

"You will not be returning to Spence. The Spence Academy for Young Ladies has obviously been a grave mistake. You'll stay here until your debut."

"But I've friends there. . . ."

Tom turns on me. "Miss Bradshaw, the penniless liar, and Miss Worthington, who is of questionable virtue. A fine lot of friends. You shall meet the right sort of girls here."

I'm on my feet. "The right sort? I've met plenty of them, and I can tell you they are as shallow as your teacup. And as for my friends, you don't know them, and I'll thank you not to speak about them."

"I'll thank you to lower your voice," Tom hisses, glancing toward the door.

Yes, wouldn't want the servants knowing our business. Wouldn't want them to know I've a mind and a mouth to voice it.

"Do you care so little about your own family, then? Do you not care that Miss Bradshaw made a fool of me—and you— by her deceit?"

"Her deceit! You were only interested in her once you heard she had a fortune."

Tom pours another splash of spirits. "A man in my position has to think of such things."

"She thought the world of you, and you treated her shabbily! Is it only ladies such as I, those with privilege, who require protecting, Thomas?"

His eyes widen. "And you would take her part against me, your own blood?"

Blood is thicker than water. That's what they say. But in truth, most things are.

Tom's narrow shoulders sag. "Believe it or not, Gemma, I do care about your welfare," he says.

"If you mean that, Thomas, send me back to Spence."

He swallows his drink. "No. I shall follow Lord Denby's sound advice, and you shall remain here, where I might watch over you."

I toss the book aside. "Lord Denby! I knew it! This is the Rakshana's doing, isn't it? They mean to control me yet."

Tom points an accusing finger. "This is exactly the sort of behavior I mean. Listen to yourself—you're prattling on about things that make no sense at all!"

"Do you deny that you've joined the Rakshana? If so, tell me the name of your gentlemen's club."

"I don't have to tell you anything about it. It is a gentlemen's club, and you are not a gentleman, though I've no doubt you'd wear trousers if you could."

I let his barb pass. "But you wear the Rakshana's pin!" I point to the skull-and-sword insignia on his lapel.

"Gemma," Tom growls, "it is a pin! There is nothing malevolent about it."

"I don't believe you."

Tom twirls his tumbler and the beveled glass catches the light, sending spectrums of color dancing on the wall. "You may believe me or not, but it is the truth."

"What is the name of your club, then?"

My brother loses his snide smile. "Now, see here, Gemma. That is my affair."

It is the Rakshana. I'm certain of it. They mean to keep me a prisoner until I give up the magic, and they've recruited my own brother to their purposes.

Tom shoves his fists into his pockets. "You and I, we must carry on, Gemma. I cannot afford the luxury of love. I must marry well. And now I must look after you. It is my duty."

"How noble," I snarl.

"Well, there's a fine thank-you."

"If you wish to suffer, you do so of your own free will, not on my behalf. Or Father's or Grandmama's or anyone's. You are a fine physician, Thomas. Why is that not enough?"

His jaw tightens. That boyish lock of hair falls into his eyes, shadowing them. "Because it isn't," he says with rare candor. "Only this and the hope of nothing more? A quiet respectability with no true greatness or heroism in it, with only my reputation to recommend me. So you see, Gemma, you are not the only one who cannot rule her own life."

He tilts his head back and drains the last of the spirits. It's too much and he could do with a hearty cough but he holds it down. No hint of vulnerability will escape him. Not even a cough.

I wander to the window. There's a carriage waiting outside. It is not our carriage but I recognize it. The black curtains, the funereal aspect. A match is struck and brought to a cigarette. Fowlson.

Tom's just behind me. "Ah, my driver. I have a rather important engagement this evening, Gemma. I trust you'll not burn the house down while I am away."

"Tom," I say, following him down the stairs to the foyer, "please don't go to the club tonight. Stay here with me. We could play cards!"

Tom laughs and pulls on his coat. "Cards! How thrilling!"

"Very well. We needn't play cards. We could . . ." What? What have my brother and I ever shared other than a few games in childhood? There is precious little that holds us together but the same unhappy history. Tom is waiting for my offer, but I have nothing.

"Right, then. I'm off."

He grabs his hat, that silly affectation, and checks himself in the mirror by the door. I've nothing left to venture but the truth.

"Tom, I know I shall sound like one of your patients at Bedlam, but please, hear me out. You mustn't go to that meeting this evening. I believe you are in danger. I know you've joined the Rakshana—" Tom tries to object but I hold up my hand. "I know it. Your gentlemen's club isn't what you imagine them to be, Tom. They've existed for centuries. They're not to be trusted."

Tom stands uncertainly for a moment. I can only hope I've reached him. He bursts into laughter and applause. "Bravo, Gemma! That is, without a doubt, the most fantastic story you've concocted yet. I do believe it is not I but Sir Arthur Conan Doyle who is in danger. For your stories may surpass his in intrigue and dastardly deeds!" I grab his arm and he brushes me away. "Have a care with that coat! My tailor is a good man but also a costly one."

"Tom, please. You must believe me. It isn't a story. They don't want you; they want me. I have something they want, something they would do anything to get. And they would employ you to get to me."

A terrible hurt flickers in Tom's eyes. "You're just like Father, aren't you? Doubting me at every turn. After all, why would anyone want Thomas Doyle, his father's constant disappointment?"

"I didn't say that—"

"No, but you thought it all the same."

"No, you're wrong—"

"Yes, I'm always wrong. That's the trouble with me. Well, not tonight. Tonight, I will become a part of something larger than myself. And they asked me, Gemma. They want me. I don't expect you to be happy for me but at the very least you could allow me to have my happiness."

"Tom . . . ," I plead, watching him walk out the door. The maid holds it open, trying to avert her eyes from our argument.

"And for the last time, I don't know what you mean by all this Rakshana business. I've never heard of them." He wraps his scarf about his neck with flair. "I bid you good night, Gemma. And please, stay away from those books you devour. They are putting the most fantastical tales into your head."

Tom strides down the walk toward the carriage. Fowlson gives him a hand into it, but his wicked smile is all for me.

CHAPTER FIFTY-NINE

FATHER'S ROOM IS LIT ONLY BY THE SMALL LAMP BESIDE HIS bed. His breathing is labored but he is calm. Dr. Hamilton has given him morphine. It is strange how a drug can be both tormentor and comfort.

"Hello, pet," he calls in a drowsy voice.

"Hello, Father." I sit by his bedside. He reaches out a hand and I take it.

"Dr. Hamilton was here earlier," he says.

"Yes, I know."

"Yes." He closes his eyes for a moment, then startles awake. "I think . . . I think I see that tiger. The old fellow's back."

"No," I say quietly, wiping my cheeks. "There's no tiger, Papa."

He points to the far wall. "Don't you see his shadow there?" There's nothing but the murky outline of my father's raised arm. "I shot him, you know."

"No, Papa," I say. He's shivering. I pull the linens to his neck, but he pushes them down again in his delirium.

"He was out there, you see? I could not live . . . with the threat of it. I thought I killed him, but he's come back. He's found me."

I blot his brow with a damp rag. "Shhh."

His eyes find mine. "I'm dying."

"No. You only need to rest." Hot tears burn my cheeks. Why are we compelled to lie? Why is the truth too bright for our souls to bear?

"Rest," he murmurs, settling into another drugged sleep. "The tiger is coming. . . ."

If I were braver, if I thought the truth would not blind us forever, I would ask him what I have longed to ask since Mother died: Why was his grief more powerful than his love? Why couldn't he find it within himself to fight back?

Why am I not enough to live for?

"Sleep, Papa," I say. "Let the tiger go for tonight."

⁂

Alone in my room, I beg Wilhelmina Wyatt to show herself once again.

"Circe has the dagger. I need your help," I say. "Please."

But she will not come when called, and so I fall asleep and dream.

Under the shade of a tree, little Mina Wyatt sits drawing the East Wing of Spence. She shades in the side of a gargoyle's mouth. Sarah Rees-Toome blocks the sun, and Mina frowns. Sarah crouches beside her.

"What do you see when you look into the darkness, Mina?"

Shyly, Mina shows her the pictures she has secreted in her book. Trackers. The dead. The pale things that live in the rocks. And last, the Tree of All Souls.

Sarah traces her fingers lovingly over it. "It's powerful, isn't it? That's why they don't want us to know about it."

Mina flicks a glance toward Eugenia Spence and Mrs. Nightwing playing croquet on the lawn. She nods.

"Can you show me the way?" Sarah asks.

Wilhelmina shakes her head.

"Why not?"

It will take you, she scribbles.

Suddenly, I'm in the forest in the Winterlands where the damned hang from barren trees. The vines hold them fast at their necks; their feet dangle. One struggles, and the sharp branches press into her flesh to keep her.

"Help me," she says in a strangled whisper.

The fog clears and I see her face going gray.

Circe.

CHAPTER SIXTY

For two impossibly long days, I'm trapped in our house in London with no way to get word to Kartik, Ann, or Felicity. I don't know what is happening in the realms, and I'm sick with worry. But each time I become brave enough to draw on the magic, I remember Circe's warning that the magic has changed, that we've shared it, that it might be joined to something dark and unpredictable. I feel the corners of the room grow threatening with shadows of what I may not be able to control, and I push the power down, far away from me, and crawl, trembling, into my bed.

With no plan of escape in sight, I've been resigned to the life of a cosseted young lady of London society as Grandmama and I pay calls. We drink tea that is too weak and never hot enough for my liking. The ladies pass the time with gossip and hearsay. This is what they have in place of freedom—time and gossip. Their lives are small and careful. I do not wish to live this way. I should like to make my mark. To venture opinions that may not be polite or even correct but are mine nonetheless. If I am to be hanged for anything, I should like to feel that I go to the gallows on my own strength.

I spend the evenings reading to Father. His health improves a bit—he is able to sit at his desk with his maps and books—but he will not be well again. It is decided that after my debut, Father will travel to a warmer clime. We all agree that this will restore his vitality. "Hot sun and warm wind—that's what's needed," we say through tight smiles. What we cannot bring ourselves to say seeps into the very bones of the house until it seems to whisper the truth to us in the stillness: *He is dying. He is dying. He is dying.*

On the third day, I am nearly out of my mind with worry when Grandmama announces that we are to attend a garden party in honor of Lucy Fairchild. I insist that I'm not well and should stay home—for perhaps I can sneak away to Victoria and a train back to Spence whilst she is gone—but Grandmama won't hear of it, and we arrive at a garden in Mayfair that is blooming with every sort of beauty imaginable.

I spy Lucy sitting alone on a bench under a willow tree. Heart in my mouth, I sit beside her. She ignores me.

"Miss Fairchild, I—I wanted to explain about Simon's behavior at the ball," I say.

She has the good breeding to sit very still. She holds her temper as tightly as she does the reins of her horse. "Go on."

"It might have seemed that Mr. Middleton was too familiar with me that evening, but that was not the case. In truth, when my chaperone was momentarily away, a gentleman whom I did not know, and who had had far too much to drink, pressed his suit to the point of being improper."

Believe me . . . please believe . . .

"I was quite frightened, naturally, being all alone," I lie. "Fortunately, Mr. Middleton saw my dilemma, and as our families are old friends, he took immediate action without thinking of the consequences. That is the sort of man he is. I thought you should know the true circumstances before passing judgment upon him."

Slowly, her face loses its misery. A shy hope presses her lips into a smile. "He sent the most beautiful flowers round yesterday. And a clever silk box with a hidden compartment."

"For all your secrets," I say, suppressing a smile.

Her eyes light up. "That is what Simon said! He told me he's nothing without me." She puts a hand to her mouth. "Perhaps I shouldn't have told you so private a sentiment."

It stings to hear that and yet I find it does not sting quite as much as it might have. Simon and Lucy are the same sort of people. They like things pleasant and untroubled. I could not abide such an arrangement, but it suits them.

"It was quite all right to do so," I assure her.

Lucy fiddles with the brooch Simon gave her, the one he once gave to me. "I understand that the two of you were quite . . . close."

"I was not the right sort of girl for him," I say. I am surprised when I realize that it is not a lie. "I daresay that I have never seen him merrier than he is when he's in your company. I hope you will find every happiness together."

"If I should forgive him." Her pride is back.

"Yes. That is solely within your power," I say, and it is truer than she can know. For I can't change what has happened. That is the path behind us and there is now only the course ahead.

Lucy rises. Our visit is at an end.

"Thank you, Miss Doyle. It was good of you to speak to me."
She does not extend her hand, nor would I expect her to.

"It was good of you to hear me out."

⌁⌁⌁⌁

In the evening, Tom leaves once again for his club. I try to dissuade him from it, but he refuses to speak to me. Grandmama has met with her friends for a game of baccarat. So I sit alone in my room, trying to devise a plan to return to Spence and the realms.

"Gemma."

I nearly shout as a man steps out from behind my drapes, and when I see it's Kartik, I'm overcome with joy.

"How did you get here?"

"I borrowed a horse from Spence," he explains. "Well, I stole it, actually. When you didn't return . . ." I cover his mouth with mine and silence him with a kiss.

We lie beside each other on my bed, my head resting on his chest. I can hear his heart thrumming, strong and sure. His fingers trace patterns on my back. His other hand is linked to mine.

"I don't understand," I say, enjoying the warmth of his fingers traveling the length of my spine and back again. "Why hasn't she shown me how to save Eugenia?"

"Could Wilhelmina have been aiding Circe? You said yourself they were close." Kartik kisses the top of my head.

"Why would she betray the Order and Eugenia?" I say. "It doesn't make sense. None of it does," I sigh. "The key holds the truth. It's a phrase that recurs in my dreams, my visions, Wilhelmina's book. But what does it mean?"

"There was no key inside the leather pouch along with the dagger?" Kartik asks.

"No. And I thought perhaps the book was the key." I shake my head. "But I'm not certain of that. I think . . ."

I'm remembering the pictures Wilhelmina drew for *A History of Secret Societies*. The Hidden Object. Guardians of the Night. The tower. I've deciphered them all save one—the room with the painting of boats.

"Yes?" Kartik prompts. His hand wanders to my breast.

"I think it might be a place," I say, reaching up to kiss him.

He moves on top of me, and I accept the weight of him. His hands slide down my body and mine push down the broad expanse of his back. His tongue makes small explorations in my mouth.

There's a knock at my door. I push Kartik off me, panicked.

"The drapery!" I whisper.

He hides behind the drapes as I quickly arrange myself. I perch on my bed, a book in hand.

"Come in," I call, and Mrs. Jones enters. "Good evening," I say, turning the book right side up. I can feel the flush on my cheeks. My heart thumps in my ears.

"A parcel has come for you, miss."

"A parcel? At this hour?"

"Yes, miss. The boy just left it."

She hands me a box wrapped in brown paper and tied crudely with string. There is no name or card with it.

"Thank you," I say. "I believe I shall turn in. I'm very tired."

"As you say, miss." The door clicks shut, and I lock it, exhaling loudly.

Kartik comes up behind me and wraps his hands around my

waist. "Best open it," he says, and I do. Inside are Tom's ridiculous hat and a note.

> *Dear Miss Doyle,*
>   *You possess something of great value to us. At present,*
> *we possess something of great value to you. I am certain*
> *we may come to an agreeable arrangement. Do not be*
> *tempted to use the magic against us. At the first hint of it,*
> *we shall know, and your brother will die. Mr. Fowlson is*
> *on the corner. Do not keep him waiting.*

The Rakshana have Tom.

The Rakshana mean to take my magic, and if I deny them, they will kill my brother. And if I attempt to draw upon my power now to save Tom? I cannot say that it is solely my power, and I may do more harm than good. I've nothing at my disposal tonight but my wits, and they seem little aid just now. But at present, it is the only hope I have.

"I'm coming with you," Kartik insists.

"You'll get yourself killed," I argue.

"Then it's a good day to die," he says, and it makes my stomach flip.

I put my fingers to his lips. "Don't say that."

He kisses my fingers, then my mouth. "I'm coming with you."

CHAPTER SIXTY-ONE

FOWLSON IS WAITING FOR ME BY HIS SLEEK CARRIAGE. HE flips a coin high, catching it neatly each time. When he sees me coming, he stops the coin on his arm with a slap.

"Awww, look at that—tails. Bad luck, luv." He opens the carriage door for me. I see Kartik sneaking around the back.

"Tell me, Mr. Fowlson, will you always do their bidding? And when, pray, will they reward you for your efforts? Or will it always be like this—they dining at the feast, you off doing their dirty work?"

"They'll reward me in time," he says, pulling a blindfold from his pocket.

"No doubt that is why you are here instead of sitting with them. They needed a driver."

"You shut it!" He glowers, but there's a small ember of doubt in his eyes, the first I've seen.

"I shall make you a bargain, Mr. Fowlson. Help me, and I shall take you into the realms."

He laughs. "Once we 'ave the magic, I'll be there all I like. No, I don't fink I'll be makin' bargains tonigh', luv."

He secures the blindfold over my eyes more tightly than is necessary. He threads rope around my wrists and ties it to something—the door's handle, I think.

"Don't go nowhere," he calls, and laughs till he coughs.

The carriage starts with a jolt. The horses' hooves strike the pavement in quick rhythm, and I hope Kartik is holding fast.

We do not travel far. The horses come to a stop. Fowlson's fingers work to loosen my bindings, but the blindfold remains in place. A cloak is thrown over my head.

"This way," Fowlson hisses.

A door is opened. I'm half dragged, down, down, around and around, and when the blindfold is removed, I find myself in a room where candles line the periphery. My brother sits in a chair. His hands are bound, and he appears drunk. A cloaked man stands behind him, his knife at the ready near Tom's throat.

"Tom!" I run for him and a voice booms out from above.

"Stop at once!" I look up to see a gallery that runs about the room. Men in cloaks stand watching, their faces hidden. "If you touch him, he will die, Miss Doyle. Our man is quick with a knife."

"Gemma, don't worry," Tom mumbles. "It's my ini . . . inish . . ."

"Initiation," Kartik shouts, coming to my side. "Call it off."

"Brother Kartik. I'd been told you were no longer living," a voice calls. "Mr. Fowlson, you will answer for this."

Fowlson's face drains of color. "Yes, m'lord."

"Let my brother go!" I shout.

"Certainly, dear lady. Just as soon as you give us the magic."

I glance at Tom, who is helpless under the executioner's knife.

"I can't do that," I say.

Tom screams as the knife presses a bit closer. "Stop," he says in a strangled voice.

"Please, I need your help!" I cry. "Something terrible is happening in the Winterlands. We're all in danger. I believe those creatures mean to come into our world."

The room breaks into polite laughter. Beside me, Fowlson laughs hardest.

"I have seen Amar in the realms!" I shout. "He was one of you once. He warned me that it was coming. 'Beware the birth of May,' he said."

The laughter dies away. "What did he mean by it?"

"I don't know," I say, keeping an eye on my brother. Tom is starting to come around. I see it in his eyes. "I thought it meant the first of May, but that day has come and gone. It could be another day—"

Lord Denby steps out of the shadows. "I don't know what manner of trickery this is, Miss Doyle, but it will not stand." His finger lowers, and the cloaked figure presses the knife harder to my brother's throat. "He will die."

"And what if you kill him?" I say. "What bargaining power will you have then?"

"Your brother will die!" His voice thunders in the room.

It's as if some fog has lifted, and I see clearly for the first time since this all began. I will not be intimidated, not by them. Not by anyone.

"And you will have nothing then," I shout, sure and strong.

"Nothing to shield yourselves from *my* power. And I will unleash it, sirs, like the hounds of hell, if you should harm one hair on his head!"

Lord Denby's finger waits at the ready. The executioner's knife also. For the longest moment, we all wait on the precipice.

"You're a woman. You won't do it." He lowers his hand, and I don't stop to think. I summon the magic and the knife becomes a balloon that slips from the man's grip.

"Tom, run!" I shout.

Tom sits, confused, and Kartik makes a grab for him and pulls him away as I vibrate with the power I've suppressed for too long. It speeds out of me with new purpose. And no one's eyes are wider than my brother's as I send the walls crawling with flames. Phantoms swirl overhead, shrieking. It doesn't matter that it's only illusion; the men believe it.

"Stop!" Lord Denby cries, and the flames and the phantoms are gone. He stumbles to the railing. "We are reasonable men, Miss Doyle."

"No, you're not. And so I must speak very plainly, sir. You are never to approach my family again, or there shall be consequences. Do I make myself clear?"

"Quite," he gasps.

"What about the realms?" Kartik calls out. "Do you forget that we have long been its guardians? Will you not come with us into the Winterlands?"

The men mumble to one another. No one comes forward for the ardous journey.

"Very well," Lord Denby says. "I shall assemble some foot soldiers for the task."

"Foot soldiers?" I ask.

Kartik folds his arms. "Men like Fowlson and me. Men who won't be missed."

"Yes, take Mr. Fowlson with you," Lord Denby says as if suggesting a servant for hire. "He has a way with a knife. You're a good chap, aren't you, Folwson?"

Mr. Fowlson accepts the statement like a blow he will not return. His jaw clenches.

"As it is my choice, I *shall* have Mr. Fowlson. We understand one another. And he does have a way with a knife," I say. "Untie my brother, if you please."

Mr. Fowlson loosens Tom's bonds. He shoulders Tom's limp body, and we move toward the door.

"The blindfold!" a man bellows.

I throw it on the floor. "I don't need it. If you wish to wear it, be my guest."

"Gemma! What the devil is going on? What did you do?" Tom demands. He's beginning to unravel, and action must be taken.

"Hold him still, will you, please?" I say to Kartik and Fowlson, who take hold of Tom's arms.

"Here now! Unhand me at once!" he insists, but he's a bit too groggy to struggle.

"Thomas," I say, removing my gloves, "this will hurt you far more than it will hurt me."

"What?" he says.

I give him a good, clean punch to the mouth, and Tom is unconscious.

"You're a hard one," Fowlson says to me, propping my brother up in the carriage.

I settle my skirts over my legs properly and pull my glove

neatly over my aching hand. "You've never taken a carriage ride with my brother when he is in such a state, Mr. Fowlson. Trust me, you will thank me for it."

~~~~~~

When Tom has recovered his senses—what sense he has, that is—we sit near the embankment. The streetlamps cast pools of light onto the Thames; they run like wet paint. Tom's a mess: His collar sticks out like a broken bone, and the front of his shirt is spotted with his blood. He holds a wet handkerchief to his bruised face while stealing glances at me. Each time I meet his gaze, he looks quickly away. I could call on my magic to help me here, to blot all traces of this evening and my powers from his mind, but I decide against it. I'm tired of running. Of hiding who I am to make others happy. Let him know the truth of me, and if it's too much, at least I shall know.

Tom moves his jaw gingerly. "Ow."

"Is it broken?" I ask.

"Nuh, jus huhts," he says, putting the handkerchief to his bloody bottom lip and wincing.

"Don't you want to talk about it?" I ask.

"Tal' abou' wha'?" He glances at me like a frightened animal.

"What just happened."

He removes the handkerchief. "What is there to discuss? I was given ether, taken to a secret hideaway, bound, and threatened with death. Then my sister, the debutante, who is supposedly away at school learning to curtsy and embroider and order mussels in French, unleashed a force the likes of which I've never seen and which cannot be explained by any rational mind or laws of science. I shall commit myself come morning."

He stares out at the murky river that snakes through the heart of London. "It was real, all of it. Wasn't it?"

"Yes," I say.

"And you're not going to, em . . ." He makes a hand motion like waving a wand, which I suppose stands for "unleash magical forces that frighten me."

"Not at present," I say.

He winces. "Can you make this pain in my head go away?"

"Sorry," I lie.

He puts the wet cloth to his cheek and sighs. "How long have you been . . . like this?" he asks.

"Are you sure you want to hear it—all of it? Are you ready for the truth?" I ask.

Tom considers for a moment, and when he answers, his voice is sure. "Yes."

"It all began last year on my birthday, the day Mother died, but I suppose, in truth, it began much earlier than that. . . ."

I tell him about my powers, the Order, the realms and the Winterlands. The only thing I don't divulge is the truth about Mother killing little Carolina. I don't know why. Perhaps I sense he's not ready to know that just yet. Maybe he never will be. People can live with only so much honesty. And sometimes, people can surprise you. I talk to my brother as I never have before, trusting in him, letting the river listen to my confessions on its path toward the sea.

"It's extraordinary," he says at last. He stares at the ground. "So they really did want you, not me."

"I'm sorry," I say.

"It's no matter. I rather hated their port," he says, trying to cover the injury to his pride.

"There is a place that would have you if you would have them," I remind him. "It may not be your first choice, but they are sound men who share your interests, and you may come to like them best over time." Then, changing the subject, I say, "Tom, there is something I must know. Do you think that I could have brought Father's illness on, when I tried to make him see . . . with the magic . . . "

"Gemma, he has consumption, brought on by his grief and his vices. It's not your doing."

"Promise?"

"Promise. Don't misunderstand me—you are quite vexing." He touches his tender jaw. "And you hit like a man. But you didn't cause his illness. That is his doing."

Farther down the river, a ship's horn makes a mournful cry. It's plaintive and familiar, a howl in the night for what one has lost and can't get back.

Tom clears his throat. "Gemma, there's something I need to say to you."

"All right," I reply.

"I know you adore Father, but he isn't the white knight you imagine him to be. He never was. True, he's charming and loving in his way. But he's selfish. He's a limited man determined to bring about his own end—"

"But—"

Tom grabs both my hands in his and gives them a small squeeze. "Gemma, you can't save him. Why can't you accept that?"

I see my reflection on the surface of the Thames. My face is a watery outline, all blurred edges with nothing settled.

"Because if I let go of that"—I swallow hard, once, twice—"then I have to accept that I am alone."

The ship's horn howls again as it slips out toward the sea. Tom's reflection appears beside mine, just as uncertain.

"We're every one of us alone in this world, Gemma." He doesn't say it bitterly. "But you have company, if you want it."

"We stayin' out 'ere all nigh'?" Fowlson calls. He and Kartik lean against the carriage like a couple of stoic andirons in need of a fire to guard.

I offer Tom my hand and help him up.

"So this magic of yours . . . I don't suppose you could make me into a baron or an earl or something like that? A duchy would be nice. Nothing ostentatiously grand—well, unless you care to make it so."

I push that one rebellious lock from his forehead. "Don't press your luck."

"Right." He grins and his lip cracks open again. "Ow!"

"Thomas, I intend to live my own life as I see fit without interference from now on," I tell him as we press toward our carriage.

"I shan't tell you how to live it. Just don't turn me into a newt or a braying ass or, heaven forbid, a Tory."

"Too late. You're already a braying ass."

"God, you'll be insufferable now. I'm too frightened to say anything back," Tom says.

"You don't know how happy that makes me, Thomas." Fowlson goes to open the carriage door, but I get there first. "I have it, thank you."

"Where are we going?" Tom asks, brushing past me and settling himself inside without so much as a care for the rest of us. Order has returned.

"A place where you're wanted," I say. "Mr. Fowlson, take us to the Hippocrates Society, if you please."

Fowlson folds his arms across his chest. He won't look at me. "Why'd you do it? Why'd you ask fer me?"

"I trust them slightly less than I do you. And it would seem that I believe in you slightly more."

"They wouldn't leave me behind," Fowlson says quietly.

Kartik scoffs.

"Do you believe that enough to stake everything upon it?" I ask. "I will not be threatened any longer. They have no power over me. This is your chance to be heroic, Mr. Fowlson. Don't fail me. Don't fail *her*," I say meaningfully.

"I would never," he says, looking down. And I realize that even Mr. Fowlson has his Achilles' heel.

⋏⋏⋏⋏⋏

When we arrive at the Hippocrates Society, Mr. Fowlson bangs hard on the doors until they swing open.

"What is it?" a white-haired gentleman demands, several of his compatriots at his heel.

"Please, sirs, it's Mr. Doyle. We need your help."

The gentlemen push out in a haze of cigar smoke. Nursing his bruised face, Tom wobbles from the carriage with Kartik's and Fowlson's help while I follow.

"Doyle, old boy. What has happened?" the white-haired gentleman exclaims.

Tom rubs his sore jaw. "Well, I . . . I . . ."

"As we returned from dinner, ruffians set upon our carriage," I explain, wide-eyed. "My dear brother saved us from those who would have done us harm."

"I . . . I did?" Tom's head whips in my direction. I plead with my eyes: *Don't muck this up.* "Right! I did. Terribly sorry to be delayed."

The men fall into shouts and questions. "You don't say!" "Fantastic tale—how did it happen?" "Let's have a look at that jaw!"

"It—it really was nothing," Tom stammers.

I tighten my hold on Tom. "Don't be so modest, Thomas. He dispensed with them single-handedly. They didn't stand a chance against such a brave and honorable man." To say this, I must fight the giggle that shouts "Ha!" from my stomach.

"A splendid display of courage, old boy," one of the gentlemen says.

Tom stands blinking in the light, rather like an old dog without the sense to come in from the rain.

"Don't you remember, Thomas? Oh, dear. I fear that blow to your head was more severe than we thought. We should take you straight home to bed and call for Dr. Hamilton."

"Dr. Hamilton is already here," Dr. Hamilton says. He steps out, a brandy snifter in his hand and a cigar clenched between his teeth.

"Single-handedly?" the white-haired man asks.

Another gentleman, with thick spectacles, claps Tom on the back. "There's a good man."

A younger man takes Tom's other arm. "A warm brandy is all you need to get you back on your feet."

"Indeed. I should like that very much, thank you," Tom says, managing to look both sheepish and proud at the same time.

"You must tell us exactly how it happened, chap," Dr. Hamilton says, ushering Tom into the small but cozy club.

"Well," Tom begins, "in our haste this evening, my driver foolishly took a shortcut near the docks and was lost. Suddenly, I heard cries of 'Help! Help! Oh, please help!'"

"You don't say!" the gentlemen gasp.

"I counted three—a *half dozen* men of dubious character, brigands with eyes devoid of all conscience. . . ."

I see I am not the only one gifted with imagination. But tonight, I shall allow Tom his glory, however much it vexes me. A kindly gentleman offers assurances to me that my "heroic brother" will be well looked after, and I'm quite sure that after tonight's tale, his place in that society is assured.

"Tom," I call after him. "Mr. Fowlson will carry me on to Spence, then?"

"Hmmm? Yes, of course. To Spence with you." He waves me away with his hand. "Oh, Gemma?"

I turn back.

"Thank you." He grins, bloodying his lip once again. "Ow!"

Fowlson gets the carriage under way. Kartik sits beside me. London rolls past us in all its grit and glory: the chimney sweeps soldiering home with sooty faces at the end of a hard day, their brooms balancing on their shoulders; the solicitors in their finely brushed hats; the women in their ruffles and lace. And on the banks of the Thames, the mud larks sift through the filth and the muck, searching for what treasures may hide there—a coin, a fine watch, a lost comb, some bit of glittering luck to change their fate.

"Beware the birth of May, beware the birth of May," I intone. "How could it have been about Circe? She didn't know I would come to her then," I say aloud. I repeat the phrase a few more times, turning it over in my mind, and something new comes to me. "A birthday. The warning could be for a birth date. When was Amar's birthday?"

"July," Kartik says. "And yours is June twenty-first."

"Nice of you to remember," I say.

"First day we met."

"When is yours?" I ask, realizing I don't know, have never asked.

"November tenth," he says.

"Leaves you out, doesn't it?" I say, rubbing my temples.

I hear the boats in the distance getting closer. We're near the docks. There is something familiar about this place. I felt it when Kartik and I came to meet with Toby.

"'Upon the wharves of sorrow,'" I say, repeating a line of the Yeats poem I found in Wilhelmina's book. The illustration opposite it: the painting of the boats on the wall. What if that wasn't a painting but a window?

"Fowlson!" I shout. "Slow the carriage!"

"You don' wanna do that. Not 'ere," he calls down.

"Why not?"

"It's as rough a place as you could 'ope to find. The Key's full o' prostitutes, criminals, murderers, addicts, and the like. I should know. It's where I'm from."

My stomach flutters. "What did you call it?"

He states it emphatically, as if I were a foolish child. "The Key. And you're mad if you fink I'm stoppin' this fine carriage 'ere."

CHAPTER SIXTY-TWO

"Don't like this," Fowlson mutters, turning up his collar to the sticky damp as we make our way down slick cobblestones in the dark. He keeps his switchblade palmed like a talisman. A fetid smell blows off the river.

"You're sure this place is called the Key?" I ask. The houses—if they could be called such—are narrow and as crooked as a poor woman's teeth.

"That's wot we always cawled it. For the wharves and the docks. Spelled 'quay' but sounds like 'key.' 'Down in the Key,' we say."

"Yes, thank you for the lesson, Fowlson," Kartik mutters.

"Wot's that mean?" Fowlson grumbles.

I interrupt. "Gentlemen, let's keep our heads about us. There will be time enough to play cock of the walk later. I hope."

We travel the dark streets as they twist and turn. As Fowlson has warned, there are rough sorts moving in the shadows, and I don't want to look too closely.

"Customs House ain't too far," Fowlson says.

"Brigid said that when Wilhelmina came to London, she was lost near the Customs House for a week. What if this was a place that was familiar to her? Where she felt safe, oddly enough?"

We turn another corner and another, until we come to a few dilapidated buildings that look out onto the old wharves. I hear the ships calling to each other; there's a fine view of the boats.

"It's here," I say. "I recognize this from my visions. Come on, Wilhelmina," I whisper. "Don't fail me now."

And suddenly I see her before me in her lavender dress.

"Do you see her?" I ask quietly.

"See 'oo?" Folwson asks, his knife in front of him.

"I don't," Kartik says. "But you do. We'll follow you."

Wilhelmina passes through the wall of a miserable tenement suitable only for tearing down.

"In here," I say.

Fowlson draws back. "You barking?"

"I may be mad, indeed, Mr. Fowlson," I answer. "But I won't know until I go inside. You may follow me or not."

Kartik kicks the rotting door, and I step first into the decaying, abandoned building. It's dark and smells of mold and salt water. Rats scratch in the corners; the sound of their busy claws puts a shiver up my spine. Kartik is at my side, his knife at the ready.

"Bloody 'ell," Fowlson mutters under his breath, but I feel his fear.

We climb a rotting staircase. A man more dead than alive lies unconscious at the top of it. He smells of spirits. The walls peel from the moisture and decay. Kartik takes careful steps down the dark corridor with me just behind. We pass an open door and I see several people lying about. One woman's head rises for a moment before her chin comes to rest on her chest again. The stench of urine and waste wafts out of the room like an overpowering perfume. It assaults my nose, and has me choking till I am forced to breathe through my mouth. It is all I can do not to run screaming from this place.

"Please, Wilhelmina," I whisper, and then I see her just ahead, glowing in the murk. She passes through the last door. I try the handle but it's rusted shut. Kartik throws his shoulder against it but it won't budge.

"Stand aside," Fowlson says. He flicks open his knife and meddles with the lock until the door gives a bit. "'E said I was good wif a knife."

"So you are, Mr. Fowlson. Thank you." I push the door open; it screeches as if angry to be wakened. The room is dark. The only light comes from a small window with a view of the Thames and the ships—what I took to be a painting of boats in the illustration. There's no doubt: This is the room from my visions.

"Wot is this place?" Fowlson says, coughing against the damp.

"We're just about to find out," I say. "Have you any matches?"

Fowlson pulls a small box from his waistcoat pocket and hands them over. I strike one, adding the smell of sulphur to the others in the room. The match flares, and in the sudden brightness, I spy the table and a lantern covered with cobwebs. A small nub of candle remains. I light it, raise the lantern, and the room is flooded with light.

"Blimey," Fowlson gasps.

The walls. They're covered in words. And in the center of one is a drawing of the Tree of All Souls, bodies dangling from its branches.

The marks are faded by time, but I read what I can. "'I see into the darkness. She has become the tree. They are one and the same. Her noble power is corrupted.'"

"'She has deceived us all,'" Kartik reads. "'A monster.'"

"'The most beloved of us all, beloved no more. My sister, gone,'" I read. I stare at the tree. "Eugenia," I whisper.

Fowlson crowds behind me. "You tellin' me Eugenia Spence is now . . . that?"

"'The Key holds the truth.' That's what she said. And I'm ready for it now." I put my hands to the walls and call out to Wilhelmina. "Show me."

The lantern's brightness grows, the walls fall away, and I'm in the Winterlands on the night of the fire. A hard wind blows black sand and snow. A huge beast of a tracker in a black cloak as long as the Queen's robes holds tightly to Eugenia Spence's arm. She is on her knees as she throws her amulet to my mother. "You must close the realms! Go, now! Hurry!"

Dutifully, my mother drags Sarah toward the East Wing, and Eugenia begins her spell to seal the realms.

The tracker hovers over her. "You cannot close us out so easily, Priestess. Just because you deny us does not mean we do not exist." He hits her hard across the face and she falls. Her blood spills across the ice and snow like the petals of a dying poppy. And she is afraid.

Another tracker arrives. "Kill her!" it snarls, revealing sharp teeth.

"Do it and we shall have her magic, but not the magic of the Temple! We'll still have no means into their world," the first tracker snaps back.

"We shall not sacrifice you. Not yet. You will help us breach the other world."

Eugenia staggers to her feet. "I shall never do that. You will not break me. My loyalty is without question."

"Whatever is without question is most vulnerable." The tracker smiles. "To the tree."

They drag her to the Tree of All Souls. It is not quite as majestic as the tree I have seen. One of the Winterlands creatures slices Eugenia's hand. She cries out in pain and then in terror as she realizes what they mean to do to her. But her cries are meaningless. The creatures force her blood onto the roots of the Tree of All Souls, and within seconds, the branches crisscross over her legs and up her body.

"When her blood is spilled, she must join with the tree."

The roots continue their march, devouring Eugenia, and then she is part of the tree, her soul joined to it.

"Let me go, please," she begs in a whisper.

I see Eugenia trapped inside the tree, her mind splintering over the years. I see the first day she asks the creatures for a sacrifice and the smallest sliver of red shows in the roiling clouds of the Winterlands.

In awe, the creatures bow before her. "We are lost and require a leader. A mother. Will you guide us?"

The tree's limbs stretch out, and wrap themselves around the Winterlands creatures like protective arms. And Eugenia's voice drifts from the tree like a lullaby. "Yes . . . yes . . ."

The fog grows heavier. The tree speaks again. "There is one

who comes, and she holds great power. She will give us what we want."

"We'll spill her blood at the tree!" a tracker thunders to great cheers.

"But first, I must pave the way for our return," the tree says.

The scene shifts to the music hall. Wilhelmina Wyatt writes upon her slate: *You must restore the East Wing and take the realms again. The Order must prevail.*

Tears of joy flood Wilhelmina's cheeks as she receives the message from her beloved Eugenia. She shows it to McCleethy, and the plan is set in motion. For how could the Order ignore a message from their beloved Eugenia?

But Wilhelmina can see into the darkness, and soon, she knows. I'm back in the room, watching Wilhelmina scribble her desperate message on the walls. And when the knowledge is too much to bear, she slips the needle under her skin and sinks into oblivion. I see her trying to warn the Order through letters and entreaties, but the cocaine and her fear have made her increasingly unstable; she frightens them and they dismiss her. And when she writes her book—a last, desperate attempt to reach them—they see her as a traitor and a liar.

Lost to the drug, Wilhelmina makes one final effort. She hides the dagger in the slate and walks out into the cold night. Her mind is frayed, and she sees haunts—trackers and beasts—in every shadowed corner. A carriage thunders down the lane, and in her mind, it is ghostly. She runs to the wharves, where she slips, hits her head on the pier, and falls into the Thames. And when the rivermen pitch her lifeless body back in, the darkness Wilhelmina feared surrounds her, but she is beyond caring. She sinks slowly into the deep, and I follow.

I break away from the vision with a loud gasp. Kartik is beside me, stroking my hair. He looks worried. "You've been in a trance for hours. Are you all right?"

"Hours," I echo. My head aches.

"What did you see?"

"I need air. Need to breathe," I pant. "Outside."

Out on the wharf, the damp air of the river hits my face, and I am right again. I tell them everything.

"No one killed Wilhelmina," I say, looking out at the boats bobbing on the water. "It was an accident. She slipped and hit her head and drowned. Stupid, stupid." I might as well be speaking of myself. I've let it all get away from me.

No, not yet. I can still stop it. There's time.

"Mr. Fowlson," I say, "we must fly to Spence at once. How quickly can you drive us there?"

He smirks. "Quick as you like."

"Let's be about it, then," I say.

We race to the carriage, which is still there, thank goodness, and Mr. Fowlson speeds us toward the east, and Spence.

"Amar tried to warn me," I say to Kartik.

"Gemma, he's lost. There's no need—"

"No, he did. 'Beware the birth of May.' It was a birthday. Wilhelmina tried to show me the headstone. Eugenia Spence was born May sixth. That's tomorrow."

Kartik looks out the carriage window toward the rising dawn. "That's today."

CHAPTER SIXTY-THREE

IT IS DAY BY THE TIME SPENCE COMES INTO VIEW, RISING from the deep green land like a mirage. A storm is moving in from the east. The wind's a demon, whipping leaves off trees. Far in the distance, a dark shadow sits upon the sky like a cat on its haunches ready to pounce. The first splats of rain have begun to fall. They leave ugly wet marks on my dress.

I do not stop even to remove my gloves. I tear through the school, searching for Felicity and Ann. I tell them everything and ask them to wait for me. Then I go in search of Mrs. Nightwing. I find her in the kitchen, instructing Brigid on household matters.

"Miss Doyle! We didn't expect you. How is your father—"

"Mrs. Nightwing, please, I must speak with you in the parlor. It's rather urgent. I require audience with Miss McCleethy as well."

The exigency of my tone has Mrs. Nightwing's full attention. She does not even chide me for my lack of manners.

Moments later, she enters the parlor with Miss McCleethy in tow. Miss McCleethy blanches at the sight of Fowlson.

"Mr. Fowlson. What a surprise."

"Sahirah. You should have a listen," he says.

"I know about the secret plan to rebuild the East Wing and enter the realms again. The plan Eugenia Spence left for you," I say.

Miss McCleethy sits as if commanded. Her expression is one of shock.

"She told you that if you built the turret, you would be able to connect to that door and enter the realms again. But I have already opened the door."

Miss McCleethy's eyes widen. Mrs. Nightwing looks from McCleethy to me to Kartik and Fowlson, as if waiting for someone to provide her with an explanation.

"It doesn't matter that I went in first—the plan was a lie. Eugenia betrayed you. 'She is a deceiver'—that's what Wilhelmina said. She tried to warn you but you thought her a liar," I say, pacing before the fireplace. "Eugenia was in league with the creatures all along. Restoring the East Wing opened the seal between worlds, and my magic gave it power. She didn't mean to give you a way into the realms; she meant to give those creatures a way into our world."

Mrs. Nightwing gasps. "That's not possible."

"Wilhelmina tried to tell me. I had visions of her. Both she and Amar told me to beware the birth of May, and I thought it was the first of May, but she wanted me to beware someone *born* in May. She meant Eugenia Spence. Eugenia betrayed her. She's betrayed us all. I know I sound a lunatic, but I'm telling the truth."

Mrs. Nightwing looks as if she's been slapped. Fear flits across her face.

"Do you mean to suggest that Eugenia Spence, one of the greatest priestesses the Order has ever known, betrayed her own sisters?" There is murder in Miss McCleethy's eyes. I've taken away her god, and she could kill me for it.

"How could she have done so?" Mrs. Nightwing asks.

I take a steadying breath. "There is a place in the Winterlands—the Tree of All Souls. Have you heard of it?"

"I have heard of it, yes. It is a legend, a myth," Miss McCleethy fumes. "The creatures have no source of power of their own. That is why they have tried to take the Temple's magic—"

"Listen to me, please!" I beg. "You're wrong. They—"

"Eugenia herself told us it wasn't real!" Miss McCleethy insists.

"Because she feared it!" I shout. "That's why she burned Wilhelmina's drawings. Why she denied its existence. But I assure you it is very real indeed! I have seen it."

"You've been to the Winterlands," Mrs. Nightwing whispers. She's as pale as cheese.

Miss McCleethy's expression is one of pure fury. "You stupid, stupid girl!"

"Perhaps if the Order hadn't been afraid of the Winterlands, if they hadn't made it forbidden all those years, you'd know more about it!"

"We know what we need to know about the Winterlands and those filthy creatures: that they must be controlled or destroyed."

"You'll never destroy them. It isn't possible. The creatures are feeding souls to the tree—the souls of the dead and the living. They've been coming into our world through the secret door and taking them back. That's what happened to Miller's men, to the mummers, to Ithal. They were taken! Those horrible things I saw—I thought I was going mad. Eugenia told me you would make me see things, illusions, that I would feel mad, and I believed her."

"You *are* mad!" McCleethy growls, her voice rising.

Fowlson holds out a hand. "Sahirah, what if—"

Her eyes flash. "Don't." And Fowlson, the bully, quiets like that frightened boy in his mother's kitchen. "Eugenia Spence was the most loyal member of the Order who ever lived! And you are the daughter of the one who nearly killed her. Why should I believe you?"

Her words sting, but I have no time to be wounded. "Because I'm telling you the truth. When Eugenia sacrificed herself for Sarah and Mary, they fed her soul to their god, to the tree. She became a part of it—her power joined to its. And over time, they've become something new, something enormously powerful. She isn't what she was. She isn't the Eugenia you knew."

"Sahirah, you said it would be safe," Mrs. Nightwing whispers.

"Lillian, she's invented this tale. It's ridiculous! Eugenia Spence!"

"Are you so desperate to be right—to admit no cracks—that you would ignore my warning?" I say.

"Miss Doyle, why don't you admit the truth—that you are loath to share the power, and that you would do anything to hold on to it?" McCleethy turns on Fowlson. "And how could you believe her?"

Fowlson lowers his eyes. He turns his hat in his hands.

Miss McCleethy's gaze is cool. "We gave you a chance to join with us, Miss Doyle. You refused. Did you think one girl could hold us back?"

It is not a question to be answered, so I say nothing.

"Our plans will continue with or without you."

"Please," I say, my voice raw. "Please believe me. They need my magic to complete their plan. They mean to sacrifice me today, May sixth—Eugenia's birthday. We must find a way to stop them."

"I've heard enough." Miss McCleethy rises.

A flicker of worry passes over Nightwing's face. "Perhaps we—"

"Lillian, remember your place as well." The door closes behind McCleethy with barely a sound.

I've never heard anyone speak to Mrs. Nightwing in such a manner. I wait for her to dismiss me, to resume being Mrs. Nightwing—imperious, commanding, never wrong.

"Sahirah . . . ," Fowlson says as he follows his lover out. I hear them arguing in heated whispers beyond the door, Miss McCleethy's mumbles sounding hard and quick, Fowlson's slower and defensive.

"I am not of the Order," Mrs. Nightwing explains to Kartik and me. "My power did not take, you see. Within months, it faded. I was not destined to continue. I left Spence for a life outside the Order, for marriage. And when the power of that faded, too, I came back to help. I chose a life of service. There is no shame in that." She rises. "Women have fought and died to preserve the sanctity of the realms. Perhaps you could bend just a little."

Mrs. Nightwing's skirts whisk stiffly across the floor, and

then Kartik and I are the only ones left. Soon morning will creep into afternoon. Dusk will fall. And then night.

Felicity and Ann rush in, out of breath. "We were listening at the door earlier," Ann explains. "Before McCleethy shooed us away."

"Then you know they don't believe me. They think I'm mad, a liar like Wilhelmina Wyatt," I say. "We're on our own."

Felicity puts a hand on my shoulder. "Perhaps you are wrong about this, Gemma."

And for once, I sincerely hope that I am. For if they come, I don't know how to stop them.

CHAPTER SIXTY-FOUR

THE RAIN SPITS ITS RAGE AT OUR WINDOWS. THE WIND'S A persistent howl, an animal begging to be let in for the night. Felicity and Ann have begun a halfhearted game of tiddledy-winks to keep their nerves at bay. They flick the colorful circles at each other, but neither keeps score. Just outside, front and back, Kartik and Fowlson keep watch. Miss McCleethy's furious about it, but Mrs. Nightwing insisted, and I'm glad. I wish Inspector Kent were here, but he has taken Mademoiselle LeFarge to London to visit his family.

I peek out the windows at the angry wind. My tea sits untouched. I'm far too troubled to drink it. Brigid is in the large wing-back chair by the fire, regaling the younger girls with stories, which they devour, begging for more and more.

"Have you ever *seen* pixies, Brigid?" one of the little girls asks.

"Aye," Brigid says gravely.

"I've seen pixies," a girl with dark ringlets says, wide-eyed.

Brigid laughs like an indulgent aunt. "Have you now, luv? Were they stealing yer shoes or leaving the biscuits flat?"

"No. I saw them last night on the back lawn."

The hair on my arms rises as quickly as a flash fire.

Brigid frowns. "Talking nonsense, you are."

"It isn't nonsense!" the child insists. "I saw them last night from my window. They bade me come play."

I swallow hard. "What did they look like?"

Brigid tickles the girl. "Oh, go on! You're telling stories to your old Brigid!"

Mrs. Nightwing's face shows true fear. Even Miss McCleethy is listening with interest.

"I promise," the girl says in earnest. "On my life, I saw them—riders in black cloaks. Their poor horses were so cold and pale. They bade me come down and ride with them, but I was too frightened."

Ann takes hold of my hand. I can feel her fear pulsing under her skin.

Alarm creeps into Mrs. Nightwing's voice. "You say this was last night, Sally?"

"Lillian," Miss McCleethy warns, but Mrs. Nightwing ignores her.

The little girl nods vehemently. "They had one of the mummers with them. The tall, funny one. They said they would come back tonight."

The wind howls, rattling my teacup on its saucer.

"Sahirah?" Mrs. Nightwing's face has gone ashen.

Miss McCleethy will not let this fire catch among the girls; she'll put it out, just as Eugenia tried to long ago. "Listen to me, Sally. You had a dream. That's all. A very bad dream."

The little girl shakes her head. "It was real! I saw them."

"No, you didn't," Brigid says. "Dreams is funny that way."

"I suppose it could be a dream," the girl says. They've made her uncertain, and that's how it's done; that's how we come to doubt what we know to be true.

"Tonight, you'll have a nice glass of warm milk and there'll be no dreams to trouble you," Miss McCleethy assures her. "Now, Brigid's got to see to her duties in the kitchen."

Amidst the girls' protests for just one more tale, Brigid hurries out of the great room.

"Gemma?" Ann asks, her voice tight with fear.

"I don't think I'm wrong after all," I whisper. "I believe the Winterlands creatures were here. I think they're coming back."

Mrs. Nightwing takes me aside. "I have always been loyal and followed my orders. But I fear you are right about the door, Miss Doyle. These are my girls, and I must take every precaution." She dabs at her neck with her handkerchief. "We cannot let them in."

"Have the Gypsies left yet?" I ask.

"They were packing to leave this morning," my headmistress answers. "I don't know if they've gone."

"Send Kartik to their camp for Mother Elena," I say. "She may know how to help."

Moments later, Kartik helps a frail and frayed Mother Elena into the kitchen. "The mark must be made in blood," she says. "We will work fast."

"I'm not listening to this," Fowlson growls.

"She's trying to help us, Brother," Kartik says.

Fowlson swaggers forward, sneering, and his old self is on display. "I'm not your brother. I'm a proper representative of the Rakshana—not a traitor."

"A proper thug, you mean," Kartik rejoins.

Fowlson steps forward till he and Kartik are nose to nose. "I should finish wot I started wif you."

"Be my guest," Kartik spits.

I step between them. "Gentlemen, if we survive this evening, there will be plenty of time for you to have your little boxing match. But as we've more important matters to attend to than your glaring at one another, we shall have to put aside our differences."

They back down, but not before Fowlson gets off a parting shot. "I'm the man in charge 'ere."

"Really, Hugo," Miss McCleethy chides.

"Hugo?" I say, wide-eyed. I see a grin pulling at Kartik's lips.

Fowlson's face darkens. "Promised you wouldn't call me that."

"The dead come. They come, they come . . . ," Mother Elena mutters, bringing us back to the terrible task at hand.

"How do we keep them out?" I ask.

"Mark the windows and doors," she says. "And still it may not be enough."

"We can't possibly mark every door and window," I say.

"We'll do what we can," Kartik says.

Mother Elena has us mix chicken blood and ashes, which she pours into bowls and gives to us all. When the doors to the great room swing open, we sweep in, our faces grim with purpose. The girls gasp upon seeing Mother Elena and Kartik with us, fascinated by the old Gypsy woman muttering to herself, as well as the handsome, forbidden young man at her side.

"What is happening?" Felicity asks.

Ann peers into the bowl of blood and ashes in my hands. "What is that?"

"Protection," I say, shoving it at her. "Follow Mother Elena's lead."

We spread out along the sides of the great room, moving quickly from window to window, checking each of the latches. Mother Elena dips her finger into a small metal char pot. She hurries as best she can, painting each window with bloody ashes, moving to the next and the next. Mrs. Nightwing, Ann, Felicity, Kartik, and I do the same. Brigid tucks tiny sprigs of rowan leaves onto the sills with one hand and holds fast to her cross with the other.

The girls watch them with morbid fascination.

"Brigid, what are you doing?" a girl in a large pink hair ribbon asks.

"Never you mind, dearie," she answers.

"But, Brigid—"

"It's a game," I say brightly. Brigid and I exchange glances.

The girls clap in excitement. "What sort of game?"

"Tonight, we'll pretend the pixies are coming. And to keep them out, we must mark all the doors and windows," I answer.

Brigid says nothing but her eyes are as big as saucers. The girls squeal with delight. They want to play the game too.

"What is this?" Elizabeth stares into the pot and wrinkles her nose. "It looks like blood."

Martha and Cecily turn up their noses.

"Really, Mrs. Nightwing. It's unchristian," Cecily sniffs.

The younger girls are enthralled. They scream, "Let me see! Let me see!"

"Don't be ridiculous," Mrs. Nightwing scolds. "This is nothing more than sherry and molasses."

"Doesn't smell like molasses or sherry," Elizabeth grumbles.

Brigid pours the foul mixture into small cups. "'Ere, we'll all help." The girls take the cups doubtfully. They sniff the mixture and come away with wrinkled noses and curled lips. But each girl dutifully paints the mark on a window and soon it becomes a merry competition to see who can complete the most. They laugh and jostle for position. But beads of sweat appear on Brigid's forehead. She wipes at them with the back of her hand.

With everyone's help, we seal and mark every door, every window. Now all we can do is wait. Dusk slips too quickly into night. The pinks and blues of day shade first into gray, then indigo. I cannot will the light to stay. I cannot hold back the dark. We peer out at the violent night. The lights of Spence blind us to the shadows of the woods.

The air has gone still as death. It's warm, and my skin's moist. I pull at my collar. By nine o'clock, the younger girls have grown tired of waiting for the pixies to show themselves. They yawn, but Brigid tells them we're to stay together in the great room past midnight—it's part of the game—and they accept it. The older girls share disapproving glances about Gypsies in our midst. They gossip over their needlework, small stitches to match their small talk. I am alert and afraid. Every sound, every movement terrifies. Is that them? Have they come for us? But no, it is only the creak of a floorboard, the hiss of the gas lamp.

Mrs. Nightwing has a book in her hands, but she's not reading a word of it. Her eyes dart from the doors to the windows as she watches, waits. Felicity and Ann play whist in Felicity's tent, but I am far too agitated to join them. Instead, I hold Mother Elena's hand and keep watch over the mantel clock as if I can divine the future there. Ten o'clock. Fifteen after. Half past. Will this day pass uneventfully? Have I been mistaken again?

The second hand moves. To my ears it sounds like the firing of a cannon. Three, *boom*, two, *boom*, one. By eleven o'clock, most of the girls have fallen asleep. Kartik and Fowlson keep steady watch by the closed doors, stopping occasionally to glare at one another. Beside me, Mother Elena has drifted into fitful sleep.

Those of us still awake sit straighter, alert to danger. Mrs. Nightwing places her book on the end table. Brigid clutches her rosary beads. Her lips move in silent prayer. The minutes tick past. Five, ten, fifteen. Nothing. Outside, the dark is quiet, undisturbed. Half past eleven o'clock. Only a half hour left in the day. My eyelids have begun to feel heavy. I am slipping under sleep's spell. The clock's rhythm eases me into rest. *Click. Click. Cli . . .*

Silence.

My eyes snap open. The clock on the mantel has stopped. The great room is as quiet as a tomb. Kartik draws his dagger.

"What is it?" Brigid whispers.

Miss McCleethy shushes her.

I hear them too—the faint sounds of horses outside on the lawn. The sharp caw of a crow. The color drains from Mrs. Nightwing's face. Mother Elena has stirred from her slumber. She clutches my hand tightly.

"They have come," she says.

CHAPTER SIXTY-FIVE

THE ROOM IS UNNATURALLY STILL. SWEAT BEADS ON MY upper lip. I wipe it away with a trembling hand.

"They can't get in," Brigid whispers. "We've marked every door, every window with a seal of protection."

"Their power is strong. They will not stop until they have what they want." Mother Elena looks at me as she says this.

"Let's not jump to any conclusions," Miss McCleethy says. "A horse. A crow. It could be nothing."

"You promised there would be no danger," Mrs. Nightwing says again, almost to herself.

"I am not convinced that there was danger at all save for what has happened to Miss Doyle's mind."

From outside I hear again the sounds of restless horses, birds.

"What is it? What's the matter?" Elizabeth says sleepily.

"Mrs. Nightwing, can't we please go to bed now?" one of the girls asks.

"Shhh!" Mrs. Nightwing says. "Our game will end only after midnight."

"Mr. Fowlson, would you check?" Miss McCleethy asks.

With a nod, Mr. Fowlson peeks behind the drapes. He turns around, shaking his head. "Nuffin'."

Brigid breathes a sigh of relief. It is so warm in the room.

"We shall not move from this room until after midnight," Mrs. Nightwing whispers. "Just to be certain. After that . . ." She stops, frowning.

"What is it?" Felicity asks.

Mrs. Nightwing is staring at the column in the center of the room. "It . . . it moved."

My heart gathers speed. Instinctively, I back away. The hiss of the lamps grows louder. The flames quiver in their glass cages as if even they are afraid. We're listening for them, for some sound to betray them. I hear the ragged cadence of our breathing. The scratching of branches against the panes. The hiss and pop of the lamps. They make for a strange symphony of terror.

Before our eyes, the creatures on the column stretch, pushing out of their stone forms.

Brigid's eyes are wide open in horror. "Sweet Jesus . . ."

The nymph is freed first. She falls to the floor with a thick plop, an insect being born. But she rises to full size quickly.

"Hello, darlings," she hisses. "Time for the sacrifice."

The others begin to break free—a fist here, a hoof there. Their whispers tumble into a spine-chilling chorus: "*It is time for the sacrifice, sacrifice, sacrifice . . .*"

The room brightens till my eyes ache. Inside the lamps the flames expand. They press against the glass and lick the walls.

With a great roar, the lamps explode, sending a shower of glass raining down on us. The girls awaken with screams. The naked flames flicker angrily along the walls, making us seem like apparitions in a magic-lantern show. But what I see coming off the column is no illusion. The creatures are no longer imprisoned there. They take shape in the room, hissing and laughing.

"*Our sacrifice . . .*"

"Mrs. Nightwing!" two small girls scream as a satyr reaches for them, narrowly missing.

"Run! Run to me!" Nightwing shouts over the din, and the girls make haste for her.

"Bloody 'ell!" Fowlson says in awe as a hideous winged beast swoops about the room.

"Hugo! The children!" Miss McCleethy barks, and immediately, Fowlson grabs the two girls nearest him and shoves them toward the great room's massive doors and away from the column. Kartik clutches my hand and pulls me away just as the nymph makes a grab for me. I reach for the fireplace poker and use it as a sword to fend her off. Brigid prays her rosary loudly as she pushes the younger girls out into the relative safety of the hall.

"Gemma! Come on!" Felicity and Ann beckon from the hall. Kartik and I have the expanse of the room to travel. Kartik has his knife at the ready, and I've got the fireplace poker.

"Gemma, your right!" he shouts.

I turn to my left, and the winged beast clutches at my hair with its claws.

"Ahhh," I screech. Turning quickly, I jab it with the poker. Injured, it pulls back, and Kartik drags me toward the doors, which we shut behind us with the full weight of our bodies.

Ann grabs an umbrella from a stand and shoves it through the handles. I place the poker through the other side.

"I . . . said . . . your right," Kartik pants.

"Mary, Mother of God," Brigid mumbles. Several of the little ones cling to her skirts. They cry and whimper, say they don't like this game anymore.

"There, there," Brigid says, trying to give comfort where there is none.

Cecily, Martha, and Elizabeth cower together, their screams uniting into one long howl.

"Gemma! Use your magic! Gift us to fight them!" Felicity pleads.

"No!" Mother Elena yells. "She mustn't. It cannot be trusted now. There is no balance to the dark. No balance." She pricks her finger and uses her blood to mark the door. "It will not hold long but it will give us time."

"What do we do now?" Ann asks.

Kartik answers. "We stay together and we stay alive."

<hr />

The hall is dark. Every lamp has been extinguished. Mrs. Nightwing and Miss McCleethy light two lanterns. They cast long shadows that dance devilishly on the walls.

"The chapel. We should be safe there," Mrs. Nightwing says, casting an uncertain glance toward the doors. I've never heard her so afraid.

"We shouldn't go out there," Kartik says. "That's what they want. They could be waiting."

The girls tremble and whimper, huddling together for protection. "What is happening?" Cecily asks through tears.

Mrs. Nightwing responds in the voice that tells us we

should wear our coats and eat our turnips. "It is part of our pixies game," she says.

"I don't wish to play anymore," Elizabeth cries.

"There, there. You must be a brave girl. It's only a game and whoever proves bravest shall have a prize," our headmistress says. Mrs. Nightwing isn't a good liar, but sometimes a bad lie is better than having nothing at all to hold. The frightened girls want to believe her. I can see it in their quick nods.

The creatures inside the great room begin to break through the doors, and the girls scream anew. Sharp teeth show themselves in the wood; they get to work, biting a section into splinters.

"We can't stay here with those things," I say to Kartik and Nightwing.

"Follow me to the chapel, girls!" Miss McCleethy says, taking the lead.

"Wait!" Kartik says, but it's no use. There's another loud crash from inside, and the girls run for Miss McCleethy. They join hands with Brigid and Fowlson. In a long snaking line, they follow Miss McCleethy as if she were the Pied Piper of Hamelin, and my friends and I fall in behind.

⁂

I have traipsed across Spence's lawn and through its woods hundreds of times, but never have they seemed as frightening as they do now with only Mrs. Nightwing's lantern and our fragile courage to light the way. The air is so still it is suffocating. I wish my mother were here. I wish Eugenia had stopped this twenty-five years ago. I wish none of this had ever happened. I wish it had not fallen to me, for I've failed so horribly.

When we reach the woods, my fear rises. A thin layer of frost covers the ground. The flowers are dead, strangled on their stalks. We can see our breath in the dim light.

"I'm cold," one of the girls says, and she is shushed by Brigid.

Kartik holds up a hand. We hold our breath and listen.

"What is it?" Fowlson whispers.

Kartik nods toward a copse of trees. The shadows move. My hand strays out, searching for the trunk of a tree, and it comes away covered in frost. A snort comes from just behind the tree. I slide my eyes toward the sound. A horse's nose peeks out from behind the large fir. Steam pushes out its nostrils. There is something odd about the horse. It's as if I can see its bones glowing beneath its skin. It pulls forward, and I can see the faint outline of its rider. A man in a billowing cape with a hood. He turns toward me and I gasp. I cannot see his face, only his mouth, and the hint of jagged teeth there. He points a bony finger at me.

"*The sacrifice . . .*"

The horse rears high, its hooves dangerously near my head, and I scream for all I am worth.

Mrs. Nightwing's shout pierces the night. "To the chapel! Go! Go!"

The tracker howls in rage as Nightwing throws the lantern at them. The candle is snuffed out, and the sudden darkness is confusing.

"Gemma!" On my wrist I feel Felicity's hand, strong and sure, pulling me forward. Mrs. Nightwing cannot keep pace. She begs us to go without her, but we refuse to leave her behind. Felicity and I take her arms and pull her along as best we can. It is a quarter mile to the chapel. A quarter mile with no place to hide. The fog has come up. It would be easy to lose our way.

The riders seem to come from nowhere. They thunder after us, darting through the trees on horses not of this world. Ann screams as the hooves of one of the beasts nearly trample her. Cut off, we dart to the left, but they have thought of that too.

Screeching comes from above. I look up to see the gargoyles descending. The riders shriek and cover their faces. One of the gargoyles falls, trampled by the rider. I recognize the majestic gargoyle who saved me from Ithal.

"This is our battle. Run!" He points to a break in the fog and the path to the chapel. We waste no time. Felicity, Ann, and I push through the chapel doors, and everyone stumbles in after us. Mrs. Nightwing sinks into the back pew, gasping for breath.

"Close—close the doors," I stammer.

The chapel darkens, and I hear the bolt click into position.

Miss McCleethy rushes to Nightwing's side. "Lillian, are you all right?"

"The girls," Mrs. Nightwing says, struggling to her feet. "Is everyone safe?"

Cecily approaches us. "Mrs. Nightwing, what is happening?" Her eyes are large and her voice trembles.

"Let's not fall to pieces," Mrs. Nightwing manages to say, but there is none of her usual stolidity. "Come on. See to the younger girls." Dutifully, Cecily does as she is told. Anything to ignore the growing panic that all is not as it seems. That she is right to be afraid. That she will never feel safe again.

The screams and the shrieks cut through the panes of the windows. I do not know what is happening outside, who is winning.

Miss McCleethy sits beside Nightwing in the pew, her head in her hands. "How could this have happened?"

"I told you before—Eugenia has become part of the Tree of All Souls. Part of the Winterlands," I say.

Miss McCleethy shakes her head.

"I thought I was going mad," I say.

"They will fight. They will come more and more," Mother Elena mumbles. "There is no protection now."

"My girls," Mrs. Nightwing murmurs. "I must protect my girls."

"There must be some hope," Ann says.

Felicity looks to me, begging me to say something that will make it better, end it.

Outside, the screeches of the trackers blend with the growls of the gargoyles—the death cries of one or both, it is hard to tell. The girls hold on to one another. Some cry; some rock. They are petrified.

"We have to cut it down. We have to go to the Winterlands," I say.

Kartik steps away from the door. "You can't go into the realms with every creature hunting for you."

"She's no safer here," Nightwing says. "It must be stopped."

"I'll do it," I say. "But I'm going to need help. The door is across the lawn, through the woods. And somehow, we've got to make it there."

Felicity whirls around. "You really *are* mad! We can't possibly get through that way!"

"We cannot simply wait!"

"Perhaps the gargoyles will protect us," Ann says.

Kartik stands beside me. "I will go with you."

Miss McCleethy is on her feet. "The Order banished the Rakshana from the realms. You cannot take them in!"

"I already have," I say, nodding at Kartik.

McCleethy shakes her head in disbelief. "Extraordinary. Is there anything you've managed not to make a mess of, Miss Doyle? That is strictly forbidden by our rules—"

"Don't you understand? There are no rules anymore! I shall do as I bloody well see fit!" I hiss. My words reverberate in the chapel, drawing shocked gasps from the other girls.

"I should point out that I am no longer a member of the Rakshana," Kartik adds. "And Miss Doyle can, in fact, do as she bloody well sees fit."

Felicity takes my hand. "I'm in as well."

"And me," Ann says, taking my other hand.

"I'll accompany you on behalf of the Order," Miss McCleethy says.

"Right, well, I'm not waitin' around," Fowlson says.

"Someone must stay and protect Lillian and the girls," Miss McCleethy chides.

Mrs. Nightwing stands firm, adjusting her skirt. She glances at the girls huddled together. "I shall hold fast here. Mother Elena will make the mark on the doors when you leave, and then we shall not open them again until morning."

"You've got a bit of protection should you need it," I say.

Mrs. Nightwing follows my glance toward the stained-glass windows, where the warrior clutches the gorgon's head.

"The windows?" Cecily screeches, overhearing.

"You'll see," I answer.

Cecily cowers on the floor, holding fast to Martha and Elizabeth. "We'll see what? I don't want to see anything more!"

Tears stream down her face, mixing with the mucus that runs from her nose, unchecked. "This is all your fault, Gemma Doyle. If we survive, nothing will ever be the same again," she chokes out.

"I know," I say quietly. "I'm sorry."

"I hate you," she wails.

"I know that, too."

Another shriek pierces the night, rattling the windows and sending the girls squawking like frightened geese. The battle between the gargoyles and the riders is fierce.

Mrs. Nightwing rises unsteadily to her feet. Her hymnal shakes in her hands. "Come, girls, take up your hymnals. We shall sing," she commands.

"Oh, Mrs. Nightwing," Elizabeth cries. "How can we sing?"

"They'll eat us alive!" Martha joins in.

"Nonsense!" Mrs. Nightwing shouts above the din. "We are perfectly safe in here. We are English, and I expect you to behave as such. No more crying. Let us sing."

Mrs. Nightwing's deep voice booms out, the notes tremulous. More hideous screams echo in the woods, so she sings more loudly. Brigid joins in, and soon, the girls do as they are told, their terrified voices a temporary wedge against the horror outside.

Kartik's expression is grim. "Are you ready?"

I nod, swallowing hard. Felicity, Ann, Fowlson, and Miss McCleethy fall in behind me. A band of six to face an army. I can't think of it or my courage will surely fail me.

Kartik opens the door a crack and we slip as quietly as possible into the night. Mother Elena bids Kartik hold out his hand. She pricks his finger.

"Mark the door from the outside," she advises. "I shall mark it from the inside. Do not fail."

The chapel doors close behind us, and Kartik scrapes his finger over the door. I hope it will hold. The gray-white fog is thick; it bleaches the woods of color. We've not brought a lantern for fear the creatures will see our light, so we navigate by memory. The shrieks of the riders and the fierce howls of the gargoyles locked in battle float through the fog so that we cannot tell where they are—near or far, behind or ahead. For all we know, we are walking into the fray.

We clear the woods safely, but there is still the lawn to cross. My heart thumps fast and hard. Fear brings a clarity I've never felt before; every muscle is a spring pushed down, ready to release. Kartik holds up a finger and cocks his head, listening.

"This way," he whispers.

Quickly, we follow him, trying not to lose each other in the dense fog. The howling screams grow closer. To my right, I see a flash of a stone wing, a glimpse of a skeletal arm. A gargoyle swoops over my head and into the fight, startling me as he descends. I turn my head only for an instant but it is enough. I have lost the others. Panic takes hold. Do I run left or right or straight ahead? *Go, Gemma. Move quickly.* I rush into the fog, pushing against it with frantic hands as if I can clear it away. I hear small choked noises—bitten-off sobs—and I realize they are my own, but I'm helpless to stop them.

A gargoyle is locked in fierce battle with one of the ghastly riders. The gargoyle takes the advantage, and the rider sinks to his knees. That gruesome skeletal face, with its red-black eyes, makes me gasp. The gargoyle turns to see me, and in that second, the Winterlands creature takes his chance. With one swift, cruel move, he slices through the gargoyle's belly with his razor-sharp claws. The gargoyle staggers toward me, bloodying my cape.

"To the Winterlands," he gasps. "Take down the Tree of All Souls. It is the only way."

The great stone beast falls at my feet. The rider opens his mouth and screams, piercing the night with a call to arms.

I run blindly ahead. I am so drunk on fear I do not hear my own cries, my calls to the others to run. I am beyond reason.

"Gemma! Gemma!" It's Felicity's voice.

"Felicity!" I call back.

"Gemma, here!"

A hand takes shape in the fog and I grab for its warmth. Felicity embraces me. We pull each other along. We reach the turret first. Fowlson, McCleethy, Ann, and Kartik follow soon after.

"This is it," I gasp. "The secret door."

"Get on with it," McCleethy pants.

I reach out my hand, and then I see the crow. Its caw is like a shriek from hell. A warning. A battle cry. Within seconds, there are a dozen of the terrible birds. They transform before my terrified eyes, shifting into the mummers who visited us. But that is only a disguise. I know who they are: Poppy Warriors.

The tall one removes his hat and bows low, and when he rises, I see the dark rings around his eyes. The inked poppies running up his arms.

"Hello, poppet. Such a nice evening for our sacrifice."

The other birds shimmer off their shiny black wings and become those gruesome knights, and I shudder to think of the broken cathedral they call home. The wicked games they like to play with their victims.

"Going somewhere, hmmmm?" the tall one asks, grinning like a death mask. His grimy fingernails are as long as talons.

"I—I—" I stammer.

Kartik has got his dagger in his hand, but it won't be enough against these fellows.

"'Kin 'ell," Fowlson gasps. "Wot pit of 'ell did 'e crawl out of?"

Miss McCleethy puts herself between me and the Poppy Warrior. Her arms wrap round me like a mother's, but this only makes the filthy creatures cackle.

"Won't work, m'lady," the one with three teeth growls.

"Ladies and gentlemen!" a Poppy Warrior shouts like an impresario. "Tonight, we've a most impressive show for your pleasure! The story of a maiden sacrificed to a nobler cause: to ensure the freedom of the Winterlands and bestow all power to its inhabitants. To open forever the borders between worlds. Is there no one who will save this fair maiden?" His grin turns feral. "No. I think not tonight. For the script has been written, and she must play her proper part."

"Run!" I shout.

As quickly as I can, I dash for the school with the others in pursuit. The Poppy Warriors give chase, rising into crows behind us. We fall through the kitchen door, with its fading blood mark, and collapse on the floor, breathing hard.

"Are we all here? Gemma, are you hurt?" Kartik says.

"What the 'ell were those things?" Fowlson asks.

"Poppy Warriors," I say. "You do not want to play with them, Mr. Fowlson, I assure you."

"They . . . they know. They're coming after us," Ann says.

"How will we reach the door now?" Felicity wails.

The light of the kitchen is weak but I can see the fear in Miss McCleethy's eyes. A crow's wings beat against the window. It signals our whereabouts to the others.

"We can't stay here," I say. "If we make it to the turret, we might be able to sneak back that way."

On the other side of the door, the long hall is dark and threatening. Anything could be hiding at the end of it. Anything. Kartik draws his dagger. Miss McCleethy leads the way, with Kartik and Fowlson just behind. Felicity and Ann, holding fast to each other's hands, follow a pace behind. I am the last, turning every few steps to keep an eye on the dark behind me.

We travel the length of the hall without incident. But to reach the stairs, we shall have to pass the great room, with its newly freed inhabitants. One door remains closed, but the other is open. I don't know how we can avoid being seen. We flatten ourselves against the wall and listen.

Kartik nods toward the stairs. Miss McCleethy moves stealthily toward them with the rest of us following. Keeping low, we make our ascent. Through the bars of the banisters I see the creatures making a mess of the great hall. The floor is littered with the glass from the lamps, the stuffing from pillows, pages ripped from books. They tear the scarves from Felicity's tent, ripping them to shreds. It is terrible to see. But there is no time to mourn. We must reach the safety of the realms, though it is not truly safety, only a temporary reprieve.

At the East Wing, we abandon caution and stumble in. We stand on the half-finished turret, hidden by the ragged stone. Across the lawn, I see the riders fanning out, blocking all hope of escape. They call to the Poppy Warrior who guards the secret door.

"They are inside," he shouts gleefully.

"Then they are trapped," one of the trackers whispers fiercely. He rides toward the kitchen door we opened earlier. He'll find us soon. And he'll bring the others. We are well and truly stuck.

"Gemma," Felicity says, her eyes wild with fear.

There is scratching at the entrance to the East Wing. They wait on the other side of that door.

Kartik takes hold of my hand, squeezing it. Fowlson joins hands with Miss McCleethy.

"I won't let it get you, Sahirah," he says.

I hear Ann's breath catching on her fear.

"Wish I had my sword," Felicity whispers. Then she adds a soft prayer under her breath: "Pippa, Pippa, Pippa . . ."

"Take my hands," I say.

Kartik is puzzled. "What—"

"Take my hands and don't let go!"

"Do not employ the magic now, Miss Doyle. It isn't wise," Miss McCleethy says.

"We've no choice," I answer. "I shall try to summon the door."

"But you've not been able to do it these months," Ann says.

"It's time to try again," I answer.

The shrieks from the lawn shudder through us. "What if you can't?" Felicity whispers.

I shake my head. "I can't think about that. I shall need everyone's help. Put your hands on mine," I say. When I feel the weight of them, I close my eyes and concentrate, marrying my need to my purpose. "Think of a door of light."

I hear the scratching at the East Wing doors. The caws

overhead as the crows beat near. They've found us. *Purpose, Gemma. The door of light, the door of light, the door of light.*

Soon, the familiar tingle begins. It is but a halting trickle at first but it grows to a hum and then a racing whoosh that makes every part of me come alive. The force of it blows my hair back from my face with its warm breath.

When I look, the door of light is there, waiting.

"You did it, Gemma," Felicity says, looking relieved.

"No time for congratulations," I say. "Go!"

I open the door and we race through nearly in a clump just as the trackers break through the East Wing doors. They howl and it makes my blood turn cold.

"Gemma!" Ann shouts.

"Close now!" I call on the magic once again, and thank goodness, it doesn't fail me. As the door of light disappears, the last thing I see is the rider in his long, tattered robe, his teeth bared in a chilling snarl. "Rot in hell, you miserable beast," I pant.

"It's already *in* hell. We have to keep hell from getting any closer," Kartik says, pulling me on.

We run into the realms as fast as we can. "We don't have long. They'll get through the other way. We must go to the garden and find Gorgon," I say, trying to catch my breath. My lungs are on fire.

"Wait!" Kartik says. "We don't know what we'll find there. Perhaps I should run ahead to see."

"Agreed," I say. I would carry on, but there is truth to what he says, and I can scarcely breathe. Corsets were not meant for running.

"I'll go wif you, mate," Fowlson says, looking around in wonder.

Grudgingly, Kartik nods, and the two of them run ahead.

Exhausted and peevish, we sit and wait, hiding under the cover of a large rock. Ann hasn't left the comfort of Felicity's side. It is tenuous comfort but she craves it. Weary from the chase, I settle myself on the ground and stare out at the bleeding horizon.

"Why did you not tell us you'd seen such things?" McCleethy says, gasping for breath. But it is a rhetorical question. She knows why. Her dark hair is half free of its bindings. It blows wild in the gusty wind. "We created order out of chaos. We made beauty and shaped history. We kept the magic of the realms safe in our grasp. How has it come to this?"

"You've not kept it safe. You've kept it to yourselves."

She shakes her head to dismiss the thought. "Gemma, you may still use the power for much good. With us to help you—"

"And what, pray, have you done to better the lot of others?" I ask. "You call each other sisters, but are we not all sisters? The seamstress ruining her eyesight to keep her children in porridge? The suffragists fighting for the vote? The girls younger than I who would ask for a living wage, whose working conditions are so deplorable they were locked in a burning factory? They could make use of your precious help."

She holds her head high. "We would have done so. In time."

I snort in disgust. "It is daunting to be a woman in *any* world. What good does our power do us when it must be kept secret?"

"You would prefer bold voices to illusion?"

"Yes."

Miss McCleethy sighs. "We may shape the course of that struggle. But first we must secure our power inside the realms."

"There will never be security here! Everywhere I turn, some-thing new crawls up from the very rocks, grappling for this power! No one can remember where the magic came from or why; they only want to possess it! I am sick of it—sick to my very bones, do you hear?"

"Yes," she says solemnly. "And yet, it is so very hard to let it go, isn't it?"

She is right. Even now, knowing what I do, seeing what I have seen, I want it still.

Miss McCleethy grips my arm; her face is hard. "Gemma, you must safeguard the magic at all costs. That is our only con-cern. Many have fought and died to protect it over the years."

I shake my head. "Where does it end?"

The men return from their lookout. Kartik's face is grim. "They've been to the garden."

"What do you mean?"

"It's gone," he says.

CHAPTER SIXTY-SIX

WE MAKE OUR WAY THROUGH A GARDEN THAT IS NO longer lush and familiar. The smell of scorched earth greets us. The trees have been burned to ash. The flowers have been trampled into mud. The silver arch that once led to the grotto has been battered and ripped from the ground. The swing I fashioned from silver thread hangs in tatters.

Tears bead in Miss McCleethy's eyes. "I dreamed of seeing it again. But not like this."

Fowlson puts his arm around her shoulders.

"What is happening?" Ann asks, cradling a handful of broken blossoms.

"Most High!" Gorgon slips into view on the river. She is alive and unharmed. I've never been happier to see her.

Fowlson takes a step backward. "Wot the 'ell is that?"

"A friend," I say, running for the river. "Gorgon, can you tell us what is happening? What you've seen?"

The snakes of her hair hiss and writhe. "Madness," Gorgon says. "All is madness."

"It's war, then?" Miss McCleethy says.

"War." Gorgon spits the word. "That is what they call it to give the illusion of honor and law. It is chaos. Madness and blood and the hunger to win. It has always been thus and shall always be so."

"Gorgon, we must get to the Tree of All Souls. We mean to take it down. Is there a safe passage to the Winterlands?"

"No place is safe now, Most High. But I shall take you down the river all the same."

We set sail. The river does not sing softly today. It doesn't sing at all. Some places have escaped the ravages of the Winterlands creatures. Other spots have not been as lucky. In those places, they've left terrible calling cards—spikes with bloodied flags, reminders that they will show no mercy.

When we pass the Caves of Sighs, several of the Hajin peek out from their hiding places. Asha waves to me from the shore.

"Gorgon, over there!" I call.

We pull to the shore and Gorgon lowers the plank so that Asha may board. "They ride everywhere," Asha says. "I fear they have ridden to the forest folk."

⋏⋏⋏⋏

"What is that?" Kartik asks as we near the golden veil that protects the forest folk from view. Black clouds stretch across the river like a scar.

"Smoke," I answer, and my heartbeat quickens.

We crouch low on the barge, holding our hands over our mouths and noses, and still we gag in the thick, dark air. Even the veil is choked; it scatters gold-flecked soot on our bodies. And then I see: The beautiful forest is aflame. The huts burn and smoke. The flames ravage the trees till they seem to bloom leaves of red and orange. Many of the forest folk are trapped. They scream, not sure where to turn. Mothers run for the water with crying children in their arms. The centaurs gallop for those left behind, scooping them up and heaving them onto their backs as they run for their lives.

"They can't see," Kartik says, coughing. "The smoke is too heavy. They are confused."

"We have to help them!" I scream, trying to stand. The heat is fierce. It sends me gasping back to the floor of the ship.

"No, we must reach the Winterlands and chop down the tree!" Miss McCleethy shouts. "It's our only hope."

"We can't leave them like this!" I yell, but even as I do, a wayward spark finds my skirt and I must beat at it frantically to put it out.

I hear a splash. It is Asha. She is off the ship and walking through the water toward the shore. Bodies are thick here, but she pays them no mind. "Here!" she calls, waving her arms so that she can be seen through the smoke. The forest folk run for her and the safety of the river.

Under the heavy layer of smoke, they are able to find their small boats. They board them and paddle out to the river and away from the ruins of their once beautiful homeland.

Philon rides to the edge of the water, and Gorgon brings us closer. "The Winterlands creatures came. They rode fast and hard."

"How great is their army?" Kartik asks.

"Perhaps a thousand strong," Philon answers. "And they have a warrior with the strength of ten."

Kartik kicks the ground. "Amar."

Fowlson narrows his eyes. "Amar's fightin' for those creatures? I'll cut 'im apart."

"No," Kartik says.

"'E's not one of us anymore, brother. Let 'im go," Fowlson says, and it is almost kind.

Asha pulls a body from the river. The creature is injured; she vomits water as we pull her onto Gorgon's ship. It's Neela.

"Let me alone," she croaks, seeing Asha's hands on her arms. The creature shifts from her dusky lilac form to Asha to me to Creostus and back to herself effortlessly. It's as if her body cannot control the function.

Asha's voice is firm. "You were the one who killed the centaur, weren't you?"

Neela coughs up water. "I do not know what you say. You lie."

Philon's eyes gleam in understanding.

Asha will not let go. "You put the Hajins' poppies in his hand so that we would be blamed."

This time, Neela does not try to deny it. "What of it?"

"Why did you do it?" Philon demands. The blaze from the forest flickers shadows across the high planes of that extraordinary face.

"We needed a reason to go to war. You would not have gone without it."

"So you invented a purpose?"

"I did not invent it! The purpose has always been! How long have we lived without magic of our own? How long would you let them deny us? They hold it all. And the filthy Untouchables were put above us! But you would not strike. You have always been weak, Philon."

Philon's eyes flash. "You wish it so deeply you would kill one of our own?"

Neela struggles to sit. "There is no progress without cost," she says defiantly.

"The cost is too great, Neela."

"One centaur for the rule of the realms? It is a small price to pay."

"We might have been alert to true danger rather than chasing shadows. And now we are without a home. Our people dead. Our integrity ruined. Before, we had that at least."

Neela shows no remorse. "I did what was necessary."

"Yes," Philon says grimly. "As I must now."

Neela shakes and shivers; her lips turn as light as the skin of grapes.

"She's suffered a terrible shock," I say. "Someone must stay with her."

"Let her die," Philon says.

"No," I say. "We can't allow that."

"I shall stay with her," Asha says, volunteering.

"What if the Hajin kills Neela?" one of the centaurs asks.

Philon's answer is as cool as those glacier-like eyes. "Then that is the price she pays for her crimes."

I look to Asha for some reassurance that she will not harm Neela, but her face betrays no emotion.

"I will stay with the shape-shifter," she repeats.

"Will you safeguard her, Asha?" I ask.

There is a moment's pause. She bows her head. "You have my word."

I let out the breath I was holding tightly.

"I will care for her even though I do not wish to," she adds, orange flames dancing in reflection in her dark eyes. "And when you make your choice, Lady Hope, we Untouchables would have a voice in it. We have been silent too long."

We gather our numbers, small though they are, perhaps forty in all. Philon and the forest folk take what weapons they have. It isn't much—a crossbow, two dozen spears with blades at each end, shields, and swords. It is like trying to take down Parliament with only a thimble of gunpowder. I dearly wish I had that dagger.

"What is our best approach?" I ask.

"They ride toward the Borderlands," Philon says.

Felicity gasps. "Pip."

"You can't save her," Kartik says.

"Don't tell me what I cannot do," Felicity snaps.

I pull her aside. We stand by the water where two small boats still sit. "Felicity, we must get to the Winterlands as quickly as possible. We can see to Pip later."

"But that may be too late! She doesn't know what she's up against," Fee begs. "We have to warn her!"

"Dear Pippa," Ann echoes.

I think of the burned garden, the bloodied flags we've seen marking the shore, the forest folk carried away. I would do anything to save Pip such a fate. But the risk is great. The Winterlands creatures could be lying in wait there. And for all I know, Pippa has joined with them.

"I'm sorry," I say, turning away.

"You're cruel!" Felicity screams after me. She starts to cry. I know I've done the right thing but I couldn't feel worse about it, and I suppose that is part of what it is to lead.

I march beside Philon as the forest folk and the Hajin ready for battle. They carry weapons onto the ship. An Untouchable hoists a quiver of arrows onto his twisted back, and one of the forest creatures helps secure it. The centaurs offer their backs to whoever will ride.

Ann runs to me, out of breath.

"What is it?" I ask.

"She told me not to tell you, but I have to. It's Felicity. She's gone to warn Pippa."

One of the small boats is missing.

"We have to go after her," I say.

"We can't," Kartik warns, but I'm already in motion.

"I won't lose Fee. We need her. I need her," I state.

"I'll accompany you," Miss McCleethy announces.

"And I as well," Ann says.

Kartik shakes his head. "You're mad if you think I'll let you go without me."

"Yes, I am mad. But you've known that for some time," I say. He starts to object, and I silence him with a sudden kiss. "Trust me."

Reluctantly, he lets me go, and the three of us push off in the remaining dinghy. Kartik stands on the shore, watching us drift out on the river. With the smoke and the fading flames behind him, he looks slightly unreal—a ghost, a flickering image in a magic-lantern show, a star falling to earth, a moment that can't last.

I have the urge to turn the boat around and run back to him. But then the current catches us and we're moving, carried swiftly toward the Borderlands and whatever waits for us there.

CHAPTER SIXTY-SEVEN

THE SKY BLEEDS RED OVER THE WINTERLANDS. IT CASTS an eerie light on the Borderlands, turning it the colors of a bruise. In the distance, the castle nestles in its robe of vines, like a pale hand hidden in the folds of a dress. I'm relieved that it's still intact.

"Do you see Fee anywhere?" I whisper.

"No," Ann answers. "I don't see anyone."

Carefully, we part the thorns in the bramble wall and slip inside. Miss McCleethy takes in everything with a nervous glance. "You've been coming here?"

I nod.

She shivers. "What a dismal spot."

"It was very merry for a while," Ann says sadly.

We step quickly and quietly through the blue-tinged forest. The branches seem to be plucked of almost every berry, and what is left hangs in mealy clumps, forgotten. Maggots eat their way through the abandoned fruit. It makes my stomach turn.

Whoo-oot. Whoo-oot.

"What was that?" Miss McCleethy gasps.

"Don't move," I whisper.

We stay as still as statues. The call comes again.

Whoo-oot. Whoo-oot.

"Come out, come out, wherever you are." Pip's voice.

She steps out from behind a tree and is quickly flanked by Bessie, Mae, Mercy, and others I've not seen before. They fan around her like soldiers, carrying torches. It's as if every bit of breath has been knocked from me. I'm forced to keep my hands behind my back, out of sight, to hide their trembling. She has marked her face in the blue-black juice of the berries. The others wear similar markings that give their faces a skeletal appearance.

In the firelight, Pip's eyes change from one state to the other, from violet to white, inviting to terrifying. "Hello, Gemma. What brings you here?"

"I—I was looking for Fee," I say.

She frowns playfully. "You've lost her, have you? Tsk-tsk, Gemma. How careless. Well, I suppose you'll have to come have a look inside, then. Follow me."

Pippa takes us to her castle like a conquering queen. She's still lovely. She has the magic working for her, but she has not shared much of it with her disciples from what I can see. They ride behind her, tattered and torn, their skin going gray and ruined.

"Bessie," I start, and she gives me a sharp shove.

"Keep movin'."

The castle is as neglected as the forest. The vines crawl up the walls unhindered and drape across balustrades, hanging down in claws of green. Snakes thread through their mossy abundance.

"Where's Felicity?" I ask again.

"Patience, patience." Pippa hums while lining up goblets of berries along the altar.

Bessie sneers as she appraises Miss McCleethy. "'Oo's she? Yer mum?"

"I am Miss McCleethy, a teacher at Spence Academy," McCleethy answers.

Pip claps, giggling. "Miss McCleethy. You're the one giving Gemma such trouble. You shall not give me any trouble at all."

"I shall give you a great deal of trouble if you do not tell us where to find Miss Worthington at once," Miss McCleethy insists.

"Don't," I warn.

"She needs a firm hand," she whispers.

"She's beyond that now," Ann urges quietly.

"Shush!" Pippa says. "This is my castle. I am queen here. I make the rules."

Mae reaches for a cluster of berries and Pippa shakes her head. "Mae, you know that is for the ritual. They must be consecrated first."

"Yes, miss." Mae smiles, seemingly happy to have been upbraided by her god.

"Felicity!" I shout. "Fee!"

The castle's walls creak and groan as if they shall fall in on us. A vine tightens across my boot and I yank my foot free.

"She's in the tower," Mae says. "Fer safekeepin'."

"Pip," Ann pleads, "you have to let her go. The Winterlands creatures are coming."

"Not you too, Ann." Pippa tuts.

"Pip . . . ," Ann starts.

"All I need do is offer a sacrifice. I tried with Wendy, but she made for a poor sacrifice, being blind. And then you came back, and I knew. . . . I knew it was fate; don't you see?"

Miss McCleethy steps in front of me. "You can't have her. Take me instead."

"What are you doing?" I say.

"Gemma," Miss McCleethy whispers, "whatever may happen, you must put aside your fear and safeguard the magic."

Whatever may happen. I do not like the sound of it.

"Sometimes we must make sacrifices for the greater good," she says. "Promise me you'll keep the magic safe."

"I promise," I say, but I don't like it.

Pippa hums to herself. "A willing sacrifice. That's very powerful magic indeed. I accept."

The factory girls drag Miss McCleethy toward Pip.

"Unhand me, you little hooligans!" she snarls, not so willing after all. She slaps Mae hard across the face, and Bessie responds with a blow of her own. Miss McCleethy falls to the ground, her ear bleeding, and the other girls join in with kicks and punches.

"Stop it!" I start for them, but Miss McCleethy holds out a bloody hand.

"Gemma, don't!" she warns.

"Yes, that is enough," Pippa says, as if she were waving away a second helping of soup. "Bring her to me."

They half drag Miss McCleethy to the altar and tie her hands behind her back. Her lips bleed, and I see fear in her eyes, the dawning realization that she has sorely misjudged these girls.

"Will we suffer unbelievers?" Pip calls.

The girls answer with a clamor of nos. In their faces, I see such hate. It chills me to the bone. They no longer see us as human; we are the other, the threat that must be killed.

Pippa turns to Miss McCleethy with a sigh. "I'm afraid there is only one punishment for those who will not follow us."

Bessie produces a shining sword. Its edge gleams in the light. The girls whoop and screech. Their primitive cries make a deafening clamor. Miss McCleethy struggles.

"No!" she shouts, kicking and trying to get away. But Mae and Mercy hold her fast, forcing her over the altar so that her head hangs free. My heart hammers against my ribs.

"Pippa, what are you doing?" I say, running for her.

Pippa blows me back with the force of her magic. Caught off guard, I fall to the floor in pain. The girls push Miss McCleethy's head forward and expose the flesh of her neck.

"No!" I stagger to my feet, and before I can call the magic, Pippa unleashes hers. This time, I clatter to the ground like a toy. Miss McCleethy closes her eyes tightly; her mouth is set in a determined line. The blade is raised.

"Protect the mag—" she shouts just as the sword comes down with lightning swiftness.

Beside me, Ann screams and screams, her desperate shrieks blending into the crowd's exultant shouts until it is impossible to tell where one leaves off and the other begins. I feel as if I shall vomit. My breath is ragged and tears prick my eyes. Ann sits perfectly still and stops screaming, shocked into total silence.

With a syrupy sigh, the vines wriggle forward and claim the headless body of Miss McCleethy. The girls kneel, hands clasped as if in prayer. Pippa stands before them, behind the altar. She raises a chalice over her head and brings it down again, mumbling words I cannot hear. She pulls a fat berry from the cup and places it gently into the waiting palms of Bessie. Slowly and solemnly she moves down the line, handing out a berry to each girl bowed before her.

"Who is the way?" she bellows.

"Mistress Pippa!" they respond in unison. "She is the chosen one."

"What is our task?"

"To eat the berries and stay in paradise."

"Amen," she says.

As one, the girls bring the berries to their mouths. They gobble them up.

Pip turns to us with her arms spread, her mouth open in a delirious smile. "I am sorry about your teacher, but she wouldn't have been able to join with us. But I have faith in you. After all, you've come back. But you must be as we are, my darlings. Those who would follow me must eat the berries."

I find my voice at last. "Pip, please listen. The Winterlands creatures mean to take over the realms. If you kill me, I cannot fight them."

Bessie takes the steps to the tower and returns with a struggling Felicity, who kicks and screeches. She attempts to take a bite of Bessie, and Bessie hits her hard.

"Oh, Fee! You're here. That's jolly," Pippa says as Fee looks at her in horror.

Pippa saunters over to us and places berries in our hands. She gives Ann a kiss on the forehead. "Ann, darling, why do you shake so? Are you cold?"

"Y-yes," Ann whispers. Her lips tremble with sheer terror. "Cold."

"Do you believe, darling? Do you believe that I am the chosen one?"

"Yes." Ann nods, sobbing.

"And will you eat the berries? Will you accept my grace?"

"If you were truly the chosen one, you would not need to intimidate your believers," I say. If I am to die, I will not go without a voice.

Pippa strokes my hair. "You've never liked me much, Gemma. I think you are jealous."

"You may think what you like. We are in danger. All of us. The Winterlands creatures mean to rule the realms. They have already killed many of the tribes. They ride without mercy, taking the souls of those who will not join them."

Pip frowns. "I've heard nothing."

"The creatures are on their way here now. If they sacrifice me at the Tree of All Souls, they will have all the power of the Temple and rule the realms."

"They cannot rule the realms!" She laughs. "They cannot because I am chosen. I hold the magic. It grows in me. The tree told me so! If they plotted, I should know it."

"You don't know everything, Pippa," I say.

She brings her face toward me until it is inches from mine. Her lips are still purple from the berries. Her breath smells of vinegar. "You're lying." A slight smile pulls at her mouth. "Why don't you use your magic against me?"

"I don't want to do that," I say, my voice cracking.

Pippa's face lights up. "You've lost it, haven't you?"

"No, I haven't—"

"That's why you couldn't stop me—because I am the true chosen one!" Pippa thunders.

Bessie grabs me hard by the arm. "Let's prove it to the unbelievers! Let's take 'em to the Winterlands!"

"No!" I shout.

Pippa claps. "That is a splendid plan! Oh, yes, let's!"

Felicity takes Pip's hands. "Pippa, if I eat the berries, if I stay with you, will you let them go?"

"Felicity!" I shout.

She shakes her head and gives me the tiniest of smiles.

"Will you? Will you let them go?"

A glimmer of recognition flashes in Pip's eyes, as if she is remembering a favorite dream. She leans down, the black of her hair weaving into Felicity's blond strands, a tapestry of light and dark. Sweetly, Pippa kisses Fee on her forehead.

"No," she says harshly.

"Pip, you don't understand; they'll hurt you," Felicity implores, but Pippa is past human reason.

"I am more powerful than they are! They don't frighten me. I am the way! I am the one! Bessie, we need another volunteer," Pippa commands.

I am pulled from my seat and up to the altar, where I fear I may meet the same fate as Miss McCleethy. Pippa forces more berries into my hands.

"Eat, for I am the way."

The berries stain my palm. I said I would safeguard the magic, but I have no choice: I must use it. We must break free.

I draw deeply on my power and it surges through me with renewed vigor. Pippa locks her arms with mine and we are joined in struggle. The magic feels new and hard and terrifying. My mouth tastes of metal. It's as if my blood is no longer in my control. It pulses out of time, rushing through my veins till I shake. I feel everything inside Pippa—the rage, the fear, the desire, the longing. And I know she feels what is in me as well. When I find the secret wound, Felicity, a look of terrible sadness passes over her face.

"Let me go," she croaks. "Let me go."

"Only if you let us go," I say.

She unleashes her power in full, and I am blown back against the wall of the castle. I fall into a crumple.

"Stop!" I shout. And when I let loose, she falls to her knees. But I can feel the magic turning, and I dare not be without my wits now. I have to rein in my power a bit, and in that moment, Pippa lets hers soar, pinning me against the wall, where the vines begin to crisscross over my hands and feet.

"Pippa!" Felicity shouts, but Pip is beyond caring now.

"I am the way!" she shouts.

Felicity swings the flat of the sword against her, knocking her over. The magic's hold loosens.

"Fee?" Pip says, eyes wide. And then she sees the gash in her arm, her blood trickling down into the velvety vines. With a mighty groan, the castle shifts and bucks till we tumble one over the other.

"What is happening?" Mae Sutter shouts.

The vines whip about, reaching for whatever they can grab. There is a deafening roar as the ancient stones begin to tumble. We run for the doors in a panicked clump, dodging the falling debris.

"Pip!" Felicity shouts. "Pip, come away from there!"

But Pip's face is alight with some terrible joy. She lifts her arms to the sky. "There is nothing to fear! I am the way!"

"Pip! Pip!" Fee screams as I yank her away.

We watch, helpless, as the desperate vines find Pippa, pulling her down hard. "No!" she shouts. "I am the way!" But the sky is raining stone. And then the great castle falls in on itself completely, entombing Pippa deep within its broken walls, silencing her forever.

Felicity, Ann, and I barely escape. We are left panting in the grass as the castle sinks back into the earth—the land reclaiming its own, and Pippa along with it. Bessie and Mae have escaped, as have some of the others. Mercy has been buried along with Pippa.

The girls stare at the spot where Pippa was standing.

Mae smiles through her tears. "She meant it to be this way," she says in utter rapture. "Don't you see? She sacrificed 'erself. For us."

Bessie shakes her head. "No."

Mae grabs her skirts. "We have to keep doin' what she told us to do. Keep eatin' the berries. Follow her ways. Then she'll come back. Pray with me, Bessie."

Bessie shakes her off. "I won't. It's done, Mae. Get up."

"She was chosen," Mae insists.

"No, you're wrong," I say. "She was only a girl."

Mae will not see it any other way. She grabs handfuls of rotting berries and swallows them, calling Pippa's name like a prayer after each one. She holds fast to her belief; she doesn't want to know that she's been misled, that she's abandoned here, alone, with no one to guide her but her own heart.

Bessie runs after me. "Can I come?"

I nod. She's a brawler, and we might have need of one.

I catch up to Felicity.

"Fee . . . ," I start.

She wipes her nose on her sleeve, turning her head away from me. "Don't."

I should leave her to it, but I can't. "She was gone for some time. You were the only force that kept her from turning completely. That's magic. Perhaps the most powerful I've seen."

CHAPTER SIXTY-EIGHT

GORGON HASN'T WAITED FOR US TO RETURN. SHE HAS sailed after us, and now she waits for us on the river. Kartik takes one look at Felicity's tear-streaked face and lets well enough alone. He and Bessie size each other up, and she moves onto the boat without a word.

"It's done," I tell him. "Gorgon, steer us toward the Winterlands."

Fowlson hurries to my side. "Wait! What do you mean? Where's Sahirah?"

"I'm sorry," I say quietly.

I'm afraid he might scream. Howl. Curse us. Hit something. Instead, he sinks silently to the floor of the ship, his head in his hands, which is somehow so much worse.

"What can we do?" I whisper to Kartik.

"Let him be."

Gorgon guides us along the river. Small fires burn upon the water. They blaze brightly in their smoking bowers. The flames leap and crackle, threatening us with their heat. The wind blows, peppering us with a choking ash. It is like entering the mouth of hell.

Lightning pulses behind the twisting, churning red clouds over the Winterlands.

"We are near," Gorgon says.

Ann gasps, puts a hand to her mouth. She's staring at the water, where the lifeless body of some unfortunate soul floats past, facedown. It bobs there for a moment, a grim reminder of our task, and then the current carries it away. But it will stay in my memory forever. The rest of us fall silent. We are crossing out of the Borderlands. We are entering the Winterlands, and there is no turning back.

⌇⌇⌇⌇⌇

Gorgon eases into the pool where we first met the army of the dead. Upon the tops of the craggy cliffs, blazes have been set. I do not want to know who set them or what might be used as fuel. The forest folk and the Hajin have pulled their boats ashore. Philon turns those cool eyes to the cliffs, searching for something.

"Which is the way to the tree?" the creature asks, shouldering a shimmering ax.

"There is a passage that way," I say.

"Where is the teacher?" Philon asks.

"We lost Miss McCleethy to the Borderlands," I say.

Fowlson has taken off his belt. He sharpens his knife against the leather in faster and faster strokes.

"I fear that is just the beginning," Philon answers.

Weapons in hand, our ragged band sets off for the narrow

passage that leads to the heart of the Winterlands. I plead with Gorgon one last time.

"I wish you would join us. We could sorely use you."

"I cannot be trusted," she insists.

I lean closer to her than I ever have before, as if I might embrace her. One of the snakes rubs over my wrist, and I do not pull away. It flicks its tongue and moves on. "I trust you."

"Because you do not know me."

"Gorgon, please . . ."

Pain shows in her eyes and she closes them to hide it. "I cannot, Most High. I shall await your return."

"If I return," I say. "We are outnumbered, and my magic is unreliable."

"If you fall, we are all lost. Destroy the tree. That is the only way."

"Will she come with us?" Ann asks when I catch up to them.

"No," I say.

Philon glances at the unmerciful landscape—the clouds streaked with red, the unforgiving passageway ahead. Harsh, cold winds kick gritty sand into our faces. "Pity. We could use her warrior strength now."

We crowd into the narrow canyon. A slick, pale creature slides its slimy hand from behind a rock, and I have to place a hand over Ann's mouth to silence the scream there.

"Just keep walking," I whisper.

Kartik squeezes back down the ranks. "Gemma, I don't think we should come out as we did before. We're exposed then. There's a small tunnel that leads to a ledge behind the cliffs. It's narrow, not easy, but from there, we can watch them, protected."

"Agreed," I say. "Lead the way."

We creep along a crumbling ledge with a severe drop into nothingness. It makes my blood pound, so I keep my eyes trained on Philon's ax glimmering just ahead. At last, we push out of the tunnel, and Kartik is right: There is a spot behind the cliff where we might hide.

"Do you hear that?" Kartik asks.

In the distance is the sound of drums. They echo off the mountains.

"I shall see," Kartik says. He scrambles up the craggy mountain as if born to it. He pokes his head above the cliff's edge, then hurries down again. "They're gathering on the heath."

"How many?" Philon asks.

Kartik's face is grim. "Too many to count."

The pounding of the drums resonates in my bones. It fills my head till I think I shall go mad. It is easier not to see their numbers, not to look on the horror of them and know. But I must know. I must know. Gripping tightly to the rock, I pull myself up and peek over the rough crags that protect us for now.

Kartik did not lie. The Winterlands army is vast and terrifying. At the fore ride the trackers in billowing black capes that flap open to reveal the souls trapped inside. Even from this distance I can see the glint of their jagged teeth. They tower over the others, nearly seven feet tall. The Poppy Warriors in their matted chain mail transform into enormous black crows and circle over the fields. They caw with a chilling persistence; more and more of them rise till one patch of the sky is a blur of black and the air crackles with their cries. I pray they will not fly in this direction and spy our hiding place. Behind them is an army of corrupted spirits—the dead walking. Their eyes are hollow and unseeing or the disquieting blue-white of Pippa's. They follow without question. And in the center is the tree, taller, mightier than the last time I saw it. Its limbs stretch out in all directions. I swear that I can see the souls slipping under its bark like blood. And I know that in its dark heart hides Eugenia Spence.

Drummers bang out a thundering rhythm.

"How will we fight them?" Ann asks, and I feel her fear within my own heart.

"Look, down there," Felicity says. One of the Poppy Warriors pulls Wendy along with him. She stumbles, exhausted, but she is intact. Eating those berries damned her to a life here, but it must have saved her from being a fitting sacrifice. The Poppy Warrior licks her cheek, and Wendy recoils. I hate to think of her chained to such a horrible beast.

The drums stop, and the silence is almost more terrifying.

"Wot are they about?" Fowlson asks, his knife already in his hand.

"I don't know," I say.

The tree speaks. *Have you brought the sacrifice?*

"She is here somewhere," a tracker answers.

I have waited so long for you, the tree murmurs in that voice that first drew me in. *Do you know me? Do you know what we could be together? That we could rule this world and the other? Join me. . . .*

The words wrap themselves around me.

Gemma . . . come to me. . . .

It is my mother. My mother stands on that field in her blue dress, her arms waiting to hold me.

"Mother," I whisper.

Kartik pulls my face to his. "That is not your mother, Gemma. You know that."

"Yes. I know." I look back, and the image flickers like a picture made of gas and flame.

"They can make us see what they want us to see, believe anything," a Hajin woman with deep brown eyes reminds me.

"How will we fight them?" a centaur asks. "Let us have some of the priestess's magic!"

"No," Philon says, watching me. "If she draws upon the magic now, the tree will surely sense it, and I fear what that will mean."

Fowlson has a hard look. "We've got to get to that tree, mates. Chop it down."

"Yes, that is our purpose," Felicity says. She's got her sword and she means to use it.

A small argument breaks out among our contingent. No one can agree on a plan. Down on the plain, I see those hideous wraiths, the tree that carries Eugenia's soul. But I also feel my mother, Circe, Miss McCleethy, Pippa, Amar ... so many names. So much lost.

"Centuries of fighting, and for what?" I say. "Today it ends. I can't live in fear any longer. I've cursed this power. I've both enjoyed and misused it. And I've hidden it away. Now I must try to wield it correctly, to marry it to a purpose and hope that that is enough."

A centaur starts to speak, but Philon silences him with a single finger held high.

"Dr. Van Ripple told me that an illusion works because people want to believe in it. Very well, then. Let's give them what they want," I say.

Philon's eyes narrow. "What is your plan?"

"They are looking for the chosen one. What if she is everywhere at once? What if I can cast my image on the ledge of this mountain and farther afield? They'll see me at every turn. And how will they make a sacrifice of someone who does not exist?"

Philon rubs a hand thoughtfully across those thin lips. "Clever but risky, Priestess. And what if we are discovered?"

"We only need enough time to confuse them while we draw closer to the tree and take it down."

"And what of the dagger?" Felicity asks.

"Leave that to me," I say.

"How do we know that chopping down the tree will end this?" a centaur asks.

"We don't," I say. "But it's the best we have if everyone is in agreement."

There are nods and ayes all around.

"Mr. Fowlson, Felicity, you will lead the charge. Ann," I say, looking at her brave face, "try to get Wendy away from that beastly Poppy Warrior."

"And me?" Kartik asks.

Stay with me.

"Someone shall have to look out for Amar. He is very powerful," I say sadly.

"Gemma, we're to be fighting, side by side," he says, and I know he's thinking of his dream.

"It was only a dream," I say, swallowing hard, waiting for him to say his bit like a joke we'll carry on long after this has finished, but he only nods, and that adds to my fright.

"What if they should find you after all?" Philon asks.

I shall die here. My soul will be forever lost to the Winterlands. The realms and our world will be ruled by the Winterlands creatures. "You mustn't try to save me. Get to the tree. Take it down. I can't say whether this is a good plan or not. But we must do something. And we can only accomplish it together."

I put out my hand. It is the longest moment of my life, the waiting. Kartik places his hand on mine. Felicity and Ann follow quickly. Philon's long fingers come down next. Bessie and Fowlson. The Hajin. The Centaurs. The forest folk. Hand over hand, we join together, every last one of us. I must concentrate hard to keep away all thoughts but my own. It would be easy for the thoughts of the Winterlands creatures to intrude, for the tree to slip inside my mind. I feel the magic flow from me into the others, one by one. And when I open my eyes, it is like standing in a carnival's hall of mirrors. Everywhere I look, we are the same. Everyone wears my face. How will they find the chosen one if we are all chosen?

"We've no time to rethink it now," I say. "We will be discovered any moment. Let's not be taken unawares."

The drums start again. My blood quickens in my ears. We fan out along the tops of the cliffs. Down below, the horrible trackers point and screech. They run to arms but so do we. We run toward the field. Swords are drawn. The clash of steel against steel sends a shiver up my spine. A hail of arrows flies from the centaurs on the cliffs. An arrow sings past me and finds its target in a wraith dangerously close.

"Aahhhhhhh!" A fierce war cry splits the air. I see one of us brandishing a sword as if born to wield it, and I know beneath that illusion beats the heart of my friend Felicity.

I can scarcely believe my eyes. Coming toward us at a furious pace is the gorgon, a sword in each of her four hands. She staggers as she moves, unaccustomed to the feel of her legs after so long without the use of them. But it is no matter. She cuts a magnificent, terrible figure, a green giantess striking blows left and right. The snakes atop her head writhe and hiss.

She shrieks above the din. "If you wish a battle, I shall give it. I am the last of my kind. I shall not lie down without a fight."

In all her glory, she is a sight to behold. The snakes move in a frenzy about her head. I am both in awe of her majesty and frightened of her terrible power. Some creatures turn to stone at the look of her; others she cuts down with the strength of her sword. It is as if she no longer hears or sees us. She is lost to the battle, so much so that she raises her sword against one of us by mistake.

"Gorgon!" I shout.

She turns on me at once. And, oh, the hideous intent of those yellow eyes now that she is free. It is a horror from which I cannot look away. I am falling under the gorgon's frightful spell. My feet have hardened to stone. I cannot move. The world spins away. The sounds of battle are gone. I hear only the gorgon's seductive hiss. *"Look at me, look at me, at me, at me, look and be amazed. . . ."*

The stone creeps through my blood. "Gorgon," I say, my voice strangled, but I don't know if she has heard or not.

Look at me, look at me. . . .

Can't breathe.

The snakes hiss wildly. Gorgon's eyes lose their bloodlust. They widen in horror. "Do not look, Most High!" Gorgon screeches. "Close your eyes!"

With what strength I have left, I do. Immediately, the trance is broken. My limbs go limp with relief and I drop to the ground, gasping.

Gorgon helps me to my feet. "You must not look upon me now, for I am not the one you know. I am my warrior self. Guard yourself. Do you understand?"

I nod fiercely.

"I could have killed you," she says, shaken.

"But you didn't," I gasp.

I hear a moan. One of us has fallen. By accident, a wraith has drawn blood. The false Gemma falls to the ground.

"Fool!" Amar shouts. "If you shed her blood here, her soul cannot be ours!"

But the body on the ground is no longer an illusion of me. The magic falters and fades. My face is replaced by the face of a Hajin woman. Her brown eyes stare up at them.

The creature howls in anger. "They deceive us! This is not the one!"

"Find the one. The true one."

"Over here," one of us calls.

"No, it is I. I am the chosen one!" another shouts from the battlefield.

"I'm the one you want," comes yet another voice.

The creatures screech. "They confuse us! How can we see when they use the realms magic against us?"

A Poppy Warrior shouts, "It is that one by the rock!"

"No, it is this one near me, I tell you!"

We are everywhere, and it is too much for them. They fall into fighting each other.

I shout over their din. "Why should you fight for the tree's glory? For the trackers'? They will let you die and take all the magic for themselves. The tree will rule you as the Order did."

The creatures eye me narrowly, but they listen.

One of us calls, "You will still be slaves to someone else's power. Do you honestly believe they will share it equally with you?"

Amar paces on his white steed. "Do not listen to them! They are deceivers!"

A skeletal creature with long shredded moth's wings shakes his spear above his head. "Why should we give the power to them, when we can have it for ourselves?"

"What will you promise us?" another man asks. His skin is as gray as rain.

"Silence!" The trackers open their hideous cloaks to reveal the screaming souls within. "You see what we wish you to see."

The Winterlands creatures cower and fall again under the spell of their leaders.

She works her enchantment against us. Find the girl, the true girl, the tree says. *Do not let them deceive you. She will be the one they try to protect.*

A tracker races for Gorgon. Gorgon fixes him with a stare, and the thing sinks into a trance. The sword swings high. It screams down, and the tracker falls like a sapling in a mighty storm. Whatever is left of him, some force within, spirals out of his body like a dust storm and into the Tree of All Souls. The tree accepts him with a terrible scream. With a loud crackle, the branches reach out farther and taller; the roots dig deeper into the frozen wasteland. The tree glows with new energy.

"Gorgon!" I shout over the hail of arrows and the shrieks of battle. "We must stop!"

She does not dare to look at me. "Why?"

"The more we kill, the stronger the tree becomes. It takes in the souls! We're not defeating them; we're strengthening them!"

I search the battlefield, and I spy Kartik running for his brother. It is Kartik free of his disguise, his dark curls framing his face like a lion's mane. He runs with grace and strength. I look about and I see glimpses of Felicity and Philon coming through. The magic is not holding! It is only a matter of moments before our plan is uncovered and I am found, and then . . .

I hear Philon's cry. The tall, elegant creature has been injured by a tracker. His ax has been thrown aside. There is no time to think. I have to get to the tree.

Pulling up my skirts, I run as hard as I can, grabbing the ax. I nearly slip on the ice and the blood, but I do not break my stride. I run straight for the tree.

She comes! the tree screeches. Its roots reach out and tangle round my ankles, bringing me down hard. The ax skitters from my hand and lands just out of reach.

"Gemma . . ."

I look up. Above me in the tree's maze of branches, Circe is wrapped in a cocoon of twigs and vines and sharp nettles. Her face is gray, and her mouth is blistered and swollen. In her hands is the dagger.

"Gemma," she calls in a strangled voice. "You must . . . finish it . . ."

The twigs tighten round her neck, cutting off her warning, but not before she drops the dagger to the ground below. I scrabble for it in the thick roots.

Gemma, would you give this all up? For what? What will you return to when you have finished me? the tree intones. *A careful little life? No longer special? No longer anything at all?*

"I shall be different," I say.

That is what they all say. The tree laughs, bitterly. *And then their magic grows less and less. They grow up, away. Their dreams fade like their beauty. They change. And when they finally know that they would like this, it is too late for them. They cannot come back. Will this be your fate?*

"N-no," I say, turning away from the dagger in the vines.

"Gemma!" Kartik is calling me. But I cannot look away from the tree, can't stop listening.

Stay with me, it says sweetly. *Like this, always. Young. Beautiful. Blooming. They will worship you.*

"Gemma!" Felicity's voice.

Stay with me . . .

"Yes," I say, my hand reaching toward the tree in longing, for it understands me. I press my palm to the bark, and suddenly, everything vanishes. It's only the tree and me. I see Eugenia Spence before it, regal and sure. I look for my friends, but they've gone.

"Give yourself to me, Gemma, and you will never be alone again. You'll be worshipped. Adored. Loved. But you must give yourself to me—a willing sacrifice."

Tears slip down my face. "Yes," I murmur.

"Gemma, don't listen," Circe says hoarsely, and for a moment, I don't see Eugenia; I see only the tree, the blood pumping beneath its pale skin, the bodies of the dead hanging from it like chimes.

I gasp, and Eugenia is before me again. "Yes, this is what you want, Gemma. Try as you might, you cannot kill this part of yourself. The solitude of the self that waits just under the stairs of your soul. Always there, no matter how much you've tried to be rid of it. I understand. I do. Stay with me and never be lonely again."

"Don't listen . . . to that . . . bitch," Circe croaks, and the vines tighten around her neck.

"No, you're wrong," I say to Eugenia as if coming out of a long sleep. "*You* couldn't kill this part of yourself. And you couldn't accept it, either."

"I'm sure I don't know what you mean," she says, sounding uncertain for the first time.

"That's why they were able to take you. They found your fear."

"And what, pray, was it?"

"Your pride. You couldn't believe you might have some of the same qualities as the creatures themselves."

"I am not like them. I am their hope. I sustain them."

"No. You tell yourself that. That's why Circe told me to search my dark corners. So I wouldn't be caught off guard."

Circe laughs, a splintered cackle that finds a way under my skin.

"And what about you, Gemma?" Eugenia purrs. "Have you 'searched' yourself, as you say?"

"I've done things I'm not proud of. I've made mistakes," I say, my voice growing stronger, my fingers feeling for the dagger again. "But I've done good, too."

"And yet, you're still alone. All that trying and still you stand apart, watching from the other side of the glass. Afraid to have what you truly want because *what if it's not enough after all?* What if you get it and you still feel alone and apart? So much better to wrap yourself up in the longing. The yearning. The restlessness. Poor Gemma. She doesn't quite fit, does she? Poor Gemma—all alone."

It's as if she's delivered a blow to my heart. My hand falters. "I—I . . ."

"Gemma, you're not alone," Circe gasps, and my hand touches metal.

"No. I'm not. I'm like everyone else in this stupid, bloody, amazing world. I'm flawed. Impossibly so. But hopeful. I'm still me." I've got it now. Sure and strong in my grip. "I see through you. I see the truth."

I spring to my feet, and suddenly, the illusion Eugenia has crafted is broken. I see the battlefield awash in blood and fighting. Hear the clang of steel against steel, the cries of vengeance, of fear, of principle and power lust, of desperation, of pure valor and unmerciful righteousness—all of it blurring into one terrible roar that drowns out every voice, every heart, every hope.

"Well done, Gemma," Eugenia says. "You're very powerful, indeed. Pity you won't live long enough to make more of those glorious mistakes."

I raise the dagger. "Right. Let's end this properly."

The tree's many arms stretch and groan. Its surface roils with those devoured souls. I try to see clearly, but this is no illusion. This is terrifyingly real, and I fall back as the tree rises taller, looming over me.

"Gemma, do it," Circe moans in agony.

I summon every bit of magic I've got, channeling it into the dagger. "I free the souls trapped here! You are released!"

I close my eyes and try to plunge the dagger into the tree. One of the branches knocks it from my hand. With a gasp, I watch it drop below. The tree shrieks and howls, calling the attention of every person on the battlefield.

"Her blood must fall!" the tree commands.

"Gemma!" Kartik calls, and I hear the alarm in his voice.

Amar comes for me. He spurs his horse forward, picking up speed. I scramble loose of the tree's grip and race for the dagger, just out of reach. For a moment, time slows. The roar of battle dims to a hum. There is only the sound of hoofbeats matching the pounding throb of my blood in my ears. I see Kartik running after his brother with a fierce determination in his eyes. And then the world spins into time.

The roots trip me. I fall to the ground. Gasping, I crawl toward the dagger, but Amar is quicker.

"No!" Kartik shouts, and then I feel a sharp pain in my side. When I look down, the dagger is there and my blood spreads across my white blouse in a widening stain.

"Gemma!" Felicity screams. I see her running toward me with Ann just behind.

I stagger forward, and when I reach the tree, I pull the dagger from my side with an anguished cry.

"I . . . release . . . these souls," I repeat in a whisper.

I plunge the dagger into the tree. It screams in pain, and the souls slip from its skin, pushing out of the branches like leaves of fire, and then they are gone.

My eyes flutter. The land goes wavy. My body trembles till I cannot stop it. I'm caught in the tree's embrace. And the last thing I hear as I fall against the cradle of the branches is Kartik shouting my name.

CHAPTER SIXTY-NINE

THE MIST IS THICK AND WELCOMING. IT KISSES MY FEVER-ish skin with a coolness, like a mother's caring lips. I cannot see what is ahead. It is just as in my dreams. But now a yellow glow is cutting the gray fog. Something is coming through. The glow comes from a lantern hanging from a long pole, and the pole is attached to a barge bedecked in lotus blossoms. The Three have come, and they've come for me. Behind me in the mist, I hear a familiar voice: *Gemma, Gemma.* It moves through me all whispery soft, and I long to return to it, but the women beckon with their hands and I move to meet them. Their movements are slow, as if they take great effort. I am slowing as well. My feet seem to sink into the mud with each step, but I'm getting closer.

I step onto the barge. They nod to me. The old one speaks.

"Your time has come. You have a choice to make."

She opens her hand. There rests a cluster of deep purple

berries, much darker in hue than the ones Pip ate. They sit cupped in her palm, as bright as jewels.

"Swallow the berries, and we will ferry you away to glory. Refuse them, and you must return to whatever awaits. Once you choose, there is no turning back."

For a moment, I hear my friends calling me, but they seem far away, as if I could run and run and never catch them.

"Gemma." I turn to see Circe behind me. She has lost the gray pallor she wore earlier. She looks just as she did the first day I saw her at Spence, when she was Miss Moore, the teacher I loved. "You did well," she says.

"You knew Eugenia had become the tree, didn't you?" I say.

"Yes," she answers.

"And you meant to save me?" I ask hopefully.

She gives me a rueful smile. "Have no illusions about me, Gemma. I meant to save myself first. To have the power second. You were a distant third."

"But I *was* third," I say.

"Yes," she says with a little laugh. "You were third."

"Thank you," I say. "You saved me."

"No. You saved yourself. I only helped a bit."

"What will become of you now?" I ask.

She doesn't answer.

"She will roam here in this mist for all time," the crone tells me.

The choice is before me in her palm. The cries of my friends grow faint in the fog. I take one plump berry and place it on my tongue, tasting it. It is not tart. Rather, there is only a pleasant sweetness and then nothing. It is the taste of forgetting. Of sleep and dreams with no waking. Never to long or yearn, to struggle or hurt or love or desire ever again. And I understand that this is what it truly means to lose your soul.

My mouth goes numb with sweetness. The berry sits on my tongue.

Felicity carrying goldenrod in her arms. Ann's voice, strong and sure. Gorgon marching through the battlefield.

I have only to swallow the berry and it is done. That is all. Swallow the berry and with it all struggle, all care, all hope. How easy it would be to do.

Kartik. I left him at the tree. The tree. I was to do something there.

So very, very easy . . .

Kartik.

With a tremendous effort, I spit the berry from my mouth, gagging as I try to rid my tongue of the sugary numbness. My body aches as if I have pushed a heavy rock uphill forever, but now I am rid of it.

"I'm sorry. I cannot go with you. Not now. But I am to have a request, am I not?"

"If you wish it," the crone says.

"I do. I should like to offer my place to another," I say, looking toward Circe.

"You would give it to me?" she says.

"You saved my life. That must count for something," I say.

"You know I abhor self-sacrifice," she replies.

"I know, but I'll not have you wandering in the mists. Too dangerous."

She smiles at me. "You've done very well, indeed, Gemma." She turns to the Three. "I accept."

Circe steps onto the barge.

The crone nods to me. "You have made your choice. There is no turning back now. Whatever shall happen you must accept."

"Yes, I know."

"Then we wish you luck. We'll not meet again."

I step onto the muddy, mist-shrouded shore as the maiden pushes the pole against the bottom of the river and drifts off into the fog and Circe retreats into the shadows. I move slowly till my legs remember how to walk quickly, and then I am running, running with all my strength, pushing through the mist with greedy, determined steps until it feels as if I am flying. I feel the hardness of branches at my back, a sharp pain in my side. I press a hand to it, and when I pull my hand away, it's soaked in blood.

I'm back where I was on the frozen ground of the Winterlands.

"Kartik. Kartik!" My voice is raw and weak. What little magic I have left is ebbing.

His eyes are wide with alarm. "Gemma! You mustn't move. If your blood falls on the ground of the Winterlands—"

"I know." With a great effort, I plunge the dagger in to its hilt and fall back, trying to get away from the tree's muddle of roots. I keep my hand to the wound and blood trickles over my hand. The tree sways precariously. The Winterlands creatures shriek to see its mortal wound. With an enormous crack, it splits open and the magic inside bleeds out.

"Step away!" Gorgon calls, but not soon enough.

Every bit of the tree's power flows into Kartik. His body

receives the magic like one hundred blows. He falls to the ground, and I fear it has killed him.

"Kartik!" I scream.

He staggers slowly to his feet, but he is no longer Kartik. He is something else entirely, a being etched in shadow and light, his eyes shifting from brown to a terrifying blue-white. He is so bright it hurts my eyes to look. All of the tree's power—the Winterlands magic—now lives inside him, and I do not know what this means.

"Kartik!" I reach for him, and my blood drops into the frozen soil.

"It begins again!" a tracker cries to the shouts of the others.

The injured tree's roots come alive. They twist themselves round my ankles and climb up my shins. I scream and try to move away, but I am being devoured.

"We didn't kill it," I gasp. "Why?"

"It cannot be killed," Amar thunders. "It can only be changed."

Felicity and Ann race to pull the roots free while Fowlson hacks at them, but the new shoots are strong.

"I told you that you would bring her to us, Brother. That you would be the death of her," Amar says sadly.

Kartik glows with power. "You told me to follow my heart," he says to Amar, and some shred of Amar, whatever remains of him, hears it.

"So I did, Brother. Will you give me peace?"

"I will."

As swiftly as a tiger, Kartik grabs Amar's sword. Amar raises his arms, and Kartik pushes it through. Amar gives a great howl. The light is piercing, and then he is no more. Kartik puts his hands to my side. The magic flares to life, and we are both bright with light, dark with shadow. His strength flows into me till the Winterlands magic mixes with the Temple magic. And for one brief moment, we are a perfect union. I can feel him inside me, me inside him. I can hear his thoughts; I know what is in his heart, what he means to do.

"No," I say. I try to break away but he holds fast to me.

"Yes, it's the only way."

"I won't let you!"

Kartik pulls me closer. "The debt must be paid. And you are needed in the world. I've waited my whole life to feel a sense of purpose. To know my place. I feel it now."

I shake my head. Tears burn my cold cheeks. "Don't."

He smiles sadly. "Now I know my destiny."

"What is it?"

"This."

He draws me to him in a kiss. His lips are warm. He pulls me tighter in his embrace. The roots sigh and release their hold on my waist and the wound in my side is healed.

"Kartik," I cry, kissing his cheeks. "It's let me go."

"That is good," he says. He makes a small cry. His back arches, and every muscle in his body tightens.

"Stay back!" Gorgon shouts, her eyes cool.

"Blimey," Bessie says in awe.

The magic takes hold of Kartik, and now I see what he's done. He's let the tree claim him in exchange. Ann and Felicity reach out to me. Fowlson tries to hold me back, but I break away.

It's too late to reverse the magic. The Winterlands have accepted Kartik's bargain.

"If I could go back . . . undo it . . . ," I say, sobbing.

"There is never any turning back, Gemma. You have to go forward. Make the future yours," Kartik says.

He kisses me sweetly on the lips, and I return his kiss until the vines twine themselves round his throat and his lips go cold. The last sound I hear from him is my name spoken softly. "Gemma . . ."

The tree accepts him. He is gone. Only his voice remains, echoing my name on the wind.

The trackers point. "She still has the Temple magic! We might have it yet!"

I push them back with the force of my power. "This is what you would fight for? Kill for? What you would try to hoard or protect? No more," I say, my lips still warm with Kartik's kiss. "The magic was meant to be shared. None of you will hold it! I will give the magic back to the land!"

I put my hands to the broken earth. "I give this magic back to the realms and the Winterlands, too, that it may be shared equally among the tribes!"

The trackers shriek and howl as if in pain. The souls they have captured push through me on their way to wherever it is we go from here. I feel their passage. It is rather like the swoop of a carnival ride. And when they have gone, there is no one to lead the others, the dead. They stare in wonder, no longer sure what has happened or what will be.

The pale things that hide in the crevices and the cracks of the Winterlands crawl closer. The tree's warmth melts a small patch of ice at its base. Thin shoots of grass struggle up through the new earth. I touch them and they are as soft as Kartik's fingers on my arm.

Something in me breaks open. My face is slick with tears. So I do what I yearn to do. I sink into the burgeoning grass and cry.

ACT V

Morning

You must be the change you want to see in the world.
—MAHATMA GANDHI

CHAPTER SEVENTY

MRS. NIGHTWING WAITS FOR US IN THE CHAPEL, WHERE she cradles the body of Mother Elena.

"The creatures?" Ann asks, her voice ragged with the screams she's spent.

Mrs. Nightwing shakes her head. "Her heart. She didn't fall to them. There is that, at least."

Mrs. Nightwing counts us as we file past—Felicity, Ann, Fowlson, me.

"Sahirah . . . ?" she whispers. "And—"

I shake my head. She lowers her eyes, and nothing more is said.

The girls of Spence sit huddled together. Their eyes are wide and frightened. What they have seen tonight is beyond teas and balls, curtsies and sonnets.

Mrs. Nightwing puts her hand on my shoulder. "There is nothing more I can tell them. They've seen and they are frightened."

"They should be." Is it my voice that sounds so hard?

"They can't know what has happened."

She wants me to take what magic I have left and blot every memory of this evening from their minds. To make them forget so that they can carry on as before. There will always be the Cecilys, Marthas, and Elizabeths of the world—those who cannot bear the burden of truth. They will drink their tea. Weigh their words. Wear hats against the sun. Squeeze their minds into corsets, lest some errant thought should escape and ruin the smooth illusion they hold of themselves and the world as they like it.

It is a luxury, this forgetting. No one will come to take away the things I wish I had not seen, the things I wish I did not know. I shall have to live with them.

I wrench away from her grip. "Why should I?"

⅄⅄⅄⅄

I do it anyway. Once I am certain the girls are asleep, I creep into their rooms, one by one, and lay my hands across their furrowed brows, which wear the trouble of all they've witnessed. I watch while those brows ease into smooth, blank canvases beneath my fingers. It is a form of healing, and I am surprised by how much it heals me to do it. When the girls awake, they will remember a strange dream of magic and blood and curious creatures and perhaps a teacher they knew whose name will not spring to their lips. They might strain to remember for a moment, but then they will tell themselves it was only a dream best forgotten.

I have done what Mrs. Nightwing said I should do. But I do not take all their memories from them. I leave them with one small token of their evening: doubt. A feeling that perhaps there is something more. It is nothing more than a seed. Whether it shall grow into something more useful, I cannot say.

When it is time for me to visit Brigid, I find her awake in her little room. "That's awl righ', luv. I don' care to forget, if it's all the same," she says, and there are no rowan leaves at her window anymore.

⚓︎⚓︎⚓︎

There is an ancient tribal proverb I once heard in India. It says that before we can see properly we must first shed our tears to clear the way.

I cry for days.

Mrs. Nightwing does not force me to go downstairs, and she doesn't allow anyone, not even Fee and Ann, in to see me. She brings my meals on a tray, placing them on my table in the darkened room and leaving without a word. I hear only the rustling of her bustle as she treads the old wood floors, back and forth. Sometimes when I wake in the early hours, I feel as if I am emerging from a long, strange dream. The velvety light softens every edge in the room, bathing it in possibility. In that blissful moment, I expect a day like any other: I shall study French, laugh with friends. I shall see Kartik coming across the lawn, his smile filling me with warmth. And just as I begin to believe that all is well, there is some subtle change in the light. The room takes its true shape. I fight to go back to that blissful ignorance, but it is too late. The dull pain of truth weights my soul, pulling it under. I am left hopelessly awake.

CHAPTER SEVENTY-ONE

THE MORNING WE ARE TO LEAVE IS AS BEAUTIFUL A SPRING day as I've seen.

When the time for goodbyes comes at last, Felicity, Ann, and I stand uncertainly on the front lawn, our eyes searching for the dust on the path that signals the coach's arrival. Mrs. Nightwing flips down the collar of Ann's coat, checks to be certain that my hat is pinned securely and Felicity's case is latched properly.

I feel none of it. I am numb.

"Well," Mrs. Nightwing says for about the eighteenth time in a half hour. "Have you enough handkerchiefs? A lady can never have too many handkerchiefs."

She will be Nightwing, regardless of what horrors occur, and just now, I am glad of her strength, from wherever it springs.

"Yes, thank you, Mrs. Nightwing," Ann says.

"Ah, good, good."

Felicity has given Ann her garnet earbobs. I've given her the ivory elephant I brought with me from India.

"We shall read of your admirers in the papers," Felicity says.

"I'm only one of the merry maidens," Ann reminds us. "There are other girls."

"Yes, well. Each of us must start somewhere." Mrs. Nightwing tuts.

"I've written to my cousins and told them not to expect me back," Ann says. "They were awfully angry."

"As soon as you've become a sensation on the London stage, they'll be clamoring for tickets and telling everyone they know you," Felicity assures her, and Ann smiles. Felicity turns to me. "I suppose the next time we meet, we shall be proper ladies."

"I suppose so," I reply.

And there's nothing more to say.

A cry goes up from the younger girls crowded on the lawn. The carriage is coming. They nearly trample each other to be the first in with the news.

"Enough," Felicity grouses, and slides into the carriage away from the throng.

Ann's trunk is secured with ropes. We embrace and do not let go for the longest time. At last, she climbs the steps into the carriage for the trip to the train and London and then the Gaiety Theatre. "Goodbye," she calls, waving from the carriage's open window. "Till tomorrow and tomorrow and tomorrow!"

I raise my hand in a half wave, and she nods, and we let that be enough goodbye for now.

Within a few hours, I'll be back in London at my grandmother's house, preparing for the dizzying whirl of balls and parties that comprise the social season. Come Saturday, I shall curtsy before my Queen and make my debut in society while my family and friends look on. There will be supper and dancing. I shall wear a beautiful white dress and ostrich plumes in my hair.

And I couldn't care less.

CHAPTER SEVENTY-TWO

THE CARRIAGE COMES TO CARRY US TO SAINT JAMES'S Palace. Even our housekeeper cannot hide her excitement this evening. For once, she looks at me instead of around me. "You look quite beautiful, miss."

"Thank you," I say.

The seamstress is just putting the finishing touches on my dress. My hair is piled high upon my head and crowned with a tiara and three ostrich feathers. I have long white gloves that reach the tops of my arms. And Father has presented me with my first real diamonds—in a delicate necklace that shimmers against my skin like dewdrops. "Lovely, lovely," Grandmama pronounces until she is presented with the bill. Then her eyes grow large. "Why on earth did I agree to those roses and beads? I must have been out of my mind."

Tom gives me a peck on the cheek. "You look wonderful, Gem. Are you ready to take that long walk?"

I nod. "I think so. I hope so." My stomach flips.

Father offers me his arm. He is very frail, but charming. "Miss Gemma Doyle of Belgravia, I presume?"

"Yes," I say, laying my hand upon his, my arm at the proper angle to my body as I've been taught. "If you say so."

We wait in the procession with the other girls and their fathers. We're all as nervous as new chicks. This one checks to be certain her train is not offensively long. That one holds so tightly to her father's arm I fear he shall lose the use of it. I do not see Felicity yet but I wish I did. We strain our necks for an early glimpse of the Queen on her throne. My heart is beating so very fast. *Steady, Gemma, steady. Breathe in.*

We move forward by excruciating inches, the courtier calling the name of each girl in the procession. One girl wobbles slightly, and word snakes back through the line in terrified whispers. No one wishes to be singled out.

"Courage," Father says with a kiss, and I wait my turn to be alone in the chamber of Saint James's Palace. The doors are opened. Down at the end of a very long red carpet sits the most important woman in the world, Her Majesty, Queen Victoria. She is rather stern in her black silks and white lace. But her crown sparkles so that I cannot look away. I am to be presented to Queen Victoria. I shall proceed as a girl and return as a woman. Such is the power of this ceremony.

I feel I shall faint. Oh, I shall be ill. *Stuff and nonsense, Gemma. You've faced worse. Stand tall. Back straight, chin out. She is but a woman.* Indeed she is—a woman who happens to be Queen and who holds the entirety of my future in her wizened hands. I shall be ill. I know it. I shall fall upon my face and live the rest of my days, disgraced and odd, in a hermitage in the south of England, accompanied by fourteen cats of varying size and color. And when I venture out in my old age, I shall still hear people whisper, "There she goes . . . the one who fell. . . ."

The courtier calls my name, loud and strong: "Miss Gemma Doyle!"

The longest walk of my life is under way. I hold my breath as I travel the stretch of carpet, which seems to lengthen with each step. Her Majesty is a solemn monument of flesh and blood in the distance. She is so very like her portraits that it is startling. At last, I reach her. It is the moment I have both wanted and feared. With as much grace as I can muster, I lower myself like a soufflé falling in upon itself. I bow low to my Queen. I do not dare breathe. And then I feel her tap upon my shoulder firmly, compelling me to rise. I back slowly from her presence and take my place among the other girls who have just become women.

≺≺≺≺

I have done what they expected of me. I have curtsied for my Queen and made my debut. This is what I have anticipated eagerly for years. So why do I feel so unsatisfied? Everyone is merry. They haven't a care in the world. And perhaps that is it. How terrible it is to have no cares, no longings. I do not fit. I feel too deeply and want too much. As cages go, it is a gilded one, but I shall not live well in it or any cage, for that matter.

Lord Denby is suddenly at my side. "Congratulations," he says. "On your debut and on that other matter. I understand from Fowlson that you were quite magnificent."

"Thank you," I say, sipping my first glass of champagne. The bubbles tickle my nose.

Lord Denby lowers his voice. "I also understand that you

gave the magic back to the land, that it exists as a resource for all."

"That is true."

"How can you be certain that this is the right course, that they won't misuse it in the end?" he asks.

"I can't," I answer.

His horrified expression is quickly replaced by a smug one. "Why don't you let me help you with all that, then? We could be partners in this—you and I, together?"

I hand him the half-empty glass. "No. You do not understand true partnership, sir. And so we shall not be friends, Lord Denby. On that one point, I *am* certain."

"I should like to dance with my sister, if you please, Lord Denby," Tom says. His smile is bright but his eyes are steely.

"Of course, old chap. There's a good man," Lord Denby says, and drinks the last of my champagne, which is as much of me as he shall ever have.

"Are you all right? What an insufferable ass," Tom says as we take a turn on the dance floor. "To think I once admired him."

"I did try to warn you," I say.

"Will this be one of those ghastly 'I told you so' moments?"

"No," I promise. "And have you met your future wife yet?"

Tom waggles his eyebrows. "I've met quite a few promising candidates for the position of Mrs. Thomas Doyle. Of course, they will have to find me charming and utterly irresistible. I don't suppose you could aid me in that pursuit with a little bit of . . . ?"

"I'm afraid not," I say. "You'll have to take your chances."

He twirls me a bit hard. "You're no fun at all, Gemma."

Later in the evening, I approach my father before he can slip off with the other men for brandy. "Father, I should like to have a word, if you please. Privately."

For a moment, he regards me warily, but then his apprehension seems to be forgotten. He does not remember what occurred the last time we had such a talk, the night of Spence's party. I did not need magic to take that memory from him; he has denied it to himself.

We duck into a musty sitting room whose draperies smell of ancient cigar smoke. There are many things we could speak truth of just now: his declining health, the battles I have seen, the friends I have lost. But we shan't speak of them. It will never be any more than this, and I suppose the only difference now is that I know that. I must pick my battles, and this is the one I have chosen.

"Father," I begin, my voice quavering. "I ask only that you hear me out."

"That is an ominous tone," he says with a wink, trying to lighten the mood. How easy it would be to forget everything I mean to say. *Strength, Gemma.*

"I am most grateful for this evening. Thank you."

"You're welcome, my dear. . . ."

"Yes, thank you . . . but I shan't attend any other parties. I don't wish to continue my season."

Father's brows knit together in consternation. "Indeed? And why not? Haven't you been given the best of everything?"

"Yes, and I am most grateful for it," I say, heart hammering against my ribs.

"Then what is this nonsense?"

"I know. It makes no sense. I'm only just coming to understand it myself."

"Then perhaps we should discuss it another day." He starts to rise. Once he does, the conversation will end. There will not be another day. I know this. I know him.

I put my arm on his. "Please, Papa. You said you would hear me out."

Reluctantly, he sits, but already he has lost interest. He fidgets with his watch. I have little time to make my case. I could sit at his feet as I did when I was a child, let him stroke my hair. Once, it was comforting for us both. But this is not a time for comfort, and I am no longer a child. I take the chair opposite him.

"What I mean to say is, I don't imagine this life is for me. Parties and endless balls and gossip. I don't wish to spend my days making myself small enough to fit into such a narrow world. I cannot speak with their bit in my mouth."

"You've quite a dim view of them."

"I mean no harm."

Father sighs, irritated. "I don't understand."

A door is opened. Music and chatter from the dance intrude on our silence until the door is mercifully closed again, and the party is no more than a dim murmur on the other side. Tears prick at my eyes. I swallow hard.

"I am not asking you to understand, Papa. I'm asking for you to accept."

"Accept what?"

Me. Accept me, Papa. "My decision to live my own life as I see fit."

It is so quiet that I suddenly wish I could take it back. *Sorry, it was only a terrible joke. I should like a new dress, please.*

Father clears his throat. "That is not as easy as you make it sound."

"I know it. I know I shall make beastly mistakes, Father—"

"The world does not forgive mistakes so quickly, my girl." He sounds bitter and sad.

"Then if the world will not forgive me," I say softly, "I shall have to learn to forgive myself."

He nods in understanding.

"And how will you marry? Or do you intend to marry?"

I think of Kartik, and tears threaten. "I shall meet someone one day, as Mother found you."

"You are so very much like her," he says, and for once, I do not wince.

He rises and paces the room, hands behind his back. I do not know what will happen. Will he grant my wish? Will he tell me I am foolish and impossible and sentence me back to the ballroom, with its whirl of satins and fans? Is that where I belong? Will I regret this tomorrow? Father stands before a large portrait of a rather grim woman. She sits, hands in her lap, an unreadable expression upon her face, as if she expects nothing and will likely get it.

"Did I ever tell you the story of that tiger?" he asks.

"Yes, Father. You did."

"No, I didn't tell you everything," he says. "I did not tell you about the day I shot the tiger."

I remember the moment in his room after the morphine. I thought it nothing more than ramblings at the time. This isn't the story I know, and I am afraid of this new story. He doesn't wait for my answer. He means to tell it. He has heard me; now I shall hear him.

"The tiger had gone. He did not come around again. But I was a man possessed. The tiger had come too close, you see. I no longer felt safe. I hired the best tracker in Bombay. We hunted for days, tracking the tiger to the mountains there. We found him taking water from a small watering hole. He looked up but he did not charge. He took no notice of us at all but continued to drink. 'Sahib, let us go,' the boy said. 'This tiger means you no harm.' He was right, of course. But we had come all that way. The gun was in my hand. The tiger was before us. I took aim and shot it dead on the spot. I sold the tiger's skin for a fortune to a man in Bombay, and he called me brave for it. But it was not courage that brought me to that; it was fear."

He drums his fingers on the mantel before the grim-faced portrait. "I could not live with the threat of it. I could not live with the knowledge that the tiger was out there, roaming free. But you," he says, smiling with a mix of sadness and pride, "you faced the tiger and survived."

He coughs several times, his chest heaving with the effort. He pulls a handkerchief from his pocket and wipes his mouth quickly, then hides the linen safely in his pocket again so that I cannot see the stain that is surely there. "The time has come for me to face my tiger, to look him in the eye and see which of us survives. I shall return to India. Your future is yours to shape. I shall prepare your grandmother for the scandal of it."

"Thank you, Papa."

"Yes, well," he says. "And now, if you don't mind, I should like to dance with my daughter on the occasion of her debut."

He offers his arm and I take it. "I should like that very much."

We fall into the great continuing circle of dancers. Some leave the floor, tired but giddy; others have only just arrived. They are eager to wear their new status as ladies, to be paraded about and lauded until they see themselves with new eyes. The fathers beam at their daughters, thinking them perfect flowers in need of their protection, while the mothers watch from the margins, certain this moment is their doing. We create the illusions we need to go on. And one day, when they no longer dazzle or comfort, we tear them down, brick by glittering brick, until we are left with nothing but the bright light of honesty. The light is liberating. Necessary. Terrifying. We stand naked and emptied before it. And when it is too much for our eyes to take, we build a new illusion to shield us from its relentless truth.

But the girls! Their eyes glow with the fever dream of all they might become. They tell themselves this is the beginning of everything. And who am I to say it isn't?

"Gemma! Gemma!" Felicity is pushing through the crowd, her chagrined chaperone struggling to keep up as the dowagers look on, disapprovingly. It is only an hour into her debut and already she has them spinning like tops. And for the first time in days, I smile.

"Gemma," Felicity says, catching up to me. Her words tumble over each other in a torrent of excitement: "You look beautiful! How do you like my dress? Elizabeth tottered a bit—did you see it? The Queen was magnificent, wasn't she? I was terrified. Were you?"

"Utterly," I say. "I thought I might faint after all."

"Did you receive Ann's cable?" Felicity asks.

I received a lovely telegram from Ann this very morning, wishing me well. It read:

REHEARSALS ARE SPLENDID STOP THE GAIETY IS
THRILLING STOP BEST OF LUCK WITH YOUR CURTSY
STOP YOURS ANN BRADSHAW

"Yes," I say. "She must have spent her future wages on it."

"When the season ends, I am to accompany my mother and Polly to Paris, then stay on."

"What of Horace Markham?" I ask warily.

"Well," she begins, "I went to him. By myself. And told him I didn't love him and didn't wish to marry him and that I would make a perfect fishmonger of a wife. And do you know what he said?"

I shake my head.

Her eyes widen. "He said he didn't want to marry me, either. Can you imagine? I was rather wounded."

I laugh a bit, the first laugh I've had. Feels odd and near a cry.

"Paris, then. What will you do there?"

"Really, Gemma," she says as if I don't know anything and never will. "It is where all the bohemians live. Now that I've my inheritance, I might take up painting and live in a garret. Or perhaps I shall become an artist's model," she says, delighting in how scandalous this sounds. Her voice drops to a whisper. "I've heard there are others like me there. Perhaps I *will* love again."

"You'll be the toast of Paris," I say.

She grins widely. "Do come with us! We could have such a merry time together!"

"I think I should like to go to America," I answer, the plan forming with my words. "To New York."

"That's grand!"

"Yes," I say, brightening a bit at the prospect. "It is, isn't it?"

Felicity holds more tightly to my arm. "I don't know if you have heard the news, but I would tell you before anyone else does. Miss Fairchild has accepted Simon's suit. They are betrothed."

I nod. "That's as it should be. I wish them happiness."

"I wish her luck. Mark my words, Simon will lose all his hair and be fat as Fezziwig before he's thirty." She giggles.

A new dance is called. It brings fresh excitement to the crowd. The floor fills as a lively tune gives new life to the party. Holding hands, standing together in a crush of silk and flowers, Felicity and I watch the dancers moving as one. They spin about like the earth on its axis, enduring the dark, waiting for the sun.

Felicity squeezes my hand, and I feel the slightest hint of realms magic pulsing there. "Well, Gemma, we survived it."

"Yes," I say, squeezing back. "We have survived."

CHAPTER SEVENTY-THREE

On Friday, Thomas and I accompany Father to Bristol, where the HMS *Victoria* awaits, ready to take him home to India. The docks are awash in well-dressed travelers—men in fine suits, ladies in wide-brimmed hats to keep out the rare English sun, which has obliged them by shining brightly today. The boards are stacked with trunks bound with twine, stamped for other destinations. They stand as testament that life is a constant heartbeat, pulsing everywhere at once, and we are but a small part of that eternal ebb and flow. I wonder where Ann is at this moment. Perhaps she is standing center stage at the Gaiety, ready to embark on a path where nothing is certain and she can be whoever she wishes. I should like very much to see her in this new life.

Father has spoken to Grandmama about my decision. She is scandalized, of course, but it is done. I shall go to university. After that, I shall have a modest allowance upon which to live, administered by Tom, who has done his best to convince Grandmama that I shall not fall to ruin in the streets. But if I truly desire independence, I shall need to work. It is unheard of. A black mark. Yet I find that I am excited by the prospect of having my own pursuits and earning my own keep. At any rate, it is the price for my freedom, so there you have it.

Father is wearing his favorite white suit. It is not snug the way it should be; he's far too thin. But he cuts a dashing figure anyway. We stand on the docks, making our goodbyes, as people push past in a flurry of excitement.

"Safe voyage to you, Father," Thomas says. He and Father shake hands awkwardly.

"Thank you, Thomas," Father says, coughing. He must wait for the spasm to subside before finding his voice again. "I shall see you at Christmas."

Tom looks down at his feet. "Yes. Of course. Till Christmas."

I embrace Father. He holds me a moment longer than usual, and I can feel his ribs. "Thank you for seeing me off, pet."

"I'll write to you," I say, trying not to cry.

He releases me with a smile. "Then I shall eagerly await your letters."

The ship's horn bellows its deep warning. Stewards raise their voices, giving the final call for all passengers to board. Father mounts the plank and makes his way slowly to the edge of the ship amidst a crowd of other travelers waving goodbye. He stands tall, hands on the railing, face forward. The sun, that great magic lantern, casts its illusory light, catching my father's face in such a way that I see no lines, no pallor, no sadness. I do not see the shadow of what is to come sitting in the hollows under his eyes, slowly thinning the planes of his cheeks. There are some illusions I'm not prepared to give up just yet.

As the ship pulls slowly away and out to the blinding sea, I see him as I wish to: healthy and strong and happy, his smile a bright, shiny promise of new days, whatever they may bring.

⌁⌁⌁

Mademoiselle LeFarge's wedding is to take place on the last Friday in May. I return a day early, Thursday, and carry my trunk to my old room. The trees have grown such a full coat of leaves that I can no longer see the lake and the boathouse from here. A hint of color flickers in the ivy beneath my window. I throw open the sash and reach down. It is a fragment of the red cloth. Kartik's signal to me. I pluck it free and tuck it into the waist of my skirt.

A new crew of men is hard at work on the East Wing. The turret takes shape nicely. No longer a wound but not quite whole. It is between, and I've come to feel a kinship with it. The door into the realms is closed just now, giving us all time to think, to take stock. When I return from university, we—the tribes of the realms, my friends, Fowlson, Nightwing, and I, and all who wish to have a say—shall work together to forge a constitution of sorts, a document and a government to guide the realms.

Not that it matters much where I am concerned. It seems that, rather like unruly red hair and skin that will freckle, my ability to enter the realms is a part of me. So on a beautiful last Thursday in May, I sit on my old bed in my room in Spence and make the door of light appear.

⌁⌁⌁

The realms are not the place of awe I remember from my first days here; nor are they a place of fear. They are a place I have come to know and would know more of.

• 802 •

Gorgon is in the garden, hoisting the silver arch that leads to the grotto back into position. It is battered but unbroken.

"Most High," she calls. "A hand would be most appreciated."

"Certainly," I say, pulling on the other side. We push until the arch catches in the dirt. It wavers for a moment, then stands.

"I wish to see Philon," I say.

"My legs are weak from years of imprisonment," she says, leaning against a tree for support. "But my spirit is strong. Come, I shall take you there."

She leads me to the river and the boat that was her prison for centuries.

I back away. "No. I couldn't ask you to become one with this ghastly ship again."

She arches an eyebrow. "I only meant to steer."

"Yes," I say, sheepish. "Carry on."

Gorgon takes the wheel like a proper captain, setting a course for the home of the forest folk. We pass through the golden mist and I let it shower me with jewel-like flecks. Some land on Gorgon as well. She shakes them free. The shore comes into view. It is not as verdant as it once was. The creatures' damage was great. Burned trees stand like spindly matchsticks, and the earth is as tough as leather. Many of the folk are gone. But children still laugh and play along the shore. Their spirits are not vanquished easily.

Several of them approach Gorgon shyly. They are curious about the great green giantess striding through their homeland. Gorgon turns on them quickly, letting her snakes hiss and snap. The children run away screaming with a mixture of dread and delight.

"Was that necessary?" I ask.

"I have told you before. I am not maternal."

We find Philon overseeing the building of huts. But it is not only the forest folk who raise beams and hammer roofs. They stand side by side with the Untouchables, the nymphs, several shape-shifters. Bessie Timmons hauls water, strong and sure. A shape-shifter girl follows her, admiring her strength. I even spy one of the Winterlands creatures brushing shimmering pitch onto the roofs. In the forest are souls of all sorts; creatures of every imagining; mortals, too. Asha offers water to Gorgon, who drinks it and returns the glass for more.

"Priestess!" Philon greets me with a clasp of hands. "Have you come to take your place beside us?"

"No," I say. "I've only come to say goodbye for a while."

"When will you return?"

I shake my head. "I cannot say just yet. It is time for me to take my place in the world—my own world. I am to go to New York."

"But you are a part of the realms," Philon reminds me.

"And they shall always be a part of me. Do look after things. We have much to argue about when I return."

"What makes you think we shall argue?"

I give Philon a knowing look. "We've the realms to discuss. I don't delude myself that it shall go smoothly."

"More tribes have heard. They will come to sit with us," Philon says.

"Good."

Philon reaches into the burned leaves and blows on them. They spiral and flutter until they form an image of the Tree of All Souls. The image lasts for only a moment. "The magic is in the land again. In time it will come back a hundredfold."

I nod.

"Perhaps we shall visit you in your world sometime. Your world could do with a bit of magic."

"I should like that," I say. "But you will behave yourself, won't you? No taking mortals for playthings."

Philon's lips twist into an enigmatic smile. "Would you come after us?"

I nod. "I would indeed."

The creature extends a hand. "So let us remain friends."

"Yes, friends."

⌇⌇⌇⌇⌇

Gorgon accompanies me as far as the Borderlands. "The rest of this journey is mine alone, I'm afraid," I say.

"As you wish," she says, bowing. Her snakes dance about her head in a merry halo. She does not try to follow me, but she doesn't leave, either. She lets me leave her. By the time I have crossed into the Winterlands, I no longer see her, but I feel her all the same.

Tiny blossoms have sprouted on the branches of the tree. Their defiant colors push up through the gnarled bark. The tree blooms again. The land is not what it was before. It is strange and new and unknown. It pulses with a different magic, born of loss and despair, love and hope.

I rest my cheek on the Tree of All Souls. Beneath the bark, its heart beats sure and strong against my ear. I stretch my arms round the tree as far as they will go. Where my tears hit, the bark glistens silver.

Little Wendy steps up shyly. She has survived. She's pale and thin and her teeth are sharper. "It's beautiful," she says, admiring the tree's majesty with her fingers.

I step away, wiping my eyes. "Yes, it is."

"Sometimes, when the wind blows through them leaves, it sounds like your name. It's like a sigh, then," she says. "The most beautiful sound I ever heard."

A gentle breeze catches in the branches then and I hear it, soft and low, a murmured prayer—*Gem-ma, Gem-ma*—and then the leaves bend down and trail delicate fingers across my cold cheeks.

"Wendy, I'm afraid I can't help you cross over now that you've eaten the berries. You will have to remain in the realms," I tell her.

"Yes, miss," she says, and she doesn't sound sad. "Bessie and me, we're stayin' on, makin' a go of it. Can I show you sum'thin'?" Wendy asks.

She takes my hand and leads me to the valley where our battle was recently fought. Amidst the patches of icy snow, unexpected plants grow. Their roots burrow deep under the ice; they grow despite it.

"Tell me what you see," she says.

"Lovely shoots sticking up. Like early spring," I say. "Did you plant these?"

She shakes her head. "I done only this one," she says, fingering a tall plant with thick, flat, red leaves. "I put my hands in the soil, and it was like I could feel the magic there, waitin'. I put m'mind to it, and up it grew. And then, it's like it took hold, and the rest come up all on their own. It's a start, innit?"

"Yes," I say. The valley stretches out long and far, a mixture of color and ice. The injured land struggles to be reborn. It is a very good start.

A man approaches me timidly, his hat in his hand. His

terror shows in his shaking limbs and searching eyes. "Beggin' your pardon, miss, but I was told you be the one to help me cross on to the next world."

"Who told you this?"

His eyes widen. "A fearsome creature with a head full o' snakes!"

"You mustn't fear her," I say, taking the man's hand and leading him toward the river. "She's as tame as a pussycat. She'd probably lick your hand given the chance."

"Didn't seem harmless," he whispers, shuddering.

"Yes, well, things are not always as they appear, sir, and we must learn to judge for ourselves."

⌁⌁⌁⌁⌁

The ones who need my help come out here and there: This one wants to tell his wife he loved her, as he never could in life; that one is sorry for a falling out she had with her sister, a grudge she held till the end; still another, a girl of perhaps eighteen, is frightened—she cannot walk away from the past so easily.

She holds tightly to my arm. "Is it true what I hear, that I do not have to cross? That there is a place where I might live on?" Her eyes are wide with a desperate hope fanned by fear.

"It is true," I answer. "But it is not without cost. Nothing is."

"But what will become of me when I cross over the river?"

"I cannot say. No one can."

"Oh, will you tell me which path to take, please?"

"I cannot make that choice for you. It is yours alone to make."

Her eyes well with tears. "It is so very hard."

"Yes, it is," I say, and hold her hand because that is all the magic I can muster.

In the end, she makes the choice to go—if I will accompany her across the river on the barge steered by Gorgon. It is my first journey of this sort, and my heartbeat quickens. I want to know what lies beyond what I have already seen. The closer we get to the shore, the brighter it grows, until I have to turn my head away. I hear only the knowing sigh of the girl. I feel the barge lighten and I know she has gone.

My heart is heavy as we turn back. The gentle laps of the river's current are but the whispered names of what has been lost: my mother, Amar, Carolina, Mother Elena, Miss Moore, Miss McCleethy, and some part of myself that I shan't get back.

Kartik. I blink hard against the tears that threaten. "Why must things come to an end?" I say softly.

"Our days are all numbered in the book of days, Most High," Gorgon murmurs as the garden comes once more into view. "That is what gives them sweetness and purpose."

When I return to the garden, a gentle breeze blows through the olive grove. It smells of myrrh. Mother Elena approaches, her medallion shining against her white blouse.

"I would see my Carolina now," she says.

"She's been waiting for you across the river," I say.

Mother Elena smiles at me. "You have done well." She places a hand to my cheek and says something in Romani that I do not understand.

"Is that a blessing?"

"It is only a saying: To those who will see, the world waits."

The barge drifts, ready to carry Mother Elena across the

river. She sings some sort of lullaby. The light grows, bathing her in its glow till I can no longer tell where the light ends and she begins. And then she is gone.

To those who will see, the world waits. It feels like much more than a saying. And perhaps it is.

Perhaps it is a hope.

CHAPTER SEVENTY-FOUR

I WAIT FOR SOME TIME TO SPEAK PRIVATELY WITH MRS.
Nightwing. At five minutes after three o'clock, the door to her
room opens, admitting me entrance to the inner sanctum. I'm
reminded of the first day I arrived at Spence, in my black
mourning dress, lost and grief-stricken, without a friend in the
world. How much has happened since then.

Mrs. Nightwing folds her hands on her desk and gazes at
me over the tops of her spectacles. "You wished to speak to me,
Miss Doyle?" Good old Nightwing, as constant as England.

"Yes," I start.

"Well, I do hope you shall be quick about it. I've two teachers to replace, now that Mademoiselle LeFarge is to be married
and Miss McCleethy . . . now that Sahirah . . ." She trails off,
blinking. Her eyes redden.

"I am sorry," I say.

She closes her eyes for the briefest moment, her lips
trembling ever so slightly. And then, like a dark cloud that

only threatens rain, it passes. "What was it you wanted, Miss Doyle?"

"I shall be most grateful for your help in the matter of the realms," I say, straightening.

Nightwing's cheeks redden with a true blush. "I don't see what assistance I could possibly offer."

"I shall need help maintaining the door and keeping watch, especially while I am away."

She nods. "Yes. Certainly."

I clear my throat. "And there is one more thing you may do. It is about Spence. And the girls." She cocks an eyebrow, and I feel it like a gunshot. "You could truly educate them. You could teach them to think for themselves."

Mrs. Nightwing does not move save for her eyes, which she narrows to suspicious slits. "You are in jest, I trust?"

"On the contrary, I have never been more in earnest."

"Their mothers shall be overjoyed to hear it," she mutters. "No doubt they'll race to our doors in droves."

I bang my fist on the desk, rattling Mrs. Nightwing's teacup and Mrs. Nightwing in that order. "Why should we girls not have the same privileges as men? Why do we police ourselves so stringently—whittling each other down with cutting re-marks or holding ourselves back from greatness with a harness woven of fear and shame and longing? If we do not deem our-selves worthy first, how shall we ever ask for more?

"I have seen what a handful of girls can do, Mrs. Nightwing. They can hold back an army if necessary, so please don't tell me it isn't possible. A new century dawns. Surely we could dispense with a few samplers in favor of more books and grander ideas."

Mrs. Nightwing is so very still I fear I may have stopped her heart with my outburst. Her normally commanding voice is but a squeak. "I shall lose all my girls to Miss Pennington's."

I sigh. "No, you shan't. Only ninnies go to Penny's."

"Most ungracious, Miss Doyle." Mrs. Nightwing tuts. She places the teacup exactly so on its saucer. "And you? You will forgo your season for a university in America. Are you truly prepared to turn your back on all of that privilege and power?"

I think of those ladies in their stiff gowns and forced smiles, drowning their hunger with weak tea, trying hard to make themselves fit into such a narrow world, desperately afraid the blinders will slip and show them what they've chosen to close out.

"Privilege is not always power, is it?" I say.

Mrs. Nightwing nods slowly. "I will offer you every assistance in the realms. You may rely on it. As for the other matter, that shall require more thought than I care to give it at the moment. The sun still reigns in the sky, and I've a school full of girls awaiting my instruction and care. I have my duties, too. Is there another matter to discuss, or is that all for today?"

"That is all. Thank you kindly, Mrs. Nightwing."

"Lillian," she says so softly I nearly miss it.

"Thank you . . . Lillian," I say, tasting her name on my tongue like an exotic new curry.

"You're welcome. Gemma." She shuffles some papers on her desk and pins them beneath a silver box, only to remove it and shuffle them again. "Are you still here?"

"Right," I say, rising quickly. In my haste for the door, I nearly topple the chair.

"What was it you said about Miss Pennington's?" she asks.

"Only ninnies go to Penny's?"

She nods. "Yes, that was the phrase. Well. Good day to you, then."

"Good day."

She does not look up or see me out. I am no more than a few steps from Mrs. Nightwing's room when I hear her repeat to herself, "Only ninnies go to Penny's." It is followed by the strangest sound, one that starts low and moves high. A laugh. No, not a laugh—a giggle. It is a giggle full of high spirits and merry mischief, proof that we never lose our girlish selves, no matter what sort of women we become.

⁓⁓⁓⁓

The next morning dawns pink and hopeful and sweetens into a glorious late-spring day. The rolling green fields behind Spence are alive with bursts of hyacinth and bright yellow flowers. The air is perfumed with lilac and rose. The smell is heavenly. It tickles my nose and lightens my head. Clouds roll lazily upon the blue horizon. I do not believe I have ever seen such a lovely sight, not even in the realms. Mademoiselle LeFarge shall have a splendid wedding day.

It is a good half hour before the wedding, and Felicity and I spend it in the gardens, gathering wildflowers for the last time together. She tells me of the new suit of trousers she vows to have fashioned in Paris.

"Think of it, Gemma—never to wear a petticoat and corset ever again. That is freedom," she says, shaking a daisy by its stalk to emphasize her point.

I pull a rose from its leafy nest and tuck it gently into my sack. "You'll be the talk of the town; that's certain."

She shrugs. "Let them talk. It's my life to live, not theirs. I've my inheritance now. And perhaps, in time and with my influence, ladies in trousers shall be all the rage."

I am not brave enough to give up my skirts just yet, but somehow I know that Felicity shall wear her trousers with aplomb. With a wicked grin, she reaches into her sack and tosses a handful of mixed blossoms at me. Not to be outdone, I toss several at her. She retaliates, and soon, it's war.

"Will you behave?" I say, but I'm laughing. A true laugh.

"Only if you will." Felicity giggles, getting in one more handful.

"Truce!" I screech.

"Truce."

We're coated in flowers but our sacks are nearly depleted. We try to salvage what we can. The blossoms are rumpled but they smell divine. I pull a trampled rose from the ground and hold it to my mouth. "Live," I whisper, and it blooms a majestic pink in my hand.

Felicity smirks. "You do know that won't last, Gemma. Flowers die. It's what they do."

I nod. "But not just yet."

On the hill, the chapel bells peal, calling us to our duties. Felicity brushes the dirt smudges from her skirt with a quick whisk of both hands.

"Bloody weddings," she mumbles.

"Oh, do be happy. How do I look?"

She gives me barely an appraisal. "Like Mrs. Nightwing. That is what comes of befriending her."

"Charming," I sigh.

Felicity removes a petal from my hair. She cocks her head, examining me. The corners of her mouth turn up slightly. "You look just like Gemma Doyle."

I decide that it is a compliment. "Thank you."

"Shall we?" she asks, offering her arm.

I link mine through hers, and it feels good and sure. "Let's."

It is a lovely, small wedding. Mademoiselle LeFarge is resplendent in a suit of blue crepe the very color of sapphires. We girls had rather hoped for a gown befitting a queen—all lace and bows and a train as long as the Thames—but Mademoiselle LeFarge insisted that a woman of her age and means shouldn't put on airs. In the end, she is proved right. The suit is perfect, and the inspector beams at her as if she were the only woman in the world. They say their vows, and Reverend Waite exhorts us to stand. "Ladies and gentlemen, I present to you Mr. and Mrs. Stanton Hornsby Kent."

"I don't see why she has to give up her name," Felicity grumbles, but the organ's sudden off-key warbling of the recessional drowns her out.

We follow the happy couple out the chapel doors to the waiting carriage Mrs. Nightwing has provided. Brigid blows hard into her handkerchief. "I awlways cry at weddings," she says with a sniffle. "Wasn't it luvly?" And we have to agree it was.

The inspector and his new bride shan't escape unscathed. With laughter and shouts of "Good luck!" we let sail our orange blossoms. They're showered with sweet-smelling flowers. The carriage pulls them down the dirt road that leads away from the chapel, and we race after it, throwing our petals to the wind, watching them float on the first heady promise of summer.

The sun bathes my back in warmth. The dirt from the carriage's wheels whirls above the road whilst some of the younger girls still try to keep pace. My hands are stained with the pungent fragrance of orange blossoms. It all reminds me that at present, I am not between worlds. I am quite firmly here, on this dirt path that winds through the flower gardens and the woods to the top of the hill and out again to the roads that carry people wherever they must travel.

And for the moment, I do not wish to be elsewhere.

CHAPTER SEVENTY-FIVE

IT IS NOT AN EASY VOYAGE TO AMERICA.

The winds are high. The ship—and my stomach—are buffeted by waves even my magic cannot quell. I am reminded that there are limits to my power, and some circumstances must be borne with as much grace as one can muster, even if it means spending several days in abject misery, clutching a pan like a life preserver. But the seas do calm. I am able to sip the most glorious cup of broth I have ever tasted. And at last, seagulls flutter overhead in lazy circles, signaling that land is near. Like everyone else, I rush on deck to catch a glimpse of the future.

Oh, New York. It is a most marvelous city—deliciously sprawling and filled with an energy that I can feel even from here. The very buildings seem alive. They are not tidy and tended as in Mayfair; rather, they are mismatched odds and ends of brick and mortar and humanity all pushing against one another in some strange, glorious syncopation—a new rhythm I long to join.

Fathers hoist pinafored daughters and sailor-suited sons onto their shoulders for a better view of it all. A little girl dwarfed by an enormous hair ribbon points excitedly ahead. "Papa! Look!"

There in the city's steam-and-smoke-smudged harbor is the most extraordinary sight of all: a great copper-clad lady with a torch in one hand and a book in the other. It is not a statesman or a god or a war hero who welcomes us to this new world. It is but an ordinary woman lighting the way—a lady offering us the liberty to pursue our dreams if we've the courage to begin.

<hr />

When I dream, I dream of him.

For several nights now he's come to me, waving from a distant shore as if he's been waiting patiently for me to arrive. He doesn't utter a word, but his smile says everything. *How are you? I've missed you. Yes, all is well. Don't worry.*

Where he stands, the trees are in full bloom, brilliant with flowers of every color imaginable. Parts of the ground are still scorched and rocky. There are hard, bald patches where nothing may ever grow again. It is hard to tell. But in other spots, tiny green shoots struggle their way up. Rich black dirt smooths over the surface of things. The earth heals itself.

Kartik takes a stick and digs in the soft, new soil. He's making something but I cannot tell what it is yet. The clouds shift. Shafts of sunlight peek through, and now I can see what he has drawn. It is a symbol: two hands interlocked, surrounded by a perfect, unbroken circle. Love. The day is breaking free. It bathes everything in a fierce light. Kartik is fading from view.

No, I call. *Come back.*

I'm here, he says.

But I can't see. It's too bright.

You can't hold back the light, Gemma. I'm here. Trust me.

The water washes over the riverbank, erasing the edges till there's nothing. But I saw it. I know it's there. And when I wake, the room is white with the morning sun. The light is so bright it hurts my eyes. But I don't dare close them. I won't. Instead, I try to adjust to the dawn, letting the tears fall where they may, because it is morning; it is morning, and there is so much to see.

ABOUT THE AUTHOR

LIBBA BRAY is the author of the *New York Times* bestselling novels *A Great and Terrible Beauty* and *Rebel Angels*. She has never lived in the Victorian era, is not British, and has no superpowers, though if she did, they would involve being able to eat her weight in Swedish fish without feeling the urgent need to shave her tongue afterward. She lives in Brooklyn, New York, with her husband, their son, and a cat of questionable intelligence. Feel free to visit her at her Web site, www.libbabray.com.